DERRY

ANTRIM

RONE

gh

BELFAST

Armagh

DOWN

ARMAGH

Downpatrick

Monaghan

MONAGHAN

Dundalk

AN

LOUTH

MEATH

ar

Trim

DUBLIN

DUBLIN

KILDARE

Kildare

h

WICKLOW

Wicklow

IS
X)

Carlow

CARLOW

nny

ENNY

WEXFORD

Wexford

ford

IRISH
SEA

IRELAND

IRELAND

A NOVEL

FRANK DELANEY

HarperCollins*Publishers*

HarperCollins books may be purchased for educational, business, or sales promotional use. For information, please write: Special Markets Department, HarperCollins Publishers Inc., 10 East 53rd Street, New York, NY 10022.

FIRST EDITION

Designed by Joseph Rutt

Printed on acid-free paper

Library of Congress Cataloging-in-Publication Data
Delaney, Frank
Ireland : a novel / Frank Delaney.—1st ed.
p. cm.
ISBN 0-06-056348-6
1. Ireland–Fiction. I. Title.

PR6054.E396I74 2005
823'.914—dc22
2004054202
05 06 07 08 09   NMSG/RRD   10 9 8 7 6 5 4 3 2

Ed Victor gave me the gift of writing this book and
thus the opportunity to rediscover my own beloved country;
he initiated the novel, waited for, guided, and guarded it.
For that and for myriad other reasons, it is dedicated to
him with great affection and gratitude.

AUTHOR'S NOTE

Beneath all the histories of Ireland, from the present day through her long troubled relationship with England and back to the earliest times, there has always been another, less obvious reporter speaking—the oral tradition, Ireland's vernacular narrative, telling the country's tale to her people in stories handed down since God was a boy.

This fireside voice took great care to say that imagination and emotion insist on playing their parts in every history, and therefore, to understand the Irish, mere facts can never be enough; this is a country that reprocesses itself through the mills of its imagination.

But we all do that; we merge our myths with our facts according to our feelings, we tell ourselves our own story. And no matter what we are told, we choose what we believe. All "truths" are only our truths, because we bring to the "facts" our feelings, our experiences, our wishes. Thus, storytelling—from wherever it comes—forms a layer in the foundation of the world; and glinting in it we see the trace elements of every tribe on earth.

IRELAND

Wonderfully, it was the boy who saw him first. He glanced out of his bedroom window, then looked again and harder—and dared to hope. No, it was not a trick of the light; a tall figure in a ragged black coat and a ruined old hat was walking down the darkening hillside; and he was heading toward the house.

The stranger's face was chalk-white with exhaustion, and he stumbled on the rough ground, his hands held out before him like a sleepwalker's. He looked like a scarecrow deserting his post. High grasses soaked his cracked boots and drenched his coat hems. A mist like a silver veil floated above the ground, broke at his knees, and reassembled itself in his wake. In this twilight fog, mysterious shapes appeared and dematerialized, so that the pale walker was never sure he had seen merely the branches of trees or the arms of mythic dancers come to greet him. Closer in, the dark shadows of the tree trunks twisted into harsh and threatening faces.

Across the fields he saw the yellow glow of lamplight in the window of a house, and he raised his eyes to the sky in some kind of thanks. With no fog on high, the early stars glinted like grains of salt. He became aware of cattle nearby, not yet taken indoors in this mild winter. Many lay curled on the grass where they chewed the cud. As he passed, one or two lurched to their feet in alarm and lumbered off.

And in the house ahead, the boy, nine years old and blond as hay, raced downstairs, calling wildly to his father.

The stranger's bones hurt, and his lungs ached almost beyond endurance. Hunger intensified his troubles; he'd eaten one meal in three days. The calm light in the window ahead pulled him forward in hope. If he held their attention, he might get bed and board for a week—and maybe more. In the days of the High King at Tara, a storyteller stayed seven days and seven nights. Did they know that? Nobody knew anything anymore.

With luck, though, the child in this house would help. Children want stories, and the parents might stretch their hospitality, fired by the delight in the boy's eyes. Unlike last night's billet; high up on a hill farm, he had slept in a loft above the cows, where the east wind got at his bones. The ignorant people there, who had no use for stories, gave him no food and closed their fireside to him. It happened more and more.

But this house would surely prove better; and it was, after all, Halloween, the great time of the year for telling stories, the time of All Souls', when the dead had permission to rise from their graves and prowl the land.

Over the last few hundred yards the fog dispersed into flitters and wisps. At the house, a small white gate opened from the lane into a country garden, which in summer would shine with bunched roses and morning glories and tresses of sweet pea. The tall man in the black coat rapped twice on a brass knocker. Immediately, the husband of the house opened the door.

"Aha!"

The stranger and the householder exchanged a solid handshake, eye to eye. Behind his father, the boy waited in the hallway, jigging from foot to foot.

"God save all here," said the stranger; he hunched his shoulders nervously.

Over the years, his voice had grown deep and rotund. His manner and speech had an unusual formality, with trace elements of stately English from an earlier century and a hint of classical learning. Consequently, his language rang generally more colorful than the speech of the people he met every day.

The man of the house smiled and stood aside.

"Come in. You brought clear skies to us."

"With your permission, I'll bring clear thoughts too."

"Your coat is wet—let me take it."

The man extended a cold, bony hand to the boy peeking around his father's waist.

"A fine boy. God save you too, ma'am!" called the Storyteller to the woman of the house.

She looked irked, and he guessed that he, this stringy, unwashed man, with skin like canvas, would disrupt her rigorous household; nonetheless she set a place for him while her husband, pleased and comfortable, poured the visitor a drink.

The boy watched the stranger attacking the food like a tired hound. He sensed that the man's hunger fought with the man's decorum. Nobody spoke because the newcomer seemed too famished to be interrupted. The boy examined the man's face, saw the long, thin scar, wondered if he had been in a knife fight, perhaps with a sailor on some foreign quayside.

And the sodden boots—in his mind he saw the stranger fording streams, climbing out of gullies, traversing slopes of limestone shale on his endless travels across the country. Did he have a dog? Seemingly not, which was a pity, since a dog could have sat guard by the fire at night. Did the man ever sleep in caves? They said that bears and wolves had long been extinct in Ireland—but had they?

That evening, in that white house among the fields, a boy's most passionate dream came true. His father had long talked of the traveling storytellers. He said they possessed brilliant powers; they brought the long-gone past to life vividly, without what he called "the interference of scholars. Those professors," he said. "They dry out history in order to put it down on paper." In his father's view, a tale with the feeling taken out of it had "no blood and was worth very little."

But the old stories, told by traveling storytellers round the fireside on winter evenings—they came hurtling straight down the long, shiny pipeline of the centuries, and the characters, all love and hate and fire, "tumbled out on our own stone floor." So said his father. "They're still among us. I wouldn't be surprised if one of them came here one day. He'll probably be tall and old, with boots and a hat, and he'll enchant us all." And now such a storyteller had finally arrived.

He was the last of his breed. Figures like him had trudged the countryside for twenty-five centuries, telling the story of Ireland in one form or another. In the old days, they were beloved; a visit from one often gave a village its brightest moment of the year.

They had counterparts all over the globe—India, South America, China. Such travelers wandered into a village, spread a rug under a shady tree, and began a daylong tale of the country's old times. They called up dragons and fire and mountains and maidens and gods. Wary villagers who drifted forward to hear what was being said always stayed to the end. Whatever the topic, the audience knew they could be assured of vitality and drama—great events told in bright colors with huge spirit. Thus the traveling storyteller and his oral tradition shaped much of the world's culture and character.

The Storyteller tongued the last crumbs from behind his teeth. He moved to a chair by the fire, where he prepared to smoke a pipe. From a yellow oilcloth pouch he offered a fill of tarry, black tobacco to the husband, who thanked him and said he didn't smoke. The stranger filled his pipe, picked up the iron tongs, plucked a tiny ember from the fire, and planked it on top of the pipe. After much sucking and tapping, the tobacco glowed, and blue smoke drifted forward in search of the chimney.

He leaned back in his chair. The boy had settled directly opposite him, on the cushions of a long wooden bench beside the hearth. With teeth tall and yellow like a horse's, the Storyteller smiled at the boy, who still gazed huge-eyed at this sorcerous creature.

"D'you know what an architect is?"

The boy looked at his father for approval before he answered.

"A man who causes buildings?"

"And d'you know where Newgrange is?"

"Up in county Meath?"

"Sure enough. May we ask on the banks of what river?"

The boy glanced again at his adored father.

"Isn't it the Boyne?"

At a noise from outside, the Storyteller swung his head hopefully. The door heaved open; a man and woman ambled in with two daughters, aged about twelve and eight. One was blond and one red-haired, and they wore flowered pinafores. The younger girl was directed to join the boy on the high bench by the fire, where she sat watching the Storyteller with wonderland eyes.

A coal fell forward on the hearth. The Storyteller sucked vigorously on his pipe, and it made a little dottle of noise. Next moment, the audience increased again—another couple strolled in from across the lane with their young daughter.

Word had obviously spread. Perhaps someone among the farms had earlier seen the tall stranger's descent through the misty fields and guessed who or what he was. So he would have an audience tonight. Whether he would have one tomorrow night—or a venue—would depend on him.

"What would you like in your whiskey?" asked the host.

One neighbor said, "More," and they all laughed.

After some minutes of talk and smiles, everyone settled down. No electricity in the houses in those days; an oil lamp in the window and another with a glass sconce on the wall laid gilded shadows into the room. The firelight played on the Storyteller's long face. He jiggled his pipe, eased back in his chair, spread his shoulders, and began.

EVERY WORTHWHILE STORY BEGINS WITH THE immortal words, "Once upon a time." Never did a phrase ring so true as it will this evening. I have come to this hospitable and decent house to continue my life's work, to do what I do every night of the year. And that is, to tell the story of Ireland.

The tale I shall render you this evening concerns the most brilliant Irishman of all time. He was the architect of Newgrange—but, as all stories should, this one begins before its own beginning. And that was a long, long time ago, before there was ever a place called Newgrange, before there was ever an architect to build its famous work, even before there was a country called Ireland.

So: once upon a time, the ground upon which we walk was no more than a lump of stone down at the center of the earth. It was part of the thick shell containing that furnace that rages down there night and day. And that thick shell was always kept cool by the oceans that covered it. But in the early days of our planet, the shell was weak in places. The flames burst through again and again, and vast layers of rock were flung up into the seas.

This boiling volcanic surface spread over the prehistoric oceans. It split and re-formed into wide lands of nothing but black rock. And these split and re-formed and cooled and split again until, two thousand, five hundred million years ago, there were five continents. These continents became all the countries of the world.

And so, every land on this planet is the child of ocean and rock, water and stone. Every day and every age since then, some rock or island somewhere crumbles and breaks off at the edge of some landmass.

Many of those fragments still retain the shapes of the countries and continents to which they were once joined. On the maps of my schooldays, some of them look like couples who have gone to sleep close to each other and then floated gently apart in the night. Tomorrow, take out your atlas and look at Ireland and Britain. Together, they look like a child curled up asleep near a larger child, who is then curled up in the lee of the parent continent, Europe. That's how our own country and our most important neighbor began life—as stone born of fire and cooled by sea.

Some of that ancient rock is with us still. I can take you to a place far down on the east coast where you can see and touch it. Near Wexford there's a stone, which, the locals will tell you, dates to two million years B.C. Two hundred miles higher up the coastline, as the crow flies, there's another such rock, in Antrim. I've looked closely at these two items, and I could see the specks of quartz sparkling inside them. They looked like the eyes of little creatures who saw the mighty flames that imprisoned them in the rock long, long ago.

So the fact is, when the volcanic earth had mostly stopped heaving, Ireland amounted to nothing more than a cold field of stone. Much, much later, sediment from the universe floated over and settled on this stone acreage and spread and thickened there like a primal silt.

Gradually, gradually, across those hard plains, there rose an island of rich loam and gentle hills, where today quiet rivers flow through green woods down to seas full of glimmering fish, where shiny horses and their foals gallop across the meadows in a bountiful and misty land flowing with milk and honey. That's how the world thinks of us today, and we're glad of the compliment, which is accurate enough—but it isn't the whole story. Before the land finally settled, before the final phase of seeds blew in on the wind and fertilized it, and before the birds and the insects again made their homes here, we were also born of another great earthly power—the direct opposite of fire. We were born of ice.

Four ice ages attacked Ireland, one after another, and the ice took possession of everything. It destroyed any fertility that had been established, ruined any progress that nature had made. Wherever it met rock, the ice's freezing edges gleamed like the starched frills of folded cloth. It found hidden flaws in the mountains, ripped them open, and filled them—they're what we call glaciers, and in time they became today's rivers. In the largest rock faults, the ice cut channels wide enough to turn into eventual seas, and that's how Ireland was cut away from Britain.

All the hills and highlands and all the ravines and hollows and gullies and gulches and every wrinkle and creek and punchbowl of the Ireland we know today was carved by the cruel hand of ice. They say that great ice takes hold slowly. It begins when the sun grows colder and the land bends under an endless chilling gale. The temperature sinks without mercy, and over the bald clay of the plains and valleys a deep rime forms, squeezing out all plant and animal life.

Across Ireland, one such pulverization followed another until the countryside became a carpet of impenetrable cold. That all happened in the accumulations of the first three ice ages. And then, just as things were thawing out once more, a last northern marauder settled Ireland's final shape—the savage Fourth Ice Age.

Twelve thousand years ago, a vast sheet of compacted and frozen snow broke away from the Arctic Circle, which surrounds the North Pole. It was thousands of feet thick and hundreds of miles broad, and when it finally rode down the curve of the planet, it looked like a floating country.

They say that ice on the move sounds like the beginning of the world. With shouts louder than the voice of God, its shelves heave and crack. The intensity of its light alters every color it meets. Ice, they tell me, is never pure white, never a fixed or lone shade. It is ivory, it is silver, it is chalk, it is salt.

Except that—according to the polar explorers, and I've met more than one of them in my own travels—ice isn't white. Close up, it handles as white. At certain distances, it stands as white. But those who know it well, who have stood on it, lain on it, even fallen through it—they say that ice in bulk glows blue.

Does it take its cue from the sky, as the sea does? Or is it a trick of the light? Maybe it has struck a pose to show how chilly it is, how menacing? Perhaps the blue is clothing, cladding, a gift of nature—as we know, she has all the best tricks. Whatever the cause, the ice that broke away and sailed down those high Atlantic latitudes twelve thousand years ago was as blue as a lady's gown.

But it had other colors too. Do you know the names of the noble metals? Gold, silver, and platinum. All ice shines like those noble metals, and all color, as we know, is determined by where the light falls. As this island of ice moved south, I wonder how many shades of gold the sun sparked from it. Yellow and bronze and copper. Amber and brass and saffron. And then, at night, under the wind-whipped moon, thousands of new shades glinted, mostly silver, soft or piercing or ominous or benign.

So there it was, sinister in its bright lights and content in its own power. Its noble metals flashed. The sound of its great creakings and crackings echoed across the waters. And the whole glimmering mass headed relentlessly down the northern seas like some great, glowing ocean liner built for a nation of giants.

It was the biggest iceberg ever seen, a thousand times bigger than the one that sank the *Titanic*. It was its own landscape and its own geography. The fierce weather of the north had polished it like glass. And the harsh winds of the east had ruffled it and etched little furrows on the plated surfaces. These shales looked like ruched fabric or ebbing sands, and the whole mass had hogbacks and crests and headlands and forelands, all sharp-edged, jagged, and crystal.

The bow of this great vessel formed itself into a fierce and concentrated spearhead. It slammed forward in slabs and reefs so wide that the very horizon seemed made of ice. And it attacked Ireland with spikes half a mile high and half a mile wide.

The first white prow crashed into the cliffs of our northernmost counties, Antrim, Derry, and Donegal. Huge chunks of foreland fell away into the ocean and formed today's bays and harbors. Higher wedges of ice scythed out deeper inlets—you can gaze up at those cliffs today and some of them look as if a great hand descended with a sharp knife and cut a sheer slice from the rock.

After it came ashore, this great iceberg plunged south across the country. It kicked rocks and even hills out of its path, and it scooped out valleys and glens that had never existed before. A few peaks and ridges were higher than the ice-cliff, and they continued to raise their spears above the ice. You know them; mountains like Errigal in Donegal, Galtymore in Tipperary, Croagh Patrick in Mayo, where pilgrims after the Ice Age climbed to be nearer their gods, and do so to this very day. But along the lower slopes and in the deep valleys and ravines, the ice fought every fold and won every groove. A new cold gripped the mountains so tightly that its chill penetrated to the stone's deepest core.

The wisest men tell us that everything, sooner or later, changes. And all change commences with a specific moment. We say to our-selves, "I won't do this again, I must become different." And we suc-ceed—eventually.

One day, even the mighty ice changed—it started to shrink and retreat. One single day, ten and a half thousand years ago, Ireland's climate began to alter. The chilling gale that came with the ice blew itself out. Softer breezes floated in from the west. Gentle and warm sea currents came from the southwest. A hot African wind rode up past the coast of Spain and caressed our southern shores.

Gradually these warm forces loosened the ice's awful grip. Its edges frayed by an inch at a time—and then by a yard—and then by a mile. Soon, like the pink-brown skin in the healing of a wound, the native earth of Ireland began to appear again.

I've described to you how the ice had ripped into the terrain on its advance. Well, it did so too on its retreat. Large melting slabs of ice gouged out caves and fjords and chasms. The ancient stone foundations of our land shook, undermined by the desperate, slip-ping ice. Rocky glens opened again as their walls crumbled. The clay began to breathe. Hills and mountains shone in the new sun, and down their slopes poured ribbons of new, silver waters. When you gaze at a mountain from a distance, and you see a shining river that looks like the spoor of a snail, you can be sure that was an Ice Age stream.

That final loosening sent boulders sliding down mountainsides and hurled stones down into valleys, as the ice ripped them away from their rock bodies. These "glacial erratics," as they're called, loiter to this day across the Irish landscape, some of them big as houses. I myself have been glad of their shelter many times. And they lie at the core of the story of Newgrange.

As though to collect breath, the Storyteller halted.

Puffs of steam rose from his wet boots as they dried in the heat of the fire.

In the pause, people stirred. The boy looked anxiously at his mother to check her mood—and she seemed calm. His father took off his spectacles and polished them with a little amber cloth. Without his glasses, his sky-blue eyes sparkled.

The boy pushed down his stockings and rubbed his shins, now hot and mottled from the fire. Nobody moved from where they sat; one or two of the men had taken off their jackets and sat shirtsleeved. Their faces glowed, with pride as much as heat; this epic account gave them the story of their own ancestry, the origins and magnificence of their own country. The women seemed more placid, less intense in their enjoyment—but nonetheless enthralled. Nobody reflected the magic of the hour as much as the children, whose faces glowed like lamps.

As the Storyteller gathered strength for the next installment, he curled one hand around the bowl of his pipe and raised the forefinger of the other hand commandingly. He drew three, four, five, silent puffs on the pipe and took it from his mouth.

THIS PLACE, NEWGRANGE—HOW MUCH DO YOU know about it? You might have read in the newspapers of this great and mysterious edifice under the ground in county Meath. It's not far in from the coast, and it's northwest of Dublin by about thirty miles or so. I've been there myself, and it's a mighty place, in rich land on a hill above the river Boyne. The local people know all about it because over the centuries many gentlemen and scholars have examined it, guessing at its history and building a good body of lore. A kind woman who lives on the hillside took me into what she called "our cave." She lit a stub of a candle, and the flame was enough to display great wonders to me.

This marvelous, immortal structure was built five thousand years ago, before Stonehenge in England, before the pyramids of Egypt. Every person in the world should visit it, because it tells us how amazing were the ancestors of man. It's a very inspiring place, and while I was there, I came to consider a great deal about it and the person who built it—and this story entered my mind.

The Architect of Newgrange was a young man, possessed of a tall and thin physique, above which his wild head of tawny hair looked like a tree on fire. His deep-set eyes frightened the children, and his manner took no account of courtesy—which is to say that he treated people abruptly. Until the events occurred that I am about to relate to you, he had spent much of his life in silence, speaking only when spoken to, never offering friendship, and generally avoiding the burden of conviviality. His was the life of the aloof. If we wish to excuse someone for being like that, we say, "Ah, they're shy," and I do believe he was a shy child and grew up a shy young man.

At one stage of his life, this remote and strange individual began to invest a deep interest in the observation of stone—and by stone, I mean those rocks I've just described to you that were cast down the mountains when the ice melted.

To most people, a stone is a stone—nothing more and nothing less than a rock. But this young man grew to love stone the way farmers love cattle, the way women love children, the way boys love pretty girls, the way the waves love the shore. To him, stone seemed to speak; he didn't hear a voice, but he understood it just the same, because deep in his mind a picture formed—of the world as it must have been long, long ago, before there were trees with leaves or animals with fur. Stone brought the past to him and brought him to the past.

Now, this man's people, who commanded the hill of New-grange—they lived handsomely. Their land of rich, brown clay was left behind ten thousand years ago, a great, wide silt after the ice melted. Like all such terrain in Europe, it was discovered by travelers coming over from the east in search of a fertile living.

In Ireland they found a good and pleasant home. Hazel and rowan trees already covered the plains and grew down the mountainsides and into the valleys. Wide, slow rivers took the voyagers in from the coast on the logs of their simple rafts. And they discovered that if they cleared the trees, they could settle almost anywhere, because the earth was so easy to cultivate.

Hillsides proved the best places. They could live off the fine land and cast an eye over the surrounding countryside for approaching dangers. Newgrange proved ideal—a high hill with good soil overlooking a placid river. People settled there very early, six thousand years before the birth of Christ, and they began to work the earth of the Boyne Valley.

In those far-off days, everyone on such a hillside labored hard. From the age a child could lift or scrabble to the oldest man or woman able to drag or push, they hauled and parted and combed the clay. The soil they tilled was warm and deep and full of different colors—honey or red-gold or mahogany. Scatter seeds there, and something always grew.

And every year they turned the soil, they sowed their seeds, they welcomed the rain, they hailed the sun, and they were happy.

Yet for all their prosperity and for all their good fortune, they made slow progress in life—because they hadn't yet discovered anything better to work with than stone. They depended upon it for their weapons and tools, and they handled it well. In their hands, stone made stone; using stone tools, they hammered out new stone implements—knives and chisels, copied from shards of stone that they found among the occasional little beaches of shale on the banks of the river.

They also established what you might call local factories. These were places to which they hauled the rocks that they found strewn in the countryside. Hacking into such boulders with stone axes and sledgehammers, they cut javelins, arrows, more hammers, and better stone axes.

Every stone in the world has a cutting point, a place on the stone where the cleanest break may be achieved. The men who made those weapons knew how to find that fault line, how to split a stone as neatly as a slice. As every stonemason has understood since the gods were born, when you add edge to weight, your cutting power doubles. And once they had mastered how to use it, nothing resisted their stone; the skull of a foe, the neck of a beast, the crest of a slope—everything yielded to it.

And that is how our young man with the wild tawny hair and the deep-set eyes first came to such a closeness with stone; he found that he had a gift for using it expertly. He understood economy—how to get strong results from controlled circumstances. His weapons and tools seemed neater, more efficient, more powerful than anyone else's because he realized that no dagger need be too long, no axe too heavy—a weapon's power only springs to life in the hands of its user, and those he made for himself always had perfect balance.

His gift with stone saved the young man's life once. One day, breaking branches in the trees where the forest had been forced back from the hill of Newgrange, he heard a noise. He looked up and saw a bear glaring at him from the ferns. She probably had cubs nearby—because bears, by and large, tend to leave people alone unless they fear for their young.

He had no intention of troubling this creature, but the bear didn't know that. The brown fur stood up at her neck; he could see the red-pink of her gums, the white spikes of her teeth, and the rage and terror in her eyes.

On the ground near his feet, his bare toes felt a heavy rock shard, long as a short sword. He stood very still, watching the bear carefully, his feet teasing the shard of stone into position. With a great roar, she rushed toward him. He bent swiftly, snatched up the shard, and drove the stony spike high into the bear's throat.

The force of his thrust almost broke his hand, but he had enough strength to twist the weapon. He saw blood on the stone, not much, enough to tell him he had wounded the animal. The bear stepped back and collected herself to attack again. But the young man lunged forward, this time roaring wildly. The bear recoiled farther; the young man struck—again and again, until the bear keeled over backward. He jumped on her and hammered the shard into her neck over and over until she was dead.

Now: the people of Newgrange had their own government—Elders and Eldresses who passed the laws and made the decisions that regulated life on the hillside. They addressed all spiritual matters too, such as when, why, and how to make sacrifices to the gods.

One year, as the leaves turned gold, the Elders held a special meeting. The harvest had again been abundant, and as they blessed their fortune they began to discuss, in the warmth of the moment, finding a way to thank their ancestors, honoring their dead. The Chief Elder, his face very serious, said, "We must build something that we will be remembered for. We must build a structure that will not only respect our forefathers but will also preserve the spirit of our people."

A great meeting was called, to which almost everyone on the hillside came. But the arguments grew so heated that they had to con-

vene again, and again, and again. To and fro the discussion raged—
what will constitute an eternal honor, and how is it to be done?

I've said that almost everyone on the hillside attended those
debates. One voice didn't speak—our wild young man stayed away.
Nobody uttered surprise at his absence, and many expressed relief.
They'd always found him a little odd; he didn't say much to many,
but in the previous few years they'd avoided him even further,
because they'd begun to fear him. With good reason—one day, he
had suddenly and openly killed two men. His status as a warrior
may have placed him above punishment, but his deed caused the
hillside fear; folk evaded him, didn't meet his eye, chose not to
work alongside him.

What they didn't know—and he never told them—was the reasons he had killed the two men. The day after the bear's death, the
young man had grown despondent with remorse; he couldn't
endure the fact that when he had killed the bear, he had also
orphaned her cubs. So he took off into the forest to bring them back
and try to rear them. He never found them. Three, four, five days he
searched, checking lairs, taking risks—but no cubs.

When he returned to Newgrange, he came upon a commotion. A
bunch of lesser men had found the cubs, had killed one, and were
burning the second cub on the spit. The young man raced up the
hill and arrived as the squealing cub, two months old, shuddered
and died, blood oozing from its eyes, its fur scorched black.

He killed the man who was holding the cub. With an axe lying
nearby he split the fellow diagonally from shoulder to hip, and
then he pounded a hole in the man's forehead. The first cub was
already being skinned by one of the men—a nice fur cap for the
winter. He killed him too, this time not bothering with attacking
the body—he just split the man's head wide open. The bystanders,
who, a minute earlier had been laughing at the sport with the bear
cubs, scattered like chaff in a wind. But from that moment, everyone avoided the young man.

He made it easy for them. The incident filled him with dreadful
feelings, and he took off into the forest again. Thereafter, his taste

for lone roving grew larger. He also knew that his rage had been released, and he knew that when that happened, he had no way of reining it in. So whenever he felt angry, he vanished for days or weeks at a time.

While he roamed, he looked at everything he saw in the world and tried to imagine its origins. That was how he came to love stone. Everywhere he went he scrutinized some new boulder or slab, relishing the sight and bulk and feel of it. And who's to say he didn't now and then run his tongue over a rock and taste one of life's joys—a fresh little pool of rainwater in the hollow of a crag immediately after a shower?

Came the day of the last big meeting. No matter what the wild young man's reputation, regardless of how rough or dangerous or foolish he was generally thought to be, a number of Elders believed in him and began to raise his name as the man for the job. He might seem unsteady at times, they agreed, perhaps a touch mad, and his rages might cause havoc, but the Eldresses perceived in him the potential of a great doer as well as a dreamer. And the Chief Elder believed him the best weapon maker, the most intelligent of the farmers, and something of a visionary—and so he persuaded him to come to the final meeting. This was to be the day of decision.

From early afternoon the people began to assemble in the Long House, the Elders' parliament building. A great, wide fire lit the darkness of the windowless chamber. Men, women, and children squatted on skins scattered across the mud floor. The Chief Elder spoke first. He announced that, although he wanted to hear further argument, he hoped they would now decide as to how, and with what, and where, they would build this great eternal monument. So far, all they had agreed was that they should use wood.

The wild young man had come in late and stood near the door. He kept his head down, looked at no one. The Chief Elder, who had personally invited him and asked for his views, called him forward; reluctantly he came up to where the Elders stood, coughed to clear his throat, and spoke.

He began by addressing the sacredness of the mighty project. They all claimed, he said, that they wished nothing less than the finest possible memorial. "Our dead," he said, "will always be with us—therefore we must honor them with something that will always be there. And we can't say that of wood. Wood doesn't last."

Yes, he agreed, wood was beautiful, a child knew that. But wood rotted; a child knew that, too—maggots ate into the wood, and the rain did the rest.

"There's only one thing that lasts," he said, "and that is—stone."

He held out the fingers of one hand and counted. One, stone was magnificent in appearance. Two, it came from the ancient world. Three, it would last to the end of time. Four, it could be shaped. Five, it would accept carved messages of respect and belief.

Then he closed his mouth and sat down on the floor.

People stared at the wild young man, their mouths gaping. They turned to each other, dumb with wonder, their faces reflecting unasked questions. And then, from every corner, in the safety of their numbers, voices began to attack him. What did he know? How could he be so foolish, so impractical? They could easily ferry wood, but how could anyone transport stone? Beneath each complaint and accusation lay an ignoble question: Who was he, a moody killer, to tell them they were wrong? Their words danced like sparks across the shadows of the Long House.

He rose and spoke again. His high-pitched voice sounded something like a girl's, and he looked lean and disturbing. He didn't say, "You fools!" but his tone conveyed it.

"Don't you understand? Stone is unyielding but not unfriendly. The marks we make on it will last forever. What could be more suited to remind us and our children's children of who has gone before?"

But he was speaking to people who had never thought deeply of stone. To them stone was like air or water—no personality until you do something with it, and it lies out there in the fields, doing nothing and with badges of moss all over it. What more was to be said of it, except that it yielded a good axe now and then?

The young man had little concern for what Newgrange thought. Like many great people, all he cared about was what he felt and what he wanted to do. The force of his passion made everyone peer at him, and the light from the fire made him look more mysterious. His head of tawny hair seemed to flare wilder. The wrinkles on his frown grew darker, his deep-set eyes lost in the shadows of his face.

Slamming one fist repeatedly into the palm of the other hand, he made point after point.

"I sense more things than I can name. I understand more than I can describe. Visions come to me and flashes of light that I can't explain. But all of you—you all have such feelings. Look for them in your heart."

In a voice powerful enough to fight off all comers, he told them that one of life's greatest mysteries lay within stone. No matter how it was approached, whether attacked, caressed, or cut wide open, stone never surrendered the story of its origins.

"As with ourselves," he said, "we don't know where it came from. It must have belonged to the beginning of the world."

His listeners shivered. They felt the same uncomfortable wonder as he did—because the young man had touched a dim, half-true knowledge. In his passion for stone, he had placed his hand on something inside every one of them—and now he tightened his grip.

"Sometimes at dawn, sometimes in the dead of night, sometimes when a breeze feathers the waters of the river, we tremble inside, and we wonder: What power that we cannot see, but we can feel, guides us? What great spiritual authority governs our lives? That's the force of our ancestors. We mustn't commemorate them with anything that's less than immortal."

In the awed silence that followed, the Chief Elder stepped in and said that he proposed to appoint the wild young man as architect. The young man didn't react at all.

One of the Elders, though, sensed the discomfort among the people, and he felt that many might think they had been ridden over roughshod. This man had suave ways and a silky voice, and he knew how to persuade folk to his point of view; we shall call him the Silken Elder. If he spoke to you, his voice never rose. When he stood conversing, he held his hands folded on his stomach. And a little pursed smile always danced on his plump mouth.

In fairness, he himself had much distinction. This was the Elder who took responsibility for all the rituals practiced on the hillside— the praising of the rain, the warning of coming storms, the songs to the sun. If some unusual act of nature, such as lightning or a whirlwind, drove fear through the people, he was the one who uttered smooth words to fight the danger. He was the man who taught Newgrange how to make offerings to the skies, the trees, the river, and he worked all this so calmly and soothingly that many people liked him. But this Elder was himself a dangerous man; in short, he was a liar, an untrustworthy and shifty man, insincere.

The Silken Elder decided that it would be to his advantage to speak for the people who disagreed with the decision they had just heard. Smoothly he began to question the young man.

"What are you going to build?" he said. "How long will it take?"

"I will create something the world has never seen, something it will always consider extraordinary."

This astonishing reply quieted the room somewhat. Even the Silken Elder was taken aback, but, he hurried not to show it, attacked afresh.

"How do we know you won't abandon the job before it's finished?"

That insult sent a hiss of wonder through the crowd. The young man looked calmly nowhere and never said a word.

So the Silken Elder tried again.

"Do you intend to be answerable at all? These folks—this room— these are your people. Will you answer to them? To your Elders? To anyone?"

Our young man never moved, never spoke. The questions drew none of his blood. He knew enough to wait. Soon the Silken Elder fell silent, appealing to the audience with raised arms, as if to say, "I don't know what we can do about this fellow."

The young Architect of Newgrange turned around and walked across to where the Silken Elder stood. As though it were a lamp, he thrust his big, tawny young head forward. Six inches from the Silken Elder's face he shone the beam of his eyes straight at the man. Like two boxers they glared at each other for a long moment.

The Silken Elder broke first. He stepped away.

"I can understand," he said, "why you mightn't wish to disclose your plans in detail. But it isn't enough to hear your love of stone. You refuse to tell us anything else. Therefore, to protect ourselves in case you fail us on such an important enterprise, we should declare ourselves entitled to Recompense."

Recompense! A blood oath! Recompense was the payment for failure to deliver on a vow—and it guaranteed a slow, humiliating death. First the offender was pegged out like a hide to the hillside. There he lay for twenty-four hours. At noon on the next day a warrior came and cut off the offender's right arm at the shoulder; on the third day at noon, the left arm; slaves staunched the blood with mud, leaves, and skins to prevent the offender bleeding mercifully to death. On the fourth day at noon the warriors cut off the right leg; at the fifth noon, the left.

On the sixth day at noon they prized out his eyes, sliced off his ears, pulled out his tongue; and on the seventh day they filleted his body like butchers. Some weeks later, when the wind and the rain had washed all the flesh from the skeleton, the whitening bones would be collected by the lowest bondswoman on the hillside and cast out into the countryside for the wild animals to gnaw. That was Recompense, a dreadful matter; the word chilled the spine of every man, woman, and child in Newgrange. All chatter, all murmuring, all noise, in the Long Room died. Every eye watched the clashing pair.

The Architect had seen the Recompense more than once; he had even been called upon to participate in it. At last he nodded slowly, like a man thinking aloud, and turned to face the people.

"I understand," he said. "But—if you, all of you, eventually agree that I have accomplished a satisfactory and eternal commemoration, then"—and he spun around to face the older man—"I will take your Elder's robe. And you'll pay the Recompense."

A soft roar came up from the people. This young man knew the laws of Newgrange. A person threatened with the Recompense had the right to turn it on his challenger, even an Elder. In the shocked hush, the Silken Elder had no choice.

"I agree," he said, soft-spoken but very angry.

He tried to recover his position a little, using all the powers of his silken voice.

"What can you tell us about how long—"

"I will tell you nothing," interrupted the Architect, and he left the Long House abruptly. The meeting broke up, and there wasn't a man or a woman there who didn't feel astounded.

From that moment, one September day fifty centuries ago, the Architect began to plan the great white circular building on the hillside at Newgrange above the river Boyne. And from that moment he knew that the Silken Elder would plot every day to cause his downfall and wreck his project, because any time a great man tries to do a wonderful thing, lesser men will try to stop him. That is one of the laws of life.

Now—there lived on that hillside a certain lady. She was tall, she had thin brown hair, and she was known as the Angry Woman. Her husband was dead, killed by a mad elk—spiked on its horns one morning when he was blinded by the sun and unable to measure how close the animal had come. Some said that the goring of her man had made this woman angry. Others claimed she had always been angry, except with her own child, a red-haired girl, eight years old, whom she loved as a tigress loves her cub.

Since the end of her mourning this Angry Woman had desired a new husband, and the mate she wanted was our young man. If, wild or not, he seemed eligible before, now he became a prize. She had watched him for some time, studied his mixture of tenderness and anger, saw the efficient way he dealt with things round and about the hillside, and observed above all his impatience with fools. Shrewd women (and she was shrewd) always value intelligence in a man, and here was a fellow who had the brains and the handsome looks. And now he had power. She didn't care that he was moody—she was moody herself.

Once or twice she had approached him, knowing she risked his snub. At a feast she filled his plate; he never even looked at her. And one day she rushed to help him when he was building a hut. The rooftree fell, she grabbed the pole, and for a moment they stood side by side, arms touching, until they could haul the beam upright. Again, no acknowledgment came from him.

When he left the meeting that day, the Architect went alone down the hill; he had a walk like the lope of a wolf. Behind him, the crowd lingered, chattering like sparrows on a roof. At the doorway of the Long House the Angry Woman stood for a moment, looked down, and saw the man of her desires striding toward the river. Her heart still raced at the excitement she had just witnessed. She wanted to talk to him in his moment of triumph—but she didn't wish him to know how she felt.

Once again she faced the difficulty of this man; when she met him or spoke to him, he improved the way she felt, he enlarged her life, he made the day bright and bearable. But he gave her no direct or tangible evidence that she had any effect, of any kind, on him.

After a moment's thought, she followed him. To disguise her intention, she took a different route. Where he had gone to the south, she headed west, to the reed beds, and began plucking rushes to cover the earthen floor of her home.

She hoped that he would see her, and soon he did. When she lifted a sheaf of the green, wide blades from the water's edge, the swing of her white arms caught his eye.

The Architect gestured to the Angry Woman and began to walk toward her. She stopped building her rush pile and waited for him; anxious, she ran her tongue along the back of her upper teeth. Our young man held out his hand, and she took it. She could see he was agitated, she could see that he had difficulty controlling his mood. So she stroked his bare forearm and led him into the grove along the riverbank. Inside the trees, where nobody on the hill could now see them, they lay down on the grass.

She began to talk to him; she said that he had been given a great honor, that nobody would carry it off better than he could, that should he need any help, he had but to ask her. Slowly but surely she calmed him down—and through it all, he never said a word.

In a clear western sky, the sun shone. Some time passed. And the breeze ruffled the water. The couple lay on the ground, hugging each other tighter and tighter. Eventually the Architect stood up and walked silently away. From the edge of the grove he turned to look at the Angry Woman, who sat up. He walked back to her, bent down, and stroked her hair kindly. Then he helped her to her feet, and they went their separate ways.

Along the riverbank little areas of mud rested, where the water sometimes flooded in and ebbed away. Over one of these the Architect crouched and began to think. Behind him, on the water, two men worked on a raft, repairing it. One fixed a loose log while the other held the raft steady.

From the folds of his deerskin tunic the Architect took a small pointed stone. With this, he began to etch patterns in the soft black mud. Nothing he drew satisfied him, and he leaned back on his haunches.

But when he looked up, his eye caught the cross-sectioned face of the log on the raft, and he saw the rings that tell the tree's age, a circle for every year—a tree grows a new ring in twelve months. He looked at this pattern for several moments and then etched again in the ground. This time, he drew a series of whirling circles not unlike the face of the log.

Getting restless, he rose, walked further along the riverbank, and began to sketch on a different patch of mud. This time, he drew a picture of the hill of Newgrange. Like any painter, he looked up now and then to check the proportions. Even though it was composed of very few lines, this picture took him several minutes. When he had finished it, he stood to his full height in order to look down on the drawing at his feet. Then, his mind's eye filled with this new perspective, he stared up at the hill again, assessing the shape and depth.

At that moment the Angry Woman came back to the edge of the wood and, her arms full of rushes, stood where he could see her. She smiled cautiously at him and walked forward to where he could see her better. In doing so, she stepped into a pool of sunlight, and her smile turned to gold.

There's an old saying, "Man's love is of Man's life a thing apart— 'tis Woman's whole existence." The way the Angry Woman smiled at the Architect was important to her, but not to him. He saw her all right, he even gazed at her—but he didn't smile back.

Instead, he turned away, crouched again, and in the mud drew a beautiful sketch; he drew a wide circle, then a thick, single line entering this circle, and at the end of the line, inside the circle, he drew a rough cross. By now, his entire body quaked with excitement, especially when, in four last strokes, he made a clear drawing of a small rectangular box.

The Architect stood up, exhausted. He knew he had just had a wonderful inspiration; he knew he had decided what this great monument of Newgrange would be and what it would look like. The thrill of it, the brilliance it contained! And it was such a simple idea! But he also recognized that it would be very difficult to achieve. Quite simply, the Architect of Newgrange had decided to make the sun in the sky do his bidding.

Genius, you know, works in many ways. In some people it comes at the end of years spent thinking deep and endless thoughts. With others, the brilliant idea flashes into the mind from nowhere, the way a hawk attacks with the sun behind it. That afternoon, the Architect felt his mind climbing higher and higher. He was brave to the utmost, brave as brave can be, thinking thoughts of great daring and then swooping to draw exactly what he wanted to express: "Can I," he had asked himself as he drew his pictures in the mud, "can I capture the sun to keep our dead warm?"

Seeking an answer to the question, he had looked back over his shoulder at the flowing waters of the river Boyne, had seen the sunlight on the Angry Woman's smiling face, and his imagination announced to his brain, "Light also flows."

If there was any true justice in the world, that shining moment, the arrival of that idea, would have inspired the Architect to go over to where the Angry Woman stood, take her in his arms, and thank her profoundly for what was arguably the most brilliant idea that he or any Irishman, before or since, would ever have. But he didn't do that—he turned away.

That very night, the Architect chose his first team of workers, five people; four men of Newgrange, and the Angry Woman. No plan did he divulge to them, no schedule of works, no path of progress; instead, he said, "You must tell nobody, ever, anything of what we do. Do you understand?"

They understood all right; they understood that he might kill anyone who betrayed his confidences.

To keep the matter entirely secret, he never showed them—or anyone—those final pictures he had drawn in the mud. He memorized them so thoroughly that whenever he wished, he could draw the images again in a few seconds—the circle, the long-legged cross, the simple, rectangular box. Like all great drawings they had no unnecessary lines.

Next morning, he led his workers westward, out into the deep countryside. Carrying nothing but food wrapped in leaves, the five-strong team walked silently behind him for two hours. At last, he stopped by a grove and pointed down a steep slope to a large flat stone half hidden in the ferns. It measured four times the width of his body and twice his height.

"Bring this back to the hillside."

The four men of the team looked at each other. Impossible. First they must ease it from the earth or, more likely, dig it out; and a stone like that could go down ten yards deep—it might even be a mountaintop. Then they must transport it, over hills and through gullies, up, down, and across mixed terrain, back to the hillside. Did it have to travel whole?

"No stone you bring back may be broken. So—tell me how you will accomplish it."

And the four men looked at each other and thought, No, this isn't possible.

All day, these four men had been perpetrating a nasty injustice, because they hadn't spoken a word to the Angry Woman. It's true that they feared her a little; but more than that, they didn't respect her cleverness, and it irked them that she had been included as an equal member of their team. In their disrespect they made their position more foolish—because when the men failed to offer a solution, the Architect raised an eyebrow to the woman.

"What would you do?" he asked her.

She looked all around—at the ferns, at the trees, at the steep hill down which they had scrambled to reach this rock. Her hair had been washed in the river that morning and shone like light. A thin red line marked her face where a branch had slapped across her cheek and eyebrow.

"I know what to do."

The four men looked at her suspiciously, but the Architect nodded. One man opened his mouth to say, Explain—but she quelled him with a look that might kill a bull. From that moment the Angry Woman became the team's leader.

The Architect left his team prizing loose their stone and went back to Newgrange. He asked the women to assemble the children of the hillside—he said he needed helpers, and he chose teams of boy-and-girl pairs.

Next day, he led the first pair, a ten-year-old boy and the Angry Woman's young daughter, out into the countryside. Both children carried small bunches of pointed twigs. When he found a stone he wanted to build with, the Architect directed one of the children to plant a pointed stick beside it.

Some days later, he went back to find the Angry Woman and her coworkers. They had lifted the stone and left the grove; all he saw was a wide, shallow crater of brown earth. He followed the trail they had gouged in the earth with their big rock, and at last, from a hilltop, he saw them down at the river. The Angry Woman had thought to cut down trees and use the trunks as rollers across the country-side. Now, at the riverbank, she had ordered the men to build a lit-tle pier of smaller rocks and tree branches. They'd rolled the stone onto this jetty and then lashed the logs together and made a raft. She'd made them double the structure, building one raft on top of another with some overlaps to guarantee buoyancy.

"It'll float better," she said.

Her calculation worked. As the Architect watched, they eased the stone onto the raft and no catastrophe occurred. After a slight dip and some shaky moments, the raft with the rock sat afloat the river Boyne. All four men stood in the water, ready to guide it, and the woman climbed onto the stone on the raft.

They moved as fast as the river's current. The Architect kept pace with them along a ridge above the riverbank. What a pleasing sight! A great, flat, sand-colored rock sitting like a captured animal astride a raft of tree trunks tied with soft, springy branches—and the Angry Woman lying face down on the stone, using her hands as oars.

And so, after many hours, they came safely to Newgrange, where, with much commotion, they rolled the great stone up the hill. The Architect and his workers put it in place, and that stone now stands at the entrance to his mysterious structure.

For the next twelve years the people of Newgrange made hundreds of these journeys for stone. No idle day passed; every morning, hail, rain, or snow, parties of workers left the hillside, traveled to some distant rock marked by the Architect and his child helpers, and hauled it back to the hill.

In the process they developed the first roads in county Meath. A team hauling a stone through the countryside would come across a great brown scar in the earth, and they'd know it was the mark left by a previous team hauling a rock. If they followed this trail, it would lead—often, but not always—to the water. By the end of the first year, three hundred people were employed hauling stones from distances of up to thirty miles away.

Most of these workers came from the ranks of the least skilled. The Architect thought of them the way a queen bee thinks of her drones. He gave them miserable lives, using them as he wanted, with no consideration; indeed, he scarcely seemed to regard them as human. In his eyes they all had only one purpose—his purpose. No allowances were made for age or sex; a girl of fourteen worked as rough and raw as an old man of forty-four—and forty-four was old in those days.

They suffered frightful injuries. In the cold weather their hands froze to the surface of the stone. They slipped on the rocks, and the bindings made of thin branches ripped their flesh. Flash floods on the water left them gasping and terrified—or dead on the riverbed. Hauling stones across the steep landscape, their bones snapped, their backs broke. Many of them, men, women and children, became cripples for life.

The hazards increased. As the Architect developed the site, he chose larger and larger stones. Some rocks fell on the laborers, pinning or shattering an arm or a leg. Or a boulder keeled over, bringing instant death through a crushed skull or rib cage. When that happened, he ordered the corpse hauled to one side and left there for the family to collect. Nothing, he said, must interfere with the work. A hard man when young, he grew harder with age.

He reserved his tenderness for his materials. When a new rock arrived, he paid it as much attention as a cat to her kitten, stroking, measuring, examining each side, each surface, each little ripple. When he supervised the final placing of a stone, people nearby observed that he spoke more quietly than his normal, high-pitched rasp.

And while he hardened at work, he seemed, in himself, to have become a somewhat happy man. Certainly a fulfilled one—he'd embarked upon a great enterprise and felt himself succeeding at it. Away from the site, he seemed more approachable, and some people surmised that he might have softened, perhaps changed; he looked easier, less tense and hostile.

The Angry Woman's admiration for him grew and grew. She thought him wonderful. He possessed qualities she wanted in a man; he was strong, he was decisive, he was inspired. So she stayed near him, and without ever asking him, she appointed herself his closest helper.

When he forgot to eat, she brought him food. When he looked exhausted, she suggested rest. If some good news reached the hillside, she brought it to him first. And she tried not to allow herself to feel slighted when he retired to his house at the end of every day without inviting her, sometimes without seeming to see that she existed.

She told herself, "I shall ignore the hurt. I shall be patient. I shall content myself to wait. Then one day, when all this has been completed, he'll take me into his life."

He made one gesture that encouraged her to bide her time. Six years into the enterprise, her daughter reached the age of fourteen, old enough to work as a messenger. The Architect appointed her into his service. The girl was delighted—but not nearly as pleased as her mother. After all, no one knew him as well or saw more of him. She knew his moods, his tempests.

What she didn't know was the fear under which he worked. Everywhere he went, he could see the sleek face of the Silken Elder, watching him, eyeing him, always calculating. The fat man had taken great care to assess constantly what the hillside thought of the Architect. Every adverse or envious word added grist to his mill, and he repeated them willingly to all who'd listen. The Architect never heard these scraps of calumny or gossip because he kept himself so aloof, but he never doubted what the Silken Elder was doing—he was plotting.

And all the while, those magnificent rocks continued to arrive on the green slopes of Newgrange like some breed of strange animal. Some gleamed like flowers in the sun. Others seemed darker—but if you looked closely, you could see they had souls.

The most beautiful specimens went straight to the carvers. In the beginning the Architect declared that certain stones would bear messages to their ancestors—words of gratitude, symbols of praise. This work would take as long, he said, as the building itself. He

chose the most skilled men and women to make these designs—
and remember, their only tools were stone.

They tapped and leveled and etched and caressed; each day
brought a small advance or a giant leap—a tendril materializing, a
whorl beginning to uncoil; the Architect drew the design in the
mud, they copied it. They alone never feared the Architect, and in
return, he made them into an elite group of Newgrange society.

By the end of the twelfth year most of the construction work was
done, as the Architect had promised. But now he came to a stand-
still, facing a sharp and important challenge. He wanted different
stones, beautiful stones, for the front of the building, the facade,
but he didn't know where to find them—and already he had gathered every significant rock within a radius of forty miles.

Fortune rode in, as fortune will for those she favors. One day a little round boat, like a bowl made of cowhide, bounced up the river
Boyne. Inside it sat a small man with no hair, who looked up and
admired the great work-in-progress, all those huge stones forming a
wonderful giant ring embedded in the earth of the hill.

To him, a stranger, the edifice seemed astounding. Indeed, it
seemed no less amazing to the people of Newgrange, who had
watched it rise stone by stone. Whether shown naked in the light
after rain or shrouded in the mists of the dawn or casting long shadows down the hillside's evening, the building had a power to make
you stop and look at it many, many times every day.

Now the little bald man in his bowl of a boat saw it and couldn't
take his eyes off it. Then he told the people of Newgrange that, where
he came from, he had seen stones that looked as white as the moon.

The Angry Woman rushed to tell this news to the Architect, and
the next day he and she set out from Newgrange. In the boat with
them sat the little bald man, and they towed his coracle behind them.
When they reached the moment where the river Boyne joins the sea,
they sailed five days south. Then they entered the mouth of another
river and followed it inland. That journey came to more than seventy
miles.

Out of the boat they climbed, and the little bald man led them over two hills down into a large hollow. There was grass overgrowing everything, but when they scrabbled at it they found underneath precisely what the Architect wanted—loose rocks of all sizes, stones so beautiful that he believed they had been hidden there for him to find. They did indeed look like the moon—they looked like silver dipped in cream, pearls that the gods had hidden in the grass to be stumbled upon like treasure. The Architect knelt to look at them, stroked them, examined them; it was the only time the Angry Woman ever saw him close to tears. Now he believed that his great task was slowly coming to a wonderful end.

So for the next three years, when the leaves came back on the trees in the spring, a hundred boats took to the waters of the Boyne and disappeared round the bend in the river to fetch those wonderful stones from Wicklow. After the first few trips, the Architect rarely went again—because he had yet to face the biggest challenge of all.

One sunlit morning, the people of Newgrange looked across at the distant ridge and saw a man behaving strangely. Sometimes he stood and made a frame of his arms against the sun, or he turned to face the four corners of the world. Soon they realized that the distant figure was the Architect. But what was he doing, they asked themselves—inspecting the world?

As they watched, he descended the ridge and returned to the hillside, where he also stood and framed his arms to the sun. With an array of sticks, long and short, with stones placed at intervals along the ground, he took measurements, paced out distances, eyed levels. He directed some of the children to gather a collection of small but long stones. Each stood perhaps no more than a foot high, and he built a little corridor of these, covered it with a tunic, and knelt before it, holding a rush light, then a torch under the tunic.

They thought he was trying to measure the length of the sun's rays on the grass. That is indeed what he was doing, and more than that: he was measuring the effect of light upon everything—on his fingers; against stones of various heights; amongst the shadows of the trees, upon the ridge of the hill. Sometimes he came down to the work-places or the dwellings, took hold of the first person he saw, and made them stand still while he measured their shadow on the grass. To their intense curiosity, he would walk in a circle around them, or crawl on the ground by their feet, grunting and thinking.

Naturally, nobody asked him what he was doing; by now they'd learned not to. But in front of their eyes, a great idea was being born. Every morning, afternoon, or evening, on every slope of the ridge or every level of the hillside, where he held his hands to shade against the sun or measured the different lengths of a woman's shadow and that of her child's, he advanced the cause of science and therefore Man's understanding of the universe.

At last, at long last, came the day when everything seemed ready. All his measurements were taken, all his calculations were sealed. Now the building was finished. Now the carvings had been com-pleted. And now the last stones were set in place. What a long trial it had been, the mornings of extracting one more effort from the builders, the afternoons of preventing one more whorl from crack-ing in the last throes of its carving, the evenings of despair that not enough stones had yet been found and ferried, and the nights of fear that nothing would come of it all.

In recent months the Architect had allowed himself to stand halfway up the hillside and look at his work, and he even began to permit himself to admire it. As he did so, others often drifted by, notably some of the Elders, who finally—but cautiously—asked if he could set a day for the opening ceremony. He replied, with a blitheness that surprised them, "Of course."

But he had known since the beginning of the project what day he would choose. It had always been his intention to have the monu-ment unveiled only on the December solstice, the shortest day of the year. No other day would do.

He had never told anyone this, lest his experiments fail him. Had anyone known his intention, they would have called him foolish beyond belief—because the risk he had taken, the idea into which he had plunged all his efforts and fifteen years of his people's hardest labor, was something that had, at best, a very difficult chance of succeeding. He and he alone knew that, for the success of his project, he required this midwinter day deep in December to dawn with bright sunshine.

Was he mad? Would the sun shine at dawn, without fail, in the middle of winter on a foggy island in the northwest of Europe? If anyone had guessed his plans, they'd have dismissed him as even crazier than he so often seemed.

Of course he was the only one who knew the magnitude of this gamble. The Elders merely professed their pleasure at his choice of date—a great feast day, the moment of the year when their forefathers slept deepest. But the Architect—he felt nothing beyond a dull numbness. Men had died, babies had been born, new people had come to Newgrange, others had left to venture into the interior of Ireland, and still he went on building his monument. Now the end had almost arrived; tomorrow his great inspiration would be put to the test in front of everyone.

He wasn't yet excited at the thought of all his planning and experimentation bearing fruit. Nor did he dwell on what the Silken Elder would do to his body in the Recompense if everything failed. Instead, memories came pouring back, especially when he thought of the most delicate and sensitive part of the building—a box of four flat stones placed above the door.

This was the same rectangular box whose picture he once drew in the mud—more frame than box, four sides with no lid and no base. Two of the stones were about four feet long and three feet wide, and the smaller two were three feet by one and a half. Not until almost every other aspect and detail of the building had been completed would he add this crucial detail, the most important single component.

Twice he had had to stop the builders filling the space for the box; twice he had had to explain that, yes, he wanted, he needed, a rectangle above the doorway, that he had a personal detail to complete, without which the building wouldn't be finished. They looked at him as they often did, somewhat vacantly, and they had to accept what he was saying.

To make the mortar, he chose, nabbed, and killed the calf himself, a russet and lively two-month-old; he slit its velvet throat while its mother lowed in anguish a hundred yards away. Then he pulled back the head and drained the blood, with the Angry Woman holding the stone basin. Next, two of the horses on the hillside yielded much of their tails to his knife, and he then mixed the mortar of blood and horsehair himself. Finally, he erected the box with his own hands, would trust nobody else with it.

So, late in the afternoon, on the eve of the great day, reviewing all of these memories, the Architect decided he would take one last look. The hillside teemed like an anthill—tables out, pigs roasting, women and children building fires to stay alight all the next day and night. At the entrance to the building, he climbed up to look at the four flat slabs in the mysterious rectangle. The guards at the door, one old, one young, looked away lest he see them staring at him. He climbed down, and stooping his great head and shoulders, he walked into the tomb.

You remember the momentous day he made his drawings in the mud of the riverbank? You recollect the diagram he etched in the mud—a round structure with a long line ending in a cross? This building of his was what archaeologists and historians call a passage tomb, and now, finished, it completely represented the Architect's drawings come to life. The line he etched was the passageway, and it led to the cross that he drew—a wide chamber at the very heart of the tomb.

Along the passageway he went, between the slender rocks, toward the chamber. Before the gloom became too dense, he let himself admire the handiwork. He loved the way his masons had merged the carved stones into the sidewalls. And he acknowledged how faithfully the mud patterns had been carved into the rocks or, in some cases, embossed.

Here and there he stopped to caress the shapes. He stroked stern triangles and merry whorls, geometric chevrons that looked like worried frowns, smiling triskelia and swirls, a little rippling field of diamond patterns, sweet presences on and in stone. They reflected the world around Newgrange—the triangles made by the hilltops in certain phases of light; the rings on a tree's trunk; the eddies and whirls of the river Boyne.

The Architect reached the inner chamber, where the building's heart opened out into a domed room. Earlier in the afternoon he had placed a small bowl of fire, a rush light, in the chamber entrance. He picked this up and raised it to inspect the highest points of the chamber—more symbols carved into the stones, the juts on the walls, the domed shape deriving from methodical corbeling, which imitates the way a crow's upper beak protrudes over, and is supported by, its lower beak. And as you know, another word for "crow" is *corby* in Scotland, or, in France, *corbeau.*

Walking round and round, looking at every stone, checking, touching, feeling all the surfaces, all the notchings, all the symbols, the Architect came to a stop at the back of the chamber, directly in line with the passageway. Carefully, with great reverence, he dropped to his knees.

Inside the chamber lay a huge, round, smooth dish made of sand-colored stone. To achieve its glossy finish took more days than anyone could count. Initially, the Architect selected a flattish stone and told the Carvers to hollow it out. Then he watched over them as they polished and polished with their primitive tools. This was his massive vessel for the cult of his people's dead.

He placed the light bowl on the floor and began to inspect the huge stone dish. Still on his knees, he bent low, almost sniffing its smooth, curved rim. He leaned right in, deep over it, the better to see its heart. Then he lowered himself to the ground until he lay flat prone, his chin almost at the dish's rim. He squinted across the rim into the passageway and narrowed his eyes for a long time, assessing and thinking. When he rose, he dusted himself down and bowed respectfully to the dish.

One last time he walked around it, stopping here and there, always looking from the passageway to the dish and back again. He shook his head many times, as if marveling at what he had found in here. What was the dish for? He and he alone knew. Tomorrow,

everyone else would know—if the skies stayed clear. A big *if.* He left
the chamber.

The wind had freshened, and he immediately looked up at the sky,
hoping, hoping—so far, so good. His messenger hovered outside
the entrance, waiting for him. He found this odd. The girl's value
lay in the fact that she did her work soundlessly and almost invisi-
bly. Yet every place he had gone that afternoon, she seemed to be in
front of him. Now he looked closer at her; there must be something
wrong. She held up a hand and beckoned him. Suddenly he saw
that she seemed very concerned, and he followed her as she led him
out of the guards' earshot.

"Sir, you must hear what I have to say."

Her voice was full of breath, but she spoke the words as directly
as her mother would; then she walked past him very quickly.

"At the top of the hill," she said. "Where they spread the skins to
dry."

He nodded—and what she said next astonished him.

"Go up there, sir. I will meet you. Order the older of those two
guards to join you. When you're among the trees, kill him immediately."

The girl looked terrified. She was now in her twenties and very beautiful; the Architect had known her long enough to trust her completely.

She ran off on a deceptive path, across the hill in the opposite
direction, giving the impression as she went that she pursued some
errand on which he had sent her.

Strolling to the doorway of the tomb, he commanded the
younger guard to fetch four men, whom he named. He waited at
the door until they arrived. Then he gave them their orders—guard
the entrance with their lives, let no one in—then stood down the
junior guard and beckoned to the senior one.

In single file they walked quickly up the steepest part of the hill,
past the Long House. At the top, he veered right, hearing the guard
breathing heavily behind him.

Up on the high slope, men and women worked on the skins,
scraping and cleaning. The stench, which everybody else found

appalling, pleased the Architect in some way he never quite understood. All the skinners rose and stood respectfully, their backs turned, as he passed by. Ahead, he could see the gap in the trees.

The senior guard lurched awkwardly and dropped his stone axe. That was a serious offence for a guard—a slovenly matter, like a soldier dropping his gun. The man scrambled for the axe and began to yammer to himself. Fear had struck him. He and the Architect cleared the far side of the bank and walked into the shade of the trees.

Then the guard moaned, a low moan; he was growing hysterical. Suddenly, in a little open space ahead, the messenger appeared— and the guard screamed.

The blow that struck the man in the knob of his throat drove his head back so far that it seemed to hang down his spine. For the rest of her long life the messenger remembered the sound of that blow—a kind of dull crack, like a stone hammering down on a smooth log. The Architect had delivered the blow with the edge of his hand.

He went forward, to hear what she had to say.

"The Elder," she said, trembling. "You know which one. He's been talking to that guard. They have people waiting up here."

"People?"

Other than lone travelers, such as the little bald man in the coracle, few people visited Newgrange. Those who did come by never surprised the residents; the view from the hill revealed the river east and west for long stretches; and the hillside's peak offered a view for miles.

"Beyond the river bend. I'll show you. Where the black rocks are," she said.

That was the one place whence someone could approach Newgrange unseen. As they trotted forward, she said, "They're to come in early tomorrow. Before dawn. They have many, many weapons."

"How do you know?"

"I followed the Elder. That's how I saw them. And I heard him telling them. The guard saw me"

"Why didn't you tell me earlier?"

"I've only known since noon. And I'm so afraid of you, sir, I can't speak easily to you."

He reached out and patted her hair. They stopped whispering and trotted on through the wood.

As they climbed out of a gully, the girl dropped to her haunches and pointed. Ahead, two men stood under a tree, guarding the path.

The Architect signaled her to hide. From a small canyon she watched him slink like an animal into the bracken. In a moment or two she saw him again—on the top branches of the largest tree. She had known that men were required to endure severe trials before warriorhood; one of these required them to move through the woods without disturbing a leaf or breaking a twig. Many of the boys and girls discussed these tests endlessly and tried to imitate them, hoping they too would join the warrior elite. Few of them made it. Now, she was watching this power at work.

The Architect flattened himself along the thickest branch of his tree and looked down. Below him, the two sentries stood close together, blocking the narrow path. The Architect edged along his branch and eased himself onto a much thicker bough, directly above the two guards. Nothing in their behavior suggested that the guards heard anything more than the breeze through the leaves.

Many times in her life the girl told the story of what happened next.

In each hand the Architect held a stone larger than his own fist. Then, as lazily as a man waking from a warm sleep, he rolled his body around and dropped from the branch. Against the sky the girl saw his body fall, his hair like a lion's mane—and she saw his hands connect with the guards' heads. They were dead before she heard their skulls crack.

The Architect picked up each body and pitched it into the undergrowth as though tossing a log on a fire. That a man capable of such delicate calculation, sensitive enough to judge the force of the wind and the brightness of the sun, should also possess such massive strength made her marvel evermore at the mention of his name.

The girl didn't move forward to join him until he beckoned. Now they ran on, and she led. Presently, she darted to the left and led him up rocky and dark ways where there was no path.

High on a hill, where brambles and briars clustered in the deep furze, she dropped to her hands and knees, as did he. She pointed, then watched him lean forward and look down.

Below them, on the flat stones by the river, a wide camp of armed men made preparations to destroy the Architect and his work and his people and his life. In their midst stood his old enemy, the fat and sleek Silken Elder, talking to a big-eared stranger.

The Architect and his messenger eased back from their hiding place and ran home without stopping. He warned her to speak nothing of what she knew. His hands on her quaking shoulders, he said, "You've done better than any man."

In Newgrange, all warriors lived and worked in the House of the Axes. They spent many of their days making new weapons and sharpening old ones. The Architect went there now. For the next three hours he explained the enterprise and supervised the preparations for an attack.

"Swiftness and silence—that's what I want, above all. Be vicious. Be silent. Be swift. I will lead you."

They stripped down to the minimum of clothing. They greased their bodies with pig fat. They checked their weapons: stubby, pointed hazel sticks, charred for hardness; the short stone axes preferred by some of the younger warriors; and leather slings full of fist-sized rocks that had been shaped into jagged spikes.

Into the night the Architect led a force of eight men and six women. They stole down to the river by a pathway where nobody on the hillside would see them. The six women fell in directly behind him, two by two, each one fearsome in battle. Then came the eight men, and everyone ran light as dancers over the ground and clambered into the boats.

The Architect could see dimly behind him the shape of each boat. His orders to them had been to keep as close to the near bank as possible. Although the leaves had all gone, overhanging branches gave them good shelter.

He checked the skies again. From tomorrow, he would no longer have a crick in his neck from looking upward. Every day recently, and sometimes it seemed to him every minute of every day for the last fifteen years, he had stared at the sky. Tonight all was clear; no moon, with stars sprinkled everywhere.

"Stay bright," he whispered up to the heavens. "This night of all nights! This coming dawn of all dawns! Stay bright!"

The gentle slap of the oars in the water, the lapping of the river against the nearby bank—the world wished to calm him. Behind, his boats paddled in the lee waters of the riverbank with the gentlest of sounds. The black stones of the promontory began to show. Further along and in from the water, he saw the glow of a dying campfire.

But—no guards on the river! What kind of fighters or wild raiders were these? Were they arrogant? No—they were careless. And had they not yet missed the two western sentries whose skulls he had loved cracking?

He said to himself, "I'm lucky tonight. My messenger brings me good luck. Maybe I'll be lucky tomorrow, too."

His boat nudged ashore with a tiny crunch, and he eased himself out. Behind him, all the others disembarked and, as he did, crouched on the flat stones right by the water.

Stay close! his gestures told them. Stay for the moment. He ran forward crouching, searching for the heavy shape of the Silken Elder. Nothing but embers remained of the fire. Bodies lay slumped all across the camp. These were mostly young men, and young men make heavy sleepers. No matter where he searched, he found no trace of the Silken Elder's fat bulk.

His comrades arrayed themselves in two lines either side of him. Crouching, he went forward again, the others tiptoeing with him. Within a moment or two he came to the first sleeping body. Reaching down, the eyes of the others watching him, he stifled the man's mouth and nose with a fierce hand and swiftly cut the throat with his sharpest bone knife. It took less than two seconds. The man sagged back with a gurgle. The Architect held the head until it stopped writhing—the man never knew how he died.

Nearby lay two other sleeping bodies; he directed a woman and a man to kill them in the same way. Again, not a sound. He and his warriors slipped like shadows from body to body, cutting and killing and, in some cases, strangling.

Nobody made a noise—until almost the last sleeper. He woke, sat up close to the dying fire, saw them, and shouted. But the man died as he yelled—one of the warrior women rammed a stone into his mouth and down his throat. A last man also started to shout—an axe in the Adam's apple killed him. Afterward, the raiders darted here and there like cats, checking that each body was truly lifeless. Others tested the camp's boundaries in case sentries had been posted out there.

The Architect himself went to the fire and threw on a log, made it brighter. Where was the Silken Elder? He wanted to silence that smooth, insulting voice and bring him home to expose his treachery. No sign of the man—not on the ground, not among the many bodies. He picked up one enemy weapon, a knife, then another, a spear. These had been made of something different—not stone, but something just as hard. But these weapons felt lighter, and very much sharper, and they gleamed in the glow of the fire.

The Architect instructed two of his fighters to collect all the raiders' weapons, which made a clanging noise, the way their own stone knives and wooden spears never did. Soon all the swords and knives and spears lay in a pile by the rekindled fire at the feet of the Newgrange warriors.

Flames from the campfire lit their triumphant faces. Excited eyes and greased bodies glinted in the dark. One laughing woman wiped a splash of blood off her bare shoulder. They began to chatter as all excited people do, but the Architect held a hand up to silence them. He had heard something.

Before anyone else could move, he grabbed a knife from the pile, turned, and ran to the water. Someone had stolen one of the boats. The Architect swam to it and caught the stern. Turning, the escaper tried to lash out with the paddle, but the Architect grabbed it and dragged the fugitive into the water.

His fighters raced to the flat stones to help their leader. All looked shocked when they recognized his captive—the Silken Elder. Smooth as ever, the fat man began to babble. The Architect grabbed the man's face, forced open his mouth, and rammed in a fold of wet hide. He then tied a strip of the hide around the Elder's mouth. They trussed the man with skins and dumped him into a boat.

When they got back to Newgrange, it was past midnight. Music and laughter carried on the wind; torches and bonfires blazed. On the riverbank, the Architect praised his warriors. At his direction, four men carried the Silken Elder by a dark route to the Long House and hid him, bound and gagged, under a pile of skins at the rear.

Bowing one by one to their leader, the other fighters scattered. The Architect turned away from them and walked toward the great white shape that dominated the hillside—his creation, his master-piece.

"Not long now," he murmured, and looked at the sky; it was clear as a night could be. "Not long."

Back in his house, his messenger lay asleep, and he trod softly in order not to wake her. She had left some meat and milk on the floor by his bed. He ate and drank. The girl woke, rose, and came forward silently. She had never so deeply resembled her mother—but without the angry face. He reached to her face and put both his hands to her cheeks, the most coveted gesture of approval.

Then the Architect placed his hands on her shoulders and embraced her, and from that moment she knew that if all wishes came true, she would spend the rest of her life by his side and bear his children. He lay down on his own bed and closed his eyes, but he didn't sleep. The girl sat by, watching over him, knowing that this might be the last night of his life.

Exactly one hour later, lit by a single rush light, the Architect stood in the center of the Long House and told the Elders what had happened in the night. He described his messenger's discovery, the attack on the two sentries, the verification that an enemy party had gathered, the night raid, the trussed betrayer, the remarkable new weapons. The Elders, without saying so, knew what had to happen next: the fat man had to die—but in accordance with custom he would be allowed last words to the people, because he was an Elder.

They decided to untie him, take the leather gag from his mouth, and let him stand before the people; then he would be denounced and killed. Four guards fetched the disheveled man—who hadn't surrendered any of his suave manner. The Chief Elder addressed him and summarized the man's offenses. He told him that he'd be granted his right to speak. After that, the Architect would deliver the Recompense—which was also the punishment for treachery.

In his smoothest voice the Silken Elder began to protest. "Don't believe these lies about me," he said, but the Chief Elder turned away.

The procession of the Elders formed up and went outside. What a great sight they saw! All along the hillside, the people stood by their bonfires, and they waved and called to the Elders to visit them. Everywhere, the children held out gifts of food and drink. The Elders, including the fat man, walked among them, accepting something from everyone, stroking the children's heads, praising the gifts—all in flickering, firelit darkness. Skin drums beat rhythms, reed pipes played; boys and girls laughed.

Slowly and joyously, winding by every bonfire on the hill, this procession at last reached the entrance to the circular white building, and the Elders turned to face the chanting, swaying crowds. Behind them, the white high walls of their mysterious and great monument reflected the firelight.

Easily the tallest among them, the Architect stood at the edge of the group. His Elders' pride in him showed—the Eldresses touched his arms, his hands. Someone tapped his shoulder and he glanced around—the Angry Woman. He looked at her as though expecting reproof; once the building work had been finished, he had seen little of her, and he expected that she grieved. But instead she clasped his hand, looked into his eye, and said, "Thank you for the trust you've placed in me and mine." And she slipped back into the crowd to enjoy the Architect's triumph.

Tawny and strong, like a lion in his pride, he looked all around Newgrange—at the happy people, the piles of food, their bowls of drink, the lights reflecting on the dark river flowing below. For this moment he had devoted every ounce of spirit he could find within him, day in, day out, every minute, every second, every hour, every breath of the last fifteen years.

The Chief Elder made a grand gesture with his arm, and the Speakers came forward. At large gatherings long before megaphones or public address systems, Speakers, men chosen for their loud voices, relayed the words of the speech throughout the crowd. When the orator spoke, the Speaker nearest to him called it out to the crowd around him, where the next Speaker picked it up and relayed it onwards—and so on, until everyone there had heard every word the orator had to say.

Off to the east, a long stripe of lemon light began to paint the sky, and the Architect knew they must hurry. On a wood pipe the Caller blew what sounded like an everlasting note, and he didn't stop until silence had fallen across Newgrange. At intervals down the hillside, each waiting speaker looked to the Chief Elder. From his place at the heart of his semicircle of Elders, the old man began to speak. Beside him stood the Silken Elder, who had the right to speak too, even interrupt.

"My people!"

"My people!" the Speakers echoed.

"In a moment you shall hear the voice of another Elder. You shall know that he is speaking because it's the last right of anyone who betrays us to tell us his thoughts."

The Speakers looked so surprised that some of them almost failed to relay these words. A moan of wonder rose from the crowd.

"The Elder was found to have befriended a party of invaders. They intended to capture all we own and make us their slaves."

The moan from the crowd became a shout—which the Speakers quelled with warning gestures.

"But"—the Chief Elder turned to his right and pointed to the Architect—"this man, who in the coming dawn will honor our dead with this great new monument, discovered the treachery. He and our warriors killed the raiders, and brought back the betrayer to face death."

Cheers rose, and the warriors who had been on the raid raised their bare arms and shook their fists to the stars.

"Therefore"—now the Chief Elder pointed to the betrayer—"you know what will happen to him. He'll give Recompense."

At this the crowd fell silent. Those among them who had seen such a fate talked of little else for months afterward.

Some voices protested, "No!"

The Silken Elder stepped forward two paces, setting himself up in a more prominent position than his Chief, who spoke again.

"But I shall begin with the words chosen for this great day. I shall reveal to you Blessings which shall be ours and our children's and their children's."

The Speakers relayed these words, and the Silken Elder stepped forward another pace. Now he stood near the front edge of the crowd. He looked all around, like a man seeking a way of escape. Yet he made no move; he waited until all the Chief Elder's words had been passed on, right down to the crowd at the lowest level, down to the bonded, the slaves, and the unsound, whose place was by the water. Then he spoke.

"And today, I shall reveal to you curses under which each of you and each of your children's children shall labor forever."

The Elders muttered. If they could have done so, some would have killed the man then and there. But the Chief Elder, who knew that a man's own bitterness condemns him, said, "We shall always be blessed with a land full of milk and honey, the riches of the earth."

The betrayer countered: "But quarrels over land will set father against son, brother against brother, husband against wife."

The crowd began to shift, uncomfortable and confused.

"Our descendants," intoned the Chief Elder, "shall be men of strength and wisdom, women of beauty and love."

The fat man waited, then cried out, "But we shall abuse and disrespect our children without reason."

"Never!" shouted angry people on the slopes.

By now the Chief Elder wished this to end. He spoke his next blessing; "Though strangers may come among us and attempt to defile us, they shall not prevail."

"You shall be conquered again and again," roared the Silken Elder. "Your seed, breed, and generations shall be made subject to others."

The Chief Elder spoke again.

"Our fighting men will become feared wherever water flows or birds fly."

"Your fighting men will destroy the root of thought, the soul of reason."

The betrayer's voice carried much farther than that of the frailer Chief Elder. And he spoke his words much more fiercely. But suddenly, he stumbled. His hands trembled, and his knees shook.

The Chief Elder spoke again. "Our ancestors shall bless us. They shall visit us here, on this hillside, again and again."

The Silken Elder recoiled, stumbled once more. For years he had tried to discover what lay at the core of the Architect's plan—he had always feared that the Architect would outwit him by forging some new connection to the past and would indeed create, as he had promised, something wonderful. Now the rage he'd contained for fifteen years attacked him. His chest felt on fire—he could scarcely speak, he was so angry.

"Our ancestors," he cried, shouting so loudly that no Speaker felt the need to carry his words forward, "will be misrepresented. Men will use the power of the past to give themselves the power of the future!"

He screamed the final words and drew himself up and back, like a man suffering a mortal blow. Those nearest to him saw that his face grew as pale as the stones from the quarries of Wicklow.

The Chief Elder knew what was happening. A year ago, the Silken Elder had come to him and said he had been suffering pains in his chest. Cures were offered and taken. Nothing further had been said. Now the Chief Elder smiled benignly at the betrayer.

"I have a last and most wonderful blessing. In time we shall spread our breed and our blood. To other lands. To other people. Everywhere we go, we shall always be known to come of this land. And we shall be known as people who bring bright light wherever they go."

He stepped back. A cheer began—a cheer that would and should have been mighty. But the Silken Elder staggered forward and began to speak. His voice had grown so weak that two of the nearest Speakers ran to his side to hear what he had to say. These were his words.

"It shall indeed be the case that your children and their children and their children's children forever will go to other lands and be among other people. But your descendants will leave because this land will drive them out, drive them away. Will not be able to sustain them. Will not be able to give them enough food and drink—"

He stopped, incapable. His words had been uttered with such passion and feeling that the Speakers who relayed them gave them a respect close to fear. The last voice of the last Speaker, echoing down by the reeds and the rushes, died away. In complete silence every eye watched the torchlit events on the hill.

The Silken Elder raised himself for one last time to his full height. He had something else to say. While his right hand clutched at his chest, he held out his left hand and used the index finger as a rigid pointing arrow, which traveled round the semicircle of the Elders. He lurched forward, intending to stab his pointing finger into the Architect's chest. But he made no more than a few steps before he collapsed on his face. His forehead struck the stone step at the entrance to the tomb so loudly that the crack echoed in the dawn.

Somewhere a night bird called, a warbling, melodic sound.

Nobody ever knew what killed the Silken Elder—was it the pain in his chest or the cracking of his head on the wide, thick, flat stone? All the watchers saw was a fat man who had been one of their chosen number, now revealed as a traitor, lying dead at their feet in the entrance to the tomb. Blood began to seep from his nose onto the stone. In the silence the Chief Elder gestured the guards to remove the fallen man's robe and take away the corpse. And in the silence the Chief Elder draped the robe on the shoulders of the Architect.

A baby cried somewhere. The Architect turned to look at the ridge, and as brightening light seeped upward from the east, he beckoned the Elders into the mouth of the monument. In total darkness they followed him tentatively, heads bent slightly so as not to hit the stones of the roof. Ahead they could see the flickering lamp. When their eyes became accustomed to the gloom, they began to admire the rocks, the structure, the carved symbols.

They reached the central chamber. The Architect arranged the group in a semicircle behind the polished stone dish. For a moment he held up the small lamp so that the Elders could inspect the chamber. Each felt overcome with wonder at the magnificence, the elaborateness, the enormous magic of it all. When the Architect blew out the light, total darkness fell, black as a mine—and outside the dawn began to spread across a sky as clear as joy.

Nobody spoke. One or two coughed; the Chief Elder breathed heavily. Someone shifted from one foot to the other. Soon the breathing of the group melded into one rhythm, as though they had all fallen asleep standing up.

The Architect never took his eyes off the passageway. He waited and waited. Not for a moment did he fear the Elders' impatience. The earlier events had dismayed them, but what they were about to see would renew them as never before. He stared toward the passageway, and his heart began to sing.

"Look," he told the Elders. "Look toward the door!"

That morning was the winter solstice, the twenty-first day of December. Outside the tomb, the upper rim of the sun's disc had begun to peep over the top of the ridge. Without mathematical instruments, calibrations, or any of our scientific tools, no compasses, setsquares, sextants, or slide rules, the Architect had calculated that, each December solstice, the people of Newgrange would

invite the rising sun to enter the tomb through the little rectangle
of the four flat stones above the door. If the sun accepted the invitation—that is, if the clouds permitted—the sun's ray would travel
along the passageway as the sun rose, and when fully risen would
come to rest in the stone dish.

Imagine his judgments: from the stars, from the skies of winter
and summer, from the speed of the sun's rising, taking into account
the height of the hillside, the depth of the building, the color and
thickness of the stone, the length of the passageway. He had calculated miraculously.

At the farthest end of the tomb, red-gold colors tinged the edges
of the rectangular aperture, making it look like a box full of light.
Next, a shaft of sunshine slid through the box and lit the floor, just
inside the entrance.

The Elders watched this glow and became transfixed. Not a word,
not a sound, did they make. Outside, the sun had started to climb
over the ridge. Inside, the shaft of light, beaming through the narrow little box over the door, began to travel slowly toward them.

Steadily, with no jumps, no lurches, the light filtered down the
passageway. Its golden yellow beam, thick as a man's arm, flowed
slowly, slowly—it was as though the sunlight was honey from a
bowl that someone had tipped over and spilled into a long, pleasant stream.

The Architect could scarcely breathe. It had worked! After all,
after everything, the rain, the blood, the deaths, the cracked bones,
the stone, the fatigue—it had worked! He clasped his hands tight to
his chest, a rare display of feeling.

When the sunbeam reached the edge of the chamber, its yellow-
orange light began to glow upward into the gathering, gilding the
Elders' faces. The ray seemed to hesitate for a moment. And then it
surged forward until it splashed into the great stone bowl. It began
to fill the dish—and it filled it exactly. Not a drop of sunshine
slipped over an edge—not here, there, or anywhere. The final resting place of the sun for that brief moment was precisely within the
full circumference of the bowl, leaving no area of the bowl's stone

surface dark or cold. It lay there like a golden sphere. Outside, the rising sun had just cleared the ridge.

"Here in this dish," pronounced the Architect, "we will warm again the bones of our beloved dead."

The Elders, one and all, began to weep. In the fire of the visiting sun their faces shone like the faces of children lit by a golden lamp. And then, as gently and as miraculously as it had come, the sun began to retreat, slipping down the passageway and finally sliding back out through the box of light to warm the rest of the world.

In Ireland since that morning, on every clear-skied December solstice except for those centuries when grass and foliage overgrew the tomb, that wondrous ray of light has responded to the Architect's great invitation and entered the building. When it lies in the stone dish, it looks as though the sun, the greatest god of our skies, now rendered mellow and sweet, has come to Earth for a golden moment—by wondrous invitation from the Architect of Newgrange.

And that's the end of my story tonight.

The Storyteller leaned back and surveyed his audience. Had he done well enough? The adults nodded their heads, smiling at each other in the shared experience. And the boy? He hugged himself with delight. No eyes in the room shone brighter; no stage drama or circus tent or cinema epic had matched this thrill.

"Well, well!" the boy's father said. "That's a tale and a half. You'll stay, I hope? And give us another story tomorrow night?"

As the room dispersed, the boy remained seated, watching the Storyteller's every move. This had reached far beyond any expectation or hope; in the color of the tale and the power of its narrator, the boy knew that he had met great, rare magic. And more than that—again and again, the Storyteller's eyes, dark as a gypsy's, had looked straight into his.

He went to bed in something of a trance—and with little chance of sleep. In the darkness he began to wonder if the Storyteller had come specifically for *him,* to seek *him* out, to tell *him* his tale—because it felt as though the Storyteller had addressed the story of Newgrange to him and him alone. Was this what people called "Fate"? What was the other word for it—*Destiny*? Would he, one day, leave this house and become a storyteller himself, traveling here, traveling there, welcomed in people's homes up and down the land, telling magnificent tales?

The year was 1951; the boy was named Ronan O'Mara—and even though he was only nine, he was ripe for change. He lived in a household where a blanket of seeming calm covered emotional tumult. An only child among three adults, he loved his father more dearly than anyone; John O'Mara told his son, "When you were

born, you had a round, serious face, with big eyes. Most babies look
like boxers—but you looked like a little seal, which is what the
name Ronan means." Ronan felt his father's warmth every day.
Some gesture, some new joke, some touch, some word, bound them
deeper. He still rode occasionally on his father's shoulders; during
mealtimes he often ate off his father's plate. At night, his father's
was the last face he saw and the last voice in his ear. Every morning
he heard the same warm words, "Come on, sleepyhead—the sun is
up before you."

They grew together like dear friends, rather than father and
child. A stick to be cut, a toy to be fixed, a wooden sword to be
made—with never a curt word the father taught the son every
skill a boy needs. He came to know the smell of his father's jackets, the gristled rub of his father's beard, the burls of his father's
hands.

The mother cast a darker shadow; she caused Ronan fright, confusion, and dismay. Where his father always smiled, his mother
seemed to frown every time she saw the boy. Alison was twenty-
eight when Ronan was born. Her young son was given to understand from an early age that he was her seventh and final and only
successful pregnancy; the previous six had miscarried. All his life he
never recalled how that information had come to him; from an
early age he merely knew that he knew—and that, as a consequence, he must demand little of her.

But he hoped eternally that she might cherish him more. Indeed,
as he grew older he often heard that an only child was a child
beloved of its mother. Not, it seemed, in his case, and as a young
adult he constantly asked himself: Why? Had she been afraid while
carrying him? All those previous stillbirths? Was he imperfect in
some way, a disappointment? Had she wanted a girl?

There had to be something—far from cherishing him, she acted
as though she found him irritating. She made him feel superfluous,
always getting in the way; he might have been one of ten children,
instead of the one and only. Her distant and almost hostile stance
baffled all who watched it, and her son most of all.

Ronan tried everything to please her; nothing worked. By the time he was five years old, he had learned not to bring her flowers from the fields—it embarrassed her. At six he bought her chocolates for her birthday; she said she had "gone off chocolates." And then came the scarf.

Red, and knit, it seemed, of gossamer, he had saved enough money from birthdays and visitors to buy it. His father whistled at the price and praised Ronan's prudence. The woman in the shop joined in the conspiracy and gave a discount.

"She'll love this. Red's grand with your mother's coloring, the black hair. And this is a one-and-only. Like yourself. A one-and-only. Like all of us, I s'pose, we're all one-and-only, aren't we?"

That night before supper, Ronan handed the package to his mother. She looked at it; he stood by, blinking a little.

"Open it," urged John quietly.

"Now?" she said.

"It's for your birthday," said Ronan.

"I don't need anything."

She opened the package. Ronan watched, and for a moment, Alison flickered. He knew he had struck gold—and then she recovered herself; "But—I have so many scarves."

That was all she said. He never saw the scarf again.

But sometimes, when Ronan was asleep, she slipped into his room and gazed down at him with a tenderness and a look of longing as deep as the sea, as though some wound in the relationship between woman and boy proved beyond her reach or repair.

The third adult in his life gave him love more abundant than life. Kate, his mother's younger sister, lived with the family, and she always smelled of some sweet thing. She hugged and kissed Ronan from infancy as though he were a small bear. He often awoke in her bed, where he had wandered in the night, and the world had no safer haven. As he grew older, she loved him even more demonstratively, and he relished all contact with her; she rewarded his every breath with a response as warm as his mother's was cold.

Kate chose his clothes, bathed him, wrapped him against the cold; Kate cured where the wasp stung him, collected jokes to tell him. She also taught him songs; perched high on the piano, he watched for her nod to join in, and she and his father laughed with delight when he hit his cue.

Nineteen when Ronan was born, Kate had turned twenty-eight a month before the Storyteller arrived. Without her, life in his mother's orbit would have been immeasurably colder. Kate took charge of his day-to-day worldly education—how to tie his shoe laces, how to use a toothbrush, how to wash his hair, how to count slowly to a hundred, breathing in and out so that he calmed down. And, born lovely, Kate stayed that way all her life.

Ronan O'Mara's life thus ricocheted from adult to adult. Consequently, he daydreamed lavishly, making himself the center of a world he had himself invented. For many of his free hours, especially when hurting from a clash with his mother, he roamed the countryside; he made the outdoors a second home.

All the terrain welcomed him. A deep wood rode down the hill almost to the backyard and became a secret universe. It teemed with wildlife; he watched foxes, badgers, rabbits, and birds. And deer; he learned their traces and scouted where they had lain. They left marks where they nibbled the trees, and he followed their trail to pools where they drank.

Upwind and downwind became his friends. He learned how to gauge the direction of the breeze by wetting his finger and holding it to the sky. When the rustling ground told him the deer were drawing near, he became a Sioux or a Cherokee and flitted from tree to tree. He held himself ready to trap and kill and return in triumph to his village with the buck draped over his shoulders. Or he chose to startle them and watch their high, sable bodies undulate like brown clowns across the rough ground.

Mostly he identified with them. They also held themselves distant, alert, ready to run at the slightest disturbance and escape along their private trails.

Ronan's bedroom faced south, over green countryside stretching to the distant mountains—the same lands through which he had watched the Storyteller come stumbling to the house. A broad and ancient riverbed coiled across the nearest field, and in wintertime Ronan dammed and redirected the nearby stream so that the wide, shallow gully filled with water and attracted marsh birds. When it occasionally froze, it offered a long, safe skating rink. Then, in summer, the riverbed dried up again, and larks nested there. He learned to step carefully so that he never trod on the tiny eggs.

Nobody else knew or shared this outdoor inner life, because he had no friends whom he trusted enough with such secrets, and he also feared breaking the forest's spells. Now and then he would form an intense friendship with some boy or girl at school, but it rarely survived their first argument. Typically, Ronan withdrew, fled the school as quickly as the rules allowed, and raced back to his own stamping grounds and his private games.

On such days if his father had reached home before he did, the sun shone again.

"Well, Champion, how's the whole wide world today?"—and from his pocket his father would pull a treat; a wooden gewgaw or a chocolate bar or newspaper cutting he knew Ronan would enjoy—a man has died of senility in France, aged only seventeen, or a calf was born in Wales with two heads, or how a lightning bolt in Arizona had split a tractor in two.

Sometimes, and these were the best days, his father brought Ronan a package with English postage stamps. John had an addiction to mail order, and he sent away for what he called "things." One contained a "Seebackroscope," which John explained to Ronan: "Put it to your eye, and it's like a backward telescope—you can see what's happening behind you as well as in front." Either the thing didn't work, or Ronan couldn't master it. And there was the Ventrilo, a small, metal half-moon that, if placed in the roof of the mouth, helped you, said the catalog, to "throw your voice and become a great ventriloquist." That didn't work either—but Ronan never complained. As for the book that said "Become an Immediate Juggler," which came with three red-and-green rubber balls, not even Kate could master the instructions.

Kate taught in a school some miles away, and Ronan listened

each afternoon for the swish of her bicycle tires on the gravel. She always greeted him first, John second, and Alison last. For Ronan she had a special backward handshake. He had to twist his arm to get it right, and Kate followed it with a slow ruffling of his hair and then a grabbed hug to her bosom. The game didn't end until he squealed a muffled, "I can't breathe!"

All his teachers remarked upon Ronan O'Mara's high intelligence, but found he had difficulty separating fantasy from fact. He proved best on subjects that made pictures in his mind—history, geography, literature. The morning after the Storyteller's arrival, he went to school with a radiant brain. "Newgrange!" He rolled the word in his mouth. Like a spotlight on a stage, that miraculous shaft of light shone down into his mind, and he asked himself over and over, "Where will he take us tonight?" Perhaps to Ulster, he hoped—powerful, magical Ulster, with its knights and courts and intrigues? Or the wild coast of the west, where men launched boats into Atlantic gales?

Throughout the day, he carried the Storyteller inside him, like a startling, marvelous secret. And after school Ronan raced home and lingered near the barn, hoping for a glimpse—but the stranger stayed in bed, still resting.

The house, however, held the man's traces. A smell of tobacco hung somewhere in the air. Josie Hogan, the O'Maras' housekeeper, had stuffed newspaper into the Storyteller's great battered boots to finish drying them. Then she polished them to a shine, and they stood inside the back door, ransomed, healed, restored, forgiven. Across the yard, his ancient shirt flapped on the clothesline, wan as a ghost in the late afternoon light.

Just as the sun was going down, Aunt Kate arrived like a lovely, happy bird. She had missed the first night—staying with friends— and Ronan's words cascaded over her. He told her about the Architect and the bear and the Angry Woman and the dish of sunlight and the Silken Elder. Kate whooped.

"We'll go to Newgrange!"

She whirled him round and round.

That evening, the Storyteller looked almost glossy—no more an ashen-faced scarecrow. He now wore a faded shirt of soft blue wool; Ronan recognized it as one of his father's. From his shining boots peeped some gray socks that Kate had knitted too big for anyone they knew. Under the long black coat he wore the same black trousers with legs like drainpipes. And under his black jacket he had a black waist-coat like a gambler's vest, across which looped a tarnished silver watch chain. He had shaved the gray stubble from his chin.

No longer did he seem famished or desperate. Until he was served, his hands lay folded in his lap; no elbows on the table. He listened for opportunities to contribute to the conversation. Kate and John asked about his travels; each of his replies added value to the question. Alison spoke little, and never directly to the old man. With Ronan, though, the Storyteller engaged as an equal; he asked Ronan's opinion, looked him in the eye, included him in all that was said.

At the meal's end the two women rose, and the Storyteller stood respectfully.

"May I offer my compliments," he said. "Many meals satisfy— but few nourish. I have been well nourished this evening, in body and mind."

By now the word had gone out—a storyteller had "landed" (as though from an alien shore) at the O'Maras'. When eight o'clock chimed in the hallway, twenty-five people had gathered round the hearth.

Some of the men asked where he came from.

To one he said, "It's a sort of truth that I'm from anywhere." And to another, "I was born up the country, but now I'm from every-where."

Ronan shared the bench with the same girl as the previous night; all other children sat on the floor. The men accepted dark bottles of stout or small glasses of amber whiskey. All the women sat together except for Ronan's mother; Alison, as ever, stayed at a distance, her eyes roving over every face in the crowded room as she supervised food and drinks.

Kate rubbed her hands with excitement; Ronan wore his Sunday-best clothes. On his forehead the cowlick of hair above the freckles was dark with water where Kate had again tried to paste it down. His father's cheeks glowed.

The Storyteller looked slowly around the room.

"How many of you heard me last night?"

Numerous hands rose, including Ronan's. The Storyteller beamed with satisfaction—everyone from the previous night had returned.

"Do any of you offer an observation on my tale?"

A man murmured, "D'you know, we never found out the Architect's name."

And the Storyteller replied, "Sadly, we'll never know it. There are no words carved at Newgrange—only symbols."

He smiled to soften the disappointment of his answer, arranged himself in his chair, and took a deep breath. Legs curled under listeners. Bodies settled down.

"Tonight"—he cleared his throat—"tonight, we shall thrust forward from Newgrange, forward by many, many centuries. I'm going to tell you a story about the king of Ulster."

Ronan felt his hair tingle. Ulster?! The Storyteller had read his thoughts.

"As we all know, Ulster is the most northerly of all our provinces. And it's the one with the most drama in its history. The events in this tale occurred on a night not unlike this one. It all took place in a few hours—in more or less the same time it will take me to tell you the story. Which, like all my tales, is true and tells you how our forefathers lived in Ireland before Jesus Christ was born. So—make way for a foolish and beloved king."

KING CONOR OF ULSTER SUFFERED FROM TOOTH-
aches, which occasioned in him a tendency toward the
morose. A stocky man, he stood neither short nor tall; he
was what the police like to call "of medium height." He possessed
an uneven mind, which swung between flashes of quick thinking
and the pace of a snail; either he grasped an idea immediately, or he
had to have it explained to him over and over. His heart experienced similar variations, by which I mean that he trusted some
people too much and some people too little.

As to his temperament, it was very difficult to measure; he was a
man who often had opposite moods in him. His eyes filled with
tears at any tender story, especially about a child or a dog. But more
than once he had turned a whole family out of their farm—they
gave him a gift too small, perhaps, or hadn't brought enough farm
produce to the court.

Conor knew he suffered from these conflicts, and by way of
acknowledging them, he always yoked his chariot to two horses. He
could have traveled perfectly well drawn by a single horse, but
when asked about it, he answered that the horses represented the
two sides of his nature: "That's why one is always black," he said,
"and one white."

If asked to explain, he'd turn the question back: "What are you
like inside? Don't you have feelings where you love everyone, and
at the same time you hate everyone? Or—don't you have times
when everything goes the way you want, but nothing feels good or
right? That's what I mean," he'd say, "about my black horse and my
white horse." And he'd add, "And maybe I mean more than that—
but I don't have the words for it yet."

No matter what he was like, the people of Ulster loved their king. They often discussed him and his little vanities, such as his fineries. He liked bright cloaks, ornamented with embroidered animals—a wolf, his horses, a hound; one cloak had a picture of a great sword with a jeweled hilt. His sandals, they knew, had to be made of calves' leather, with the softest straps. And around his mouth he often had green stains, from the herbs that he chewed to quell those toothaches.

The court of Ulster was like a village. Some people knew some of what was going on. Some people pretended they knew all of what was going on. Most knew very little, and what they didn't know they made up, as folk do everywhere—that's part of what we call "gossip." Some gossip is often accurate—because it's based on a little information and inspired guessing. Another kind of gossip is no more than a rumor, started by someone who hopes to see it come true. The best gossip of all, though, comes when something new and mysterious happens that nobody had expected and that nobody knows anything about.

Therefore, one day King Conor's subjects and his courtiers went wild over some new gossip.

What the gossip was saying was this: King Conor was about to announce a decision that might cause, not two horses, but two women to divert his life. And, they said, you could be sure of one thing—these two women mightn't always be pointed in one direction as easily as his two horses.

Two women? What did he want two for? He already had a wife—his queen, the mother of his little children—so what was this about another woman? Someone said they knew for sure that a high-ranking woman was coming to the palace "by appointment." It was long known that the king wanted a new chancellor, in place of his old uncle, who had died the previous year. But could it be possible that he'd appoint a woman? Yes—here indeed was food for gossip.

They prattled and they prattled, wagging their tongues up and down and in and out: a juicy question, a plump little theory—they were like birds picking berries off a branch. And they all said the same thing: What a strange decision! And not only a woman but a widow. And not only a widow but a young widow, and into the bargain, very beautiful.

What was wrong with that, you might ask? Conor, being a sensible man, liked beautiful women. However, there was the matter of the queen; she, being sensible too, also liked beautiful women, but she liked them not very much—and only when they kept their distance from her husband the king.

All the people—the courtiers, the tenants, and all the maids and men and servants and slaves of Ulster—puzzled over every aspect of this appointment. How well did the king know her? Dana was her name, or so it was said. Where did he meet this Dana, and why had she impressed him so much?

They had a few details. Dana came from the west; one brother was a druid, priest to a rich chieftain; one was a bard, who did his job well, entertaining the court with good poems (but his satires, they said, never rang bitter enough). Beyond that, they struggled to find illumination.

Someone recalled that the king had been a guest in this woman's territories the previous year, at a stag hunt. Was that where it all began? This Dana had ridden well, they said, and had ridden closer to the king than any of the men would have dared, risking a breach of protocol.

After the hunt, she'd invited the royal party to her house for a banquet. Conor, never impressed by a woman merely because she could handle a horse, didn't take up her invitation. He suffered from loneliness in social gatherings, and he longed to return to his own home and table. So it can't have been her cooking or her hospitality.

No: this is how Dana first came to the king's attention.

Six years earlier, Conor had paid his annual visit of respect to the High King of Ireland, who lived south from Ulster on the hill of Tara, not far indeed from Newgrange. On the long ride back north, Conor was caught in a thunderstorm. He rode hard ahead and lost four of his six household guards, who couldn't keep up with him. Conor and the other two champions, as they were called, took shelter in a wood. Not the most sensible place, I'd say, when lightning strikes—another piece of evidence, perhaps, that the beloved king of Ulster mightn't always be completely wise.

A party of bandits came upon the royal group. It was broad daylight, but teeming with rain so heavy that it leaked through the trees. The king and his two champions, all of them in hunting regalia, looked like wet hens. However, there was one thing you always knew about Conor—even those who had gone swimming naked with him in the river when he was a child said this—no matter where he was, or how he was dressed, he always looked like a king.

The bandits who entered the wood saw that too. But instead of backing off, as they might have been expected to do, they attacked. Nobody could dream of attacking a king and surviving; there was no hiding place on the island of Ireland for such a villain. They must have been desperate men or true ruffians—and they attacked viciously.

First, they fired their spears across the clearing. Three spears went astray, but two struck the horses of the escorts. One animal, hit in the chest, died under his rider, whose leg was crushed when his steed fell. The other horse took a spear deep in his flank, and that poor animal reared in pain. It unhorsed the champion riding it and crashed into the king, who barely managed to steady his own mount. Conor was now the only one fit to fight back; one of his guards lay on the ground, rolling in agony under a dead horse, and the other was staggering around, concussed from a heavy fall.

The five bandits came in close, drawing their long swords. The king and his men had only worn short swords, which became a serious disadvantage; it meant that the attackers had a longer reach.

Conor unhooked his beautiful round shield from his saddle. This had a jeweled boss—that's the round knob at the center. He wore it mainly for decoration, an ornament, to show respect to his High King. For fighting, he would have preferred his long, oblong shield, which protected his body from chin to knee. Nevertheless, he went forward on his horse, his shield on his left arm, the sword in his right hand cutting circles of light in the forest clearing.

The outlaw leader, a scarred man with one eye, tried to duck under Conor's swinging sword but had to pull back. One of the champions half recovered and came to help, but two of the outlaws seized the man. One clawed his head back by the hair, and the other cut his throat. And that same two bandits now attacked the other guard, the one whose horse had fallen on top of him. They dragged him clear and with one swipe of a sword almost severed his head from his neck.

All five villains could now turn their undivided attention to the king. Two of them got under his shield, grabbed his left leg, and managed to drag him off his horse. Conor, though, had always been a remarkable fighter, and even though they manhandled him to the ground, he wounded one grievously in the throat, caught another in the eye with the boss of the shield, and got to his feet again.

In his exertions, the king's mouth began to froth with saliva. He'd been suffering from a bad toothache that morning, and he'd been chewing herbs, so that it began to look as though his mouth foamed green.

Very disconcerting, you might think—but not for the ruffians, who were gaining the best of things. While one fought Conor from the front, two tried to get behind him. Conor stayed as close to his horse's flank as possible, but they began to stab the horse in the rear. The poor creature bucked and reared, and Conor tried to decide whether to cling to the horse or fight his way out of the circle of his attackers. There was little he could do—the horse screamed in pain, kicked out, and broke away, leaving Conor utterly exposed.

At that moment, two horsemen, strangers, galloped into the forest. They too had come there by accident, also sheltering from the storm, and they recognized that this man fighting for his life was a king—and that the odds were unfair. They stopped, took stock of the situation, and decided to act.

With great force and style, the newcomers routed the bandits, killing one immediately. The pair whom Conor had injured ran off—and now there were two. The strangers jumped from their horses and with their swords slashed the chest and stomach of one more, leaving Conor to face the bandit chief alone.

Both strangers stood back a little to allow a king to recover his honor. The bandit chief, even though he wielded a long and mighty sword, proved no match for Conor's skill. With the delicacy of a dancing master, the king ran rings around the ruffian, piercing him here and here and here, the face, the stomach, the chest—swift, thrusting blows that drew spurts of blood. He then disarmed the bandit chief with a dreadful blow on the villain's sword arm. Finally, in the great gesture of all fighting kings, Conor killed him with the man's own sword.

Then and only then did he turn and thank his rescuers. One of the king's two saviors on that rainy day was a landowner out on a hunt—and the husband of Dana.

"I'm a lucky man," said Conor to him. "Thank you very much."

The gentleman shrugged it off.

"We all deserve a bit of luck. I'm a lucky man too," he told the king. "I was lucky enough to marry a wonderful wife, and you must come and meet her."

And it was true—no man knew more love from a spouse. Dana thought her husband the core of the world, a man from whose eyes the sun shone in the morning and the moon at night. The servant women in that house could scarcely keep up to the standards of attention Dana wanted for her husband. When the king met her— she was part of her husband's party that day—he agreed; this was a grand young wife.

But some years after the king's rescue, that fine man died in a fall from a horse during a helter-skelter hunt. Such a tragedy! People thought Dana might die too, of grief. At the graveside, nobody could get through to her on account of her wailing and weeping. Young though she was, nothing girlish marked her mourning—hers was a powerful, adult grieving.

Then, the day after the burial, she called her brothers, sisters, parents, friends, and household to a meeting and told them that she'd mourn for the traditional period of a year and a day. She said that on the last day of that year she'd fill a small silver cup with her tears, and at dawn on the following day, the "day" of the "year and a day," she'd empty the cup of tears on the stone cairn that topped her dear husband's grave.

All of this she duly did, and when she emerged from her black chrysalis, people said she looked lovelier than ever—stronger, if not yet serene.

On the night of our story, Conor came to his banqueting hall to dine. Aware that everybody was talking about him, he could almost hear the whispers; "Is it true? Who is this woman, Dana? Does the queen know her? Would the king do such a thing?"

It was true. Out of all the wise counselors at court and out of all the experienced men in the surrounding chieftaincies, the king had chosen for his new chancellor the young widow of his rescuer.

You have to understand the power he was giving her. At a nod of the king's head, she'd now gain the third most powerful position in the kingdom, with intimate access to the workings of the palace and the royal estates. She would know, as the king and queen already did, where every coin came from and where every coin went. She'd decide how much the king would spend on improving the palace buildings; she alone would determine rights of way through the kingdom; she'd assess who'd supply the palace with corn, who with potatoes, who with baked soda bread, whether the existing palace staff were good enough, and so on.

About the only powers she wouldn't have—for they belonged solely to the king and the queen—were the power of royal decree, the power to make laws. Nor would she have the power to execute somebody for a crime, nor the power to declare a man and woman husband and wife, nor the power to act in a dispute over land.

No wonder everyone watched Conor more closely than usual as he sat to dine. Not only that—this was the night Dana was supposed to arrive.

Gossip can bring on a fever, a fever of excitement. As usual, many people had gathered to dine in the palace; but they drifted in much earlier than they normally did, and they began to whisper in gales.

Someone heard that the queen might be absent, she hadn't returned from Armagh, where she had taken offerings to a river goddess. She spent a lot of her time at shrines or plotting the stars in the heavens. This didn't gain her many friends—and she could have done with some, because she also had the reputation of a sharp tongue. Unless you had your remarks prepared when you met her, she'd jump on what you said and query it. She wasn't so extreme as to question someone who said, "Good morning, Your Majesty." But if you said something careless, such as, "D'you think we'll have a better harvest this year, Your Majesty?" she'd come back at you and say, "What was wrong with last year's harvest?"

And that was the kind of thing the gossips seized upon, the same whisperers who claimed that the queen's absences and maybe even her sharp tongue had caused the king to turn to this woman, Dana, for help and, maybe, sympathy. Nobody mentioned the fact that this Dana had a reputation among her own people as a foremost breeder of great cattle—and the herds of Ulster had been failing a little.

With all this gossip going on, the king sat in his great chair. Everybody thought he looked anxious and moody. But the sixty people who rose to greet him had no real appetite for food. Each of them was agog—courtiers, champions and their wives, visiting neighbors, farmers who were tenants of the king, and the many servants. What a night they expected—and what a night they got!

Soon after the king was served—first, as usual—the vital moment came. Those nearest the huge wooden doors heard the rattling clatter of hooves in the courtyard. Somewhere, a horse gave a loud, trembling whinny. Every diner in that great room looked in two directions—they looked at the door, and at the king. He gave an order with a waved hand.

A servant man hauled up the big, thick wooden bar that locked the great doors together. Another rushed to help him. Together, they dragged both doors open at the same time. And there, framed in the entrance, astride a glossy horse, was Dana—a tall, dramatic woman with shining hair the color of a blackbird's wing.

She had timed her arrival precisely. The full moon, newly risen, hung over her right shoulder like a big, round, silver lamp. Nobody else could be seen; she had evidently told her traveling companions to stand well to the side of the doors so that she could have the stage to herself.

Wooden buildings have no silence. Timber creaks and groans, as the old sailors knew well. That night, though, the wooden walls and ramparts of the court of Ulster were quiet as the moon in the sky—and just as watchful.

Conor rose to his feet. On his face two emotions fought for control, the same way his two horses fought for control of his chariot. Dividing him to the heart and soul, one feeling conveyed deep and furrowed anxiety. But the other emotion spoke of passionate joy; he was looking at a woman he already loved—or was about to love.

Dana dismounted. The diners couldn't yet see her face—too much shadow, and the moon too bright behind her. But her silhouette was graceful and tall, and she gave the impression of being firmly anchored, a woman sure of her place in the world. Remember now that some men in the court had already seen Dana; they had ridden a stag hunt with her. However, when it comes to describing such a woman, men reflect only what they think of her, how they react to her—they forget the details. Send a man to a wedding or a funeral, and his wife will never be satisfied with the report he brings home. Send a woman, and her listeners will be able to see the leaves on the trees in the yard of the church. Therefore, the womenfolk, the true makers of opinion in a household, were astounded. Nobody had conveyed to them the full force of this young widow's presence.

An invisible hand led her horse away to one side, and Dana stood in the exact center of the big doorway. Framed against the night and the moon, she prepared her entrance like an actress to a stage; she threw back the skirts of her cloak and spread out her mane of hair.

As she paused, a certain man in the banqueting hall also looked at her keenly. He was a big young fellow with a thick beard who sat on the left-hand side of that room, not far from the king. His name was Dermot and he was the blacksmith. An important man, he made horseshoes for the king's stables, he manufactured and repaired the court's harness pieces, and he forged the champions' weapons.

Dermot's work had brought him much wealth. Consequently he farmed some of the best land in the province. He farmed it well, too; with his skill he had made a horse-drawn plow—five, ten times faster than a man opening the ground with a spade.

Many people thought Dermot an awkward man. He took offense easily. Being near him felt like standing on a box of eggs: a wrong shift, and something would smash. Therefore people took care in his presence. This meant that he didn't hear all the court gossip—in fact, he only overheard snatches, and he never knew any of it fully. Yet at the same time, some people had experienced great kindness from him. The children, especially, loved him. They brought him little gifts, and he made things for them, toys and gadgets.

When the commotion of Dana's arrival had first begun, Dermot had been leaning back on some large cushions. Now, like everyone else, he sat up and stared. Dermot had a more crucial reason for scrutinizing her; he had a powerful and unfettered devotion to the queen. Nothing improper, nothing forward, nothing indelicate or disrespectful—he simply believed the queen was saintly and unique. Nobody dared to utter a wrong word about her in Dermot's presence, and ever since he had heard the first rumors about this Dana, he had been concerned that the queen might be usurped.

This didn't mean that his devotion to the king stood in doubt. Quite the contrary; by every blade and every hilt, by every ring, bit, and buckle, the king knew that his blacksmith loved him. The gorgeous harness pieces Dermot made, the weapons he forged and decorated—they'd have graced any court in the world. But the difference was this: duty governed Dermot's loyalty to the king, whereas blind devotion dictated his fealty to the queen.

Naturally, Dana knew nothing of all this when she stepped forward and began the long walk up to the king's chair. In her stride, her great cloak billowed its train behind her.

Among the red-haired, green-eyed girls and the blond, brown-eyed girls, Ireland has always bred a kind of Irishwoman who looks almost foreign, more like a woman from a Balkan country, Czechoslovakia or Yugoslavia, or somewhere farther east, with high cheekbones and eyes dark as the Black Sea. Dana looked like that—and with that mane of raven hair and those dark eyes, no wonder she had been a chieftain's wife.

Ireland at that time was a place where the valleys bulged with grass and grain, the land of Ulster truly was full of milk and honey, and (according to some who kept secrets), gold was to be found in the corners of the hills. Tillage yielded well, and the animals grew plump. The people had warm clothing, woven from the white and shaggy fleeces of their sheep or cut from the hides of their horses and cattle. Their houses had separate rooms; their women were skilled at baking and sewing—in other words, they knew something of comfort and how to create it. And they had pets: dogs and cats and little songbirds.

A successful way of life had evolved, of strong families sharing widely and helping each other and their neighbors. The father of the house, usually the oldest son of his own father, ruled—but not without his wife's agreement on important matters. Their place in the world was judged according to the size of their landholding; the bigger the farm, the more senior the family, and the greatest landowners stood closest to the king, who was the most senior of all.

By the time of King Conor, the brain of the country had also developed. Many strangers arrived from Europe and brought with them interesting ideas. These could be expressed as thoughts in conversation, or as verses in poems, or as decorations on weapons and pots and pans, or as styles of dress, or as stories they had heard in their own houses. When Conor ruled Ulster, the Roman Empire was exerting its power in all corners of Europe and as far as Africa.

And then there were the people of Greece, with their wonderful poetry and benign rules for living. They had long impressed anyone who encountered them; men came to Ireland who had met Greeks and talked with them, and when they recounted those conversations, many a lively debate arose as to politics and families and heroes and gods.

The country was governed by means of a hundred and fifty petty kingships—"petty" as in the French word *petit*—and five large kingships. These petty kingships were really prominent families with land, names like Murphy and Dolan and MacCormack and Foley and MacCarthy and O'Brien. Were he not a king, Conor would have been addressed as no more than "Conor O'Conor"— Conor of the family of Conor. Another king of Ulster, also first-named "Conor" and later than the man I'm telling you about, was the son of a man called Nessa, so he was called "Conor MacNessa." But you know all that already, the difference between *O* and *Mac;* in Irish names, *O* is "coming from" or "the family of" or, some say, "the grandson of." And *Mac* means "the son of."

The kingships owned this green and beautiful island, and they hired the ordinary people or enslaved the bondspeople to work their land. Or they leased acreage out to tenant farmers. Others provided important services, such as butchering or making cheese or milling grain to make flour.

There were five major kingships: the High Kingship at Tara, and then the rulers of the four provinces—Munster in the south; Leinster in the east; Ulster in the north; and Connacht to the west. So the king of Ulster was a figure of great significance and standing, not a man to be disrespected or taken lightly.

When he—or any king—invited someone to dine, that person truly dined. It was no small invitation. On most evenings the banqueting hall contained the king's most important chieftains—and therefore his biggest tax contributors—plus some traveling nobility or rich tenant farmers, with perhaps a druid or two, a poet or a singer or a passing musician; and, always, a storyteller. In other words, the evening's dining brought together all sorts of people under the king's hospitality.

They were pleased to be invited; it made them feel rewarded for their loyalty and hard work. Their day began with a first breakfast, maybe at five o'clock in the morning when they rose to get the first fresh air of the day and care for the animals, milk the cows, feed the horses, and so forth. Then they had a second breakfast at nine o'clock, when all the milk had been taken to the dairy and the day's cheese and butter making was commenced.

After the second breakfast, as the men attended to the cattle or the tillage, the women cooked or sewed. The meal at midday was usually brought to the men in the fields, and it often contained the proceeds of the morning's baking.

So by eveningtide, everybody prepared to rest, and most ordinary folk in their homes sat around their kitchen tables and ate the produce of their fields—except on those special evenings when they were invited by the king to one of his nightly banquets. If you were a member of the court, however, like Dermot the blacksmith, you went to the banquet more often.

Now: Dermot the blacksmith had no wife. So, when Dana, Ulster's new chancellor and purse-keeper, continued her long walk up that banqueting hall, it became Dermot's turn to show conflict on his face. Across his countenance, as it were, two horses began to gallop. One had a black coat—the dark concern that such a woman might supplant the queen in the king's affections. The other shone bright—the fire that glows across a man's forehead and eyes when he sees for the first time the woman with whom he will fall in love forever and whom he wants to make his own. As Dana approached, Dermot rose to his feet and stared openly at her.

And still the queen hadn't appeared. As everyone watched Dana, a new question arose in their minds: Which woman was the more beautiful, the queen or this newcomer? Dana's tall, they muttered—the queen's short; Dana's figure is like the letter S—the queen loves food; Dana is dark with smoldering eyes—the queen is as gold as a June morning, with eyes blue as the flowers of flax.

So it was that in Ulster on a moonlit night long, long ago, the king, a decent if anxious man, had one strong and beautiful woman already in his life and now introduced a second. And, as if that might not prove troublesome enough, Dermot the blacksmith decided to tell the queen.

She, at that moment, wasn't far away. On her return from Armagh, she had taken, as she sometimes did, an early supper in order to be with her two little children. Typically, she'd now join the king for the music and poems and stories that often came after the evening meal. As yet, though, she hadn't entered the banquet hall.

But Dana had. A stately procession of one, with every eye watching her, she reached the top of the room. The king rose to greet his new chancellor. Dana bowed and kissed the king's hands in the correct homage. She sat down by his side, and he waved to the harpers to play.

But she sat in the queen's chair! Well—every man and woman in that hall, whether rich, poor, or bonded, gasped. Some all but stood on their own chairs to look. Older wives, who knew about these things, put their hands to their mouths. What's going on? they asked themselves. The king has allowed a strange woman to sit in his wife's place! Has the queen been ousted? Is she gone? Is that why this Dana has taken her chair? Or worse—does the queen not know yet, and will she only grasp that things have changed when she sees that her chair has been taken by another woman? And a beautiful, younger woman at that?

The king didn't seem to notice. From the expression on his face, a star might have fallen from the skies into the palm of his hand. Perhaps he looked like that when he first met Dana, and perhaps he invited her to become his chancellor because he had fallen in love with her. Or maybe it had only happened at that exact moment, when the king saw how Dana's beauty glowed inside the walls of his own palace.

Or maybe it had been happening all the while since he had met her. It's sometimes the case that people are best regarded when we're away from them. Whatever the truth of it, no doubt could exist in anyone's mind that King Conor of Ulster found this beauty special.

The servants brought food, and a conversation opened up between Dana and the king, as naturally as could be expected between a well-mannered guest and a civilized host: Did you have a safe journey? I hope it hasn't fatigued you. Was the weather clement? It's been very nice weather here lately. And so on.

All around them, people pretended to busy themselves with their own conversations, but they never took their eyes off the king and his new friend. Dermot looked at them too, he looked for one long moment—and then hurried from the hall.

In the corridors of the palace the blacksmith found the queen. She had heard the commotion outside and seen the horses gleam in the moonlight. Next, she had recognized the huge sound of the wooden doors being opened, which never happened except for a special visitor. As a result, she had begun to make her way to the king.

Although Conor hadn't shared with her his appointment of Dana, the queen had heard the rumors and much of the gossip. But she decided not to raise it with her husband—undisclosed knowledge is often a source of power.

When Dermot saw the queen walking toward him in the long wooden corridor, he began to run to her, and she noted his agitation. She liked Dermot; she appreciated that he showed her proper respect, and it's possible that the queen might have thought of him as a potential husband, should any catastrophe fall from the sky and hit the king on the head. Nor would she have been marrying beneath her; blacksmiths had an honored place in early Irish society.

Dermot spoke, trembling a little.

"Madam, I think the king misses you at table."

"I'll go there now."

"Madam, I'm happy to escort you to your rightful place at the king's side."

Blacksmiths are famed for their strength rather than their social delicacy. Dermot landed heavily everywhere, with his tongue as well as his feet. When the queen fell in step with him, a small, blond figure at the side of this big, black-bearded man, the timber floors of the palace corridor shook under Dermot's boots. His next remarks had the same heavy touch.

"Madam, a woman has arrived, and all Ulster's talking about her. Your husband invited her. And if you want my opinion, the king should never have asked her to come here and when you see her, you'll know what I mean."

Small people need to possess significant gifts, especially when faced with large people. In this matter, the queen had many—one of which was the gift of ice. Without breaking her stride, without saying a word, she let Dermot know that he had overstepped the mark. When the queen assumed this demeanor, it was as though a halo of frost surrounded her head and face, like a ring around the moon. Yet Dermot was too indelicate and, in any case, too far above her physically to feel this cold force, and so he sailed on blissfully beside his queen.

But the servants along the corridors saw the icy halo and thought that the night might prove even more interesting. They were right, though not in the way they imagined.

One entrance from the domestic quarters to the banquet hall led from the corridor through a heavy curtain. Here the king and queen had a special, private alcove, a breathing space, in which they might pause for a moment before facing their guests. Then they went through another great curtain and emerged immediately behind their two chairs at the head of the table.

The blacksmith and the queen came to this curtain. Now Dermot had a dilemma; he wanted to be back among the banqueters when the queen first saw Dana. So he counseled the queen to take a little rest between the curtains. She, still furious with him, never said a word.

The moment she disappeared behind those curtains, Dermot ran like the wind. His shiny curls shaking and shifting on his head like a little nest of black snakes, that enormous man raced like a great, hairy hound down the long palace corridor. The rush lights on the wall flickered as he passed, and it was said the following day that one of them actually blew out in the wind of his wake.

At the door of the hall, he slipped, didn't quite fall, hit the edge of a table, knocked over someone's goblet, and clattered his way noisily to his chair near the king. Nobody around paid any attention to this—they were used to the noise of Dermot crashing through life. Dana, however, started a little, turned her head to see where the clatter came from, and looked straight into Dermot's face.

Everybody there that night remembered the scene all their lives. The tables had been decorated with great bunches of flowers and greenery. In front of each guest stood a drinking vessel of bright silver. Women wore little gold balls as decorations in their long, silken hair, or had wide golden combs pinning up their braids and tresses. Their gowns hung from shoulder to ankle in brilliant yellows or deep greens or soft reds.

As for the men, they wore tunics of darker colors, deep blue or brown, sometimes tied with gold pins. Some wore the torc at their necks; this ornament, hammered from a lump of gold into an almost closed circle, protected its wearer from the blow of a blade on the back of the neck. Tonight the torc was for decoration; none of the men had a sword—in King Conor's court, weapons couldn't be worn at table. He believed that people should eat without fear, and he also knew that, with drink taken, some of the champions could get a bit flighty.

That was the gowned and decorated scene that greeted the queen as at last she slipped from behind the curtain into the hall. Then she saw the king—gazing at this tall woman, whose eyes were as deep dark as that bitter little berry we call the sloe. And now the people all over the room at last saw what they were waiting for—the small, pretty blond woman in the crimson gown, their queen, a thin gold band around her forehead. And she was looking straight at Dana.

We must understand the nature of an Irish monarchy at that time. In all the province of Ulster, the king and queen ruled no more than a few thousand people. Parts of the region had yet to be cleared of bears, forests, and wolves. Roads didn't exist.

All communication was personal. Everything went from the mouth of one person to the ear of another. Where you have that kind of communication, information is given and received with great intensity. The gossip about the king and Dana had now been a powerful and important part of Ulster life for a matter of weeks.

The queen walked forward to her husband's side, prepared for the greeting that all Ulster longed to see and hear about. Her name was Sorcha—the English call it Sarah—and she grew up in a family related to the king of Leinster. Her mother died when she was six. The father never remarried, and he raised Sorcha and her younger sister with the help of servants. A distant man, he never gave his older daughter the attention she wanted and, indeed, deserved. The younger daughter had a sweeter nature, and the bereaved father felt it easier to deal with her. This made the older girl feel she had to fight for everything. The one good thing about that characteristic was the fact that she learned to fight subtly.

As she did now. She knew what had been tripping off the wagging tongues. And now she saw for herself that this woman, Dana, fell not one inch short of all that queen Sorcha had heard—stately, elegant, calm, and exquisite. Being shrewd, the queen immediately took stock of the ingredients she had to mix so that her cake didn't burn, so to speak.

She couldn't repudiate the newcomer. That would look cheap, jealous, and premature. Dana had done nothing wrong; she had merely—and quite properly—replied to an invitation from a monarch. Nor could Sorcha show anything but support for her husband, the king; otherwise, she'd undermine him and give him the right to rebuke or isolate her. Furthermore, she was the hostess of the evening, and in Ireland the laws of hospitality have always been sacred; no matter who the guest or what their behavior, the welcome must be gracious. There had to be a solution—and Sorcha found one.

Her eye fell on Dermot the blacksmith. He's a hasty man, she thought, sometimes incautious—but he's also handsome, and even magnificent; and of course he's very strong, muscles on his arms like small ropes. Sorcha also knew that few people spoke to Dermot on account of his abruptness. She reckoned, though, that he wasn't rude but shy. Which all meant that Dermot was probably lonely. And she was right. Nobody asked for his company. The farmers and their servants feared him. And the champions excluded all but other champions from their group.

The queen knew that this made Dermot feel bitter. All fine for them, he felt, to draw on his best skills for making their weapons or crafting a beautiful hilt on a sword—but not as much as a goblet of mead did they ever offer him, not as much as a word of praise, not a jot of social respect.

She then turned her thoughts to the worst possibility of all: Will this beautiful stranger, she asked herself, gain greater influence with my husband the king than I already have? Followed by this thought: And if I give her a moment's foothold, doesn't that mean the battle is joined—and I mightn't win?

In short, she reasoned that if she didn't take action there and then, she might as well give up.

There's an old Irish saying: If you don't use your power, it will leave you for someone who will. Queen Sorcha had considerable powers, and now she drew on one of them. A rule in ancient Ireland decreed that a man without a wife and a woman without a husband could have a marriage arranged between them by a king or a queen. Sorcha stepped forward, smiled the warmest of welcomes, and accepted Dana's outstretched hand; and she nodded graciously at Dana's curtsy.

Then she looked at her husband, Conor, and understood at last why he had made this appointment. She had been out riding with him in his chariot earlier that week, and now the answer came to her: this appointment couldn't be described as something the king *did*—it was a reflection of who the king *was*. He needed a woman for each side of his nature—the queen his white horse, Dana his black horse. That was why her husband had extended this invitation without discussing it with her, his beloved wife.

When women feel danger, they look to strong men. Privately, the queen always thought her husband was a little weak. So she beckoned to the strong man gazing anxiously at her across the tables—the blacksmith Dermot.

He came over. The queen took his hand and placed it on Dana's.

"I propose," said Queen Sorcha, "that you, Dermot, my husband's blacksmith"—she looked into his eyes, then turned to Dana—"take you, Dana, my husband's chancellor, to wife."

Well, well, well! The gasp of wonder nearly blew out all the candles. Such a solution! The courtiers of Ulster looked at each other and laughed. The king would have his dark horse and his white horse—but only after a fashion. Dermot would certainly fall in love with Dana, because Dermot would have fallen in love with any half-decent woman who gave him a kind glance—and he'd kill any man who tried to take her away. And what better arrangement than to have the new chancellor married to the royal blacksmith, who would always be devoted to his queen and who would therefore advise her if anything ever came amiss in the king's behavior—financial or otherwise?

Dana, who was no fool, curtsied again to the queen. Yes, she could work as the king's chancellor; for her, it meant protection, status, and a new husband. Looking at Dermot, she thought he was probably a slightly foolish man, but she'd bend him into a good shape.

And thus the queen, who already took responsibility for the spiritual health of her husband's kingdom, now got control over the court and finances. Above all, she tightened her grip on the man she loved, her own husband, the head of her household and her people.

But wait! The king felt a toothache coming on. He saw what had happened; he knew his wife had trumped him, and this wasn't the first time. What could he do? To accept it meekly would make him look a little silly, and he was too vain a man for that.

Conor had flashes of brilliance, including gifts of anticipation. He guessed that the queen must have heard the gossip, and he'd

been wondering how she'd react when Dana arrived. And he fig-
ured that she'd started making her own plans in plenty of time.
He'd observed, for example, that when Dermot came over one
morning with a new gold buckle, the queen asked him several questions—Who prepares your food? What do you do about sewing?
And so on. Conor put two and two together, and he made four—the
queen had known in advance about Dana the beautiful young
widow, and always intended to match her with Dermot.

But Conor wanted to come out on top, and he had made his own
arrangements. Behind him every night at dinner hung a large
bronze gong, and carved on it was the great emblem of Ulster, the
red hand. Conor picked up his eating dagger and with the hilt
struck the gong three times. Everybody thought he meant to make
a speech; everybody was wrong.

For the second time that night the great wooden doors opened,
and down the wide aisle, two grooms backed the king's chariot,
with the black horse and the white horse yoked to it. They stopped
a few feet from the king's chair; the horses pranced a little, snorted,
tossed their heads. Dana looked on, mystified, her hand in Dermot's huge paw; the queen guessed and smiled to herself.

King Conor of Ulster jumped into his chariot and galloped out of
the banqueting hall, driving his black horse and his white horse.
Long after he was out of sight the banqueters could hear the horses
snorting with effort and the harnesses rattling and the hooves
pounding—and then there was silence.

Did the chariot take off into the night sky and land him on the
moon? Well, it had about as much chance of doing that as Conor
ever had of outwitting his wife. So that's the end of this moral tale—
of a king who thought he could outsmart his queen, who thought
he could defy all the known wisdom about two women living easily under one roof, and in the end found that the best he could do
was control his two horses, one black and one white.

The Storyteller clapped his hands three slow times—
his tale had ended. A neighbor's infant stirred in her mother's arms
but didn't quite wake. The adults rose from their chairs and rubbed
their eyes. Little by little, everybody in the room returned to the
year 1951. Someone opened the door, and a billow of November fog
blew in like a giant's breath. Ronan gazed into the flames of the fire
and sighed because the tale was over.

The neighbors said good night.

"How d'you remember it all?"

"It was like being back in that time."

And, "Will you be here again tomorrow night?"

"I hope so. I'm at my host's pleasure."

Soon the last few steps faded from the stone-flagged yard.

The Storyteller sauntered to the door after them; John stopped
him, handed him a full glass of whiskey. Ronan jumped from the
bench, ran over to his father, and tugged his hand.

"Dad!" He danced from foot to foot. "Dad!"

John bent down. "Dad, listen! This is the best thing ever, ever
happened." He squeezed his eyes almost shut and shifted his feet
again.

The Storyteller patted Ronan's head and went quickly out into
the night.

But Alison O'Mara stood waiting by the table; her eyes had
hooded, and her high cheeks flushed red. She was coughing her
"annoyed cough," and Ronan heard her saying that she didn't at all
like the direction that story took. "Who was he getting at?"

Kate said, "But you're being ridiculous," and Ronan caught some
of his mother's words—"don't want him hovering around here too
long" and "bad influence." Earlier in the day she had asked in her

sharp voice whether the Storyteller would go to mass tomorrow morning.

Kate snorted—"The man's probably still a pagan"—and John said, "Some people have their own gods."

Alison looked as though she relished neither remark.

Ronan climbed the stairs, dimly aware of a rising problem. Worried that something might somehow be his fault, he curled up in bed and arranged the pillows so that the arguing voices blurred.

His father arrived.

"Well, champion?"

Ronan said, "Wasn't it grand? D'you think he'll stay?"

His father tucked in the blankets. "It's cold outside."

"Dad, are you able to decide what you dream about?"

John said, "Only when I'm awake. Are you?"

Ronan thought for a moment. "I think so."

"And you'll dream of—what? Horses?"

John blew out the candle.

Next morning they drove to Sunday mass in the black Ford, John's pride and joy. Kate held Ronan's hand; Alison stared ahead. At their pew she looked all around the congregation, twice. From the menace in her glance, Ronan somehow knew she was searching—and in vain—for the Storyteller.

After mass, neighbors crowded round, and many asked whether they might invite themselves that night. John welcomed all, and a young farmer handed Kate a bag of apples, which caused much teasing in the car on the way home.

Breakfast over, Alison folded her hands; she had been rigid all morning.

"It's time," she said to John; and to Ronan, "Go and ask the gentleman to join us."

The Storyteller had long surfaced; he had eaten breakfast while the O'Maras were at mass. Ronan entered the barn and looked up to the loft.

"Sir?"

The old man came to the top of the ladder.

"I suppose you're talking to me." He smiled down and smoothed his black coat.

"My mother wants to see you, sir."

He came spryly down, snapped to attention, and saluted like a soldier.

"Lead on, Macduff!"

Ronan looked at him, alone with the magical man for the first time.

"Thanks for your stories," he said with the bravery such an effort costs a child.

"I appreciate your remark," said the Storyteller, as though speaking to an adult. "What did you like best so far?" and he stooped to listen, folding his hands.

"I liked Dermot the blacksmith."

"And Newgrange?"

Ronan said, "Oh. That was the best. My aunt said we're going there this summer."

"Good, good," said the Storyteller, in no hurry to break off this conversation. "And would you like to learn how to tell stories?"

Ronan felt his neck go cold.

"I'd—love that, sir. A lot. How would we do it?"

"This is what we'd do." He rubbed his hands together. "First of all, we'd pick a time, a moment in Ireland's history. It might be about a man who owned a wolfhound, or a woman who lived on an island in a river, or a boy who kept a secret horse. Whoever it was, the story would be about that person—because people always want to know about other people, that's the heart of all stories."

"Ronan!"

They started in fright at Alison's call, and Ronan led the Storyteller across the yard. Despite his mother's tone, he felt comfort and irresistible peace walking in the old man's shadow.

"We'll talk again, you and me," the man whispered.

Alison had left the door wide open. The Storyteller spoke his greeting. "God save all here!"

"And you," said John O'Mara.

"God's name warrants more reverence," Alison said, attacking immediately.

"Oh!" said Kate.

The Storyteller opened his mouth to draw breath. Ronan winced and blinked—as he always did before tears. He recognized this force too well.

"I've something to say to you," Alison continued. "In this house, stories must have a good moral code? D'you understand?"

The Storyteller had taken off his hat in respect, and he held it in his hands like a supplicant. His fingers shook as he pleated the brim.

"Ma'am—"

"You know what I'm talking about. Why did you come here?"

"Ma'am, I never meant—"

"I don't care what you meant."

"Easy," said John O'Mara, blinking hard. "Alison, c'mon now, easy."

"John!" She rapped the table hard, and he fell quiet.

"Ma'am, I never meant to do anything but tell a story—I never meant any harm."

"I'm not interested in your excuses," said Alison, her face closed in a rictus of anger. "This is a respectable house."

She brought down a cold silence as she scrutinized the tall old man, head to toe. Ronan chewed his hand—the Storyteller had begun to cry. Tears filled the dark eyes, and slow fat drops rolled down the weathered cheeks. Ronan could hear his own mind whimpering for the man, and he wished desperately to hug him. Kate turned away. Alison rode on through the disorder she had triggered.

"Today is Sunday. You weren't at mass."

"Ma'am, I've been walking for weeks—"

"Don't interrupt me! Even you must observe the Sabbath day. So, tonight," she said, "you'll tell a story about Saint Patrick."

"But I was going to tell a different—I mean, ma'am, stories are my trade." The Storyteller began to sweep at his tears with his big frayed cuff.

"Take it or leave it," Alison said.

John came forward and took the man by the arm.

"C'mon. Go for a walk. I'll come over to see you later. It'll be all right."

"I never meant to jar anyone," said the Storyteller, his great voice cracking. "Never. No. Not a bit." Then he turned and looked John in the eye from a pace away. "You know—you tell her—go on, tell her—tell her I'm all right."

John stopped him with haste—"C'mon, c'mon. Let things settle"—and steered him away.

The two men left the house. Ronan sat down hard on the wooden bench, bewildered, no breath in his throat. Kate looked at Alison.

"You can be some bitch!" said Kate. "You and your bloody nonsense. Jesus!"

She saw Ronan's breathing change, and his chest begin to heave; she went over, sat beside him, and took his hand.

"Now—count. To a hundred. One. Two. Slowly. Three."

Alison stormed upstairs and slammed the bedroom door.

When John returned, Ronan broke off counting at eighty-five.

"Dad, why didn't you stop her? Dad?!"

John said, "It'll be all right. It will." He soothed Ronan's hair. "We'll have another story tonight. He'll be here."

He picked up the Sunday newspapers and began to read.

Ronan whispered to Kate, "Why didn't Dad stop her? He's the only one can stop her. Why didn't he do it? He said nothing."

"Shhhhhhhhh," Kate said and stroked his hair over and over: "Shhhhhhhhh."

When they were courting, John O'Mara received this letter from the girl with whom he had fallen in love.

I want you to know everything about me, so we had better start with my name. "Alison" comes from "Alice," which descends from "Adelaide," and it means "noble" and "kind." As for "MacCarthy," it

means "the loving one," and some say it is connected to the Roman
name "Caractacus" and the Welsh name "Caradoc." Our fortunes
ebbed and flowed down the centuries, but we retained Kilcarthy
House, and I think that makes me an Irish aristocrat. You know how
the English upper classes call themselves "bluebloods"—meaning
that there's no black or dark breeding, i.e., no slaves among them,
because their veins glow blue? Well, I reckon that I'm a "greenblood."
What are you?!

The year was 1934, and she was twenty. Her education had been far
more privileged than almost anyone's in Ireland at that time. Her
boarding school in Dublin, nicknamed "the Little Sisters of the
Rich," also had an English convent. There she spent two years, of
which six months were taken in Montreux. By the age of seventeen
Alison MacCarthy spoke Swiss French, when many of her Irish
neighbors had barely stayed in school long enough to read and
write. Then she went to the Sorbonne.

If you studied art in the Paris of the 1930s, you were presumed by
many to have tasted nectar. Alison remained demure, an observer
of the demimonde, never a participant. But the sights that she saw
loosened her stays, and John O'Mara did the rest; from the moment
she met him, she would have given anything he asked of her. Two
years her senior, emotionally twenty years older, he reminded her
of her own father, whom, in her puberty, she had lost to a hunting
accident.

Jacob MacCarthy had local fame as a fearless rider. The first in the
county to make his horse clear wire fences, he came down one day
jumping onto a road. He made it home, lamenting that his horse
had to be put down. But the doctor had himself been damaged—a
piece of grit sliced into his scalp. The infection killed him in ten
shivering days, baffled that he could not heal himself.

On the night he died, twelve-year-old Alison never went to
bed; she walked a hundred circuits of the house and gardens. At
dawn, she took her father's leather-bound notebook from his desk,
and wherever she traveled for the rest of her life, the notebook went

with her. Already a "difficult" child, now she became unmanageable—she ate no food, went missing for days at a time, stayed silent.
The mother, also inclined to be catatonic, sent the girl to boarding
school, whence eventually, via Paris, she fell into John O'Mara's
arms at a party one Easter in Dublin.

With him, she loosened, eased, laughed. From the night they
met, they kissed like libertines. He wanted her, and she wanted
him, and that desire gingered every day of their lives. The relationship's deeper power, though, came from his care of her emotions.

When pressured, when lonely, when oppressed more than usual,
Alison headed for the gates of silence. Early in the relationship, John
instinctively sensed these moods and trained himself to wait for her.
If one of their dates proved silent, with Alison's mouth pleated in
gloom, he canceled their plans, took her to bed—profoundly against
the conventional mores—and held her.

It always worked, and in time they survived all their jolts, such as
a pregnancy three months after they met. They coped with this by
agreeing to wed, and when she miscarried, they married anyway. By
then Alison had decided: John O'Mara or no other.

He felt ideal to her; he even looked a little like her father: same
dislike of confrontation; same refusal to flap in a crisis; same size,
over six feet; similar large ears and large hands. Same touch of the
debonair, too; John, though never pretending to be anything other
than a country town lawyer, groomed himself like a dandy—perfect
tweeds and varsity tie with white collars on striped shirts. For days
in court he wore dark three-piece suits with foaming white handkerchiefs.

And he was and remained his wife's only lover; smart, resource-
ful, amusing—and strong as a horse in the hips.

As Ronan grew up, he too thrilled to his father's style. So ardently
did John O'Mara fight for his clients that nobody bore him grudges,
not even in the lawsuits he lost. He liked saying that only one client
had ever failed to speak to him again—a man who was being sued
for Breach of Promise. John advised him that he would certainly
lose his case, and when the man felt coerced into wedding the

woman he had tried to jilt, he blamed John. The story made great telling.

"I knew he was a problem the minute he came to the door," John would say. "He didn't knock—he kicked."

When he came in, he refused to sit down and grabbed John's hands.

"I'm possessed by the devil," he said.

"Then it's an exorcist you need."

"No, this is her"—and he showed John an advertisement for a local hairdressing salon where the "devil" worked.

"And did you ask her to marry you?"

"I did—but I didn't mean to."

John wheezed when he laughed—and Alison could never hear enough of that wheeze.

Other than that one "failure," everybody loved John O'Mara. His clients weighed him down with gifts—geese, turkeys, chickens, hams, bottles of drink. Some of the parcels arrived anonymously—salmon stolen from a licensed river, pheasants shot on a preserved estate, a hunk of venison, the fur still attached. Always wrapped in newspaper inside thick brown paper and usually leaking by the time they were delivered, John always knew who had sent them.

Whatever cards John was dealt, he played easily. An outstanding sprinter, he should have represented Ireland at the 1932 Olympics. But he got peritonitis that January, and once he met Alison, he never returned to training. He concentrated instead on building a career in law, and when his hair turned prematurely white, he called it a gift; "I'll win all my cases now—I look venerable."

John inherited his uncle's practice, in a small town near the new border with the North of Ireland. Alison never felt comfortable there, so he sold out and came down south to her territory. Within a year the MacCarthy relatives had sent him more business than he could handle; he bought an excellent old house, and car number 500 in the country.

Their lives became, to his mind, splendid. His journey to the office took twenty minutes along beautiful roads across a ridge;

morning and evening the sun blessed the valley. On Saturdays he finished work around noon and met Alison for lunch in the town's one hotel or took food into the office. Always they drank wine, and always they jumped into bed when they came home. He made her laugh—and laugh—and laugh.

For pastime John gathered local history and sent it to the Folklore Commission in Dublin. In many a dark farmhouse or cottage kitchen, Ronan sat eating currant bread hot from the oven with melting butter as his father collected a family's long-held cures or transcribed old people's accounts of their parents in the Great Famine of 1846 or gathered ancient, homespun prayers.

A shrewd hobby, the folklore; recording people's histories brought John O'Mara new business. When someone had finished talking about the past, he'd ask, "What about the future?"

To the inevitable blank look, he said, "I mean, you should make a will."

Alison never went on those folklore trips. She knew she was much less popular than her husband, she knew that she rode on his coat-tails. Afflicted with her mother's haughty touch, she was only welcome in the houses they visited because of their affection for John.

But, obsessively private, she never gave them a chance to accept her on other terms. They knew nothing of the playful, cuddling Alison that only John saw, who hugged him each night in bed and held on and on and on; or the thoughtful Alison who sent anonymous gifts of food to a grieving neighbor; or the conscientious Alison who cared so tenderly for a manipulative and ungrateful mother, even overcoming her own tense fastidiousness to perform appallingly intimate nursing.

The rural Irish always liked to go out on Sunday nights; consequently the Storyteller's next audience grew by thirty people. Most had to stand, leaning against the walls. Ronan retained his prime seat on the fireside bench.

John O'Mara had laid in cases of liquor. Early in the afternoon, Josie Hogan and Aunt Kate and Mrs. Dowling and Mrs. Condon and

Mrs. Ryan toiled at sandwiches and baking. Alison eventually joined them.

At seven o'clock the house began to fill. Everyone helped to hand around food and drink. By a quarter to eight Alison had seated herself directly across from the Storyteller's chair. He had not appeared for his evening meal, and sandwiches had been sent; Ronan offered to bring them over, and was denied by his mother, who had insisted that Ronan remain within her sight all day.

Eight o'clock saw the large room packed. Children squatted on the stairs, and men sat on the floor. Five minutes went by, then five minutes more.

At a quarter past the hour, John O'Mara walked out of the house and closed the door behind him. Ronan looked anxiously at Kate while Alison chatted with those near her. At half past eight John came back and stood still. The room grew quiet; for a moment Ronan feared the old man had fled—until he saw his father smile.

With what seemed like pride John said, "Here he is."

He stepped into the kitchen and beckoned. The Storyteller stooped a little as he entered the doorway, and doffed his hat briefly to all.

In that reticent society nobody applauded. But the buzz of interest and the murmured words of welcome would elsewhere have translated into a standing ovation.

"Oh, now, isn't he tall?"

"God bless him, hasn't he the look of a traveled man?"

"How are you, sir, 'tis very nice to meet you."

"The whole place is talking about you."

People moved aside to let him reach his chair. Women reached out and shook his hand. Kate stepped forward with a glass of whiskey for him and a warm pat on the arm. A man from down the valley offered him a fill of tobacco.

Then the Storyteller saw Alison, her arms folded, all pearls and formality; he faltered at her show of power and focused on wresting his pipe from his pocket. Next, though, he saw Ronan, and this seemed to give him courage; he raised his hat courteously to Alison.

Yet when he sat down in front of her, his hands trembled and the whiskey quavered in his glass. He tried to clear his throat, but it became a coughing fit. People chatted among themselves again until he had recovered enough to speak.

His pipe, his main prop, eased his way. He fiddled with it, filled it, and prepared to light it.

"Tonight being Sunday night," he said, slow in his speech and his pipe filling, "And the seventh day being the day on which God rested, and the Sabbath day, which we are obliged to keep holy, I'm going to tell you another story about the formation of Ireland. Is there anyone here who's been with me since the first night?"

Among many, Ronan's hand shot up.

"Well, you'll know by now that the stories I've been telling can be used to trace broadly the history of Ireland and the Irish people and the way our ancestors lived. Tonight's story is part of all that—but there's one mighty difference. And it's this."

As he warmed, he calmed. He settled himself more firmly in his chair, but never seemed as though he would have the courage to look Alison in the eye.

"From tonight onward, we're in real history. D'you understand what that means? I'll tell you. Every word out of my mouth so far in this decent house has described a time when no history was written down. Tonight, though, we enter the realms of record. I knew a man once, he was a town clerk up the country somewhere, and he was very fond of 'the realms of record'—that is to say, he preferred facts to anything else. Whatever facts are. And that's an argument for another night."

The match flared, and he puffed until smoke billowed.

"So tonight I'm going to tell you about the patron saint of Ireland—Saint Patrick, Saint Paddy, Saint Pat. Now you all know certain things about Saint Patrick. He wasn't yet a saint, of course, at the time I'm talking about. So we'll refer to him simply as 'Patrick,' and this is about the way he walked among us. I'm going to tell you how he converted the country from paganism. And then I'll tell you how he banished snakes and drove the devil out of Ireland."

If YOU LOOK AT THE MAP OF SCOTLAND, YOU'LL FIND a town on the west coast called Ballantrae; it's just across from the northeast of Ireland. One morning, in the year four hundred and three, a little flotilla of Irish boats sailed into Ballantrae and moored there. The men who disembarked were big and wild-looking. They had long hair piled on top of their heads or braided like ladies or free like the mane of a horse. And they were armed to the teeth with swords made of iron.

Near the town of Ballantrae stood a Roman house owned by a wealthy man called Colpornius, who was the son of a man called Potitus. I tell you this to emphasize the fact that even though they lived in Scotland, they were Romans, because at that time Britain was part of the Roman Empire.

The Romans never came to Ireland. They say that eighty years after the birth of Christ, a Roman general called Agricola stood on the shores of Scotland, looked over at the distant headlands of Ireland, and boasted that he could take us with one legion. Observe, however, that he never tried, and so Ireland was the only country in the west of Europe that never became a Roman dominion.

That's not to say the Romans were unknown in Ireland. Many an Irish raider or trader brought back from Roman Britain a lovely goblet for himself or a brooch for his wife, and some say that Roman boats occasionally came up the rivers as far inland as sixty or seventy miles.

Now: this man Colpornius in Ballantrae had a son called Patricius, not an uncommon name among the Romans in Britain in those days. It means "noble" or "of the ruling classes"—the Romans gave their children Latin names that had a practical meaning. If a

Roman seventh child happened to be a son, he was most likely called Septimus, which means "seventh," or the third child, Tertius, the fifth child, Quintus, and so on. Sometimes they still do it; I lived in Italy for a while, and I had a friend who called his oldest son Massimo, meaning "Maximus—the greatest."

Anyway: Patricius was sixteen years old when the raiders in the boats arrived. These fellows were looking for anything of value that they could rob—including human beings that they could turn into slaves. Slaves were free labor and could be sold on the open market.

When they reached the gates of the villa, the men split up into two groups. The first gang attacked the house and terrified everyone inside. Weapons, wine bottles, jewels—anything they wanted, they took. The other group went to the gardens, where they might find slaves working. And there sat Patricius—we'll call him Patrick from now on—he was reading a book in the sunshine. They grabbed this big, strong lad and ran him back to the shore at the point of a sword. He was pitched into the bottom of a boat with several other captives and taken back to county Antrim.

Patrick became a swineherd, on the side of that bleak mountain called Slieve Mish or Slemish. For the first few weeks he lived in a frightened daze, not quite able to understand what had happened to him. He had no warm clothes, they gave him no good food—often he envied the pigs what they ate. The other slaves were pitched into a rough and bewildered life too, except that Patrick got one of the tougher jobs because he looked robust.

He slept on the mountain in all weathers, trying to keep the pigs near places where he could best shelter, and managing to raise his spirits when a day dawned clear and mild. In summer, naturally, life was a bit more enjoyable, but in winter those cold northern winds found every bone in his body and turned the marrow to ice.

However, Patrick had been raised to use such resources as he had; the Romans were an advanced people. Therefore he made sure to try and extract whatever benefit he could from his difficult circumstances. One of the tasks he set himself was to learn the local speech, the Irish language. A shrewd decision; not only did it help him to understand what was going on around him, it became a great asset to him later.

Altogether he spent six bitter years up there among the pigs, a hard life, full of despair, lonely, dangerous, and without hope. Later in his life he wrote about his experiences, a kind of autobiography they call "Patrick's Confession." In it he described how, hail, rain, and snow, he prayed and prayed on that mountain, to whatever gods he knew, that his burdens might be lifted.

One night, while he was sleeping wrapped in his rough cloak, his life changed for the better. He had a dream in which a wonderful voice told him, "Patrick, Patrick—your ship has arrived." He was a little scared at first, and then very puzzled. But when he thought about it, he believed this must be an answer from one of the gods he had been praying to, and he assumed it meant that he should now try to escape and get back to his own people.

He didn't rush matters; he thought it all through very carefully, and then one day Patrick said good-bye to his pigs, slipped away from the mountain, and headed out into the countryside. Some say he went southeast to Waterford, some say he went southwest to Dingle, some say he went northwest to Derry. All we know is that in some Irish seaport, a captain allowed him on board a rough ship, where Patrick had to quarter with the cargo, a pack of dogs.

The ship sailed from Ireland, and after a long and hard journey down the Bay of Biscay, the captain landed Patrick far south in France. From there, he journeyed slowly back, getting work where he could in order to eat. At last, after many, many months, he arrived home in Scotland, where his parents were understandably delighted to see him. They gave him a wonderful welcome and, deep in their home, took care of him with all the warmth they possessed.

He had barely recovered from these long and difficult adventures when, one night, he had another dream. He dreamed that a man called Victor approached him with a handful of letters and started handing them over one by one. When Patrick began to read the first letter, he also heard a ghostly chorus of the people who wrote it. This

became known as the famous "Vox Hibernicorum," as Patrick called
it in Latin—"Voice of the Irish"—and the words they chanted were,
"O, holy young man, we beg thee to come here again and walk
among us." Of course, he knew who they were because he had
learned to speak the Irish language.

Patrick accepted the message of his dreams. He left his family in
Ballantrae, went to Europe, and embraced Christianity. Very soon
he entered the priesthood and trod the long and sometimes tedious
road of the seminarian. After his ordination he embarked upon a
career in the church, and while still a young man he was made a
bishop, which gives you some idea of how he impressed his superiors; bishops are not generally young men.

Then the great time of Patrick's life began. He returned to Ireland
with a powerful mission—to bring to the Irish people the word of
the Christian God. It was the year four-thirty-two, and Patrick had
quite a task facing him.

Although it hadn't yet reached our shores, the Christian faith
had grown very clear in itself. It proclaimed no other gods except
the one—and in that one true God dwelt the Trinity of Father, Son,
and Holy Ghost. The carpenter from Galilee, Jesus Christ, was born
the Son of God to a chosen girl, Mary, and he died on the cross of
Calvary so that the word of God would be carried around the world.
That was what the apostles preached after the crucifixion of Christ,
and that was the basis of the Christian religion.

But the Irish, in common with all pagan countries, had many,
many deities. Gods lived in the trees, the rivers, deep in the earth,
high on the mountains, up in the sky. Also, they knew their gods
well; they knew who they were dealing with.

If it takes some skill to make any one person change his beliefs, it
takes a remarkable man indeed to convert a whole country. By
then, though, Patrick's own life had shaped him very well for the
job in hand. He came from a noble family and therefore mixed easily with nobility; he knew how their lives worked. Remember too
that he had been a slave; therefore he knew what life was like at the

bottom of the heap. So: can you imagine a man better qualified? Especially when you consider that he was also able to translate the Latin and Greek of Christianity into the Irish language.

And he had other assets; one of them—you'll be surprised at this— was sin. Now, we're all aware that sin isn't exactly what you'd call an asset, but Patrick turned it into one. He let everyone know that when he was a young man he had committed a great sin; he says so in his own writing. Nobody knows what the sin was—he never specified. Some writers guess that he stole. Others say he killed a man. And it might have been something else altogether, something we don't talk about in mixed company.

Whatever it was, Patrick said how it weighed on him. He also exploited it—because it enabled him to meet people on an equal footing. He was able to say, "Look, I'm not above you. I have my faults, too. I've done terrible things." Just because someone had once sinned, he said, didn't mean they were bad through and through. And that was part of his work in life—to show that people might sin and still go on to live good lives.

His next great asset was love. He was a man who loved every- thing under the sun—the flowers, the birds, the clouds, animals, the day, the night. And he loved the Irish people; even though his earliest times here had been miserable, he truly loved us and our country. He also understood that when you show people that you like them, they tend to like you in return—not always, but it often works.

His most important asset of all, though, was that he had a plan. He had worked out what he was going to do and how he was going to do it. The task of conversation, as Patrick saw it, boiled down to two factors—who would be the most effective people to whom he could first preach, and how could he get his message across?

The shrewd man aimed to convert the kings and chieftains first. People like being loyal to their superiors, and he knew that example is the best leader; if he could sway a king, he could convert every- body else along the scale, right down to the slaves. A good and pru- dent strategy, and it worked by and large—but it truly succeeded because of *how* he preached to them, the examples and the oratory he used. Patrick developed a particular tactic, and I believe it accounts for why his conversion of Ireland was so successful.

This is what he did: he knew he had to come to terms with the pagan gods, to whom, as I say, the Irish were deeply attached. But if he could keep them comfortable with what they already had, and if he could use what they already knew, he'd succeed.

The result was, he reinterpreted what they knew as "pagan" and called it "Christian." He didn't dismiss what they had called "holy"—he included it. If there was a tree where people worshipped, that became a holy tree. We have all seen such trees or bushes, festooned with rags where people made offerings to a local saint. They existed in Patrick's time too, but where the people had been worshipping a pagan god at that tree, he now made it the shrine of some saint.

Or if there had been a sacred stone so large and peculiar that ancient people believed a god dwelt in it, Patrick said mass on that rock, and thereafter they called it Patrick's Rock. If it was a well where a demon lived, he blessed the water and turned it into holy water, and it became known immediately and forever as "Patrickswell."

In other words, he reached deep into the land, into the countryside, into the natural life where the gods had been living. And he told everyone that the world was made by the sole Christian God, and that they and everything they saw were part of God's greater glory.

The best example of this gave us one of our national symbols, the shamrock. Patrick was trying to explain how the Christian trinity of God the Father, God the Son, and God the Holy Ghost worked—three persons in one God. He could tell from their faces that his listeners were finding it difficult, so he bent down and picked up a stalk from the shamrock that grows everywhere in Ireland.

"Look," he said. "Three persons in one God, three leaves on one stem."

Not a totally satisfactory symbol in my view, especially when you consider that folks are always looking for a four-leafed clover. But the people grasped it, and shamrock became Patrick's own sacred symbol.

My favorite example of his preaching had to do with his teeth. A few miles from here is the place you all know as Kilfeakle. Well, on the left side of his jaw, Patrick had a bad tooth. When he looked at its reflection in a bowl of clear water, he could see that it was black, and when he held it between thumb and forefinger, it wobbled. And it was sore.

One night, his mission party stopped in a field not far from here, where Patrick's followers built for him a shelter of poles and leafy branches. It was dark, and Patrick's tooth was driving him crazy. He gripped it between his thumb and forefinger, to see if he could make it wobble enough to come away from the gum.

Not looking where he was stepping, Patrick stumbled, and his hand jerked the tooth out. He was delighted—and he proclaimed that in honor of God he would build a church on that very spot. Now, as you know, the Irish word for church is *cill* or *kil,* and the Irish word for tooth is *fiacail* or *feakle,* and that's how the hill of Kilfeakle got its name. Of course, if he founded a church every place the word *feakle* appears, the man must have been a dental wonder. Or he lost all his teeth in Ireland, which is, of course, entirely possible.

So that's how Patrick converted our ancestors to Christianity. He preached here, there, and everywhere, on riverbanks, hillsides, and mountaintops, under trees, standing on flat rocks, at the doors of great houses. He told the story of Christ to the Irish people—to kings and queens, farmers, milkmen, slaves, servantmen, and dairymaids. He told them the miracles. He told them the parables. He told them the mysteries. He told them Christ was the grandest man who ever lived. And of course he told them Christ was God, too, and was also the son of God, and that he lived everywhere.

But, unlike the days when they had to remember which god they were appealing to—this single, great God, Patrick said, had created them and knew them intimately and would recognize who they were when they prayed to him. They loved it, they embraced it, they sank on their knees to introduce themselves to this great God of all, who loved them and who wanted them to be with Him when they died.

And that's the same faith preached in every local church in Ireland every Sunday throughout the year. It came straight down from Patrick, and most of Ireland continues to live by it—even though the English tried their best to kill it. Content in this new faith, our forefathers turned the soil, tilled the earth, said their new prayers, and were happy.

Now: I said I'd tell you how he drove the snakes—and the devil—out of Ireland. And I will. Both matters happened in the same hour and at the same place, and a great relief it has been to us all ever since.

One day, Patrick and his followers came to this fine house out in the open countryside, right in the middle of Ireland, in the county that today we call Offaly. The house sat on a high, grassy mound, a manmade fort. A river flowed past the gate, and birds floated on the water, happy and chirping. Children played and men worked, just like you'd find in a farmyard today.

This was the house of a man by the name of Gara. He sat at the top of the social tree, because he was a farmer of some wealth, which was measured by how many cattle a man owned. Gara had many beasts, and he fed and clothed his family from what he produced on his own land; he was an independent man.

If you walked into Gara's house, you wouldn't be able to see at first on account of the darkness. And just as you were getting used to the dark, the smoke would sting your eyes, because those houses had no chimneys, only a hole in the thatched roof to let out the smoke from the fire. But smoke isn't biddable, it doesn't always rise up in a straight blue column—it likes to meander before it escapes. As a consequence those houses were very smoky.

Hanging over the hearth, you'd probably see a large iron pot being licked by the flames from the logs; and near the fire sat several other such pots, of varying sizes. Over by the window would be a bench with all kinds of tools—knives for skinning; a scythe for cutting down the straw and the rushes with which to repair the building; a round stone kept in a bowl of water and used for sharpening the knives and scythes; a bucket of milk under the table, and a cat eyeing it. Gara was a wealthy man, and his house had everything it needed.

And he was more than just a farmer. Gara also dealt in cowhides, very important for making shoes and other leather goods. Besides that, he bred horses, as any worthy Irishman always wants to do.

He also sat as a judge. We called our judges "Brehons" in the old days, and many of the laws they set down still control our dealings in land—rights-of-way, ownership, boundaries, and the like.

At that time Ireland had no elected parliament, as we know it, no central organization to make laws and govern the people of the whole island. Kings made the rules, but in due time the kings looked to these judges. If a king in a neighboring province heard of a law that he hadn't passed—perhaps it concerned grazing rights, or injury due to an accident, or some such civil matter—he'd observe its usefulness and relevance. And then he himself would pass the same law, or something like it.

Gara was renowned for lawmaking and for intelligence in such matters, and therefore he had wide influence, which made him important to Patrick, whom he now welcomed.

"I'm very interested in hearing what you have to say."

Patrick said, "Do you know who I am?"

"It's a small world, and I receive many visitors. They tell me you have been sweeping across the land like a wind from the south—warm and good."

Patrick never traveled without a considerable retinue of men and women, and sometimes their children. Many of the followers wanted to look after him, fetch his milk, toast his bread at the fire, cook his meat, wash his clothes. Others, who did less work, wanted to hear him every time he preached the word of God, because they themselves longed to go and do likewise.

And there must have been one or two who enjoyed the excitement—because it was thrilling, following this tall, white-robed man with his long beard, with his five-foot wooden staff and the motley who went with him, all jostling to get closer to him, to hear him, to get his attention. And everyone seemed happy and inspired.

By now Patrick's name was growing famous throughout the land, and the people he had not yet met—such as Gara—had a great eagerness to see him.

Gara called his wife, his family, and his servants out into the open fort. The weather smiled on them, and they made arrangements to feed all these strangers—chicken and beef and lamb and pork, bread made of wheat and goblets of ale and warm milk, all set down on a long wooden table. Patrick sat at the place of honor on Gara's right hand and began to tell Gara and his family about the seven days of Creation. They loved hearing about the making of day and night, about separating the earth from the ocean and the instant growing of the herbs and the fruit trees and the making of the morning and the evening and the birds of the air and the creatures of the sea and the beasts of the fields and the creeping things and so on and so forth.

Then he told them the story of Jesus Christ. They grew wide-eyed at the miracle of the loaves and fishes, the healing of the sick, the raising of Lazarus from the tomb. What manner of man was this, who could walk on water? That was the question Patrick always planted in the minds of his listeners so that they'd reach by themselves the conclusion that the carpenter from the shores of Lake Galilee wasn't just a mere man, he was a god too.

Patrick concluded with the five phases that ended Christ's life: the agony in the garden of Gethsemane; the scourging at the pillar by the Roman soldiers; the crowning with thorns; the carrying of the cross up to the hill and the crucifixion on Good Friday, when at three o'clock in the afternoon the sun darkened and the earth trembled as Christ died. When he finished, Gara looked at him, tears in his eyes.

"And they did all this to him just because he was a good man?"

Patrick replied, "The good are a danger to the corrupt. So it is now; so it has always been."

All around that long table, even among Patrick's followers who had heard him tell of these events many times, the tears shone in the people's eyes. Even the very young children remained quiet long after Patrick had finished.

Gara sighed. "Your God is for me," he said. "And I think I speak for everyone in this place. I've never heard anything as powerful. No wonder all Ireland is talking about you."

Patrick placed a hand on the good man's head and blessed him, and within an hour Gara and all his household had embraced the new faith. Drawing water from the crystal clear well outside the ramparts, Patrick baptized them all, leaving Gara until last.

The good man, with the waters of christening streaming down his face, said to Patrick, "I want to give something back to you. But it's a strange gift. It'll ensure for you the following of all the people of the south."

Patrick said, "I'd welcome that."

"South of here," says Gara, "about three days of traveling at comfortable speed, you'll see ahead of you a big flat mountain. That'll be the most important place you'll ever come to in Ireland."

"Why so?" said Patrick.

All of you here tonight know which mountain Gara meant—the Devil's Bit. About twenty-five miles north of this house as the crow flies, near the town of Templemore, the mountain rises alone out of the plain with no other hill near it.

"On this side of that mountain," said Gara, "stands a cave. Inside that cave, if I understand my new faith, lives a great force of evil."

"And who might he be?' said Patrick.

"He's been living there for some time," says Gara. "He makes all kinds of mischief among the populace. Murder and thievery and assault and"—he lowered his voice—"difficulties with ladies and so forth. He makes bad liquor, he cheats at gambling, slaughters animals at night, destroys crops in the fields."

Patrick said, "He'll flee before the word of God. I'll confront him."

"As you go," said Gara, "take one of my musicians with you. My drummer—you'll find him helpful."

•   •   •

I want you to stop for a moment and fix that picture in your minds. The year is four hundred and forty Anno Domini; the sky is blue; the river ripples by. In the middle of this circular fort, standing in front of his rectangular house with its thatched roof, stands a man of about fifty years old. He has a shrewd face, now soft with emotion. Beside him stands his wife, a handsome woman with blond hair that's turning gray; nearby, his married daughter, her husband, and their two children, and all around them, men and women and children, the farm stewards, the servants, and their families.

They're all wearing more or less the same type of clothing—a tunic of linen that comes down as far as the knee and a pair of sandals, made by the simple expedient of cutting out a foot-shaped piece of leather and making eyelets in it for laces or thongs that tie around the leg. Were it a harsher day, most of them would also have been wearing a large, square, woolen cloak, big enough to wrap many times around the upper body and fastened with a great ornamental pin—I'm sure you've all seen pictures of the Tara Brooch. If you haven't, it's a very big pin attached to the back of a jeweled circle.

Patrick was similarly dressed. Ever since he had been a shepherd, he felt the cold and tended to wear a longer tunic than most, and so, winter and summer, hail, rain, or snow, he wore a cloak. His garments, like those of many missionaries, tended to be white, and his followers had begun to copy the way he dressed.

And there they all stood, Gara's household and Patrick's retinue, talking and laughing and rejoicing. Finally, after many good-byes and promises to return, the travelers left the house of Gara. Well fed, laden with new provisions, and with good wishes hanging in the air like sweet little white clouds above their heads, they felt powerful and brave. So they should have; they were traveling in the company of one of the most interesting and successful men the world had known up to that point.

Consider for a moment the challenges Patrick had overcome. Kidnapped at sixteen; made to work as a slave in conditions foreign to him in every sense; a daring escaper whose voyage to freedom must have been full of hardship—yet he came back to the land that had kidnapped and abused him, to bring it what he believed was the greatest salvation ever.

That was some man. So what if he was a little bad-tempered? So what if he fell asleep too easily after a mug of ale? So what if he could be rude and unfeeling? This was a man among men, devoted to the cause he had taken up and for whom no hardship was too great. And remember, he was also a man who found time to write as he traveled the road. It's no wonder Ireland took to heart what he had to say. And he brought us into contact with a wider sensibility, with European religion and the Middle Eastern mysticism of the early church, in a way that had never happened before.

The roads in Ireland at that time were no more than drovers' trails. As advised by Gara, Patrick and his followers headed due south. Knowing a great deal of the enemy ahead, that is to say, being highly aware of the nature of evil, Patrick sent many of his supporters scattering in all directions, looking for reinforcements. They arranged to meet two days later, about half a day north of the infamous cave.

In the meantime, Patrick strode on with the few people left to him, and he ate well and he drank well, and they all prayed and sang, sleeping under the stars, wrapped in their cloaks. Next morning, the people in the fields waved to them as they walked by; some, it was said, even laid down their tools and joined the march.

The two days passed like two hours, and at the appointed moment Patrick climbed a small hill. To the south of him sat the mountain Gara had described, flat as a table. A little to the west of it, and much nearer, a small clump of rocks, topped by a little grove of trees, stood out in the landscape. From Gara's description, Patrick knew this must be the devil's cave. And, as he looked at it, shading his eyes against the sun, he could see smoke rising.

Patrick turned away, his lips grim as a whip. But then he started in surprise. Bearing down behind him, across the open plain, came crowds and crowds of people, divided into bands as orderly as the regiments of an army, each group led by one of Patrick's followers. He couldn't count how many people—maybe a thousand.

He thrilled to this sight; this crowd was beyond anything he expected. They'd all heard of Patrick, accepted the invitation from his followers, and they determined to make the whole business memorable. Therefore they had dressed in their finest, and in Ireland of those times their finest amounted to something wonderful.

Linen tunics of red and green and violet and orange, and woolen cloaks of heliotrope and vermilion—colors like pretty girls—waved and shimmered in the distance like beautiful visions.

Some men played pipes and drums; the others danced along to the music. It was an army of jollity spread out across the countryside like a great, wide, sweet, colorful tide. They laughed when they weren't singing, and they sang when they weren't laughing, and they had only one aim in their souls—to support Patrick, to be as good and helpful and cheerful as any people could ever be on the face of this earth.

When he saw this crowd coming to help him, the tears shone like diamonds in Patrick's eyes. He waited on the little hillock until they reached him, and then each of his own people, one by one, left the group they were leading and came across to Patrick. They all said the same thing to him, as if they had rehearsed it.

"We've gathered these people who want to help. And afterward they want to hear the word of God from you."

"And indeed they will," said Patrick. "They can be sure of that. I won't preach to them just now because I need to conserve my strength. But tell them that I'll address them after I have dealt with this vile creature."

"Do you want us to help in any way?"

"Let's march closer," said Patrick. "But only I and I alone will approach the cave."

They set out, Patrick at the head of this wonderful throng. And the people in all their finery loved walking after this famous man as he strode out across the country under the clear blue sky.

Patrick assumed the demon to be Satan himself, and he knew as much as any man on earth about the adversary facing him. But he didn't know three crucial things.

First he had no idea what the Devil looked like. He had heard that the Prince of Darkness changed his shape as often as he wished. Secondly, he had no measure of how powerful Satan might prove face-to-face, or what force his powers could rise to. And thirdly, he didn't quite know how to drive him out of Ireland. But Patrick had learned to depend on himself since the day he was kidnapped into slavery, and he had no doubt that he'd cope with this too.

They reached their destination quite soon, and Patrick observed that as they drew closer to the black cloud, the musicians in the multitude behind him stopped playing, one after another. The singers fell quiet too, and soon all he could hear was the *swish-swish* of people's legs walking fast through the grass to keep up with him.

Now he began to observe something else. The black cloud spread wider and farther than he thought, and as they reached the wisps at the edge of it, people behind him started to cough. Patrick himself coughed, and then the smell hit his nostrils—as foul as a boneyard set on fire with manure, the worst smell in the world, the smell of hell itself.

Patrick turned to face his followers.

"Go back," he said. "Go back until you can't smell this anymore."

All turned and retreated. Except one woman; she ran forward and handed Patrick a little bundle, a cloth package in blue pleated linen, all neatly wrapped. Patrick took it.

"Hold it to your nose, sir," said the girl, lovely as a smile.

It smelled of flowers from a meadow. Patrick thanked her. Turning, he headed for the cave, the little package pressed to his nose. It took him about five minutes to get there, because—a curious thing—the ground grew rockier and rockier on the way, although from the distance it had looked smooth to the eye. Soon he stood at the edge of the copse; he could see the mouth of the cave and, deep within, the glow of a fire. The smell, even through the nosegay, almost made him drop.

But there he stood, this noble, upright man with his white beard, his staff in one hand, and the blue linen package pressed to his nose.

A noise just ahead, at about the height of his right knee, disturbed Patrick. Then he heard another noise, at about the height of his left knee. He looked carefully. In the shadows he saw what he first thought to be two sticks or very thick reeds, except that they were weaving and swaying, over and hither, in the air. He took a step forward, and one of them made a louder noise—a real, vicious hiss, and a rattle to follow it.

They weren't reeds or sticks—they were snakes! A pair of big black snakes guarded the cave, and when anyone drew near, they rose in the air as though a snake charmer played his pipe. Their venom could kill a man, and they could spit it thirty yards and more.

Patrick stood stock-still to get his fear under control. There's nothing braver than a man who knows fear and conquers it. Taking a deep breath, he poked his long staff forward, and the first snake struck at it. With a fast circular whip of his staff, Patrick coiled the snake around the stick and slammed it down on the ground. He jammed his foot down on the snake's face and then grabbed the reptile just behind the head, a tight and close grip to avoid being bitten on the hand.

Patrick picked the snake up in the air—a difficult thing to do, this was a heavy snake, five feet long and five inches thick. Like a man using a slingshot, he whirled and whirled and whirled the snake over his head and flung it as far as he could out into the open country. The snake flew through the air like a black, flying coil. It landed on a rock and broke its head.

While all this was going on, the second snake darted over at Patrick, twice as menacing as the first. He spat—a mouthful of green venom like a little missile hurtling through the dark air. It missed, and Patrick caught him too, and flung him farther and in a different direction. The serpent went higher and higher in the sky, so high that he looked like a black circle spinning and wheeling, and then he landed with a crash.

But he didn't land on his head, and therefore he didn't die. He scuttled across the countryside, headed for the port of Wexford, sneaked on board a ship, got away from Ireland, and spread the word that no snake should ever come here; it was too dangerous. And there have never been snakes in Ireland since that day.

Patrick stepped forward to the mouth of the cave. He peered in but could see nothing. Suddenly a voice greeted him, a well-spoken voice, a little trace of a strange accent, but an educated speech—this was someone well traveled. The voice spoke in Latin, but I'll translate it for you.

"You shouldn't abuse the property of others."

"Well, you know all about that," said Patrick, stepping in a little farther until he all but blocked the mouth of the cave.

"I know who you are."

"And I know who you are," said Patrick.

"But you have only one name and a dull name at that. I have many names, all of them exciting."

"I need no more than one name," said Patrick, "I have nothing to hide."

"In that case, I pity you. Life is more interesting my way."

"Out! Come on!" said Patrick. "Go! You cause nothing but trouble."

He tried to step inside the cave, but something stopped him. It felt like a barrier that he couldn't see, and yet he also felt as though some force held him back from behind.

But he could now see everything inside the cave; it was a lavish place, hung with all manner of beautiful cloths. He could see nobody inside, and yet the voice came from straight ahead.

"Do come in," said the drawling tone again. "Or d'you feel incapable?"

"I'm never impressed by tricks," said Patrick.

"This is no trick—this is power. Don't you know the difference between trickery and power?"

"I've no interest in such matters," said Patrick. "My concerns lie in making the good defeat the bad, in giving the sacred its rightful power over the profane."

"You know who I was. You know the kind of power I had."

"Yes," said Patrick, "You're the angel who fell, the one God threw out. God in his wisdom, I might add."

"But I had true power—and that felt like nothing you'll ever know, old man. You have no power of your own."

"God is my power," said Patrick.

"But I have power over people's lives. I can make men kill their own children."

"Why is that useful?" said Patrick.

"I can make women drool over such men."

"And how does that improve the world?"

"I can make children mad."

Patrick stood resolute as a statue in marble.

"But can you make someone feel the world all around loves them? Can you make them feel the rain is for cooling them, the wind is for drying them, the sun is for warming them?" He reached down and plucked a tall blade of grass. "Can you make something as infinite, as beautiful, as perfect as this? Look at its shape, its edge, its lovely color, the way it curves. You've never made something as eternally wonderful as this blade of grass—you never could, and you never will."

Not a word came from that cave. A sound came, yes. But not a word. The sound had impatience in it, maybe even a little tinge of anger. Patrick sensed that his blows had landed.

"Can you lead to dignity a man abused by his employer? Can you give hope for a new life to a woman whose infant has died? Can you guide an oppressed people to freedom and power? The God of my heaven can do those things."

Something now happened inside the cave. Patrick saw a movement—he never afterward felt competent to describe exactly what it was; just a movement, a flicker of light, nothing more. The inside of the cave changed color, grew hazy, reddish pink, and shimmered before Patrick's eyes.

The languid voice spoke again.

"For all your preaching, old man, you can't say that you were there when it began. But I was. And I'll be in at the end, too, like I was at the beginning. After all, what are you? A tall man with a beard who can walk fast and tell innocent people stories about a carpenter from a country they never heard of. What use are you?"

Patrick had to rein in his anger, for which he had by now something of a reputation. The cool voice from inside the cave irritated him, and he recalled how he'd learned to use his fists as a slave. But he held fast.

"I give people hope."

"Ah! But I give people enjoyment—which they much prefer. And anyway, you live by promising them something whose existence you never have to prove."

"Not so," said Patrick, who had heard that argument from some of the Irish and never felt he answered it well.

The voice from inside the cave picked up the uncertainty and sharpened up.

"If you weren't traveling among ignorant people, nobody'd listen to you. If you preached where people have education, they'd expel you. Go to Greece. Go to India. See what they think of your nonsense there."

Patrick's blood began to boil like water in a pot; he ran his hand through his hair and clenched his teeth.

"I know all about you," said the voice from inside the cave. "I knew about you up in Antrim. And I know what you did there. Isn't it hypocritical, telling people they should behave, given the secrets of your past?"

Like a man driven by fire, Patrick dove into the cave. But a kind of black sheen whipped across the entrance, like a curtain made of steel, yet shining like satin. It stopped Patrick dead—he had never seen anything like it before, and he bounced off it. And then he had to endure a hoot of posh laughter coming from inside the cave. For a moment he knew not what to do.

However, help approached. While Patrick had been arguing with the languid creature, Gara's drummer had grown concerned. Watching from a distance, he had seen the snakes being thrown into the sky, and now he had seen Patrick forced back as he tried to get into the cave.

The young man came forward silently. So that he would not strike the drum accidentally if he stumbled, he spread grass all over the drumhead. On and on he came, tiptoeing across the open ground toward Patrick, whom he could see up ahead. His master, Gara, had whispered to him as he left the house, "Use your drum as magic. If you see things going badly, strike up a rhythm that'll inspire people."

The drummer came to within fifty yards of Patrick, just in time to hear the cackle of mockery from inside the cave and to see Patrick lunge forward a second time. But again he was repelled by something invisible.

Just as Patrick was about to leap forward a third time, the drummer brushed the loose grass off his drum and set up a slow, steady, powerful beat. It started like an insistent whisper. They say that mushrooms whisper up from the grass, asking to be picked. It was that kind of whispering beat, so soft only the keenest ear could hear it—in fact, so soft that only Patrick could hear it.

He stopped. Some people waste their smiles by using them too often. Not Patrick. He rarely smiled—but when he did, his face shone like the sun after rain. In a flash he understood the drummer's lovely beat—it was keeping time to his own heartbeat, the most powerful rhythm in us all. Patrick turned around and smiled at the musician—a young man of twenty-five years or so, good-looking lad, touch of red in his hair. The drummer kept up his lovely, steady, tranquil rhythm.

Behind him, from inside the cave, the voice called out, "And listen! Your God claims to be 'all-merciful,' and he claims to be 'all-just.' He can't have it both ways. To be merciful, he can't be just. To be just, there'll be times when he mustn't show mercy. What's your answer to that, old man?"

I told you earlier that Patrick had left behind some writings, and one of his most famous works was something many of us learned in school called "Saint Patrick's Breastplate," a kind of a cross between a hymn and a poem. It came into his head now. His brain started to keep time with the drum, and he stood there, a glowing smile on his face, nodding his head. To the rhythm of the drum he began to speak the words of the "Breastplate."

"I rise this day. Through Heaven's strength. Lit by the sun. Bathed by the moon. Gloried by fire. I have the speed of lightning. I am swift as the wind. I am deep as the sea. I am stable as the earth. I am firm as stone."

Suddenly, he heard from the cave a great whoosh! of sound. Still smiling, still chanting the words of the "Breastplate," he looked back at the cave and saw that the black satin screen had disappeared. A bright orange light glowed inside, and in the entrance he could make out some shape, not quite an outline or a ghost—what I shall be content to call a shapeless shape—and it gave off a very frightening air.

Patrick, still nodding his head to the beat of the drum, turned fully to face the cave, and now he stepped far forward.

"God's power will support me," he chanted. "God's wisdom will advise me. God's eyes will look out for me. God's ear will listen for me." He walked steadily forward. At that moment, the cave went dark as coal. "God's hand will guard me. God's shield will protect me."

As fast as a cannonball, the shapeless shape hurtled past Patrick, at about head height; a strange-looking article, it looked like a flying goat.

"I call up," cried Patrick, "all God's power between me and the forces of evil."

The wild shape got bigger—and bigger—and bigger. It flew just over the drummer's head; the lad ducked—and the next thing that went past him was Patrick, running like the wind, extraordinary for a man his age.

The drummer stood and watched. He saw this great, ugly creature in the sky, steaming and enraged, traveling in a southerly direction, and Patrick chasing after it so fast he nearly caught it. The drummer waved to the crowds behind him, and they began to run in pursuit. Within minutes this great colorful crowd of people began to stream across the lovely plain that lies just north of Templemore.

At this point in the chase, Patrick seemed faster than the Devil, whose goat's tail had changed its nature. The tail grew and grew, and eventually it became thick and strong as a bullwhip, with a point like an arrowhead on the tip.

Yards from each other, they raced to the flat top of the mountain. Patrick reached out to grab the Devil's tail. He caught it but had to let it go again because it was red-hot—it felt, he said afterward, like grabbing an iron from a blacksmith's fire.

At that, the Devil became desperate to get away. His way was blocked, so he bit a big chunk out of the mountaintop and carried it off in his mouth. Patrick, stunned at the size of the hole in the mountain, hesitated for a moment, and lost his advantage. By the time he looked up, the Devil had gone too far ahead to be caught. Patrick gave up the chase.

Up ahead, at Cashel, the Devil stopped for a rest, and he dropped the stone out of his mouth. That stone became the Rock of Cashel, the most famous sight in Ireland. If you knocked down all the ancient buildings on the Rock, took up the stone, and hauled it back up to Templemore, it would fit exactly into the slot on the mountain they call to this day "The Devil's Bit."

Lucifer—for it was he, the Fallen Angel, once God's favorite—looked back, and he saw coming toward him across the open countryside not only Patrick but this huge crowd of happy, vividly garbed people, clapping their hands to the rhythm of the drummer. He knew he had lost, and as fast as his legs could carry him he ran to the nearest port—which was Waterford. He changed his shape into that of a gentleman and got on a boat to England, where he lives to this very day.

And that's the story of how Saint Patrick drove the snakes out of Ireland forever and banished the Devil to England. Some people say that explains why there has always been such trouble between England and Ireland. The Devil stirs it up.

The Storyteller's mouth had grown a frill of saliva, a surf on the tide of his words. Ronan saw the man grow larger in his chair as the black coat swelled to the size of a conjuror's cloak, and all the characters in the story sprang from its folds.

Clearly the Storyteller was making up none of this; the old man had lived in the world of his tales. He was there, on a clifftop, when the ice floes broke over the coast of Donegal. And he must have been hidden in the ferns when the bear attacked the Architect. Where was he when Dana stood at the door of the palace? In the shadows outside, near the horses? Or just inside the great doors?

Tonight proved it. Everybody knew the Devil's Bit; everyone in the room had seen it, and many had even climbed it. Ronan had seen it himself hundreds of times. And, of course, the Rock of Cashel adorned postcards and calendars. All true, every word—and Ronan, still sitting on his bench, sipped his bedtime milk.

Somewhere in the midst of these delighted thoughts a new tide of unease began to swirl. It flowed from the usual source, his mother and he turned to look down the large room.

All guests now gone, Alison looked venomous. Her mouth had tightened; she arched her neck a little; she rubbed her knuckles together. Kate's cheeks grew rosier, and she wagged an angry finger at her sister. His father sat still as a pool, head bowed against the fierce murmurs. After a moment he rose and began to pace the floor. When he caught Ronan's eye, he smiled and raised an eyebrow to suggest bedtime. Then, as Ronan climbed the stairs, John turned back and tried to cope again with his wife's feral state.

•   •   •

Alison O'Mara adored her husband, and he worshipped her. But their undiluted passion for each other meant that she kept getting pregnant—at increasing and serious risk to her health. Contraception did not exist: it was banned by the church, outlawed by the state, because, as every Irish Catholic knew, sex between man and wife could only have one purpose—procreation, not pleasure. That's what the church taught and the law supported. Consequently, Alison O'Mara could not and would not use contraception, nor would she let John discuss it.

They had only one course of action available to them—abstinence. If they abstained from each other, they committed no sin, nor did they put Alison at risk—a tough choice in a relationship founded on delighted nightly contact.

In the early days, when Alison and John sat reading, their arms or hands or knees had always touched; sooner or later, Alison would put aside her book, lean her head on his shoulder, and doze while he stroked her hair. When she woke, she invariably smiled up at him and said, "I'm ready for bed."

A few times a year they went out and danced. Together they shimmered across the dance floor, glamorous, bright-eyed, perfect in each other's time. Back at the table, even among friends, their eyes recorded only each other. More liquor, the romantic and clawing intimacy of the homeward car journey, and the playful climbing of the stairs—all helped to prime the mood and build toward heaven.

And then the long arms of the priests and the doctors reached in and pulled them apart. Slowly they saw the ardor of their bedroom cool. Steadily, the freedom that had once delighted them was stifled. Inevitably, the erotic fun of the dance, the car, the fields, the woods, evaporated; caution hurts eros.

As pregnancy after pregnancy failed, and all impulse was handcuffed, they tried the one remedy known to work for others. The church allowed itself a tolerance of the "safe"—i.e., infertile—period; pregnancy was assumed a risk only on certain days of the month. At first they had high hopes—but it embargoed anything sudden; where formerly they had devoured each other, asking only "How?" now they drew up calendars asking "Whether." In the end they found that no regularity could be depended upon, and the sixth miscarriage almost took Alison's life.

Only she and her husband knew how the frustration played out in their souls—and they handled it in different ways. Where John took a resigned view, she turned to prayer and a new zeal for her faith. At every level available she became the church's local advocate. Volunteering for parish duties, she stoked her own piety; the flowers, the cleaning, the music, the choir. She enlisted other local women to help polish the floors and furniture of her beloved God's church. If they failed her standards, she whipped the broom from their hands and waded in deeper.

The practical waterfront covered, Alison next commandeered moral high ground and appointed herself a protector of her community. With one hundred percent of the parish attending church on Sundays, she acquired the force of an abbess, insisting that there was an example to be set. Thus the O'Maras said nightly prayers, nominally led by a dragooned John but driven by Alison. In an open crusade she exhorted all families in the neighborhood to kneel on their farmhouse floors and finger their beads every night. Within months she could be confident, for example, that every family who came to hear the Storyteller had said a rosary before leaving home.

This fervor made her erratic. On the one hand, Alison was first in the world to help any girl "guilty of mortal sin"—pregnant outside wedlock. Yet, of those who stigmatized such a creature—i.e., the church or its pillars—she brooked no criticism, on any level, in any form.

Imagine, then, her view of the Storyteller on Patrick. He had mightily transgressed; "He called our national saint a sinner"; why had she not intervened?

Kate tried to protest, "It was only a story."

Alison countered with, "The Bible is a story."

To which John said, "Dear, you can't have it both ways. Are you dismissing the Bible as a story? Or are you supporting it? If you dismiss it, then tonight was harmless. If you support it, then tonight's story had its own validity."

Alison bit hard on her lip and said, "Stop being such a bloody lawyer. I'm not dismissing the Bible. I'm merely saying that stories have their own power, especially over impressionable people. And he vilified Saint Patrick's character. He called him a sinner."

Kate said to her, "What Saint Patrick did was his own business."

"Most certainly not!"

"He wasn't saying Saint Patrick was bad," said John.

"John, it's our duty to cherish and defend our saints. They guide us morally through life. They are our protectors and spiritual guardians. We owe them our support."

"I bet Saint Patrick was bad-tempered," said Kate. "With teeth like that."

"This is no time to be frivolous," said Alison. "That man believes what he says, and he wants us to believe it. That's my worry—the belief he creates. It's degenerate. He's degenerate. People have left our house thinking Saint Patrick was a deeply flawed man. And that Lucifer actually lived in this country. Here. A few miles away! The nerve of it!"

"Some days I think he's around still."

"Don't blaspheme, Kate! He actually said sin was an asset."

"It was only a story," said John. "Anyway, what do you propose we do about it?"

"You have to talk to him in the morning. Tell him that this house fears and loves God, and we'll not have the good name of God's holy saints interfered with here."

"But this is crazy—"

"Keep out of this, Kate! Well, will you tell him?"

John O'Mara shrugged. "If you want me to tell him, I'll certainly say something. But I've told him he can stay for the week."

"Well, he can't."

"This is such arrant nonsense."

"Kate—that's enough!"

After which they fell silent.

John O'Mara shrugged. "I'm not asking him to leave. You're the one feels strongly."

"But you're the head of the household, aren't you?"

"This is rubbish! If people knew—"

"Kate!"

In this sullen air they drifted apart, blowing out lamps and candles and heading, one by one, for the stairs. Ronan raced ahead of them, worried to the heart. Did this mean no more stories?

He awoke later than usual; his father had not called him. Josie Hogan made breakfast, singing as ever and blinking behind her owl's glasses.

"Where are they all?"

"Your father's gone to work."

"Already?"

"So's Kate."

"Where's Mama."

"In the land of dreams," said Josie.

"Did you see any sign of—"

Josie shook her head.

"Not hide nor hair. Wasn't he good last night?"

"D'you believe him, Josie?"

"About the Devil's Bit? 'Course I do."

In the barn the Storyteller's boots stood like monuments at the bottom of the stair. He reached in, touched them, and exhaled in relief. The old man wasn't gone—he must be staying.

But by the time he got to school, he began to worry afresh. The Storyteller had no one at the house to protect him from another attack. Should he go home? If only he could slip out . . .

Miss Burke looked preoccupied. Ronan clambered from his desk and made for the door—no good.

"Ronan O'Mara. No toilet break until half past ten."

With a swerving finger Miss Burke directed him back to his desk.

•   •   •

Alison had seen Ronan leave for school. She had long been dressed, waiting for a clear coast. Downstairs she sent Josie to the barn with a tray of breakfast—and instructions to tell the Storyteller to come to the house when he had eaten.

An hour later, she received him in the parlor. Immaculately groomed, severe as a lady in an old photograph, she said, "Close the door, please."

He stood before her with his hat in his hand and his fear on his face. And he recoiled as Alison went straight in.

"You mentioned Italy last night. How did you come to live in Italy?"

He straightened up, a little surprised, and composed his answer as firmly as a man expecting praise.

"Irish College in Rome, ma'am. Six and a half years."

But she struck with the speed of a snake.

"A spoiled priest?"—the scathing term for a failed seminarian.

The Storyteller defended.

"Spoiled, yes, ma'am. By all these lovely people up and down the country listening to me through the years. Priest—no. And never would be."

"So if you failed to go through, how can you presume to speak about Saint Patrick?"

"Probably, ma'am, because he, like me, was one of God's creatures. And he's my native saint, too."

Whatever the bravery of his face, his soul felt as thin as a playing card.

He could never have won. With a disdaining finger and thumb Alison handed him an envelope. He stood back, unwilling to take it, and she thrust it until he gave in.

"Please go. We can't have blasphemers in this parish."

"No, ma'am, no, I'm no blasphemer—"

"You'll not undermine what we stand for here. Go. And go now."

"Ma'am—your husband, there's an understanding—"

"My husband's not here. Do I need to summon help?" said Alison.

Her viciousness chilled him. He wheeled around and left abruptly, never looking back. In his wake she winced in every bone at the hurt she knew Ronan would feel.

From his desk Ronan could see part of the village street. The man swept past the gate, walking like a machine, and Ronan shot out of the classroom—too fast for Miss Burke.

"Sir! Wait!"

The boy ran headlong, and the Storyteller guessed who called him. Still racked by Alison's force, he held up his hands as though to ward Ronan off; then he walked even faster. In a moment the steepness of the hill would hide him from the village and the shame.

At the top of the slope Ronan caught up. The Storyteller's stride was too fast, and he longed to grab the frayed, black sleeve, but his nerve failed. For a moment the old man glanced down at the boy, and then he looked away again, as though he dare not engage. He began to talk, more to himself than to Ronan.

"I've been well treated. She gave me money. It's all right!" He ended each sentence with a whimper, a kind of upward *Nnnnh*. Then he paused and said again, "She gave me money."

"You can't go! I'll tell my father!"

That was always Ronan's greatest threat—but the Storyteller pressed on. However, his head had lifted a little, even if his face still bore anguish.

"Your father's a decent man."

"He'll want to know where you are. And what'm I going to tell my aunt?"

On the narrow country road the tall man strode ever faster while he tried to shake off the blond boy running by his side.

Ronan sprinted several yards ahead and turned so that he could look at the Storyteller's face. But he then had to trot backward, because the man would not slow down. In the distance another figure appeared on the slope. Deirdre Mullen, a girl from the senior classes, had been sent by Miss Burke to fetch Ronan back to school; she held out his coat.

Ronan renewed his plea.

"Please stop! Please come back home with me! Sir?!"

On the previous night, as he lay in bed after the Patrick story, Ronan had come near to panic. What if he lost the Storyteller forever? The man had become his personal wizard, had taken Ronan into his magic life. An arched eyebrow, a little nod that others never saw—he made Ronan feel he had traveled across the globe to these fields, to this village, to the O'Mara fireside, just to meet him. Now, on the pillow, he decided: If Mama sends him away—run away with him! Become his apprentice. Learn how to tell stories. After all, the man promised to teach him.

"Sir! Sir! I'm coming with you."

The Storyteller hesitated, then strode faster, out of sight of the village now. With Ronan still backpedaling, entreating, Deirdre Mullen began to run, beckoning harder. The boy began to weep.

"Sir? Please let me. I'm never any trouble!"

Deirdre Mullen caught up. The Storyteller realized they had a pursuer and turned his head.

"Hallo," he said to her. "They've come for you," he said to Ronan and stopped.

"I don't care. You could come back to my house now. Or the school, Miss Burke'd love to see you. I know she would, she asked me all about you. And then I could go with you."

Deirdre Mullen stepped carefully around man and boy. She was (and to this day still is) level and calm. Ronan flapped his arms up and down, a sign of distress. When he did it at home, Kate and sometimes his father put arms around him quickly and held him. Neither the Storyteller or Deirdre Mullen moved. They waited for Ronan to subside. She wore a broad green ribbon in her frizzy hair.

After some moments, she eased the coat levelly onto the boy's arms and stooped to button it. The Storyteller moved in on her success.

"If I tell you one last story, will you go back then?"

"No! Not a last story!"

"All right. One *more* story?"

"Now? Here? Where?"

"There's a gate." He pointed to the tree-shaded limestone pillars of an old entrance. Light rain began to fall. "We can shelter."

Ronan hesitated. Deirdre Mullen finished buttoning his coat and led him by the hand to the sheltered gate. The Storyteller followed.

"When I tell you this, will you go back?" said the Storyteller, when they had settled on the wall.

"He will," said Deirdre Mullen. "Won't you?"

Ronan nodded. He had too many tears on his breath to speak clearly.

Fifty years ago, every country road in Ireland saw a simple and pleasing morning sight. Most farms kept cows, milked morning and evening. One or two pails, still warm and creamy, went to the kitchen for the family's use. The rest, in shiny aluminum cans shaped like tall, fat cones, were taken to the local creamery on horse-drawn carts; consequently, a monthly check, a farmer's salary, underpinned the rural economy. From eight o'clock every morning, Ronan awoke to the sound of carts trundling by and looked out of his window at the gleaming creamery churns.

Along the road now, coming toward the village, he saw the first of the returning farmers. Dan Collins, his face a mottle of freckles, called Ronan (and all small boys) "Captain." He stopped when the Storyteller asked him for a light.

"You're the man they're all talking about?" he said.

The Storyteller smiled. "We're telling one more story."

"I'll listen so. If nobody raises a parliamentary objection," said Dan Collins. "Slow, Beauty," and the horse duly lowered her head to graze on the roadside. Another cart appeared and another, and soon seven more farmers had reined in their horses on the damp November lane.

The Storyteller lit his pipe with Dan Collins's matches. Blue smoke roamed the gray morning. He eased the old black cravat from his chicken's-neck throat.

"This tale has special meanings for you," he told Ronan. "Your first name, as I'm sure you know—it means 'little seal,' and your last name, O'Mara, means 'coming from the sea.' So listen carefully, because this is a story about a great sea voyage—and a little seal from the sea should know about such things."

W E MUST REMEMBER ALL OUR LIVES TO RAISE our heads and be aware of the horizon. A boy may achieve great things in his life by casting his gaze abroad; that's how he will find the wonders that the world can offer. And anyone who looks out to sea on our western coast may see ancient visions, sights from the long-ago. This story confirms that point.

It's a known fact that the Irish got to America long before Columbus or Amerigo Vespucci or any of those characters. How else can you explain that the North American Indians who greeted Columbus offered him a drink of "usquebah"? Listen to the word: "usquebah." Doesn't it sound like the Irish term we pronounce as "ish-keh ba-hah"? Which means "the water of life"—and your ear will tell you that the word *whiskey* comes from *uisce,* the word for "water."

One morning a long time ago, on the rocky shores of Kerry, where the relentless Atlantic waves beat green and wild on the beaches of the southwest, a very respected monk by the name of Brendan stood and looked out at the horizon. A long time he gazed, the salt seas flecking his beard and his eyes narrowing against the gleam of the sun on the waters.

Some weeks earlier, a nine-year-old boy had asked him whether great palaces rose from the sea. Then, a few days before that, when he was visiting another monastery at Clonfert in county Galway, a very old monk, named Barrind, told Brendan that if he sailed westward he would come to "a Promised Land which God will award to his chosen souls when Time ends."

Brendan had sailed the seas frequently, but always to other parts of Ireland or Scotland or Europe, and in his travels he had come to believe many things about God. He believed, for example, that God keeps his most beloved creatures in the deep of the ocean. And—to answer the little boy's question—he also believed that golden palaces lay out there, beyond the line where the sky meets the sea. On days when the light on the waves shone brilliant as blue gems, on nights when the world had a quiet so deep you could hear the lobsters breathe, he had watched how the sky lit the sea and looked at the serrated gleams of the silver fish in their shoals.

A woman once asked him what it was like to understand the spirit of the sea, and this is what Brendan said:

"When I rise out of my bed and take in the first air of the day at my door, I can smell the sea. And when I smell the sea, I also see it—in my eyes and in the eyes of my mind. When I feel the waves lift my boat, I feel in my bones the pulse of the tide. And I know that my heart and soul shall not be at peace with each other until I am once again afloat like a prayer on the swell of the waves."

Brendan, as you know, is called "Brendan the Navigator." The word *navigator* comes from the Latin word *navis,* meaning "ship," and Brendan carved out for Ireland and the Irish the greatest path in our history—the path to America. Every morning of the year, all along the shoreline of the Atlantic seaboard, men have stood and gazed west across the sea as Brendan did all those centuries ago. They do it still, in the counties of Kerry, Clare, Galway, Mayo, Sligo, and Donegal. What were they looking for, those coastal ancestors of ours? What do they look for now?

It has been called many things—the lost city of the sea, the golden country in the ocean, the Land of Youth. Some people have referred to it as Hy-Brasil and believed that the gilded towers rising out of the waves were in Brazil. But the explanation of Hy-Brasil has a greater simplicity; in the ancient languages of Europe, *brasil* means "fortunate" or "abundantly rich."

When I was at school, I learned a poem which began, "On the ocean that hollows the rocks where ye dwell/A shadowy land has appeared, as they tell/Men thought it a region of sunshine and rest/And they called it Hy-Brasil, the Isle of the Blest." In the poem, a man decides to set out in his boat and find these gorgeous palaces, these cloud-capped towers, and he sails and he sails and he sails. But he never draws nearer—the gilded city stays far ahead of him, and the last line of the poem is, "And he died on the ocean away far away."

My story describes how Brendan the Navigator, braced by the love of his God, set out to find Hy-Brasil or the Promised Land of Saints—and found it. I believe that Atlantis or Hy-Brasil or whatever you like to call it has always been the coast of America. And they do say that if you sail into New York up the Hudson River in the early morning, the sun gilds the skyscrapers until they look as though they're made of gold.

The year was five-forty-six Anno Domini, that is to say, five hundred and forty-six years after the birth of Christ. Patrick had been dead almost a hundred years, and Brendan, born on the sixteenth of May four-ninety-three, had pursued devoutly the teachings of Christianity, which Patrick had brought to Ireland.

Brendan was a strong man, over six feet tall, with deep brown eyes; he made all others chuckle when they heard him laugh. As a young man he had embraced Patrick's teachings with joy. He examined his own life in the light of this new God whom he had learned to love, and he understood that the search for God must be seen as never-ending.

So he became a holy man and established monasteries where the word of God, as taught by Patrick, could be kept vigorous and spread anew. To do this, he called upon his own particular skills as a superb boatman. Using his control of his boat and his knowledge of the ocean, he sailed up the west coast of Ireland and established monasteries that lasted for many centuries.

On the morning in which this tale begins, Brendan acknowledged to himself that he had been restless for some time. The monasteries he had founded prospered under the abbots he had appointed; they didn't need his attention, and so he longed for a new quest. When the young boy asked him about the horizon and what lay beyond, and then when the old monk Barrind told him about the Promised Land in the ocean, Brendan took all this as a sign from God that he must set out to find the place. To guarantee the success of his mission, he fasted forty days and forty nights, and when his fasting ended he began his new work.

In the monastery at Ardfert, he gathered the fourteen monks who formed his usual crew. He had three helmsmen, each of whom would work sixteen hours a day: one steering, one the lookout, the third sleeping. Eight other men would handle the great leather mainsail, which in heavy weather became as unmanageable as an elephant. A doctor and two cooks completed the crew. All of them loved and respected their great skipper, Brendan.

Of course, he had taught each of them the skills they needed for sea voyages. The helmsman could also cook, and the doctor could repair a sail or patch the leather keel of the boat if it was torn by a reef or a shark.

Brendan met the men in the monastery chapel. All those buildings were made of wood in those days. They sought to form monasteries quickly, to bring together their monkish communities as fast as possible. Abbeys made of stone would not be built in Ireland for some centuries yet. As the fourteen monks knelt in prayer beside Brendan, each felt the rush of excitement he always brought to their lives when he summoned them. They had sailed with him up the broad, slow-flowing rivers of Ireland, through the fogs around the coast of England, and into the placid estuaries of Brittany.

In rain or under hailstones the size of plums, scorched by yellow suns or tossed by winds that blew from the throat of the world, in freezing storms where the ice hurled itself at them in particles as big as golf balls, they rowed, they steered, they sailed, eager to be in the company of this wonderful man who made everyone feel so good and so capable.

Now, when their prayers had ended and Brendan had implored God's blessing and a serene voyage, they crowded around him, full of excitement: "Where are we going this time?"

Brendan told them of the two conversations—with the young boy, and with the old monk. The sailor monks smiled and laughed; one or two clapped their hands. Then, almost as one voice, they told Brendan, each and every one of them, that they too had often stood on the shore, gazed out to the light of the west, and asked themselves—and God—what lay beyond.

These men loved Brendan. They loved his kindness, they loved his immense capability aboard a boat, and they loved his love of the sea. When they sailed with him, they each tried to be awake for the moment, every dawn, when Brendan dipped his hands in the ocean, brought the salt water to his lips, tasted it gently with his tongue, smiled, and said to them, "How fortunate we are—how fortunate!"

He never failed them in this little ritual; he performed it every dawn, and then he blessed them with the water.

Now he told them what he knew of Hy-Brasil—that on certain days of the year, due north and west of where they now stood (in other words, directly due west from the center of Ireland), great towers rose slowly from the sea. Witnesses had reported that on clear days they had actually seen the shelves and ledges of these towers as they rose out of the ocean, and the billows of the waves as they fell back from them.

At first, said all who had seen them, the buildings seemed dark, in shadow. But as the sun swung around on its slow course across the heavens, its golden rays soon lit the towers, and they seemed more wonderful and more expertly constructed than anything ever seen. And the spray from the billows caught the light and looked like diamonds in the sky.

Brendan told his crewmen that he himself had never seen this city of the sea. Nor had any of them; one helmsman, however, a slim and quick-footed man with muscles of iron, told them all that his grandfather, who came from farther up the coast, from south Galway, had seen it. They pressed him for details, with Brendan the most eager. The helmsman said that his grandfather reported great clouds of wonderful birds flying in circles above these towers. And in front of them, spouting whales sent hundreds of fountains into the air.

Most notable of all, said the helmsman, was his grandfather's feeling—and this too was held in common with all who reported sightings.

"Every sighting brought my grandfather a wonderful, gentle peace. For over a week or so afterward, he felt calm and good. He slept deeply at night, he awoke untroubled and placid. And every day he came down again to the shore to see would the towers reappear."

Brendan loved this report so much that he asked the helmsman to repeat it. Once again they all listened, as enthralled the second time as they had been the first. Then Brendan pronounced that he suspected God of having put in his mind the idea of looking for this place. Something so wonderful, he believed, must have been created by God for a specific reason. They needed to find that reason, and when they had found it, they would have also found some more of God, something new.

So they left the monastery of Ardfert and set out on their great voyage. All the monks gathered to watch them depart, rowing away in a flimsy boat.

Their first port of call was the Aran Islands, to visit Brendan's old friend Enda, whose advice everyone valued. At the end of the third day, Enda had confirmed to Brendan that a trip to the west across the ocean would surely honor God. Brendan and his boat left for their next stop, an island up the coast of Mayo. There, he and his crew began to build a new boat, a big version of the curragh, the fishing boat they still use on the west coast of Ireland today. This new boat would be the greatest of them all, made by sewing together the hides of forty cows, and each had to be perfect when taken from the cow—no holes made by warble fly, no damage to skin caused by ulcers. All of them set to work, including Brendan; he had a rule that he never asked anyone to perform a job he wouldn't do himself.

But the most immediate task wasn't boat-building. Brendan took a helmsman, the tallest of the fourteen crewmen, to a point high on the clifftop, above where the island's boats lay on the sand. He told the man to spend every day before their departure gazing out to the west, in the hope of sighting the rising towers. Straight away, the helmsman began his vigil from dawn to dusk.

Now the crew began to build the great boat. They knew exactly what to do, but nevertheless they understood that it would take many months, even though all the materials they needed for the building were ready to hand in the surrounding countryside. First, they chose the skins they wanted, forty cowhides supplied by the nearby farmers, and they stitched them together with thread made of flax. Linen comes from flax, and the core of the flax plant is a very strong fiber.

Next they searched for a tree to make the mast, and they found a tall ash from the northernmost side of a forest, where the living is hardest. They cut down this tree, skinned it clean, and weathered it in brine; and every day they checked it for any sign of rot or decay. When the mast passed their examination, they unrolled the sail they had made and spread it out upon the broad white sand. All the men knelt in a row on the leather and moved forward in a line, peering minutely at the fabric one last time. This was a most important inspection; if the sail had suffered a small perforation, a high wind could turn that little gash into a great rent and thus imperil the voyage.

No holes were found, not even the size of a pin, yet Brendan decided to proceed with another test. Section by section, four of them held the sail up, slacking each portion into a kind of belly. Then Brendan poured water into this billow and dropped to his knees, peering underneath to see whether water leaked or—equally dangerous—seeped through the leather. This scrutiny took many cumbersome hours, but in the end the sail seemed utterly watertight, and everybody praised and thanked God.

Just for safety, they did one more thing. Monasteries raised sheep so that they could get the wool for the monks' robes. When you shear a sheep, the fleece has grease in the wool. That grease makes wonderful waterproofing and elasticity. The monks had tubs of such grease for the specific purpose of making their hide boats waterproof. The crew smeared the boat with this grease, and by the time they were finished they must have smelled so rancid that the dogs barked at them.

Brendan allowed a week for stocking the boat with supplies. They also carried sufficient materials to make two more boats. At the end of that week, he had his last consultation with his watchman on the clifftop.

He, in answer to Brendan's questions, reported, "I have seen the white gannets making themselves into spears as they dive beneath the waters to come up with fish in their beaks. I have seen the small puffins by my feet, unafraid and inquisitive. I have seen the guillemots trying to save their eggs from tumbling down the cliff side. I have seen the shearwaters fly like small, dark angels. And I have seen the clouds wipe the face of the sun. But I have seen no gilded towers nor whale fountains, no great flocks of birds in the sky."

He also reported that the wind had swung a little to the southeast and would favor them. And so things became plain to everyone, and Brendan knew they must set sail next day.

For fifteen days they sailed out to the northwest, never knowing where they were going, never controlling where the winds blew them. From time to time Brendan himself took a turn at steering, but even he could not determine the direction of his boat. After fifteen days the wind dropped. Not so much as a sigh filled the great sail, and the men took out their oars and rowed. That was how their voyage continued, sailing and rowing, rowing and sailing, and they began to make fine progress across the wide straits of the Atlantic Ocean.

Have you ever been at sea? This is what you can expect. The sky assumes an importance it never receives on land. At sea, you have only two landscapes filling your eye, one above and one below. The one above can be gray or blue or white or hidden by fog. And the one below will be green and gray and black and blue, sometimes all at once. Above you, all will be stillness and unmoving vista, save for the days when clouds pile across the sky like pillows of down taken from giant geese. The landscape beside and below you, namely the sea, will heave and chug and pull and splash. No portion will be still—even if it appears to be. Every particle of it will be in motion, every second of the day.

Nothing on the surface or in the deep sits still. All heaves and shifts; the sea moves this way and that, shunting and slipping and slopping, here, there and everywhere.

But if you look very closely at the sky and the sea, you begin to understand that all is not air and water. Sometimes above your head, like a dark flake or a faint pattern, a flight of birds will pass, intent on a migration to or from Africa. They may be swifts, who sleep on the wing; they may be swallows or martins. Sight of them does not necessarily mean you have neared landfall, as happened to Noah and Columbus. All you may be seeing is a flock of birds traveling onward.

And if you look down at the waters, you begin to see other wonders in that green-green race that sloshes past your leather hull made from the hides of forty fat cattle. Is that a jellyfish you see there? A great mauve blob shimmering just below the surface of the sea? Or did you glimpse a creature fly up out of the water, describe an arc above the surface, and then fall back again with almost no splash? In which case, here be dolphins. Or porpoises. Or basking sharks. They bring good luck, and mariners welcome their attentions, especially the dolphins.

We do well to remember dolphins. If a dolphin ails, then others come alongside and nudge him gently through the waters; because a dolphin must keep moving in order to keep breathing. We all have need of our dolphins alongside us from time to time.

And in those North Atlantic waters, two other great sights might have greeted our beloved Brendan and his fellow mariners. Somewhere out there, among the billows and the surges, great green creatures mosey along, offending nobody and feeding many others.

These are the whales of the North Atlantic, and if you are very lucky, you will hear them sing—they sing deep, vast, musical sounds, like melodic foghorns, like church organs in deep caves, like the sound of the earth before Man was born.

Lastly, your eye will be dazzled by something extraordinary. It will not be something to sail near; it will be a thing to avoid, as the whales do. You will not be able to escape looking at it; because you will never have seen a color so white in your life. This will be an iceberg—and then, if you draw near, you will find that the ice, that white, white ice, whiter than snow or hoarfrost or the freshest milk, is, inside itself, blue. But some of you already know that.

Those sights were there in Brendan's day—and when they set sail across the North Atlantic, he and his men saw a multitude of other wonders too.

The first place their boat came to had high cliffs. Streams of fresh water poured like waterfalls straight over these cliffs into the sea. The mariners had run out of food, and they needed desperately to find some people who would supply their boat. But they sailed and they sailed around that high rocky island and couldn't find a place to land. Then on the third day Brendan himself saw an entry, by chance, in a sudden flash of sunlight. He thanked God for the vision, and they sailed straight in.

When they disembarked, a dog came up to them, wagging his tail. He seemed to be leading them, and Brendan believed the dog was a messenger that God had sent. So they followed the dog, and they came to a town. The dog led them to a great house where the walls were hung with drinking vessels and harness pieces. They had evidently reached the home of a wealthy man. No people appeared, but miraculously, food and drink were placed on the table, and basins of water were laid out for them to wash their poor feet.

After a grand meal of excellent fish and wonderful bread and all the drink they needed, Brendan and his crew took to bed in very comfortable accommodation.

During the night Brendan had a dream. Now I should have mentioned that, as they were sailing away from one of the islands near

Ireland, three monks came forward and begged Brendan to take them with him. He did so, but with considerable reservations because there was one of these monks whom he didn't trust. That night, Brendan dreamed that he saw a devil enter this monk's heart.

They stayed in the great house for three days and three nights, and then the time came to set forth again. Before they left, he warned the monks not to steal anything. They all cried out, "Oh, no! Never!" but Brendan looked at the man he didn't trust and called the man forth from the rest of the group.

He said to him, "Last night the Devil gave you something. Where is it?"

The unfortunate monk looked astounded. He reached into his tunic and pulled out a silver bridle that had been hanging on the wall. At that moment everyone saw a little devil leap from the man's chest and flap away, complaining bitterly. The thieving monk fell down dead, and they buried him on the island of the flowing waterfalls. Back in those days, that was the way of the world, and the ways of the world were various.

After many days and many nights on the wild wasteland of the ocean, they reached the next place—a lovely island. Brendan called it the Isle of the Sheep because when they went ashore they saw flocks of sheep, all white in color, and many of the sheep had their little lambs with them.

Now—conjure to your brain the picture of that day. The sun shone with the clear and bright light of the North Atlantic. Under blue skies, with an occasional little riffle of cloud like the tail of a mare, the big leather boat was rowed by these strong Kerrymen to a small, sandy harbor. Not only was it rowed, but a favorable wind came behind them and greatly assisted them, bulging their big leather sail.

See them in your mind's eye. The boat edged up on the sand with a pleasing, crunching noise. Out climbed the monks, led by Brendan. They stood on the pretty little shore and stretched their arms and legs, this group of rough-hewn and warm-hearted men in their long whitish cassocks. All of them had beards—because how could they have shaved at sea? Their faces had been creased brown by the winds, and some had blisters on their hands from the rough wood of the oars.

But they slapped each other on the back, they joked and roared with laughter—and they bowed their heads in gentle prayer led by Brendan.

All of them knew what time of year it was. Easter had arrived; they had landed on the Isle of Sheep in time for Holy Thursday. Brendan instructed his men to capture a spotless lamb so that it could represent the Lamb of God as they celebrated Easter.

Next morning, Good Friday, a man approached, and he recognized at once that his island had been graced by the presence of a wonderful holy leader. He threw himself at Brendan's feet and declared himself honored to have been chosen by God as Brendan's next supplier. You might say that both men had a very good knack for conducting business! They all celebrated Easter, and they left the Faroe Islands weighed down with almost more supplies than the boat could hold. Yes, the Faroe Islands—out there in the Atlantic, those were the Isles of the Sheep.

What came next was in some ways the most surprising thing that ever happened to Brendan—or indeed to any Irish monk, or perhaps any Irishman. They pushed out to sea again, intending to sail, following the directions of the Faroe Islander, to a place he called "The Paradise of Birds." Now this, they felt, was getting a little more like what they had hoped to find—an exotic place as described in the legends of the Promised Land of the Saints. But long, long before they could reach it, the boat ran aground.

They looked out over the side, down at the ground that had halted them. It had no grass. All they could see on its surface was some driftwood; it was a scrabby sort of a place, uninteresting and gray, harsh to the touch, with barnacles and seaweed. Some of the crew got out and tried to push the boat off the place where it had grounded. They found themselves unable to do that, so they were reduced to sitting down and eating their supper. A few reflected surprise that Brendan stayed in the boat and never climbed out. Brendan, however, knew something about the island, something secret and frightening, and he did not want his monks to know.

That night, some monks slept in the boat, and some slept on the island. Next morning, the crew decided to cook some of the raw meat from the supplies. They lit a fire of the driftwood on the island, and to their horror and amazement, the island began to move. At top speed, they scrambled back into the boat, abandoning the burning fire and the pot sitting on it. Brendan held out his hand to help each and every man aboard, and he told them to hoist the sail as fast as they could.

They hoisted the sail; it bellied with the wind. But as the boat pulled out from the island, the island seemed to slip away from under the boat. Amazing! Each went in different directions, with the island sailing away much faster than the boat. They watched it for one, two, three miles, with the fire still burning on it.

This crew of innocent men was very puzzled by this matter until Brendan explained: they had not been grounded on an island— they had come to rest on the back of a great whale!

By now the North Atlantic had truly begun to open up to them. But it's important to remember that Brendan did not undertake this great voyage for any personal esteem. He sailed out there for the greater glory of God; for him it was a form of worship, a long and arduous prayer. At the beginning of the voyage he had pledged himself to follow God's instructions as they reached him and as he interpreted them. And so things became plain to everyone.

The Paradise of Birds, their next port of call, looked marvelous. Flowers grew there, so abundant and multitudinous that it looked as if part of the island was one great colorful carpet. Once again they sailed all around the shores until they found a place where they could land. A silver river exactly as wide as the boat turned out to be their avenue of entry. But it proved too shallow for the draft of the boat, so all the crew climbed out and stood in the bright river, with only Brendan remaining aboard.

Two monks hitched ropes to the prow; they lowered the sail, hauled the boat inland along the stream, and came to rest not far from the source of the river. On the bank stood a tree whose trunk was thicker than anything they had ever seen, as thick as one of the famous American redwood trees through which men have cut roadways.

In the branches of this great tree sat so many white birds that it looked as though the tree had white leaves. Brendan found this image so profound that he prayed to God for a sign that would tell him what it meant. As soon as he had finished his prayer, one of the white birds flew down from the tree, and the noise of her wings sounded like the ringing of a little silver bell. The bird sat on the prow of the boat and began to speak.

She told Brendan and his amazed crew that all the birds on the tree were spirits who had been released by God at the fall of Lucifer. Ever since then, they had traveled the world advising people how to celebrate God—and their favorite resting place was this tree.

The white bird now told Brendan she had a task: to tell him where he and his crew must celebrate the great holy days of the year. They were to stay on the island of the birds until Pentecost was over, forty days after Easter. Then they were to travel on to the island of a saint called Ailbe, where they should celebrate Christmas—and then back to the Isles of the Sheep for Easter, and then Pentecost again with the birds. And they had to do this for seven years before they would be released to find America.

When she had imparted this information, the white bird flew from the prow of the boat up into the tree. As she landed there, all the other birds began to sing hymns and psalms, and they kept time to the sacred music by beating their wings. The sound made a melody that could be heard a thousand miles out to sea.

After spending the allotted time of forty days and forty nights on the Paradise of Birds, Brendan and his monks set out with heavy hearts for the island of Saint Ailbe. Getting there was no easy matter. The summer sun burned them, and the sudden squalls and

great gales of the ocean buffeted them here and there, but finally
they found the island. When they landed on it, an old monk
met them, but he never said a word. It soon dawned on Brendan
that this was a silent community where, for the love and honor of
God, nobody ever spoke.

Then several other monks arrived, carrying candles. With gestures they invited Brendan and his men inland and confirmed that
this was indeed the island of Saint Ailbe and that the Irishmen were
to stay there for Christmas. They led the sailors to the chapel to
pray. Inside the church, which was a perfect square, the abbot broke
his silence and told Brendan that this was an island on which
nobody ever grew old.

As they knelt there, a burning arrow flew in through the window
and lit all the candles in the church. Brendan and his men dropped
to their knees in wonder. And they stayed there while the monks of
the island turned the earth, tilled the soil, and were happy.

Bear in mind now that Brendan had received an instruction from
God to sail the ocean for seven years before he could find the
Promised Land of the Saints. When his first spell ended on the
island of Saint Ailbe, that is, when Christmas had passed, he and his
crew took to sea again. Now, in the remainder of the seven years,
they wandered to and fro. Between the island where the white
sheep lived, the island of the birds, and the island of Saint Ailbe,
they had rare adventures.

One island they came to had a well, and they were parched with
thirst. So they drank long and deep from the well, and they all fell
asleep. The man who had one drink of water slept for one whole
day, the man who had two drinks slept for two days, and the man
who was greedy and had three drinks slept for three days. But eventually they all woke up and went on their way.

And then they came to another island where they could hear the
sound of a sledgehammer on an anvil. Somebody on the land saw
the boat, and a blacksmith came running out with rage on his face.
In his hand he held huge iron tongs, and in the teeth of the tongs

blazed a lump of coal. He threw this coal at the boat, and it fell sizzling into the water a few feet from where the oars touched the sea. Other islanders came out and also threw burning coals, but luckily they missed, and the boat sailed on.

After this, they were traveling along merrily, when suddenly they observed that the sea seemed still and thick and no matter how they rowed, they couldn't seem to get themselves out of it. But they rowed for forty days and forty nights, and eventually they pulled clear.

As soon as they did, a great sea creature began to pursue them, steam blowing out his nose. They were terrified and tried to row as fast as they could, and get every last puff of wind into the leather sail. But closer and closer the creature came, until they could feel his hot blowing breath on their faces and see his bulbous eyes glaring red and green at them, and the foam of his nose steaming.

They prayed to God, oh, they prayed and prayed in anguish, and after the third prayer went up like a sigh, a new creature appeared on the opposite side of the boat. He had long teeth with edges like saws, and he swam round the stern as smooth as a spear. In deadly silence he attacked the dragon that was following the boat, and he bit the vile creature into three bloody chunks, and the monks went on safe and sound, thankful to God that their prayers had been heard.

For months and months they sailed to and fro on the ocean, and then it became years and years. Each Easter they found the island with the sheep, each Pentecost the island of the white birds, and each Christmas the island of Saint Ailbe, with its silent monks and the people who never grew old. Soon it was time for their reward.

One morning, with the sun shining over their shoulders, they at last sailed due west. Little white waves pranced on the surface of the sea, and little white clouds danced on the floor of the sky.

The watchman cried out, "Look! Look ahead!" and everybody turned so fast the boat almost keeled over. There, on the waves, sailed a wondrous tower of crystal. It was so high they could not see the top of it, and it went down so deep into the water that they could not see the bottom of it, even though the sea was as clear as glass at that point.

Furthermore, the tower was wrapped in a great, silver net whose meshes were so wide that the boat was able to sail through it. And sail through they did, and out the other side, under a sort of natural bridge in this icy crystal tower, and when they had sailed through it, they somehow knew they were on course for the magical country they had hoped to see.

Soon they sighted land, and their hearts told them that this was their destination as promised to them by God, as suggested to Brendan by the aged holy man, his friend Barrind. But suddenly a great fog came down. Just as everybody began to fret, Brendan recalled that one of the holy men he had met had told him they would sail into their promised land under the protection of a fog.

Sure enough, the fog lifted, and there they were—on the coast of America! They drew the boat up on the shore, and on the white sands knelt to thank God for their great success.

This country was the biggest place they had ever seen; they could tell this from the great mountain ranges in the distance. They walked up and down on the shore and the dunes looking inland, where they could see trees heavy with fruit and leaves turning a wonderful gold. Yes, this was indeed a promised land.

After they had rested, Brendan heard a voice shouting what he hoped was a greeting. He looked up and saw a band of men coming toward them. Fine-looking men, tall and handsome, they had painted their bodies and wore great headdresses of feathers. Their leader raised his hand in the air and with the palm held outward and flat said to Brendan, "How."

Brendan knew this was some kind of greeting; because he could see that the flat palm meant the man didn't conceal a weapon. He bowed to the man and offered him a drink of Irish whiskey from the leather flask that they carried on the boat. The gentleman took it and loved it. Brendan taught the man how to pronounce its name—"ish-keh." In gratitude, the man, with a wide sweep of his hand, indicated the country behind him, as though suggesting that Brendan was welcome to visit—or indeed own—any part of it.

But Brendan, with the gracious air that caused people to love him, declined. He had accomplished his mission, and if this was the Promised Land, then God had kept his word, because it looked wonderful. There might not have been any gilded towers inland or tall fountains of water or circling flocks of multicolored birds—but the earth was obviously fruitful, and the inhabitants obviously welcoming.

After a few days, Brendan decided to return to Ireland and his monastery in Kerry. So he and his monks loaded the boat with provisions and accepted the gifts of precious stones given them by the man with the feathers, who then plucked from his headdress the most brilliant feather, taken from the wing of a great eagle, and handed it to Brendan, his special gift. Brendan promised to send many more countrymen from Ireland to this Promised Land. He kept his promise many million times over.

Brendan the Navigator sailed home, where all the people of Kerry turned out on the shore to greet him. And that's the story of how Saint Brendan discovered America. As for Hy-Brasil and Atlantis, who needed to find them when he had seen such wonders? And anyway—aren't they all one and the same place?

Heavier rain swept in. Another tale had ended. The carters shuffled their reins and chatted to themselves in that same shared delight that the Storyteller had generated up and down the country for so many years. Ronan slid down from the wall. Red Indians! Sea creatures! The Storyteller had aimed this one last story more at him than anyone else.

During the telling, Miss Burke had arrived. She neither scolded nor objected. In shelter near the gate pillar, she folded her arms and listened. At the end, the Storyteller looked at her apprehensively and held out a hand for her to shake. She took it.

"I'm to blame," he said. "Blame me."

"No blame," she said, a thin woman with wire-rimmed spectacles and tense curly hair close to her head. "Only a brute or a fool would interrupt a story."

Ronan said, "Where are you going, sir?"

"I'm going where I always go. On the road."

"Sir, where'll you be tonight? My father'll drive me to meet you." He twisted his fingers round and round.

"Listen," said the Storyteller, bending toward Ronan. "I'm a hard man to find. Here."

He took Ronan's hand and spoke so that no one else could hear.

"You're an important boy. That's what you are. And you'll grow to be an important man."

The Storyteller straightened up, then stepped fast away from the group and never looked back.

Ronan said, "Listen! Sir! Wait!" He started to follow—then held back. "Oh, God!"

The tall dark figure headed east, walking so fast and smooth that he seemed like a man on wheels. Behind him on the little hedge-lined road, everyone stood watching the lone walker.

Dan Collins broke the silence; "Hop up, Captain."

Deirdre Mullen helped Ronan onto the cart. He looked back—but all he saw behind him was the lumbering file of horses and carts. Rain veiled the distance.

After school Ronan set about his mother.

"Did you send him away? You did, you did!"

"Behave, please."

"He was the best thing ever happened. And you're not going to stop him telling us stories. And I'm going to find him."

His disturbance became worse than anything Alison had seen in him. She hauled him screaming to his room, locked the door. He lay facedown and churned the bed in a weeping, raging hurricane.

John O'Mara came home and heard Alison's complaint.

"Appalling. If it had been a mere tantrum—I was almost afraid of him."

"Well, you know why—"

"Are you saying we should condone it? Really, John!"

"Look, Allie—I also wanted him to stay. Not just for Ronan's sake—"

"I don't want to talk about it, I don't want to know about it."

John went upstairs, unlocked Ronan's door. For a moment he worried whether he should call a doctor; Ronan lay in a heaving wheeze, still in hysterics. After several minutes of soothing talk, water helped, taken in sips with John holding the glass for him. But the anguish broke out again, and John listened to his son's gasping-for-breath tirade, saying nothing, nodding his head, holding Ronan's hand, stroking the boy's hair.

Again Ronan lay down, this time less angry but still weeping in a helpless way. John asked him questions, invited recollections, tried to talk him out of it.

"That picture of the Devil at Cashel. His mouth full of rock, Patrick on his heels. I thought of it all day."

No response, no let-up.

"In all the stories, what was the thing you liked most?"

The weeping continued, a sound of genuine loss.

"C'mon, champion. It'll be all right."

Kate arrived. She lifted Ronan's upper body from the bed and held him tight. Not quite crooning, she nonetheless made soothing sounds and rocked him in her arms, looking over his blond head at John's concern.

It took an hour and more; eventually Ronan began to tell them, as best he could, the story of Brendan the Navigator's great voyage; from time to time the echo of a sob tripped his breath. Kate brought food; all three had supper in Ronan's room; he did not go downstairs again that night. Neither did Kate.

She said, "He'll be back one day."

John waited to comment until Ronan was ready to sleep and said, "Try and turn bad into good."

"What does that mean?"

"Find him. Learn more about him. Become his friend."

Later that night, Alison lay in John's arms and wept at her own actions.

"Why can't I stop myself? Why?"

He said, "Shhhh. Let it pass."

"Kate's right. I can be such a bitch. I don't mean to be." The tears poured down.

"Shhhhhhh. Easy, easy." John stroked and stroked her hair—and the matter ended there.

Ronan never mentioned the Storyteller again in Alison's presence. But, long accustomed to an inner world, he now created his greatest secret yet. As methodically as geometry, as driven as an underground movement, he began a plan to find the Storyteller and make the man part of his life. From that moment, even though he was only nine years old, he built a core system known to many men—three lives, public, private, and secret. In Ronan's case they comprised school and the neighborhood; home and its curious ramifications; and, deep inside him, his secret quest for the man in the long black coat.

He began by contacting every person who had heard the Story-teller in the O'Mara house. What with children and carters, neighbors and wives, women who had helped prepare food and drink, this amounted to over a hundred people.

Schoolmates gave him the first guidance, that is to say, the first measure of difficulty. Ronan altered his behavior to get what he wanted; he stopped quarreling and developed a facile, pleasant manner.

"Did you ever hear where he went?" he said to Deirdre Mullen.

"My father thought he wasn't going far."

"How far?"

"Maybe ten miles. Maybe twenty."

"Where would ten miles take him?"

Deirdre said, "Which direction?"

This flummoxed Ronan, made him think again. He had assumed the man would follow the road to a logical place—a town or a village.

Deirdre's friend cut in. "My brother said he heard the man got a lift to Dublin."

"That far?"

Deirdre said, "Ronan—he could be anywhere."

After that arresting thought, Ronan decided to establish patterns: whether the man came to the same houses year in, year out; whether the Storyteller had previously been in Ronan's neighborhood; whether anyone had met him anywhere. One or two neighbors thought they had seen him in the past, but couldn't be sure.

He made all his inquiries sound casual, and in due course, he met every adult who had been to the storytelling sessions. Some lived nearby, and he could easily ask innocent questions. He got a bicycle for his tenth birthday, and on this he traveled the countryside.

People responded generously. They liked discussing the stories, told Ronan what they remembered, rehashed them as they did great sporting events.

"That woman, arriving at the palace in the moonlight, what was her name?"

"Ah, but what about that shaft of light? We should all see that."

"The devil's tail—the heat off it."

On and on it went, lively and vigorous memory, pleased reminiscence with people happy to be reminded.

Two years Ronan spent, of weekends, vacations, and long summer evenings, two years of pondering, looking at maps, measuring distances—and sometimes fighting off anxiety; could the old man still be healthy? But not one answer took him any closer—no address, no connection, no trace. By then, however, he knew so many lanes, fields, and hidden avenues, and these too became the secret places of his mind. He also traveled inwardly; over and over again he revisited the four tales he had heard from the Storyteller, and he felt that he knew them by heart; Newgrange, Ulster, Patrick, and Brendan.

So far as he could tell, nobody had yet sensed his search. He grew daily closer to his father and Kate; if they guessed at his great enterprise, they never pried. At the same time, to protect it—and himself—he drew further and further from Alison. He learned not to inflame her with a tantrum nor touch any of her numerous flashpoints.

Indeed he ensured his distance from her in an ironic fashion—by doing something he knew she dearly wanted. He enlisted as an altar boy, in crimson soutane and white surplice. On Sunday mornings he lit candles, answered the Latin prayers of the mass, brought forward the altar wine. Alison's pleasure at his newfound "piety" doused some of her ire at him; his careful distancing did the rest. Ronan gained doubly—by her approval and by a new visibility in the parish; if anyone heard anything about the Storyteller, they knew where to find Ronan.

About six months into his search, Ronan developed a parallel, separate passion. He became imbued—and soon obsessed—with his country's past. His private games changed. No longer Hawkeye, he became a warrior, a champion. He borrowed entirely different books from the library; no more Jack London or Zane Grey—now he took out Celtic myths, old sagas, accessible history books, and collections of folk tales. Following his father's mail-order gene, he spent his pocket money on secondhand books from catalogs: *Annals of the Fair Isle, Ulster's Champions, Ancient Irish Warriors.* He traced Celtic scrolls in special notebooks.

Night after night he followed a driven course; homework, supper, and then a long, glorious delve into the past. He taught himself every legend of the long-ago. Ancient family names and their meanings; places of magical fame; the birthplaces of heroes—they went into another notebook. He learned the weapons that Champions bore, the curses witches cast, the evils of shape-shifting goddesses—such as the Morrigan, harbinger of war who sometimes appeared as a bird and sometimes a bride. Great duels, fights to the death between famous warriors, love affairs, elopements, intrigues—he escaped into a past that not only satisfied his huge thirst for story but affirmed him in the deepest way.

"This is what I come from," he said to himself—a short step from, "This is what I am."

His passion for the past brought him nothing but advantage. Such reading had a scholarly appearance, and it also kept him in touch with his search as he traversed the same ground—and more crucially, breathed the same atmosphere—that he had heard from the Storyteller's lips. He read Saint Patrick's *Confessio*; he found Brendan's *Navigatio*. In effect he became the complete bookworm, content to live in his room.

He paid no price. The social life of his peers had never been important to him; he had never mixed much, and now he never missed it; his inner force drove him like powerful twin engines. Best of all, he was left alone to pursue it. The adults in his life approved his studiousness; they endorsed it, even indulged it. His head deep in piles of books, lit by a single candle, he frequently had to be reminded of bedtime by Kate or John.

On the broad surface of the world, Ronan's life seemed little different from the norm. Primary school ended when he was eleven, after which he went to a higher school in the town where his father worked. On most mornings Ronan cycled the five miles, his imagination calling giants down from the hills or seeing fields as battlegrounds. During bad weather he traveled in the car with his father and, later in the day, did his homework in a corner of the law office. The staff made a fuss of him, especially the unmarried ladies.

Every Thursday, he had lunch with his creature-of-habit father, either in the office or at McGuane's Hotel. Sometimes acquaintances joined them. If the opportunity arose, Ronan asked whether they had ever encountered a traveling storyteller. The question usually triggered a discussion, but in all of his enquiries he learned nothing of the man in the long black coat. Nobody knew his name, whence he came, or where he went.

He might have vanished completely. The police had no trace of the Storyteller nor knew how to track him; they defined such a person as "of no fixed abode." No other house in the parish had ever accommodated him, not before, not after, his time at the O'Maras'. No farmer or carter or truck driver had been known to give the man a helping hand on his journey. None of the doctors—in the town or in the country parish—had ever treated him. Nor had anyone reported food missing or traces of a stranger sleeping in their barn, as sometimes happened with tramps or men caught on a journey with insufficient money.

At last, in December 1954, three years after the visit, Ronan asked his father to help. Not caring to divulge the passion of his hidden search, he broached the subject elliptically.

"Mr. Cronin was teaching us the history of Newgrange today."

"Oh?"

"He was wondering when educational tours might start."

His father put down the newspaper and began to gaze through the window.

"Wasn't the Storyteller remarkable?"

"Better than the pictures," said Ronan.

"Better than the cinema, yes."

Nothing else was said for a moment as father and son reflected.

"He looked so ill," said Ronan. "D'you remember? When he came here first?"

"Ye-es," said his father.

"I wonder if he's still alive? I mean—we could go and see him, couldn't we? If he was in a hospital?"

John flinched. "D'you know 'The Twelve Days of Christmas'? Kate was playing it on the piano last night. D'you know why that carol's interesting?"

Ronan looked at his father: Why this swerve, this blunt change of topic? He waited.

John said, "If you add up all the gifts, they come to three hundred and sixty-four, one for every day of the year except Christmas."

Yes: a definite change of subject. Ronan opened his mouth to make the challenge—but he recognized the finality with which his father returned to the newspaper.

Three weeks later, though, Ronan heard once more the voice for which he so longed and ached.

Traveling storytellers prospered best in undeveloped times. They triumphed before print, before mass communications. In Ireland they had occupied a special niche—storytellers in a land of stories. Here too, however, time eventually defeated them, with books, then newspapers. The hammer blow, though, came from their own idiom, words spoken by the fireside: in the late 1920s Ireland acquired radio.

John O'Mara bought a set when he and Alison married. It sat on a table in the parlor, covered with a brocade cloth like a household god. John alone knew the controls—the volume, the tuning, the exotic, mysterious wavelengths: Hilversum, Berlin, Kobenhavn, Bergen. On the shelf beneath the set, the great batteries sat in a stout box and lasted many months, because the family used the radio so rarely. They listened to a daily news bulletin and—for Alison—an occasional papal broadcast from Rome.

•   •   •

On New Year's Eve, 1954, the O'Maras visited friends. Ronan, as usual, declined.

From the hallway John, departing, said, "This might be a good night on the wireless."

For the first time he showed Ronan the controls.

"Don't move the dial. It's always on Athlone."

The moment they all drove away, Ronan turned on the radio, and the god's green light glowed like an eye.

Half listening, Ronan sat rereading *The Ancient Irish Warrior.* He had long tried to run through a wood without rustling a leaf or treading on a twig, jump a bar set at the height of his own head, pluck a thorn from his foot while running at top speed; all the old warrior trials from the tale of Newgrange had cropped up repeatedly in his reading. The radio droned a distant mixture of speech in Irish and English, punctuated by dance music.

Suddenly, Ronan heard the words "oral tradition" and a word that sounded like "shana-quee," which he recognized as *seanchai,* the Irish term for storyteller. Heart racing, he rushed to the set— God! Is it?! Yes! It is!

"No, I've never separated history from myth," said the great voice. "I don't think you can in Ireland."

No mistake, no possible doubt; the Storyteller had evidently answered a question.

Another question: "Where do you get your stories from?"

Answer (after a pause): "That's like asking a star where it gets its light. Or a lark where it gets its song. But I can help you a little. Whenever I'm visiting a house in an important or famous place, I always try to have a story about that place. Not long ago, I found myself in the vicinity of Slievenamon, the Mountain of the Women. Decent people there gave me bed and board, and I told them a story of how the mountain got its name. And since you invited me here to tell a story, I'll offer it now to you."

THE GREAT IRISH WARRIOR, FINN MACCOOL, HAD the longest arms and the fastest legs and the fairest hair and the bluest eyes and the broadest shoulders and the soundest digestion of any man ever living. He was a god, a leader, a warrior, a hunter, and a thinker.

And he was a poet. One day, when they were all discussing the sweetest music on earth, one of Finn's warriors said it was the sound of hounds baying as they pursued a stag. Another claimed it must be the rushing of water over a weir when fishing for salmon. A third said it was surely the flutter of a woodcock's wings as it rose from the brush before the archer.

The argument raged back and forth, with every warrior giving his opinion. Finally they all turned to Finn, who hadn't said a word.

"Finn," they said, "what do you think is the sweetest music in all the world?'

Finn didn't answer for a minute. He looked into the distance, where the mountains were turning purple in the light of the sinking sun—and then he spoke.

"The sweetest music of all," he said, "is the music of what happens."

Make of that what you will.

Anyway, it came to pass once that Finn MacCool was searching for a wife. You would think he knew how to find the right creature; after all, hadn't he tasted the Salmon of Wisdom? You remember that, as a boy, he met a man on the banks of the river Boyne, who asked him to tend a salmon the man had caught and was boiling on the fire.

"But," he said to Finn, "on no account are you to taste it."

He knew, you see, that he had at last caught the Salmon of Wisdom, and he also knew that whoever tasted it first would instantly acquire all the wisdom there ever was or would be. That was why he wanted the fish in the first place.

Young Finn watched the salmon cooking, and to his alarm he saw a blister rise on the salmon's skin. He was worried in case this meant that the fish was burning, so he pressed his thumb down on the blister. But it burned him, and he put the thumb into his mouth to cool the burn. At that moment he saw all the wisdom in the world. And that's why we have wisdom teeth—because that was the tooth where Finn pressed his thumb.

Now: when Finn grew up and wanted to marry, he knew what he was looking for; the wife he wanted to marry had to be beautiful and capable, exactly what any man wants in a wife, only some want her to be wealthy as well. And they want a woman who other men admire—but don't admire too much.

Finn was a very eligible bachelor, so, as you can imagine, once he let the world know he was in the market for a wife, it was as if the heavens opened and girls came down like rain. So many lovely, sweet-natured, competent lassies were brought by their mothers to see Finn that he had to work out some way of dealing with it. Drawing on his wisdom, he decided on a solution, as follows.

He asked them all to meet him at a place where he used to enjoy hunting, on a mountainside in county Tipperary. Good deer ran there, and some wild boar, and down the slopes poured mountain streams, bright as molten silver, cool and refreshing to wash a hunter's face at the end of a great day's pursuit.

Hundreds and hundreds of girls arrived with, needless to say, their mothers, and in many cases their entire families, all recruited to the cause of marrying Finn. The great man lined them up to inspect them, and they all smiled big wide smiles at him. Some of them were as blond as flour, and some were as dark as blackberries, and some were as red-haired as rage. And they were all raising their eyebrows at him and saying "Choose me! Choose me! I'll make the perfect wife for you." Some of them had even brought apple cakes that they had baked, because Finn MacCool was known to have a mighty appetite for apple cakes.

Looking at this variegated throng, Finn didn't know what to do. Any man faced with that gorgeous array would have to admit bewilderment. This was his solution: Finn got them all to wait at the foot of the mountain, and he organized a race to the peak; he would sit up there, and the first girl to reach him would be his bride.

He told them the rules of the race. It could only be conducted in daylight. There was to be no movement during the night, in case some girl got her father and her brothers to carry her near to the peak while everyone else was asleep. He would blow his hunting horn to start the race, and again to call a halt each night. And he told them, "As it's a very steep mountain, with rough ground and wild thorny bushes, I expect that the race will take up to three days."

He left them, climbed the mountain himself in seven strides—calling, of course, on his powers as a god—found a comfortable place to sit, and blew a long blast on the horn. It echoed among the valleys and the woodlands; it scared the deer and the mice and the songbirds—and it started the race. Hundreds of girls in their pretty colors scrambled and clambered up through the heather and over the stones of this rough old slope.

Now Finn MacCool hadn't tasted the Salmon of Wisdom in vain. He'd given them the hardest test of their lives. Some fell into the streams; some cut themselves on stones and started to cry; and some got so badly scratched by the heather or bitten by the horseflies, because it was a very hot summer day, that they stopped and could carry on no more.

But by the first nightfall, there were still several hundred girls left in the race, and they had reached about a third of the way up the mountain. Finn blew his big hunting horn, and that was the signal to tell them that the race was over for the first day. He watched over them from the mountain peak as the girls all settled down slowly to rest. In most cases their fathers or their brothers or their uncles had followed them up the mountain to bring food.

Some who had come alone had brought no food—after all, nobody had expected a race—and they were invited to share with those who had lashings to eat. They might all have been rivals, but every woman was on her best behavior, because they also wanted Finn to see how nice they were. At nightfall, as the shadows finally darkened over the mountain, the sight Finn saw was one of happy people settling down and eating well.

Next morning, when the sun had fully risen and Finn had consumed his breakfast of berries and wild honey, washed down with the water of a sweet mountain stream, he blew a loud blast on his horn. As he peeped over the edge of the crag on which he sat, he saw the race begin again. The girls in their gorgeous colors set out on the long climb, and such leaders as had been at the front the previous day now led once more. This day grew much hotter than the previous one, and many fell by the wayside, in tears, berated by their mothers for not making a greater effort. It felt like an act of charity when Finn blew the horn at the end of the second day.

After much bathing of bruised feet and much feeding of hungry mouths, the mountainside at last fell quiet as the exhausted girls fell fast asleep. Finn sat high above them and listened to the music of the night's happenings—the occasional soft cheep of a little bird dreaming in its nest nearby, or the sudden cry of a small creature caught by an owl, or the snuffle of a badger rooting food for its young.

Now: when all the girls had been lined up in front of him on the day they arrived, Finn had noticed one above all the others. She was a red-haired girl from Kildare, with a lovely wide smile and a shy and gentle eye. He had tracked her journey during the day, and he saw that she had done well and was robust enough to keep in among the leaders of the race. Everybody had responded well to her; even the most ambitious of the mothers had smiled if the girl spoke to her.

On that second night, when Finn was satisfied that all the ladies were sleeping, he crept down the mountain. Being a god and a great hunter, he had eyes that could see in the dark, and he began to inspect the sleeping beauties. He was searching for the girl from Kildare.

And he found her; she was asleep like a baby on a bed of heather. Finn reached down, picked up her up very gently in his great arms, and carried her to a place near the peak of the hill. He placed her down at a spot not so far up the mountain that anybody would think she cheated, but not so far down that she could be overtaken.

Next morning, when the sun had cleared the hill, Finn blew on his hunting horn for the race to start, and the girl awoke. She blinked her eyes, saw where she was, rose, and started running up the slope. It takes little imagination to realize that she was the first to reach Finn's arms.

On the first day of the next quarter the Kildare girl became Finn MacCool's bride. It was the greatest wedding ever seen in Ireland. There were seven men wielding seven shovels for seven days, stripped to the waist and sweating—and they were only mixing the mustard for the sandwiches.

And that's how the place got its name; the Irish word *Slievenamon* means "the mountain of the women." Now—is that myth or history? Some will tell you that it's a myth, meaning fanciful—but I'd say it has to have some truth. Why else would we have a place called Slievenamon?

Music broke out; no announcement, no thank-you, no name. Ronan waited for the tune to end, but—nothing: no reference back, no comment. Ronan's elation gave way to dismay. Could he reach the man? Where did the broadcast come from? Dublin? Over a hundred miles away. Nearest telephone? The doctor, but that's three miles. And anyway, what number to call? He sank back on his knees to consider. Then, gathering his resolve, he rose, went to the table, and wrote the story down as best he could.

Next morning Ronan said, "Dad, where do they make the programs on the wireless?"

He wrote to Dublin that day. After some weeks a letter came back from the Director of Radio, saying they could not put listeners in direct touch with contributors, but if Ronan cared to write a letter, they would forward it. "However, in the case of your inquiry there seems little point, as we believe the gentleman in question lacks a permanent address."

Disappointment again—but there was a straw to grasp; at least he knew that the Storyteller still walked the land; the search was worth keeping up. As long as the Storyteller still traveled, Ronan had some chance of finding him; if the man came off the road, it probably meant illness and unthinkable death. Every day now he checked the radio program list in case another appearance should be heralded, and every day he revised his knowledge of this new tale.

The writing down of the story—having a tangible record—brought such comfort that he then transcribed the other stories he had heard. Sometimes he checked details with his father or Kate, and he wrote and rewrote again and again, fine-tuning and adding and shaping, until he felt he had fully echoed that beloved voice from his head.

Just under two years later—on his fourteenth birthday, in October 1956—another written reward came his way. John came home from work, slipped into Ronan's room, and took a letter from his pocket, written on blue paper.

> *Dear Mr. O'Mara,*
>
> *I have something of interest for you here. Your name was suggested to me because it is known that you collect folklore, and we have recently had a Storyteller visit us. He told a long tale that entertained us all. My daughter is attending secretarial college, where she is learning to be a secretary. She took down the story in shorthand and typed it out. Her teacher said she typed it magnificently. When the gentleman found out that there would be a record of what he said, he mentioned your name and that of your son, Ronan, and he seemed most anxious that your boy would receive this story. Knowing the way things can get lost, I don't want to put it in the post, but if you would care to visit us some Sunday, I'd gladly hand it over.*
>
> *Yours truly,*
> *Madge O'Callaghan (Mrs.)*

On the following Sunday, they drove thirty miles to the house of Madge O'Callaghan (Mrs.). Ronan, who had not slept the night before, pulled all talk in the car back to the Storyteller.

"I wonder how long he stayed with them?"

"What stories did he tell?"

"He was very near us."

"I wonder, did he know them before?"

Kate said, "Why do you ask that?"

"On the map they're east of us, and when he left us he went east."

John said, "But that's five years ago. How can you remember so clearly?"

From the back seat, Kate said, "Ronan remembers everything about him."

The house had a thick and safe thatched roof. On a windowsill cooled a loaf of fresh bread. A dog wagged his way to them, licking Ronan's hand. Inside, everything shone, including the stone floor.

Madge O'Callaghan (Mrs.) welcomed them. On the table sat crockery and a deep apple pie. Ronan's patience dwindled as Mrs. O'Callaghan fretted about other things—the government, the weather, "the state of the country."

"We have too many elections altogether," she said. "I'm beginning to think we should have no government. We should do the job ourselves."

At last John asked the aching question.

"Now tell us about your Storyteller?"

"Well, he came in here one night a few months ago and I wasn't best pleased to see him let me tell you because I knew that he'd disturb the whole house and those old men they always want to stay for a week but this man said no that he was never again going to stay in any one house for more than two nights that way he could do no damage that's what he said."

Madge O'Callaghan (Mrs.) practiced unusual punctuation.

"So anyway he arrived and we fed him and he sat down and it was like having a magician here we were all speechless when he told us the story of how the monks wrote the Book of Kells and my husband said afterward that wasn't the truth of it how could they write the Book of Kells like that and we all said to my husband what does it matter if the story is as good as that?"

She looked at Ronan.

"He asked if we knew you and he told us about you." She stopped and, uncertain how to continue, looked at John and Kate.

Ronan said, "Was he all right? I mean, his health?"

"My daughter sat alongside him and she has the shorthand she can write down a hundred words a minute imagine that a hundred words a minute and she took it all down and she typed it out and her teacher said it was magnificent the way she did it."

Large, placid Madge O'Callaghan went to a dresser in the corner of her large, placid kitchen. She drew out a manila envelope and handed it to John, who handed it to Ronan, who placed it on his lap. The farm wife smiled at him.

"Oh, another thing I said to him, 'Sir, how fast can you walk?' and he said to me, 'Missus, my height, when I don't stoop, reaches to six feet and three inches. Often have I contemplated whether my long legs count as an advantage, and I've concluded that they do. Because,' says he, 'I've looked at small men hurrying and they have a great deal more work to do than me. In answer to your question, I took to the road in nineteen-twelve and I believe I've been walking at least thirty miles a day for the past forty-four years. In any one year, I hope to spend an average of two successive nights in the same bed, that is to say, when I arrive at a house, I hope they'll put me up for as long as they can. Some people manage ten nights, some manage none, and I calculate that it averages out at two. If, therefore, I average five walking days a week—that means I walk for two hundred and sixty days a year. Multiply that by an average thirty miles a day, and we come to a sum total of roughly eight thousand miles a year. For a period of forty-four years I reach a total of, miles walked, over three hundred and forty thousand. I seem to recall that the circumference of the earth is twenty-four thousand nine hundred and two miles, and if my poor mathematical gift doesn't fail me, I assess that I have walked round the globe nearly fourteen times.' My husband calculated it afterward and said it all worked out."

Suitable wonder lit all faces.

"Three hundred and forty thousand miles," said John and looked sad. Ronan had a picture of the Storyteller as a tiny figure walking along the equator on a huge globe of the earth.

Mrs. O'Callaghan said, "He told us he knows most of the barns and overhanging sheds and warehouses and unguarded premises on the island of Ireland and he said he even knows one or two trees where a hollow in the trunk gives him shelter."

John, rising from the table, said, "The things people know."

• • •

Ronan carried the typed document home reverently. He locked his bedroom door, opened the envelope, and flicked through the pages—a clutch of foolscap papers pinned in the top left-hand corner with a brass staple.

First (in the "magnificent" typing) he read the heading: "A story told by a Travelling Storyteller at the house of Mr. and Mrs. Michael O'Callaghan of Mullinahone on the evening of Tuesday, the 5th of August, 1956. Taken down in shorthand and typed by Madeleine O'Callaghan, second daughter of Mr. and Mrs. Michael O'Callaghan." Beneath came the title, "How The Monks Wrote the Book of Kells." Lower still were the words, "Madeleine O'Callaghan, Typist."

Familiar ground; a school project had required Ronan to trace one of the great "carpet" pages in the Book of Kells, where the art was as intricate as an Afghan rug. Next year's school visit to Dublin promised to visit Trinity College Library and see the book in its glass case, a page turned per day. His father liked telling the story of how Queen Victoria viewed "the greatest treasure of the early Christian Church in Western Europe, and what did she do? She called for a pen and wanted to sign it like some kind of Visitors' Book."

His hands almost unsteady with excitement, Ronan turned over the facing page, read the first words and again heard the unmistakable voice: "I have a story tonight that will inform you as to what an artistic country Ireland was, twelve hundred years ago."

LONG, LONG AGO WHEN THE GEESE WENT BARE-foot, in the days before men thought they descended from apes, two monks dwelt inside the walls of an abbey. Other monks lived there too, many, many of them—but these two had a distinction that set them apart, and their colleagues in prayer seemed happy to acknowledge it.

You should know the names of these two men; our names are often all we own, if we can be said to own our names. They were called Annan and Senan, and folks could easily tell which was which, because Annan was tall and thin as a string, whereas Senan was short and buttery, a little tub of a fellow. At the time of our story these two benignant and genial men had lived in this abbey for exactly the same number of years each—twenty-five years, a quarter of a century. Everybody loved them, and they loved the world.

It came to pass in the wheel of Time that the old abbot died. The mourning bell rang out sincerely. He had been an unusual man, broad in his views, and he combined kindness with relentlessness of discipline. But he was old, and we all have to move on. He left behind him a successful, well-run abbey—and a great question: Who's going to be the next abbot?

As you know from your schoolbooks, an abbot presides over a monastery with the greatest power and importance, and some abbots have even become cardinals. This departing abbot had been hailed by the pope in Rome as a man of singular ability and honored with a papal medal.

To everyone's surprise—and out of the ordinary for such establishments—the dying abbot had chosen not to settle the question of his succession. In this day and age, that kind of question is resolved by the pope or the head of the order of priests represented in that monastery. But in those days they had different rules.

For a start, the abbey didn't feel as attached to Rome and the pope as Rome and the pope thought they should feel. Those monks believed in choosing their own abbot and would not take kindly to a man imposed on them by the pope. Actually, all the Irish abbeys maintained a powerful independence from Rome and only came into line around the year six-sixty-four after a great argument at a place called Whitby on the eastern coast of England. But that's another story for another day, maybe when the sun rises higher in the sky and the birds are a bit happier about the weather.

Annan and Senan and their brother monks knew that the choosing of the next abbot would have a certain urgency. Not only that, there were others who had something to say on the matter. When the monks first came there, they received the land to build their monastery from a local farmer, a wealthy man who had been baptized by Patrick himself. This man's son, grandson, great-grandson, great-great-grandson unto fifteen generations—if twenty years makes a generation—had all continued the bequest of the family lands to the abbey. They had made only one stipulation—that they be comfortable with the choice of each abbot. Therefore, it came to pass that, in effect, they chose the abbot—or certainly helped in the appointment.

At the time the abbot died, the landowner was a widow. Her husband's death had been premature, but he left her well off, and she took control of everything. She had great capabilities, and she also possessed the rare gift of common sense. So she knew that an abbey without an abbot would be like a ship without a skipper. And by virtue of the deal done thirty years ago, when her husband had renewed the gift of the land to the monks at the appointment of the last abbot, she had the major say in who should be the next one.

This lady also knew that the two best candidates, in everybody's eyes, had to be Annan and Senan. At the abbot's funeral she ran a careful eye over them and saw how excellently they got on with each other and with all the monks, and indeed with everyone. As to which would be the better leader, that was most confusing; impossible to tell. Every day for a week she tossed and turned the question back and forth; Annan or Senan; Senan or Annan? The poor woman couldn't make up her mind, and she became severely addled.

But how could anyone distinguish between the two men? Each had excellent qualifications; each received much respect. It used to be the case that the abbot of a monastery got chosen very simply—whoever seemed the most devout, the man who prayed the deepest and longest, that was the man deemed the holiest, and that was the man they elected. But these two equaled each other in mighty praying—as they did in everything else. And while this problem became the daily topic of conversation in the abbey, the monks turned the soil, they welcomed the rain, they hailed the sun, and they were happy.

The lady at the heart of this decision was named Delia, and she was known to all the monks. She often came to mass in the abbey chapel, and she had her servants bring gifts of food and extra wool, from which the monks wove their robes, even though they had their own sheep. Nobody had any fears as to the decision she might make; they trusted Delia, and they all thought it a good idea that she should have such a say in the choosing of the next abbot.

It often happens that when two perfectly qualified candidates go for the same job, neither of them gets it. The post goes to a third person. He might not be ideal; he might not be as clever, say, or as popular; but it's a way of breaking a deadlock.

In the case of Annan and Senan, such a compromise would have meant that each man should distance himself from the idea that he might be the next abbot and agree that some other monk, perhaps not as well liked or as well qualified or indeed not as devout or as leaderly, should get the job. But the thorny problem was, no other suitable monk could be found. Not one. They were either too young or too careless or too hasty or too—well, we mustn't use the word *stupid* about holy men, but you know what I mean.

Delia, the landowning woman, knew she had to make a decision. Yet all her mental efforts had failed to bring her to a point. So she fashioned a different kind of compromise, an unusual one but potentially full of delight—she decided to hold a competition between the two men. Her decision sprang from the fact that this monastery had grown famous for its scriptorium, the most renowned in all the Christian church.

The word *scriptorium* comes from Latin, and it has to do with writing. A manuscript, for example, takes its name from two Latin words, *manus,* "the hand," and *scribere,* "to write."

In a scriptorium, monks wrote and painted those wonderful, colored holy books to illustrate the hymns, antiphons, and psalms transcribed in them. Scholars refer to them as illuminated manuscripts, but they were in fact books of sung or spoken prayer, or copies of the Bible and the Gospels, and they stand as the hallmark of early Christian Ireland's most golden moment, when we were rightly known as the Island of Saints and Scholars.

All of them were illustrated by hand; this was long before printing was invented. The pains taken by the monks in those books show a society that knew its own soul and how to express its feelings and beliefs. Other countries had their illuminated manuscripts too, but the Irish ones have the greatest renown.

These weren't books as we know them today. Paper hadn't yet been invented; therefore, each book had to be made of parchment—the skin of a goat or a sheep, specially thinned and stretched so that you can write on it. Their books consisted of many sheets of this vellum, and this made it very heavy, so they fashioned covers for the book, of board and sometimes of metal.

These weren't light articles to carry around. But the monks often had to haul them from one abbey to the next, because sometimes an abbey would have one book but not another, so they would borrow one and copy it. And the busiest work of all was the copying that abbeys did for their own use, because they needed enough prayer books and hymnbooks and study books to go around.

They worked mainly in Latin, the language of the fallen Roman Empire. Inside the abbeys here in Ireland, young men dedicated their lives to God and were schooled in Latin and Greek, for these had been and continued to be the languages of the church, the languages of sung and spoken worship.

Very fortunately for all of us, as well as copying out the holy books of Christianity, they also wrote down other things. They had learned from the Gospels that the life of Christ had been written by people who traveled with Jesus or knew him at that time, eyewitness accounts.

Following this example, the monks not only transcribed sacred texts, they also became the first people in Ireland to write down accounts of what the land was like, which families owned it and ruled it, who came to visit, and how many cattle they all owned. They believed people should know these things, and that's how the first histories of Ireland came to be written.

It wasn't that some monk sat down and said to himself, I'm going to write down here everything I know about what happened in the past of Ireland. That kind of book, which you learn from in school, didn't happen for many, many centuries. No, it was just that they wished to preserve the records of their own communities from which they came. And the monks also wrote down, alongside those details of who owned what, stories not unlike the stories I make my living telling up and down the length and breadth of this island.

Above all else, when they had written out a hymn or a psalm, they then ornamented it in the most delightful way, all tracings and drawings and tendrils, in lovely colors. You'll hear more of that presently if you keep your hat on.

One fine morning, Delia the landowner rode her horse across the fields to the abbey. She forded the same river that the first monks had diverted to release a piece of high ground for building, and she trotted into the monastery yard. Monks rushed to help her from her horse and then led the animal off to give it some feed.

Delia sat on a low wall by the cloisters and asked to see Annan and Senan. Both men were found at prayer in the chapel, but they came immediately to see Delia, whom they respected and liked.

"I can't decide which of you excellent gentlemen should be the next abbot. Can you help me?"

Blinking in the sunshine, Annan said, "He should," pointing to Senan.

And Senan said, "He should," pointing to Annan.

Delia laughed, then sighed.

"Just as I feared. You have no clearer solution than I do. But I didn't expect you to have. So this is what I have decided. Both of you gentlemen have for some time been jointly in charge of the scriptorium. You run it very well, and everybody works hard, because they all know that whatever you ask them to do, you can do it better and faster yourselves."

Annan looked at Senan, and Senan looked at Annan, and perhaps they blushed—but they never answered. Maybe they felt embarrassed because monks do not receive very much praise; it runs contrary to the austere spirit of the religious life.

"Therefore," said Delia, "I'm going to decide this matter by setting a competition between you."

"A competition?" said Annan.

"A competition?" said Senan.

"I want each of you to make me a page of a holy book. You may decide what text it should be. Then each of you must decorate your page with those wonderful illuminations for which this abbey is famous, the drawings, the colors, the scrolls. You each must do your work in secret, and when you have finished, arrange for the two pages to be manifested in the refectory. The abbey can vote for the page the monks like best. Whosoever emerges with the largest number of votes shall be the next abbot—and I myself shall have a vote."

Annan looked at Senan, and Senan looked at Annan. They said, "That all seems fair."

"Will six months be a sufficient time?" she asked. "I dislike that the abbey must be without an abbot."

They nodded.

"In the meantime, both of you can run the place together."

They said, "We never quarrel."

And soon enough matters became plain to everyone.

They thanked Delia, who called for her horse and rode back home across the ford, pleased at a job well done. She could sit back now and wait for the results to come in.

Tall, stringy Annan and little buttery Senan sat down on a wall and looked at each other.

"Well, now!" said Annan.

"Well, indeed!" said Senan.

"I suppose we have to have some rules."

"You're right. We have to observe the secrecy."

"Suppose we lend each other things—brushes and tools and the like?"

Annan said, "But I suppose we can't lend each other paints or colors."

Senan said, "And may I put something else to you?"

The two men held their heads close together and soon could be observed in the deepest and most animated, whispered discussion. So intensely did they converse that the other monks began to wonder why.

In due course they attributed it to the contest whose details had just been announced. The word spread through the abbey, and all were delighted. They thought it a fair and honorable way of managing things, and they also knew that the two pages when finished would provide glorious inspiration. That night, the evening meal buzzed with talk.

However, Annan and Senan had been discussing something else and something greater, which they never divulged until the contest had ended. In that powerful conversation, they agreed that the task they had been set should form the basis for a very great book, a large and brilliant work of art. Instead of being pressed into everyday use, this book would be employed to enhance the altar of the abbey on special days, a sacred ornament.

As a first step, they agreed on the text—nothing less than the four Gospels in Latin: Matthew, Mark, Luke, and John. Next they said that every page of this book would receive decoration, and some pages would bear no text, would exist only as sheets of beautiful painting in deep and lovely colors.

Then they considered the size of the book, both its number of pages and its bulk. The length had to remain undetermined, because it would depend on the height and size of the letters in the writing. But they reckoned that they should be able to measure that factor very soon after the entire scriptorium began work, and indeed they would specify the size of the lettering to be used.

As for the physical dimensions, they wanted something very noticeable, and they began to cut their parchment to a measure they thought fitting and respectable for such an important work. Having looked at big, little, and smaller pages, they chose to make the book rectangular. Eventually, when written on, cut, and trimmed, each page measured just over a foot high and nearly ten inches wide, and the book grew to be the size of a biggish dictionary. When finished, it contained nearly seven hundred pages, only a few of which had no painting.

Each of the four Gospels, they decided, would begin in exactly the same way—with three special pages. The first page would contain the four portraits of the Evangelists; the next would show the face of the Evangelist whose Gospel then followed; and the third page would have the opening words in Latin of that Gospel. They would now, in their competition, create that first and second page.

Annan and Senan had different skills. In Annan's case he liked to make the parchment take on the appearance of metalwork, so that his pages with their glinting colors always looked as if they had been made by a goldsmith or silversmith. If you met Senan, however, you would observe that he peered closely at you; Senan loved looking at people, and therefore he liked to draw portraits.

The rest of the skills for the total book would come from the body of the scriptorium. Neither Annan nor Senan had any interest in doing pages of lettering, and that is why some of the pages had no words, no script. For instance, the page Annan now decided to create consisted only of glorious decoration, whereas Senan would create a page of the Evangelists' shining faces.

Both monks sought an effect that sacred art intended to achieve. It was said that if you couldn't read the prayers in Latin, and yet you wanted to pray and let your spirit ascend in order to get as close to God as you could, you need only concentrate your gaze on one of those illustrated pages, and it would send you into a kind of holy trance. Getting to that point of artistry was one of the great achievements of the past.

They started work right away. That very night Annan tidied his cell, brought in his workbench from the scriptorium, and set it up under his window, where he could get plenty of light. Senan did the same, and as their cells adjoined each other, each knew his friend sat on the other side of the wall, working hard. For six months they labored while the ships sailed the seas and the clouds sailed the sky.

To the abbey slaughterhouse they sent for special parchment, the best they could get, taken from the skin of the finest sheep they bred in the abbey farm. Good vellum has to be strong enough not to break, yet thin enough to let the light through. You should be able to see its veins and notches when you hold it up to the light. To get it right so that the letters look perfect on it, you have to stretch it, as you'd stretch a sheet of canvas to make a painting on.

They stretched their sheets on little wooden frames, and they prepared their paints. I do not know whether it can be quite accurate to call them paints—they were a kind of cross between ink and paint.

They had various substances from which they drew color. For a certain kind of blue, they had the powder of lapis lazuli, which came from the mines of Afghanistan. When they wanted a brilliant red, they had the crushings of an insect that came from Mexico, where it feeds on cactus, and that color is called cochineal. For green, they pulped nettles and mixed in a little butter or goose grease to hold the mixture firm. Their yellow came from a streak of sulfur in rocks not too far away and a yellow clay with which they mixed it.

Then they had the many vegetable colors they took from the plants they grew in the monastery garden, all pulped and crushed and mixed in water or sour milk, until they had prepared all the colors of seven rainbows. To keep these firm for the purpose of painting them on the parchment and to make sure the colors did not run, they mixed in some white of egg, which stiffens the mixture, as everyone knows who has ever baked a cake.

They made their brushes out of all manner of things—feathers, both the quill end and the fluffy end; hairs pulled from a squirrel's tail, or a badger's neck, where the hairs are especially strong; pointed twigs, iron pins, shards of slate. On each drawing table they set out little balls of moss, to wipe off the excess ink.

No magnifying glasses in those days, no spectacles; these men worked with the naked eye. Sometimes they polished a piece of metal so that it shone and shone, and they reflected the sun's light from the metal to the page; that way, they saw more detail, and their work could be tiny and intricate.

In the beginning Annan and Senan only concerned themselves with color and fine detail. When transcribing a text in the scriptorium, the writers used the feathers of the monastery geese and cut a sharp angle across the quill. Depending on whether they wanted the letters of their words fine or broad, they would cut the point narrow or wide. And they never crossed something out and started again—they could not do that on parchment. Every letter of every word had to be carefully thought about and then set down, in beautiful big, sacred letters, each black as a crow. And the colors had then to be controlled so that they didn't run in little leaks across the thin membrane.

So there they sat, Annan and Senan, all their brushes and pens laid out on one side of the table and their piles of colors sitting in seashells on the other side. Each man had experience of creating colored work in sacred books.

Annan set out to make a page the way he knew best, and his first page consisted of a dense and tiny pattern woven into a greater picture of eight circles or discs inside a strong rectangle. Not a square inch of the surface remained undecorated—powerful straight lines and perfect curves dominated it.

First, he drew the outline, and for this he used a compass and other geometrical instruments. Then, he mixed much red and yellow and soft green and brown, and on the page laced it all into curls, coils, and complexity, lacework and tracery, arabesques and bobbles and curlicues. Anyone who looked closely at the page, he thought, must be drawn in deeper and deeper, must get passionately lost in the intricacies and beauties of these tiny details. He pored and pored over his page of parchment, with his badger hairs and his squirrel tails and his tiny quills of soft sparrow feathers and his colors.

Everywhere you go in the world today, wherever ancient Irish art is mentioned or displayed, the little spirals and ovals and leaves spring into the minds of those who know. The inspiration for this work lay easily to hand. These monks lived close to nature. Outside the windows of their cells they saw the trees and the leaves, the birds and the branches and the silver river winding by. All their patterns came from nature, animal, vegetable, or human, and in their own estimation they celebrated God by drawing attention to, and re-creating, his beautiful works.

At the same time, however, now that our wider world is better known, it is possible to see all sorts of traces from other civilizations in these pages. Echoes of Armenia and the Orient, Egypt and Ethiopia, the Greeks, the Germans, the Etruscans—their tracks are to be found like little footprints on every page. Did they all know each other? Or did this work simply come up out of the pool of life like a face from the Family of Man? Annan, by the way, suffered greatly from indigestion and had to be very careful with belching when he was actually drawing.

Senan's page looked not at all like Annan's, and yet it seemed related—brothers of the same tribe. He built a structure of the four Evangelist portraits and the ancient symbols by which they were known. In the top left-hand corner he drew a portrait of Matthew, the only Evangelist always depicted as a man. Across from him comes Mark, portrayed as a lion, and the lower two pictures he made for Luke, whose symbol was a calf, and John, the eagle.

To say he drew them is a big understatement—the page was brilliant. Senan gave the man of Matthew a clear face and a pair of gentle, fluted wings. Mark's creature has a long curled tail, and his body is rendered in the blue of the sky and the gold of the corn. The calf of Luke has a spotted face. John's eagle has a proud glare and a great, blue, broad wing. General soft reds and yellows and browns and brilliant blues gave the page a kind of light that came from inside, like true beauty. The same tradition of lacy tracery tiptoes all over the page, and there are animals with curious expressions and indignant and swishing tails and feathers. Each portrait has a firm border, as though Senan contained all his talent within a most capable and responsible spirit.

His page was more playful than Annan's, and in due time that gave the monks in the scriptorium a kind of permission to be amusing. Soon they drew little faces on their parchments, hidden in among the letters of the prayers, and they also drew kittens and butterflies and calves and the abbey dog and frogs and ducks and corn before the harvest, all wavy and yellow. Someone painted a wood, and when you looked into it closely, you could see the sun shining on the earth between the trees. Other monks added posies of flowers peeping out through the arms of letters and filled in a capital letter with the face of a little pig. Thus, because they had taken care with the tiniest detail of their works, Annan and Senan paved the way for one of the most delicate and human works in the world.

The two monks had a pact—that on the day one finished, he'd rap on the wall with a stick, seven raps, seven being an important number, because we have seven openings in our heads; two eyes, two ears, two nostrils, and a mouth.

One Wednesday morning, just before noon, with three days left of the six months, they knocked on the wall together at the same identical moment. Then they rushed out in the corridor and embraced each other.

Annan said to Senan, "I can't wait to see your page."

And Senan said to Annan, "And I can't wait to see your page."

Soon it reverberated through the abbey that the two men had finished the competition, and the excitement ran through the air like good news.

When Senan saw Annan's page, he almost burst into tears of delight. And when Annan saw Senan's page, he wished to swoon. Each seemed dazed. Very carefully, as though they were carrying babies, the two monks took their work to the refectory, where a special stand had already been set up to display the two pages side by side. Annan set up Senan's page, and Senan displayed Annan's. Then they shook hands with each other and stood back to let the other monks see.

For an hour and more, until the bell for lunch rang—they had to ring it again and again—the monks of Kells Abbey stood looking at the two pages. Men wept, they laughed, they marveled. One thing they knew—nothing so captivating as those two pages by Annan and Senan had ever been made in that scriptorium.

And then they knew another thing—how could any mortal choose which should win? One page was as brilliant as the other.

They sent for Delia, who arrived in tremendous excitement. She loved the pages more than anyone. After congratulating the pair, she organized the secret vote.

Not counting Annan and Senan, that community had two hundred and nine monks. Plus Delia's vote. Nobody expected Senan and Annan to vote. Therefore there was an even number of two hundred and ten, and the possibility of a tie. But since this was going to be a secret vote, they felt that they'd probably get a clean result.

Two boxes, marked "Page One" and "Page Two," were placed on an oak table in the darkest corner of the refectory. Beside the boxes sat a large bunch of colored feathers, taken from three pheasants;

the boxes and the feathers were covered with a tapestry. Every voting monk had to go to the table, lift the tapestry, choose a feather,
and, making sure no one saw him do it, place the feather in the box
of his choice.

One by one, youngest first, the monks voted solemnly. Nobody
spoke. All you could hear was the shuffling of their sandals. Delia
went last. After she voted, you could cut the tension in that room
with a knife. The oldest monk, who was in charge of the voting,
was about to lift the two boxes and count the feathers when Delia
called out.

"Wait!" she said, this fair-minded woman. "Annan and Senan
should vote. They're monks too. Isn't that only fair?"

Everyone agreed, and the two friends made their way to the
table; one after the other they voted. Their feathers brought the
total to two hundred and twelve votes.

At last the old monk lifted the box marked "Page One" out to
the main table, where everyone could see it. Slowly, slowly, he
counted the feathers in the box, and slowly, slowly, he counted
them again. The watching people looked at each other in amazement; the box held far more feathers than it should have.

"What's going on?" they murmured—because the old monk
announced, "Page One gets two hundred and eleven votes."

Which either meant that the monks had put all the feathers into
one box by mistake—or that everybody except one person had
voted only for Page One.

Annan and Senan looked baffled. Delia cleared her throat to
speak and said in a kind of a hushed voice, "We must see the second
box."

Everybody looked at her very strangely, unable to understand her
reasoning. Surely the result was now known? The creator of Page
One had been elected abbot, hadn't he?

The old monk now lifted the box marked "Page Two" up to the
main table and raised his hands in the air.

"Glory to God!" he said. "The box is full of feathers."

"Please count them, Brother," said Delia.

"I will," said the old monk, and he began slowly to count aloud the feathers in the box marked "Page Two."

Everybody watched him, holding their breath.

"Twenty-one, twenty-two, twenty-three, twenty-four . . . ," and soon, "Sixty-seven, sixty-eight, sixty-nine," and eventually and excitedly, "Two hundred and eight, two hundred and nine, two hundred and ten, and—the last one—two hundred and eleven."

He looked baffled, but he said in his quavery voice, "Page Two, two hundred and eleven feathers. And that means that Page One and Page Two each got the same number of votes."

A hubbub broke out that made Babel sound like a whisper. Did you know, by the way, that an Irish monk went to the Tower of Babel, took the best bits of all the languages he heard there, brought them home with him, and made them into the Irish language?

At Delia's insistence, the old monk counted all the feathers again, in both boxes—and got the same result. Someone else counted them. Then Delia counted them herself, and she made it two hundred and eleven each. She counted out loud.

"Two hundred and nine monks. And myself. That's two hundred and ten. Plus Annan or Senan. That's two hundred and eleven. That means," she said, "that almost everybody voted twice." Then she blushed red as riches and said, "I know I did."

Everybody applauded her. Delia looked at Annan and Senan.

"But I was hoping," she said, "that you'd break the deadlock."

Annan grinned. "I voted for Senan."

And Senan grinned. "I voted for Annan."

"In that case," says Delia, "the two of you can continue as you are; you can run the abbey together. Instead of one abbot, we'll have two."

And that goes to show that things of great beauty can sometimes come out of awkward situations and that people, if you leave them alone, know how to make their own decisions. It also, according to some people, gave the Irish people the habit of voting often at elections.

The room had long darkened when Ronan finished.

He read the last few pages at the bedroom window as the evening star brightened.

"If only he'd signed it," he said half-aloud. "Then we'd have a name."

Insofar as he could at the age of fourteen, he tried to reach the Storyteller through the dry pages. He visualized the evening in the O'Callaghan household. Which chair—the chair his father had sat in? Or Mrs. O'Callaghan's? Did he turn his hat in his hands? Light his pipe?

If it had been a visit for one evening only, how large was his audience? If small, was that sad for a man who liked to be heard? Ronan also wondered whether he detected a certain fear in the story, a desire on the Storyteller's part to praise the men of God. He winced to think of his mother's rage. Why had she been so fierce?

He fingered the pages again, observed their numbers typed neatly on the top right-hand corner, the indentations for paragraphs, the heavy letters unevenly inked where one key received a stronger finger than others—the *k*, the *s*, the *u*.

Now a new problem rode in. Kate had raised it on the way home.

"Where will we keep that story?"

Alison opened all letters to the house, even Kate's.

"The office?" said his father.

"I can—" Ronan stopped, about to say the word "hide." Then he said, "It'll be all right."

"Are you sure?" said John and Kate together.

They obviously knew that Alison searched Ronan's room. He himself laid traps—tiny strings on drawers and doors, a pen placed at a specific angle, all the tricks he'd learned from adventure stories. Not that Alison attempted to conceal her visits; if she found reading matter that she deemed unsuitable, she removed it and sometimes replaced it with a work on the lives of the saints. But she left his history books untouched.

Two years previously, Ronan had decided he would bury his treasures. Therefore, at specified points in the woods and fields, he engineered deep caches. In them he buried tin boxes; they stored the entire proceeds of his search for the Storyteller. Most correspondents had replied to him at school because his letters suggested an educational project; on his way home through the woods he stored them underground.

Next day, Ronan went to the rocky corner of the high woods and moved a pile of stones. The tall oblong can, wrapped in old raincoats, came up easily; after a struggle the rusting lid yielded; he eased in the Annan and Senan typescript and replaced everything with care.

On the following Thursday, the school had a football game. At home Ronan lied, said attendance as a supporter was mandatory. He went on the bus, but not to the game. A five-minute walk from the field took him to the main street—and a gray door. Inside, a woman with fat arms halted him.

"Yes?"

"I have a message for Madeleine O'Callaghan."

"Give it to me, and I'll give it to her." She slid back a glass panel.

Ronan said, "I have to give it to her in person."

"Her class finishes at four. You can call back."

"May I wait?"

"Ooh," the woman trilled. " 'May I?' 'May I' indeed? Around here we can only manage to say, 'Can I?' And where d'you think you'll wait, Mister May-I?"

"Outside," and Ronan retreated to the hallway.

Nothing happened in the next twenty minutes, nothing at all. No one came and no one went, and all Ronan saw was the bare staircase and the walls painted an exhausted municipal green.

At four o'clock a bell rang. The woman with the fat arms frowned as Ronan came back.

"Will you point her out to me?"

"Huh. You'll know her straight away. She's like a flagpole that has long hair on it. Someone should cut that hair for her, I would if she was my daughter."

A throng of chattering girls poured up the stairs like Finn Mac-Cool's women. With giggling come-on eyes they pushed past Ronan. Near the back of the crowd, a remarkably tall girl chattered to two others who hung on every word. And yes, she did look like her mother, though much thinner.

"Are you Madeleine?"

"Yes."

"I'm Ronan O'Mara. You know. The story you typed."

"Oh! Howya? I wasn't there Sunday, my cousin had her appendix out, I was bringing her grapes, did you bring it back? My mother said she gave it to you for keeps."

Madeleine had her mother's punctuation.

"I wanted to ask you about him."

"Wasn't he quaint? And the hat and the pipe, my father said he was as quaint as a cottage. I'm famished for a cup of tea, come over to the bus stop café."

Ronan asked question after question.

"How was his health? Did he seem happy? What did he wear? How long did he stay?"—and, the most crucial, "Where did he go?"

Madeleine had the chatter of a bird.

"Not a thing wrong with him except the odd wheeze. Aren't these cakes quaint? I love anything coconut. Oh, he was very lively, laughing like a donkey and puffing away at the pipe and lowering the glasses of whiskey like he was afraid the source was drying up, and the black coat and the tight old pants and the hat, talk about quaint. He wouldn't stay the night and we had a fine room for him, the overflow room, we keep sacks of flour in it, they often use it after a party or something, but no, he had to be off."

Madeleine ate a third cake, and Ronan called for more. A coconut flake clung to her upper lip.

"Where did he go?"

"We never saw. All we know is that he walked out the door at midnight like some sort of magic man and he was gone, no flashlight, no torch, nothing, not even a match. Where he stayed we don't know and my father asked people but nobody saw him anywhere and no one met him on the road the next day. Maybe he's a ghost."

The extra cakes arrived; Ronan was still within his pocket money. Madeleine ate three out of the four, her braided hair swinging like a bell rope.

"But I'll tell you something we heard. D'you know who I mean by Barry Hanafin? 'The Poet Hanafin,' they call him—probably because he's actually a poet. I heard that when times are rough with the old man, he goes to stay at Barry Hanafin's, they have a pub too, so he'd like that. Tell me, did you ever kiss a girl?" She had started to tease him. "We're all talking about kissing these days, it seems to be in fashion or something."

"No," said Ronan, startled. They left the table.

"Well, you'll have no bother when you want to. I know a slew of girls who'd find it very easy kissing you. Including myself. Bye now," and Madeleine O'Callaghan waved an airy hand.

Ronan trotted after her.

"Where does he live?"

"He doesn't live anywhere. You know that."

"No, Barry Hanafin."

"County Clare. He's near the Burren, bring a clothes pin for your nose. And don't forget what I said—about what's in fashion."

She winked.

Two of Barry Hanafin's poems ranked high on Ronan's course. "The Tuber" laid down images of the potato famine that swept Ireland in the 1840s and lingered (the point of the poem) in folk memory: "My father's hospitality/Never overcame his embarrassment/He disliked all mealtime callers/In case their board had more or less than his."

The English teacher, Andrew Hogan, made much of the "dynamic eight-ten syllabic structure." Ronan felt much more at home with "My Own Personal River." He memorized all fifteen stanzas for pleasure and often ran them through his mind; "When you leave the outskirts of our poor town/You never look back but travel on down/Through meadow and woodland, forest and lea/'Til you pour your spirit into the sea.'

In the coach returning from the football game, with the school team unvictorious (again), Ronan contrived to sit beside Mr. Hogan.

"Sir, how many poems do we have to learn?"

Water glistened in thin nostrils. Andrew Hogan possessed not one follicle of visible hair.

"Poems we have to learn? In life or this year?"

"On the curriculum?"

"On the curriculum? Do you feel taxed, O'Mara? When I was your age, I learned a thousand lines of Greek a month. And still helped to milk the cows for my father."

"I was asking about favorites, sir?"

Mr. Hogan sipped his own saliva.

"Favorites? They all become favorites if you accommodate them."

"But aren't favorites mostly old or dead?"

"They don't have to be. Look at Barry Hanafin," and Ronan's mind cheered; his plan was working. Everyone knew how Mr. Hogan bragged of his friendship with the poet.

Ronan began to murmur, "Rise from a pool where the ferns are dark/Over the banks where the rocks are stark/And the mountaintop whose lightning crags/Hang over the land where the river drags . . ."

As he hoped, Mr. Hogan took up the refrain.

"Its sullen youth, bubbling and hissing/Giving no hint it will one day glisten/And sparkle and shimmy and prettily dance/Down from the hills through the lands of romance."

Mr. Hogan clapped his hands.

"Don't you love the way Hanafin makes the stream feel like a flapper—d'you know what a flapper was? They were the girls in

Chicago who danced in black dresses with fringes on them; they wore silver little headbands, and they used to do dances called the Charleston and shimmy their hips."

No, Ronan didn't feel the poem said anything about Chicago or shimmying girls, but he didn't say that to Mr. Hogan.

"What do poets look like, sir?"

"Poets look like? Poets look like poets, ordinary people, I s'pose, though some of them have a kind of shaggy twist. Have you never met a poet?"

"There aren't any living near us, are there?"

"Living near us? Not quality, no, a few go-the-road balladeers with rhymes that have no arse to them. But they're not poets, their work is dung."

Next day, Andrew Hogan, in his unnaturally shiny gray trousers, called Ronan across the yard.

"The first Sunday of the month I have to go to Clare, and I've to see Barry Hanafin. Would your father drive us?"

Mr. Hogan and John O'Mara knew people mutually, and on their way to pick up his teacher Ronan began to tell whom Mr. Hogan liked—they were "pillars" or they were "dross." Kate sat with Ronan in the back seat, unable not to laugh. From time to time she scribbled a note; Kate collected "choice remarks."

Mr. Hogan, when they found him, was talking on the street with Ronan's history teacher, David Cronin; John climbed from the car and joined in. Kate and Ronan heard them through the open window.

"John, I love teaching him," said the correct Mr. Cronin. "He has wit and instinct—and such a sense of history's purpose. And he always grasps the point."

In a sudden movement Kate turned her head. Had there been any reason, Ronan would have sworn something had made her cry.

John stopped the car at a pub near an old castle. Men in tweed caps sucked at black drinks. Kate emerged from the toilets laughing and held the door open for Ronan to see. On either side of the bowl stood piles of pigs' heads, a great delicacy on the menu. No wrapping could be seen, just the flat and leather-snouted heads and the little eyes peering brightly, as though they had lost none of their wisdom in slaughter.

After an hour of ale odors, cheese sandwiches, and noise, they set out again. Twenty minutes later, across the white rock moonscape of the Burren, they drew up at Hanafin's Select Bar. A white goat on a long chain eyed them with a marbled glare.

Andrew Hogan strode ahead. Ronan's heart boomed, his ears roared. What if he's here right now? Sitting just inside that red door? He hung back a moment. No Storyteller, though; in the gloom he blinked at the disappointment, bit hard into a fingernail.

"The bard himself. How're you, Barry? God, the shine on you."

"Galloping Hogan," said the red-haired, tufty man behind the bar. He saw Kate. "Who's your lady friend? Jayzez, she must have bad eyesight."

Ronan started at hearing the acid Mr. Hogan being mocked.

The poet Hanafin needed thorough washing.

"Girl, you've lips on you like flowers, what's your own name?"

"Kate McCarthy, and proud of it," she said, laughing.

Mr. Hogan said, "This is my friend, John O'Mara; he'll help you make your will if you want to."

"Where there's a will, there's a lawsuit," said Barry Hanafin, his face like a crushed truck. He shook hands with John, took his hand away, and scrutinized it. "Hold on, now. One, two, three, four, and the thumb. All present and correct. When you shake hands with a lawyer, you have to count your fingers, isn't that what they say?"

Ronan came forward, drawn by Kate and John. Hanafin looked at him, looked at John.

"H'm. I see. What are you—fourteen? Let me look at you. Are you married? No. You look too shrewd for that. H'm. I see. Well, well."

They settled to drinks, Ronan on lemonade. Andrew Hogan smoothed Hanafin's edge. Eventually they got to his poems, with Ronan the bait. Hanafin became half a teacher, the other half a performer for Kate. She timed things well, asking, "Where's the link, would you say, between poetry and the oral tradition?"

The poet bloomed like a lover.

"Funny you ask," he said. "I've a man comes here, sometimes he stays with us, a very distinguished man." He stared hard at Ronan. "He's the last Storyteller in Ireland. And I don't know how long more he'll last."

Ronan blinked.

Kate said, "Is he not well?"

"It isn't only that. People throw him out; they don't want to hear the old stuff. They only want Clark Gable and Errol Flynn and them lads. This man's better than any of that crowd."

Hanafin watched Ronan as he spoke.

"When was he last here?" asked John.

"Three weeks ago. I heard he's a hundred miles away now. He went up north—Donegal or Carnlough or somewhere like that."

"And did he tell you a story?" asked Kate.

"Ah, hasn't he me annoyed with stories?" Barry Hanafin stopped and wondered at something. They waited for him. "But he did tell me this last time a great story about how the Irish discovered poetry. He made it all up, of course. Or—I don't know. Maybe not."

John had a skill at prompting reluctant witnesses.

"I suppose it was too long to remember?"

"No, faith," said Barry Hanafin. "I've a good memory for that sort of a thing. Even though he's a hard man to do justice to. If he'd only put his shoulder to the wheel, he'd make a better poet than most of them that calls themselves poets, they'd give you warts on your arse. I wrote down most of him, and I filled in the rest from remembering it."

Ronan said, "Did he light his pipe?"

"Like a chimney. Or a furnace. We'd a crowd of people in that night, and they were all around him; they love him. He sat on that chair over there, where he always sits."

Hanafin poured himself two drinks—a large black pint of Guinness and a smaller glass of whiskey. He reached for a sheaf of rough papers from behind the clock on the shelf and began to shuffle through them. When he had arranged them in the order he wished, he drank from the Guinness, then the whiskey. As he opened the top button of his tieless and formerly white shirt, he closed his eyes and inhaled; he looked as though he was winding himself up like a clock or some great hairy toy. At last he began to read.

AS YOU PROBABLY KNOW, NOBODY CAN ACTUALLY *write* a poem. There's no such act as *writing* a poem. That's not how poems are made. Oh, yes, there's the physical business of pen, ink, and paper—but that isn't whence the poem comes. Nor may you send out and fetch a poem from where it's been living. No, like it or like it not, you have to wait for a poem to arrive.

The people we call "poets," by which I mean true, real poets— they're merely very keen listeners who've learned to recognize when a poem's dropping by. Then they copy down what the poem's telling them in their heads. After that, they tidy up the writing, ask their wives, sisters, or daughters to type it out for them, and so the poem's finished, next to be seen on the pages of some august publication in the Northern Hemisphere where they pay you minus tuppence per line and hope you don't visit them naked roaring for more cash.

The thing about true poets is—they never have to wait. Some people are born lucky. They long to eat a hazelnut, and next thing a man walks past their front door with a bag of nuts and he offers them one. Or a woman who likes the fruit called "mango" stands at her window, and below in the street she sees a dark and handsome stranger who holds up his hand and offers her the only mango this side of Rangoon.

Poets are like that with poems. No sooner do they listen out than a poem swoops down, whispers something to the top of their heads, and they feel it flowing down into their brain, down along their arms, into their fingers, and out onto the page in black letters.

And poems are like angels. They visit often, but you've to be watching out for them, and you've to believe in them to benefit from their gifts. Ireland has a great many poets because we've a quiet country here, with empty fields and silent lanes, where it's very easy to hear poems when they come by. But where did full poetry start here—I mean, that wasn't religious or prayers? Well, according to my friend the Storyteller, it was all typically Irish. It started because of a husband, his foreign wife, and a lawsuit.

A long time ago, there was a man who lived in the mountains of Galway, in the year of Our Lord nine-twenty-five. A big bucko, with broad shoulders and dark curly hair, he had looks so handsome that when ladies saw him, they wanted to swoon and throw themselves down on his boots. And many of them did.

His name was Jem, and what the ladies truly admired were his hands. With long, strong fingers and skin like ivory, each hand spread the breadth of a shovel. He could bunch them into fists that would protect any woman, or he could use the soft skin of his palms to caress a lady's flowing locks.

Naturally, therefore, as is the way of the world, many men didn't care too much for Jem. But men who made his acquaintance or became his friends enjoyed his company.

One man, however, formed a great dislike of Jem. This man's name was Leary and he suffered from fear. He had no reason to—he had wealth, some good looks, and many capabilities. Fear, however, answers to no logic; some ungifted and stupid men, who should know fear, feel none whatsoever. And some men, gifted and safe, are the most fearful of all.

The reason for Leary's fear lay partly in a lack of assuredness with ladies. He had dull words, and he couldn't bring a sparkle to the eye of a star. His compliments came across as ham-fisted. He once said to a lady from Longford, "The last time I saw hair like yours was on a horse my father owned."

The woman took offense. No girl wants her hair to be compared with the coarseness of horsehair. What she didn't know was that the horse in question, a champion racer much beloved of Leary, had a floating, glossy tail.

To another woman this man Leary said, "I was thinking of you last night when I was feeding my pigs."

She nearly swiped him across the face, but what she couldn't have known was Leary's affection for his pigs and their sweet pinkness and round little cheeks and high intelligence.

His fear, therefore, as you may now understand, had two fountains—that he'd never gain the heart of a woman, and that if he did, she'd be taken from him by some honeyed fellow such as Jem.

Well—as the smooth wheel of Time rolled onward, fearful Leary found a lady whom he liked very much. Her name was Gloria, she lived in the wooded valleys of Hampshire in England, and she had a round face thought by many to be beautiful. Gloria came to Ireland with her father to buy a horse, and she met Leary at a fair. He showed her how to be careful when buying.

"If the man selling the animal walks toward you, leading his beast, look at the man's legs carefully. If you think he's limping, then he's trying to disguise the fact that the horse is lame."

He also told her, "When a man won't let you open his horse's mouth because he's afraid the horse'll bite you, then you'll know that the horse has no teeth."

As a result of this sound advice, Gloria bought not one but two fine beasts. Being English, she didn't take umbrage when Leary said to her, "You have eyes like my dog, Koko"—she could see that Koko had dark and faithful eyes. Englishmen are so dreary that English women will kiss anything that sounds like honeyed lips.

To cut a long story short, Leary proposed marriage. He had a fine farm, thirty-five pigs, an old servant woman with no insolence, a large milking herd, and two bulls—one for his own cows, and another for the neighbors, so that they'd not sully his good bull with their common beasts. Gloria moved to Ireland, married Leary, and settled down.

Sometimes, the very fact of fearing something is enough to make it happen. Six months married, Gloria met shiny Jem, the handsome man with the big hands. It took place at a fair where Gloria had gone to buy hens. Leary, the new husband, went with her to show off this treasure. He took her here, he squired her there; people shook her hand and complimented him. Never in his life did the man enjoy such popularity—and as I say, he himself was by no means horrible to look at.

They were talking to a cattle drover from Carlow when Jem wanders over, bright as day. He saw Gloria's legs and thought she was choice. She looked at him, and before the day was over, they had contrived to meet at the bridge below the town. Handsome Jem was a fast mover, and so, we have to agree, was round-faced Gloria.

When they met under the bridge, Jem shook Gloria's hand, and Gloria returned the handshake with both hands and didn't let go; Englishwomen have never been backward in coming forward. They swooned for each other. Jem was smitten by Gloria's cool way of talk, and Gloria was thrilled at Jem's hands. They said, "We must meet again," and they went their ways.

Their next tryst took place on a mountainside above Gloria's new home. Leary, by the way, couldn't have been a kinder husband; he genuinely loved her and wanted to give her the best. Despite that, one Saturday morning, when Leary was off somewhere birthing a calf, Gloria met Jem under a tree behind a rock.

Jem asked her why she married that droning insect, Leary, when she could have married him. He said he'd been looking for a wife just like her since the day he realized women had been put on earth by God to make men's lives a joy.

Her heart singing like a linnet, Gloria went back down the mountain to her life with Leary, and that night he saw that she had fallen very moody. He did the sensible thing—he kept out of her way, except to bring her a drink of hot whiskey before bedtime. Every night before then, these newlyweds had slept like a pair of spoons made by the same silversmith. This night, though, she turned her back on him, hard as a coconut, and went to sleep without as much as a whisper.

Two days later, she met Jem on the mountain again. He lived thirty miles distant, and he complained about the rough ride. Gloria got a fit of fear. She swung herself up into Jem's saddle and said, "Take me with you."

There's an old saying, "Be careful what you wish for—because you may receive it." Jem felt a bit taken aback. Fun had been his highest motive, but here he was now, landed with a large bundle called Gloria. My mother used to say, "Fun is fun till someone loses an eye."

But he looked at Gloria, and he thought, "She's good to look at, and her father's rich, and I can train her into the idea that I don't have to be at home every night of the week." Jem, for all his talk, didn't know much about women. And so the two misbehavers rode off.

When Gloria didn't return, Leary grew frantic. He searched the mountain, and he searched the vale. All night he wandered through the heather, holding up a big lighted torch, calling Gloria's name. He feared she'd been taken by a wolf or had fallen down a cave.

"Gloria!" he called. "Gloria, my love!"

The hills yielded nothing but the echo.

For two days and two nights the poor, distraught man looked high and low for his missing wife. Finally he assembled a great search party. They gathered in the farmyard on their horses and ponies and donkeys, thirty men and boys; Leary's concern for his wife had washed away much of their dislike for him.

Their compassion grew further at what happened next. Just as Leary told his volunteers from the yard to go north, south, east, and west, a young man rode by.

"What's the commotion?" he said. They told him, and he looked uncomfortable.

"Is she an Englishwoman with plump cheeks and black hair cut short as a boy's?"

Leary rode forward.

"Did you see her? Where? Where is she? Is she all right? How is she?"

"She looked fine," said the young man. "She rode down through the White Valley two days ago on the same horse as Jem the handsome man. And they say she's living in his house."

The embarrassment of that! There's humiliation! But Leary knew like doom it was true. Nevertheless he thanked his searchers and fed them ale.

Now there's long been in Ireland a law we call "criminal conversation." It applies where one man takes away another man's wife. The injured party may sue for damages and is often very successful. It doesn't, so far as I know, apply the other way round—sometimes Justice's blindfold is too tight. "Criminal conversation"—that's it, hardly criminal and a cause of great conversation.

Leary decided he'd sue Jem for taking his wife. When that news spread, the buzz of the gossip could be heard on the moon. The case came forward for judging, a date was set, and everyone wanted to be at that trial.

In those days, if you sued somebody, you had to plead your own case. Leary grew rightly worried at his lack of words. He reckoned that Jem and Gloria had a better chance of persuading a judge than he had, poor slob. Jem had a renowned sweet tongue, and Gloria had unusual and pretty speech.

Like a lot of men who feel inadequate, Leary got occasional bouts of inspiration, and a few days before the trial was due to begin, he had a wonderful idea. He'd take advice on how to conduct the trial—but he wouldn't ask a man. Who better to advise on the heart of a woman than another woman? And since judges are reckoned to be wise, a woman who also had that reputation would be doubly useful.

Well, there lived all over the countryside in those days, and right up to my father's time, a number of creatures who went under the description "Wise Woman." They are thought to be the origins of midwives, and some confusion also exists as to whether they were what witches became.

Certainly they helped to deliver babies into the world. The *witch* word clung to them because as part of their medical contribution they mixed potions and because they usually lived in peculiar circumstances, distant from the rest of the community. Also, to add to their impression of necromancy, many of them were believed to see into the future.

Leary chose a woman who lived in a cave five miles away from his home. Bearing the gifts he had been told this woman liked—a pitcher of cream, a flitch of bacon, half a dozen duck eggs, and some red currants from his garden—he rode to the mouth of the cave. As he had been advised to do, he waited until she called him. He expected that he'd enter the cave, sit by her fire, and listen as the old hag crooned some strange melody and peered into a dish of mixed items.

That isn't at all what happened. The Wise Woman turned out to be forty years of age, with red, frizzy hair tied up behind her head in a yellow ribbon. Buxom and spotlessly clean, dressed in a gown a lady would have been honored to wear, she bustled out of the cave so lovely and spry that Leary asked himself why she had no husband.

"I chose not to marry," she said, answering his unspoken thought.

I have to be careful what I think, thought Leary.

"Yes, you have. Get down off that horse and talk to me. Aha! smoked bacon? I knew I'd get some this week"—and Leary unwrapped his parcel.

"Now, you've come about your wife."

"Yes."

"You want me to help you with the trial?"

"I hope you will."

"And I will," said the Wise Woman. "Normally I'd never help a man oppose a woman. But in this case you've been treated disgracefully. You behaved better to that woman than most men—because most men are clods. Her kind of behavior gives all women a bad name and licenses others to do worse. But I can see that you want her back, and I'll help you."

She walked Leary round the corner of the crag to a beautiful divan under interlaced willows that grew out of the ground. From a silver pitcher she poured a blackberry drink. Leary drank it and felt better than he had for weeks.

For the next three hours she schooled Leary in how to conduct his trial. He told her of his twin hopes—to win the judge's verdict, and to make Gloria think him more valuable than Jem.

I don't want to spoil the story by telling you too much in advance, but I will tell you the most significant piece of advice the Wise Woman gave Leary.

She said to him, "People can't hear what one says. If you walk into that court and say to the judge, 'Judge, I loved that woman and treated her well and this man took her away from me,' the judge will think, I've heard all this before.

"And if you look across the court at Gloria and say, 'I love you and that's why I asked you to be my wife and why I promised to cherish you,' she'll say to herself that she hears much sweeter words from Jem—and, no denying it, women do like sweet words, it's one of the many paths to our general downfall."

Leary listened as he had never done; the blackberry drink helped him to concentrate.

She said, "You've to devise a means of being heard. It's like making up a different language. And I know you're not good in the tongue department. But I'll show you where you'll get wonderful words."

Up she rose from her divan, took Leary's hand, and led him out into the open air. She pointed to the sky.

"There," she said. "Up there. That's where the words you need will come from, the words that'll say what's in your heart—that's where they live."

Leary looked understandably puzzled, and the Wise Woman clarified what she meant.

"Every word that was ever spoken or sung has gone out into the air. They're all still up there. Oh, yes, they may be jumbled up but that's the beauty of the thing. Since words have their own lives, they can choose which other words they'll associate with. They're always looking for a good home, and a poem is about as good a home as a word can get."

Leary looked doubtful. He looked very doubtful indeed.

"But," he said to the Wise Woman, "I'm a farmer. I'm not a poet."

"Huh-ho, my fine man, many's the poet has been a farmer."

"But," said Leary, "I've no turn for poetry."

"What do you think a poet needs?" she said. "You're thinking a poet needs stanzas and rhymes and meters and cadences. No, no, that's not how it works. By and large, words will arrange themselves, thank you very much. Yes, they may need a little help here and there to get settled into the right place in the right line and so on, but that's easily learned. What a poem needs by way of a good home is a heart of fire and a spirit of honor. Poems won't come to rest in a place of baseness. No self-respecting poem would think of entering a soul of perfidy."

Just as Leary was about to say, "I'm afraid I don't know what you're talking about," the Wise Woman said to him, "You may not know what I'm talking about today, but you'll recognize it when it happens."

He shook his head impatiently.

"Don't shake your head like that—it makes it difficult for me to pick up what you're thinking," she said.

Leary rose, walked to the entrance, turned around, and held out his hands in a hopeless way.

"I want you to listen very carefully to me," the Wise Woman said. "The words you need will have to be expressed as poems. Listen out for a voice that's sweet and strange. Listen out for a voice that has the heart's own tune. Listen out for a voice without vanity or contempt. And think of all the wonderful words that must be up there—all of them can come to your aid, if you will only let them."

Leary said, "I never put too much store—"

"—in words," she said, finishing his sentence. "The point about words is—the better you use them, the stronger is the thought that wears them. You know what your thoughts are—you want to win back your wife. If you let the words of the skies come and help you, they'll dress your thought so beautifully, so kindly, so tenderly, that people will stand aside in admiration and let you have what your heart wants."

•   •   •

Leary went away fuddled, not at all sure of his course. He rode his horse over the mountain and watched the birds wheel in the sky and the rabbits scamper down the slopes. But he heard no voices, nothing but the wind muttering in the trees and the water blabbering in the streams.

And his house felt lonelier than ever. Even though the old servant woman who never answered back made him a very fine supper of pork and cabbage with a pitcher of ale and apple tart with cream to follow, Leary still couldn't cheer up.

"Sir, a word to you?" she said as she cleared the kitchen table. Leary nodded.

"The good heart," said the old woman, "tells what matters."

Leary looked at her, trying to figure out what on earth she meant, but she went out of the kitchen, and he didn't have the energy to follow her.

That night he lay awake, irritated and sleepless. People were telling him things he didn't understand. He tried to make sense of the Wise Woman's advice—but it meant nothing to him. And he tried to interpret what his servant woman meant by "the good heart," and he was baffled. The poor man tossed and turned and turned and tossed until the bedding resembled a hank of onions.

For three days and three nights he got no rest. He stood out under the sun and he stood out under the stars, his ear cocked to the sky in the desperate hope that some sound, some whisper, some murmuring cloud, would provide him with the words he needed to win back his wife and the respect of his neighbors. But nothing came, even though he had sharpened his hearing to a point where he could hear the smoke leaving the chimney.

Came the morning of the court, and he dressed in his finest tunic and his grandest boots. He looked exhausted as he mounted his horse. The servant woman stood by the door and said to him, "Sir, don't forget—the good heart." He was too tired to snap at her.

The court lay twenty miles away, and he arrived in good time. As he rode into the town, he could see a crowd ahead of him outside the courthouse, and as he drew nearer, he saw that they had come there as Jem's supporters. In the midst of them, joshing and jostling, stood Jem, smiling and glad-handing, all grinning, hand-rubbing, back-slapping, hail-fellow-well-met.

Leary's heart sank and then dropped to the bottom of the world—there was his Gloria, primped and preened on the steps of the court. But at the same time his heart raced; he still loved her. In fact, he loved her even more now that he had lost her, and in some strange way that he didn't understand, he gladdened to that thought.

Someone in the crowd saw him approach, and they began to mock him. Awkward Leary didn't know what to do, and yet he had to brave them. He tied his horse to a tree and walked slowly to the courthouse. Jem stepped toward him.

"My old friend," he jeered. "Old friends share everything, don't they?"—and he tried to throw an arm around Leary.

At that moment something happened; some strange vapor came down into the air. Leary stopped where he stood, looked handsome Jem right in the eye, and began to speak. Now Leary was quite a well-known man in the neighborhood, and as I have said, nobody really liked him. He spoke little and smiled less, although in the sympathy that had risen for him in the Gloria business, a surprising number said he'd been a very obliging neighbor.

Suddenly—and this is how they reported it afterward—Leary altered in front of their faces. A kind of light came into his eyes, and he seemed to grow taller. He looked up into the sky, so straight above his head that they thought he might topple backward. Then he opened his mouth to speak and surprised them all.

"I think a friend's a man of thought
Who'll always hold out his decent hand,
To give as true friends surely ought.
He'll take away not a grain of my sand,
Nor any blade of my greenest grass,

Nor a leaf from any of my apple trees.
He lets all slights and insults pass,
And he says to his friend, 'You are me.' "

Jem stood back—or, rather, he fell back. He tried to make some joke of things, but he was stricken by the dignity and power with which Leary spoke and the light on Leary's face. There was sudden quietness in the crowd.

While Leary had been speaking, Gloria came forward. Like everyone else, she found Leary's words and his sincere manner very moving. Jem attempted an answer, but he was tongue-tied. Gloria turned on her heel and ran into the court. Leary walked serenely after her.

This courtroom could accommodate a crowd of about five hundred people. But that day, three times as many tried to get in. Criminal conversation always draws a big crowd. The clerk barked like a dog—he was a North Tipperary man and they sound like that over there.

When the judge appeared, Leary stood in front of him as the plaintiff, and Jem came forward as the defendant.

The judge summarized the case: "That you, Leary, complain you were damaged by him, Jem, on head of the fact that he lured your wife away, thereby denying you the pleasure and comfort of her company and the value she brought to your life."

Leary nodded, back to his old, somewhat dreary self again.

The judge, who had white hair and looked a bit like a seagull, said, "And I have to determine two things here: one, did Jem entice your wife away from you? Two, if so, how much should he pay you—if anything? The 'if anything' part comes when we consider whether you behaved in any way to make your wife feel unhappy or seek what might have seemed to her more decent company."

Now the judge turned to Jem. "How do you intend to plead?"

Jem looked at the body of the court where all his supporters sat, and he gave them a wink as broad as a gate.

"Judge, I intend to plead with eloquence, style, and a little daring."

"That's enough of that sort of chat in my court," said the judge. "Do you contest this case?"

"With a lion's strength and a hero's force," said Jem.

At Jem's eloquence Leary's heart sank again.

The judge turned to Leary.

"Were you ever married before?"

"No, judge."

"Therefore you mightn't have fully understood the nature and contract required of marriage?"

Lo and behold—it happened again! Once more the strange, invisible vapor came down and enveloped Leary. People who had seen it out on the street trembled in wonder and leaned forward to hear what would come out of Leary's mouth this time. Leary paused—and then words poured out of him like a stream of silver coins.

"Of marriage? Judge, I want to say,
It's deep and homeward, safe and soft,
As evening birds make to their loft,
Or horses to their beds of hay."

The judge looked a little startled, but not dangerously so; judges in Ireland have a latitude other judges don't have, probably because one or two of them have been poetic, even in their sentencing.

Leary spoke in a steady and measured tone, his voice full of mellifluous inflections, and if it hadn't been a place as serious as a court of law, it could well have been that people got mesmerized. They didn't, as it happened, and he continued pleading his case.

"Of women I knew nothing deep;
I lived alone and worked my fields,
And fed my cattle, milked their yields,
And nightly, wearied, laid to sleep.

But I believed that man needs more,
And so I set myself to learn
Of marriage, everywhere I turned,
By watching couples evermore.

I saw young men with beardless cheeks
Dancing with their shining brides.
I saw old gray-haired men besides
Look fond as though they'd wed but weeks.   •

And then I thought and thought so much
Of what Life needs to make it pure,
I understood man must be sure,
Yet tender with his loving touch,

And never coarse and never mere,
Watchful that he do his duty,
Husband, lover, to his beauty,
Trusted guardian of his dear.

I thought and thought of how I might,
Love a woman who would give,
Her hand to me and come and live
Beneath my roof from morn till night.

I found a woman, sweet and pretty,
Good of nature, clear of eye,
Kind in spirit, soft of sigh,
Who didn't need me to be witty,

Who knew that I could love with force,
Who judged my feelings were sincere,
Who sensed that I would hold her dear,
Who saw I was an untapped source

Of kindness, warmth and deep affection,
Care and conscientious thought,
Who believed a true man ought
Give his wife his best protection.

She married me, I married her,
A day of days, the sun shone brighter,
Our hearts, we found, were never lighter,
And then I knew it—love's the spur."

Jem began to fidget. For the first time, he saw that the case might go against him. He never expected such glory out of Leary's mouth. Added to that, he saw Gloria staring at Leary, doe-eyed and trans-fixed.

Jem raised his hand to get the judge's attention. He didn't have much to say to the judge, but he hoped to break Leary's stride. The judge raised a hand to halt Leary and turned an inquiring eye on Jem.

"This man is holding the floor for a long time," said Jem. "Is nobody else to get a word in?"

"You're worried by his eloquence, aren't you?" said the judge. "And you should be. You'll get your turn—if you'll want it by then." And he said to Leary, "Carry on."

After a gulp of water from the leather flask he carried, Leary took up where he left off.

"For the short time we were married,
I did my best to love this girl,
I never grizzled like a churl,
And always made sure that I carried

Heavy weights, like sacks or logs
Or furniture from room to room,
I combed the horses with the groom,
And fed the cats, the birds, the dogs.

The other matters that I tended,
Sweeter things that women need,
A lovely flower, a glass of mead,
A smile to praise a garment mended.

I ate her food with hearty joy,
I chose for her the finest leather,
For boots to brave inclement weather,
Loved her hearty or when coy.

If I came into the house,
And she stood there, unawares,
I chased her laughing up the stairs
And kissed her neck, soft as a mouse.

Every night I held her close,
Stroked her softly, caresses deep,
Smoothed her forehead, and in sleep,
Held her safely till she rose.

As I speak these words this morning,
It must sound as though I brag,
But my motive is to drag
My hurt heart out of its mourning."

A shout stopped Leary. Jem had wined somewhat before the hearing, and even in the courtroom took a covert nip.

"Make your point, man!" he yelled. "This is so dreary."

The judge looked down along his beak of a nose.

"Silence there! If you're unruly,
I've the power to shut you up.
Losing is a bitter cup,
And I'd say you'll taste it truly."

Well! The court nearly fell down in amazement. The people listening knew what had happened. Leary spoke so hypnotically that
his rhythm had infected the judge. And the women there—and it
was mostly women—concluded that it was now only a matter of
time until Leary won back his wife.

But Leary wasn't finished. He had some more powerful things to
say, and he meant to say them.

> *"The truth is, judge, I lost my lady*
> *Not to any man who's moral.*
> *Pretty soon he'll pick a quarrel,*
> *And he'll dump her somewhere shady.*
>
> *But if she'll come and take my arm,*
> *I'll so love her, so regard her,*
> *Do my best to work much harder,*
> *Even try and learn some charm.*
>
> *I may be dull and somewhat boring,*
> *But I love her perfect skin,*
> *And the way she tilts her chin,*
> *And her little whispered snoring.*
>
> *I love the way her tiny hand,*
> *Can crack a nut, or milk a cow,*
> *I love above all that she knows how*
> *To draw pictures in the sand*
>
> *Of faces, insects, beasts, and birds,*
> *And writes rhymes that never scan.*
> *She whistles better than a man;*
> *I love her sense of the absurd.*
>
> *We dwelt quietly on a hill . . .*
> *I'm an ordinary man . . .*

Her body's soft, much softer than
A fledgling's—God, I love her still."

Leary ran out of steam. His speech halted, and he sat down with a jolt, a man from whom all the energy had suddenly drained out. He had tears in his eyes. The judge sat back, closed his eyes, and breathed very deeply. He kept sending his hand across his smooth, seagull's head.

Before he could sit up again, a tiny noise could be heard down in front of him. Gloria had turned away from Jem; she faced Leary, and as sincerely as a woman in love—which is the truest sight on earth—she held out her tiny hands and began to applaud him.

Behind her, another woman began to clap her hands, and then another, and then another. Soon the whole courtroom was clapping and cheering, making the place as merry as a carnival. The judge did nothing to quell this noise—most unusual, because judges are known to love banging their gavels and shouting, "Silence in court!"

Leary sat there, a little dazed. After a moment he looked up and saw the lovely face of Gloria a few feet away from him, clapping her hands toward him with all her might and crying like the rain. Handsome Jem stood there too, but his face was as black as a cloud over a hill. After a few seconds, he darted away from Gloria and slipped out through a side door. People said he was never seen in the area again.

Gloria came over to Leary and laid her palm on his cheek. He caught the hand and kissed it.

"I'm sorry I hurt you," she said.

"I'm sorry I was a dull husband," he said.

"You're not dull. How could a dull man make words dance in the air above our heads?"

"No, that's where the words came from," said Leary.

Gloria looked puzzled.

"I'll explain it you," said Leary. "But it'll take me the rest of my life."

"I'm listening already," she said.

They were carried shoulder-high from the courtroom. The judge fell asleep on the bench, as judges famously do.

Leary and his Gloria went back to the farm, and the old servant woman who never answered back, and never was there such jam made or such chickens stuffed.

Barry Hanafin's little audience grunted. Two or three drinkers drifted over and nodded.

"Good stuff."

"Powerful, Barry."

The poet raised his eyebrows and half-closed his sleepy eyes in embarrassment; it made him look like a tortoise. He said, "More power, says old Power, when young Power was born."

"Always an old proverb to hand, I see," said Andy Hogan.

"I learned that saying from my grandfather," said Hanafin. "Too rural for you, I suppose." He turned to Ronan. "Well, young shaver, how did that go down with you?"

Ronan nodded. "Very well, thank you."

"I hope you're teaching him right, Andy?" said the poet.

"Ask him," said Mr. Hogan. "Come on, young O'Mara. You know what to say."

Kate smiled encouragement, and Ronan began to recite a poem to its poet: "For the lands of romance are the fields of gold/Where the earth we have is the wealth we hold/Greened and watered by each little eddy/Fruitful each year with the seasons steady."

Andy Hogan joined in. "And home to the coots and the pairs of swans/Who nest in the reeds or glide along/Searching for trout or gleaming salmon/Those citizens . . ."

Hanafin, embarrassed, cut in; "You fellas must have little to do with your time."

When the good-natured laughter died away, Ronan said, "When is the Storyteller coming back?"

"Apropos that," said the poet, "and by the way, did you ever notice how people always say 'apropos *of* that,' which is all wrong, that's like saying, 'arising from from that,' the second 'from' is totally and completely unnecessary, utterly unnecessary—"

"Barry, you never repeat yourself," said Mr. Hogan, now feeling the length of the liquor inside him. "Look at me, too. I never, never repeat myself. No, I never, ever, ever repeat myself."

Ronan wished they would both be quiet. He shuffled his shoes.

"What I'm really asking, Mr. Hanafin, is—if you know when he's coming back here, I'd like to come and meet him."

Barry Hanafin walked away. "I'll be back in a minute. Don't steal anything."

One of the younger men in the bar, with ragged yellow-blond hair, edged up to Kate.

"How well do you know him, the story man?"

Kate said, "He came to our house five years ago."

"I got talking to him a few times," said the young man. "I'm Kieran the tractor mechanic," and he pushed for a space beside Kate on the bench. Ronan had to move along.

"Hallo, Kieran the tractor mechanic," said Kate.

"He's most interesting," he said, pronounced it "inter-*est*-ing." "He walks twenty-five thousand miles a year."

"Does he?" said Kate, smiling.

Hanafin came back. "Ah, Jayzez' sake, how could he walk that much? What about bunions?"

Ronan said, "What's his name?"

Kieran looked surprised. "Barry, what's the story man's name?"

Hanafin looked morose. "He has no name. I asked him once and he told me to call him 'Mr. Everyman.' I said to him, What kind of a name is that, sure that's no kind of a name to have."

"Was that all he said?"

"Kieran, if he said any more than that, I'd tell you, wouldn't I?"

"But what kind of a name is that? Everyman? Every what man? Everyman who?"

"Jayzez, Kieran, I told you. Why don't you listen? I said—no kind of a name."

Kate tried to cool the heating air. "It's medieval. The figure of

Everyman is a medieval figure. Everyman is a no-name person who makes a great journey."

"Aah!" said Kieran, not totally familiar with morality literature and eyeing Kate ever more keenly.

"The Man with No Name," said Hanafin. "Like a gunslinger. The Wild and Wooly West."

"Did you know," said Kieran, "that Barry's a direct descendant of Brian Boru? His mother is one of the O'Briens of Thomond."

Kieran placed his thigh alongside Kate's, who moved to get away. Ronan asked another question.

"Is there any way of knowing where he comes from?"

"Brian Boru?" said Hanafin. "He's from here. Everyone knows that."

"No, Barry," said Kieran. "He's talking about the story man. The wind, that's what he told a girl here in the bar one night. The Man Who Comes from the Wind."

Kieran the tractor mechanic nuzzled closer still to Kate, who laughed and slid away from him. With jerky movements, Barry Hanafin poured two more drinks for himself and said, "There's people here who believe he's a ghost."

"A ghost?" said Andrew Hogan.

"These your own legs?" said Kieran, patting Kate's thigh.

"No, I bought them in Cork."

John laughed at Kate's riposte and moved toward her; she rose from the bench. Hanafin's face had gone slack as a hammock.

"There'sn't a thing wrong with ghosts. They can—you know— Jayzez, a ghost can do you a favor now and again. If you grease his palm. Or his wing, I suppose it'd be."

He leaned back, closed his eyes, and fell asleep standing up. Nobody disturbed him.

On the journey home, Mr. Hogan now sat in the back seat beside Ronan.

"Of course," said the teacher, his voice bleary with drink and bad sandwiches, "that was all a myth. I wonder, you know, if it isn't a bit dangerous putting out a story like that about poetry. We'll have people trudging the country, their heads cocked, listening for words to come down to them out of the sky."

John O'Mara winked at Kate.

"But, Andrew, how d'you know he's wrong? We weren't there to witness the moment poetry first happened."

"There to witness the moment? Is that a lawyer's approach?" asked Mr. Hogan.

"What do you think, Ronan?" said John.

"We should be allowed to believe anything," said Ronan, awkward in the presence of his teacher.

"The key word, 'believe,' " said Mr. Hogan. " 'Believe.' What makes us 'believe' something must be the truth? We can 'believe' events that actually happened. We can 'believe' things that eyewitnesses reported. The truth'll be in there, at the heart of those occurrences, that's why we 'believe.' "

"Not if you practice law in a country town," said John. "I've seen people believe what they've been telling me even though a dozen others contradicted it. But Andy, tell me; the way he said poetry was invented—did you ever think of teaching something like that?"

"That poetry happened like that? Heresy," said Mr. Hogan. "Utter heresy. You can't teach as fact something that is a man-made myth."

"Don't tell my wife that," said John. "And you'd better not tell the archbishop either."

"Did you know," said Andrew Hogan, "that if a penguin falls backward on its back, it can't get up again?"

Next moment, they heard him snore, which saved them asking him what he was talking about.

Ronan rose at six next morning to begin writing down the poetry tale. The verses tantalized him; he could remember many but forgot crucial rhymes. Should he write to Barry Hanafin? What if he took the day off and tried to recall? He decided not—and decided well; school that day brought a new dimension to his life.

The history teacher, David Cronin, called Ronan to the front of the room. He turned him around to face the class and said, "Now, Mr. O'Mara, I hear you've been to county Clare. And we've been studying King Brian Boru. So, I want you, in a tale of your own words, to tell us his story."

Ronan's mouth went dry. Andrew Hogan had evidently talked. But the challenge roused him; he had so much inside him that he could bring to this. He licked his lips and reached for general facts.

"As we've learned, Brian Boru was a great Irish king, and we've learned too that he was the first king in Ireland to repel a foreign invader."

He surveyed his classmates. Would they smirk—or worse? To his surprise their faces encouraged—as though they genuinely expected a good story well told. Ronan hesitated, then leapt to the task.

A S YOU WELL KNOW, THE ANCIENT PROVINCE of Munster, in which we live, consists of the six southernmost counties on the island of Ireland. Waterford, Cork, Kerry, and Clare are all maritime; Limerick has its big estuary of the river Shannon flowing to the sea, and Tipperary is the only county entirely inland.

In the first thousand years of this calendar, that is to say, the ten centuries since the year one Anno Domini, Ireland, and especially our southern province, prospered. It was our country's best era, and some say it was the most important time the Irish ever had. The good land made the farmers rich, and Ireland was a peaceful place most of the time, except for those local kings and chieftains who made war in order to take land from their neighbors. We weren't invaded in any dangerous way until the eighth century, and this gave the country time to grow rich.

Part of this wealth included big monasteries, and because they were supported by their neighborhoods, the monks had enough time and skill to make beautiful and valuable books. As well as books, they made objects of gold and silver, with jewels inserted as ornaments.

Our first invaders came here in longboats, and they wore metal helmets with horns that made them look very fierce. These were the Danes, part of the Viking people who lived in Scandinavia, and they were the best sailors in the world. They were also very savage, and they wrecked many of the places they invaded. Mostly they attacked the monasteries and abbeys because these buildings usually stood on the banks of rivers, so that the monks would always have enough water for their cattle.

Monks, however, hadn't much of a fighting tradition. Therefore, when the men from the north came in with their longboats, the monks greeted them as guests. The abbot of a monastery would stand out on the riverbank, his monks assembled behind him, and watch these open boats with high, curved prows come up the river. As the boat docked, the abbot probably raised his hand in greeting. The Norsemen poured ashore with their horned helmets and their wild blond hair. Often their first sword cut off the upraised hand of the abbot, and the blood spurted up like a fountain from the stump of his forearm.

Then the raiders ransacked that abbey and took every valuable thing they could find. First of all, they grabbed all the food and loaded it into the boats; they came back for the chalices and the other sacred vessels. Then they tore the jeweled covers off the Bibles and threw what was left of the great illuminated books into the rivers. We don't know how many of these beautiful volumes were simply thrown away.

After the pillage the Norsemen went off, leaving everybody behind them dead. When the first of these catastrophes was discovered, the word spread, and abbots everywhere were advised to welcome nobody unless they knew them.

The monasteries began to build a safeguard—what we now know as the famous Round Towers of Ireland, several of which are intact. These tall, narrow buildings reached seventy feet off the ground, and they had their entrance doors thirty feet up. The towers had two functions; they served as watchtower belfries and as refuges. When the monk on watch duty rang the bell to say he had seen the Viking boats approaching, the brothers raced to gather up every valuable they hoped to preserve. Then they climbed to the high door and pulled up the ladder.

Sometimes, because they were fearless warriors, the Vikings tried to scale the walls. But the monks prepared vats of boiling oil that they poured down on any Danes climbing up. When the boiling oil hit them, it roasted their heads and their necks. It slid down the metal helmets and blistered their eyes and burned their faces. The

Danes couldn't fight the oil; they usually went away again, and the monks thanked God for their safe release from danger.

Many of the coastal places in Ireland were overrun by the Danes, mostly on the south and east coasts. They took control of Waterford, Wexford, and Dublin and settled down there, marrying into local families. In most other places they raided and ran, but enough of them stayed to mix and marry with the Irish, so that they became a noticeable part of the people. And those that stayed and married and had families eventually contributed in large ways to the life of Ireland.

But others still raided our shores, and finally it became too much for the Irish kings, who were supposed to rule their people and therefore protect them. They banded together and tried to merge their armies and defeat these terrible people. But they couldn't agree among themselves very often, and when they were supposed to be fighting the Danes, they wound up fighting each other instead.

All through the ninth and tenth centuries, one wave of Norsemen after another raided and settled down. Finally, around the year nine-ninety, one king got tired of all this, and he decided he'd bring an end to the Norse raids. His name was Brian Boru, and he held court in county Clare, in a place called Kincora. His name, "Boru," came from the Irish word for a tax on cattle, which was one of the ways Brian made money for his kingship. In the year nine-seventy-six, when his older brother was killed, he had become king of the Dalcassians, a tribe from county Clare.

Brian had great ambitions. He wanted nothing less than to rule all of Ireland, and he watched very carefully to see would such an opportunity come along. All the time he was growing up, most of Ireland was controlled by the ruling family of Ulster, the O'Neills. No decent Munsterman would want to be ruled by an O'Neill, so Brian set out to find out everything he could learn about them.

The main thing he discovered was how they had acquired so much power. They did it by military force, and Brian decided that he would do the same and try and get control of all Ireland—in other words, that he would no longer wait for an opportunity; he would create one.

Starting with the families who killed his brother in battle, he made war on many tribes. He agreed peaceful settlements with others, especially the ones who were afraid of him. Then he subdued the Vikings of Limerick and several Irish clans north of there. When he marched further up the country, the people of Leinster proved a difficult enemy, and they even enlisted the help of the Danes to fight Brian.

In spite of great opposition, Brian fought hard and also worked a lot of politics, and in the year ten-oh-two he became High King of all Ireland. He ruled wisely and well, and by two different means he made sure that everyone obeyed him.

First of all, he continued to maintain strong armies, and he needed them to keep under control the many warlike kings up and down the country. Secondly, he took a keen interest in the affairs of the church, and as king he insisted on appointing many of the abbots and bishops. This gave him a powerful influence over the church, who had to speak well of him, because he gave many of their leading figures their jobs. Thus he was able to get the church to tell the people he was a good leader, a factor that has been useful for leaders in Ireland up to the present day.

About ten years after he became High King, it became apparent to Brian that the Norse threat seemed to be increasing again. The raids on coastal settlements became more numerous, and in some of these forays the Vikings even attacked their own people who had settled down. Many chieftains who had suffered and many abbots whose monasteries had been pillaged came to Brian and asked him, as High King of Ireland, to fight off the Danes.

Brian had just subdued another king, his former enemy Malachy, part of the O'Neill family, who had fought Brian's attempts to take over all Ireland. He approached Malachy and suggested that together they should fight the Danes and defeat them for once and for all. Malachy agreed, and Brian let it be known that he and Malachy were marching on Dublin to fight the toughest Viking of them all, King Sigurd.

The battlefield was set in Clontarf, a name that means "valley of the bulls." Brian arrived with a large army, and the Vikings had already prepared their tents. On the eve of battle, as Brian sat in his tent with his generals, going over the last details of the battle plan, a messenger asked to see him, saying it was urgent. Brian asked to see the man personally, and the messenger, who was very embarrassed, told Brian he came from King Malachy, and the message was that King Malachy had decided that day to withdraw his army; he would not be fighting the Danes with Brian on the morrow.

No reason was given, and after ordering that the messenger be given food and drink before returning to his own people, Brian went out and addressed his troops.

"Listen," he said to them, speaking from the saddle of his great white horse, "We're alone tomorrow. Our allies have decided to turn and run. The men of the north, King Malachy's soldiers, obviously fear battle. So we'll have to show them what it's like to fight and win. It means that we'll have to be twice as strong, twice as swift, and twice as fierce. But we shall be twice as victorious."

Brian's men, who knew that he was a wonderful general, cheered and cheered.

Next day, the Vikings were still laying out their arms when Brian's army attacked. It was a surprise raid; Brian wanted to use their own tactics against them. He reasoned that they had achieved their conquests in Ireland mainly through surprise. So he selected small bands of his best fighters to race across the grass, twelve at a time, attack the Danes, and return as swiftly as they came.

The strategy proved very successful. Man after man from Brian's army killed at least two and sometimes three and four Vikings before they had time to put on their horned helmets. One of their soldiering tricks was to look for a man with his back turned, tiptoe up behind him, and drive the point of the sword into the nape of his neck. It was very successful.

Then Brian sent a messenger to King Sigurd, and asked him did he want to surrender. King Sigurd roared that he didn't want to surrender to an old fool of a king like Brian, and he would have killed

Brian's messenger except that there was an unwritten law guaranteeing the safety of messengers.

Brian then sent all his troops into battle, long lines of them across the low-lying fields of Clontarf. Both armies of soldiers had long swords and big, round shields. They were very evenly matched, and the battle raged all day. Brian, who by now was not a young man, rode up and down the battlefield, exhorting his troops and occasionally taking a swipe at a Viking. He took off one man's nose, and he split another right through the forehead. By four o'clock in the afternoon, he could see that his army was winning. After one last exhortation to his men to take no prisoners—in other words, to kill everybody they could catch—he retired to his tent.

It was a beautiful afternoon, and after some refreshment, Brian stood outside to watch the last moments of the battle. When he could see that the Danes were finally routed, he dropped to his knees on the grass and prayed his thanks to God. But a Norse soldier, fleeing the battlefield, came running by, saw the old king at prayer, and attacked him. Brian almost succeeded in defending himself—but, as the Viking soldier cut off Brian's head, Brian's heavy sword cut the man's legs off at the knee.

When Brian's royal attendants came running, they found their king dead and a legless Dane beside him, whom they killed immediately. They roasted his body on a spit in revenge, and then fed it to their dogs.

As you can imagine, the celebrations after the battle weren't as lively as the soldiers had hoped they would be—everybody was very glum. A few weeks later, King Brian Boru was buried at Armagh, very near Saint Patrick's grave. The funeral gathering went on for seven days and seven nights.

As he spoke the last words, Ronan's self-consciousness returned. It proved needless; his classmates crowded around him. Boys who had mocked him, smirked at his books, jostled his bike—they changed. Some asked for help; one offered to pay if Ronan would write his essays—and a chorus called out to Mr. Cronin, "Sir?! Sir?! Can he do it again?"

The teacher agreed, and with Ronan developed the exercise; either the horn-rimmed master wanted an unusually vivid piece of history retold as a story to energize the class, or he wanted a complex passage to be unravelled and spread out like a map.

On such occasions he paid Ronan the unusual compliment of tutoring him personally in advance. When they finally brought it to the classroom, Mr. Cronin set out the dates and characters elegantly on the blackboard, and then asked Ronan to tell it as a colloquial story.

When Ronan told Kate about this, she commanded a performance, calling it grandly, "The True Story of Brian Boru." And she praised him for staying within the bounds of history while embellishing for the sake of color; "Makes it so memorable," she said.

His father also heard and brought the story home. This concentration upon history went down well with all three adults. His father's interest in folklore and Kate's background—she had taken a history degree—connected with his mother's sense of the past never having ended; Alison repeatedly told family stories that sounded recent, but on examination came from as much as a century earlier. Thus it surprised none of them that, in school and state examinations, Ronan scored highest in history. It seemed unavoidable—predestined, almost—that he should pursue it at university and beyond.

•   •   •

Ronan O'Mara passed into adolescence smoothly. He had no skin eruptions, no wild behavior—nothing beyond an increased fastidiousness and a rising interest in his own appearance. The tension of the household never arrested his maturing; John's and Kate's warmth, plus his own good management, wrapped him against Alison's frosts.

Puberty passed like a short season. Yes, he had a greater awareness of girls; school functions introduced him to the locals, but he liked very few. One or two, home from expensive boarding schools and thus a touch exotic, gave off some spark, but he never felt like kissing anyone.

Many tried to get to him. They set up friends to say that such-and-such had fallen "terribly in love" with him (the phrase came from a novel they were all reading), but he took none of their bait. And they felt the loss more sharply because their mothers urged them toward Ronan. He was tall, clever, famously studious, well-mannered, and handsome—future perfect, so to speak, as a potential son-in-law.

How he tantalized them, not just with his reserve but because he had one extra quality that the mothers adored—ambition. He enthused about people who reached pinnacles; he discussed their achievements with passion; he had heroes. They all knew that he too would aim for success—and they guessed he'd succeed at anything he went for. Adding everything up, he had the makings of a true "catch," even at the age of seventeen. Yet, no matter how the mothers fed or feted him, he slipped past the arts of their daughters.

It wasn't that he didn't want to kiss them, which was what the girls claimed; nor did he lack interest in girls, as they also hinted. In fact they had long ago entered his secret life; through Kate's fashion magazines, he knew about amazing underwear. In newspaper advertisements some of it seemed like armor, but in the women's magazines it felt more intimate and immensely thrilling.

Hollywood in the Alexandra cinema raised the stakes—form-fitting slips, akimbo thighs, devastating bosoms; Lana Turner proved helpful, Jane Russell more urgent. And Barbara Stanwyck walked naked (rear view only) into a river in *Cattle Queen of Montana*. And in a laneway not far from the school he had found a mildly lewd magazine called *Confidential Detective,* which contained many photographs of tough-looking American ladies in black negligees or swirling, conical brassieres.

Where he differed from the usual boiling adolescent boy was in his control. He filtered all thrills through a disciplined brain, in which his Storyteller quest still absorbed him. Every day he did something toward finding the old man: a letter to someone, a newspaper cutting of a discovery from the past, a poem he felt the Storyteller might like. And every month he visited a new phase of Irish history, selected for color as much as for fact. If he had to measure, he might have said that the history now outweighed the search—until the thirteenth of August, 1960, when his life changed again.

Autumn came in gorgeously that year; wood smoke in the air; hazelnut bunches under leaf clusters; a smell of apples and fall, and the chuckling of pheasants in the woods.

The Saturday afternoon began vividly, and heightened. Ronan set out for one of his hiding places—a disused badger sett, over which he had dragged a flat stone and ancient branches. On his way from the house, he came down through the high wood, where the wild strawberries grew every summer like small red gems. Ahead of him on a rock stood an iridescent blue-green bird, unafraid and resting, wings puffed. Ronan guessed immediately—a homing pigeon, fallen out of some race or blown off course by a storm out at sea forty miles away. Sometimes the seagulls drifted this far inland, and his mother prayed, "Heaven help the sailors on a night like this."

He dropped to his haunches and edged toward the pigeon. The bird showed little alarm, merely hopped a few feet away. Ronan saw but could not read the green ring on its leg. He waited and watched; the pigeon ducked its beak into a small pool on top of the rock.

Ronan then knew the bird had measured its own safety; pigeons need to rest and drink, then they resume the journey home. He walked away, content.

A hundred yards on, as he cleared the wood, he saw the hawk. It wheeled, fawn and lethal. Climbing, climbing, it made its point high above and hovered, wings shimmering on some thermal pad. Then it dropped like stone propelled by rockets. Suddenly Ronan understood and dashed back—but too late; the hawk had taken the pigeon. One small blue feather floated in the pool of rock water.

As he stood there and swore, his wider sight picked up a movement. The hawk had not taken off again but stood in the ferns fifty yards away, holding down the pigeon with one talon; Ronan registered the classic pose, the steady, violent glare, the rich mottled gauntlets. All the same, he ran at the hawk. The predator took off, carrying the pigeon, but couldn't rise far.

Ronan lost sight of them in the thickets but kept running along the line of flight. In the deeper woods he saw the hawk again, now attacking. On the pigeon's breast feathers sat one drop of blood, a dark bead. Ronan picked up a dead branch and threw it lightly. The whirling stick caught the hawk on the side of the head and forced him off the pigeon. As the hawk turned to assess Ronan, the pigeon rose amazingly and flew out of the wood. It wheeled two large circles in the sky, determined a direction, and flew away to the north.

When Ronan turned back, the hawk thought to attack but instead lurched deeper into the wood. It had trapped itself in a dense bramble; there it sat, pinned, one wing splayed. Ronan knew he had to gamble; he wanted to release the hawk, but he might be attacked—and, he argued with himself, the hawk might eventually free itself anyway.

However, the more he scrutinized it, the deeper seemed the hawk's trap; coils of briar had snared the splayed wing. He asked himself what his father would do, or want him to do. And so, though rightly afraid—hawks attack the head and eyes—he moved behind the bird and began to ease the bush. He got so close, he could have stroked the feathers; instead, he forced the branches apart, and the hawk struggled free. The bird soared to a safe, high bough, and Ronan felt a surge of power, a dizzying self-approval.

He returned to his task and reached the cache. As ever, he studied the exterior to see whether it might possibly have been uncovered. The branches had been moved—animals could have done that. And the stone? Had it? Not sure. He hauled it back. Inside, wrapped in the remnants of an old leather satchel, lay some of his treasures; the radio director's letter about the Storyteller, his copy of *Confidential Detective*—and now, something else. An ancient shirt nestled under the leather satchel, and something was wrapped inside it.

Who had been here? Impossible! Nobody knew of this cache. He opened the shirt without removing it from the shallow pit. Inside, he found a small clutch of papers, undated, unsigned, and written at random, some inscribed on the lined sheets of school notebooks or on scraps of the blue writing paper that Irish people once commonly used for correspondence; two pages were jotted down on a brown paper bag. A few of the entries seemed almost indecipherable; water stains had made the ink run. Ronan weighed them in his hand. The papers felt thin and haphazard—but they had ragged physique and a power.

He took them out in the open air, shielding them from the sun as though they might rot. Sitting against the warm brick walls of an old kitchen garden, he sat and read.

I AM WRITING THESE PASSAGES IN A BARN IN RATH-drum, county Wicklow. Outside, the rain is pouring down as straight as stair rods, and the raindrops are hopping like frogs off the stones in the yard. I am reasonably comfortable, thanks to a hospitable man and his wife here, Mr. and Mrs. Dunne, whose only note of doubt was a warning to me not to let my candle burn down to the straw or, to quote Mr. Dunne and his vocabulary (unusual for a Wicklow farmer), "We'll all be immolated."

Tonight I told them one of my stories, and as often happens, I cannot now sleep. My mind is galloping with details I might have included and errors I made in the telling. Every night, I am despondent at such failures; if I perform in a way that does not grip my listeners, I'm out next morning. Additionally, I take my life's work very seriously, and that is why I want to write down why I became a storyteller, and what it means to me.

First a note on a most important aspect of my life—the business of walking: Pace is all. Rhythm is master. Consistency is your friend. In the morning, setting out for a new destination, I take five or ten minutes to find my legs, so to speak. I will trot a little, followed by a saunter; or I'll stride to warm the tendons and then slow down, then speed up again. Soon, I will have found that day's speed, although days can vary, and then I settle into it and do not deviate from that speed for five or ten miles.

Stopping, or rather the control of stopping, has an importance. I walk at the rate of four and a half miles an hour. After one and a half miles, that is to say twenty minutes, I always stop to empty my bladder and feel pleased that I can return a contribution to the earth. But I learned not to make this stop a long one, because the concentration required of walking, once lost, cannot easily be recovered.

Within seconds, I have hit my stride again and have found my rhythm. The regular movement has small qualities of what I imagine hypnosis to be—a pleasant feeling with a gentle hint of what a trance might feel like. This comes best on a level surface such as a good road; in a field, the rough ground can jolt one's concentration—and can assist it too, so that an ankle is not twisted or a sinew forced.

The first wave of fatigue comes early in the third hour, at about the ten-mile mark. At that moment, a decision is always called for— how considerable is the destination, and how sensible to press on? In other words, should I divert to some nearer place or keep going? By now I know a considerable number of destinations, although I have a principle of adding some new houses every year. This has its dangers; what do I do if it proves not merely an unfriendly house but one hostile to me and my tradition, and worst of all, one who knows my story?

As I walk along, I think of my own past. We were poor people; my father worked in a seed and grain store, and my mother tended a smallholding of reeds and thin pasture. We lived in Leitrim, the poorest county in Ireland, a land of marshes and that evasive bird, the snipe.

I was an only child, and as I grew up, I found that I loved the sky. I believed that certain clouds came by on certain days; I was sure that I recognized their shapes. In those clouds I first saw other worlds. Sometimes I look into yet another fire on yet another hearth in yet another home, and I see enthralling pictures. Likewise in the heavens; in the skies above Leitrim I saw the great animals of Africa, the hippopotamus and the rhinoceros and the giraffe, and I repeated their names to myself for the music of the words, just as I murmured "portmanteau" and "mellifluous" and "Abercrombie" long before I had any sense what such words meant. Also in the clouds, I saw palaces—great, olden Irish palaces with wolfhounds and chariots and warriors and beautiful women.

Then when I looked down, I found beneath my feet different treasures of the world; grasses that look like blades of silver; reeds of deep red and with a sweetness of nectar in their taste; pink, struggling worms made of rings; beetles with shiny black backs. I encountered the bulrush, that tall plant that grows wild near water, its top-heavy pod made of brown velvet. And I found the ferns, wide and hospitable, ready to shelter underneath their untroubled fronds the chrysalis of a moth—or a small, dreaming boy.

In there too stood the wonderful rocks. I thought of them as people or as animals; because many of them had wrinkles, like old men's faces or the hides of elephants. They wore little brooches of green moss, like ladies walking about on Saint Patrick's Day. Sometimes the water from the last shower lodged on a rock and sat there like a magic pool in which you might see a face from a legend.

Next, I met the birds and grew to know them by sight and by sound. The blackbird warbled a message to me of dawn and another of dusk, thereby setting the boundaries of my day. And the wren taught me protection; the wren builds three nests each year, and two of them are decoys, so that predators will never find wren chicks in their little mossy igloo with the round door halfway up one side. And of course the snipe—I saw her as she rose from the marshes and flew in a darting line across the watered lands; that is how I learned necessary evasiveness.

Then there was the cuckoo—or rather, the effects of the cuckoo. By a nest I would find dead baby birds on the ground far below and know that, if I looked in there, I should find a young, strapping chick, black and brown, of no resemblance whatever to the species of bird who had built, laid, and hatched that nest. No, the cuckoo, up from Africa, and heard in far corners of distant fields, had laid her egg in some other bird's nest, and that chick had then ousted the rightful heirs. From that, I learned that as soon as one acquires a position, one has created the danger of being ousted.

But I also came to know the thrush. As I attempted to peer into her nest, she came diving through the sky at me, whizzing over my head so closely I could feel the breath of her wings and see her angry face. From her I should have learned to leave well enough alone. She taught me that all property must be protected, that it is natural to fight for what you love, and that new life is all.

And so I wandered here and there, never without determined purpose, looking all around me and learning the world. Every tree taught me something; the horse chestnut gets its name from the little hoof at the end of each twig; the sycamore casts its seeds in the form of little whirling propellers.

In every pool and stream I learned something. I watched beetles careen across shiny surfaces, like ambitious men going too fast through life. In still waters beneath the banks of rivers I saw pike lying in wait. Watching the fish rise at dusk or at dawn on silent, unattended rivers taught me that for every fish, there is a bait, and every man has his price.

Although I lived in an ordinary practical world where food was eaten and liquid was drunk and clothes were worn and beds were slept in, I also saw, heard, smelled, tasted, and touched another life. Sometimes I got into this world through a practical gateway. For instance, I recall sitting in our kitchen as my mother served what we called stirabout—others call it porridge or oatmeal—and I began to think of the farmer who harvested the oats. Did he have a beard, and was he tall, and had he red hair and a great hat? I never had seen a human being so bizarre, yet I found this picture within me.

Next I imagined the harvesting of the grain—but I also saw the rabbits and little mice who fled the blades of the mowers. In an instant I was within their tiny homes under the earth, where they had created snug and warm safety into which they would welcome a small boy who promised to behave.

When I think of that boy now, I sometimes wish to weep. He— meaning, I—had a kindness, a soft way; never intended harm; only wished to wander an easy path through life, "looking at things and leaving them so," as the old expression says.

Ronan searched the papers for clues, but they offered no trace whatever of their origin. He felt no fear, only wonder, that his hiding place had been discovered and breached—but not violated. Instead he had received, through some mysterious means, a rich and marvelous gift. There and then he accepted it as part of the general magic of his life associated with the Storyteller. He read the papers again, much more slowly, and allowed some of the emotion to reach him. Then he put them back, stored away in the cache. Already he knew enough about himself to delay his responses and digest for hours on end what he had just read. He walked home, feeling he lived in a marvel.

The day ended significantly, too. That night his father announced major plans; they had rented an apartment in Dublin, where Kate had found a new teaching position. Ronan would study, and she would run their lives.

John spooled it out; three years of history for a bachelor's degree; a year more to a master's; then a three-year doctorate study.

"Then you'll get a distinguished chair of history in some university, and your doctorate thesis will be the first of a long list of brilliant publications."

Ronan looked across the table. Leaving home? He would greatly miss his father—the interest in every topic; the constant good humor. But he nonetheless felt the bolts of satisfaction click into place.

One Sunday morning in late September, John drove Kate and Ronan to the Dublin train. Inside Ronan's leather suitcase lay a tender world of new clothes bought by his father; shirts, sweaters, underwear—and John's own treasured university scarf. Alison said good-bye at the house, awkward and reserved; Ronan saw her turn away, her hand to her mouth in woe.

They had half an hour to chatter, with John checking his watch against the calm, big-faced clock. He intercepted the lone attendant.

"Billy, is the Enterprise running to time?"

"Sir, you'll have to ask the driver," said Billy McGrath.

"Doesn't that defeat the purpose?" said John when the porter had gone.

As they laughed, the green and red signal arm dropped—five minutes. John spun away and walked to the farthest end of the bare platform, distinct in his tall gray coat, his gleaming black shoes.

"Your father's in tears," Kate said. "Look. The handkerchief."

Like a white flag it emerged from John's pocket. After much business, he stowed it and came back to them, composed, as the train steamed in.

"Remember," he said to the two beloved faces crowding the carriage window. "No drinking out of wet glasses. No betting on slow horses. No—" The jokes died in his throat. "Oh, Jesus God Christ, what am I going to do without the two of you?"

He turned away, bleak with loss.

They clanked through fields of yellow stubble, and they swung through autumn's leaves. Ronan and Kate sat by the window, facing each other. Such conflicted feelings—the loneliness of a receding past and the excitement of a new life ahead; so much to say, so little said.

In Dublin, the apartment occupied an entire floor, with rooms to spare. They ran from door to door like newlyweds. The huge bathroom had its original claw-footed Victorian tub; Ronan's desk overlooked a park; and in Kate's room a pair of closet doors opened out into a major surprise—a theatrical dressing table, ritzy with lights.

They ate the food they had brought from home. In the kitchen cupboards they found blue china, and in the drawers, bone-handled cutlery. Kate opened linen napkins, and she had packed Ronan's own drinking glass.

"Begin as we mean to continue," she said and posed a little, swanking and swaying. "The highest possssss-ible social standards."

They ate potato salad moist with homemade mayonnaise; cuts of cold lamb on which Kate daubed filaments of mint; small planks of crumbly brown bread that Ronan slathered with salty yellow butter. Kate heaped thick cream on the deep-dish apple pie that she had baked and zested with cloves.

From their separate rooms they called fresh and excited thoughts to each other as they unpacked. Kate chattered her way in and out of the bathroom.

"Don't forget to write down the names of your lecturers, or it'll take ages to remember them. And make sure you register for as many societies as you can—they're all run by girls. Get to Registration early tomorrow, or you'll be there all day. I wonder if you'll have any of my old professors. Some of them were mad."

Suddenly she said, "Come here," and raised her hands to his face. She kissed him on both cheeks. "I'm so proud of you. But not as proud as I'll yet be."

Ronan had never slept in a bed outside his own home, and he scrutinized everything: a mattress that sagged a little; an ornate lozenge of orange marquetry on the polished headboard; the green light cast by the lampshades. Sleep took him by surprise, and a dream led him through fields of huge-eared corn in which strolled very tall men with high-legged dogs. This vision switched to a land of lakes where a troop of plumed, ornamented horses, like some posh circus, plodded along a hillside, while he and Kate—or someone like her—watched from a window.

Next morning he registered in a great, echoing hall, where everyone talked loudly at the same time. Within an hour he sat in his first lecture; thirty tiers of curved amphitheater benches. He looked around at the other young men and women—sixty of them, all under twenty; some looked casual, some nervous; some, airy and grinning, carried no books of any kind; most of the girls were festooned with pens.

Enter the wizened face of academe: T. Bartlett Ryle, a famous professor of history. His nasal chant preceded him through a side door, and within seconds of the professor's opening remarks Ronan felt a whole flood of new delight.

THE MOST DISGRACEFULLY NEGLECTED PERIOD of Irish history stretches from the year seven-ninety-five to the year eleven-seventy. Those dates are in what many people call the Dark Ages. I am not one of those people. And I sincerely doubt that any of your teachers has clearly defined the centuries of the Dark Ages, so let us strap them down here and now. Most of the stuff that's spoken about that era is good enough to grow roses in.

I dislike the term *Dark Ages*. Day by day, ancient texts and archaeology's finds are brightening those centuries, and it may well prove to be the case that one day the Ages won't deserve to be called Dark anymore. The word you should be searching for is *medieval*. In my lectures you'll hear only the terms *early medieval, high medieval,* and *late medieval*. Let me see nothing else in your essays. You may write about the sexing of chickens—there's deep sympathy around here for that sort of thing. You may write about the effect of drought upon a toper. You may write about the fate of maiden ladies who work in bishops' houses. But you may *not* write about the Dark Ages.

All-right-very-well-so: Let us address them now, one by one. "Early medieval" covers, in my view, the beginnings of literacy in Ireland, that is to say, from the *Confessio* of Patrick circa four-sixty to the flowering of the great manuscripts such as the Book of Kells four centuries later. "High medieval" commences—again, in my view, and no other view need concern you—from the middle of this so-called Golden Age, that is to say around the eighth century, to the end of the fourteenth century. And "late medieval" takes us into, but not beyond, the year sixteen hundred, after which behavior and its record have begun to change significantly.

Many people disagree with me. That's their problem. You have no such privilege, and you should by now be taking notes. These notes shall become your moorings for the entire course of study with me. I advise you never to permit the wide, flat—and as yet empty—barges of your intellect to drift far from the notes you take in my lectures.

Therefore, thereby, and thereupon, let us now address the significance of those two dates—the year seven-ninety-five and the year eleven-seventy. They represent two of the most important moments in all the history of Ireland. In seven-ninety-five, the modern island—"modern" being a term relative to the many millennia of prehistoric Ireland—the modern island received its first wave of outside attackers who had the capacity to establish a lasting presence in our country. This spells out our historic vulnerability to colonization, the inherent weakness in a small but fertile land.

By "outside attackers" I refer, as you know, to the Scandinavian mariners, whose oceangoing skills brought them to these shores. After the usual daily round of rape and pillage, they then settled here, and in due course they intermarried with the natives. Nothing surprising in that.

They're not our concern this morning. Their incursions more or less halted after the battle of Clontarf in ten-fourteen, when the southern king, Brian Boru of Thomond, inflicted a military defeat upon a massed army of Norsemen. But this was mostly a symbolic victory—it proved that the Norse were vincible. It didn't get rid of them—they had been too long ingrained here. Indeed, by then they had developed this city of Dublin, in which you now sit and I now stand.

So Clontarf was, in many ways, no more than a family fight. When it was over, and Brian was dead, the resident Vikings and the longstanding Irish all got together and got drunk, and they fought and intermarried some more, and they traded and generally got on like neighbors. That, to oversimplify everything, was the long-term outcome of the invasions that began in the year seven-ninety-five.

As to the second date, the more astute of you will recognize it as the time of the people we call Normans.

The Normans came here from across the Irish Sea, from England and Wales; sadly, they didn't come from their own original province of Normandy in northern France. Had they done that, then the history of Ireland would have been very different.

For one thing the food would have been better—we, the Irish, would have been conquered by the French and not the English. And who wouldn't prefer a piquant béarnaise to the brown sauce of the English commoner?

The arrival of the Norman knights in Ireland is popularly seen as the first invasion of the English. Is that accurate? Well, in common with the ambiguity of all things Irish, it is and it isn't. (I once asked my good friend the professor of theology here if he believed in God, and he answered me, "Some days I do, and some days I don't.") It used to be said that the Normans came here to make Ireland the king of England's granary, just as Julius Caesar conquered France to do ditto for Rome. No, not so; they weren't as clever as that. But it is true that, by and large, they came here at the request of the king of England, Henry the Second—he was also the ruler of Normandy, and the men who came here were his knights—and that he later arrived to augment them.

Those of you who have managed to understand me this far have probably been told already that all history is a matter of interpretation, mostly by the victors. In the case of our little island it has been rather different, because the history of Ireland was also written by the vanquished—the repeatedly defeated, the hung, drawn, and quartered, the kicked and beaten. And haven't we made the most of our victimhood? There's an English gentleman called Chesterton, a decent fellow by all accounts, quite ample around the waist, who says that "the great Gaels of Ireland are the men that God made mad. For all their wars are merry and all their songs are sad." He's entitled to his opinion.

So: old Irish, Vikings, and Normans—three people on one island; my purpose here is to pick a way for you through that mixture and give you a teaching of our history since the Normans that'll render you fit to go forth, marry decently, raise a family, live to a ripe old age, evacuate your bowels no more than once daily, cultivate your garden, or if you prefer, spend your life in low dives, gambling on two flies climbing up a wall while drinking cheap liquor imported from Rumania. I hope you're still with me—in spirit if not in spite.

All-right-very-well-so: now let me offer you the first and most powerful fact of the Norman invasion. It had as its objective—religious domination. Are you listening to me? Religious. Domination. The good priests, brothers, and nuns in your well-run schools won't have taught you this. But it's nevertheless true. And the domination that was sought was by Rome, who wanted to slap down a few stroppy Irish bishops.

Pope Adrian the Fourth was the only Englishman ever to sit on the Vatican throne—a British pope is as rare as a hen's tooth. He became aware that the church in Ireland, which had always been inclined to go its own way, showed signs of taking little interest in what its guiding fathers had to say. Its immediate guiding fathers dwelt in England, in Canterbury, whose archbishop to this day presides over the Church of England, and in those days Canterbury was a kind of suboffice to Rome.

But—you're saying to yourselves—hold on, here. Isn't the archbishop of Canterbury a Protestant?

As I look at your faces, I am thankful to find few struggles there, because you all seem to realize that this was some centuries ahead of the Reformation, before which there was no such thing as a Protestant. Some of you may long wistfully for that day—but that's a matter between you and your God.

In eleven-fifty-two the archdiocese of Dublin had a heady moment and decided flat-out it wanted nothing whatsoever to do with Canterbury. Dublin was still sore at having lost the church politics of these islands in the Synod of Whitby six hundred years earlier.

Also, the church had become rather temporal in its outlook; the monasteries had built up huge power, and in many cases the abbots controlled all the money for themselves and their cronies and their wives and their flocks of snotty-nosed children and their concubines. Now—be warned! There are some who will accuse you of blasphemy or heresy or something equally racy and thrilling if you're heard to murmur, "Has nothing changed?"

In short, the Christian church in Ireland had dissipated much of its own glory in exchange for money and power, and Rome first, then Canterbury, became agitated. Some Irish priests and monks tried to improve matters from within, but they only succeeded in making the whole boiling a great deal messier, and they're too insignificant to bother with here. A poor professor of history has few powers—but one of them is the right to ignore those who he thinks made no difference to the spin of the earth.

In eleven-fifty-five, the same Pope Adrian, whose maiden name, if you grasp the expression, was Nicholas Breakspear, gave Henry the Second a Papal Bull requesting him to bring Ireland into line. Many people believe it wasn't a Papal Bull, that it was all bull, if you get my meaning—in other words, that the French-speaking English king had the crucial document forged. Such convenient penmanship crops up often in the history of England's dealings with Ireland.

In any case, whether the Papal Bull was forged or not, it had balls, and you know how big a bull's balls are; Henry was armed with the moral authority to tackle Ireland. But Henry was a busy man. He had wars to fight in his French provinces, and he had England to govern, and he knew that Ireland was never a country the English could manage; it always was and would always be a country the English could only subdue. So he sat on his Papal Bull, so to speak, and did nothing—even though he not only wanted control of Ireland, he needed it, because he had several sons to settle down, to get other kingdoms and lands for.

When politicians and those who observe them consider matters, they frequently fall into the trap of assuming—hopefully or desperately, depending which side they're on—that a status quo may last forever. They forget what changes things—events. That's what all politics are changed by—events. And eleven years after the ink dried on the behind of the Papal Bull, events here gave Henry his way into Ireland.

From the west, the great Rory O'Connor expanded his kingship of Connacht and became the High King, to whom all others should acknowledge loyalty. In order to become High King, he had had to defeat a gentleman called Dermot MacMurrough, the king of Leinster, a prime and driven man, who was no easy foe.

Now, the general interpretation you'll have been given in school is like this: "Dermot MacMurrough was the greatest Irish traitor who ever lived—because he and he alone invited the Normans, i.e., the English, into Ireland and actually led them in here."

That makes it sound as if Dermot had gone over and sold his country, lock, stock, and foaming barrel to the people who became the British—the slithering son of a bitch. No, no—that's not how it was.

First of all, he went abroad because he was deposed as king of the eastern province of Leinster and banished from Ireland by the High King, Rory O'Connor. The fact that he had abducted the daughter of the High King and the wife of O'Rourke of Breffni, a passive sort of a dame called Devorgilla, had no small part to play in this. But the real reason he went is that he was simply trying to raise an army and regain his kingship of Leinster.

How many of our singers and whistlers, whose idea of patriotism is to hate England and all things English—how many of them would have been out of a job if Dermot had gone, say, to Belgium or to Morocco looking for help? But he didn't. No, ladies and gentlemen, he did what any pragmatic man would do—he went to the nearest possible port of call.

As for Dermot MacMurrough being the traitor who sold out our glorious Isle of Saints and Scholars to these grunting barbarians— nonsense. Long before then, people from England were in and out of here like a fiddler's elbow. No doubt about it, folk went back and forth between the two islands like a weaver's shuttle, but that idea would, of course, rob Irish history of some of its drama. And heaven forfend that we do that—there'd be many people out of a job.

Anyway: Henry the Second gave Dermot permission to recruit such gentlemen as would be willing to embark upon an Irish adventure. Dermot's method of recruitment was to read aloud, at markets and meeting places, a letter from the king. In Wales, where the land was poor and the king had long ignored the local gentry, some Norman knights living there heard the call and climbed aboard Dermot's bandwagon in the years eleven-sixty-seven, eleven sixty-nine, and most powerfully in eleven-seventy.

According to popular opinion, that's the time when Ireland's doom at the hands of England was commenced and sealed. Popular opinion? What I suggest you do with popular opinion is morally questionable and biologically impossible. But it is true that platoons of soldiers arrived in Ireland, on the coasts of the southeast, led by Norman knights, and that surely and not so slowly they overwhelmed the incumbent people, mostly old Irish with some Viking intermarriage.

Ironically, in terms of colonization, the two cities first conquered by the new invaders had the Viking word *fjord* as suffixes to their names—Wex-fjord and Water-fjord—because they had been established by Norse raiders.

Within the first years of the Norman presence here, there began the great assimilation, which later caused the Normans to be accused of growing "more Irish than the Irish themselves." And that, ladies and gentlemen, is where your course of study begins—in the year eleven-seventy, with the arrival of a very superior Norman gentleman by name of Richard FitzGilbert de Clare, the former earl of Pembroke; he will be more familiar to you by his nickname, "Strongbow."

In the unlikely event that any of you has an imagination seeking further stimulus concerning this passage of history, some additional illumination may be derived from the very fine painting, *The Marriage of Strongbow,* by my distinguished relation, Daniel MacLise.

It hangs in the National Gallery in Merrion Square, and admission is free. The costar in this epic, as you will see if you bother to go and look at it, is Strongbow's wife, Aoife or Eva, the daughter of Dermot McMurrough.

All-right-very-well-so: somewhere in my desiccated frame I harbor an irrepressible humanitarianism. Does anyone among you understand a syllable of that sentence? Ah, why should you, straight from the bogs and backyards of our green and bilious land? What I'm saying is—I always cut the first lecture short for first-year students in case you get brain fever or wind. This is the last concession you'll get from me. Go now, explore the seamy delights of our capital city, which once had more whorehouses than Bombay, and make sure you're back here, disease-free, in time for the next lecture.

T. Bartlett Ryle had halted in mid-flow. He swung
right around, faced the wall for a long moment, then swung back
again and peered up at the ascending rows of students.

"H'm," he said—and nothing more.

Placing his long feet carefully ahead of him, he stalked from the
podium like a stork in tweeds.

Ronan eyed his fellows jostling from the lecture. How many of
them truly loved history? No point in talking to those who didn't.
A tall girl, gathering her books into a Red Riding Hood basket, eyed
Ronan back.

"A scream, isn't he?" she intoned. "A riot. A chuckle. A chortle. A
hoot."

Ronan laughed. "You sound like him."

"If this is what he does to me in half an hour, I'll be in tweed
britches by Christmas."

"Great, though, wasn't it?"

"Was it?" She cocked her head to one side and tried to look like
an owl. "If I don't know yet, how do you know?"

Ronan shrugged. "He's—exciting."

She nudged her spectacles farther up on her nose.

"You'll do well. If you suck up to him like that."

Ronan protested. "No. I meant it. He was funny. He's different."

"H'm," Red Riding Hood said. "Wait till you hand in an essay.
They say that fella marks in blood."

Kate had arranged to meet Ronan for lunch. She laughed at his
account of Bartlett Ryle and asked merry questions.

"Did he have snuff stains down his lapels?

"And was he wearing a grey speckled tweed suit? The leather patches on the elbows, the cuffs?

"And did he have a dirty white shirt? I mean, very dirty? And a polka-dot bow tie?"

Ronan said, "Did you ever see such scratching?"

"You know, don't you, that he was giving that lecture in your father's time? And your father asked me these same questions after my first lecture."

"I loved it."

"His books are wonderful. He debunks everything. The bishops hate him." She patted Ronan's arm. "You're going have a great time."

In 1960, Kate was thirty-seven—old now for marriage, even in slow rural Ireland. Yet she looked wonderful, brown eyes and hands of ivory. She herself disliked that her right ear protruded more than her left and she mostly arranged her black hair to hide it. With the looks came sweetness and light; a readiness to laugh; a gift for listening. Her speech was quick, and during conversation she groomed constantly, drawing strands of hair through her fingers, fixing a sleeve or a collar; sometimes, when very animated, she grasped the forearm of the other person.

Good with money (and with a sizable inheritance), she bought expensive clothes a notch above her friends' taste. Waisted jackets that shaped her figure and long skirts over high boots gave her a Russian look years ahead of fashion; with a taste sharpened by fashion magazines, she wore black turtleneck sweaters and even owned cocktail dresses; high-complexioned, she rarely used cosmetics.

She also had a secret life. To the great disapproval of her sister, Kate spent much of her money on underwear. She shunned the armor of the day, all that rubber and whalebone; she wore light fabrics in dainty colors. And she made it all part of her mood; the more dismal a day's prospect, the more sensual the underwear—silks and satins next to her skin. With some added wit: she wore her spicier pieces on Sundays.

Ronan paid for lunch out of his allowance, and Kate taught him how to calculate the tip. She waited outside, and the cashier said, "Hey, your girlfriend left her hat."

"We both win," said Kate. "It means that you look older than eighteen, and I look younger than thirty-seven. What do you want to do now?"

"How about 'the distinguished relation, Daniel MacLise'?"

Nobody else entered the National Gallery during their visit; no other footsteps clicked the solemn floors. The only sound came from a square-built lady attendant who sucked her teeth. When they were out of her earshot, Ronan began to suck his teeth, and Kate punched him on the arm.

Heroic, on a vast canvas, gory and epic, *The Marriage of Strongbow and Aoife* by Daniel MacLise "ignored metaphor and irony"— according to Kate, who moved into lecture mode.

"But it has two principal values. It arrests time seven hundred and ninety years ago. Even though it can't have the impact of an eyewitness record, it gives an artist's impression. Which has a kind of truth. And secondly, it shows a moment in Ireland's history of art, when a painter like MacLise used his skill and technique to say that his country needs its history."

"You're beginning to sound like Professor Ryle."

"Seriously. Look at it. This might be mistaken for a classical scene, the great building and the tableau of the marriage, the corpses everywhere. And see the way Aoife is concentrating on getting married? She doesn't care that her bridegroom has just slaughtered all these people—her own countrymen, for heaven's sake. There's blood running down the streets, and she loves the man who spilled it. This painting says that we too, on this little island, we have our own heroic past to match Greece and Rome."

•   •   •

All that first week, Kate waited for Ronan in Saint Stephen's Green, always in the same deck chair. They ate sandwiches as he told of his morning, and like everyone else, they fed the ducks with the crumbs. Her freckles swarmed in the sunshine. Everywhere they went, she took Ronan's arm; man after man, Dublin turned its head to look at her.

Soon the term settled down for her too; she was the only woman on the teaching staff of Belvedere College, a Jesuit school for boys. And the household developed a routine; Ronan had late lectures two evenings; Kate always reached home by five o'clock; after supper Ronan studied, every night of the week. He resisted all social life—whether pushed by Kate or pulled by peers.

Toward the end of their second week, a letter arrived from John. After what he called "a casual inquiry," the Folklore Commission had replied to say they had made a recording in county Cavan of a storyteller. If Ronan would care to contact them, they would try and arrange a playback.

Ronan cheered. "They'll know where he was—they'll know where to find him!"

From her school, Kate telephoned. That afternoon, she and Ronan sat in a small booth in the Folklore Commission's offices with Sean O'Sullivan, the director, a man of quick dark eyes.

"The Scandinavians much admire us," said Mr. O'Sullivan. "In fact, we're the model for many countries who want to preserve their own history." His voice seesawed in the accents of the far southwest. "Now, we don't know if the man on this tape is the same man you're interested in. Your father thinks it might be."

The director instructed his technician to switch on a large green machine.

First, they heard the hissing that haunted all tape at that time. Through the sibilance echoed a hesitant voice: "Field Recording made on Sunday the nineteenth of July, nineteen-fifty-nine, at nine-thirty P.M., in the home of Mr. and Mrs. Kevin MacKenna of Cootehill. The recordist on behalf of the Irish Folklore Commission is Daniel P. Kelly."

Then Daniel P. Kelly said, "You're comfortable there, sir?"

Next, they heard the unmistakable voice: "Is that thing listening to me?"

"That's the microphone—I'll hold it here, and you just talk into it."

Ronan quickened; this was the voice he wanted to hear every day of his life. It felt almost like a dream now—all the times he thought of the stories; all the days he wondered where the old man was. At the simplest level, this tape was a kind of breakthrough in his search—if this had been made fifteen months ago, the man was probably still alive. How many times had Ronan speculated the worst? Pneumonia; tuberculosis; age.

After some rustling and clearing of his throat, the Storyteller began. A few phrases in, and Ronan's heart raced once more with the feeling that the old man spoke directly to him and him alone.

I'M GREATLY DRAWN TO EPIC PEOPLE. THE HEROIC in man is something for which we should all reach in ourselves. If we find we don't possess our own heroism, we should respect it wherever we come across it, in friend or in foe.

This subject came to my mind last week when I was treading the low sand hills of the southeast, where the maritime counties of Waterford and Wexford meet. It was a sunny day, as it often is down there, and I began to think about a hero whose first contact with us was by way of the sea.

When you live in a country that's surrounded by water, you think about things in a way that's different from other countries, where the sea isn't as important. Here in Ireland, nobody lives more than seventy miles from great water. This island is a hundred and forty miles wide at its broadest—and I make it about two hundred and seventy from top to bottom. So: in olden days when somebody came to us from foreign parts, they first had to deal with the sea.

Now, down around the tip of Wexford, the waters are mostly benign. I'm thinking of Kilmore Quay, where every Christmas the local families sing private hymns that are hundreds of years old. And I'm thinking of the Saltee Islands, where the birds bask in sunshine so sweet that some days you would think the place Mediterranean.

Therefore, if you wanted to send a raiding party to Ireland, that is probably the best coast on which to land. The point I'm coming to is this—and some people say it's the most important point in all our Irish history.

Once upon a time, on a summer day, a robber baron landed on

that serene, sunny coast. He was a Norman, from Normandy in France, but he had lived many years in Wales, sixty miles across the sea from us. When he came here, he was already an epic figure, and when he left us for the next world, he was more than epic—he was a leading light in our history. Because from that robber baron's arrival flowed everything that the outside world knows of Irish politics, if it knows anything. This man's story is my tale tonight—his name was Strongbow.

Strongbow landed at Baginbun. You all know the old rhyme; "'Twas at the creek of Baginbun/Old Ireland, she was lost and won." It was the first of August, eleven-seventy, the day that changed Ireland forever. Strongbow was tall amongst men of that time, which means that he was probably about five feet ten inches. If you look at the crusader knight in armor lying in Saint Michan's Church in Dublin, you'll marvel at how small were the men of long ago—but not Strongbow, with his broad shoulders and big head. He had other fine knights with him that August day, and a goodly array of strong and varied troops. Their mission was simple—their soldiers were under orders to capture land.

Now, long before Strongbow arrived, many Normans had already been here—men with names like Fitzgerald and de Prendergast and then, in May eleven-seventy, a fellow called Raymond le Gros, Raymond the Fat. He was the advance party for Strongbow, and he made camp on Bannow Island, a sandy bank by Baginbun Creek, which has long since been inundated by the sea.

Strongbow had been invited here by the king of Leinster, a man called Dermot MacMurrough, over whose character we must cast some grave doubts. But Dermot is a tale for another night, when the dogs have stopped barking and the birds have gone to sleep.

Now: when I'm making a story, there's one thing I have to do, or it won't come out right. I have to open wide the eyes of my mind and let my imagination do the work. So as I sit here in this decent house, full of decent people, I close the eyes in my head, and I open the eyes in my mind, and what do I see?

I see the sun shining and the birds in the trees singing their small sweet songs. Next, I see the shimmering waves beating and retreating along the empty shore. And now I find myself standing there, all those centuries ago, and I look out to sea.

What do I behold? I see dots on the horizon—and they're coming nearer and clearer. What are they? They're sails; I look harder, and the sails draw nearer. Unlike the ship bringing Iseult to her dying Tristan, these sails are neither black nor white—they are red, red as blood, and beneath them sit rows of men with great oars whose efforts scatter little white waves across the surface of the water.

But what else do I see? Along the sands, ranks and ranks of soldiers already wait, camped by moored ships, and waddling to and fro among them I see a man with a big stomach, his armor bulging out against it. One hand is resting on his sword's hilt, and the other hand's shading his eyes from the sun. I assume this man to be Raymond le Gros; he certainly looks fat enough for such a nickname.

I follow the direction of his gaze, and next I see, from my place in the low sand dunes, that the ships, and there are many of them, are now coming gently into the shallow waters. Soldiers jump out and wade ashore, and last of all comes a tall man to whom everyone defers. He is clearly a chief among chieftains—he is Richard FitzGilbert de Clare, the man they called "Strongbow."

Strongbow was once the earl of Pembroke, but for political reasons he had been stripped of his title by the king of England, Henry the Second. Since no man likes being humiliated, the baron was pleased enough to come to Ireland, where he might make a fresh start. Dermot MacMurrough had approached him, because he himself had been deposed as king of Leinster. He said to Strongbow, "You put me back on the Leinster throne, and I'll make you my successor."

"Fair enough," said Strongbow, and over he sailed.

Dermot made another promise too, but I'll come to that in a moment.

Not many people wanted Dermot back in Ireland. He was a well-respected soldier, but he was a terrible man. After a battle one day, he saw the head of an enemy lying on a pile of severed heads, and he said to one of his soldiers, "Bring that over here to me."

With a curl of distaste on his lips, the soldier obeyed the order. Dermot reached out, took the head by the hair, held it up, and turned it this way and that.

"D'you know what?" he said. "I hated this fellow when he was alive."

So, with everybody watching, he took a big bite out of the cheek on the dead man's face. Dermot MacMurrough was not a man you'd lightly invite to your home.

Right: Strongbow has landed, and everything is set up and waiting for him. On that fair August day, the army of Strongbow and Raymond le Gros set out from Baginbun and marched due west through the rich fields to Waterford, where the citizens barricaded themselves in. Strongbow's archers breached the walls, Waterford fell, and the Normans tore in and killed a great many people. The blood, it is said, ran like streams down the streets of the city.

Dermot arrived with reinforcements—and more than that. He brought with him the other half of his promise to Strongbow—his own beautiful daughter. Her name was Aoife, and she was Dermot's declared heiress—she would one day inherit a great parcel of land. Strongbow was a widower and the shrewd Dermot had promised him Aoife's hand in marriage.

See how this suited the parties? Strongbow would get a wife who owned land. Dermot would get a son-in-law with a strong army. And Aoife, if anybody considered her, would get a powerful husband to protect her and maybe give her children.

Such marriages of convenience were not unusual or surprising in those times—indeed, they happen to this very day. It never happened to me, but what woman would have a nomad like myself? And anyway, I believe you can't organize and control the random passions of the heart.

Except—sometimes in marriages of convenience great love is born. It happened to Aoife, who in the midst of all this planning and arranging took everybody by surprise with her reaction. After one look at Strongbow, this fine Frenchman in his shining armor and his chain mail and his great bow made of the wood of the yew tree and his dark eyebrows that met in the middle of his forehead and his rich French accent, she fell in love with him. He thought her the prettiest girl he had ever seen. There and then, on Tuesday, the twenty-fifth of August, in the year eleven-seventy, they were married in Reginald's Tower, which you can see to this very day standing, big and round and proud, on the quays of Waterford.

There was the blood of the city swirling around their ankles, there were men moaning and groaning from their wounds, there were other men trying to pluck the arrows from the breasts of the fallen—the French are very thrifty, they always use something more than once if they can—and there were distraught women weeping and mourning and beating their breasts in anguish because their husbands and brothers and sons and sweethearts had been killed in the defense of their native city. Nevertheless, that is where and when the great wedding took place, while the clouds sailed the sky and the ships sailed the seas.

The Storyteller stopped speaking, but the tape continued to hiss. Ronan and Kate could hear sucking noises, and they grinned at each other.

"My pipe's gone out, and I forgot to get matches. Is there a man here with a light? Ah! Decent man, I thank you, sir, I'll make sure you get them back."

They heard the scrape of a match; a short pause, more sucking and puffing, then a deep breath.

NOW, THIS IS A GOOD MOMENT TO TELL YOU something you'll all recognize. The Normans, as we all know, were here to stay. And they never left. I'm sure there are Normans among you in this room tonight. How would you know? Well—listen carefully.

What's in a name? You're descended from a Norman or from a family who came in with them if your name is one of these; Prendergast, Cogan, Fitzgerald, Barrett, Lacy, Cullen, Bermingham, Devereaux, Condon, Walsh, Power, Bolger, Eustace, Barry, Tyrrell, Keating, Codd, Neville, Roche, Cummins, Furlong, Colfer, Stafford, Carew, Hayes—and there's a lot more that I haven't mentioned.

I think I gave you twenty-five names there, and you should think about some of them. Down around Wexford you can't throw a stone without hitting a Devereaux or a Bolger or a Colfer or a Codd or a Stafford or a Roche or a Furlong. Next door in county Waterford, there are as many Walshes and Powers as there are leaves on a tree.

The line of history is very short. From eleven-seventy to say, next year, nineteen-sixty, that's a stretch of only seven hundred and ninety years, no more than forty generations, if we call a generation twenty years. We all know people who went to Parnell's funeral in Dublin in eighteen-ninety-one, our lost leader, God be good to him. My father was there, and, he said, so were a million other people.

And in nineteen-thirty, when I myself was forty-two years old, I met two old men up in the west whose grandfathers saw the French under General Humbert land at Killala in seventeen-ninety-eight, their blue uniforms shining as they came up from the beach on the twenty-second of August—a Wednesday, I believe. How is it that all Irish invasions seem to happen in August? I wonder, could it be anything to do with the weather?

All I'm saying is that if people with the names I'm telling you here tonight came over with Strongbow and his barons, and people with the same names still live in the countryside where he landed and ran his first campaigns—that is not coincidence. They are direct descendants of the Normans.

Now—Waterford has fallen, and so has Wexford, which is once again in the hands of Dermot MacMurrough and the knights who helped him. Strongbow and his bride, Aoife, seem as loving a couple as ever tied a knot.

The next target was obvious—the biggest Viking city in Ireland, Dublin. By the time he left Waterford, Strongbow must have had five thousand men with him—and up in front, beside himself and Aoife, rode her father, Dermot MacMurrough, and the stout man, Raymond the Fat. Five thousand men is a big gathering at any time in any place. In Ireland in eleven-seventy, where the population was still fairly sparse, you'd think you couldn't keep an army like that a secret. Well, they did.

To begin with, the Normans weren't like Irish soldiers, who were a bit ragged, to say the least. No, these foreign men were armed and disciplined; they didn't slouch along, they marched. The cavalrymen rode big horses, they carried lances, and they had heavy armor because they were easy targets. And alongside them trotted the elite—the archers of France, deadly with their yew longbows and their arrows. Behind came the provisions, wagons of food and drink, and the civilians in charge of them.

Not many in Ireland would ever have seen a crowd that large. The people in the counties along the southeastern side—Waterford and Wexford, Kilkenny and Carlow and Wicklow and Kildare— they came out to watch these fine marching soldiers and all their equipment. Women stood at doorways, wondering who they were. Children either hid from them or ran after them, marching in step, as children like to do. Men in the fields put down their spades and watched the soldiers in no small amount of fear.

Other people heard they were passing through and traveled many miles across the country to view them from a hilltop or watch as they forded a river, their armor glinting in the sun, the wheels of their carts trundling in the ruts of the mud. This, you'd have thought, was no surprise attack. You may be sure that the word got out—there's an army marching north, and they must be heading for Dublin.

And in case it didn't, horsemen saddled up and rode ahead of this army, looking back over their shoulders. Their intention was to ride forward and warn the city, hoping to be paid for bringing such bad news; never a good idea—people often shoot the messenger.

But then something very surprising happened—Strongbow and his army disappeared. They had been marching through Kilkenny and Carlow, and there was wide, open country between them and Dublin—but they vanished. Disappeared. Not to be seen. Was there a door in a mountain? Did they fall down a hole?

This is what happened. Being a shrewd general, Strongbow wanted as much advantage of surprise as he could get, so he had Dermot MacMurrough's guides—local men—lead them on a secret route through the passes of the Wicklow mountains. The weather must have been very fine, because even today you'd never get an army of five thousand men through Glendalough if the weather wasn't good. But in they went, into the forests and through the ravines, and nobody saw them for days. Dublin heard they'd gone away, and everybody breathed again.

But it's no more than thirty miles from the foothills of Wicklow to the outskirts of Dublin, and Strongbow was at the walls before they knew it. The citizens rushed to defend. They raised extra fences of wattle; huge spars locked the gates; they chopped down trees and tried to barricade the river Liffey. No good. All in vain.

Now I open my mind's eye again, and I see myself standing outside the old walls of Dublin, if we can call them walls. It was early on a

September morning, when the light in Ireland is as lovely as in heaven. For a long time nothing happened. A dog barked; a child peered out from behind a fence to look at the Norman knights in their wonderful silvery armor and their thousands of men, ranked up neatly on a sward of green grass. The main gate opened a little, and out slipped a respectable gentleman, who walked briskly toward where Strongbow sat on his horse.

This was the archbishop of Dublin, Laurence O'Toole. He saw the great man at the head of this impressive troop, and then his eyes went to the figure riding alongside Strongbow.

"My God in heaven," he said to himself. "Dermot MacMurrough is back!"

He hesitated for a moment, then walked on.

"Is there any justice in the world?" said the archbishop, still talking to himself. "That barbarian!"

It was at that moment the bad name of Dermot MacMurrough was forever set, the reputation that branded him Ireland's greatest traitor. Laurence O'Toole surmised that Dermot went off to get help and didn't care what happened to whom.

As befits the conventions of war, Strongbow greeted the archbishop with a courteous salute, even though he didn't understand a word the man said; Strongbow spoke a combination of English, French, and the old Celtic language, Welsh.

Dermot translated the archbishop's words. The people of Dublin wanted no trouble. Of any kind. It was well over a hundred years since the battle of Clontarf. In the meantime Dublin had been settling down nicely. We all get on well here, Irish and Viking. And Archbishop O'Toole wanted to know, Was there anything they could do for this strange, strong band of men?

Dermot put it plainly. He was coming back to claim his Leinster throne; Dublin was his capital. Whatever man was now calling himself the king of Leinster should step down immediately, and there'd be no bloodshed. The knight in armor beside him was no less a figure than the personal emissary of King Henry of England.

The archbishop gritted his teeth and said to Strongbow, "What terms would you want in return for not attacking Dublin?"

Strongbow said, "Complete surrender."

The archbishop said, "Out of the question," and he turned to go back inside the city, where he'd tell everybody what a traitor Dermot MacMurrough was.

The moment he walked away, Strongbow's two leading officers, Raymond le Gros and Milo de Cogan, who was a very clever general, gave the order to storm the city. Dublin fell that morning, and Milo de Cogan opened the gates for Strongbow and Aoife to ride in triumphantly. There was a king there, Hasculf, a Viking; some say he was an ancestor of Shakespeare's Macbeth, who, like Hasculf, was a man from Orkney. Anyway, Hasculf fled to those northern isles he came from, and we'll return to his part in the story in a moment.

Meanwhile, Strongbow and his Normans took over Dublin and got to work. They did what all conquerors do—they got a tight grip on the people they conquered, and they set up for themselves the best of everything; fine food and drink, the nicest clothes, comfortable beds.

So began in earnest the Norman conquest of Ireland. When the city was under control, and Dermot had been restored to the throne, and daily life was back to normal, they set out to take over the surrounding counties. Their ventures took in a circle from Louth in the north all around to Meath and Kildare to the west and Wicklow in the south. And of course the sea gave them an eastern defense.

They were organized and careful; they were tough; they had come to get land, and they meant to get that land. Day in, day out, they did more and more to dig in. They built stone castles and strong bridges, they extracted vows of loyalty and taxes from the Irish chieftains, and they began to construct the boundary known as the Pale. That was the fence to keep out the native Irish— so if anything is said to be "beyond the Pale," it's wild and uncontrollable.

In eleven-seventy-one, a year after the fall of Dublin, Dermot MacMurrough died. They said he had a horrible death—that his flesh began to melt off his bones, and he died screaming. When this news went abroad, Hasculf the Viking came back from his northern climes to besiege Dublin, and he brought with him a terrible weapon.

You are familiar, no doubt, with the word *berserk*? Haven't you often heard that a man "went berserk"? The word refers, as we know it, to a state of mind producing awful behavior. But it comes from a Scandinavian word, in Norse, meaning first of all a man who wore a coat or a shirt made from a bear's skin, and secondly, a certain kind of fighter. Presumably a man who could kill a bear and take his coat and wear it wasn't a lily. Some Norse kings used to wheel cages of these Berserks onto battlefields, and when things got bad, they opened the cages and let them out.

That's what happened in Dublin. Hasculf brought Berserks with him, and the Normans were nonplussed by these crazy warriors, especially by a big, wild man called John the Mad. He was the greatest fighter Hasculf could find; he carried a huge axe, which he swung in circles around his head, and God help anyone who came within range of it.

And he had one special trick. Remember—Norman cavalrymen wore armor and chain mail. But John the Mad would aim his axe at a cavalryman's thigh, cut through the armor, and sever the limb so that the Norman's leg fell down on one side of his horse, and he himself fell down the other side—where John the Mad immediately cut off his head. John was what you'd call a definite sort of fellow.

The battle for Dublin between Hasculf and his Berserks and Strongbow and his generals was probably the fiercest and most prolonged battle ever fought on the island of Ireland. Once the Vikings got back in, they linked up with the local people, who hated Strongbow. The native Dubliners showed Hasculf's soldiers all the lanes and alleyways, and from these they would jump out and attack the Normans. Soon the entire Viking army was within the walls and rampaging through the streets. They took their cue from

John the Mad, whom they could see up ahead, hacking men down left and right.

Strongbow's generals had to do something; this is what they did. That clever man Milo de Cogan led his troops out through one of the city gates, giving the impression that he and his soldiers were in retreat. But they weren't; he rode back in by another gate, came up on the Viking rear, and cut the tail off the dragon.

That was the end of it. Three Norman knights killed John the Mad. It was like cutting down an oak—they hacked and hacked with their swords, and John the Mad's blood spurted, they said, high as the leaves on the trees. Raymond le Gros captured Hasculf and marched him to Strongbow, who listened for a few minutes to an earful of Norse defiance and then had him executed.

After that, Strongbow and Aoife ruled as king and queen of Leinster. It's often said that life brings the most difficulty to newlywed couples in their first year. Certainly, Strongbow and Aoife had no easy time of it. Out there, in the wilds of Ireland, in the counties not yet under Norman control—beyond the Pale—tribes were assembling armies and heading to attack Dublin.

As long as Milo de Cogan and Raymond the Fat were around, Strongbow could be sure that things would remain reasonably safe and level. But soon another problem arose.

Word began to reach King Henry the Second of England that Strongbow had done very well for himself in Ireland. He had taken Dublin, become king of Leinster, married an heiress, and repelled all invaders. Not only that, it seemed as if he had used his Norman army to extend his reach.

Henry had difficulties himself trying to rule England and at the same time keep an eye to his dominions in France. The last thing he wanted or needed was the island to the west of him in control of someone he hadn't treated very well. He remembered that the pope had asked him to make the Irish bishops behave themselves, and he took this excuse out of his cupboard, spruced it up a bit, and set forth for Ireland.

By the time he arrived here in October of eleven-seventy-one, he had thought out a shrewd approach. His informers had told him that the Irish chieftains were afraid of the Norman barons, who were making raids all the time and seizing their land. So Henry set himself up as the savior of the native Irish.

That was how he got control of both sides. Strongbow had no choice but to offer homage to his king, who, by the way, had come with a large army. "Speak softly," it is said, "but carry a big stick." In return, Henry told Strongbow that he could stay king of Leinster for as long as he lived. When most of the other Irish kings and chieftains saw Henry's power, they agreed to offer their loyalty to him too. He allowed them to keep their land but now, for the first time, they were answerable to an English king, not an Irish one.

In the six months that he stayed here, Henry effectively made himself king of Ireland, and by the time he went back in eleven-seventy-two, we were changed for ever. Bit by bit, Henry doled out Irish land to Norman generals like Milo de Cogan. The Irish chieftains and kings resisted the loss of their land, but the truth was the power of old Irish kingship was over.

Strongbow lived for another four years. He died in June eleven-seventy-six, and they buried him in a great funeral at Christchurch Cathedral in Dublin, where you can see his tomb to this very day. His kingdom of Leinster was given to Henry's son, John, who annoyed the Irish chieftains—for some reason he derived great amusement from the length and shape of their beards, and they thought him disrespectful. In time he became King John, and thereafter English kings and their sons and daughters ruled Ireland until we got them out of most of the country after the rebellion of nineteen-sixteen.

We're all taught to think that history happened a long time ago—as if "that was then," so to speak. I don't find it to be the case. When I'm in a place that has had a strong history, it's the same to me as if it happened yesterday. And that's what makes my life so interesting—everywhere you go in Ireland, there's a vivid piece of history; it's the great advantage of being born in a small and storied land. I think of Strongbow when I'm in Wexford and Waterford, and I especially think of him when I'm in the city of Dublin. And I see a man who carried himself and his sword well, whose shining helmet had a tongue of metal that came down and covered his nose, and whose wife looked up at him with adoring eyes.

And that's my story for you tonight.

The technician switched off the tape machine; Ronan stood up; Kate clapped her hands in applause.

"The coincidence," she said to Mr. O'Sullivan. "He's studying that period."

Ronan weighed in.

"D'you know his name?

"Is he still traveling?

"Where is he now? Or when was he last seen?"

For nine years he had been asking the same driven questions.

The Director walked away, then said over his shoulder, "Did you know that the park of Saint Stephen's Green was given to the city of Dublin by the Guinness brewery? Wasn't that a most decent gesture?"

"Where did he go?" Ronan raised his voice. "Did you pay him? We could trace him that way."

Mr. O'Sullivan said, "All folklore contributions are voluntary. Do you know the origin of the word *lore,* as in *folklore*? It comes from the word *learn,* and here's a theory. Generally *learn* is regarded as a word from northern European, old German, and the likes; those isles around Frisia generated a trunkful of language."

The Director's neat hands ushered them from the room, while he spoke fast to fill every space.

"But I have a friend who says it comes from the Latin word *lira,* which means a furrow in the field, and that *learn* derived from *lira* because we furrow our brows when learning."

Taking control, Kate said, "Do we have any way of tracing the gentleman?"

Ronan chipped in; "Of finding out who he is?"

The director did not wish to seem rude.

"Give my best to your father, will you? I believe he knows the gentleman, doesn't he?"—and he eased away from them.

On the street outside, Kate said, "Wasn't that something?"

They walked silently home, side by side. The quiet mood between them continued until they had finished supper.

"You're very quiet," Kate said. "Speak."

Ronan pushed back his chair. He sent a hand across his hair, took a breath.

"Listen. The night he came to the house. You weren't there, that first night, Halloween. He walked in as though—as though he came from the Far East. Somewhere exotic. His face was a sort of yellow white. And I remember his hands were so cold and bony—God! Hearing that tape now. It brought it all back."

"I remember how you cried," she said, "the day he left. We were so worried about you."

Ronan pressed on.

"He came into the kitchen. Dad welcomed him. Mother was displeased but tried not to show it—she made him a meal. He had shaken my hand in the hall, and I was afraid to let my hand touch anything in case the magic was rubbed off. Do you believe in predestination?"

"Oh, my!" said Kate. "What a question. I'd need a week to answer that."

"But do you believe in it?"

"Your reason for asking would help me to answer."

"Well—I know this is crazy. But I believe that I have—that I was born to have—some connection with that man. I mean, some important connection. I'm not talking about something easy, like meeting him again. There's something more."

She said nothing; knew enough to let him talk.

"Kate, you'll think I'm a lunatic."

She shook her head. Ronan put his hands to his face, passionate with youth.

"When he came through our door, he already knew I lived there. I know he knew. I know it. And—this is the crazy part. I felt as though he had come for me—as though he wanted me to do something for him."

Kate remained level, nodding and watching.

Ronan shook his head. "Mad, isn't it? This—this 'thing' that I feel he wanted me to do—it's protective in some way. But how can a boy of nine, as I was then, protect a man as old as that?"

"I'm sure you wouldn't have felt it unless it had some truth," said Kate.

"It got worse. All along the line, every time I drew close to him—every time I met someone who had contact with him—the feeling was reinforced. There's nobody else in the world would understand this except you." Ronan stood, hands clasped behind his head. "And one other thing. Did you see today how the director deflected my question about the Storyteller's whereabouts?"

Kate said lightly, "He has excellent tact"—and they laughed.

"But everybody behaves like that. In that same way. If I ask a direct question about where I might find the man, nobody answers me. Even Dad's the same."

"When you say, 'in that same way,' is there a pattern? You know how keen your father is on observing patterns."

"Yes! Either they evade the question, or they deflect me with some interesting titbit. That O'Callaghan woman—she never answered. Barry Hanafin glared at me. Dad told me about the twelve days of Christmas, the carol, you know, 'my true love gave to me.' And this man today told us about the Guinness brewery and Stephens Green and then about the word *lore*. It's as if they're all trying to throw me off the scent."

"Or," said Kate, as though speculating, "acknowledging that they weren't in a position to tell you. If they knew. Which they might or might not. And yet they don't wish to be ill-mannered. In fact, if they wanted to throw you off the scent—as you suspect—they did so by honoring you very sweetly. They could have told you lies. Or they could have told you to mind your own business."

"Yeah, they could."

•   •   •

Dear Kate,

Your sister is in the bath hosing herself down, I hear her singing! Josie has gone after another day of work avoidance, and I'm sitting here writing to you and Ronan. They say that it's unmanly to speak what you feel, we're supposed to keep what the English call "a stiff upper lip," but hell's bells, I miss you both.

Are you well? How is Ronan faring? Do you think he has stopped growing yet? I didn't until I was twenty-two. And is he eating well? And not staying out too late at night? Do you think there's any danger he'll turn into a drinker? So many students do, but I know you'll keep an eye on him. I hope he won't be a burden to you.

Is there any chance of you coming down soon? There's a big surprise here, but I won't tell you what it is until you're here. The house is empty without the two of you. Tell Ronan I found a good secondhand edition of Gibbon's Decline and Fall *in a shop in Limerick. Let me know if you'd like to come down, and I'll organize train tickets, etc.*

With affection, John.

"What d'you think's the big surprise?"

"A new car?" said Kate.

"No. It's something else—I wonder what it is."

John talked a great deal, very hearty and fond; he laughed at Ronan's version of Bartlett Ryle.

"What's the surprise, Dad? We thought it'd be a new car."

"You'll have to wait and see. With the emphasis on *see.*"

Alison looked preoccupied—and exhausted—but denied that she was. She had prepared lavishly, as though for special visitors. Ronan's experiences at college dominated the meal.

"Okay," said Kate at last. "We've waited long enough. What is this surprise, where is it?"

John led them to a small sitting room that Alison used as a study.

"Take a good look. And in point of fact, that's what you're supposed to do."

He flung back the door. In the corner of the room stood a tall wooden cabinet like a polished icon.

"They've started test transmissions." He tugged cables, twisted switches, opened doors. The television screen glowed blue and then fizzled with snow. Soon an image materialized, bumping and shimmering. "We'll leave it on for a while."

They sat there, John, Kate, and Ronan.

"Look at us," said John. "Watching nothing happening. We'll try again tomorrow night. They say there's fog coming in. That's always good for viewing, a foggy night. We can get the BBC very clearly from Wales."

At midnight, Ronan heard whispers on the staircase; was it an argument? He climbed out of bed and peeped. Kate and John stood outside Kate's door; her head rested on John's shoulder, and he stroked her hair repeatedly.

"No, no. It'll be all right," he said over and over. Ronan barely made out the words. "It'll be all right, it will, I assure you, it'll all work out."

Ronan knew from her shoulders that Kate was deeply upset.

John stepped away, his hand resting briefly on her cheek. Kate chewed her own hand and wiped her tears.

"Kate, it'll be all right, it'll be all right."

One more time John stroked her hair and her face, walked upstairs, came back, and held out his arms. She leaned in to him and seemed helpless. He left her again—and closed his bedroom door behind him.

Kate slumped against the wall of the landing. In her doorway she hesitated, then turned and tiptoed the few steps to Ronan's ajar door. He raced back to bed. She came into the room and stood beside him. Ronan pretended sleep. She put her hands on his hair and stroked and stroked, then returned to her own room. Ronan never moved—and lay awake for hours, fear in his stomach like a weight.

Saturday felt brittle. John told many jokes; Alison disappeared repeatedly—into her room, the garden, down the lane. Ronan studied. Kate and John had quiet conversations that suddenly brightened out into innocuous topics when Ronan came upon them. He wanted to ask, "What's up?" but he dreaded the answer.

After supper, Ronan poured drinks for all—and himself: a small whiskey.

Kate never ceased fidgeting, smoothing skirt or blouse, turning an endless lock of hair in her fingers. Her eyes returned again and again to John and Ronan.

"Have you ever seen such a resemblance between a father and son?"

Alison nodded.

"Poor boy," said John. "Going to look like a bloodhound."

"Dad, I don't like whiskey much."

John said, "That's probably good news." He went to the door. "Did anyone see if there's fog? We might be lucky with the television signal."

"Dad, there was fog last night too."

John led the way to the television room. This time a picture clarified, and they watched a man talking to sheep farmers.

"I saw this once or twice—this makes a good show," said John. "They go to Wales and to Scotland and to the north of Ireland. 'The Regions,' they call it."

Ronan picked up something in his father's tone, and felt an excitement rise. Was something going on here, something about which his father had prior knowledge?

The scene changed. Over pictures of a river, the announcer said, "And now to our Northern Ireland region. Everyone knows the Irish like to talk. And such yarns as they spin, enchanting us with their shamrocks and leprechauns and their gift of the gab. Our Belfast studios have been speaking to a man who spends his life spouting the blarney. He's a traveling storyteller; we caught up with him in country Londonderry, where he was persuaded to tell a tale or two by my Ulster colleague, Sam Hanna Bell."

Ronan jumped up. "Dad! Did you know?!"

"Shhhhhhh," said John, wagging a finger.

Two men sat on a whitewashed wall. The image waxed and waned in gentle surges.

"How long have you been living this life?" said Sam Hanna Bell in his earnest tweed jacket.

The Storyteller said, "I took to the road in nineteen-twelve."

"Goodness. That's forty-eight years of walking. How many miles, d'you think?"

"I used to know. But as I get older, the notion daunts me, and I prefer to think of myself as like one of those acrobats in a circus— you know, the ones that walk on a big ball and keep it spinning under them and never fall off. That's what I'm like—I'm walking on a big ball, this Earth of ours. And so far I've not fallen off."

"And where do you get your stories from?"

"From the woods. From the mist on a hill in the dawn. From a curling wave out at sea that's coming to the shore."

"In other words," said Sam Hanna Bell, "from your imagination?"

"From a world that thinks a story is the most important thing man has. That's where my stories come from."

"And the one you're going to tell us now?"

"This is a true story—because the imagination doesn't distinguish between true and false."

"Well, sir," said Sam Hanna Bell, "we'll all sit back and listen to you."

The camera glided closer to the Storyteller's face; he looked directly into the lens—and thus into Ronan's eyes.

ERE IN IRELAND, WE'VE RECEIVED MOST OF our inner riches from Mother Nature. In olden days, the monks in the abbeys made art from natural matters. They were inspired by the sights they saw every day—a rabbit leaving its burrow; a fox running across a hillside with its red brush of a tail streaming out behind it; a horse standing in a field, its back to the rain; a hawk making its point far up in the sky. And even their painting materials also came from the nonhuman world—bird's feathers and colors from the earth.

So: all our expression, all our means of saying what's in our souls, came first from the universe that we see every day all around us, out under the air. We were not alone in this. For example, man made his first music from blowing air through reed pipes and kept rhythm by tapping a stick on another stick.

But here in Ireland we made music from one very unusual source. It's our greatest musical instrument, it's very contrary to play, and it had its roots in the sea. This is the story of how we invented—the harp.

Once upon a time, before swans learned to swim and before bears wore fur coats, the wife of Breffni O'Rourke, a Sligo chieftain, liked to walk the sands at Rosses' Point. She enjoyed looking out over the Atlantic, hoping to see whatever glories might lie far away to the west. As she walked, she listened to the crawk of the gulls, the hiss of the tide, the ocean's hush.

One morning, however, she heard a new sound. It was strange and wondrous, it was melody so tinkling and beautiful, she thought she must capture it forever. She looked around to see where it came from—but nobody walked near her; the sands stretched white and empty, and she could not find the source of these harmonies.

It was all very peculiar. The noise grew louder and then fainter and then louder and then fainter. She asked herself, What comes and goes, and then comes again and then goes again? After a moment's thought, she found the answer rising in her brain—the wind! The wind comes and goes, and comes again and goes again. So the Lady Breffni looked in the direction the wind was coming from, and she found the source of the glittering tunes.

On the sands of Rosses' Point, near the original Coney Island, lay the beached carcass of a whale, high and white like a monument. The silver noises she heard came from the rib cage, where the sea breezes danced through the bones. For many minutes the lady stood and watched and listened to sounds that moved her to tears. She returned enthralled to her castle and immediately summoned her musicians, who played every night at supper.

"Visit straightaway the sands at Rosses' Point," she instructed them, "and listen to the sound of the wind in the bones of the whale, and then come back here and devise a means of making that music."

The musicians mounted their horses, rode off to the beach, and dismounted by the carcass. They also found the sound enchanting, and they spent hours there that day, scratching their heads, walking north, south, east, and west of the white shape, trying to divine how the music was caused. What structures, they asked, what tensions, would be needed to create something so lovely? Like scientists, somber and grave, they debated and they questioned and they considered.

On their return to the court, they began work immediately with Breffni O'Rourke's carpenter. Some weeks later they produced a very large, ponderous-looking wooden instrument with long, thin staves running from top to bottom across a frame curved like a whale's rib cage. They wheeled this contraption into the castle yard, and as good fortune would have it, the wind blew from the west that very day. To their great delight, their instrument made sounds even more beautiful than the carcass of the whale.

Next, they wheeled it around to the front door of the castle and sent a messenger to tell the lady her music was ready. She emerged at once and could hear the melody as she approached; in fact all the people in the castle turned out when they heard these heavenly notes. As they stood and listened, some people felt that a miracle had come to the great house of Breffni O'Rourke.

But there were two problems. First of all, this instrument was as big as a van, and the lady pointed out that she could only listen to it in the open air; it wouldn't fit through the castle door, and like the rest of Ireland, Sligo isn't a place where you can listen to music out-of-doors all the year round. The second point she made—it was now late afternoon, and after a time, as the sun began to sink in the west, the wind dropped. And of course, the music ceased. The Lady Breffni looked at the musicians and said, "Where's my music?"

They replied quite reasonably that the instrument only played when the wind blew, to which she said, "Then how am I going to hear it when we sit to dine?"

The musicians looked at the carpenter, and the carpenter looked at the musicians.

"Place it in the yard outside an open window of the dining hall," suggested the carpenter, trying to solve two problems at once.

"But the wind may not always blow through that corner of the yard," answered the lady. "And if it does, it'll make the room too cold to sit in."

One of the musicians said, "Perhaps if the carpenter were to make some bellows, like a blacksmith uses for blowing on the fire?"

"I don't want a blacksmith's bellows inside or outside the banqueting hall," said the Lady Breffni. "Are you all dolts or something?" She was cross by now.

A child wandered forward, a boy of nine or so, blond and inquisitive. He leaned in to look at the great instrument, reached out to touch it, and drew his fingers across the long, tall staves. But he pulled back his hand with an expression of distaste on his face.

"I'm surprised the wind wants to play this," he said.

He was the son of Lady Breffni's housekeeper, and renowned in that house for his cleverness and powers of observation. The musicians knew him well because he spent a great deal of time listening to them and observing how they played; one of them had begun to teach him the tin whistle.

"What's wrong with it?" asked the carpenter.

The boy thought for a moment.

"It's too—unfriendly," he said, after struggling to find the word. "These wooden bones—they offer no welcome."

"And what would you find welcoming?" asked one of the musicians.

"Something easy, a supple thing," the boy said. "Something that would bend to the fingers. Then you wouldn't need the wind. Any of us could learn to play it."

"But how would that make music?" asked the carpenter.

"These don't make the music," said the boy, indicating the wooden slats. "The music is made down here, where the vibrations echo from the blown bones"—and he laid his hand on the broad frame of the instrument.

"He's perfectly right," said the musicians.

"And it could be a lot smaller," said the boy, "provided the box was deep enough to reverberate."

They carried the huge instrument away, removed the wooden staves, and replaced them with long strings of gut taken from the stomachs of cows and waxed with the grease of a goose. It took them no more than a few hours. They wheeled it back into the castle yard, and that night the Lady Breffni O'Rourke of Sligo sat down to dinner, listening to music that seemed even sweeter than the melody she had heard in the skeleton of a whale. Next day, they made a much smaller version, and brought it into the castle that very night. It was even sweeter than the first. And that, my friends, is how the harp was invented.

Did you know, by the way, that Ireland is the only nation on earth to have a musical instrument as its national symbol? Canada has the maple leaf; New Zealand has the silver fern; Scotland has the thistle; England has the rose; Wales has the leek; America has the eagle—and Ireland has the harp.

The program ended, and John switched off the set.

"Dad! Did you know?"

"How would I know? I merely switched on the television."

Ronan was puzzled. "D'you remember when he came here first?"

"Who could ever forget it?"

"Did you know he was coming here that night?" Ronan looked at Kate, who nodded at him to press on. "Dad, there's something you know that we don't, isn't there?"

John paced the room. "This is my advice. Go look for him."

"I wouldn't know where to begin. What I want to know," said Ronan, "is this. Is there something else here—'more than meets the eye,' or whatever the expression is?"

John deflected the question. "You know who I mean by Matt Conway?"

"The mispronouncer," said Kate.

"Yes." John laughed. "He was talking to me on Wednesday about spies who 'defecate' to the Russians. He meant 'defect'!"

"See what I mean, Kate? Dad! You're evading."

"Look. When we're next together, I'll answer any of your questions. That's a promise. I mean it."

Next day, John's high jollity prevailed, but much of it seemed forced. Ronan felt discomfort—and even more so at Kate's unusual distress when parting at the train. Halfway through the journey, she took Ronan's hand and held it tight. Finally he asked, "There's something wrong, isn't there?"

Kate shook her head. "I'm sometimes weepy."

Kate had suitors in droves. They trooped to the house; they ambushed her at school; they heaped gifts on her Sundays at mass.

The smile, the looks, the warm good humor—all men who met her fell for her; one pursuer observed, "There's money, there's fame—and there's Kate."

As the shore has waves, they advanced and retreated, some ardent, some wild, some shallow, some deep, with no end in sight to the tide. Some made hilarious proposals; one told her that his family had "the finest plot in the graveyard." Another said he was going "to bull" all his own cows himself that year. Kate, telling her friends, thought it wise to assume that he meant he would buy his own bull, rather than rely upon the animals of his neighbors.

"Because if that isn't what he means," she said, "life in this parish is about to heat up."

One man, many years older than her, asked Kate to marry him, "Because you'd be nice and warm for the winter." Another proposer said, "Your legs would always keep me in a good mood." Len Culleton drove all the way from Abbeyleix in his truck with his farm accounts—and a poignantly cheap wig.

Many offered much. Simon Nolan, a doctor from Cork, was universally liked, rare for a man with such a fortune. On all other counts he stacked up too: manners, behavior, clothes—and love, of which he gave copious proof. He kissed her in the best possible way—soft and careful, with hints of force to come.

"He holds me," she said, posing merrily to her friends, "like Hollywood." And he could sing like a soloist.

It almost worked. Kate enjoyed his company and liked his choices; a picnic deep in the woods; theater in Cork; to the coast for the sighting of a whale. She returned from each date looking more and more aglow—until she gauged the mood of the house. And it never wavered—somewhere between lukewarm and cool.

"Do you like Simon?"

Alison always said, "Yes, he's very nice."

No enthusiasm, no inflection, no further comment; and John, each time, said, "Nolan? I wonder if he's Marcus Nolan's nephew?"

Nothing more, no interest, no verve.

The same tepid responses ended a lawyer's prospects—and a farmer's and a fellow teacher's. Yet none of these men felt hurt by

Kate, and many became friends. Only one, bitter at failing to win, called her "frigid," which she was not. But his remark almost reached an insight—or two.

To begin with, though never cold, Kate had an uneven soul. Nobody in her life and times knew of the phrase *mood swings*— much less *manic depressive* or *bipolar*—and therefore such mercurial heaves swept in without her knowledge. Slowly, slowly, she came to recognize the dangerous elation. And slowly, slowly, she learned to guard against the ensuing blackness.

Secondly, she could never decide whether she had been born with this saddle on her back or whether—as she also suspected—it was a burden she had strapped on, with a little help. She knew what it was; since she was twenty she had carried inside her a tough secret, a life matter, which lay around the house like a ticking bomb. It could explode any day or hour, with damage far and wide. To intensify matters, if it didn't explode, should she detonate it herself? Some mornings a loud voice inside her said, "You must"; other days a different voice cried, "Leave it alone."

In Dublin she finally decided to unload some of this weight. But on whom? In her society all roads led to the church; God took care of everything. The priest in the confessional heard and forgave, aired the worst; all shall be well.

Not for Kate; if she was to trust any establishment with her secrets, she wanted more understanding, more debate. She shared none of her sister's blind zeal; out of Alison's sight she all but shrugged off the faith. Not out of hate—but she felt no love; given the nature of Ireland, it had to be a pastoral church, she understood that. But at parish level it disallowed all thought and insisted on its rules, and Kate believed it had no room for her issues.

Debate. Intellectual. Anti-intellectual. Pastoral. Forgiveness. Understanding. As she paraded key words across her mind, she had no illusions—and her thought process ran: I have to think my way through this. Feeling my way through it is no longer any good, I am too often too fraught. Therefore, I need someone to help me in my thinking, someone safe, someone who grasps it, someone intelligent. This problem has controlled my entire adult life. Now it has become urgent, and I need advice—and I need advice that won't judge me, won't accuse me, won't force me to do things I don't want to do, will help me to find out what I should do, will guide me to a safe place. I can't ask John for advice. Alison? Certainly not. Kate ran through the catalog of everybody she knew and found no one.

Back she went once more to first principles: Were I a "normal" Catholic, I'd be discussing this with my confessor. But I don't have a confessor anymore, because I've never liked the low level at which country priests are obliged to forgive the parade of "sin" they hear. But I can understand it from the church's point of view, the morality of it all. It's just that—well, it's not that simple. Definitely not.

Which is why she sought the job with the Jesuits. She hoped for more than employment; she hoped to find an adviser among them, someone who could be a friend, a guide. They were the Princes of the Church, weren't they? Their structures, she reasoned, would keep her on familiar ground; they were still priests, but famous for helping people to think rather than depending on blind faith. From her first day at their school she scanned them like a hiring fair.

Kate chose as her "new friend" a thoughtful man twenty years older than her. English-born, in Ireland twenty years, Father David Mansfield, as deputy head, had attended her interview with the school board.

He said to her that day, "We've asked you many questions. Have you some questions for us?"

Kate said, "Does scent threaten your vows?"

He told her afterward they laughed so much that they had to give her the job.

On Kate's first morning he invited her for tea; "I'm also teacher liaison." By the end of the second week, they spoke every day.

He came for supper, and the evening glowed. They found mutual passions—literature, history, and art; she relished his knowledge of travel; he devoured her country-life tales. No lulls in

their conversation, no awkwardness, not even a passing shyness—
their friendship took hold, immediate and firm. They ranged over
health, education, and the television she had just seen. She cooked
sublimely that night, lamb from the mountains, rosemary and
mint.

"Now," he said, "tell me about your nephew."

They had returned to the fireplace; Ronan's photograph sat on
the mantel. Kate groomed her hair, sighed, and made the bold decision.

"Well, now. Father—here's the drama of my life." She picked up
the photograph and gathered strength. "He's not my nephew—he's
my son. But he doesn't know it."

The priest raised no eyebrow, showed no surprise. His tone
sought to establish facts.

"Not at all?"

"Nobody knows—except my sister, her husband, and me."

They both looked at the boy in the frame.

"I sense a purpose. This matter was—organized?"

And Kate knew she had chosen well.

"My sister had miscarriages. Each one got worse than the one
before. She knew her husband wanted a child—girl or boy, it didn't
matter. I was almost twenty, in perfect health. That's how it happened. I mean—that's where the idea came from."

In the summer of 1941, an ectopic pregnancy almost took Alison's life. As yet her religion had not developed into raw zeal, and
she winced again at having failed John. Kate came to stay, to
lighten the household load—and Alison came up with the plan.
Were John to father a baby by Kate, no one would know. Almost all
blood requirements would get satisfied. And the MacCarthys had
precedent—this had happened at great-grandparent level, to ensure
land inheritance.

John objected—but not too heatedly, as Alison noted dryly to
herself; Kate demurred too, but at last agreed, under assurances that
she would help raise the child. After that, practicality had its cold
way. Alison had taught her young sister the facts of life and thus

knew all of Kate's rhythms. For a week in January, seven tearful nights, she absented herself with an aunt in Cork, during which Kate slept in the matrimonial bed.

Between John and Kate no awkwardness took place; they felt neither clinical nor lewd. He led; she followed, natural as light. In the mornings they smiled and carried on with the day; in the evenings they lay and proceeded with the night.

However, something occurred which none foresaw—a profound love. He felt deeply responsible for Kate, and she fell in love with him. Never admitted, never said, no further "connection" (to use John's old word) occurred between them—but the silent emotional bond ran down into both like a shaft of gold.

The secret burdened the years. Alison nursed her regret; Kate never forgot; John never said; Ronan never knew. And so, between delight in the child and recurring torment at the deceit, Kate had come to this point.

"What an intelligent solution."

"Oh?" She turned from the photograph.

"Brilliant. Everybody's happy. You've all lived together?"

"Since he was born."

"Was it easy to cover up?"

"Nobody knew anything. I went for six months to a convent eighty miles away. As you know, the nuns have homes for—well, girls like I was."

"Excellent business."

Kate had been stopped in her tracks. "Do you really think so, Father?"

The priest held out four of his very white fingers and counted.

"Practical. Loving. Efficient. Supportive."

"But—also sinful?"

"Oh, come on! Who's to say what's sinful? I have little patience with the way Mother Church manipulates her flock. Tell me more. Were you bewildered? You must have been."

"Well—as I say, I was almost twenty. It was a time of very mixed feelings. I was thrilled. I was lonely. I was delighted. I was worried. I felt—unconventional, which I enjoy. I was upset."

"Which you don't enjoy?"

"No. But not as upset as my sister. She couldn't look at the baby."

"Ohhhhh," the priest cooed. "That must have been so difficult. And the father?"

"Took it in his stride. As he does everything. He stayed calm, he taught me how to handle it all, he made the house happy—or as happy as he could make it; he was extraordinary."

The priest nodded.

"But there's still the problem—" Kate stopped.

"Of—when do you tell him?"

Kate nodded.

"Or—do you tell him at all?" The priest looked into the fire. "I mean—it seems to me that Ireland is full of secrets. The country is one vast secret—and that's typical of close-knit people. So why is this arising now?"

Kate said, "I feel I can't deceive him any longer. And it's quite urgent—because it's getting in the way of my handling him well." She hesitated. "Ronan lives here with me, but he never goes out. He sort of clings to me—he's only got me and his studies—but I think I need to push him out into the world. And I know he won't go—and I feel I can't ask much of him, because I haven't told him the truth of who he is."

"Just the two of you here?"

Kate nodded. "It's too close—too close for a boy his age."

"And you cook for him?" Kate nodded again, and the priest laughed. "I wouldn't go out into the world either, were I in his shoes. But I agree with you. This is the time when he has to grow."

Kate rubbed her hands in agitation. The priest moved to another place within the subject.

"Tell me—I've often wondered. What's it like—having and raising a child?"

She accepted the lifebelt. "It's remarkable. No, it's extraordinary. And obviously I've never felt able to talk about it. I often feel as if part of me has grown sideways and more—more . . . " She searched; he waited. "D'you know how a tree, a well-established tree, will sometimes grow a lovely branch that's complete in itself? It's a bit like that. Oh, God, this is trite, I'm not making myself clear."

Still he waited.

"When he was born, I did all the usual things. You know—the sentimental-mother things. Counted his fingers and toes, helped him develop his first grip on my little finger, looked at his little red lips, felt the fuzz of his head. The smell of him, that combination of skin and milk. And the softness of the touch—makes velvet feel coarse."

"Seems pretty wonderful."

Kate had begun to relax a little; the powerful secret had been spoken.

"It is. They're feelings like I know I can never have for an adult. I remember thinking, Kate, you don't need to do anything else with your life. It felt—sublime. God, I sound mushy."

"He's somewhat older now?" The priest dangled the question.

"I'm sure, Father, you've seen and heard so much that nothing shocks you. So—I know you'll understand when I say—it's like . . ."

Kate ran out of words. She made a helpless, profound gesture, opening her hands out to the world.

"Try. I promise not to run from the room."

They laughed.

"Don't get me wrong, Father. And I'm sure every woman who ever loved a son has had this thought. They want to hold that son, feel the strength they gave to his shoulders, run their hands around the head that contains his brain, the head they gave him, stroke the cheek he has just begun to shave. And then you look into the eyes, and you see the eagerness there. Life to be devoured and all that. Forgive me, I've never known anyone I could say all this to, and it's just bursting to come out of me."

The priest waved a hand. "I love hearing it. And—you are so right." He paused. "My own mother, she said to me about a year before she died, 'I'd have married you if it wasn't for incest.' " He laughed. "She meant it as a joke, of course, but I knew what she meant beneath the joke. And my mother was quite a reserved woman."

"The quick way it cuts into you," said Kate. "The flash of anxiety if he's minutes later than you expect. The irritation he causes when he does something clumsy or rebellious, and I could wring his neck—and the immediate regret for feeling that. The hoping each morning that nothing will hurt him today."

"And that's your great fear—that if you tell him the truth of his birth, it may hurt him more than he can bear?"

"Exactly." Kate folded her hands. "That's exactly it. And I don't know what to do."

"Could I help? Is there a way I could . . ." He left the sentence unfinished.

"I don't know. I want him to go out and meet the world feeling as secure as he can. But I'm afraid the truth will undermine him dreadfully."

"Do you have room for another person here? A relative? A room-mate?"

"Yes. Why?"

"He's an only child, and I'd suggest he needs to feel some pressure in the nest."

"But the greater problem is—"

He interrupted: "How to tell him—whether to tell him. I know."

"There's another reason why I need guidance. We went down home at the weekend. It turned out to be extremely painful. His father told me that—"

Kate stopped—because Ronan raced up the stairs, calling out, as he always did, and burst into the room. Full as ever of news to recount, he recoiled when he saw the priest; he took the introduction coolly, then focused on Kate.

"How was your lecture?"

"Lively."

Father Mansfield said, "Lively? And I gather you're reading history? You can only mean Professor Ryle."

Ronan laughed.

"Yes, Father."

The priest beamed at Ronan and Kate.

"He uses wonderful language. Do you like him? Tell me you do!"

"I do, Father," said Ronan, warming to this man.

"He's very entertaining. But he's also very civilized. And he's a good friend of mine. You'll learn a lot from him."

Ronan's next piece of learning came not from Professor Ryle but by post; a college secretary handed him a letter sent two days earlier, postmarked "Ballinamore." He fingered the bulky, rain-stained package; blue paper again; the stamp had been placed with old exactness; and there was the same mannered, breathtaking handwriting. Inside—no introduction, no address.

A JOURNEYMAN'S TRADE

A STORY HAS ONLY ONE MASTER—ITS NARRATOR; he decides what he wants his story to do. I know, I have always known, what I want my stories to achieve—I want to make people believe. Believe what I tell. Believe in it. Believe me. Belief is the one effect I'm always looking for, and I apply every device, every pause, every gesture, every verbal nuance and twirl, to that end. To achieve it, I myself have to believe; if I don't, who will? I must believe ancient Ireland was as I describe it. The swords really did ring loudly off the shields. And the armor surely gleamed in the sun.

In fact, I want my listeners to believe so deeply that I almost have them saying to themselves, "No, he couldn't have been there, that's impossible!" In order to get them close to that point, I make a great effort to close a specific gap—the gap that separates the historical fact from the invented tale. And if they are—or could be—one and the same thing, that's what I call "the magic of the past," and that's what I deal in: the magic of the past.

I know that if my listeners, with their round eyes and rapt faces— if they believe that what they're hearing actually happened, they'll remember it forever, especially if the facts are lit in bright lights. That's why I try and make every tale I tell seem like a film made centuries ago.

The need for belief also accounts for the reason why I tell such different stories. Some are history, reported by those who were there, and reembroidered by me. Others are myth, from deep in our souls, handed down by word of mouth, and I am the latest narrator. And I make up yet others—because I like the power and the fun of creating worlds.

When it's running well, the effects of a story will last as long as I remain in the presence of my audience. Then, when they shake themselves back into the present day, and by the time they cross the dark night on their way home, they know and see my sleight of hand. And I hope they talk and laugh about the evening, as they would have after watching a magician. I don't even mind if they work out how I did the trick.

In order to do my job well, to capture their hearts and spirits and minds, I have to know my audience; I have to know a great deal about them. Every day I learn something new about the Irish and about our island. Over the years this has built up into a body of knowledge that gives me a good and permanent picture of what we're like as a people.

I know all kinds of things. For example, I know that we like to fill empty spaces with words. Sometimes the words don't mean a thing; my father used to murmur every so often, "Up she flew, and the cock flattened her." Out of the blue he'd say it, no context whatever, a meaningless utterance, spoken to no one. I have no idea why he did it; and I think he merely liked to roll a lively and cryptic phrase in his mouth, to taste it like a bright fruit.

And I also know that, as a people, we generally cohere, that we're a nation of human beings with much in common. North, south, east, and west, we eat the same foods, feel the same weather, dance the same steps, die of the same diseases.

These common factors make my job easier because I always know to whom I'm speaking. All through the thirty-two counties of Ireland, most of the adults who have listened to my tales have quit school at the legal age of fourteen. That is our national pattern since the beginning of the twentieth century. Even now, I have met very few in the countryside who went to any secondary school, or who then climbed to university level and beyond. If they have done, it's always been a happenstance of their parents' view and position, rather than a general norm.

For "ordinary" people, that is to say the people who work the land and the other people who form the parish, the tradition of education has not yet returned. The next few decades might restore it to Ireland; it was killed two hundred and fifty years ago by the English in one of their many attempts to eradicate us, and it needs to be brought back to life.

By and large, we have no class structure in Ireland, except among the Protestants. Many of the Catholic Johnny-come-latelys would like to look down their noses; they'd love to be the haves lording it over the have-nots. But by dint of cheek and irreverence, and by dint of traditionally being in the same repressed, oppressed boat, Irish Jack is largely as good as his master.

So when I'm addressing such mixed audiences, I have to accommodate a width of response that ranges from illiterate to doctorate. I live by a guiding principle that I learned in Rome (of which eternal city more another time); "Never underestimate their intelligence, always underestimate their knowledge." And because I know my audience, my little extra details can send shivers through them, especially when I draw on things they know, that they've seen. If they understand that Irish people two thousand years ago lived similar lives, they grasp my story more powerfully, and they more willingly give themselves over to me.

As you'll have gathered by now, mine is mainly a rural audience. They think about cattle and meadows, saving hay and reaping corn, tanning hide and spinning wool. I can be deep in the west, in the snipe-grass smallholdings of poor Mayo, or I can be down south across the richness of Limerick and Tipperary, in what they call the Golden Vale, a seam of rich earth that carves its way across Europe from Hungary. Or I can be in a house in a town where the church clock chimes.

Wherever I am, my listeners easily recognize from their own lives my descriptions of the ancient Irish—the farmers who worked the fields, whose wives baked bread for the midday meal, and whose comfortable farmyards housed fat pigs.

Beneath its broad surface, storytelling should always work hard to say more than it seems to. When I told you the story of Newgrange, I made the Angry Woman's daughter look like a child with red hair who was there that night. If I'm describing a beautiful princess, I'll make sure nobody round that fireside matches her. The men love the account of the girl, and the women want news of her beautiful gown.

Likewise, before I describe someone ugly, I'll look carefully around the room in case I come out with an account that offends anyone. Folk are touchy; it would be easy for some man to feel that I mocked his blemish.

I also do what old storytellers always did. People need to take a rest now and then, so I make sure that I use little phrases to ease them, to tell them—and me—we can relax for a few seconds. I have composed a wide repertoire.

"And every year, they turned the soil, they sowed their seeds, they welcomed the rain, they hailed the sun, and they were happy."

"And so, things became plain to everyone."

"That is one of the ways of the world, and the ways of the world are many."

"While the ships sailed the seas and the clouds sailed the sky."

Homer the Greek had such tricks. When he said, "Dawn comes early, with rosy fingers," and spoke repeatedly of "the wine-dark sea" and "Such were the words that passed between us," his audience drew breath with him. If it was good enough for him twenty-seven centuries ago, it's good enough for me. All of us storytellers, the world over, the last few of us still traveling—we play with such chosen phrases. They allow us to change gear, and we can also use them to tighten the screw as the story begins to climb.

In some ways I'm very like an actor; this is a performance that I give, I can think of no other word for it. It takes place in a very inti-

mate theater, with no stage and no proscenium arch and no curtains and an audience that is often only inches away. To address
those circumstances, much of what I do has to be theatrical, and
every actor in the world needs his props.

My main prop is my pipe. First, I fill it with tobacco as carefully
as a man counting his money. Next, I strike the match—I love how
that little yellow flash surges. Then I suck the flame down into the
bowl until the pipe has swallowed its light. I like to think it gives
the impression that I'm inhaling the sorcery of fire. And I tamp
down the hot tobacco with my fingertip; this looks fearless, and I
want people to think, Here's a man who can touch flames and never
burn. Not a word do I say through all of this, and slowly the listeners fall silent as they wait for me to speak.

When finally I look up from the pipe, I make my eyes rove
through the audience, because I want to be sure that every person is
ready to come happily into my grasp. A storyteller has to know how
to get power over people.

I also use my hat as a prop, my old hat that keeps out the rain and
deflects the sun, on whose brim the dew settles like little pearls on
a necklace. Once it was a homburg, but it has been long bruised by
the world.

Still, it is my good theatrical friend. I take it off when I want to
build a pause or unwrap a detail. Sometimes I pass the brim through
my hands as if attempting to shape it into a consistent straight line.
Or I fiddle with the decrepit old ribbon, which slides easily around
the crown, like a belt on a man grown thin. Or I punch it gently until
the homburg shape becomes one large dome, like a comical hat.

And then with the heel of my hand I restore the soft dent in the
crown and return the hat to my head. More than one child has said
to me that they think the hat somehow shelters my tales, whose
colors would otherwise come bursting out of my cranium like the
rays of rainbows.

At the end of the story I follow a long-practiced routine. I lift my
hat from my head and replace it, as a gentleman would to a lady; I
take my dead pipe from my mouth; I lean down and tap it on the

wide hearthstone. When the small gray powder falls out—I always smoke my pipe down to the last ash—I like to think it looks as though I wrested every last fiber from the tale.

Then there is the language of the body to aid the delivery of the words. Musicians know how and when to arrange the spaces between their notes. So should storytellers. I pause and let the audience watch me, and I wait for their minds to come to me. Or I turn my head away from the room and gaze into the fire. Or I look around at the assembled listeners, almost as if seeking someone. And then I stare once more into the flames. When at last I turn to face the room fully, I know that my face seems to glow red and my eyes black with the fire I have absorbed.

All I'm saying is, I use the techniques of an actor, with my body as my tool bench and my hands alternating between my pipe, my hat, and my gestures of expression. And I have one special gesture, which I use almost every night.

As my arms open in wide movements, I make my eyes flash like a mesmerist. While my left hand grips the pipe bowl tight as desire, my right hand closes in a fist. Slowly, slowly, like the petals of some bony flower, my gnarled fingers begin to open, so that the hand becomes like a little bowl—and then the fingers flatten and extend to their lengths until the hand itself lies flat, upward and open in the air. I always make this gesture at the moment when I feel the audience most hushed.

At that moment I would not be surprised to find sitting on my hand the population of the room, silent and enthralled—and all permanently half-smiling at me and my magical words. I want them there, I want them like that, I want them to say, "He held his audience in the palm of his hand"—and all my efforts, my gestures and expressions, are directed to that aim. When they are there— they believe.

The letter ended abruptly; no signature, no trace.
Ronan turned it over and over in his hand; he peered into the
empty envelope—not a clue of any kind, other than the postmark
from county Leitrim.

He read it again—and he mimicked the hand gestures, opening
his fingers slowly like a flower, resting the palm upward. One abid-
ing thought took over: *He said he'd teach me!*

Only when he saw other students peering at him did he put the
letter away.

T. Bartlett Ryle chose to include Ronan in those few students he
tutored and hesitated not at all when pointing out the privilege of
being the professor's tutee, ". . . although some will tell you that
you're no more than the madam's favorite jack. I prefer the sultan's-
wife simile myself. Which of you takes snuff?"

Four other young men and Red Riding Hood had been called to
the sanctum.

"I don't expect you do," said the professor, "but you never know.
My grandmother took snuff, and she raved like a dope. What's your
name?" He pinched tan powder from a small leather case, and his
nostrils flared like gun barrels.

Red Riding Hood said, "Rowena Hayes, sir."

"Sounds like a weather condition. Rowena? Rowena? A trifle
Welsh for my taste. Do you know what it means, child?" The powder drifted to his white shirt collar.

"It means fame and joy, sir."

"Good. Lovely. Suits you. And we wish you both. Plus a rich husband, which I doubt you'll find among any of these gallants here.

All bollocks and no brass, I'd say at first glance. But thankfully very little acne. I hate acne, I had a student here once—between pale and acne, God, his face looked like the surface of the moon."

Professor Ryle scratched himself with staggering intimacy.

"Rowena's a Saxon name, perhaps, not Welsh—aha! Yes and no. Geoffrey of Monmouth, a scurvy tosser if ever there was one—he has a Rowena."

She said, "And there's a Rowena in *Ivanhoe,* isn't there, sir?"

"My God! There is!" T. Bartlett Ryle clapped a hand to his forehead like an actor playing torment. "Well observed, child. Christ, I love Scott. He was so blatant, always by all accounts tugging at his genitals. The Scots do that. Very energetic people, the Scots. D'you know that he pointed out one of the great truths of English literature? And do you know what it was?"

T. Bartlett Ryle surged around his study, half skidding on a pile of papers and crashing into a globe of the world.

"Sir Walter Scott pointed out that in Jane Austen's novel *Pride and Prejudice,* Miss Elizabeth Bennet showed absolutely no interest whatever in her beau Mr. Darcy until—UNTIL—she saw the size of his estate in Derbyshire. He was right. He was RIGHT! Gold-digging little bitch."

Ronan recalled Kate's—and the priest's—remarks on Ryle; he felt it was safe to laugh and relax.

"I've never read Jane Austen's books, sir."

The others looked admiring of Ronan's courage.

"Excellent for social history, O'Mara," intoned T. Bartlett Ryle. "But regrettably Miss Austen knew less than a gnat's arse about the Statutes of Kilkenny in the year of thirteen-sixty-six. The date is probably as much as any of you knows about them too."

They all tried to look somewhere between calm and wise.

"Never mind. We shall have Socratic dialogue. Excellent way of learning. Let us begin. Why did Kilkenny attract the making of such important legislation? Was it for the food? And if so, do we know what standards of cuisine prevailed in a filthy Irish city in the High Medieval period?"

Rowena Hayes said, "Because it was a Norman stronghold."

"Or"—the professor scratched again; things shifted in his clothing—"was it more than that? Was it in fact the locus of Norman power in south Leinster?"

"Yes, it was," said a black-haired boy, "and it had a cathedral; therefore it had church power too."

"And," said Ronan, feeling competitive, "it was the outer limit of the Pale."

"So Kilkenny was not beyond the Pale," said T. Bartlett Ryle. "Now, what was the name of the family that dominated medieval Kilkenny? And why were they called that?"

"The Butlers," said the black-haired boy. "I'm a Butler myself."

"In which case, polish the silver and fillet the fish," said T. Bartlett Ryle. The black-haired boy looked puzzled. "Therein lies the answer, you goose."

"The Butlers—were they descended from the man who was—the king's butler?"

"Young man," said Bartlett Ryle to the black-haired boy, "you'll go far, and pray you don't have to go soon. Like so many of our race, you're descended from a domestic servant. But who was the townsman—note my inflections carefully aspirated and separated—'the towns-man'—who was the townsman family opposite to the Butlers?"

Nobody answered. Ronan felt he was in a quiz show.

"Listen to my language. 'Towns'—the 's' is genitive—meaning "of the town"—the man of the town. Think, and when you have thunk, essay—that is one of my many reusable nostrums (or nostra, if you prefer)—think, and when you have thunk, offer me some thoughts on other words for town. Useful words, I want."

Ronan said, "Urban."

"Borough," said Rowena Hayes.

"Yesss," said Bartlett Ryle. "And from *borough* we derive—what? Think! Think! Think 'Edin-' and 'Ham'—those should help.

"Burg?" said the black-haired boy.

"Indeed. Now we have it, do we not?"

"Burke?" said Ronan.

"Indeed. Descended from William de Burgh, the earl of Kent, who hammered seven shades of shit out of the MacCarthys of Munster."

Ronan tried a joke. "My mother's a MacCarthy of Munster."

"Then she'll know what I mean by seven shades of shit—is she taking anything for it?"

The tutees laughed, Ronan most of all.

"Now, the Statutes of Kilkenny. What were they? And don't confuse me; don't tell me they were equestrian carvings or figures standing aloft, with their hands on their swords and flowers growing out of the place marked 'arse.' I said 'statutes,' not 'statues.' The Statutes of Kilkenny."

The black-haired boy almost yelled.

"Sir, they were the most vital moment in the early English governance of Ireland."

"Most vital? What about the soldiers with the swords and the lords with the lances and the longbows and the strong bows?"

"Sir, that was military, I'm talking about governance."

"Aha!" said T. Bartlett Ryle, "a splitter of hairs. Go on with your governance."

The black-haired boy hit a fast, memorized stride.

"Sir, the Statutes of Kilkenny comprised thirty-six laws or statutes intended to stop the Normans who were now governing Ireland from becoming more Irish than the Irish themselves."

T. Bartlett Ryle took over. "The laws were very particular in what they prevented, and by 'particular' in this instance, I mean that they were more personal than impersonal—the Normans were prevented from doing things that many people would regard today as too personal for legislation."

He leaned back against one of his book-lined, disheveled walls and galloped onward.

"For example, they had to ride a horse in the English fashion and not the Irish. That is to say, they had to sit on a saddle and use stirrups and not sit flat down on the horse's back with their legs stuck

out on either side like the Irish. They had to get their hair cut properly and not wear it like the Irish did, sticking up all over. They
weren't allowed to be godparents to the native Irish children, they
couldn't take Irish girls as concubines—

"By God, this is good and racy," said T. Bartlett Ryle. "Who can
continue in this happy vein? What else couldn't they do?"

"Irish musicians couldn't go and play music in the Norman
houses," said the black-haired boy. "An Irishman couldn't become
a soldier in a Norman militia. The Irish couldn't buy horses from
the Normans."

"And in your salty estimation," said the professor, "what was the
most serious statute—I mean, they were all serious, but what was
the one with the most serious implications?"

The black-haired boy thought—but for too long; Ronan nipped in.

"The change in the courts."

"Thank you, O'Mara. They changed the way disputes were settled. In the old Irish tradition, if you had a dispute with your neighbor, you simply rode over and helped yourself to some of his cattle
or his women, depending what kind of fit you were having that
day. Under the Normans, there had to be a litigation, in court,
before the ruler, and all sorts of stuff like that. What was the real significance of the Statutes of Kilkenny? And remember, history looks
forward as well as back."

This last remark puzzled everyone. With his fingernail plying like
a plectrum, the professor made a desperate assault upon his regions.

"Come on, now. That's the clue. 'History looks forward as well as
back.' You'll hear it many times from my lips."

He waited, then released them.

"It began and established a pattern of English rule in Ireland
where the state, that is to say the ruling body, that is to say the
monarchy—and later the elected Mother of Parliaments—felt and
exercised the right to interfere in people's lives in a minute way. To
put it differently, it paved the way for oppression on a personal
scale, because it struck at the personality of a people. And that is the
hallmark of true prejudice, of true despotism. The principles of
democracy as the Greeks invented it, and as it is practiced in the

least worst political systems in the world, allow room for debate as to whether government has the permission to control people's intimate existences—and to what degree.

"In Ireland, England as a ruling body has always felt it had the right to govern minutely, even down to decreeing what kind of hairstyle a man might affect or where he might buy his horses or indeed his food. But the more astute of you—if there are such in your midst—may point out to me that it was their own people, the Normans, who were affected by this intimate governing. And I'll point out to you, Yes, but when you control a man, you also control all who deal with him, whether you mean to or not.

"In the Statutes of Kilkenny, the Norman English, governing from England, denied certain areas of commerce and activity to the native Irish by saying they couldn't trade in certain spheres with the Norman Irish. Therefore and thereby, they coerced both sides.

"Above all, they introduced a certain type of government that, in time, they exercised over and over again. And through the centuries they elaborated upon it, intensified it, and made it more prohibitive and ultimately punitive and despotic. You'll uncover all the gory details in my lectures, and I expect to see them regurgitated through the inimitable kaleidoscopes of your interpretations in your various essays."

In the weeks that sped by, Ronan studied ever harder. His routine never changed—college by day, study at night. He read the course ahead; he missed no lectures. Nobody got to know him; he took no breaks; he made no friends.

By now he had begun to organize all his Storyteller material into files, and on the wall of his room he had pinned a large map of Ireland. Flags marked every place that he knew the Storyteller had visited; his own home; Mrs. O'Callaghan's village; Barry Hanafin's in Clare; Dublin, for the radio broadcast; Cootehill in county Cavan for the Folklore Commission; county Derry with Sam Hanna Bell; Ballinamore in Leitrim. None of the "sightings" had anything in common; no pattern emerged, no rhythm, no routine.

He also saw that Kate watched his every move. Once or twice she asked him whether he had joined any of the college societies.

Ronan shrugged her off.

"I've too much to do."

"But you never go out."

"I don't want to."

"Ronan, you have no friends."

"I have you. That's enough."

He wondered that she did not press further—but he also observed how she seemed so often distraught. This was new, and when he dared to ask, she pleaded work. Then came the day, the awful day, the day of dismay.

Deep in December, a week before Christmas break, Kate met Ronan at the head of the stairs.

"Pack a bag. We have to go." She checked her watch. "The last train." Her eyes burned red with pain.

"What's wrong?"

"We have to hurry."

"Kate?"

"Ronan, we have to rush. Come on—please."

She offered nothing further until under way—and he pressed hard.

"Right. What is it?"

"Your Dad."

His stomach heaved. "What?"

"He's not well."

"How do you mean?"

"I don't know enough."

"How bad—"

"I don't know! Wait till we get there."

It rained all the way, and he watched her image in the streaked window. She sat looking straight ahead, dazed throughout the hours, sometimes moving her lips in silent talk. Ronan could not rest; he fidgeted; he stretched his legs; he failed to read.

From the train they took the only cab, a car of cigarettes and rust. Kate said, "Saint Anne's"; the driver turned and looked.

"Aha—I have you now," he said, from behind green teeth. "That O'Mara man, right?"

Ronan followed a dictum that his father liked repeating: When you don't know what's happening, listen before you speak. The car drew up at a clinic.

In the hallway Kate stood square before him. "You'd better know now. This isn't good."

In a quiet corner room lay a sleeping John, his skin gray as slate. Alison watched; she looked like a woman with no face, and their entry brought her no surprise.

Ronan looked around the wide room and felt his lips grow cold; a bowl of grapes, unopened newspapers, ominous towels, a vase like a funeral urn.

"What's happening? What is it?"

"Tell him, Al," said Kate. She pleaded. "Al, we have to."

"Your father has cancer."

"Cancer? Cancer how?"

"Where," corrected Alison, looking to him for hope.

"Cancer?" said Ronan again, as though to convince himself.

"Yes," said Kate. "That's what he has." Her voice died away.

Alison said, "He's had it since—"

"Why didn't you tell me? You should have told me."

"He didn't want you worried."

Kate said, "He thought he'd get better."

"But you've known all along, you knew the last time we were down here. You should have told me so that I could come and see him—"

Kate held his arm. Alison said, "He wanted to get over it and tell you afterward."

"But he's not over it, is he?"—and when Kate said, "Shhhhh," Ronan knew he had begun to yell. He ripped himself away.

"Dad?!" To Alison, "When'll he be awake?"

"He's sedated. Painkillers."

"Dad never had a pain." Ronan stood bewildered, like a man falsely accused. "How much pain?"

He looked down at his father; mouth vulnerably loose; hair untypically lank; eyes shut as shades. Odors floated up—ointment, medicine, sweat.

"A lot of pain," said Alison. "A lot."

Ronan reached for John's hand and felt surprise at its warmth.

"A lot of pain?" he said in a half-aloud query. "Dad, are you in a lot of pain?"

"The sedation's heavy," said Kate, now sitting upright in a simple chair.

"When will he wake? Dad?"

"Shhhhh! He can't hear you." Alison looked through the curtains—she could see the town clock. "About two hours."

"Dad?"

Ronan drew back from the bed and rubbed his fingers along his eyebrows, a habit he had picked up from his father. No breath stayed in his lungs.

"Where's the doctor?"

"They'll be here soon."

He rubbed his eyebrows again. "Can they cure it?"

"He had a lump," said Alison.

"What lump?"

"There's always a tumor," said Kate.

"And the veins near it," said Alison, "when they swell, they're said to look like a crab's legs. Hence 'cancer.' Your father told me that."

"Where's the lump?"

"The liver," said Alison and began to cry soundlessly, a desperate sight. "The liver, isn't it awful?" Neither Kate nor Ronan went to her.

"Will I be able to talk to the doctors?"

Both women said, "Yes."

Ronan put his back flat against the wall, like someone being measured for height.

None of them moved. None went to the bathroom, nor into the night street to take the air. Nor did they speak much.

Alison asked about the train journey, and, "How did you know to come today?"

Kate shrugged. "I just knew."

Ronan watched his father's face. From time to time he came forward, picked up John's hands, and caressed them. At college, they had begun work on the Elizabethans in Ireland, on Ann Boleyn's father in Carrick-on-Suir; they had skirted round the small peaks of Edward Bruce and Silken Thomas and their brief, stylish rebellions. So much to report, and so much to ask; the Ballinamore letter; how to tell stories; the homburg hat.

At almost exactly the two-hour moment John woke up. Ronan sensed it first, leaped across, and clasped a hand. John took a second or two, then registered.

"You got here," he said. "I needn't have worried."

Moments later, Dr. and Dr. Kelly arrived, both tall, both austere, both immeasurably kind. The husband, shyer than the wife, shook everyone's hand; she, known universally as "Mrs. Dr. Kelly," went straight to the patient.

"Now, John. How's it this evening?"

The doctors' conduct sang of care and thought; no swift movements near the patient, everything looked at and checked, the gentlest of touches—they brought good spirit into the room.

"And the pain, John?"

"Maureen, how long is it since you saw Ronan?" said John O'Mara.

She looked across at the tall, nervous student with the dark red hair and the college scarf.

"He's even more like you now," she said. "Tell me you're sick and tired of the food, John," she continued, and said reassuringly to Ronan, "It's always a sign they're improving when they complain about the food."

Her husband came to the bed and reached for a pulse.

"I've felt weaker horses," he said.

"They were carrying my bets," said John.

Mrs. Dr. Kelly took a small wooden spatula from her bag.

"Open a little."

She inspected his tongue and withdrew.

"Is life worth living? It depends on the liver," said John in wisps of breath. "Do any of you know—how often—I've used—that joke?"

"We all know, Dad." Ronan could do nothing but observe.

Alison said, "Would you like us to leave the room?"

Dr. Kelly shook his head. Mrs. Dr. Kelly adjusted her bun of gray-black hair.

"James Harrington sent you his best. I met him in town today. The new wife was with him."

"Is it true?" said John.

Mrs. Dr. Kelly laughed. "Yes—she's at least thirty years younger." And to Ronan she said, "That's another good sign—when gossip comes back in."

Dr. Kelly said, "I've changed the liquid intake. Just a little. The nurse'll tell you. And we'll be in again at midnight."

John ate no more food, and he gossiped not a word. It only took two days, and all three saw him die.

First he said to Ronan, "There's no one like you. Not for me, anyway."

Next time he woke, he said to Kate, "That red's lovely on you."

He said his last words to Alison—"The television will be great company in the evenings."

Then he slept; the head back on the pillow; a rumble from the stomach; a small drool that Alison wiped away. One hour later he woke briefly, startled and unseeing—the hands flinched, and he died.

As Kate said afterward, "He all but waved good-bye."

Outside, a sudden shower of rain, heavy as blood, flogged down on the roof.

Ronan could touch no one. He held his hands out from his body as though frozen, then put them behind his back like a soldier at a lying-in-state and bowed his head. Once or twice he swayed from side to side; in grief, no two people behave the same.

They brought John home—to the house he had restored and loved. Her mind clear as a spring, Alison ran the wake. Teams of neighbors helped; linen draped the table; every fireplace blazed; food and drink piled up.

Kate said, "Expect five hundred people."

Alison allowed for twice that—and got it right. As the undertakers arranged the room, she called Ronan aside.

"Come here to me."

In the past, he had dreaded the phrase; this time it carried different freight.

"Now, listen. You're eighteen years old. Men not much older have led regiments, and men your age have won Olympic medals. This is your father's funeral, and I want you to comport yourself with dignity and calm. You do not allow yourself to break down, not even when the coffin is lowered. Keep your tears to yourself. Shed them when everyone's gone. You're the host of your father's funeral."

Ronan looked at her and saw again the steel on which he had been so often pierced. He said nothing.

"Agreed?" she said.

Still not a word.

"Agreed, Ronan? What your father would want?"

Ronan agreed.

They came from everywhere—silent, awkward, rich, rough; men from the town; widows with hats; strange people from the hills. Two couples came a hundred miles, one timid man from his sickbed. All stood in the hallway and praised.

"He saved our farm from the bank."

"That man won my injury claim."

"No one else would have taken the case."

All said, "Sorry for your trouble."

The legend came back to life; John had steered them through a will to protect their children; John had straightened out a boundary that had caused strife; John wrote down the stories of their lives.

Women in black, with pleasant faces and heavy bodies, said to Alison, "Ohhhh, wasn't he so handsome then, I remember when he came here first, we were all jealous he was married, and he always dressed so well, I used to annoy my husband comparing him."

For hour after hour the house refilled. More than once Ronan saw people from the Storyteller's nights. Two old foes shook hands over the open coffin, looked down, and said, "He'd like us for that." Odd people, with squints or lip defects or massive birthmarks or crippling diffidence, came forward and shook Ronan's hand; they said, "The apple never fell far from that tree," and, "If you're half the man your father was, you'll be twice the man of any of us," and, "What a fatherly son you are." When Kate explained that it referred to the resemblance, Ronan found it easier to look at his dead father's—now younger—face.

A woman whom nobody knew and no one would ever see again slid in, laid a bunch of green holly with red berries on the catafalque, and vanished. Mrs. Dr. Kelly arrived and hugged Alison without a word. Policemen shook hands, still in uniform; aged and wrinkled twin sisters wept in tune.

And at last Toby came and all but collapsed in grief. John's younger brother, he lived in Oxford; they corresponded rarely, visited less. Toby took off a thin gold ring and hooked it to a finger of John's left hand.

Four judges arrived, somber by practice, conscious of their status. They spoke only to Alison, Ronan, and Kate. When they left, the wake took courage. A man in a cap sang a song like a dirge. His brother came forward to speak ringing praise.

"Who was he? He wasn't even from here—he was a stranger from up in the north, where they have people we don't understand. But he came down here and made us his own. And what was he? As decent a man as ever pulled on a shoe. He let me go two years without paying him, and he never sent me a bill. I'd meet him in town, and I'd say, 'John, I owe you money,' and he'd say to me, 'Patsy, you'll know when you can pay me.' There's not many'll do that." When the eulogist finished, he doffed his cap to the coffin. The woman by his side sang a slow Irish song, "Kilcash," which spoke of a great house dying and the end of times that they loved.

When she finished, a fiddler began to rosin his bow, and someone unwrapped an accordion. Their first tunes came slow and sad, stately laments with mellow grace notes, and then, as drink followed drink, the music quickened. A banjo player joined in, and a man played castanets with two spoons. Finally a piper arrived; he squeezed the doleful woolen bag under his arm, and the session matured—hornpipes, jigs and reels. It went on for two hours and more; on the stroke of midnight it ended, when the other musicians held up their hands for the piper to play a slow march, "The Death of the High King."

At Ronan's elbow a tiny woman with a red nose said, on her sixth sherry, "If your father ever comes back to earth, I'll want a son like you off him."

The funeral of John O'Mara closed the town until midafternoon. From the church to the graveyard stretches a mile. All windows closed their blinds in respect. Every life along that route had been touched by the man and his work. The deeds he stamped, the contracts he drafted, the sales he closed, the letters he wrote, the lore he heard—his presence had pervaded their lives, and their memories spoke the word "good."

He had also spiced their world—and he did so now once more. Behind the chromed black hearse walked the gossip of his life— his son, his wife, and her sister. Alison wore a black coat, loose as a cape, her two rows of pearls and a pearl hatpin in her black cloche. Kate, hatless and brave, wore a fitted black coat over a fitted black dress and the brightest red lipstick. Underneath, she wore the most expensive and beautiful white underwear she owned. Both women wore stockings black and sheer; they had been prepared for weeks.

Ronan wore his father's darkest suit.

Everyone who watched knew the truth of their lives; the sisters never made such a thought conscious—or disallowed it. John, however, astride everyone's secrets, had always faced the fact; he knew better than most the things that people know but don't say. And so the funeral continued, a slow, steady pace behind a slow, steady hearse on a bright December afternoon.

Men counted the crowds and told their wives that night, "Five thousand. It took an hour," they said, "to pass the corpse's office."

Black crepe ribbon framed the shingle's polished brass: "John O'Mara, Commissioner for Oaths."

At the graveside, people jostled for space. Politicians rushed to be seen; women's heels sank; the priest and the undertaker pushed through the parting crowd. On the hillock by the grave, Ronan stood rigid, hands behind his back; Kate linked his arm; Toby stood on the other side of Alison. Everybody waited, breathing on the air; the tail of the crowd was long.

That grave was dry as a bone; the shovels had sliced it neat, a deep, rectangular slot. Ronan almost looked in but chose to gaze at the sky. The coffin rested on wooden spars over the mouth of the pit, with canvas straps looped beneath. When the priest intoned the prayers, not a sound could be held. And no bird sang.

The holy water splashed. "In nomine Patris." And the priest kept time with the splashes. "Et Filii." Which fell on the shiny wood. "Et Spiritui Sancti." He wore a white baggy cassock, and round his neck a purple stole that matched small veins in his cheeks. "Dearly beloved brethren. We'll observe a minute's silence now. To release the soul of our friend, John. May he rise to his just reward with God."

Ronan swung between two feelings—a curious sense of enjoyment and the driving pain of dismay; his body felt tight as a drum, and his eyes were sore with restraint. He joined with the crowd in a murmured giant "Amen."

Five gravediggers, faces weathered as bark, hustled forward in trained respect. Four took each end of the two canvas straps and hauled. As the coffin rose, the fifth man took away the spars, and the coffin went lumbering down, played out on the canvas loops. Kate, beside Ronan, gasped, and Alison seized her arm. Nobody moved; nobody left the place. The men replaced the spars and drew green canvas over the cut. And the priest drew away from the scene; John O'Mara was in the ground.

The crowd took its time; condolers came forward afresh. Alison, Toby, Ronan, and Kate shook hands in perfect calm. Then Ronan saw Alison start. The old cold humor crossed her face, and her lips narrowed to a thin line. What had she seen? Ronan surveyed the crowd, seeking the source of her wrath. He looked at her again; she had definitely taken an angry turn, though only her family would know. His eyes swung right and left; he saw no hostile face—and then he followed her line of sight.

High on the hill, at the top of that cemetery, stood two cypress trees. Someone had planted them thinking a graveyard should have such presence, but the prevailing wind from the west had reduced them over the years, and they lacked enough branches for grace.

Between the lonely trees stood the man Ronan dreamed of. The same long coat, the same immortal bearing—tall, powerful, and gaunt; it could have been a ghost, but it wasn't, and Ronan would have known him anywhere in the world.

He turned to Kate, "Jesus God!"

"What?"

"He's here, Kate!"

"Who?"

Ronan stepped past the grave to get through the swirling crowd. Alison grasped his arm to hold him back; he shrugged her off. But it took too long; the crowd still milled; folk tried to shake his hand; the graves gave no easy path. By the time he got clear and ran up the hill, the Storyteller had gone from the trees.

Ronan stood there, looking across the fields. On that hard, cold morning, visibility from the cemetery wall stretched for miles; he could see Grantstown Castle, he could hear the Dublin train's whistle, he watched distant flights of birds flicker across the empty sky—but he saw no long-striding man in an ancient homburg hat.

In that part of the country, farmers can afford labor; they keep their farms neat; hedges are low and trimmed. No hedgerow could have obscured a walking traveler, unless he sat down to hide. No, he had gone; inside minutes the Storyteller had vanished.

It seemed that everyone had come back to the house for lunch. Kate put Ronan "on parade"; he welcomed people, poured drinks, greeted distant kin. Thus he kept his grief at bay—and his chagrin at the Storyteller's flight.

Toby openly grieved. He wept in bursts, laughing too loudly, drinking compulsively, eating mammoth plates of food. Kate detailed Ronan to steer him to a quiet room.

"My God, how juvenile." Toby wiped a crumb from his mustache. "I'm drinking too fast. It's a sad day when a man has to learn decorum from his nephew. But I suppose it's a sad day anyhow, wouldn't you say?"

He wore a silver watch chain on his waistcoat, and at forty hadn't the age to carry it off.

"Were you there, Ronan? At the, ah'm, you know—the end? When he went? He went well, didn't he? John'd die well, he'd make a point of it." More tears.

Toby had perfect fingernails, which he scanned often.

"The thing I remember about your father—he always had money, even when we were boys, I used to call him 'the mystery man' because he always had cash, some people are like that. And I hear you're all rich now, everyone's talking about it, and for once it won't be a case of 'Where there's a will there's a lawsuit,' will it?"

"I don't know," said Ronan, truthfully.

"Buckets of it," said Toby. "Money to burn."

Someone knocked on the door. A man with wire nests of nose hair said, "You must be Ronan?"

"I am."

"You're wanted."

He led the way through the back door, down the long garden path, to the lane and a parked car. Ronan stopped him.

"Where are we going?"

"Just down the road."

"I can't go."

"You have to come."

"How long'll this take?"

"I'd say an hour."

"For what? I can't stay away."

The nose hair man said, "You'll be glad."

"No—come on. I have to know."

The man said, "I'd say, you'll be very glad." He looked excited and opened the passenger door. Ronan climbed in, as did the man, and they drove away.

"How far?"

"You'll see in a minute."

Not more than two miles away they stopped, at the cottage of a stonemason beside the river bridge.

"They're waiting for you in there," said the man with the nose hair. "I'll go back to your house and tell them you'll be away for a bit."

Ten or twelve cars stood nearby, unusual for such a modest house. A woman opened the door before Ronan knocked; with no hallway he walked directly into the packed kitchen. People turned to look at him; all had been at the graveyard; this seemed like the funeral's overflow. They shook his hand, sorry for his trouble—and they handed him deeper into the room.

His eyes got used to the dimness; something momentous was here. Two men stepped aside, and behind them, in a small space by the fireside, sat the Storyteller. Pipe in one hand, whiskey glass in the other, he looked at Ronan as no man ever had—tense and welcoming, a fearful yet delighted look.

Ronan clenched both hands and felt his mouth go dry. Every eye watched, every voice stopped. The Storyteller put his glass on the floor, stood up, and held out his hand. Ronan reached for the hand-shake—the same texture as nine years ago.

"People say you've been looking for me."

"I have," said Ronan, short of words. "How are you?"

"I guessed you'd grow this tall."

"The last time was in the rain," said Ronan.

"Brendan the Navigator. Broaden your horizons," said the Story-teller. "I'm pleased you remember."

The man of the house came forward and took Ronan's shoulders from behind; gently he steered him to a stool a few feet from the Storyteller's face. "He's just started."

Ronan tried to feel calm but reeled at the force of life. One beloved man buried, another reappeared—this was a day of fate. How to be quiet, yet exult? He settled himself by inspecting the old man.

Had he changed? Undoubtedly—older and frail now; the decade had been harsh to him. His eyes had the red of longstanding rheum, and his glance seemed less in control; the canvas of the face was stretched tighter. The voice, though, had grown more resonant, as though someone had added a bass bell to a deep chime. Ronan blinked his feasting eyes—and then sat back to listen.

B Y OUR STANDARDS TODAY, WE'D THINK HUGH O'Neill a marvelous man—so what must they have thought of him in fifteen-ninety? To some of his people he was like a god. He was their leader, their chieftain, their governor, their guardian; he was a family man, a great soldier, a forward thinker. That last bit is the most important, because it made him immortal to us. His title was the second earl of Tyrone—I prefer the name history has given him, the Last Chieftain; it's a sad name, but it has the right depth.

At the time he became "The O'Neill," as he was called, and therefore the most important man in the northern half of Ireland, the whole country was in a bad way. Hugh had done a lot of fighting inside his own family to get to the top—because he saw that if he didn't become chieftain, the O'Neill clan would lose everything to the English. Or indeed to his marauding Irish neighbors, of which there were plenty. Who needs enemies, he probably said to himself, when you have friends like mine? Once he got the power, though, the neighbors left him alone.

So he consolidated himself in his own territories, and he set out to rebel against the queen. A daring thing to do; as an Irish earl he was supposed to swear allegiance to Elizabeth or to whosoever sat on the English throne. But no, he didn't want to do that—he took the opposite course. He planned and he organized and he marched against the English, and—the most important thing he did—he gave us a military style.

I think of him often; he's one of the men I'd most like to meet. There are mornings on the roads of county Tyrone when I say to myself, "He rode past here on his big gray horse," or "He stopped on this hill to admire the view down the valley." A bearded man, as so many were four centuries ago; and a spirited man, fond of a good time; a thoughtful man and a man of deeds. And a man with twists to his life; he was known to have an eye for the ladies, and that put ink in the milk.

He'd been raised inside the Pale, where he'd a lot of contact with English families. And he'd even adopted some English ideas. In fact you could say he copied the king, because Hugh also divorced his wife—fine if you're Henry the Eighth, but a very spicy thing for anyone else to do in fifteen-seventy-four. The lady he then married, wife number two, died in fifteen-ninety-one, and the bold Hugh, at the age of forty-one, decided to elope with the daughter of Sir Henry Bagenal.

Bagenal was an English gentleman, and he didn't want his daughter marrying some wild Irish go-the-road with a reputation for unruliness, earl or no earl. He refused to give the girl, who was called Mabel, any dowry so long as she was involved with that Beelzebub, O'Neill.

In point of fact, Mabel didn't stay long anyway. Hugh's eye roved again, and he admitted to it, and Mabel went home to her mother. Her father hated Hugh O'Neill more than ever; how could he now get this daughter off his hands? "Tarnished goods," the father called her. No, Bagenal didn't like Hugh O'Neill.

So: with Mabel gone, Hugh married wife number three and, a bit more settled down, began to plot in earnest against the English. He did so in a very inventive fashion. Up to that point, Irish soldiers won such few victories as they'd had by nerve, by shouting a lot and rushing blindly into battle, cutting the head off the first thing they saw. Or they raced down out of the woods, attacked the last soldiers in a marching column, and ran back into the trees, laughing.

The O'Neill knew that this style of fighting had limited power. He wanted a more scientific army, trained soldiers rather than lads with axes who might or might not turn up for the battle on the day.

Now, you remember from your schooldays that Irish troops had two kinds of soldiers—they were called "gallowglasses" and "kerns."

The gallowglasses were mercenaries, professional foot soldiers who were hired from Scotland and the north of England. They carried heavy swords, and if they got into a battle, they often won, because they were strong, ferocious men. The kerns were light-footed and had javelins and daggers and bows. Although they could never manage the heavy, hand-to-hand jobs of the gallowglasses, they made dashing raids on the flanks of an enemy's column or fired salvoes of arrows from their bows.

Neither kern nor gallowglass had much hope, however, when faced with musket and cannon—which is what the English had and what Hugh O'Neill now brought into use on the Irish side. He surveyed his troops, and he realized they were afraid of nothing. But they went into battle with no support or protection. He saw what he had to do; he bought artillery, and he trained men how to use it.

For added strength, he forged alliances with Ireland's two old friends, Spain and the pope. The king of Spain especially promised help. He had no time for the English because Henry the Eighth had dishonored all Spain when he divorced his first wife, Katherine of Aragon. Hugh smiled at this idea, and was glad he hadn't divorced a Spanish lady.

By the fifteen-nineties, therefore, Hugh O'Neill had an army and strong alliances—all he needed now was a war. So he started one; he attacked the English fortresses in the north, and he destroyed the supply trains traveling to them. In one raid the food went into the river, and ever since, it's been called the Battle of the Biscuits.

If any of you men here in this room had been alive in fifteen-ninety-five, you might have enlisted as a soldier in Hugh O'Neill's army. There was prestige attached to it—you'd have been fighting for a very inspirational leader, and you'd have been one of the first Irish soldiers—I mean real soldiers, trained and with kit—to take on the English. We'd be singing your praises to this day. And you might have played a part in a famous victory. The week before last I walked the site of it—did school teach you about the Battle of the Yellow Ford in fifteen-ninety-eight?

•   •   •

Have you ever traveled through the county of Armagh at apple-blossom time? If you have, you'll know of its beauty and light. You can easily see why it was the Protestant prize when it came to creating the Six Counties of the North of Ireland in nineteen-twenty-one. The loveliness of that countryside, those rolling fields and those bunches of woodlands and the bushy hedges—Armagh always lifts the heart.

That's not to say the entire county's perfect. It has its share of bogland, as every Irish county does. But the bog played a part in the greatest defeat England ever suffered on the island of Ireland.

There are some who'd argue with that and say the biggest defeat England ever suffered was the day they marched out of Dublin in nineteen-twenty-two, but that's a story for another day, and that day, when it comes, will dawn bright and fair.

They called it the Battle of the Yellow Ford because of the yellow mud. It's a nothing kind of place; you can trace the battlefield easily. It's not far from Armagh, out to the northwest of the city, by a half-decent river called the Blackwater. Don't confuse it with the beautiful river Blackwater in Munster, where the salmon leap into the fishermen's hands.

One of the strongest English forts stood on the river Blackwater near Armagh. It had a garrison of three hundred and fifty soldiers who used to rob food from the local folk. They did this partly because Hugh O'Neill had cut their supply routes—and they did it because they were the local conquerors and, like many people who do bad things, they could get away with it.

Hugh O'Neill hated that there were English garrisons in his northern territories, and he was heartily sick of this particular fort. He besieged it, and he stopped its gallop—no more food robberies; in fact, no more food. After a week or so, the English rulers in Dublin heard about the siege and they sent an army north, under Hugh's old pal Bagenal.

We Irish, we've always been guerrilla fighters because with a total of under five million living on the whole island, we've never had a population large enough to make up a big standing army. Usually, therefore, when you hear of an Irish battle against the English, it was guerrilla work—hit them hard and run like blazes. Those tactics put the fear of God in the hearts of regular soldiers in uniform who have orders to fight in disciplined lines. And they say the China leader, Mr. Mao, based his campaigns on our men who fought from nineteen-sixteen to nineteen-twenty-two.

The Yellow Ford, though, was always going to be different—it was guerrilla work with conventional warfare added, a fearsome combination. Hugh O'Neill had built a chain of command that made sure every soldier knew where he was supposed to be. This was a big change from the typical Irish soldier, who had always worked by taking a look at some big enemy boy and saying to himself, "I'll have a cut at him."

On Monday, the fourteenth of August, fifteen-ninety-eight, O'Neill barricaded the last stretch of road from Armagh to the fortress. Bagenal, trying to dupe O'Neill, kept his army marching north, past where he should have turned off to get to the fort. Then he turned his army and cut down through the countryside, hoping to reach the river from a direction O'Neill mightn't have been guarding.

When he saw the state of the ground, Bagenal had his men cut branches off trees and lay them on the bogs. For a tactical move like that to work, you have to know the land well. Bagenal didn't—and anyway, if he thought he could get his cavalry, his carriages, and his field guns across an Irish marsh by laying down a few branches of heather, God help his poor head. Besides, he was dealing with a man from the north, who had grown up knowing such treacherous ground.

The English that day wore shining armor and tall helmets. They looked grand; they carried iron shields, straight broadswords, axes where the blades had deep wide edges and plenty of muskets and cannon. The Irish bore much lighter arms—their lances had handles of ash, their axes were forged of a lighter steel, they wore no armor and were equipped for fast, raiding fighting, not toe-to-toe slogging.

They had two-edged swords, bows and arrows, and sharply pointed throwing darts, with which they attacked the horses of the English cavalry. If a poor horse got one of those darts in the neck, he bucked and reared until he threw his mount.

Knowing that the English might change direction in the hope of deceiving him, O'Neill had set traps in the ground. His men dug a long, deep trench parallel to the river on the northern side—as well as wide, hidden holes scattered across the marsh. Over these pits, full of stakes and thorn bushes and water, they threw bunches of grass and scattered moss and branches to make the ground look innocent—all the full trickery of a devious general who also knew about guerrilla warfare.

Bagenal led his men down one hill toward the Yellow Ford. He rode at the head of a column about a mile long, four or six men abreast, led by the cavalry, followed by the infantry, who were protecting the wagons of supplies for the besieged fort. O'Neill had lined up his men on the far hill, behind low ramparts of thorny bushes. The Irish were raring to go. Before Bagenal appeared, O'Neill had ridden up and down his own lines saying, "Don't be afraid. They'll have armor you've never seen before, and unusual guns. And their trumpets will make a terrible noise, and they'll have many, many soldiers. But—all the more for us to rout."

Their morale was sky-high by the time they saw the first line of the English cavalry. The fine men with their armor and great steeds charged at them—and dropped into the great trench and the various wide holes. You never saw such a melee. When the soldiers in front started toppling into the traps, the ones galloping on behind didn't know what to do—by which time it was too late, and down they went too.

After a few minutes, when more and more of Bagenal's soldiers were pitching into the traps, O'Neill lifted his sword and shouted, "Open fire!" Remember—Bagenal never knew the Irish were there; they were hidden behind these false hedges they had built. With cannon that O'Neill had purchased from the English, the Irish let fly their first fusillade. The minute the smoke died away, out from behind their thorny palisades rushed hordes of Irish soldiers to attack the broken English line. There was consternation and chaos and a lot of killing.

Back to their ramparts dashed the Irish, pleased with their hundreds of kills. They hid again and waited while their guns let fly another huge salvo, and then launched a second attack. All in all, it was a total ambush, and the covering fire from the Irish artillery was every bit as powerful as the English had.

After two and a half hours Bagenal's lines were ripped apart. O'Neill ordered his men to move in. They surrounded the English and began to hack at them with swords and axes. To back them up, the Irish cavalry charged the English again and again, cutting down their cavalry, riding over their infantry roughshod.

There's an old saying, "The ball bounces for the winning team"— in other words, the victor gets all the luck. That day, the English had no good fortune at all. Their main gunpowder wagons blew up accidentally, killing several of them, throwing up clouds of black smoke everywhere, and frightening the wits out of the men and the horses and causing stampedes. Now they had no gunpowder left. And when they looked around for some desperate hope, they saw the last straw: their fort had fallen, and the Irish were riding in.

Some English officer shouted an order to retreat, and their cavalrymen didn't stop galloping until they reached Dublin. Poor old Bagenal lost his life, to a musket ball just above the bridge of his nose. It was fired at him by an Irish soldier from a range of about four yards.

On the battlefield at the end of the day, the Irish roamed here, there, and everywhere, beheading every wounded foe they found. They seized all kinds of spoils—food, weapons, personal possessions, and naturally, being Irish, the horses. In London, the queen, when she heard the outcome, hoisted her skirts in a fit and said she was very displeased: "I never get any good news from Ireland, nothing but calamity."

When it was all over and everything was reckoned, the English had lost around three thousand men and the Irish a sixth of that.

What a famous day! That battle took place in the course of what they call the Nine Years' War.

When I'm going around the countryside, one of the pleasures I get from life is the tracing of great people. I have walked down the side of the black mountain of Arigna in county Roscommon to the grave of our finest composer, the blind harper Carolan, who, they say, composed the tune that became the American National Anthem. And I've stood by the big rock that marks the burial place of Saint Patrick himself in the city of Armagh. But I'll never have the chance to honor the tomb of the great Hugh O'Neill. And this is why.

The Yellow Ford was his finest hour. Gradually the superior force of England had its way. The Spanish fared badly when they came to our aid—they were either caught in a trap by the English or destroyed by the Atlantic weather. Our own campaigns came to naught, and slowly but surely Hugh O'Neill was forced to his knees. The English pushed him back and back, deeper into his own lands of Tyrone, and all around him they built a ring of forts to hem him in, and finally they made him sign a pact. He was a giant in chains, able only to peep over his own parapet at a land full of alien men.

And after he had signed the pact, he powerlessly watched his lands, day by day almost, being handed over to English owners. In Ireland a man's land was—and still is—his authority, but only if he owns land. O'Neill endured it for several years. At last he decided to exile himself. He chose Spain, and that's why I'll never stand at his grave—he didn't die in Ireland.

Everyone in this room knows what happened—we call it the Flight of the Earls, one of our most lonesome days. On Friday, September the fourteenth, sixteen oh-seven, Hugh O'Neill, with his family, relatives, and friends, altogether a hundred people or so, boarded a French ship that had slipped into Rathmullan and sailed out of Lough Swilly.

Even then their troubles hadn't ended. A storm in the Bay of Biscay drove them ashore. They traveled over land to Rome, though some stayed in France, and to this day you can find their names on bottles of wine—Phelan, Lynch, Kirwan, Haut-Brion, or O'Brien. They say that wherever an exiled Irish chieftain fought in a French army against England, he was rewarded with a land growing vines.

Hugh O'Neill, The O'Neill, died in Rome in sixteen-sixteen at the age of sixty-six—schoolchildren always remember that date on account of all the sixes. And so ended an old order.

Today, an old order ends too. I chose to tell that story here in this parish because the passing of a good man is a moment that should be marked. And today we lost the modern equivalent of an Irish chieftain when we laid John Francis O'Mara to rest.

Someone remarked, "Well said."

Before anyone moved, Ronan rose and went to the old man's chair. Nine years—the searching, the remote contacts, the hope: what could he say to bridge all of that? And the questions: How did the Storyteller find Ronan's cache? From whom did he learn where Ronan had gone to college? The radio, the television—had Ronan found the broadcasts by chance?

In the excitement he raised none of these issues; he said, "I wish my father had heard that."

The Storyteller said, "How well do you know your Shakespeare?"

"We did a lot at school."

"When beggars die, there are no comets seen."

Ronan completed the quotation: "The heavens themselves blaze forth the death of princes."

"A chip off the old block. And he loved a good story."

"How long will you stay here? I have things I want to—to ask you."

The Storyteller stood up. People began to press close, claiming his attention, offering praise.

"You grew up well," he said, looking Ronan up and down. "D'you tell any stories yourself?"

"I have to write history essays."

The Storyteller said, "Well—that's a kind of storytelling."

"Not as lively."

"No reason it can't be."

"Will you come to my home? I know there was trouble the last time you were here, but—"

The woman of the house pressed right in and began to draw the Storyteller away.

"I promised people in Clonmel I'd stop there a while," said the Storyteller, "and there's a kind man here driving over that way."

Ronan felt panic rising. "Will you come to meet me in Dublin? Or I can meet you anywhere."

"Very well."

"But how can I get in touch with you?"

"You'll find me where I always am—on the road."

"Listen. Sir. I've looked everywhere for you."

But the Storyteller turned to go. Ronan grabbed his arm, and the Storyteller placed his hand over Ronan's.

"I'll send for you," he said. "I will. That's a promise."

People came between them like a separating tide; almost like guards a couple eased the Storyteller toward the door. The nose hair man came forward.

"I'd better take you back."

"No, hold on. I still want to talk to him."

Ronan tried to get out of the house; the door was blocked with people. On tiptoe he saw over their heads the tall figure in black on the road outside. Ronan pushed harder through the small kitchen and broke through—but a car had been waiting and drove the Storyteller away.

"Where's he gone?"

"He wanted to go," said a man. "He was very definite about it."

Ronan watched the car disappear up the hill. Jesus God! He had him, by the hand, by the arm—and he let him go! How had he allowed that to happen? He suppressed a rising fury—he felt unsafe. But one thing at least held good; the power of the old contact had not dimmed. It still felt destined, it still felt right; the Storyteller was meant for him.

Nobody back at the house seemed to have missed him. Kate and Alison spoke as though he had not been away.

"Where's Toby?" Ronan asked.

"Lying down," said Alison, sardonically.

"He's feeling off," said Kate.

Around six o'clock the party began to decline. The hired help moved here and there, cleaning and clearing and putting away. Old friends said good-bye to Alison in the hall, they more tearful than she. As the last one left, she closed and locked the door. Ronan heard the clank with surprise—Kate started too; they rarely turned that big old lock. In the hall, Alison stood with her back to the door, her face torn open with grief.

"That's it," she said. "That's it."

"What?" said Kate, wary and tired.

"John's gone now. He's—just—totally gone. Gone."

The tears came down. Alison stood and looked at them without a defense in the world. She sobbed until she had no breath and never wiped her eyes. Kate approached—Alison's hands warded her off; Ronan made no move. For long minutes the three stood there, and Alison finally stopped. She looked from Ronan to Kate.

"He'd want us to go to bed."

Ronan awoke to sunshine at nine o'clock and heard Toby coughing downstairs.

Minutes later he asked, "Will you drive me to Clonmel?"

Toby looked at him blearily, holding a cigarette.

"Huh?"

They left at eleven. In the car Toby asked, "Why Clonmel?"

Ronan told him the reasons.

"Oh? Yes, your father told me about him."

"What did Dad say?"

Toby answered deliberately, a man selecting words. "He told me he came to the house. And that you loved the stories." He coughed himself into a fit, opened the window, closed it. "Do you know you're supposed to look at the sky any time you're in Clonmel?"

There it was again—the deflection!

"You see—there's never a cloudless sky over the place because Clonmel is 'the town under a cloud.' Did you ever hear that? There was a miscarriage of justice here years ago. The English hanged a priest called Father Nicholas Sheehy—they trumped up a charge of

murder, and when the judge condemned him to death, Father
Sheehy stood in the dock and declared, 'From this day forth, a
cloud will hang over the town of Clonmel.' "

Half an hour later, they reached the top of the last long hill. The
town spread beneath them under a clear blue sky.

Without question or comment, Toby drove under the old castel-
lated tower of the West Gate and along a long narrow street. He
pulled up outside a Georgian stone house. Ronan looked at the
door, looked a question at Toby—who put a finger to his lips. They
climbed out.

"If he's anywhere, he's here."

"How do you know?"

But Toby merely pressed the brass doorbell and pulled up his
argyle socks.

A tiny girl, aged twenty or so, opened the door. She peered up at
them through thick glasses.

"Who're you?"

"We called to see Mrs. Cantwell," said Toby.

"Well, you couldn't be calling to see anyone else, for if you did,
you'd have to go to a different house."

"Yes, that's, well—logical enough," said Toby. "Is Mrs. Cantwell
at home?"

"She is when she's here. This is her home. So when she's here,
she's at home."

"I mean, is she in now?"

"Well, she didn't go out. Go straight along to the door at the end
of the passage. You can knock if you want to, but the door's open."

With crochet on her lap, an elderly lady sat by the fire, small,
brown-eyed, and plump.

"Mrs. Cantwell?"

She looked up, quick as a squirrel.

"Who have I here? Aw. Well!" She had dimples and white teeth.
"I know indeed who you are! You're Mr. O'Mara's brother."

"And this is his son. I hope you don't mind the intrusion."

"Oh, no, no, this is a welcome visit." She brought regret into her face. "But I couldn't go to the funeral, my hip is in a temper. Come over here and shake my hand," she said to Ronan.

He walked across.

"To lose such a lovely man—that's very hard. If ever you're in need of comfort, just remind yourself that you were important enough to have had such a fine father." She turned to Toby. "You're wearing a professor's socks."

"I'm not a professor yet."

"All the better. Wear the socks, and they'll have to make you one. Now, you'll have tea or a drink?" She called, "Theresa!"

Toby said, "We met Theresa at the door."

"I don't know what I'm going to do about her. She told the parish priest last week that I was in the house with no clothes on. Which I was—but I was in the bath. Dear Heaven."

Theresa brought water and whiskey and poured gigantic drinks; Ronan put his to one side.

"Tell me all about yourself," Mrs. Cantwell said to Ronan. "How's your mother? I must write to her, did she get through the funeral all right? I heard there was a crowd big as the Last Judgment."

Theresa returned with a tray of teacups and fruit cake dark as coal. Toby nodded a raised eyebrow to Ronan: Ask your question.

"Mrs. Cantwell, d'you know a gentleman who travels Ireland telling stories?"

Mrs. Cantwell set down her crochet.

"I do. When I say I know him—I've met him, he's stayed in this house." She looked hard at Toby, who shook his head slightly at her. "And I've listened to him, enchanted. He was to have been here today, but I got a message he's not coming." She saw the disappointment in Ronan's face. "I never know when he's going to be here; he's a very random sort of a man. If I ever know, I'll be sure and write to you."

Ronan said, "I'd love that."

"But if it's his stories you want—sure we all love a story, he said to me once that a good story deepens the heart."

"I've been collecting his stories," said Ronan, who until that moment had not defined it so.

"Ah! The same as your father and the folklore. Well, I can give you a tale he told me. A true one, and he told it to me because it's about a member of my own family. And I remember it the way he told it to me."

A floorboard creaked; Ronan looked around and saw Theresa in the hallway, easing herself back out of sight against the wall and preparing to listen.

THIS IS A STORY OF HOW MY GREAT-GREAT-GREAT-great-great-grandmother was responsible for the defeat of that old nuisance, Oliver Cromwell. He came over here to put manners, they said, on the Catholics of Ireland, but of course the true reason he came was to kill us and take our land, because when our chieftains all emigrated and went off to France and Italy and Spain, we had no one left here to defend us."

"No one at all," said the invisible Theresa from the passageway outside. "It was very sad."

Mrs. Cantwell continued as if Theresa hadn't spoken, and Ronan could see she was trying to mimic the Storyteller's rhythm.

"As you know, Cromwell besieged the town of Clonmel here on a Friday. It was the seventeenth of May, lovely time of the year. Sixteen-fifty, it was. Well! As you can imagine, Clonmel nearly died of fright at the news he was coming."

Theresa cut in from outside. "They'd heard what the villain did in Drogheda."

Mrs. Cantwell said, "Theresa, don't interrupt me."

"Ma'am, I know the story better than you, you always tell it wrong." The invisible voice echoed in the hollow passage.

Mrs. Cantwell shook her head in annoyance. "How'm I going to get the flavor of it right if you keep interrupting me?"

"I'll keep you right, ma'am. You forgot to say he called Cromwell a 'lanky purist.' "

"No. 'Puritan.' A 'lanky Puritan.' "

Silence from Theresa.

"Clonmel did know that he enclosed three thousand people, men, women, and children, in the middle of the town of Drogheda, nearly the whole population, and butchered them; and if any survived, he sent them off to the West Indies as slaves."

Theresa called out, "Don't forget Wexford. He did a lot worse in Wexford."

"Dth." Mrs. Cantwell, irritated, clicked a tooth. "Anyway, he killed thousands in Wexford, and it was worse because they were discussing a peace treaty. God knows, when Hitler did things like that, everybody complained."

"Tell them about Ann Maher," said Theresa. "Don't forget that part."

"Ach, how could I forget Ann Maher, isn't she what the story's about? Ann Maher was my great-great-great-great-great-grandmother, and she had the high cheekbones of all the Mahers, and that's in a big strand of my family, my late sister had the same cheekbones. And Ann Maher had blue eyes, they say, and very blond hair, as blond as you'd get out of a bottle today."

"Peroxide," said Theresa. Her tone sounded helpful.

"Theresa, they had no peroxide in those days, I told you that before."

Ronan dared not look at Toby; they would have set each other laughing. And, Ronan felt, the odd thing was—the Storyteller was somehow shining through.

"The people of the town didn't know what to do, but they had some help. Lord Ormond, a local man, was very opposed to Cromwell and he had a bit of an army here in the town, about a thousand men from the north, led by a man called Hugh O'Neill— not the famous one, he was long dead, but a descendant of his, a man with a black beard, Black Hugh, Hugh Duff. They heard Cromwell was coming over from Yoh-hel in county Cork, and they got ready. They reinforced the walls and—"

"Tell them about Youghal," called Theresa. "You always forget it. And the local people call it 'Yawl'—not 'Yoh-hel,' I was there last year."

Mrs. Cantwell sighed. "She wants me to tell you that William Shakespeare visited 'Yawwwwwwwwwwl' [she exaggerated and grinned] and met the man he turned into Shylock, a moneylender from Cork who became the mayor of 'Yawwwwwwwwwwl.' Will that do, Theresa?"

"Tell them about *Moby Dick*."

"They know about *Moby Dick*—they're not ignoramuses."

"You mean the film?" said Toby.

"Five years ago they were there, and the town is still wet from it," said Mrs. Cantwell. "Anyway, the people of Clonmel reinforced their walls where they could, to stop Cromwell from breaking in. But they knew the walls were mostly soft as putty."

"They could be knocked down with roasted apples," called Theresa.

"No, Theresa, that's what they said about Limerick. Or was it Derry, I forget? Anyway. Then they devised a clever trick; if this trick worked, it would give them control of where the fighting would take place. They made a series of false lanes into the town, making it look as if these lanes were the real entrance to Clonmel—and they made sure that the false lanes led only to the strongest part of the walls. Sure enough, the trick worked for a while. When Cromwell arrived, he couldn't knock down the walls. So, a siege began."

Theresa clarified. "Because he was attacking only the strongest part of the walls—that's where the false lanes had led him."

"Theresa, would you go to the butcher's and get the meat?"

"Ma'am, he's closed; 'tis one o'clock, and he won't be open again until two."

"Oh, dear Heaven." Mrs Cantwell sighed quietly. "And everyone else is closed too. Have you any ironing you could do?"

"I'll do it when I'm in the right frame of mind, ma'am."

"God knows when that'll be. Anyway. The siege of Clonmel went on for weeks. Cromwell attacked and attacked, and he got nowhere. And this is where my great-great-great-great-great-grandmother came in. While the siege was going on, Hugh O'Neill pulled off a second trick."

"More false building," called Theresa.

"That's right." Mrs Cantwell had begun to settle for the ranks of the if-you-can't-beat-them-join-them brigade. "This time, O'Neill built a false square—and he built it in behind the weakest part of the walls. It looked like an ordinary town square; you could see the houses above it. If you walked into it, you'd think you were in the heart of Clonmel. And then, to weaken the weak wall even more, he pulled stones out of it—but he pulled them out right in front of this false square.

"The father of my great-great-great-great-great-grandmother was watching this, and he said to his lovely daughter, Ann, 'Go out there and ask that man if he's gone mad, pulling down the wall.'

"Off she goes, lovely as the summer, and when Black Hugh O'Neill sees her, he whips off his hat and bows—because he was a gallant soldier. She asked him what he was doing, and instead of answering her he said, 'You're just what I need—I have a job for you.'

"You forgot about him falling in love," said Theresa.

"Dth. He didn't fall in love with her. That's your version."

"Well, how do you know he didn't?"

"Because she married my great-great-great-great-great-grandfather."

"But she might have broken Hugh O'Neill's heart?"

"Theresa, that's enough now. Or I'll tell them about the boy from Dublin you were running after."

A shuffle outside the door suggested that Theresa had gone away. Mrs. Cantwell listened for a moment and looked relieved.

"Supplies here inside the town were running short, and O'Neill knew we couldn't hold out much longer. That night, he sent my great-great-great-great-great-grandmother out and told her to tiptoe into Cromwell's camp and pretend she'd left the town because she was dying of the hunger. She was to tell them that part of the wall was very weak, that if they threw a roasted apple, they'd knock it down. And not only that, but that everybody was so hungry, all the soldiers inside the town were now allowed to sleep at night.

"So when it got dark, about half-past seven in the evening, she tiptoed out and went into Cromwell's camp. A sentry stopped her, and she asked him for food. He had her brought straight to

Cromwell's tent. She stood in front of him, and he looked down his long nose at her.

"Ann Maher said afterward that Cromwell had the face of a man who might have a little trouble with his stomach, and he sat very straight in his chair and stared into her eyes. He had warts on his nose, and he asked her who she was, and she gave him a false name and told him how hungry she was.

"Then he says to her, 'What kind of a condition is the town in?' and she answered him as if she was holding something back. He said to her again, 'I asked you—what kind of a condition is the town in?' and she answered by saying, 'Sir, I'm very hungry. We're down to eating rats at home.' She was playing her part well.

"Imagine that. There was my great-great-great-great-great-grand-mother, Ann Maher, standing in front of the famous English general, Oliver Cromwell, whose forces had overthrown the king himself, Charles the First, and executed him. There was a joke in my family that Cromwell's title, 'the Lord Protector,' should have been changed to 'the Lord protect us.'

"Cromwell said to his officers, 'Get this girl a plate of stew,' and he sat her down at his table and watched her eat. She pretended she was like a savage with some manners, and she carried it off well. He couldn't stop looking at her, nor could his officers, she was so easy on the eye.

"When she was finished, he said to her, 'Now, little Clonmel girl, I've been kind to you, I could have had you hung. And I might yet. But one good turn deserves another. I gave you a feed of stew, so is there anything you can tell me about the town of Clonmel that would help me to bring this foolish business to an end?'

"She looked up at him, all innocence, and said, 'Sir, I shouldn't be telling you this, but you're attacking in the wrong place. If you moved your soldiers east of here, where that very tall tree is growing—they say the wall there is so thin that anyone could breach it by throwing a roasted apple.'

Theresa had come back. "You see. I knew it was Clonmel they said it about."

Mrs. Cantwell raised her voice to overcome Theresa's presence. "Cromwell, ever the soldier, said, 'So they guard it extra carefully?'

"And Ann Maher says, 'Oh, no, sir, they're all too tired, they can't guard it at night.' To cut a long story short, Cromwell got most of his army together that night. With one cannonball they blew down that bit of the wall, and they went charging in. Well! They charged into a trap. On all three sides of the false square, Black Hugh had raised wooden ramparts and lined up all his guns. They blasted and they blazed, cannonballs flew everywhere, there were muskets and swords—the women even joined in, hitting the English soldiers on the heads with frying pans."

"And chamber pots—don't forget the chamber pots."

"Theresa, there's no need for vulgarity." And Mrs. Cantwell at last hit her stride. "Cromwell retreated as best he could. He lost two and a half thousand soldiers, the heaviest defeat he ever had. The mayor of Clonmel negotiated a peace treaty with him, and this time Cromwell had to keep to his word because his army had been badly reduced, and he didn't know how many soldiers were inside Clonmel. What he didn't know either was that, while the terms were being discussed, Black Hugh O'Neill and his army had crept out of Clonmel by a quiet route, and they lived to fight another day. This was the one battle Cromwell never mentioned in the reports he sent back to the English parliament. And he never harmed my great-great-great-great-great-grandmother—if he had, I wouldn't be able to tell you that story, would I?"

Toby went back to Oxford, inviting them all to visit.

"We will," they assured him.

Ronan and Kate stayed for Christmas—no point doing otherwise, with schools and colleges closed. And so many details to address; Alison had never learned to drive, and they found a neighbor to teach her; John's office set the will toward probate; a gravestone had to be ordered, of which Kate took charge.

Many people called to the house, and dozens telephoned. Ronan did practical things; he paid the undertaker, the drink supplier, the hotel who helped cater. People everywhere spoke to him.

"Are you going to take over the firm?"

"So sad for Christmas."

"At least your mother won't have to worry, he was a great provider."

His own emotions had to wait; too much going on, no clear look at how he felt; and at night, a kind of fractious, unrestful sleep.

He had hoped to experience sharper grief. One or two sights did pierce him; his father's pocket handkerchiefs, laid out on the bed by Alison, some polka-dotted, some with horses, some paisleys; and the paperweight of stone his father had carved with the initials "J O'M"; he asked to keep it.

Alison's grief burst through once more—briefly when preparing Sunday's meat; at which moment Kate peeled many onions to hide her own tears.

Early on a quiet afternoon, Ronan browsed his father's books. On the tall shelves he opened one, then another, looking for passages John had marked—and he found an odd assortment of items used as bookmarks; old news clippings; a flimsy red feather; and, in

John's handwriting, small sheets of song lyrics, snatches of epic poems, amusing limericks.

Each volume, however, had one bookmark in common—a photograph of Ronan at some stage in his young life; baby smiles; snapshots on beaches; a dance in rare snow.

Kate walked in to hear of his discoveries.

"Even in his own copy of *Treasure Island,* and look, the *Encyclopedia Britannica,* every volume."

He flicked the pages; the photographs fell out in sheaves. On the stepladder again, he grappled with a shelf of tall books unopened for years; *Land Law & Mountain Grazing Rights: Decisions in the Province of Munster since the Act of Union 1801.* He handed the books down to Kate.

From one volume fell a long, narrow sealed envelope. Ronan caught it, broke the red sealing wax, and looked inside—more photographs.

Kate suddenly recalled—John had photographed her pregnant. No chance it was Alison; the sisters bore no resemblance. She grabbed the packet.

"I can't bear this."

"What's in it?"

"I'll show it to you later, it's just—too sad right now."

Christmas week rolled on slowly; now the pain of missing his father began to bite in some way every day. All the things he saw and heard and thought—and now he could not share them, could no longer watch his father's shoulders shake when he laughed; once or twice he remembered what it had been like as a child to cry helplessly. The rich seam of praise had also dried up, and he found that difficult to acknowledge to himself; the quiet compliments, the steady assurances he had taken for granted.

Kate caught the flu; pale and quiet, she wished no connection to anything.

Ronan said, "The house is empty without him."

Kate said, "Yes."

Ronan tried to galvanize her. "I haven't even told you about the Storyteller. That I met him."

"I know you did."

"Who told you?"

"Toby."

"Kate, he said he'd send for me."

"Then you must go when he sends for you."

"Do you feel like going for a walk?"

"No."

"I have an essay to write."

"For when?"

"A tutorial on New Year's Eve."

"What subject?"

"The Penal Laws. But I don't know how to write it."

"Try what you talked about—put some blood back on the page. Like your dad said."

Ronan lit the tall red candle in the window, the Christmas Eve tradition of guiding home the weary traveler. No one dared speak the annual toast, "That we shall all be alive this time next year."

The dynamic of the household had begun to change; Alison, though needing attention, seemed to replicate John's behavior— quieter, encouraging and calm. Out of her earshot Kate and Ronan whispered how she had changed; she had ceased to snap or speak brusquely. Josie Hogan murmured to Kate that the house "never felt such peace."

On Christmas Day Alison led them through different rooms, revealing finds.

"He had pictures of you everywhere," she told Ronan, opening a black-lacquered Chinese box. "Look—a hundred photographs": Ronan running, Ronan tumbling, Ronan laughing. Ronan at two, four, six, eight, twelve.

From the linen closet she took a package in tissue paper.

"This was his first gift to me—I've never used it," and she

unwrapped a napkin with the word *Alison* embroidered on it. "He was very proud of it; he bought the linen raw and found a lady to embroider it. Not bad for a boy of twenty-two."

And she showed them the silver bracelet made of his mother's spoons, given to John at eighteen for whatever girl he would marry.

"He proposed to me sitting by a lake. I wasn't able to answer him for five minutes; he thought I was saying I wouldn't. And my hand hurt afterward, he held it so tight."

Ronan said, "Toby slipped a ring on Dad's finger. What was that for?"

Alison looked at him quickly; "I don't know."

Ronan said, "He seemed very upset about—"

Kate nudged him, and he dropped it. They spent Christmas night quietly; no turkey, no trimmings, no drink.

"People will expect us to mourn," said Alison. "So we might as well take advantage."

Ronan stifled an uncaused, inexplicable anger that took him by surprise.

In the midafternoon of the following day, a troupe of Wren Boys arrived. Faces painted, they bore holly bushes decked with ribbons.

John had long ago documented this pagan tradition and thought it centuries old—these mummers, rough troubadours, bore ironic homage to the tiny wren, the "King of all Birds." All had faces daubed with color; the leader wore a great cardboard mask. One played a harmonica, one a fiddle, one a concertina, and one a tin whistle; the rest danced whooping jigs and sang ballads.

Alison gave the leader money. He nodded his huge head.

"And we have to shake hands with everybody."

In Ronan's hand he folded a note, as though slipping him cash. It read, "Take to the road. Boyne Water"—in familiar handwriting.

Next day Ronan returned to Dublin alone and delivered his essay through the brass letter slot at Professor Ryle's house. At Kate's insistence he had accepted an invitation from Father Mansfield.

With much reluctance. "I don't want to be a Jesuit."

"He's not asking you to."

"Well, I don't want to go."

"Why not?"

"I don't know him."

"But you've met him. And he's good company—he's the one told me the Jesuits have magnificent humility."

The joke thawed Ronan.

They lunched in the restaurant of the Metropole cinema, a long, deep room with Edwardian airs, all paneling and pristine linen.

The priest beat around no bushes. "Are you very upset?"

"It feels like that."

"This your first bereavement?"

"Yes, Father."

"I was thirty-nine when my father died, and it knocked a chunk out of me. And I'm not sure that I even liked him that much."

He had Ronan's attention.

"Oh?"

"Well, he didn't like me very much. Did your father like you?"

Ronan looked at him open-mouthed. "I never thought he didn't."

"Then he did like you. Did you like him?"

"Better than anyone."

"Lucky you."

Mansfield had substantial gifts—of managing conversation; of knowing when to advance something and walk its terrain; of finding tactical retreats.

"Now, I want to hear about these stories you're collecting." Ronan looked surprised. "Kate mentioned them," said the priest.

Ronan told the Jesuit his long history with the Storyteller, ending with the note from the King of the Wren Boys. The Jesuit took great joy in it all.

"How extraordinary. He's chosen you. That's it, you're his Chosen One. Nothing's more powerful than being chosen. That's the connection you feel."

"Why?"

"In the old days, when a master chose an apprentice or a teacher chose a student, it was to carry something on. To keep an old power alive."

"D'you think so?"

"Oh, yes—and look at how useful it'll be. It'll bring you right up against that great question—What's the story of our lives? Is it the history that people write down from a political perspective? Or is it the closer-to-home version our grandfathers give us? Or is it both?"

"Should I go and look for this man?"

"Of course, of course."

Lunch arrived. The priest needed condiments; he looked around in vain.

"Most waiters are blind—all over the known world. The profession requires it. But good diners have the cure for waiter blindness; this is what you do."

Father Mansfield rose from his chair. Like a soldier at attention he simply stood there, without moving, napkin in hand. In twenty seconds two waiters arrived.

"They don't want trouble," he said as he sat down. "If there's trouble, they'll get blamed—that's the order of things."

When coffee came, the priest said rather shyly, "Is it difficult to tell a story?"

Ronan said, "No, Father. Anyone can tell a story."

"May I try? I should like to have your verdict on my skill."

"Who's yours about?'

"Aha! You said 'who,' not 'what'—how very interesting."

"The best stories are about people," said Ronan. "At least that's what I think."

"This one is about another Englishman in Ireland, a long time ago. Did you ever hear of Edmund Spenser?"

O NCE UPON A TIME—ISN'T THAT THE APPRO-
priate way to begin a story? Yes, once upon a time, in the
city of London, lived a man who made cloth. In fact, now
that I think of it, ah—he was, he was probably a man who, yes,
made clothes, but of course in the, ah, in the language of the time
he was called a "cloth-maker."

This man resided in, ah, what I believe I'm safe in referring to as
a, well, frankly [pause], a commercial area of the city, Smithfield,
where he married and had an appreciably large family, though not
as great as many Irish families, although in poor countries and
indeed, England was a relatively poor country, I mean well, every
place was poor long ago, I suppose. [A longer pause.] Although I do
believe the English have been rather more sparing generally in sup-
plying the earth with their progeny; perhaps we know something
about our breed—or about the earth, don't you think?

London was a rough city in those days. Very rough. I suppose
that's, ah, the right word, rough. If you were rich, and I do mean
very rich, you could afford to buy an orange and press it to your
nose as you traversed the streets—in order, of course, to, ah, how
shall I put it, to deaden the aroma coming off the streets. No drains,
you see, no drains. [Much longer pause.] No drains? How terrible.

The cloth-maker's name was, ah, John Spenser, yes, John Spenser,
and in fifteen-fifty-two, to John Spenser and his wife was born the
gift of a son. They named the boy Edmund, and through a good
family connection his parents, they, ah, succeeded in getting him
into a newly opened school that has since become very famous,
very famous indeed, it is called the Merchant Taylors school, and,
ah, you can understand the pathway, if his father was a tailor or a

cloth merchant or both. You see? Merchant. And Tailor, although of course in those days they spelled *tailor* with a *y*.

Young Edmund had the education common to many schools of the time, and oh, how I do wish we had it today. By the age of ten, like his great contemporary William Shakespeare (five years younger than Edmund, of course, and not even a neighbor, eighty miles north of him in Stratford-upon-Avon, although Shakespeare did indeed come to London as we, ah, famously know), Edmund had encountered Latin, Greek, and Hebrew and very possibly Italian, Spanish, or another one of the Romance languages. Nobody in those days believed that the thoughts of Cato or Erasmus or Homer should be beyond the power of young minds to comprehend, and I have to say I believe them to have been utterly right in this assessment. [The longest pause of all.] Utterly right.

Thus, by the age of fifteen, Edmund would have been required to perform Latin and Greek original composition according to classical rules and would have also been taught to write sonnets after the fashion of Petrarch. His handwriting would have been scrutinized to the nth degree, and his training in the courtesies required to write letters to his betters would have been assiduous.

When Edmund Spenser left the Merchant Taylors school, he entered the University of Cambridge, my own alma mater—

The priest broke off.

"This is no good, is it?"

"No, Father, I mean, yes, it's very"—Ronan searched—"It's very—relaxing."

"You mean you're almost asleep."

"No, no, not at all—"

"It's all right. I should stick to teaching. What I really wanted to tell you is that Edmund Spenser catches my heart, because he too was an Englishman who loved Ireland. He came over here as a public servant—did you learn him at school?"

"No, Father."

"Then I will personally buy you a copy of *The Faerie Queene*." And he began to recite:

> *"The joyous birds shrouded in cheerful shade,*
> *Their notes unto the voice attempered sweet;*
> *The angelical host trembling voices made*
> *To the instruments divine respondence meet;*
> *The silver sounding instruments did meet*
> *With the base murmurs of the waterfall.*

"Lovely, lovely poet! The Irish scenery we all know, and love is all over that poem. In fact, I used to think that the Faerie Queene of the poem was Ireland herself. And the poem is about all kinds of other things—it's about morality, it's about joy, it's about falsehood, it's about sin and virtue and gallantry." He looked at Ronan again. "Did you talk about poetry with your father?"

Suddenly Ronan had no answer. He looked dumbly at the priest.

"I'm sorry, Ronan, that was tactless."

They sat for some time; the priest broke the silence.

"May I—may I offer a piece of advice?"

With no words available, Ronan nodded.

"Don't cut off any of your mourning. Stifle nothing. Feel it all, let it course through you like a sluice. Mourning washes us, it cleans our recesses, it brings light to the mind. Very important."

Father Mansfield tapped his fingers on his closed mouth.

Ronan said, "I don't know how to mourn."

"What an intelligent remark!"

"Intelligent?"

"People don't know how to mourn? How could they? We spend most of our lives hoping we never have to. And—people don't know how to love, they don't even permit the word in their vocabulary. Let me ask you—you who seem more sensitive than most. Did you ever tell your father that you loved him?"

"No. It wasn't a word—in general use. If you know what I mean."

"Yes, I so know what you mean." The Jesuit shook his head. "You could do worse than turn to my friend Spenser. 'Sleep after toil, port after stormy seas, Ease after war, death after life does greatly ease.' I think poetry is written more for mourners than for lovers."

THE PENAL LAWS/BY RONAN O'MARA

I N ENGLISH HISTORY, THE TERM *PENAL LAW* describes a set of measures introduced to make sure that the Church of England remained superior to Protestant noncon-formists such as Presbyterians, Methodists, and Baptists. Above all, it wished to overwhelm Catholics.

However, when the term *penal law* is used in Ireland, it refers to those laws discussed in this essay; the English crown began to enact them almost three centuries ago, starting in 1691, and they were intended to prevent the Irish not only from practicing Catholicism but from having any customary legal rights.

These Penal Laws were expressed rigidly—and had a very personal construct. The underlying intention in crushing every Catholic had been born of the need to protect the new Church of England, which King Henry the Eighth set up after the pope condemned Henry's divorce.

No attempt was made to disguise force or intent; Penal Laws for Ireland had titles such as "An Act to prevent Popish Priests from coming into this Kingdom;" "An Act to prevent the further Growth of Popery"; "An Act for the Better Securing of the Government against Papists"; "An Act for Banishing all Papists exercising any Ecclesiastical Jurisdiction, and regulars of the Popish clergy, out of this Kingdom." This became known colloquially as the Bishop's Banishment Act, and it required all Catholic priests and bishops to leave Ireland by May 1, 1698. If any came back, they were to be arrested, hung, drawn, and quartered.

"An Act Declaring which Days in the Year shall be Observed as Holy-Days" gives a clear picture of how viciously the Penal Laws were meant. For Catholics, the Holy Days, such as Christmas or Good Friday, were as important as Sundays, but the new law declared that Irish Catholics abused such days by spending them idle and drunk. Therefore, if the authorities found or had reported to them any man who said he would not work on a Holy Day, he was to be whipped in public, and no trial would be necessary to pass such a sentence.

The Penal Laws came on to the statute books at Ireland's weakest moment. After the Flight of the Earls, with the country's morale low, England's grip tightened. The crown confiscated more and more Catholic lands until, by the year 1700, the Catholic—i.e., native—Irish owned less than 15 percent of their own country. It had been taken from them and handed on a plate to Protestant farmers, whom the English brought in from England and Scotland specifically to "plant" on Irish farms.

Cruelty accompanied such measures. It was not unusual for a Catholic man to find a stranger knocking on his door. Let us dramatize such a happening in, say, county Monaghan:

The stranger on the doorstep would ask to see the man of the house. "Are you called Thomas MacMurrough?"

Mr. MacMurrough of county Monaghan would reply, "Yes, I am he"; behind him, his wife would look over his shoulder at the stranger, and the children would peep around the corners to see who was at the door.

Then the stranger would say, "You have to leave this house now, for I own it."

"What?!" our Mr. MacMurrough would ask—but he would know well what must happen next.

"I have a piece of paper here, signed by the lord lieutenant of the county Monaghan, and it says that this place has now become my house and land."

"This house and land has been in my family for centuries."

At Mr. MacMurrough's defiance, the stranger would whistle with his fingers, and from behind the trees would march a troop of red-coat soldiers with guns.

Soon afterward, Mr. MacMurrough and his wife and children would be seen walking along the road, with no place to stay that night and no place to live in the future. Had they been lucky—or prudent—they might have possessed enough money for a passage to America. But if unlucky, harsh weather would decimate them in the rough shelters they raised on roadsides, or they would be sold as slaves to the West Indies.

This system of eviction and plantation had in fact been taking place in Ireland since Elizabeth the First ascended the English throne in 1558. Native Irish people had been losing homes in all the rich counties of Ireland. When it began to intensify through-out the 1600s, those who came in and took over the properties began to grow fearful; even though they now "owned," the land they remained much the minority of the population. They also knew that they had been tools of a gross injustice, and they feared personal retaliation. So they asked King William of Orange, a Protestant from Holland, for protection. That was how the first Penal Laws came to be passed, as a system of legislation to legit-imize what had been happening informally.

So Mr. MacMurrough was not the victim of the Penal Laws; he was a victim of the policy of plantation—which "planted" strangers in the rich land of Ireland. The Penal Laws merely made it legal to remove any farmer such as Mr. MacMurrough from his land.

Known also as the Popery Laws or the Popery Code, the Penal Laws attacked the Catholics in a most basic way, because they were designed to remove all power and influence from the Catholic pop-ulation, no matter how big it continued to be. When the first of the laws was passed, 80 percent of the population of Ireland was Catholic.

The perniciousness of the statutes also cut deep into the Irish family culture. Again, let me dramatize for the purposes of clarity.

Take a farmer in county Limerick with many good acres of land; we'll call him Mr. Kennedy.

One day, Mr. Kennedy falls ill and suspects he may soon die. He gathers his family around him and tells them so.

When everyone has stopped weeping, the eldest son says, "We won't be able to keep our land unless I turn Protestant."

They all ask, "What are you saying?"

The eldest son replies, "A new law is coming into force that says a man cannot inherit his father's land unless he be of the Protestant faith. If not, the family can be turned out in the air, and the farm given to Protestants."

Mr. Kennedy's eldest son was correct. One of the very first Penal Laws passed stipulated that if the eldest son remained Catholic, the land had to be divided among all the children in equal shares; this would have the effect of making all Irish farms small. Or it could be taken from the Catholic family and given to Protestants.

Worse lay ahead. The Penal Laws stopped all Catholics from owning a horse worth more than five pounds. Were you a Catholic riding your horse along the road, and were a Protestant to stop you and offer you five pounds for the horse, you had to sell it to him, no matter what its market worth.

Let me dramatize a further example:

Mr. and Mrs. Lynch have been married for many years, but they have always argued. One day Mrs. Lynch goes into town shopping, and she hears of a new law. She comes home late because she met some friends, and her husband upbraids her.

Mrs. Lynch turns on him: "If you don't keep a civil tongue in your head," she says to him, "I'll turn Protestant and I'll divorce you and I'll be awarded this house and farm and you'll be out in the fields."

Mrs. Lynch was right. Were you a wife who did not much care for your husband, you could turn Protestant and not only divorce him, but take all his land—that was the law.

In other countries of Europe, Penal Laws had also been passed; the Reformation had caused a great upheaval. However, marked differences prevailed. Where those European laws were aimed at the people who left their old religion and embraced the new Protestantism, the Penal Laws in Ireland were aimed at those who refused to embrace the new religion and adhered to the old. Also, in Europe the devotees of the new reform were almost always in a minority of the people, whereas in Ireland the laws attacked the majority.

All strata of the old society became targets. For instance, no Catholic could work in a government or official job or run for elected office or become a lawyer or buy or lease land or accept a gift from a Protestant or trade in any goods or open a shop or live inside a town or within five miles of a town or become a doctor or a lawyer—or vote in any election. A Catholic could not carry a gun or speak the Irish language, the native tongue which all Catholics spoke as their first language; very few spoke English.

Above all, no Catholic could practice his religion; he could only worship in the monarch's faith. All Catholic churches were closed down; many were demolished. The priests were banished—but some of them stayed and traveled the countryside in disguise, saying mass on flat rocks out in the countryside, places to this day known as Mass Rocks.

The laws denied education to Catholics, unless they turned Protestant and went to a Protestant school. No Catholic could attend a Catholic school, open a school, own a book, or go abroad to be educated. As with priests, all teachers became fugitives, a bounty on their heads. Many fled the country but some stayed and became "hedge schoolmasters"—that is to say, they taught Greek and Latin and algebra and geometry to adults and children who huddled under hedgerows in remote places.

The fugitive priests and schoolmasters hid in caves or holes in the ground so that they might survive long enough to perform their life's work. Such a life might prove short—one law said they could be shot at sight. Or a priest, if someone preferred, could be branded on the face or castrated.

These Penal Laws penetrated every corner of Irish Catholic life. Making a pilgrimage to a holy well, a popular countryside rite of worship, became a crime. The saying of the mass was banned, and this led to a colloquial practice still in force today. According to Catholic liturgy, devout Catholics must raise their eyes adoringly at the key moment of the mass, i.e., the consecration. But in the Penal days, those who attended the secret ceremonies at Mass Rocks were allowed to keep their heads down. Thus, if a Redcoat soldier asked at bayonet point, "Did you see mass today?" a Catholic could answer truthfully, "No, I did not."

The "letter of the law" encouraged a malign "spirit of the law." Governing authorities let it be known that they would shed no tears were a Catholic evicted from his land. This paved the way for the crowning humiliation—an oath that all Catholics had to take if they were not to be dispossessed. This oath renounced everything they had once believed in—the sacrifice of the mass; the sanctity of the Blessed Virgin Mary, Mother of Christ; the existence of the saints. If they did not swear this oath, they ran in danger of all the penalties the Penal Laws were intended to enforce.

It has often been observed that, as a nation, the Irish incline toward lawlessness and disrespect of authority. But they had always observed faithfully the old Irish laws. Any disrespect can be traced to the Penal Laws. These measures derived not from just and proper government but from prejudice and injustice, because the British sought to make the Irish into Britons, make them speak and dress like English people. Instead they made criminals of people for doing what they had always done—practicing their religion, exercising their rights and beliefs.

Spenser? That hoor?"

Professor T. Bartlett Ryle looked enraged.

"D'you know what Spenser did? He was one of those civil servants the English sent over here because they had no jobs for them at home. And Spenser wrote an official recommendation as to how the 'Irish problem' could be ended. He said there was no need to waste soldiers and money killing us. Cut off their means of farming, he said, destroy their food base, and one day they'll turn to eating each other and that'll be the end of them."

"Was he bad?"

"No. But he wasn't that good, either. Although he wasn't far wrong about the eating—not that we needed him to tell us to eat each other." The professor pinched snuff. "And I'll say another thing for him. He was a helluva poet."

His eyes began to dream, and he began to intone. "One day I wrote her name upon the strand/But came the waves and washed it away/Again I write it with a second hand/But came the tide and made my pains his prey."

Then he stopped. "Right, that's enough of that."

He had called in his tutees one by one; "Come and see me," he wrote in the margins of Ronan's essay—but no grade.

Rowena Hayes said, "God! I'd hate that. He gave me a High."

"That's very good."

"I wanted a Very High."

"Better than getting nothing"—and Ronan went glumly to "the Hole," Bartlett Ryle's room.

The professor picked up Ronan's essay and tapped it.

"What were you at here?"

"I thought I was writing an essay on the Penal Laws."

"You 'thought'? You know what happened to Thought; he had a glass arse, and he 'thought' if he sat down, he'd break it."

Ronan tried to figure out this aphorism and failed.

The professor peered at the pages and then said, "You're from a lawyer's family, aren't you? Did your father do this for you? The language's a bit legal."

"My father died the week before I wrote it, sir."

T. Bartlett Ryle stopped all his fidgeting and looked across the desk. Winter sunlight lit the detritus that adorned "the Hole"—old bean cans, biscuit packets, ancient shoes everywhere, across, on top of, and underneath crazy piles of books.

"Died?"

"Yes, sir."

T. Bartlett Ryle said, "Brothers and sisters?"

"No."

The professor said, "God, I'm sorry."

Ronan said nothing.

"Bloody Death. I hate the bastard. A man's there one minute with his jokes, and his hands in his pockets, next minute he's lying white and dead. I hate bloody Death. How old?"

"Forty-eight."

"Men shouldn't die when they're only forty-eight, I'm very sorry, O'Mara. I'm *very* sorry, that's lousy, forty-eight, I suppose you don't want to talk about this pisspoor essay now."

"I do, sir."

"Well, I say 'pisspoor,'—but that's because I want you to defend it. You tell me what you think's good about it, I'll tell you what I think's pisspoor about it."

"Sir, I wanted people to know what it felt like—"

"Hah! Stop there! You said it—you said the damning word. You said 'felt.' History is not about feelings. History is about knowledge."

"Does one cut out the other?"

T. Bartlett Ryle looked startled. "What d'you mean, 'Does one cut out the other'? People have to know what went on in the past and how it might still affect us and shape us—that's what history is for."

"But everything affects our feelings," said Ronan. "I wanted to understand what it felt like to have to sell your good horse to a total stranger for very little money. Or not be allowed to read or improve your mind."

T. Bartlett Ryle was arrested enough to rise and pace.

"So what's your argument?"

"My argument is this: the Penal Laws made the Irish easier to control because they destroyed our morale, and that's what they were meant to do. If your horse made you feel good every time you looked at it, and someone who had no right to it took that horse away from you—they had a better chance of wearing you down. And it's more difficult to fight back if your spirit is cut down."

The professor looked at Ronan as at a hallucination.

"I never had this conversation in my life before. There's people in my profession would shoot me for listening to it."

"Sir, I know it's an essay, and it has to obey certain rules—but what I was trying to do was this. When we read history, we get the facts, sure—but we never know how people felt, do we?"

"Can't we judge that by the way we act?"

"Sir, can people tell what you're feeling from the way you act?"

Ryle prowled like a tiger.

"I see, I see. Is this how you want to develop? I mean—if you were to become a professional historian, is this the road you'd take?"

"Sir, I don't know yet. All I know is that—when I was writing this, I was thinking, How did they feel? What was it like to lose your farm to a total stranger? And at the same time the essay tells a great deal about the facts, the Penal Laws themselves. If no one had ever heard of Ireland, knew absolutely nothing about us—they'd learn something from it."

"You can learn something off the back of a box of matches! The other thing is—if you're going to write essays, then you'd better learn how to do it. You have to call everything by its full name; you have to list your sources, your footnotes. You give the names of some of the laws here, but you don't say what date they were passed, what the full title was, how many clauses the main draft of the law had, and in only one instance do you give the date it passed into law." The professor thought at length about something, then said, "That bastard, Death. Was the funeral itself big?"

"Very, sir."

Bartlett Ryle waxed angry again. "And these people here—how do you know there was a Mr. MacMurrough who was drummed out of house and home?"

"Plenty were, sir."

"But do you know there was a MacMurrough among them? Did you find his name and his townland and its map references?"

"No, sir."

"Well, where did he come from?"

"I made him up, sir."

"You can't make up history! I mean, you can—but 'tis called something else, 'tis called 'propaganda' or 'the Lives of the Saints' or 'autobiography' or something like that. Listen. You can't use your imagination when you're writing a history essay. The imagination has no map references."

He stopped and looked at Ronan. "Jesus and his henchmen. I feel like a man who's just handed over his gun. Ignore that last remark. It's too dangerous."

He scrawled for a long minute in the essay's margin.

Bartlett Ryle had written, "In Scottish law they have 3 verdicts; Guilty, Not Guilty, and Case Not Proven. This is a 'Case Not Proven,' but if it were proven, I'd give it a 'Very High.' And a 'Very, Very Low' for academic work, e.g., footnotes, etc."

Rowena Hayes, hands on hips, said, "Well? What did you get— come on, let me see."

Ronan showed her.

"Oooh," she said, "That's a bit of a downer. You won't like that, will you? I bet that's the worst mark he's ever given."

•   •   •

Kate came back to Dublin on New Year's Eve, still fragile physically and emotionally very low. Her panic had come, not when John died, but weeks before, when she knew the likely toll; that weeping night on the stairs had brought her to the truth.

As for the question that seared her mind—"What am I going to do without him?"—of whom could she ask it? Not Alison, not Ronan. That day, the train had no heat, and an east wind had come whistling through. Kate sat in the apartment, anxious and cold—and she had a further reason for fearing the night.

Ronan walked home, mood darkening with the day. Rowena Hayes's taunt echoed, as did the nasal "pisspoor." He felt jarred and ill judged.

Other issues weighed him down. He had looked again and again at the scrap of paper—"Take to the road. Boyne Water"—and failed to crack its code. The priest's lunch had made him grieve afresh; and he felt invaded that Kate had told Mansfield about the Storyteller. Worst of all, he now knew hour by hour how empty was his father's space. If he had no one to tell, then his studies had no point; when he could no longer expect his father's laugh, Bartlett Ryle's manner palled; where on earth could he find good company now?

At least the apartment helped—the privacy, the light. As he walked, he made plans to move the Storyteller material into the spare room and make the room a proper study.

Kate heard him arrive and decided not to delay. Brittle and speaking quickly, she broke the news.

"I have something to tell you."

Ronan looked wary—as did she.

"We're taking in a tenant. Not a tenant-tenant—I mean, it's someone we know, family, sort of. Toby's brother-in-law's coming to live in Dublin for a year or so, his job's sending him here. I told Toby it'd be all right—we have that big extra room." She smiled, attempting humor. "He's very English, he'll civilize us."

Ronan said nothing, went to his desk, opened books, failed to read. Presently Kate appeared in his doorway.

"Don't you think you should say something?"

"How do you mean?"

"A reaction would be welcome."

Ronan looked out of the window. "What's the point? You've all agreed it."

"Ronan, it happened very fast."

"You're keeping things from me."

"I'm not."

"Yes, you are. Toby's ring. All of you, you all evade things. The packet of photographs."

Kate walked away–and came back. "I told you, it was too sad."

"There's some other reason."

"There isn't."

"Show the photos to me."

Her words stumbled. "I—left them with—I forgot them."

"No, you didn't. That's a lie."

"That's not very nice of you."

"It's a lie. It's a lie. It's a lie!" He roared the third line.

"Ronan, Ronan—what's all this about?"

With one wide arm he swiped every object off his desk. Screaming louder than he or the world had ever heard, he overturned his chair and stamped on the legs of it, breaking the cross rail; he smashed the desk lamp against the wall; he picked up the inkwell and sprayed its contents on floor, walls, and bed.

"It's a lie. It's a lie. It's a lie!"

"What are you doing?!"

He screamed again. "It's-a-lie-It's-a-lie-It's-a-lie!" and began hauling out the desk drawers. One by one he upturned them or swung them in an arc so that their contents scattered everywhere. He kicked the littered floor, spraying things ever farther, then hurled his father's "J O'M" piece of rock into the large mirror over the fireplace, smashing the glass into silvered flints. Next he jumped on the bed and began to trample the bedding with his shoes, ripping the fabrics and tearing at the pillows.

Kate, having first recoiled, now advanced.

"Stop this, stoppit! At once. Now. This minute. You're not a child. Stop, Ronan!"

He grew wilder; he kicked the night table, sending everything fly-ing, he swung from the ceiling light, ripping down plaster, then jumped from the bed and began to trample on the clock, smashed a drinking glass with his shoe, danced on the books—some of which he picked up and began to rip open, scattering the pages like a giant's confetti. Kate jumped at him, grabbed his arm.

He said, "Don't touch me—don't—TOUCH—me. I'll kill you, I'll kill anyone who touches me!"

From the bedroom he raced into Kate's room, where the lip of a drawer protruded. He grabbed it, yanked it out. Turning it upside down, he danced on the bright sea of colored silks and satins, kick-ing them here and there, tearing them apart with his shoes. Then he swept everything off her crowded dressing table—and broke two of the actress lightbulbs.

She stood in the doorway with a changed, icy tactic.

"Now, let me see: what else can we find you? The kitchen? The bathroom—you could turn on the taps and throw water every-where."

"You bitch—you ALMIGHTY BITCH!"

Ronan lunged at her, Kate stepped back into the hallway and sidestepped, and he crashed past her and half fell down the stairs.

"Since you've gone that far, why not keep going? The air will cool you."

Ronan's fury would have given an older man a stroke. He raced up the stairs, his eyes fixed on Kate; she ran into her room and locked the door—with difficulty, as debris blocked the path. Ronan kicked the door until it shook, but the Victorian carpenters had built well. He kicked it some more, then raced down the stairs and out into the street and ran for a hundred yards.

At a garden wall he stopped, breathing steam.

"The bitch. She's evicting me, she is, I know it." He sank back, still enraged, but with his energy fading.

He stood there for perhaps twenty minutes; people walking past looked at him curiously under the streetlamps. At the far end of the street he could see the light in his room.

An elderly woman said, "Too cold to be out without a coat, young man."

Ronan looked at her savagely. "And I'm staying out."

He meant it.

Ronan walked to the center of the city. Nobody watching would have tried to obstruct him; his head thrust forward, he moved like a force of nature. Once or twice he stopped, to think, to consider a return, but his anger swelled again, and incoherent thought swept in like a wave. At the same time he felt a liberty that elated him, a feeling that anything could happen, that he had no one to whom he must answer. It rose with a glee unlike any previous freedoms of the woods and fields.

Sudden rain lashed down and would have drenched him had he not found a vacant doorway. In the hour and more he was forced to stand there, his mood darkened further, and feelings of revenge began to fester. By the time he next walked on, he had decided he would thereafter deny them his company—Kate, Alison, everyone. At around nine o'clock, another stinging rainburst held him up yet again. And still he felt no cold, heated by his own rage.

When the rain died away, he saw what seemed like the promise of a crowd walking with purpose along Dame Street, and he followed. They led him to Christchurch Cathedral, where people had begun to gather; many drank liquor out of bottles.

"What happens here?" he said to a couple of girls.

"Ah, lissen to him," they giggled to each other.

"The New Year," said a man with a dog. "They'll be ringing the bells, you know, ringing in the new."

"There'll be more than the bells ringin', if you ask me, so there will," said one of the girls, and they wheezed with laughter, holding on to each other.

"Her drawers, that's what'll be wringin' like," said the other by way of explanation, and they could see that Ronan had not the first idea why they were laughing. Which doubled their mirth.

He fastened on them. Their gaudiness caught him on a spike; as exotic as blowfish and coarser than anything he had met in his life, they became a lightning rod for his high and excitable mood.

"I'm Carmel, and this is Yvonne. She's the wild one."

"Listen to you. I am not wild!" Their accents fascinated him, and he had a flash of reflection on how deeply sheltered his life had been.

"She's a Protestant, and I'm a Catholic—I'm a good girl," said Carmel.

"Carmel Dolan, give over, you!"

"Do you drink?" said Ronan.

"We do, and we don't."

"Which? You drink or you don't drink?"

In chorus, they mimicked him, broadening their urban vowels to try and match his accent; "You drink or you don't drink."

Carmel said, "I don't drink much."

Yvonne said, "No. She spills most of it."

"I do not! Hey, d'ja bring any butter with ya?"

"Meaning?"

"All fellas up from the country has butter with them, in their hair and that."

And Carmel said, "Yass, up from the country, isn't that where all the butter comes from. The country?" and to Ronan's bewilderment they heaved with laughter as though they had invented comedy.

More people arrived. The man and his dog had not moved; the dog ate a placid sausage from the man's hand.

"Hey, Rover," said Carmel, eyeing Ronan. "Give us a sausage, willya?"

"Isssn't him you should be askin' for a sausage," said Yvonne, and again they laughed like mad dolls.

"His name isn't Rover, and youse two is a pair of trollops," said the man with the dog.

"We weren't talkin' to youse."

"We were talkin' to him."

"And the dog. We were talkin' to the dog too, weren't we, Yvonne?"

"Hey, mister, is it a dog or a bitch, mister?"

The man said. "Youse are the bitches, a right pair, too."

"Look at youse, with the head on ya," said Carmel.

"Doncha hate oul' fellas?" said Yvonne.

Ronan tried to edge in. "You didn't answer my question."

"Wha' question?"

"Drinks? I don't know. A pub?" he said

"C'mon, so—and bring the butter with ya," and the laughing girls trotted off.

Ronan walked behind them against the tide of the gathering crowds. Under dim streetlights, he followed them to the corner of Francis Street, where they stood for a moment, still giggling. Pied pipers on teetering heels, they led him down the cobblestones. At a lighted door they stopped, looked back at him, then went in. He followed, with mixed feelings of adventure and repulsion; the girls wore seedy clothes and eye makeup black as death; the walls of Ronan's sheltered life had begun to crack.

Inside the pub, two men sat like crows at the bar. On a frayed banquette sat an old woman; she wore a hat that had once been a thrill, her face a map of red blotches. Above her head hung a long mirror hailing Power's Gold Label Whiskey; the silvering on the glass had flecked to gray. A barman, wearing a pea-green suit, edged cream off full pint glasses with a beer mat. His shirt collar curled like heated paper, and his neutral eyes inspected Ronan.

"The dog after the bone, huh?"

Ronan said, "Hallo," looked around, and saw no girls.

"They're in there," said the barman. "Follow your nose."

His gesture pointed Ronan through a doorway half draped by a fake Persian curtain. Inside, like a pair of cheap parakeets, sat Carmel and Yvonne.

"Well indeed an' youse took your time."

"We thought youse had run away."

"Would you girls like a drink?"

"I'll have a rum-and-shudder," said Yvonne.

"That's right, she'll have a rum, and I'll shudder," said Carmel.

"Dickie!" yelled Yvonne. "Bring us your legs!"

The barman appeared; his suit, when seen in full glory, had been worn to a shine; he wore lopsided shoes of mottled gray suede.

"My legs is together, not like some I could mention."

He turned chattily to Ronan. "Now what are youse? A medical? Or—I'd say law, if I have to guess. And I don't have to."

"Jaysus himself, Dickie, if youse aren't goin' to get us a rum—"

"Listen to her taking the Holy Name in vain, and she a Protestant." To Ronan he said, "Youse're well on here. A Protestant'll give youse a ride any time."

The girls whooped. "Dickie, bring him a pint. Anything to knock the starch outta him."

"If youse two want service offa him—"

"We know! Give him a brandy."

Dickie confided in Ronan. "It makes the oul' lad stand up straight, there's some calls brandy 'the hanged man' because of— what you might call 'the erectile effect,' know what I mean, like?"

Carmel said, "Mr. O'Toole."

Yvonne said, "From the Dublin Erection Company." And they both laughed again.

Ronan nodded. "I'm a history student, actually." And it became plain to the others that all the carnal references had passed him by.

"Dickie! She wants vodka, and you never got me the rum."

"History? Aw, Jayz, tough station, history, you don't know who to believe, know what I mean, like? I'm seventy next March, and sure I don't believe my own history."

Ronan sat down, and Dickie vanished, limping.

"C'mere," said Carmel. "She said to me she'd throw someone over for you."

"I did not!" said Yvonne.

"Lissen. Wha's yer name?"

"Ronan."

"Ronan? Nice ring to it, Ronan, we wouldn't be able to stomach it if you were called Percy or something, would we?"

"I want you to stop laughing and talk to me," said Ronan.

The girls looked at him and subsided.

"We're a bit giddy," said Carmel.

"How old are you?" said Ronan.

Carmel said, "Old enough to have sense."

"Youse should never ask a lady her age," said Yvonne. "Very rude. How old are you?"

"Eighteen."

Carmel said, "Oh, he's yours, Yvonne," and they laughed again.

Yvonne wore a white blouse, the ruffled collar stained with makeup. Carmel's teeth protruded, and she wore a red headband.

"Are you working girls?" said Ronan.

"We are notttt!?!" said Carmel. "The cheek of it."

Yvonne said to her, "No, he means—" She whispered something, then said to Ronan, "You mean, do we have jobs like, doncha?"

"What else could I mean?"—at which the girls pealed louder than ever.

The drinks arrived.

"Dickie, he wants to know are we working girls?"

"He's not far wrong"—but Dickie saw that Ronan had no idea what they meant. He leaned and whispered, "Round here, a working girl is a hoor—a tart, know what I mean?"

Ronan blushed bright red.

"It's all right, drink up," said Yvonne and patted him on the knee. "Anyone can make a mistake."

"If it is a mistake," said Dickie.

"Go on, you," said Yvonne. "Go back to your knittin'."

"No, no," said Carmel. "Tell us a story, Dickie."

"Dickie's always telling stories, aren't you, Dickie?"

"Oh?" asked Ronan.

Dickie effaced himself. "Ah, sure don't you hear every sort of a story behind a bar?"

"Real stories—I mean, long stories?"

"Ah, yeah, I mean some that'd go on all night and be resumed the next night. Like a follower-upper, d'you remember, in the pictures? They'd leave you with yer man on the edge of a cliff till next Saturday."

"A serial?" said Ronan.

"The very word. There used to be an old fella came in here was great at it, he'd tell the whole pub a story, and they'd have to come back the next night to hear how it ended. But he was a professional like, he used to go the roads, north and south, telling stories."

Ronan quickened. "Was he very tall, with a long jaw and an old hat?"

"He wasn't, you know, he was a small scutty sort of a lad, with breath that'd take the paint offa the walls, like a man was always eating onions. And he had a lazy eye. But he had great yarns on him."

The girls cooed.

"Tell us one, Dickie."

"C'mon, Dickie."

They sampled the drinks as Dickie searched his memory.

"Well, the one I like, it all came out near here, across the river in Fishamble Street. That was where Handel put on the *Messiah* for the first time. And this fella, this old lad with the lazy eye, he used to call it 'The Story of the Only Man who could Handle Handel.' "

I FORGET WHAT YEAR IT WAS—SIXTEEN-SOMETHING or seventeen-something, it doesn't matter, it was back in them days when tea was tea and water was water, and you had to be careful you didn't make them in the one pot. Anyway, Handel's *Messiah*—first performance thereof as aforementioned—is one of the many things for which Dublin is respectfully famous.

Dublin, of course, was always a great city for the music. The time I'm talking about, there was a man living here called Kelly who was a wine merchant and had a passable voice himself, but his son became a great singer for Mozart over in Vienna in the Imperial Theater and used to play billiards with the same Mozart, who by all accounts was a small little fellow, thin as a rake and blondy-haired and couldn't stand noise at all. That's Mozart for you. But that's neither here nor there.

The Only Man Who Could Handle Handel was a man called Jimmy Hanly—although after this story got out, he said he wanted to be known as James, more respectable, like. And that's part of the story, the fact that his name was Hanly—because when he met Handel, the great composer was carried away with how like his own name Jimmy's was: Handel and Hanly. That's how they got off to a flying start, and if they hadn't, there might never be a *Messiah* at all.

Anyway, Handel was a German gentleman, and he came over here from England, where there was a German king at the time who liked Handel's music. So, because people always wanted to be in the fashion, and the fashion in them days was always what the king liked, anyone who liked Handel was likely to be liked by the king. People can be very foolish.

So: the English people who lived in Dublin and who governed the country from Dublin Castle invited Handel here, hoping to gain the king's approval thereby. To be fair to them, they had a good reason; they wanted Mr. Handel to give concerts for the aid of the prisoners in the jails. That's where Jimmy Hanly comes into the picture—he had a young brother in jail, as had a lot of people in Dublin, because they were very poor and always stealing things, hoping to make a bit of money.

Handel came here of a Thursday, and Jimmy Hanly decides he'll go and see him and ask him to say something about the prisoners before he starts conducting, like. He wanted him to say, "Look here, ladies and gentlemen, this concert is for the aid of the prisoners, but between you and me there's a lot of people in jail that shouldn't be."

Which is what Jimmy thought about his brother, who found an orange in the street that fell off a cart, and was caught with the orange in his possession and thrown into jail without any trial.

There was no chance on this earth of Jimmy Hanly getting to meet Mr. George Handel; it was nearly like him trying to get in and see the other George, the king, in his palace over in London. He tried three or four times to get into the house on one excuse or another—delivering milk or with a message from the tailor or a gift of a special bottle of wine, which he came by lightly of course; he wasn't a man could afford to buy wine. But no go—they always sent him to the tradesman's entrance, where a butler or some lackey took whatever he was carrying and sent him away again.

Then he hung around the street for a while, in the hopes of seeing Mr. Handel walk out for a constitutional stroll, as a great many gentlemen were accustomed to doing. But he never saw him. All he saw was the Dublin streets, all mud and everything like that. You must remember now that times was desperate hard on the plain people of Dublin, that only a handful had any money at all, and they were all English—judges and earls and men who owned land. He'd see the ladies walk out in their wigs and the gentlemen in their brocade coats, and they wore wigs too, all enjoying their stroll. But no Mr. Handel. And Jimmy nearly gave up.

The day he said to himself that he'd abandon his plan—which was breaking his heart, because he loved his little brother and had been responsible for him since their father had a stroke—that was the day things changed. Bad weather came in, huge gales blowing up and down the east coast and wrecking all the ships. Jimmy knew that nobody would be sailing back to England in them kind of conditions, and he says to himself, "I won't give up yet."

Now, inside in the house he was staying in, Mr. Handel was raging over the weather. He didn't want to be stuck in Dublin just because there wasn't a ship on the Irish Sea that'd take him with waves like that. He walked up and he walked down and he walked up again, and he muttered and he spluttered and he muttered again.

"There'sn't a thing I can do, is there?" he said to himself and to everybody who heard him—by all accounts, he had a very loud voice.

Outside in the street, Jimmy Hanly had made friends with one of the maids in the house, a little girl from Stoneybatter called Rose Barry.

"How's Mr. Handel, Rose?"

"He's beside himself. We're all mad from him."

"Mad? Why so because?"

And Rose said, "He's like a bear, so he is, he's walking up and down 'cause he wants to get back to England, and the weather's too bad. And he's in an awful bad temper, and that has everyone real worried."

Jimmy didn't want anyone to say a derogatory word against his friend Handel, whom he hadn't met yet, like, but he already thought of him as a friend—Dublin people are like that.

"Ah," said Jimmy, "we all get that way betimes."

"Yeah," said Rose, "but they're all desperate worried because Mr. Handel, he had a stroke, and they're afraid he'll have another one, and if he does while he's in their house, what'll the king say? I mean—they don't care if he has a stroke and dies on the boat going back to England, so long as he doesn't die on them."

"That's not very nice," said Jimmy. And then he thought for a minute. 'D'you know what, Rose, my father got a stroke and he didn't die of it. And d'you know why he didn't die of it? 'Cause I was there. And I stopped him getting a second stroke."

"Ya did not?" said Rose, not inclined to believe him.

"Go down Henrietta Street and ask anyone, and they'll tell you," said Jimmy. "Ask 'em, did Jimmy Hanly stop his own father dying of a stroke and then stop him from getting a fatal second stroke, and they'll tell you he did. That's the God's honest truth."

Rose was a good girl, and she was well thought of by her employers, who were Mr. Handel's hosts. When she went to work the next day the German gentleman was worse than ever, pacing the place and effing and blinding or whatever they did in them days.

Rose says to her mistress, "Ma'am, a friend of mine, I hope I'm not speaking above my station, ma'am, he told me he kept his father alive after getting a stroke and he stopped him from getting a second stroke."

The woman of the house looked at her as if she was after falling down off of a cloud, and she says to Rose, "How did he do it? For I'd give a lot to know that secret."

And Rose says, "Ma'am, I'll ask him."

When she was knocking off from work that day, Rose met Jimmy Hanly outside on the street.

"Come here to me, your father and the stroke—how did ya do it?"

"Who wants to know?" said Jimmy.

"My lady," said Rose, "'cause she's only demented from Mr. Handel, he's worse every day, and last night he went without his breath for a minute, nearly purple he was."

Jimmy saw his chance. "This isn't something I can tell anyone," he said. "This is something I can only do."

Rose thought about this. "I dunno. Everybody's gone out from him, his temper is so bad. He had a clerk and secretary and a fella to copy his music, and they're all gone, he won't let them near him."

"And what's he doing all day?" said Jimmy.

"He's sitting down moping, or he's walking up and down snarling," said Rose.

"Tell everyone they've only a few days left, in my opinion," said Jimmy, "before his heart bursts with another stroke."

Rose went pale, but she reported Jimmy's words back to her mistress. And the mistress went pale, and she reported to her husband, who said, "Bring that fella in. He can't do worse than the people what's gone before him."

This was a big house with a grand staircase. If there were ten people living there, they had thirty servants; if there were twenty people, they had sixty servants—it was that kind of a place. They paid them that worked there no more than pennies a week and a share of the food, but it was a good station if you didn't mind being a servant. And it was one of the first grand houses in an Irish city that wasn't a castle nor a hut, like. It was built of good strong stone out of a quarry in Kildare, and it had been drawn up by an architect.

Rose brought Jimmy in, and he stood at the foot of the stairs. He stared all around him—at the curtains and the windows and the lovely flagstones on the floors and the chairs with their crimson brocade and the green walls and the mahogany table with the big silver urn full of flowers and the huge logs in a fireplace you could stand up in and the fire sizzling because the heavy rain outside was spitting down the chimney into the flames and the long painting over the mantel showing the man of the house leaning against a tree with a gun crooked over his arm and his two dogs beside him— and this is only the hallway we're talking about.

"What are you looking at?" said a voice, real angry, like.

Jimmy looked around him, and he couldn't see nobody, but he answered all the same, "I'm looking at these gorgeous things."

The voice said, "Are you planning to steal them?"—because Jimmy, being from a poor family, was not in the best of clothes: he was not what you might call a picture of sartorial discrimination.

"Whoever you are, sir," said Jimmy to the voice he couldn't see, but of course he guessed from the thick accent who it might be, "let me tell you that the only thing Jimmy Hanly ever stole was his own father's life. And the person from whom he stole it was Death himself."

The man with the thick voice came out of a room, big face on him.

"What's your name?"

"Hanly," says Jimmy.

"Handel?" says our man, a big stomach on him from eating truffles.

"No, sir," said Jimmy. "You're Handel right enough, I'm Hanly. But we might be related."

Handel looked at Jimmy, and Jimmy looked at Handel. He saw a heavy man with a red nose, a bit like his own father, and a man who was worried about himself. He walked slowly, he blinked a lot, and his left arm dragged a bit; that was another thing Jimmy recognized from seeing the effects of a stroke. And when Handel looked at Jimmy, he saw a tall young fellow in his middle twenties, sort of sandy-haired, with a pair of kind eyes.

"No, we're not related," said Handel, "I'm from Germany and you're not.'

"Ah, sir, sure we're all related under God."

"Leave God out of it," said Handel. "I'm annoyed with him."

"Why has he you annoyed, sir?" said Jimmy, and he took a step closer to the big man. "And what happened to your arm? Aw, would you look at that. You poor man."

Now, the thing is—great people never have anyone to give them sympathy. They get praise, sure, and they get admiration and they get patted on the back and they get the best of everything, pork and fresh herrings and mashed potatoes with cream. But they never get sympathy, because they look so successful and confident that nobody ever thinks they need it. Jimmy Hanly, though, had found out that his father, who worked on the docks and was a hard man with a bad temper, was much easier to manage when he got a bit of soft talk and compassion.

The same turned out to be the case for George Frideric Handel.

He held out his arm to Jimmy like a dog holding up a sore paw, and he said, "I had a stroke." He said it the way a small child would say, "I cut my finger."

Jimmy looked at the arm, and he saw that it wasn't too bad—it was a bit floppy, but the gentleman had some use of it.

"But that's what my father had, sir. He had a stroke."

"Your father?" said Handel. "Whose life you say you stole back from Death?"

"One and the same man," said Jimmy.

"Come in here, sit down beside me and tell me how you did it," said Handel, "for I'm half out of my mind with worry that I'll get another stroke and that it'll finish me. But I seem to be doing everything I can to bring it onto myself."

"Isn't that always the case?" said Jimmy. "We're always trying to cause the one thing we should be trying to stop."

"Let me think about that," said Handel. "That seems to me a very wise statement."

To cut a long story short, they sat on a couch cheek by jowl, and Handel said to Jimmy, "I'd ask you if you'd like a cup of tea, only there's nobody here to make it for us."

"I thought this house was full of people," said Jimmy, "and I know for a fact that my friend Rose works here, for it was her brung me in."

Handel said, "I think I've frightened everybody away."

"A nice man like you, sir?" said Jimmy Hanly. "Ah, no, not at all, there must be some other reason. I'll go find Rose."

"No. Stay here and talk to me," said Handel. "They'll have to come out of their hidey-holes eventually."

By the time Handel's host and hostess appeared, the great man had been taken over by Jimmy Hanly's charm. Now that sounds as if it was all very shallow—but it wasn't. In fact what happened was very important; Jimmy made Handel relax, made him shake off his bad humor, and made him feel better—so much that Handel said to his host and hostess that he wished Jimmy to start the very next morning as his clerk for as long as he'd be staying in Dublin.

They agreed but they tipped the wink to Rose to tell Jimmy come along good and early so's they could put a decent suit of clothes on him.

Nine o'clock next morning, after being an hour with the valets of the house, Jimmy turns up like a new pin in Mr. Handel's chamber. The German gentleman is sitting up in bed, and he's humming like a rail that's expecting a train.

"Good morning, sir," said Jimmy. "How are you this morning?"

"Is this my cousin?" jokes Handel. "I'm glad to see that you know a good suit of clothes when you see one."

"Now, sir," said Jimmy, "it's still raining out there, and the wind is howling along the street like a pair of bellows you'd use to blow the fire hot. So you can't sail today either. And into the bargain, on my way here I met a farmer from north county Dublin who's very good at forecasting the weather, and he says 'tis going to be bad for at least another week because the birds are flying upside down."

Well: instead of fuming like a giant, Handel started to laugh, and he said to Jimmy, "Flying upside down. That's very funny. You're the only one around here understands anything. The others only give me good news. If there is any. They do it to please me, but the thing about writing music is—you have to tell people the bad news as well as the good."

"Oh? Did I walk in on you, sir, while you're writing music? Because if so, I'm very sorry of the interruption."

"Ahhhh," said Mr Handel. "If only you had."

"But," says Jimmy, "isn't that your job, like? Writing music?"

"I'm not able to do it anymore," said Handel. "If I could, I wouldn't mind the bad weather so much."

"And why aren't you able to do it?" says Jimmy.

"I don't know. I've nothing to write about."

"What are you talking about? Haven't you the whole wide world to write about?"

Handel looked at him from under his heavy eyelids. "Cousin Jimmy," says he. "Isn't that why I'm annoyed with God? He won't let me do it."

Jimmy Hanly looked at Handel, and Handel looked at Jimmy Hanly, two paragons each in his own way. And Jimmy said, "Mr. Handel, I know how to fix that."

"If you do," said Handel, "I'll make sure that the next piece of music I write will be performed first here in your own native Dublin."

Well: there's nothing like pride in his own city to get a Dublin-man's faculties working. Jimmy Hanly would have winked at the big German gentleman in the bed if it wasn't disrespectful.

"My dear sir," said Jimmy, taking the liberty of sitting down on the blanket near Handel, "when a man has a problem, he should always go to what's causing the problem to find the solution."

"Them are good words and wise," said Handel, "but what do youse mean like?"

"I mean, you're saying God's not listening to you—so I say, Make him listen."

"My prayers have a broken wing these days," said Handel, "kinda like myself," and again he holds up the feeble arm.

"This is what you do," said Jimmy—and this is where he made history. "Stop praying to God and start writing about him."

"How would I do that?" says Handel.

"Suppose," says Jimmy, "suppose you wanted to tell me a story. Wouldn't it be about somebody?"

"It'd hardly be about a pool of water," said Handel.

"Or a pot of milk."

"Fair enough. It'd be about someone or his family."

"What are you driving at?" said Handel.

"I'm saying—you're having a bit of difficulty getting God's attention. So—why don't you write about his family?"

Handel looked at Jimmy. "Are you serious?"

"Yeah. Easy enough too. He had only the one son and no daughters. And the family story is well known."

Handel stroked his chin, and he looked out the window, and he stroked his chin again, and then he climbed out of the bed and he said to Jimmy, "Wherever I am during the next few days and weeks, make sure you're nearby."

He started work that very morning.

•   •   •

For three weeks George Frideric Handel worked like a nailer, a flying slave. He rose at cockcrow, he had Jimmy sharpen all his quill pens and line up piles of music paper on the floor beside his desk, and he wrote like a man with an engine. And while he wrote his nature changed—people couldn't believe the difference in him. He hummed, he sang, he laughed, and several times a day he'd say to Jimmy Hanly, "Listen to this, cousin." He'd hum a few passages, and he'd say, "Isn't that sublime?"

And Jimmy would reply, "Only sublime, sir."

Once or twice, Jimmy would put in his oar, and Handel would listen, nod, and say, "Yes, that's a good idea," and he'd scribble faster. For instance, Jimmy said, "Sir, begging your pardon like—that word there, 'disliked'—I think you'll find it isn't the same word as the scripture has."

"The scripture says 'despised,' but is it going to be a big enough word, strong enough I mean?"

"You mean—it's a bit puny, like?"

Jimmy, now, was perched on a couch, or sitting on the floor near Mr. Handel, peeling an apple or something like that.

"What about 'detested'?"

"H'm?" said Jimmy and wrinkled his nose.

"Loathed? Abhorred? Abominated?"

"He was abominated," said Jimmy, testing the word on his tongue. "Try a few more."

"Hated? Contumeliated?"

"We're getting there," said Jimmy Hanly. "D'you know—I think the first word's the best."

"I'll do that," said Handel. "I'll stick to 'Despised.' "

"You can always drag out the note," said Jimmy, "so you're doing grand."

Three weeks and a day Handel sat in that house, writing like a trooper. From time to time Jimmy'd make him stop, and he'd lead Mr. Handel over to the nearest wall of the room, and he'd say to him, "Now. Put your poor hand on the wall there and make your fingers crawl up and down." And every day he'd make Mr. Handel's hand climb a little higher—because all the time he was getting the gentleman to exercise the arm that had the stroke in it. Jimmy did it with his own father, that's how he knew. And the German gentleman could see that his hand was getting stronger and stronger, and consequently, to the astonishment of precisely nobody in particular, he composed his music better and better.

Halfway through the composition he said to Jimmy Hanly, "We're going to need a big choir."

"That's no bother," said Jimmy. "There's a grand stack of singers over at Saint Patrick's Cathedral."

And so, as the Bible says, it came to pass—a gala night, one of the most famous nights ever in Dublin, don't we talk about it still, the first night of *The Messiah*. The place was packed; everyone turned up in their finery, and so did Jimmy. Handel had him seated in a place of honor, where he could see him, and Jimmy nodded every time his German friend did a piece of extra grand conducting. And I can tell you for a fact—he gave an extra special smile when he saw Handel manage to use the bad arm if he wanted to add a bit of spice to the proceedings.

Everyone was on their best behavior. The choir of Saint Patrick's sang their hearts out like birds in a garden. There was a girl over from England, a married lady, like, an actress, and her name was Mrs. Cibber. She sang what Jimmy came to think of as the bit he wrote, which Handel added a syllable onto and turned it into "He was despis-ed."

Now being an actress in those days was only one step up from what we were calling a "working girl," no respect at all, like. But this Mrs. Cibber, she sang this like an angel, and when she was after singing her heart out, over there in the New Music Hall in Fishamble Street, Dr. Delany, who was a dean or a canon or something high up over in the cathedral, jumped to his feet and shouted out, "Madam, for this thy sins are forgiven thee."

The night was a great success altogether, and the people in the know, by which I mean the German gentleman's host and hostess, they said it couldn't have happened if Jimmy Hanly hadn't handled Handel.

And Mr. Handel himself—he said from the podium where he was conducting, "This oratorio is for the relief of prisoners in Dublin's jails so's they can have decent food. And I have to say to you—we'd need a lot less money for relief if we weren't packing the jails with youngsters who are only accused of stealing an apple or an orange. What young fella wouldn't do that if he got the chance?"

Jimmy's brother was released out of the jail the next day.

Handel, of course, went back to England and spent the rest of his life conducting his *Messiah* here, there, and everywhere. And not only that; his success with it lifted his spirits, that and the fact that he wrote it in three weeks flat. And didn't he get back nearly all the power of his left arm?

Jimmy was given a job as the butler in the house where Handel stayed, and for the rest of his life they gave James Hanly credit for helping Handel to write *The Messiah,* and as he walked the streets of Dublin, as slow and dignified as any respectable man, he was always pointed out to people as "the Only Man Who Could Handle Handel."

Ronan looked at Carmel and Yvonne to gauge their reactions; they had let their mouths fall open.

"Dickie, is that story true?" said Carmel.

"Is it?" said Yvonne.

"Ach, what's true—'course 'tis true, everything I say is true."

Dickie winked at Ronan and went back to the bar outside.

Carmel called after him, "Bring us the same again."

She turned and looked Ronan up and down; Yvonne looked elsewhere; Ronan looked at Yvonne.

"Where's your tongue?" said Carmel.

"Leave him alone," said Yvonne.

"Ah'm, where do you girls work?"

"We're machinists. Doyle's Fabrics. We call it Purgatory. We'll go straight to heaven, but she won't, she's a Protestant, they go to hell," said Carmel, as though discussing plain facts.

All three finished their drinks. Dickie reappeared with fresh supplies.

"So what about my story? Didja like it?"

"Very nice," said Ronan. "Very enjoyable."

"Very nice, very enjoyable," said Carmel.

"Stop being bitter, you," said Yvonne.

Dickie left; silence; Ronan finished his drink.

"Would you like another?"

"I'd like another of anything," said Carmel.

Yvonne nodded; "Same goes for me. I'm a bit like that, a copy cat I am." Ronan rose and walked through the curtain.

Said Dickie. "The other half?"

Ronan looked blank.

"Like—d'you want another pint?"

"Yes, please. And—" he pointed.

"Them two? Hah! Their night's going well—they found their soft touch."

As Dickie prepared the drinks, Ronan looked around the pub to try and orient himself. The lone, elderly woman stared ahead, her glass of sherry half empty. One of the two crows stabbed the other on the arm to make a point. Ronan gathered the full glasses from Dickie and brought them back to the inner room. He sat down and drank his pint glass dry.

"Look at ya!" said Carmel. "You must have a giant's thirst."

Yvonne stroked his arm and said, "Go on, get yourself another, it'll do youse good."

Ronan rose again and waved at Dickie from the curtain, who put down the flashlight he was repairing.

"Jaysus, is it a drain you've in there?"

Ronan waited the long minutes and then lurched forward to get the drink.

"How much do I owe you?"

Dickie said, "Well, that's the shortest slate I ever known. Not since jockeys used to come in here on their way home from the races. Jockeys. Short. D'ja get it?"

Ronan paid him, took the big glass, and rushed into the back room, drinking as he walked. He skidded to a halt beside the girls and sat down, gulping the black drink.

"Who's following you?" said Carmel.

He drained the glass and said, "Yvonne, may I ask you a great favor?"

"For me to grant," she laughed, mock-haughty.

"Would you walk out on the street with me?"

"Oh, Jaysus!" said Carmel. "Watch yourself."

Taking her arm, Ronan almost ran Yvonne through the bar and out on the street.

"Over here, stand over here." He strode to a streetlamp and stood, tall and nervy, in the circle of poor light; rain slanted in.

"Here, here!"—so urgent.

She walked over and stood in front of him; her head scarcely came to his chest.

"Close your eyes."

He bent and kissed her on the mouth, and Yvonne pulled back.

"Hey! Watcha!"

"This is my first kiss."

"It is?" She softened. "And what makes you think you can practice on me?"

"You have a nice face."

"You could call me beautiful, and it wouldn't hurt neither of us."

"Yes, you are beautiful."

He bent down again; she put her arms around his neck and allowed him to kiss her.

"That's not kissin'," she said when she drew away, "that's eatin'."

"I didn't know—" and he held out his hands in deep embarrassment.

"S'all right!" she said.

But Ronan turned on his heel, walked, and then ran.

Behind Yvonne, Carmel materialized at the door.

"Whassup?"

"He's very nice," said Yvonne, looking down the dim street and listening to the fading, running steps. They shrugged and headed in the opposite direction, with fading giggles and clicking heels.

Minutes later, Ronan came back and crashed into the pub. The woman with the hat looked straight ahead, the two crowlike men still stabbed the air with fingers—and Ronan said to Dickie, "May I borrow your coat?"

He never slept that night. Nor did he go home to the apartment and Kate. Wrapped in a coat rigid with stains and age, he let no timeline enter his thinking—it could take ten days, ten years, before he ever returned to the places he called home. If ever.

Mad in his mind, feeling thrilled and unclean, he walked some street somewhere as the bells of the New Year rang. Now and then his journey seemed haunted, as though stark white faces peeped from doors. The night had no reality, nothing but distant sound; sometimes a car whisked by; faraway cheering came in on the wind, and then, at last and alone, he heard the brisk sound of his own footsteps.

His mouth felt the two kisses, and his lips still tingled inside. Sour tastes lit the back of his throat, and the liquor's vague headache thumped. A yellow factory neon shone through the night; Lemons Pure Sweets. The street sign read "Drumcondra Road." A man leaned on a bridge and flicked a cigarette butt in a sparked arc.

"Excuse me."

"Yeah, howya?"

"If someone sent you to Boyne Water—where would that be?"

"No, head, this is the Tolka."

"The what?"

"The Tolka River. The lifestream of north Dublin, pure and distilled."

Ronan looked over the parapet at the narrow dark trickle below.

"But—Boyne Water, d'you think that's the same as the Boyne River?"

"Oh, yeah, that'd be up in Meath, head. The Boyne's up that way. This is the Tolka."

"And that's the same as—Boyne Water?"

"The Tolka? No, head, the Boyne's not the same as the Tolka."

"I mean, the river Boyne."

"The battle, like? Havta be, wouldn't it?"

The man began to swing his arms; he marked time and sang, " 'On the green grassy slopes of the Boyne. Where King Billy and his men fought and won.' Are you by any chance familiar with the music of the late, great Glenn Miller and his timeless melody 'American Patrol'? Same tune, head. 'Where we fought for the glorious religion. On the green grassy slopes of the Boyne.' "

"How far away is it?"

The man considered. "Two hundred and seventy years. In fact, you just missed a most coincidental conjunction—sixteen-ninety to nineteen-sixty, how's about that for arresting numerology?"

Ronan wanted to say, "What on earth are you talking about?" but the man could not be interrupted; "Up the long ladder and down the short rope, to Hell with King Billy, and God bless the Pope." And he marched off, his spine as straight as a martinet.

The borrowed coat had lost its warmth years since, and Ronan began to shake with cold. Now the night's heaviest and coldest air fell on him. No cars, little sound; a passing bicycle swished its tires on the wet streets, and with it came the jolt—he realized that he had no money, nothing but someone else's coat, some half-wet clothes, strong shoes, and a growing desperation. His anger came flooding back.

In the shelter of his childhood and adolescence, Ronan had never been taught how to recover from loss of control. As an only child he had grasped how his tantrums alarmed the adults, who had appeased him to prevent such outbursts and therefore had never taught him how to recover from them; no cures had been tried because none had been needed. Consequently he had no idea how long it would—or should—take him to cool down, and no measure of how dangerous an angry state could be.

The world teaches swiftly. Walking toward him, talking and laughing, came three boys spread across the available space. Ronan marched straight at them and never yielded—he barged through them, jolting one.

"Hey!" said the jolted one.

"Hey yourself," said Ronan over his shoulder, striding on as though in seven-league boots.

Next he felt a fist on the back of his head, turned, and got another in the face. Then a harder punch, as though the hand held a rock, landed on the side of his head, and he reeled back. Two of the three attacked, while the third looked on and laughed. A boot kicked his hip; an open hand slapped his face.

"Stop that, stop! You're hurting me!" Until that moment he had never been struck in his life. They pounded him again; he had no self-defense of any kind; they grabbed his hair, shook him like a rat, pulled his nose, and, final indignity, kicked his behind so hard that he lurched forward. Then they all laughed; Ronan, turning away from them, began to cry.

Within a hundred yards, his tears halted, gave way to anger again—but that dissolved, and he felt nothing but soreness, inside and out. Shock first, then shame, set in. He looked behind him cautiously; the three assailants had forgotten about him and were far away, although he could still hear them laughing. Now he realized fully his state—that his head hurt, that his face was probably bruised, that the coat he wore would damn him in the eyes of any reasonable human, and that, other than not returning to Kate, he had no idea what to do. With no precedent of any kind, no preparation for such circumstances, he walked faster to keep himself warm.

Kate recovered quickly from Ronan's tantrum and made as many repairs as she could to his chaos—ink stains, shards, debris. Then she took what she always considered a sensible step—a long bathtub soak. She determined that if she went to bed, she would avoid further confrontation; by eight o'clock, still nervous of his imminent return, she locked her bedroom door and fell asleep.

Two hours later she woke up and listened carefully. No sound. She checked the time, she surveyed the driving rain outside, she felt the cold. And she began to worry.

At half past ten she telephoned David Mansfield. He arrived within half an hour and heard the story.

"I'm not surprised. He needed to react. His father's death, new at college, competitive peers, maybe—all of that. And now being squeezed in the nest, so to speak."

"I know, Father."

"And he—still doesn't know?"

"About me? Oh, no, Father. How can we tell him now? If this is what his reactions are like—my goodness, I'd be afraid to think what he might do."

"Practical steps are life's cures. Where should I go looking for him? If you think hard, you'll know where he's gone."

In the small hours of New Year's Day, 1961, the roads of Ireland were empty and black. After three in the morning, no transport of any kind passed Ronan by; not another human did he see, other than some late revelers crossing their neighbor's fence to their own home with many echoing laughs.

No lights in houses; no animals in the fields; the old year had truly died, and the new one not yet come alive.

He walked faster and then slower, then faster again. His tumult waxed and waned; he tried to quell his disturbed thoughts by remembering dates of battles, names of kings, significant laws. Nothing worked; anger still dominated, plus, now, a pitying voice that began to list injustices. Dad shouldn't have died. They should have told me about the illness—they're always keeping secrets from me, they oughtn't. Bartlett Ryle's mark was unfair, he shouldn't have done that. Should; shouldn't; ought; oughtn't—the enemies of contentment.

At dawn, Ronan swung his arms in countryside brightening under a red sky. Deep in self-pity, he became aware of a car drawing up behind him and keeping pace. It stopped alongside, and the passenger door swung open.

"Ronan?"

The voice! And yes, the priest's collar.

"Dear boy. Have you ever seen such beautiful light? Though I fear that red sky. Rain, rain, go to Spain."

Without a word Ronan climbed in. The priest reached across with a handshake.

"Happy New Year." He looked more saintly than ever, the eyes calm as a cat's. "Did you ring in the new?"

Ronan said nothing. The priest looked in his mirrors, wheeled out onto the road, and began a soft patter.

"Until I came to Dublin, I always tried to be asleep before midnight on New Year's Eve—it's a melancholy night." The car interior's warmth began to reach Ronan. "But then I discovered the foghorns in Dublin Bay, and d'you know—last night, I remembered a fragment of a poem I wrote years ago. 'The foghorns are booming down in the bay and I want to go to sea, And sail through those mists that are long, long twilights, And hope that my soul will be'—" The priest settled the car's speed and sat back. "And either I forget the rest, or I never wrote beyond that point. By the way, I received your very courteous thank-you note for lunch—now how have you been?"

"They never told me my father was dying—and they should have, shouldn't they?"

The priest looked straight ahead, considering his answer.

"He was so dear to you. So dear. As you were to him. Goodness, what a blow to you. I've been thinking that since our lunch."

"They ought to have told me?"

"I'm careful, Ronan, about 'should' and 'ought'—people make errors. Often for very good reasons—perhaps to save us pain. We're all very human."

"It gave me no chance to talk to him. And he was my father, not anyone else's."

David Mansfield tapped his fingers on the steering wheel.

Ronan said, "I would have said all kinds of things to him."

"How old was he? Forty-eight, wasn't he?"

"Father, did you come looking for me? Were you talking to Kate?"

"D'you remember our friend, Spenser? 'Sleep after toil, port after stormy seas, Ease after war, death after life does greatly ease.' Nineteen-twelve, he must have been born, I'm nineteenth-oh-seven. But forty-eight's too young."

"Father, did you come looking for me? Kate knew I had to come up here."

The priest said, "Let's not discuss that until later this morning."

"I don't want to go back!"

"Understood. It's all right." The priest drove on, braking hard at every turn, a juddering driver who stared at the road as intently as if expecting to meet an army.

Ronan waited for questions—but they never came; nor did the comments on his disheveled clothing or the stale beer breath or his unshaven jaws or the bruises he felt certain had come up around his eyes. Instead—

"Here's a good question, Ronan. What would you say is the one gift your father gave you?"

The car stopped on a junction as the priest looked at the sign-posts. Ronan opened the door.

"Father, I'm getting out here. I don't mean any bad manners—"

"No, of course, of course." The priest, yet again, seemed unsurprised. "Young men have things to do. But won't you get wet? It's going to rain hard. Look—there's an umbrella in the back, priests always have large umbrellas."

Ronan wanted to refuse, but Father Mansfield insisted. Just as he was about to close the door, Ronan asked, "Father—did you know you were going to meet me this morning?"

The priest smiled enigmatically, as only a Jesuit can. "Perhaps, dear boy, yours is 'the face one would meet in every place,' eh? Make sure you keep in touch. Bless you."

And he drove away, leaving the tall young man holding a black umbrella with its huge bell above his head on an empty country road beneath an overcast sky.

Ronan had two options. One signpost led north to Balbriggan, and one west to Slane. He dithered—and then the decision was made for him. Across the road he saw a white house in need of paint; an ancient harvester blocked the yard; two old cars slouched near a barn, their wheels long gone. The nameplate on the gatepost said in white plastic letters, "Boyne Water."

Though it was only half past eight in the morning, he had no hesitation in knocking; the door opened immediately.

"Tom isn't here," said a blond young woman. "He's over at Joe Cooney's, I think they've an early lamb."

Ronan lowered the umbrella. "I was told to come to a place called Boyne Water, and—"

"Yeah. I'm Marian Geraghty, come in. D'you know Joe Cooney?"
Ronan had to concede ignorance.

"Who wants Tom, anyway? I never heard him say he was expecting anyone."

"Actually, I'm looking for an old gentleman."

"Oh, are you the lad?" Light dawned in Marian Geraghty's face. "Ahh, I see. The man with the stories. I heard Tom saying the old man was hoping to meet someone, would that have been you?"

"Is he still in the district?"

"Well, he's around somewhere, he's here three or four days now, I think he's staying over in Slane. Anyone there'll know."

In the kitchen a child lurched across the floor, grinning and wagging a toy.

"That's Gerard, he's called after Saint Gerard Majella, the patron saint of birth; if he was a girl we'd have called him Majella, but you can't do that to a boy, they'd laugh at him in school."

"Did he say where he was going next?"

"He did." Ronan's heart leaped. "He said he didn't know where he was going." Ronan's heart sank. "Are you sure you won't wait for Tom, 'cause he'll only be a while. Mind you, he broke his watch, it fell off his wrist, so he could be here any time."

Ronan thanked her—but as he left, she called from the door, "Come back, come back, there's something here you're supposed to read."

She foraged in a table drawer, hauling out coils of string, some clothespins, old letters.

"This is it. We give it to everyone who asks about the Battle—the old man wrote it out for us a few years ago because we were sick and tired of being asked things we didn't know about. But he said specially that you should get it, and he said you're to walk the riverbank and read it. Oh, and everybody brings it back to us, we'd be lost without it."

Ronan took the stapled pages of handwriting; the rain began to die, and weak sun filled the fields. He read as he walked.

M Y GOOD FRIENDS, TOM AND MARIAN GER-
aghty, live in a house whose name commemorates a
very significant event. Not a week goes by without
someone stopping at their door and asking questions about the Battle of the Boyne. One night in this house, I told them the story of
the famous day, and then they asked me to write it down so that
they wouldn't have to answer any more questions. I have never
written a guidebook, I am only a storyteller, so in advance I'll ask
the pardon of everyone who reads this, because I'm going to tell it
the way I know, in the form of a tale.

The Battle of the Boyne matters more to twentieth-century Ireland than any battle before or since. It took place along the banks
of the river, the Boyne Water, on July 1, 1690, and they say the day
has been commemorated by 365 ballads, one for every day of a
year's singing.

As battles go, it didn't differ greatly from what happened in the
warfare of the time—cannon, musketry, bayonets, and cavalry
charges. The outcome, however, was more dramatic than anything
that happened on the day. And that's saying a lot, since it was a day
of great and lively incident.

Two armies fought here. One was led by a forty-year-old Protestant
Dutchman, William of Orange, who had become King William the
Third of England in the previous year. His foe was the man he had put
off the English throne, James the Second, the Catholic-convert son of
King Charles the First, the man who was executed by our great and
good friend Oliver Cromwell. I say "great and good friend" with my
tongue in my cheek, because whosomever the same Mr. Cromwell
was a friend to, it wasn't the Irish. But that's for another night.

What happened just before the Boyne was this: The English Protestants were furious at James's conversion, and they knew the Dutch had steadfast Protestant faith. So they invited William in, an invitation to which the same man responded with an alacrity that many Englishmen thought unseemly. James ran away to France, an old foe of England's, where he hoped to gather an army.

And indeed he did, though not much of one—a few thousand soldiers—and he landed with it in Ireland on Tuesday, March 12, 1689. They sailed into Kinsale, and all of Catholic Ireland thought James had come to liberate them. As did James.

At the other end of the island, a year and a quarter later, Saturday, June 14, 1690, William of Orange sailed into Belfast leading fifteen thousand troops thought by many to be the best in Europe. They had fought on the continent; they were well disciplined, well equipped, and well fed.

During his Irish stay, James had been receiving much hospitality and enjoying hearty acceptance in such great houses as the Irish Catholics had—and he even scored a few military successes, nothing to write home about. But his jaw dropped a bit when he heard that William, the man he had run away from, was coming to look for him. James tried to raise as many extra men as he could from landowners and the like, but the Irish weren't nearly as trained as William's men; many of them were no better than lads with pitchforks, and James's officers only came across one or two who could handle a musket.

William himself stayed in the north because he was recruiting more men in and around Belfast. And to make certain of success, he sent overseas for even more regiments. When they arrived and he felt his army good and ready, he launched a few local attacks against leaders sympathetic to James. It'll come as no surprise to you to learn that he won every fight. Time now, he said to himself, to go after James.

So in the month of July, King William of Orange, confident, ready, and spruce as starch, set off on his march south; he had mustered an army of more than 35,000 men, all experienced in soldiery across England and Europe. By comparison, James had a puny spirit and an army to match it; he had fewer than 25,000 men, and of them no more than 5,000 had any military training or discipline or experience of battle. With nothing like the same verve or chirpiness, he began to journey north.

I often wish I had been a man working in the fields in the months of May, June, and July 1690. If I had been anywhere in the counties of Down or Louth, some miles in from the coast, I'd have heard a noise in the distance, and I would not have known what it was—a great rumbling noise, steady and persistent and getting louder. Suppose I was in a hill field; I'd have run up to the crest of the hill and looked north, the direction from which the noise was coming. What would I have seen? First, a cloud of dust, off in the distance; and just ahead of the dust, three men riding prancing horses. They were not galloping—they were reined back, three fine horses, held under control by their riders the way you see in a parade ring.

Next comes a small, gleaming parcel of men, nine of them riding in a tight formation, three abreast. My eye goes to the middle man in the second row—what a figure! He sits his horse with the ease of a jockey—and it's a big horse for a heavy man. A white diagonal sash goes across his body, and the buttons on his blue coat catch the sunlight. He wears a tricorne hat, beneath which I can see the curls of a white wig.

No prizes for guessing who this is—William of Orange, the dour Hollander whose greatest passion in life was winning battles through excellent military strategy. The men immediately nearest to him are his generals, whom he respects mightily because they are among the most brilliant officers in Europe.

Next comes a wonderful troop—King Billy's cavalry, a hand-picked army in itself, thousands of mounted soldiers. Each horse has been polished to a shine, each cavalryman as correct as a bridegroom, and they keep perfect and respectful time with the pace their king has set.

Behind them, also coming through the dust, onto harder, open ground where I can begin to see them, march steady lines of troops in bright red coats. Six abreast, they travel fast, officers on the flanks barking orders. And behind them rolls a tremendous array of field guns on wagons, and that's where the rumbling noise is coming from—the big wheels lurch and lumber on the uneven ground, and sweating gunners half-run, half-march at the heads of the horses drawing these cannon.

Last of all there are lines and lines and lines of mule-drawn wagons carrying food and munitions, supported by the people who, according to some generals, matter most in any force—the cooks and the other kitchen staff, who had it drummed into them that a fed soldier is a good soldier. It was Napoleon Bonaparte who said that an army marches on its stomach.

Now: suppose that I, the workman in the fields, saw that remarkable sight around twelve noon. I'd have done little work that day—because it would have taken the English army about four hours to pass me by. And I'd have said to myself, I sure wouldn't like to be fighting on the other side.

Change the picture now; instead of a field on the east coast, I'm south of Dublin, where I see the Irish army of King James on its way to the Boyne Valley. This is a totally different sight, close enough to a rag, tag, and bobtail.

To begin with, the cloud of dust is not as huge, because not only is the army smaller, it has far fewer pieces of artillery. And the cannon don't look nearly so polished and ready as the guns of King Billy. In fact the whole army looks much less snappy. Yes, there are cavalrymen, and yes, there is a quick-marching infantry, but there are also undisciplined troops at the back, and they're singing, some of them, and there are pipers playing, and altogether they seem more relaxed. I think to myself, an army has no business looking that easy—and it doesn't look anything like a match for the war machine headed by the Dutchman.

Came the day when the forces lined up to face each other on opposite banks of the river; it was the thirtieth of June. Some say that James chose the Boyne as a kind of symbolic battleground, because it lies roughly halfway down the east coast of Ireland, and if you draw a line directly west to the coast, the island will be bisected. As we all know, it has since become a symbolic border between the southern and the northern Irish, even though the actual border as we know it today doesn't begin for another forty or fifty miles north.

In the middle of the afternoon, as the soldiers were making their preparations—in full view of each other—something happened that might have changed the course of Ireland's history. King Billy rode the last leg of his journey down from Belfast and said to his officers, "We'll go and have a look at what the other side is like."

The Williamite generals didn't relish the sound of this at all, but if their chief wanted to survey the enemy lines, they thought they'd better go with him. William rode right up close to the river and sat on his horse, looking across at James's camp on the southern bank. I wonder if he was surprised at how narrow the river is—along there, not far east of the hill of Newgrange, the widest it gets is about thirty yards.

That's too close for comfort, especially if your guns are big—and one of James's Irish officers saw the English king. He gave an order to his gunners to open fire, and the cannon must already have been loaded, because William and his officers didn't have time to get out of the way. The first few cannonballs that whistled across the river killed a handful of English soldiers in front of William. Then the king himself took a six-pound cannonball on the right shoulder. It tore a hole in his coat, ripped into his linen undershirt, scraped the flesh under his arm, and traveled on. As it came down from its arc, it actually broke the butt of a pistol in the holster of an officer riding behind the king.

Now, had that cannonball been six inches to the right, you can only imagine what would have followed. The Irish side, though—they thought they had pulled off a miracle. James's officers were so certain that they had killed their enemy that the French among them sent a dispatch to Paris, where the news set the city on fire with excitement. But alas, those chickens never hatched.

The incident became so famous that, for weeks after the battle, local people, out from the town of Drogheda, visited the spot where it happened. To this day the place where William of Orange received his flesh wound is still known—King William's Glen.

Next day, the first of July, brought the battle proper to a head. In the artillery divisions, King Billy and the English brandished five times the strength of King James and the Irish. And as if that weren't bad enough, his early moves, it was said afterward, were like those of a chess player—he and his generals had everything mapped out in advance.

First of all he set out to secure the river. He sent a large force upstream, past Oldbridge, which only had a house or two in those days—it's a little bigger now. When they reached the ford at Slane, they had orders to cross the river and outflank King James's armies; William gave them about an hour and a half to get to this position. Then he tilted full into battle at Oldbridge itself; he rode up there from King William's Glen.

It was still morning. In the beginning nothing much took place at Oldbridge, just some random shots, mostly from the Jacobites— that's James's side; the Williamites were awaiting dispatches from the forces they had sent up to Slane. By the way, the dispatch riders who brought back such news were the finest, bravest riders in any army. Those boys thought nothing of jumping rocks and ditches and hedges at breakneck speed.

But even while King Billy was waiting for the good word, the fighting broke out. Not surprisingly, it happened most fiercely on the shallow river crossings.

Fierce fighting it was, too. The Williamites, with their green sprigs and leaves in their hats, were much more numerous than the Irish, who wore the white cockades of France. The reason for the cockades was to stop gunners and musketeers killing their own men when firing from behind. I'm afraid it didn't work that well on James's side—many Irish soldiers were killed by musket balls and cannonballs from their army's guns.

James's Irish and French soldiers fought like tigers—in the water, either standing or on horseback. Wave after wave of William's soldiers poured down off the northern bank into the river, and the Irish lads beat them back with every weapon they could lay their hands on. They shot, they stabbed, they hit them with their fists, they stabbed them with hayforks, they wrestled them into the stream.

By noon, all along the Boyne, on a battlefront that must have been almost a mile long, the fighting had grown intense, and there were bodies in the water and blood coloring the stream. Most of the conflict seemed to consist of musket fire, and here the Dutchman again had an advantage. His soldiers carried a new kind of gun, the flintlock, which was capable of being reloaded much faster than the older matchlock on the Irish side.

But the Irish gave as good as they got, especially in any hand-to-hand fighting, and at certain moments in the day, the tide of battle could have swung easily in their favor. Again and again they ran or rode into the waters of the river and forced their enemies back onto the bank from which they had just recently attacked.

King William, though, had the resources to stretch the Irish lines thin. James's generals had not prepared sufficiently; they simply didn't anticipate every eventuality, which is what constitutes good planning. King Billy spread his troops wider and wider, up- and downstream, until the Irish lines began to thin out and eventually disappear. And William also had the leadership quality; he himself set an example by leading a detachment into the water at Drybridge. Everybody who ever told the story of the Battle of the Boyne, every soldier who ever survived it, made two famous observations. They said it was as fierce a combat as was ever fought—and secondly they said no one ever saw a leader as recklessly brave as King Billy himself.

James, I'm afraid, didn't earn the same praise. While William did what all great leaders do—he led from the front—James spent the day hidden in a small church on the hill of Donore. "Praying for a great victory," he said afterward, when he should have been out there fighting for it. And if he had been there—who knows? The

Irish were outgunned and outnumbered, but the show of fighting they put up might easily have tipped the balance in their favor if they had only had a leader who inspired them. After all, Julius Caesar used to put on his purple emperor's robe and make sure he was seen riding among his men in the thick of the fight, urging them on. Praising them. Ordering them. Leading them.

At three o'clock, King Billy began to apply a slow coup de grace. He brought up his main force of artillery, over fifty field guns and twenty mortars, to the hill looking over at Oldbridge on the southern side. William raised his arm; the gunners raised their priming rods. The king dropped his arm; the gunners lit their fuses and set off the decisive barrage. They pounded the Irish lines, and all men of common sense, military or no, will soon understand that such barrages weaken any army; a force that cannot compare can rarely withstand. Under cover of these relentless salvoes, the Williamites now began to cross the Boyne Water successfully, and inch by inch, foot by foot, they forced the Irish ranks to fall back.

Up along the river, the expeditionary force that William had sent to outflank James was scoring a big success, and so the Irish line was first stretched, soon weakened, and finally pierced.

By early evening, everyone knew the outcome. King William the Third, William of Orange, King Billy, representing the Protestant forces of England, had outmastered King James, who represented the Catholic tradition in England and Ireland. James fled to Dublin; local skirmishing continued into the evening and night and even the following day. To the victor the spoils; the Williamite forces showed little mercy to any Irish soldier they found hiding in a wood or bathing his wounds by a stream.

As for the longer outcome—the world knows that Protestantism, already surging, became politically dominant in Ireland after that day. And each year the Orangemen in the north of Ireland celebrate the Battle of the Boyne with triumphal marches in the month of July.

The rain came in again, confirming the morning's red sky; Ronan had to tuck the papers away quickly. He peered out from under the umbrella and wondered whether he dared walk the battlefield in such weather. But he was already standing in the fields on the northern side. Braving the rain, he trudged through the wet grass until he came to King William's Glen. From there he looked across the river to imagine where the almost lucky gunner had been when he fired the six-pound cannonball at King Billy.

Poor visibility made Ronan peer, and on the southern bank he saw lights. A car bumped along a lane and stopped. Two men got out briefly, and one pointed along the river. The man who pointed—could it be the Storyteller?

He shouted: "Hey!"

No reaction; Ronan ran forward down to the water's edge—but that took them out of his sight and, he presumed, took him out of theirs. He ran back up the hill and shouted again. The men seemed not to hear him and climbed into the car, which, surprisingly, did not move off. Again Ronan ran to the river, but he had no chance of crossing; recent rains had brought a muddy spate, and the waters flowed fast and high.

Deciding to keep the car in his sights, he made for the main road. But he knew it would take him at least half an hour to get anywhere near the car. He kept running, and as he clambered out of the field, the car passed. The driver, a young man, waved a salutation—and Ronan could see another person inside. The hat, the hunched shoulders, the pale face—was it he? No doubt about it.

The road at the junction from which the car had emerged led through to Slane, the last known location of the Storyteller. Had he but seen through the rain as he walked, Newgrange would have appeared on the hill, above the road to Ronan's right. At Slane, two hours later, he stood on the bridge, looking down into the flowing Boyne.

The night had caused him shame; those girls made him wince now. He began to miss Kate dreadfully—and his mission had failed; he had glimpsed but not reached the Storyteller. The priest's arrival earlier had not been explained, and now hunger attacked, depressing him further. No father to turn to, no close friends—and no assessment that made sense of how his life had begun to hurt so hard so young. He should have stayed with Father Mansfield that morning; maybe a man so sophisticated would understand anything, would condemn nothing, would steer rather than judge.

Although the rain cleared, he continued to hold up the umbrella. From somewhere deep in the countryside a green van came toward the bridge of Slane; Ronan flattened himself against the parapet—no time to get out of the way. The van stopped beside him, and the driver looked out.

"Well, you're not local for a start."

"How d'you know that?"

"There's no one round here'd carry an umbrella when there's no rain."

He made Ronan smile, a return of courage, and he asked, "Where would I find a man called Joe Cooney?"

"You wouldn't. Not today anyway—he's gone off for a long drive."

"Is he with an elderly gentleman?"

"He is so."

So that was the Storyteller; now Ronan knew certainly that the opportunity had passed; no choice now but to regroup.

"You from Dublin?"

"At the moment I am."

"And that's where I'm goin' myself—hop in if you want to; if you don't, stay where yew are."

Ronan climbed into the van, whose inner door handle had been replaced with string.

"Pull it hard, or the door'll fall off and you'll be out on the road."

The entire vehicle shuddered with the force of the slam. Ronan started as something wet touched his ear. He turned to see a greyhound, who had a pleading look.

"That's Morning Star of Slane," said the driver. "We all calls her Judy, and she's running tonight if you want to make money."

Ronan patted Morning Star of Slane's head. The dog licked him again.

"There's only one thing wrong with Judy, she's very reticient." Ronan knew he meant "reticent" but didn't say so. "Just as you think she's goin' to say somethin', she says nuthin'."

Ronan nodded, not sure whether it was polite or impolite to laugh.

"Oh, hey, here," said the driver. "I'm Archie, by the way, Archie Halpin, my father's Archie too. You must be a student, are you?"

The same short, glottal curl—"ahhrr yew"—another new accent to Ronan's ear, a world away from the urban Dublin of last night's girls.

"History."

"Well, you come to the right place for that, we've plenty of it round here, you can't go out the door but history's hittin' you in the face. I got a fair wedge of it last night in Joe's house. How d'you know Joe?"

Ronan remarked that, in fact, he didn't know Joe.

"You don't? Jizz sure the dogs of the road know Joe. Well, I went over to Joe's last night, and who was there only a big, oul' fella with a hat on him like a dead doctor's and he telling stories like you never heard coming outta anyone. A man with no name to him, he said."

Ronan leaped in. "That's the man I'm looking for."

"Right enough, he said he was goin' off to meet someone up at the Boyne Water at twelve o'clock—Joe was goin' to drive him there—and if the fella wasn't there they were going to go off somewhere. But boys-oh-boys can't he tell stories. And a long coat on him like he was gettin' ready to wear it into the coffin."

"Into the coffin?"

"He had a wheeze goin' like a hearse horse, so he had."

"And he never said where he was going next?"

"No, I'd say 'twas a case he didn't know where he was goin'—for he told us he stayed a different place nearly every night. Do you know him itself?"

"Sort of."

Archie Halpin chattered all the way; Ronan, lost and feeling loss, scarcely heard the benign words; Morning Star of Slane, also known as Judy, licked Ronan's hand, and Ronan's low mood continued to descend. In eighteen hours he had had a tantrum that might have killed an older man, drunk unprecedented amounts of liquor, kissed a girl on the mouth for the first time ever, got no sleep, no food, felt the sharp blows of a fist on his head, and endured long, long walks in the cold rain. At the same time he nursed sufficient grievance to avoid a return to Kate, a bitter choice into which he felt forced.

Ronan had played no sports at school; Alison had decreed him too fragile for the physical risk. Therefore he had limited capacity to endure effort or privation. He began to do what all survivors must— he narrowed his thoughts to essentials, namely food and rest.

Suddenly, some miles north of Dublin's outskirts, he asked Archie Halpin to drop him on the roadside. He had to recover himself, and he believed that, exhausted though he was, he would retrieve some sense of himself by walking. Morning Star of Slane had one more lick, Archie bade him cheerful luck, and Ronan walked again. But after a mile the walking became trudging, and he stopped, giving in to the fact that he could not go on; he was, ultimately, too defeated.

He reached the outskirts of a village and looked ahead at its deadness. Across the road a clock winked in an electrical shop—it told him the time but not the place.

But last week's sign in the window advertised a pre-Christmas bazaar in a nearby school. He found the school and an unlocked window. Inside, he also found an office with a couch and an electric heater; from another office he fetched a second heater and turned them both on. He had a haven of sorts; the schools had closed for Christmas until several days into January.

The sun woke him, and the wall clock said noon; he had slept twelve hours. Every part of him ached; the hunger made him dizzy. He lay without moving, grappling with his disturbing state. Slowly, slowly, he drew his body together. The instinct to weep attacked again, and he fought it off. Still bleary with sleep and aches, he searched his pockets and reminded himself that he carried not one single possession, and the weeping threatened to attack once more.

Ronan began a systematic search of the school. He had slept, he discovered, in the teachers' room, now cozily warm. The corridors felt icy, but no door had been locked. He found the door marked "Principal" and in the large desk, after some searching, came across the box marked "Petty Cash." Not much, it yet guaranteed that he would eat. He checked the school diary—reopening in six days.

For the first time in his life he had by now strung together hours of existence that he alone defined, he alone controlled. The feeling of freedom surprised him and then almost exhilarated him. He made the teachers' room ever cozier, took some blankets from a closet, bought biscuits, chocolate, and lemonade in the village shop. Fortune was helping; no house looked into the school grounds, so his comings and goings remained undetected, and the teachers' room could not be seen from the road. Nor, more luck, did he show any public marks from his affray; his clothes hid the bruises on his thighs, hip, ribs, and arms; he had a sore but unmarked head and face and a raw seam of damaged pride.

In his first thirty-six hours at the school, Ronan ran through every emotion. Then, sleeping and waking, sleeping and waking, he grew refreshed and determined. By Tuesday afternoon he knew exactly what he wanted to do and how he would do it. That night, he telephoned his uncle, Toby, in Oxford.

"How much do you need, Ronan?"

"It has to be a lot."

"How much is a lot?"

"Enough to keep me for a while?"

"How long d'you think a while will be?"

"I don't know. I don't know." Ronan felt the waves of distress coming in. "I mean—I need food and stuff."

"Will we start with, say, a thousand?" Toby's voice grew jaunty.

"As much as that? I hadn't sort of thought . . ."

"D'you know that you're going to be rich?"

"How d'you mean?"

"Your father made a lot of money. And when you're twenty-one, you'll be the richest young man in Ireland, I'd say. There'll be girls perched on your gate. And on the mantelpiece, if you let them into the house. And then you'll never get rid of them."

"Yeah. Well." Ronan neither knew nor cared what to say. But he somehow felt the comforting hand of his father at his back.

Toby said, "You're not in trouble, Ronan, are you?"

"No—but I don't want anyone to know I phoned you."

"What about Kate? And your mother?"

"I don't want to talk to anyone."

Two days later, the money arrived at the local bank that Ronan had designated. He drew it in cash; Toby and he had agreed passwords because Ronan had no other identification. As signed for the money, the cashier reached into his drawer and handed Ronan a blue envelope; "This came for you too. A man handed it in."

Ronan did not even ask for a description of the man. He already knew from the handwriting, from the mere existence of the envelope. (And he also grasped that only Toby knew he would visit that bank.)

WHERE MY SOUL TRAVELS

THE PRINCIPAL ADVANTAGE IN THE HARD AND uncertain life of a Storyteller is the freedom of his soul. It is a freedom expressed in travel—I need not plan where I shall be, I have no need to know where I may next go. However, over the years certain principles have developed and I can look back and see two patterns in the way I have journeyed.

Mostly I go to the places where I might find—or have found—stories. I revisit them over and over, and sometimes the first story that I found in such a place changes in my mind so much that I have a new version. Or it simply returns to me ever more vividly, in which case a second story may arrive. Battlefields draw me back, and places where kings ruled and saints preached. I like to visit the houses—or the remains of houses—where great men lived or stayed on visits or the abbeys where the monks made their beautiful works, those sweet cloistered limestone ruins in the middle of the fields or often on the banks of rivers.

In short, I seem to bend myself in the direction of places where history gleams brightest. And fruitfully so; we would give our birthright, would we not, to tread in the steps of our future? But we never shall—and I would argue that the past may prove equally exciting when you step into it, a land full of battles, intrigues, heroes, and magic.

It can also be sad, full of the mournful echoing past. One year in

Mayo, deep in the west, I spent a day and more moving from foundation to foundation in the long grass. I knew I was tracing the outlines of an old village that had disappeared under the tide of poverty or misrule in the abuse of Irish land. As happened more fiercely in Scotland, landlords in Ireland evicted people because sheep yielded greater profit than tenants. Thus, few things have hurt my heart so much as the outlines of those and other abandoned houses, which, one day, must have been built in such hope and gaiety.

When I climbed the next great height, I saw the western ocean that those uprooted people had to cross in order to make a new life. Some took the rooftrees of their houses with them on the boat and set down again in the earth of Nova Scotia or Canada or Delaware or whatever newfound land they embraced.

In my second pattern of travel, I go to safe and decent houses, places where I have told my stories so well that they have appreciated me and kept me fed and warm. A fireside where the householders and their neighbors look at me with round eyes and cheeks rosy from the fire compels me back there—the actor needs his audience. To such homes I return again and again. If busy and capable men and women live there, so much the better; I find something reassuring about the company of people who accomplish good tasks in their daily lives—aimlessness distresses me.

Other than those two guiding principles, I have favorite places for specific times of the year. In the dead of winter I love to see the small birds scurry and then skate accidentally on the ice of a lake. When the new year's evenings stretch—not much, just a little— hope gathers in the lengthening sky. Sharp air dives into the lungs, and we get what old people call "pet days," when the sun unseasonably shines as warm as early summer.

One such January morning, in county Armagh, near the site of the Yellow Ford, I strode across a small stream by a hilly grove and saw two deer ahead of me. Perhaps I was downwind, or the light dazzled them—the sun in the north of Ireland does hang lower in the sky on winter days. In any case, they never saw me; they stood nuzzling each other like young lovers, which, I suppose, is what they were. I could smell the ferns and the heather—it had lately rained—but I most remember the delicacy of their hooves as each raised a foot and pawed the ground a little. So reluctant did I become to disturb their privacy that I hunkered down slowly and watched them until one mooched off into the trees, and the other followed a little haughtily.

Some farmers, especially in western counties whose shores are washed by the warm Gulf Stream, let their cattle out early after the winter. I love to watch such a herd, steam rising from their brown backs as they graze a hillside, and I know then that I am not far from a decent meal; people with fat cattle keep a good table.

The coming of spring always refreshes me. Clouds scud across the sky, and the twilight is the gentlest of all the seasons. In my earlier years I sometimes helped the farmers with their work, and one year I footed turf in a bog near Athlone, the very center of the country, a place to which I enjoy returning.

The young people have never heard the expression "to foot turf," and I am sad at that. We used an implement called a *slane* or *shlaan,* a spade with another blade at right angles to the main one. To "foot" turf, we stepped on that implement, drove it into the peat of a bog and dug out a long rectangular block—a "sod" of turf—that is, peat, which is black with wisps of white, like an old woman's hair. I find comfort in the fact that peat is congealed root and vegetable matter. To think that it lies buried there for thousands of years, and then, when we dry it out, gives us a lovely, hot fire with blue smoke and exciting images in the flames—surely those are the pictures of the past.

When the days strengthen, I usually make my way to the banks of a certain river in the south, where it meets its own little tributary. There, in the ground near the tree at the fork of the two rivers, I have a "safe." This is a tin box that contains some of my possessions, and I have many such boxes buried across the countryside. How I am to gather them all up before I die, I cannot say, and if I don't collect them, some farmers of the future shall find interesting surprises on the tips of their plowshares.

This particular place has a pair of swans, and I sit and watch them foraging in the rushes. Swans mate for life. In the farm overlooking the river bend lives a woman who tells me that she dreams very bright dreams every night of her life. After her husband died, she sat with me on the log we use for a bench, watching the rivers meet. She told me she dreamed of his death a week before he died.

"Do you dream of him now?"

"I dream of milk."

"That's to be expected on a farm."

"I dream of drinking milk, and I dream of spilling milk."

"Then," I said to her, "you are dreaming of mixed fortunes, because to dream of drinking milk foretells success, and to dream of spilling it foretells misfortune."

She took off her shoes. "My husband said he married me because he thought my feet beautiful. Did you ever hear of such a thing?"

I said to her, "I have heard of a man who married a girl because he heard her laugh beneath his window. And I have heard of a man who married a girl because she could dance a jig on a dinner plate and not break the plate, and she was not a small girl. I know a man in county Monaghan who married a girl because she could not pronounce the letter 'r,' and he found that charming."

"Things are strange," said the woman with the lovely feet. "The strangest of all would be if my husband came back to me. But he was thirty years older."

Every year I go back there and smoke a pipe, sitting at the angle of the rivers. Sometimes I meet her, and she gives me a mug of fresh milk; other years they tell me she doesn't want to meet anybody. Then I dig up my box at night, add to its contents or take some money out, tip my hat respectfully in the direction of her fine house, and move on.

I also like to be in the lakes, the bowl at the center of Ireland. Their names make music to me—Derravaragh, Gowna, Owel, sweet names for watered hollows full of reeds and the cries of birds. I have known afternoons where the silence over Westmeath had a stillness I have never found elsewhere. To lie on a grassy slope, to look down and see the lake waters reflecting a clear sky and not hear a sound other than the sudden *crawk!* of a bird—why would I exchange such a life for anything else?

The waters of the lakes feel icy, and one of them has a clear bed—like Lake Inchiquin in Clare, where the limestone floor reflects a brightness up to the surface and the lake has a clarity like an intelligent mind. These, I think, are the last of the ice pools—and I believe the ice still owns them; I cannot explain their cold in any other way. In the year in which I was forty and in which I therefore set myself a number of physical challenges—walking speeds, etc.— I attempted to stay half an hour in the waters of Lough Gowna. Ten minutes finished me—it was a bright, scorching day, yet the lake water found the marrow of my bones and invaded. On the bank I shivered for an hour.

Until a few years ago, I welcomed August more than any month in the calendar, especially those last ten days when the gold is seeping into everywhere and the high temperature of the day lingers. Heat becomes vital in your life if you have no sure bed for the night, and thus August brings some guarantees of warmth. Where it delighted me most, though, it no longer can—I have no suppleness now, and August has lost its greatest charm for me, the hard work of harvest; it is a young man's month, and now I watch them, as muscular as I once was.

This I regret, because I used to help in the many harvests. Come August, the farmers wanted all the hay in and all the corn standing in sheaves across the fields. Those golden days brought me an inner peace and happiness that I draw on now like a bank account. We worked hard, and I am old enough to have seen the manual harvesting replaced by machinery. No doubt the mechanization has proved a great saving and efficiency, but the old methods, with us since God was a small boy, brought more people to the event.

With hay, skilled men scythed in rows, and we followed, teasing out the heavy grasses. A few days later, when the swathes had dried, we moved in again, this time with pitchforks or with our hands, turning the hay so that the underside could dry.

When all had dried, we piled the hay, which by now was getting dusty, into small cocked heaps. Days later, in the greatest exercise of haymaking, these were assembled to make fewer but larger domes, called "wines" or "trams" or "pikes." Each one had the shape of a tall beehive or igloo and was tied down by a rope made of hay; that was my expertise.

I sat on the ground, a pile of loose hay at my feet. In front of me stood a child holding a stick. I then wound some strands of hay around that stick and told the child to walk backward, turning the stick round and round. The hay tightened into a rope as I fed it out in a controlled fashion. Many a strong housewife has put new seats on her kitchen chairs made of such ropes, called *sugawn* or *suggan*, depending which part of the country bred you.

The sights of the year sometimes contradict the lore. According to legend, hares leap in the spring. I beg to differ. On a hill overlooking the river Nore in county Kilkenny, on a warm September night thirty years ago, I discovered a group of stones forming a natural shelter; I have slept there many times. This is good countryside, abundantly wooded, substantially farmed. When first I stayed there, I slept like an innocent.

In the morning, when I opened my eyes, five hares danced in front of me on the hillside. I never saw anything like it—it seemed like a ritual. They leaped over each other, they ran in circles, they left the group, raced round its perimeter, and jumped back in again. Nothing will persuade me that all this was accidental. It had rhythm and method, intent and routine, system, rite, and rote. Their charming little bodies, with their high back legs and long, brilliant ears, twisted and turned and celebrated—a "magic of hares," I called them, and I think of them like that.

When you walk into new countryside, a new tract of land every day of your life, you look minutely at the things that you see. Small occurrences become memorable, hung in a frame. Memory then enlarges them; you may never pass that way again or see the same sights. If you do see them again, you can tell the miracles by virtue of the fact that they still possess the same thrall.

For example, I smile with delight when I see my own footprints in the morning dew of a field. It seems to defy logic that grass can hold a footprint, but there it is—your trail behind you, clear enough for a dog or a detective, and the green has grown darker where your foot has landed.

I like cobwebs on branches, the fine silver netting with drops of dew at the corners. In winter trees, the nests of the old year appear, abandoned and clear to the eye, and I laugh to think of all the effort the birds put into concealing them.

In all my wanderings, my mind divides my life into Time's portions: morning, afternoon, evening, and night—of spring, summer, autumn, and winter. Each period of the day has its own flavor, as does each period of the year. If you put me to sleep for a long time and then woke me up in the Irish countryside, I believe I would be able to tell you what time of year and—even blindfolded—what time of day. This is not something I can explain easily, and it is not as simple as the smell of wood smoke identifying the fall of the year. But when it comes to day and season, I know what and when.

And now and again I fancy that I would even know where I am, in which county. Often I recite their names to myself like a litany— they say that rhythmic chanting refreshes the mind. Since 1922 and the drafting of the Irish border, I have had to amend my lists; the old province boundaries are now confused. But I still recite them county by county, and I know the flavor and feeling and personality of each one. Sometimes, when I fear that my brain has begun to slacken, I call their thirty-two names aloud to myself alphabetically as I walk from one parish to the next, one uncertain billet to another. The music I make from them may not sound great to anyone else and may look ungainly on the page, but it has sustained me like a prayer many a time.

If I speak the name of each county, if I savor the word, I find myself transported there, to some aspect of its life or feeling. In Antrim, I know the glens and the deep coastline looking out to Scotland, and a certain bleakness on those northern headlands, and a suspicion that I never found there when I first walked. Calling upon an unknown house in Antrim invites a cold stare—though I have had my surprises.

One night, outside the town of Bushmills, it had begun to snow, and I knocked at a door. They invited me in, a Mr. and Mrs. Wilson; they told me they were staunch Presbyterians who had lived in county Antrim all their lives. When I told them who I was and what I did and that I never took money from anyone without giving top value, they fed me, gave me a bed, and listened to my stories. More valuably, I listened to theirs and saw new points of view, a rare occurrence on this island. An amusing exchange took place between Mr. Wilson and me, an exchange that also had a political edge underneath.

He said to me, "Can you name all the counties of Ireland in alphabetical order?" I said I could—and I did. Antrim, Armagh, Carlow, Cavan, Clare, Cork, Derry, Donegal, Down, Dublin, Fermanagh, Galway, Kerry, Kildare, Kilkenny, Leitrim, Leix, Limerick, Longford, Louth, Mayo, Meath, Monaghan, Offaly, Roscommon, Sligo, Tipperary, Tyrone, Waterford, Westmeath, Wexford, and Wicklow.

Upon which he said, "And I can name the six counties of Northern Ireland in alphabetical order; Antrim, Armagh, Down, Fermanagh, Londonderry, and Tyrone." It was wise of me not to argue that Derry should not be called Londonderry, that the "London" prefix had been added to a name older than Irish history. And I enjoyed Mr. Wilson's laugh.

I always try and get to Armagh in June for the apple blossom, but sadly I cannot travel as comfortably there as I once did. Too much of it lies along the border, and British soldiers have no time for stories. They have fear in their faces, those young boys, not knowing when they will be shot at from behind some horse cart or hedge.

Farther south, Carlow puzzles me. I have always felt it should offer me more personality, lying as it does in the wealthy plains of the east. I said this once to a Carlow man, and he answered me, "The problem is, people from county Carlow are always either going somewhere or staying at home." Many times have I puzzled over his remark, but I cannot make out what he meant.

But I do understand how the countryside changes, in quite a particular way, from county to county. I know when I have crossed a county border, not from experience but from change of texture. On a mountain road I can tell when I have crossed from Cork into Kerry; northwest of Tipperary town I know the moment I move into Limerick, near the villages of Monard and Oola.

The county personalities continue to astonish, so clearly are they defined. Mayo sits on Galway, yet they feel as different to me as two sisters with whom I have just danced. Is Clare a shrewder version of side-by-side Limerick? Waterford and Wexford fell to Vikings and then to Normans and to Cromwell, but deep within their green and rich fastnesses, they feel as if they have no closeness other than geography.

I cannot satisfactorily explain this widespread individualism, but when I try to grasp it, or discuss it with people who have been listening to my stories, I often feel that I come close to a greater understanding of the whole island; this forty thousand square miles of Atlantic land has a vivid fame the world over. What caused it? Do we talk so long and so loud that everyone hears us? Or did it come about because we put the first dent in the mighty British Empire?

Perhaps our writers did it. I would like to think that they did, because they came from my tradition—poetic, journeyman storytellers who may have twisted and fractured the forms of language along the way but who have always tried to get the flavor across.

Liken it to a stew, a tapestry—anything that draws a final impression from mixed and visible ingredients. The individual counties when melded give me the whole island. We are illogical—the man from Carlow taught me that. And how violent we are; to kill a British soldier matters not a blink to men I have met, no thought of how his eyes closed, where his blood flowed, if he tried to breathe at the last minute and found he couldn't and panicked.

A third ingredient—how entertaining we can be! I have laughed as much in a Dublin hall as in a Kerry pub, laughed at the observations of man's follies deployed to entertain us so that we can draw comparisons. Our music, too; how it grows. A man in a room will strike up a tune on a whistle. Another man will open his shoulders, ease his fiddle, and join in when the first man's spirit has become evident in the music.

Then someone will squeeze the same tune, but differently, out of a concertina or melodeon. A piper will join in next, adding his variation, his eyes tight shut as he concentrates on controlling the air he elbows through his chanters from the leather bag under his arm. Shakespeare called them "the woollen pipes," but we call them the Uileann pipes because *uile* is her Irish word for "elbow." Did Shakespeare make a linguistic error? Or was he referring to the fact that the air bag is often made of sheepskin?

And one by one, others join in, all with different interpretations of the same tune, until soon, if they choose to, they begin to cease one by one and withdraw, so that eventually the tune ends with the lone sound of the man who started it. That always brings tears to my eyes.

Maybe in the middle of all that, a couple will take to the floor, an ample man and a skinny woman, or more often the other way round, and they will dance like sprites around the kitchen, and for those few moments that farmhouse becomes an Astoria ballroom.

We are seers too—or so we say. Islands appearing in the ocean off the coast surprise no one; strange birds in farmyards portend death; ghosts stride hillsides. What I mean is—we are infinitely permissive of possibility; we rule out nothing. And while nations who have a more prosaic approach to life may find this difficult to digest, neither do they forget it.

And how we have achieved on behalf of others; we have composed the anthems of other nations, designed presidential mansions, drafted the constitutions of new states in Africa, forged chains of charity and teaching that reach across the globe. Rome or Hollywood—we have treated them equally in our glib way, our profound way, our false way, our lies and our desperate, earnest truths and our wish to eradicate prejudice because we have known so much of it. We have taught how politics can be corrupt beyond imagination; we have exported our children as though we wanted rid of them; we have hugged our land as though the very grass covered the gates of heaven or hell, and we did not know which; we have bred some of the world's best shamans.

As I write these words, a man whose great-grandparents came from down the street here (tonight I sleep in New Ross, county Wexford) will be president of the United States, a man called Kennedy, and he has the same red hair and the blue-green eyes of the Kennedys that I have stayed with near the shadowed foot of Mount Leinster. We have not yet had an Irish pope, but I have no doubt that if we can bargain, bribe, or buy it, the Vatican will one day bow its head to the raised, blessing fingers of Pope Patrick the First.

All of these things, all of these colors, feelings, moods, aspirations, capabilities—I have found them all in each county of Ireland. Sometimes the depth of the places I visit surprises me afresh. Take Meath, one of my favorite counties—from the ancient profundity of Newgrange, achieved so long ago, to the crucial Protestant victory at the Boyne Water—that is a compression of history which the very air breathes.

And such compression can be found elsewhere. Galway, the City of the Tribes, aches with memories of those who made the long— and, in those days, forced and never to be retraced—journey to the New World. Cashel of the kings rises above the Tipperary landscape like a fairy tale, and I have seen it of mornings when I wondered if the medieval household was just waking up, so realistic did it appear in the light.

And I know that those who have left such places have taken with them out into the world all the feelings and moods and remembrances of times before their times. That is the way I now explain to myself how Ireland, so small, became so famed so widely—a matter of the spirit.

For myself, I may easily say that I know all the counties and all the towns and all the villages and all the parishes and townlands and roads better than any Irishman alive, and I carry them inside me too; that is how I can tell their boundaries without requiring maps. What good it has done me, I have yet to know.

My sadness is that I do not have a fit receptacle for what I have learned. I know that one exists, but the fates and fortunes have not yet removed the obstacles between him and me, have not given me an easy access to the dispensing of such wisdom as I have where I most wish to place it. I have known of him since birth; we met when he was a boy of nine years—but I think I will likely die without the fulfillment he brings.

Ronan delayed not at all. After another, less headlong reading of this latest communication, he moved with purpose.
He restored everything in the school to the position and condition
he had found them in; he replaced the petty cash in its box—the
exact amount. If, when the teachers came back, they felt the shade
of somebody in their offices and classrooms, so be it; they would
not find any intrusive physical trace; he took some pride in this
show of responsibility.

In the village he telephoned Toby again.

"Thanks for the money. Did you know about the letter?"

"What letter?"

"A letter was waiting for me at the bank."

Toby did not ask, From whom? Or, What did the letter say? Or, I
don't know about any letter. Ronan pressed.

"You were the only person who knew I was going to be in that
bank."

"Ronan, banks have hundreds of employees. Anyone could have
seen that paperwork going through. How's the weather over there?"

Ronan felt the shutters come down. He thanked Toby again and
found a local taxi driver who took him back to Dublin, and in a
shopping district as far away as possible from Kate, he bought a
knapsack, sensible hiking clothes, and all the kit he felt he needed.
He also spent considerable time choosing a strong but portable notebook and a selection of pencils, plus the most recent road map of Ireland. With the remainder of his money he opened a bank account
and arranged that he could draw cash at any branch in the country.

In a pub-restaurant called the Comet, he changed in the toilets,
dumping his ruined and musty clothes—including Dickie's coat—

in a corner of the yard. Then he ate what he deemed the best meal he had ever tasted—brown Windsor soup, bacon, and cabbage, followed by apple pie and custard; he asked for second helpings of everything.

From that moment Ronan O'Mara began to zigzag through Ireland, full of purpose. The message of the letter seemed as clear as an order: Walk as I do, and you'll find me.

Although at the beginning he knew not where he was going, he believed the Storyteller's letter—again unsigned—gave him a sketch, if not quite a map. He decided that, as he traveled, he would try to pull together a scheme, a system of pursuit, from all he knew. The facts in his possession seemed uncomfortably disparate and slim; he had nothing concrete to work from, and he hoped, trusted, that a pattern, a purpose, would materialize as his journey went on.

He had already been to the Boyne Valley, and had read the Storyteller's account of the great battle. It also happened to be the location of the Newgrange story—but that had been told to him a hundred miles south. While on the Boyne he had also visited the Geraghty house, in which, yes, the Storyteller had stayed. Yet the other houses of which he knew were all too scattered to offer him a pattern. Nor did any connection seem possible between the houses the Storyteller visited and the stories he told there. This recent letter, and the stories he had heard so far, told him only where the old man had been, not where he would next travel, and thus Ronan still had no precise location at which he could say, "I'm starting from here."

He felt he must bring some science to his search, so he applied a principle he had gleaned from studying history—the value of firsthand witness. This, at last, gave him his point of departure; he asked himself, "What is the location of the most recent story I have personally heard, with my own ears?" It also coincided with a mention in the letter—and he headed for Armagh and the site of the Yellow Ford, which the Storyteller had told of after the funeral.

• • •

January was kind to the north of Ireland that year; Armagh had balmy forenoons after light frosts, and he wandered its roads with pleasure. In the city he stood at the rock of Saint Patrick's grave and made a note to write a description. With more than a little excitement, he listened to the strangeness of the overheard accents, faster and more inflected than in the south. A bed-and-breakfast called King William's Bower, hung with pictures of Queen Elizabeth the Second, fed him well if silently, not even asking questions.

Next morning, when he sought directions to the river Blackwater, the landlord walked to the door and pointed without a word to the northwest.

Half a mile beyond the city's outskirts, a car drew up and a woman's voice asked, "Where you heading?"

"I'm looking for an old battlefield."

"And you found an old battleaxe. Hop in."

Her name, she said, was Myrtle O'Farrell: "A Protestant first name and a Catholic second name—I suppose I should have a split personality. What's the battlefield?"

Ronan told her, and she said, "You need the man I'm going to see, my uncle. He lives in the shadow of Navan Fort, though I always tell him that it's too low a hill to have a shadow."

She had a face like a pigeon; her head scarcely rose above the steering wheel, and she drove the car with her eyebrows raised. If another car appeared, she swerved toward the roadside and braked. Soon she pointed to a narrow river in the fields below.

"That's the Blackwater there. Well named, isn't it? But I don't know where they fought the battle."

Ronan asked her if she could slow down—and Myrtle O'Farrell stopped dead, pitching forward the random contents of the back seat. He got out and climbed the earthen roadside bank. Here, on this northern side—was that where Bagenal had come charging in and fallen into the traps? And over there, on the southern side, Hugh O'Neill had lined up his troops and his new artillery—is that the same line of bushes? Such a low slope—how could it have worked so well? Ronan could almost hear the shots and shouts in his ears.

Chatty Myrtle climbed out and stood beside him, almost a foot smaller. "It was the Nine Years' War, wasn't it? Home economics is what I teach, not history. Where are you from?"

Ronan told her. She said, "Is this your first time up here? Because if it is, we'd better get going. If the police or the army come, they'll have questions for you."

"Why?"

"Ah, why? Why anything?" Her style had too much force to be called enigmatic, but she gave no fuller answer, returned to the car, and revved the engine.

He watched the line of the river until they lost it. "Is the border along here?"

"Is a pig fat? It certainly is! My uncle says he's going to write a song called 'The Particular Peculiarities of the Irish Border.' I don't think we'll hear it being whistled. But I like his point. I mean, if you look at that church—see that wee spire on the hill over there?" Myrtle O'Farrell's bosom kept her at a distance from the steering wheel (and most things in life). "There's a Protestant clergyman, he's a nice man, especially for a Protestant, he preaches every Sunday morning from the pulpit in that church. And he's on this side of the border, in the Six Counties of Northern Ireland. But the flock of the faithful, to whom he's preaching—aren't they sitting on their backsides in their pews down south in the Republic, in the Free State? And why? 'Cause the border runs straight through the church. Did you ever hear anything so nonsensical?"

Ronan twisted in his seat to look. "Is there no dividing line? Nothing by which you can tell?"

Myrtle O'Farrell's jowl wobbled with agitation. "They don't need one—the border's in people's heads. Although it hits other parts of them too. There's a man teaches in the same school as me—he sleeps in the Six Counties, and his wife sleeps in the Free State, the Republic. And they're both in the same bed. He always says they had to start an invasion to have children."

The hedges were high and the sun low, as the Storyteller's chronicle described. Ronan watched for deer but saw none. Myrtle O'Farrell asked no further questions—she ran entirely on her own fuel and talked endlessly of nothing in particular. Soon she turned off the road down a sharp slope into a cottage yard.

"This is Uncle Bob's house—our family all has English names, Robert and Myrtle, my brother is called Charles, and my father is called Nigel. I never understood why; we're as Irish as wet grass."

An elderly man came to the door, wearing a gray knitted waistcoat and gray tweed pants. He greeted his niece with a yell and said, "Is this a husband you have here?"

"What am I, Uncle Bob, a baby-snatcher?"

In the kitchen the man fastened on Ronan.

"That's a southern accent. What're you up to?"

Ronan said, "I'm looking for a man who tells stories."

"Every man tells stories," said Uncle Bob.

"And every woman," said Myrtle.

"Are you sure that's what you're after?" Uncle Bob looked suspicious. "Because you're just about the right age for trouble."

"Trouble?" said Ronan.

"You're very innocent-looking. I'm not sure about you. You're a long way from home."

"I'd say he's all right," said Myrtle. "Are you all right?" She unpacked clean laundry from a large shopping-bag.

"I think so," said Ronan.

Uncle Bob narrowed his red-rimmed eyes further. "Don't you know what's going on up here?"

"I know there's been trouble from time to time."

"Is that all you know? Well, I'll tell you what you should know. For the last five years there's been an IRA campaign all along the border. You people in the south—you know nothing. Fat as fools down there, while we get it in the neck. The IRA attacks barracks and policemen, they kill people when they can, close up if they're able, and just because we're Catholics, we get blamed. That's the kind of thing you should know, isn't it?"

Ronan said, "I sort of knew it."

Myrtle had unpacked food from the car. She poured three glasses of milk. "Uncle Bob has an ulcer, that's why the milk."

"Do you hate England?"

Ronan sat back from the question and the ferocity of Uncle Bob's eyes.

"I—I suppose I don't know."

"Well, you should know. I love my country—that's Ireland, by the way, even though I live inside the English part of it—but I don't hate England. Sure, I believe she has no rights here nor ever had. She should have left a long time ago and let us sort it all out between us. Do you think about these things?"

"I'm only a history student."

"History? Begod, I'm your man. Did you know that this border, out there across the lower field—it wasn't the first partition of Ireland."

"It wasn't?"

"No, it was by no means not. I'll tell you what was the first division of Ireland. It came from the time the people who worshipped the goddess Danu was hammered by the Milesians—d'you know about the Milesians?"

"A race of mighty men taller than Roman spears," quoted Ronan.

"Hah! You're not as green as you're cabbage-looking. Up from Spain they came thousands of years ago, thousands. And they had spears, whereas the Danu people only had spells. And a spell is like your arse—it has its uses, but not in a fight."

"I said you came to the right house," said Myrtle.

"And when the Spanish defeated them, they made a treaty, and the Milesians took all of Ireland above the ground, and the Danu took all below the ground, where they are living still—that was the first political division of Ireland. Did you know that?"

"We were taught it at school," said Ronan.

"And did you never think to question that you were taught as a historical fact that people live like sprites under the ground of Ireland?"

"No," said Ronan.

"Why would you?" Uncle Bob began to chant. "What country could be better than this land where the sun sets so beautifully? Who, but I, can find the clear springs of water here? And who, outside of me, can tell you how old the moon is? Who, other than me, can summon the fish from the ocean's deeps?" He clapped his hands to applaud himself. "D'you know what that is? That's the song of Amergin, the first conqueror of Ireland, who burst into song when he landed at Belfast. America was called after him."

"Uncle Bob, drink that milk while 'tis fresh. And it was Kenmare he landed at, the other end of us altogether. And America wasn't called after him, it was called after a fellow called Amerigo Vespucci."

"Leave me alone, I'm enjoying myself." Uncle Bob turned to Ronan. "You see—if you listen to me, you'll soon learn that we don't need to fight, because we're the greatest talkers in the world. We can argue, cajole, wheedle, like no other nation on earth; we can charm the birds off the bushes. And why isn't this remarkable power stronger than the gun? Because we talk too much."

Myrtle winked at Ronan. "Some of us do."

Ronan said, "Have you heard of a king of Ulster who had two horses, one black and one white?"

"No," said Uncle Bob, taking out his dentures and polishing them on his sleeve. "And he could only ride one at a time anyway. But the kings of Ulster lived on that hill outside the door—that's Navan Fort, where all the power was."

Ronan stayed at Uncle Bob's that night, in a tiny whitewashed room with a patchwork quilt. Myrtle made him breakfast and said if he wanted to climb the hill of Navan Fort, she'd wait for him and take him back down across the border again.

He stood on the highest point, where he hoped to imagine a king driving a chariot with a black horse and a white, and a blacksmith with hair like a nest of little black snakes.

She came from the west, he reflected; her name was Dana—and he looked westward. Trees and poor visibility defeated any possible view, and he had to content himself with believing that time had shrunken the earthen mound to less than palatial size. As he left, he puzzled again over that story of the king and the two horses. What was its place in the history of Ireland?

Myrtle dropped him back on the banks of the Blackwater. Ronan spent two more days there, walking, reconnoitering, making notes; he stood under trees during showers; he watched the sun tip gold into the river; he peered at the ground, hoping to find the ancient mantraps. Once or twice he regretted not having his transcription of the Yellow Ford story, written down in the quiet days after the funeral, with him. But he remembered it well and did not leave the area until he knew he had likely covered every yard of the battle- field.

He stayed at Uncle Bob's the next night too and listened to stories of ancient invaders or wild chieftains or local disputes about land— plus an occasional burst of polemic; "England has the worst cooks in the world," and "Did you know Churchill was drunk the entire length of the war?" and "I heard a man argue one night that the queen of England is secretly a Catholic."

But Uncle Bob suffered a drawback to his own powers of argu- ment—he kept falling asleep. On both nights Ronan went to bed, leaving the old man snoring by the fire. Before he left on the third day, he finally managed to ascertain that Uncle Bob had never met nor heard of the Storyteller.

For the next leg of his journey Ronan combined yet another careful reading of the recent chronicle with the memory of a powerful tale heard.

"Is this the home of Mr. and Mrs. Kevin MacKenna?" he said to the woman who answered the door of a bungalow in Cootehill.

She looked at him. "Kevin!"

The man who answered her call had eyebrows like frightened shrubs.

"Hallo," he said, nothing more, as he walked to his own front door and looked at Ronan.

"There was a recording made here some time ago. About Strongbow."

"Who?" said Mrs. MacKenna.

"Strongbow."

"Oh, that fella? Come in." She looked at her husband. "When were we talking about Strongbow?"

Ronan recited: "Sunday the nineteenth of July, nineteen fifty-nine, at nine-thirty p.m."

Mrs. MacKenna said to her husband, "Oh, yeah. We were, too. Dan was here."

"Aye," said Mr. MacKenna.

Ronan recited again, "The recordist on behalf of the Irish Folklore Commission was Daniel P. Kelly."

"That's my brother Dan," said Mrs. MacKenna.

"Aye," said Mr. MacKenna.

"And that's how the recording happened," she told Ronan. "My brother Dan."

"I'm looking for the man who told the story."

"He's not here. But he could be any day—he said to me that whenever he was anywhere in the county Cavan, he'd make a bee-line for us. The children love him, and I make him a big breakfast always. He's very fond of eggs."

"Aye," said Mr. MacKenna. "He's fond of eggs."

Ronan said, "When did you last see him?"

"He was here in November."

"And did he give any indication of what his future plans might be?"

"No, and he was complaining that the health was letting him down a bit—he was a bit bronickle, he said he'd a touch of a rattle in the chest. The only thing he said was that he might have to go down south for a funeral, but he wasn't sure."

"A funeral?"

"That's all he said."

"I met him at a funeral in December."

"You're more recent than us, then."

"Over the years—how often did he come here?"

"Oh, a lot. He was very friendly with Kevin's father, Kevin's father had a lot of stories. That's how Dan came into it—Dan has an electrical shop in the town."

"Aye," said Mr. MacKenna. "An electrical shop."

Daniel P. Kelly said, before Ronan could speak, "I haven't it ready yet. It'll be Tuesday."

Ronan looked at him. "I—"

Daniel P. Kelly said, "Is it a repair you're calling for?"

"No. I was speaking to Mrs. MacKenna. Your sister."

"Oh. Tess. Yeah." Daniel P. Kelly said, "She's good, Tess."

"I was wondering whether—I believe you recorded stories."

"Ah. Now I have you. Most of the stuff I sent to Dublin, the folklore people. Is that what you're after?"

"What I really want," said Ronan, "is—there's a man I'm looking for. The story about Strongbow."

Daniel P. Kelly lit up. "Him! Oh, he's massive! A massive person altogether, he has massive stories."

"Do you have any more tapes of him?"

"No—well, yeah, I do, I have one—no, maybe I don't, all his stuff goes to Dublin—but the recording on one tape, that's how I got into it, I have up-to-the-minute tape recorders here. And one tape went bad on me, it came off, I got a lot of the story, but you can't send out a thing like that."

"May I hear any tape you have?" said Ronan. "I'm collecting that gentleman's stories."

Daniel P. Kelly went into the back room of his shop and emerged with a large green and cream machine. It had a lightning flash in front, a manufacturer's symbol, and great square buttons.

"I've a tape here somewhere," he said and searched a shelf laden with unopened mail, much of it very old. He drew out a red-and-black box marked BASF, slotted the spool on the machine, and threaded the tape. Daniel P. Kelly pressed the button, and the sound "wowed" into life. The recording had evidently missed the first few words, and the harsh, short-voweled voice began in mid-sentence.

Ronan opened his notebook—but this voice was different.

"That's not the same man."

"No, that's my sister's father-in-law."

"Do you have any recordings of the gentleman I mean?'

"Well, I do and I don't." Ronan looked puzzled, and Daniel P. Kelly said, "I mean—I have a tape of him that there's nothing on, he spoke into it but it didn't take down his voice. There's a story on this one, though. Here y'are."

N O SHORTAGE OF GHOSTS, BECAUSE WHAT'S a ghost? A ghost is no more and no less than a spectral apparition from another time and place.

Well, the story I'm going to tell you is about a very strange kind of ghost that was seen many times not far from here, near the village of Ballycarron, where as we all know there's a big convent. But the convent has nothing to do with this story, although it could one day, who knows? And by the way, the same thing has happened in Yorkshire and in France and in the county Clare and in east Limerick. Which is important to know—because there's always naysayers who deny these things, and around here they claim this coach wasn't a true thing at all, and that we have it because that American fellow, Edgar Allan Poe—his family come from near here, and didn't he have a big thing with ghosts and stuff like that? So this is the story of the Black Hearse of Ballycarron, and it happened first in the year seventeen-forty.

There was a family near that village who I'll keep nameless, only because their descendants are still scattered around the place, and some of them aren't very pleasant people. Nor were their ancestors, who were given a fine parcel of land after the Battle of the Boyne. They got eight farms rolled together, and eight families were thrown out on the roadside to make way for these people, who came here from the island to the east of us, I won't say what part they came from. Anyway, they came in, and they built a fine house with grand windows and a big curving staircase and an avenue a mile long. In this story, the avenue is more important than the staircase, although that plays its part too.

Like all foreign landowners in Ireland at that time, they employed the local people at next to no wages. But some of the servants became so important to them that they looked after them better than others. This offended many, especially a man called John Philbin, who had long sideburns down to nearly under his chin, mutton chops, they're called. He was one of the farm stewards on the estate, and he was very good with the animals—he could always tell if a cow was going to be sick or why a horse was lame.

Like many men with skills, John Philbin thought he should get paid more than anyone else, only he had no gift of making himself liked. And when he heard that the chief butler, a foolish sort of a man but very pleasant and cheerful, was getting bigger money, John Philbin got very cross. One morning he approached the man of the house, and he said to him in his gruff way, "I'm worth a lot more wages than that fool you have polishing your knives and forks."

The man of the house liked neither the words nor the tone in which they were delivered; John Philbin had a habit of coming right up to anyone he was speaking to and looming into the person's face. Which he did that morning. What happened next tells you something about the treatment of servants in those days. The squire stepped back, owing to John Philbin's face up against his.

"How dare you?" he shouted, and he called to two other of his workmen fixing a wall near at hand. "Grab this man and hold him."

The two men didn't want to, but they had wives and families to feed, and so they grabbed John Philbin—whom they didn't much like anyway. While they held him, the squire horsewhipped him with a big whip—he ripped the clothes off his back with the force of the lash. I suppose he must have given him about forty or so strokes—a weaker man might have died.

When the squire finished, John Philbin stood back.

"Thank you, sir," he said to the squire, but there was a strange light in his eyes as he said it. "I'll see to it that in my gratitude to you, the carriage will come for you on time."

I should point out here that this story is often called "The Ballycarron Carriage."

The squire looked at him and presumed the man meant the family carriage to take the squire and his wife and children to the
Protestant church the following Sunday, and he walked away, shaking his head. John Philbin—

The tape began to spool off the reel, and Daniel P. Kelly jumped to his feet.

"This bastardin' thing," said Daniel P. Kelly. "I thought I fixed it."

Some of the tape had snarled; painstakingly he wound it back on its reel and finger-spooled the tape forward until the wrinkled, damaged part had been passed—and he pressed PLAY.

OOKED AT EACH OTHER, WONDERING WHAT HE was doing. The avenue had two long straights in it, one from the gate to a sharp bend, and the other from the bend straight up to the house. As they watched, John Philbin walked to the bend, turned and looked at the house, and began to walk back, his eyes fixed on the front door. When he came abreast of the two workmen, he seemed very strange in himself, and he had a mutter going on, the words of which they couldn't properly hear.

They stepped back, partly because they didn't yet know whether he bore them a grudge for holding him down during the horse-whipping, but mostly because he was giving off an air that frightened the life outta them. He walked right up to the house, stood looking at it for long seconds, turned on his heel, and went past them. As he did so they heard him say, "It'll be in tonight. It'll be in tonight."

The men went home, and they told their wives how worried they were, but none of them, husbands or wives, could figure out what John Philbin was talking about. They found out soon enough.

That night at midnight, the squire and his wife were fast asleep in their beds when one of the maids came knocking on their door so hard they thought the end of the world had come. It had—for one of them—but they didn't know that yet. The girl shouted, "Look out the window, look out the window!"

It was a fine moonlit night, and they rushed to the window in their nightgowns and nightcaps. Coming down the avenue, straight toward the house, picking up speed, was a long black carriage, like a hearse. It had two carriage lamps lighting either side on the front, and on the box sat a coachman, his hands held out as though he held the reins on a team of horses. Except—there weren't any horses. The coachman wore a black hat and black greatcoat, but he didn't seem to have a face. On and on came the black carriage; it had glass sides to it, and the squire and his wife and the maid could see that there was no one and nothing inside.

As they watched, the coach came faster and faster toward the house, the wheels rumbling and rattling and flashing in the moon-light. The closer it came to the house, the faster it seemed to travel, and it reached the point where no force on earth could stop it from crashing through the great front doors.

At the window, the three people watching stiffened themselves for the crash—but it never happened. Not a sound, not a budge. All they felt was a kind of cold air that swept through the entire house.

Well! They were amazed. Their shoulders sagged back down, and they looked at each other, trying to figure it.

"Go down," said the lady to her squire, "and see what all that's about."

She and the maid were whimpering with fear, and the squire didn't seem in great condition himself. But he went downstairs—it's a man's duty to look after his household in times of danger—and he opened the front door. Outside there was nothing to be seen only the trees against the sky under a half-moon the color of a lemon.

Back upstairs goes the squire, and into his room, where the lady and the maid are still trembling.

"Go," he said to the maid, "and bring us brandy."

"Sir," said she, "I don't mean to disobey you, but if 'tis all the same to you, I won't. Because—look!"

She pointed out through the window, and there, same as before, round the bend in the avenue, came the black carriage again. There was the coachman with his black hat and his black greatcoat and his no face, holding his hands out, driving invisible horses. Faster and faster it came; this time the moon shone straight in through the glass sides of the carriage, and the squire and his wife and the maid saw for definite that it was empty.

Up it came, right to the forecourt of the house, until they thought it was going to crash into the doors. But not a sound was heard, not a shock was felt, only a kind of dank air that swept through the room like a sour fog you'd get over marshy ground.

"I'll get the brandy myself," said the squire, and down the staircase he went. In the hallway, he opened the front door an inch or so and peeped out. Once again he saw nothing only the trees against the sky under a half-moon the color of a lemon.

The squire climbed the stairs slowly, the brandy on a tray out in front of him, and next thing he heard the servant girl shouting.

"Sir, come on quick, here 'tis again."

In he goes to the room, over to the window, and there's the coach rolling up the drive toward the house. Only this time it didn't gallop at the doors; it slowed down and turned in a circle and stopped. The coachman with no face got down offa the box and opened the carriage door. Now this was a vehicle that was oblong like a hearse, but there were seats in it too, for mourners. The coachman saluted toward the house, and someone walked across the forecourt, as if from the front doors, and got into the carriage.

In the bedroom above, the people looking down couldn't first make out whether 'twas a man or a woman, and then they thought it was someone the spit and image of the squire himself. But how could that be, since he was there in front of their eyes? The coachman closed the door, and the carriage drove away.

All three of them had a drop of brandy—including the maid, and that was rare for a servant to be given a drink by those people in that house, they kept everybody in their places.

The following day, as you can imagine, the ghost carriage was the talk of the place. Nobody else had seen it but everybody heard about it, and—

The tape broke this time, and the take-up spool spun round madly while the left-hand reel stopped with a grunt. Daniel P. Kelly dove on it, shouting, "Scutter!"

For many feverish minutes he tried to fix it; he used little pieces of adhesive tape, but each flew away when he started the machine again. Finally he gave up.

"But what happened?" said Ronan in some dismay.

"The machine broke the tape."

"No—in the story?"

"Oh. The person who got into the coach was the squire himself, and a week later, at midnight, he fell down the stairs and died."

"And that's the story of the Ballycarron Carriage?"

"Yeah, but I don't know if I have the end of it right, I might be wrong about it."

"Does it still happen?"

"It does. I think the tape gets wound too tight."

"The coach, I mean."

"Oh, yeah. Whenever one of that family is going to die, no matter where they are in the world, they see the coach a week ahead of the death, and they see themselves getting into it. John Philbin's curse."

"Have there been any reports of it?"

"There was a case of it over in Manorhamilton, last year—the coach galloped up the road, several people saw it, and the following week a woman of that blood was killed in a car crash coming home after a game of cards."

Ronan furrowed a brow. "But—don't people get alarmed?"

"I suppose they do. The drink they had on them when they saw it—that was a bit of a cushion, I suppose."

•   •   •

Ronan fought off a feeling of dissatisfaction—not just at Daniel P. Kelly and his up-to-the minute tape recorders, but at his own scheme of "last sightings." Clearly his system was not working. Would he have to settle for the compensation of merely visiting the locations of the tales he had heard in person? Hoping somehow the Storyteller would return there at that moment? Yet meeting the MacKennas, walking the Yellow Ford site, even the distressing near-miss at the Boyne—these had already buoyed him up, and he felt certain that if he traveled in hope, he would somehow arrive at the man himself.

As a bonus, his mood had improved beyond recognition; since he started on his walk, he felt lighter and less aggrieved, though still without a wish to return to any base.

With his spirits climbing, he decided that, for the next few months—at least through the spring and summer—he would behave as much as possible like the Storyteller. He would visit places he knew the old man had seen—the story locations and the clues would guide him; night by night, he would ask for bed and board in return for tales told; and day by day he would intensify his inquiries for any sightings.

This plan cheered him greatly—but a cloud came down; what if he was too late? Twice, now, he had been told that the Storyteller's health was poor; a bronchial condition (or, as Mrs. MacKenna called it, "bronickle") would hardly improve on the road; damp nights and cold dawns chilled weak chests. Could he set himself to imagine never reaching the old man? What if Death got there first? No: too awful an idea—but its fire forged in him a stronger, if still inexplicable, link.

Next day, Ronan stood on a hillside outside Ballyjamesduff and looked down on a lake. On the far shore, the windows of a white house sparkled; this would be his first attempt at the new way of traveling. He descended the hill, skirted the lake by the tall reeds, then climbed a slope to the front door. A wooden plaque read "Two Horse House."

"Hallo," he rehearsed to himself, "I'm a student—I'm traveling, learning the history of Ireland. I wonder—could you give me a bed for the night?"

The young man who answered the knock seemed not much older than Ronan. He disappeared and returned, followed by an unusually tall woman wearing a bandanna round her hair.

"Yes?"

Ronan spoke the phrase that he hoped would become his ticket; "I can tell you some stories of Ireland in return for accommodation." The woman surveyed him and opened the door wide.

"Come in. We're too trying to learn the history of Ireland."

The farmhouse had been bought by a Dutch family two years previously, and the interior had been restored to its original feeling—the hearthstone, the open fire, the rope-seated chairs.

"We called it 'Two Horse House,' " said the tall woman, "because of what happened here. You are familiar with the Penile Laws?" Ronan wanted to correct the pronunciation but dared not. "It was owned by a man called John Joe Brady, and he came from a generally strong family. But a man called Cruickshank made Mr. John Joe Brady from this house sell him his two best horses for ten pounds, as you had to do under the law, ya? So Mr. John Joe Brady went to the Protestant bishop in Cavan town and said he wanted to become the Protestant. He was made into the Protestant on the spot, and then he went back to Mr. Cruickshank and said he wanted his two horses back—but once he recovered his two horses, the same Mr. John Joe Brady was never in his life seen in the Protestant church. Is that not good? We are very interested, because like so many Dutch we are Protestants."

Ronan asked permission to write it down.

In Two Horse House, Ronan made his first true stab at storytelling. He retold the Architect of Newgrange; the next night, he did the Book of Kells; the third night brought Strongbow and Eva. In the telling he tried no more than to repeat the Storyteller's versions, which he had memorized like an actor. More than once he felt an urge brimming to tell more "history"—facts he had learned in school or from Professor Ryle. Uncertainty kept him to the versions he knew, and the Dutch family loved every moment.

The tall woman had an even taller husband and a tall daughter; together they listened rapt by the fire, and Ronan felt a return of that first power he had known in school when telling of Brian Boru. He also quaked a little at his daring at emulating the old man. To get over that fear, he told them about the Storyteller and his props and his techniques and his walking feats. And so the days he spent in the white house enriched and enlarged him; the family took to him, showed considerable respect, and called him friend.

"Now," they said to him, "you have become a man in a story that we will tell. That is a good thing?"

Reluctantly they all said good-bye. The tall daughter gave him a card with their name and address; the tall mother kissed and embraced him. Father and son drove Ronan to what he considered a good point on the road, and after many handshakes he continued his journey south. He felt rewarded and brave and strong.

Over the next weeks, no house refused him. People welcomed him, told him local stories, listened to his renditions. None thought it strange that a man so young should have such an interest, especially a history student. Some had heard of the Storyteller—and those who hadn't immediately wanted to know more. Everyone encouraged him in his search; nobody thought him ludicrous, and all responded eagerly to his writing down such tales as they themselves had to tell.

Gradually, his journey grew into something richer and more worthwhile than he had foreseen, and he felt himself calmer, almost as though he could sense himself maturing. The only surprise he registered was a pleasant one: how willingly people listened to a tale—and told one in return.

By early March, he had come down-country as far as the lakes in the county of Westmeath. At four o'clock one day, having sat by the waters for an hour in the sun, which was unusually warm for the time of year, he stopped at a house with ivy on the walls to ask directions across the fields.

"You're the second traveler today," said the woman.

Ronan instantly knew what she meant—he simply knew in his bones. With his patience on edge, he waited for her to tell him.

"We had a man staying here last night, and you never heard such stories. Of course he's very well known by now, you must have come across him."

"Not only have I come across him—I'm looking for him."

He asked all the questions: the hat, the pipe, the coat—and the health. All her replies confirmed his hopes, except the last.

"Not that good, I thought. My husband drove him to Athlone, he said something about wanting to be in the very center of Ireland, that it might be the last time he'd be there."

Urgent as pain, Ronan said, "Is he staying in Athlone?"

"I don't know. And if he is, I don't know where he's staying at. My husband dropped him outside the post office."

Ronan sped from the house, and any time he heard a car, he tried to flag it down. On other days every car and truck seemed to stop; today, none did. South of Ballymahon he asked a garage owner to drive him into Athlone and offered to pay. They agreed a fare, but the man took another hour to reappear, and every time Ronan went to the door, he heard the driver say to his wife, "Tell him I'll be ready in a minute."

By the time he got there, the post office had closed, and the neat streets of Athlone held few people. Ronan asked everyone he saw. Some did him the honor of thinking carefully before saying no; some just shook their heads. To ease the frustration and disappointment, he granted himself a night in a hotel, but the wedding party downstairs went on until four in the morning, and sleep kept itself distant until the music died.

Next day lifted his spirits again. He struck out for the river Shannon and stayed on the western bank, fully aware from his map of the treat that lay ahead. When the sun shone its highest, he reached the monastery of Clonmacnoise.

The photographs he had seen underplayed the place. Its towers looked so peaceful, with the buildings gray as doves and the land from the river to the abbey walls as green as water meadows. In air gentle as this, monks such as Annan and Senan had made beautiful books. Ronan approached almost on tiptoe, as though afraid he might tread on something timeless. Not a hostile stone did he see, nothing but ancient welcome and stately quiet among the ruins.

He walked alone; no one else came by, except the birds skimming low over the reeds. Above his head he viewed the corbels and carvings of a civilization long past, built in the love of their God eight centuries earlier. Some of those walls, no matter how ruined now, had never been touched by hands other than those that had built them. The stone varied—some had been cut smooth as silk, some rough as tweed.

The monastery, where a great saint called Kieran had lived, consisted of not one great dominant central church but many smaller chapels, all clustered together like friends. Ronan imagined that a scriptorium might have stood over there, where the morning light would have come in brilliantly; and over there a refectory, say. Where might a ford have been, which a lady could ride across to elect a new abbot? Were all the past abbots shrewd? What old monks had been buried out here in the cemetery? He found gravestones, flat decorated slabs with images that could have come from distant, peaceful planets, all whorls, tendrils, and sweeps. And didn't his father have a poem that began, "In a quiet watered land, a land of roses, stands Saint Kieran's city fair," and something about the warriors of Ireland who "slumber there"?

Deep within the ruins he turned and looked at the river below. He leaned against a wall and let the atmosphere of the place wash over him; the back of his head touched cold stone, and he allowed himself to feel it. As though an onlooker, he tried to imagine what he looked like—the dark red hair, the glasses, the dark green windproof jacket, the khaki pants, the boots, the lumpy backpack on the

ground, the large, white hands. He thought he looked both individual and lonely—a traveler with an intense love of all he saw, yet
a lonesome young man with no one to talk to.

Now the grieving truly struck for the first time. When he went
home, he would have no father to whom he would describe all this:
no eyebrows raised in delight, no eager questions, no incline of the
head, no benign listening. Ronan's breath tightened in something
close to a gasp; he exhaled and leaned his head back against the
cold wall, closed his eyes.

"Jesus God!"

He thought he stood there for as long as an hour; but his mourning reverie lasted no more than a few minutes. To bring himself
back to the world, he reached down and placed the palms of his
hands on the limestone walls behind him. Nobody had told him
about that kind of pain—nobody had ever told him about any kind
of pain. All childhood attention had blanketed him; all "difficulty"
was smothered before it blossomed, especially since the time of the
Storyteller's departure; following that event, the three adults in
the house clothed every situation in calm.

For two days he wandered around Clonmacnoise. He slept in the
monastery, not so much under the stars as within the walls. In one
of the chapels, where workmen had been renovating, canvas
draped their materials. Under the tarpaulin lay some dry sacks, and
he lifted planks from a pile, made a rough bed with the sacks, and
slept like a child. During the night, he woke to a snuffling noise;
when he shifted, something ran away, perhaps the size of a dog; a
fox, he presumed, and went back to sleep.

Next morning, he found food in a local shop and went back to
the abbey. From the riverbank, he examined the ruins as a raiding
Viking would have seen them, and in his mind he reconstructed the
plundering of Clonmacnoise and other monasteries. He then set
himself to read the tombstones, feeling disappointment at how
recent the dates seemed. Again, the sun shone, and few days in his
life had felt so texturally complete. His bed felt less comfortable

that night—but he had the reward of lying there, quite warm, looking up at the unfettered stars.

Next morning, he followed the river Shannon for most of a day, until he had to decide to go west or south.

"What county is this?" he asked a postman with a bicycle.

"Offaly. In Ireland. And you're in the year nineteen-sixty-one. And at twelve o'clock last night it got to be Thursday."

"Offaly?"

"Did I say anywhere else?"

Gara, in the tale of Patrick, had lived in Offaly.

"How far away is the Devil's Bit?"

"Go to Banagher, and they'll tell you."

Ronan was about to ask, "Why won't you tell me?" but the man looked exceedingly sour as he stood there, leaning on his bicycle, smoking a cigarette.

"Which direction is Banagher?" He expected to hear a road direction, but the postman pointed south across the fields.

"Banagher's there," he said.

At which Ronan, partly in defiance and partly in adventure, climbed into the fields and struck out south.

Half an hour later he came over a steep hill and down into a lone farmyard. Dogs barked, a woman came out, and a man, big and heavy, came running from a barn. They shaded their eyes to look—and both half ran toward Ronan. A few yards from him, they stopped.

"It's not him," the woman said.

"You're not him," said the man. And, after a pause, "So who are you?"

Ronan told them.

"He never mentioned a Ronan," said the woman. "Nor an O'Mara, that I heard."

"Did you see him?" The man looked desperate. "Did you?" He caught Ronan's forearm. "Don't say you're bringing us bad news, oh, Jesus, don't say it."

Ronan stood blinking, confused.

"Bring him in, come in," said the woman, "before anyone sees us. Are you on your own—is there people following you?"

Their urgency struck Ronan as dangerous, yet sad. They propelled him into their kitchen and then to a parlor with dried flowers in green vases and red flocked wallpaper. The table had been set for three.

"I've kept it that way since he went," said the woman. "For when he walks in."

The man said, "And you didn't see him?"

Ronan said, "I don't think I'm anywhere near understanding—I mean, I'm a history student, I'm walking the country looking for an old man who tells stories, I think he may be the last traveling storyteller."

"No, this is no good to us," she said. "No good to us at all."

The big man looked shifty—but held out his handshake.

"I'm Peter, this is Annette." Ronan felt he had broken through their haze. "Annette, explain to him."

"We got word last night," said Annette, "that he'd be here this morning. Our son—Peter Junior—you know there's the IRA thing—"

"An armed struggle, Annette—an armed struggle!"

"Whatever—up on the border, and Peter Junior—"

The big man burst in. "Peter O'Connell, like his father before him, is the commandant of the East Louth Division of the Irish Republican Army, dedicated to remove by force of arms the obnoxious remnants of the British Empire from the island of Ireland!"

Annette interjected. "And he's gone from here these months, and all we have to show for it is worry."

"Months? How many months?" Ronan looked at the woman sympathetically.

"What's your own place in the struggle?" demanded Peter O'Connell.

"He hasn't one," said Annette. "He's more sense than that."

"He should have. We all should."

"My father was against violence." Ronan thought his own voice sounded weak.

"Pacifism is a cover-up," said Peter O'Connell.

Annette flinched. "Peter, this gives this young man trouble—"

The heavy farmer with the sad eyes looked hard at Ronan.

"What she's saying is—If my son comes in now, and you see him here, because you know he's on the run, you've to tell the authorities."

"Peter, this isn't fair to this boy—"

"No right-minded Irishman would inform on another Irishman, would he?" said the farmer, looking into Ronan's eyes.

"But wouldn't it be best avoided? If I went now—he's still not here—I'm just a history student . . ."

The big man relented. "He mightn't show up at all. We often get word that he's going to be here, and he never comes, his mother is destructed from it."

"All the same, I think I'll go."

"Ah, fair enough, message understood, no hard feelings."

Ronan turned to Annette. "Look, if I come across him—I mean if I meet him and know who he is, I'll tell him the two of you are well."

She nodded, incapable of a word.

Peter O'Connell, the heavy farmer, whose son, a volunteer in the IRA, was on the run, drove to Banagher, where Ronan stayed in a bed-and-breakfast, needing to recover.

He also needed rubber footings on the heels of his boots, and next morning his landlady directed him to a shop that sold shoes.

"A young man owns it. Not a lot older than yourself. He inherited the business very recently, but they say he has no feel for it."

Ronan found the "young man" reading a newspaper; he seemed at least forty.

"Can these be fixed?"

The Young Man looked. "Dinny!" he called.

An old man emerged from the rear of the shop and picked up Ronan's boots. "Five minutes." He took the boots away.

"Big walker?" said the Young Man, now back in his newspaper.

"Yes. I'm going on to Roscrea."

"I suppose somebody has to," said the Young Man. "D'you live there?"

"No, I'm heading to the Devil's Bit."

The Young Man looked up with fresh interest. "What'n the Lord's happening up on the Devil's Bit?"

"I just want to see it."

"There'll be a crowd there."

"Oh?"

"Well, you're the second man in a week's going there."

Ronan's interest heightened. "Who was the first?"

"A German tourist. He heard the story of it, and he wants to measure the gap and then measure the Rock of Cashel to see would it fit. Isn't that very German?"

Ronan said, "So you know the story too?"

The Young Man said, "Do you know how I heard it? A pal of mine came in here the other day, he had an old lad with him, and he says to me, 'Gus, I want you to give this gentleman a pair of boots free, gratis, and for nothing.' That's what he said—straight out."

"And did you?"

"I asked him, 'Why should I?' and my pal said to me, 'Because of his trade.' So I said, 'What's your trade?' and my pal answered for the old lad, 'Oh, Gus, you'll love his product, I assure you of that, would I steer you wrong?' And d'you know what—didn't he persuade me to hand over the boots? I wasn't that happy, I can tell you."

Ronan said, "Did you find out more?"

"Oh, yeah, wait and I'll tell you. 'Now at least will you tell me what your trade is?' I said to him when he had the boots in a bag under his arm. And my gentleman pal said to me, 'He tells stories.' I said, 'What good are stories to me?' and they could see I didn't like it. My pal said, 'Look at the time. You'll be closing in fifteen minutes. Close now, and this man'll pay you for the boots with a story.' I closed—I'm always glad to close early. I banged the door shut and I closed the blinds—and I declare to God, wasn't I there for another two hours, and didn't I send him off with two free pairs of boots?"

"When did this happen?"

"Dinny, when did I give away them boots?"

Dinny called from the back of the shop, "Nineteen-fifty-two."

The Young Man said, "That's right, my father was dead a year."

Ronan paid for the rubber heels and said, "Nine years ago. So— you would have no idea at all where the man went?"

"No, but I've a cousin he always stays with, and if you're going to Roscrea, you might as well go the whole hog and go on to Cashel. He's a vet—if you've anything wrong with you, he'll fix it."

The Devil had a wide mouth. Ronan had to spend four days in the village of Moneygall, sheltering from violent rain, before he could attempt the top of the plateau. When he did, he loved it. He had no easy ascent; the ground was rough, the limestone base pocked and scarred, with little steeps and ridges. Heavy scrub tore at him, and once or twice he almost twisted an ankle. But at the top the sun came out and lit all the colors in the rocks.

To amuse himself, he tried to pace the actual width of the Bit, but brambles and awkward terrain made it impossible. He contented himself with staying half a day there, standing on each crest looking in all directions.

In Moneygall that night, they persuaded him that, were he to rise early, he could "walk to Cashel dawn to dusk" if he stuck to the bank of the river Suir; "Sure you can—that's why 'tis called the Suir—the Suir for sure."

It proved a little less sure than that. To begin with, the river seemed too small to have national significance, and he felt uncertain of his trail. Next, not a few ditches proved impassable, and in one field a menacing bull sent him on a circuit. Two nights in separate houses, one free, one a bed-and-breakfast with a dog that barked all night, half comforted him, and by now, past the town of Thurles, the river at last had status.

He reached Cashel three days later, at noon in sunshine. From a public telephone he dialed the number he had been given.

"I'd like to speak to Eddie Landers."

"The very man. Who's this?" Rich, friendly voice; broad, slow sounds. "Yeah, Gus is my cousin. I'm not as lazy as him. Where are you, and I'll come and collect you."

Ten minutes later, Ronan closed his eyes during the fastest, most perilous drive he had ever known; the veterinary surgeon's rusting car had once been green and now stank like a mortuary.

"There's two hundred thousand miles on this thing, and I've carried sheep and dogs and even deer in the back. We've to stop here."

They raced up a long, white-fenced avenue, and the vet swung into a stable yard.

"Come on with me."

They walked from the car to a large, open stable door, and inside, three people stood or crouched around something on the ground.

"Ah, how ya, Eddie, the man we want."

Greetings rang all around. They stepped back, and the vet went in among them.

"Ohhhhh, now, what's-this-what's-this?"

He dropped to his hunkers and began to stroke the flanks of a young and frightened chestnut horse.

"What time'd it happen? Ohhhh, now, now, that's a sore thing, we'll fix it, we'll fix it in a minute." He spoke to the horse as to a child.

"Just when we were letting her out in the paddock. Eight o'clock or so."

"Wire?"

"No, thank God. She kicked at the gate, and a spar tore her."

"Good girl, good girl, good girl, easy now, easy, easy."

Ronan could have sworn the horse's eyes lost their white frightened glare when the vet spoke. Or was it the caress, the genuine tenderness with which he stroked the animal's coat?

After fifteen minutes of silent work with ointments and a bandage, they freed the young horse and eased her into a standing position.

"Walk her a bit," said the vet. He stood back, watched, then walked with her. "H'm. She's not what I'd call lamed. When is she going next?"

"Gowran Park, Saturday week."

"H'm. She might do."

The horse plunged her head; the vet caught the bridle, held her down tight, stroked her nose, then released her, did this twice more, talking to her, talking—and she stood still.

"And I'll come out tomorrow again. If it swells any more, give me a shout."

They climbed into the wild car and, faster than before, the vet raced down the avenue, honked once on the main road, and exited without changing speed or looking anywhere but straight ahead.

"Horses, they're the ones worry me the most—I'm keener to fix a horse than anything."

He turned at a wild right angle down a lane, and in half a mile or so screeched the car to one side and parked it.

"Okey-dokey, we'll get out here. Now you're looking for 'Himself,' as we call him."

"I am. Is he all right?"

"C'mon, you're dressed for the fields. We're going up there." He pointed to a ruined castle ahead. "I was here with him the day before yesterday."

"What?!" Ronan almost fell off the gate he was climbing.

Eddie Landers would not be interrupted.

"And he amazed me. And since I'm a bit of a storyteller myself, I'll pass on to you what he told me—about the time the famous Dean Swift stayed here, in this castle. You know who he was? And the fellow that wrote *Gulliver's Travels* was a wild man himself by all accounts."

They climbed a steep field, Ronan took out his notebook, and the vet began to talk.

JONATHAN SWIFT LIVED IN DUBLIN—HE WAS THE dean of Saint Patrick's Cathedral, which means he belonged to the Church of Ireland, the Irish version of the Church of England. A Protestant. Unless they're Catholics, we call everyone Protestants, unless, of course, they're Jews. Technically speaking, "Protestant" should only refer to those people who dissented from King Henry the Eighth's version of the Reformation, but who weren't Catholics—nonconformists such as Presbyterians, Methodists, Baptists, Unitarians, and the like. But no, we call 'em all Protestants, and that's that. My own name, Landers, that's French.

So: in those terms, Swift was a Protestant—and a fearless man. He said he was "a clergyman of special note, for shunning those of his own coat." And the story our old friend told me—he said 'tis also a description of life in Ireland at a particular juncture in history.

It all happened on this hillside we're standing on. Swift came here because he'd heard in Dublin that the man who lived in this house spent all his money entertaining people and looking after a multitude of guests.

The whole place—that ruin up ahead—it was owned by people called Mathew, they were generally a strong family. They started well and got better. And they added on so much here that you can't see the outline of the original house—which was built in sixteen-seventy. It was simple enough in the beginning, mostly brick, built by George Mathew—his father had married a local lady. This George Mathew was a modest sort of a man, and he had been content with a good, strong two-story house and his farm of fifteen hundred acres—God, we'd all be happy with that.

Then his grandson came along—he was the man Swift had heard

about. He was so lavish in his spending and his way of entertaining that he was called "Grand" George Mathew, and he took over the house in seventeen-eighteen.

Grand George added fifty bedrooms to the place and built a theater, a banqueting hall, which was nearly twenty yards long, and other things too—I'll tell you about them in a minute or two. He hired the best gardeners he could find to make him beautiful landscapes like the king of France had in Versailles. One of the things they built was a bowling green—and that's nearly the hardest piece of gardening in the world to do. It has to be as level as a board and as soft as a carpet, and the grass has to be nearly like velvet.

Grand George also got them to build a very beautiful ornamental lake, and that was the scene of a great tragedy. You see that dwarf tree down there? At that exact spot, a child of the Mathew family died one day. That long, shallow hollow in the ground—that was the bed of the lake. The child, who was only two, fell in and drowned; and the nurse having care of the child was given the blame and dismissed from her job, a very serious business.

She said she was blamed in the wrong, and she put a curse on the place and said the tree would never grow another inch and that the castle itself, by now a very grand place with towers and turrets, would one day become no more than a nesting place for crows and jackdaws. Which, as you can see, is exactly what's happened.

However, when Swift got here, he came through the gates—they were down there, on the main road. He stayed the night before in the village of Golden, two miles away, in some sort of inn that wasn't up to much, but when he finished his breakfast in the morning, there was a coach drawn by six horses waiting to take him to the castle. And he was thrilled at that.

About fifty yards from the castle's main gate, the workmen who built the entrance had set a large flagstone in the ground. It measured twenty feet by fifteen feet, and when the hooves of a horse or the wheels of a carriage hit this flagstone, it sank an inch or two. That flagstone rested on an iron pad, which set in motion a series of levers. They operated one off the other, until the gates of the main entrance swung open slowly for the visitors to pass through without stopping.

When Swift's carriage with the six horses went through those gates, they faced pitch darkness. Each side of the avenue, which was nearly a mile long, had been planted with laurels that met in the middle, making night out of day. But when the gates swung closed behind the carriage, the visitors heard something very beautiful. All the laurels had been hung with small bells, and the air stirred by the carriage rang them. By the time any visitors emerged from the avenue at the top of the slope, the hosts of the castle had been alerted to expect them.

By the way, the carriage horses—my guess is that most of them were what we call three-quarter-breds and maybe even bigger than that, because it's a known fact that Grand George kept twenty hunters for his guests.

Anyway, the coachman swung his six horses up along the Bell Walk, as that dark avenue was known, and emerged by that grassy mound over there, which was the castle's ice pit. If you look at it now, you'll find a very well made, deep stone beehive lined with brick, and it's as cold as ice, even on a warm day like today. Our old storytelling friend told me he tried to stay in it once, thinking it an excellent place to shelter from the winds, but the cold drove him out of it.

The coach turned right at the ice pit and rattled along here, on the greensward before the castle doors. By the way, their builder called those three towers you see on the castle "French architectural spires," and they were modeled on a great chateau in Normandy, not far from where my own family name comes from.

Swift got down from the carriage—they say it was a beautiful morning. He had been charmed by the engineering of the opening gateway and delighted by the ringing of the bells; he had then been most impressed with the position and presence of the castle. And who wouldn't be? You can see that it must have been a fine building—look at the strength of some of those walls.

The Dean stood here where we're standing and looked all around him. To the north we can see the Rock of Cashel and way beyond it the Devil's Bit, where Saint Patrick chased Beelzebub out of Ireland—that's another great story our friend tells. Over to the east we're looking at Slievenamon, the Mountain of the Women, where, as everybody knows, Finn MacCool found a wife. To the south we find the gay Galtee Mountains. And west is the hill of Kilfeakle, where Saint Patrick lost a tooth and founded a church—as you already know, because I think our old friend said he told that story one night in your house.

So Jonathan Swift stood and looked at all this. And then he looked again at the castle.

"What in the name of God," says he, "is the use of such a vast house?"

One of the men traveling with him said to the Dean that there'd surely be a lot of guests here, because Mr. Mathew had forty apartments built specially for guests to stay, and that they were all probably full, except for what had been reserved for the Dean and his party. Swift climbed back into the coach.

"I'm going back to Dublin," says he. "I'm not going to mix with a crowd that big."

But however cantankerous a man he was, he also had very good manners, and he thought for a minute and he said, "No, I can't do that, I said I'd accept the man's invitation, but it means I've lost a whole fortnight out of my life and I'll just have to put up with it."

So he sat there, in a sulk. After some minutes he got a bit annoyed again because no one had come out to greet him. And yet he had heard that the hospitality of this house was unmatched in the British Isles.

"Maybe," says he, "I'm not so welcome after all."

He ordered the coachman to turn around and drive away, but at that moment a local woman who worked at the castle was passing nearby and saw the Dean. She was the great-great-grandmother of an elderly Ryan lady who lives in that house down there in the village, the little yellow house. This servant woman ran to the castle and alerted a steward, who hurried off to get the boss.

Grand George Mathew was living up to his name that day. The reason no one had seen Swift arrive was because there was a big, lavish party going on. But when he heard that his distinguished visitor was here, Grand George dashed out from the banquet and caught the carriage just in time.

He calmed the great Dean with sweet words and told him he must agree to be the guest of honor at the feast. And why wouldn't he? Swift was already one of the most famous men in the British Isles. He had written renowned books and made fierce attacks on the government and the rulers of the day. His personality dominated all his society, and people loved to tell stories about him.

For instance, he was at work one day at his writing table at the Deanery in Dublin when he heard a loud commotion in the yard. He looked out the window, saw a large crowd gathering, and called his servant.

"Who are all those people in the yard?"

"Dean, they've come to watch an eclipse of the sun."

"Go out and tell them," said Swift, "that it's been postponed."

He was a heavy sort of man, about five feet eight or nine or ten inches tall and known to be very cautious with his money. Except— whenever he left the Deanery to go anywhere, he had his pockets full of coins to give to the poor. And he had a taste for mocking pompous folk, which made him very popular with the people of Ireland.

There's another story about him that you'll hear in Dublin to this day. Swift called to see a friend of his one morning and was told by the servant that the man wasn't at home. A few days later, the same man came to see Swift—who saw him coming, opened the window, and shouted out, "I'm not at home." The visitor said, "What are you talking about? I can see you with my own two eyes." And Swift said, "Listen, mister, I believed it when it was only your servant said you weren't at home. So now when the master himself tells you he's not at home, why won't you believe him?"

He hated injustice, and even though he belonged to the Protestant ruling classes, he didn't side with them when it came to governing the people of Ireland. His attacks on the king and the government made him many friends—and many enemies.

Anyway, here he was, walking up the greensward in front of Thomastown Castle on the arm of Grand George Mathew, who said, "Let me show you the place—there's a good view of it from this gate."

They climbed this little hill and stood up there, by the ramparts, where they could get the widest view.

"That's the formal garden," said Grand George. "And there's the ornamental lake. And these here are the terraces."

He pointed to those three grass terraces over there.

Now: the Dean was a man, who, no matter how he washed himself—and there's no evidence that he washed himself much—could never look clean.

Nevertheless he said to Grand George, "Do you have bathtubs for your guests?"

"We do," said Grand George, "big tubs, you could have a swim in one of them, they're so capacious."

"And," said Dean Swift, "do you have people who can launder gentlemen's clothes?"

"We have them too," said Grand George, who was getting a little puzzled at this turn in the conversation. He had more puzzlement to come.

The Dean began to empty his pockets—his pens, his pocketknife, his notebook, all the contents—and he handed everything to Grand George, who stood there, his mouth open, not knowing what to do with all these personal possessions—a snuff box, a pipe, a book the Dean was reading, and a little tobacco pouch, a box of wig powder, a wallet, and so on.

"Stand aside," said the Dean. And Grand George and the coachman and Swift's servant, who always traveled with him, and a servant from the castle—they all stood aside.

The Dean lay down on the grass at the top of the first terrace and folded his arms to his chest. Then, like a child playing, he rolled himself over and began to roll down the first terrace, and then he rolled himself along the little plateau and down the second terrace, and then he rolled himself across the next little plateau and down the third terrace, and at the bottom of it he gave himself a few vigorous extra rolls until he was stopped by a box hedge in the formal gardens.

He stood up and waved to everyone above, and then Grand George could see why Swift had asked so particularly about bathtubs and laundry—the Dean was muddy from the top of his white wig to the ankles of his white socks. But he was smiling like a child.

Grand George walked down the terraces to meet him, and the two gentlemen went into the castle.

"I fear," said the Dean, "that by the time I've washed and put on clean linen, I may be late for your banquet."

"Not at all," said Grand George. "The banquet has scarcely started. And besides, I've other things to show you."

"Well," says Swift, "To tell you the truth, I'm not in much of a mood for a banquet right now, but I don't want to be rude."

"Listen, Dean," says Grand George, "this feasting will continue for another three days—I mean to say, the musicians have scarcely warmed up. Go in and get yourself washed and rested, and we'll talk again."

"Are you sure?" said the Dean.

Grand George put his arm around Swift's shoulder, and this is what he said to him.

"This is your castle for as long as you're staying here. Eat your breakfast at any hour you want to, be it four or eight in the morning. Eat your dinner at any hour of the day you want to. And the same for your supper. And if you want to stay in your apartment and never meet the other guests—invite anyone you like to join you. When you come down, I'll show you more."

Swift went in, took a bath, put on clean clothes, and came down the grand staircase where his host was waiting for him—he had been tipped off by the servants that the Dean was out of the bath and getting ready.

"Now," said Grand George, "come with me."

First of all he showed Swift the parlor.

"If you want to eat here, you can. There are servants on hand to take your order any hour of the night or day."

Then he let him peep into the banqueting hall, which was full of carousing people, but Swift didn't want to go in there just then.

Next he took him to two unusual rooms. In the castle, Grand George had built a replica of a London coffeehouse—they were very popular at the time—and in it he had all the things you'd expect, books and newspapers and decks of cards and chessboards and all the accoutrements of a coffeehouse. Next door to that was a tavern, just like a pub in Dublin or London, with a barman in a blue apron, and that was where a lot of guests went after dinner, even though Grand George himself wasn't a drinking man at all. And he showed Swift the billiard tables and the foxhounds and the stables and rods for fishing in the river Suir.

"Is that how you pronounce it?" said Swift. "Like 'for sure'? I always thought it was pronounced like 'sewer.' "

And they had a good laugh at that.

For the next three days Swift mixed with no one but his traveling companions and his host, Grand George, who took him out riding across the estate, where he showed off all the building and fencing and gardening that he was planning. Finally on the fourth night, the Dean took his place at the head of the table on the right hand of his host in the banqueting hall, and it became the most famous stay ever in the castle.

Remember how he complained that he'd have to lose a fortnight out his life? Well—Swift stayed for months. Two reasons caused this; first of all, he was so magnetic, he was such a great man, that Grand George let him stay longer than any guest had ever done. And secondly, the Dean felt he was being entertained so lavishly and cared for so comfortably that he didn't want to leave. The year, they say, was seventeen-twenty-three; that'd make him fifty-six. Others say he didn't come here until seventeen-thirty-five, but what does it matter, so long as he came here?

He also made good use of his visit. Think now on the times that were in it. The Battle of the Boyne was over, the Penal Laws had been coming into force at a rate of one every two years or so, each law more oppressive than the one before, and the great majority of the people in Ireland were badly downtrodden. And here, in the heart of lush Tipperary, Jonathan Swift took part in as luxurious a life as could be had in the world at that time.

In his private apartment in the castle, he had as many servants as he cared to call for; they would have washed his face for him, if he asked. Grand George granted him privacy or gaiety, as he preferred; Swift chose both. But he was also very interested in the contrast between this life here in the castle and the lives of the people who lived all around.

When the Irish were evicted from their lands, they took three pathways. The first road led to the outer world, by emigration, mostly to America in those days, because no Irishman could ever imagine a welcome could be found for him and his large family in England. That, thank God, changed a long time ago.

The second pathway proved long and winding, a path our old friend the Storyteller knows well. Some families simply took to the road and became itinerants. People called them gypsies, a term that was born of the word *Egypt,* because these travelers had haphazard clothing and colorful wagons—they looked as exotic as something that might have come from a country with a name so exciting as Egypt. And people also called them tinkers—because they sold pots and pans and other implements that they made out of tin. Nowadays we call them travelers or traveling people, and the hardness of their lives has never diminished since the day their ancestors, MacCarthys or O'Connors or Sheridans, had to leave their houses and take to what they call the "long acre," the grass margin on the side of the road.

However, many of the dispossessed couldn't bear to leave the countryside where they'd grown up and where they knew every branch of every tree, every blade of grass. So they stayed, very often on common land at the side of the road, and they built houses for themselves—if you can call them houses; as the Eskimos build igloos with blocks of ice, the dispossessed Irish built cabins with clods of turf.

Using their hands and working with stones sharp as knives, they lifted mats of turf from the ground and piled them on top of each other until they had built four walls. These walls usually formed a square or a rectangle around the bare earth from which they had lifted the turf, and therefore the cabins had earthen floors. Then they laid branches of trees across these turf walls, like a tight lattice, and across these branches they laid more lengths of turf as a roof. Eventually the little house seemed almost to merge into the landscape.

Swift saw the contrast between those people and the people at the banquet in the castle. So when he stayed here, he walked out across the countryside, looking at how the poor people lived, what they ate, how they grew potatoes on small patches of ground and cherished a hen as though it were a prize animal, because eggs also can feed a household. He found dignity among them—no bitterness that he could discern, but no future for them that he could imagine.

And he offered an interesting opinion. Everybody, said he, is afraid of being attacked by the Irish. But these people haven't the strength to revolt; they're too poor and too hungry. And there is one thing of which you may be sure: he never departed such a house without leaving behind some of his famous coins. During his time here he distributed many of them, and people grew very fond of the Dean.

Now, here's the tail of this tale. Looking due north from where we stand, this castle estate was planted with wonderful trees. It had been arranged in groves, very artistic landscape gardening, and— see!—there are still stands and regiments of lime trees from the original planting. And if you look down there by the roadside, there was an exceptionally fine beech tree, tall and broad with spreading branches; I remember it well, it was in front of that house, which is the teacher's.

On many an afternoon Dean Swift walked down the slopes of these fields to the banks of the ornamental lake. Beyond it, he came to the shade of the big beech tree and sat there for hours, reading and writing. Sometimes people walked by, and he either greeted them civilly or never even saw that they were there; he was that kind of man.

Many words of debate have been squandered since seventeen-forty-five, the year Swift died, as to whether he went mad. He did leave money in his will to found a lunatic asylum in Dublin—as he indicated in the bequest, he believed no country needed it as much as Ireland did. But that doesn't necessarily prove he was insane; indeed a lot of people would argue it proved the direct opposite!

What is true is that the beech tree was called Swift's Tree, and not just because he sat under it on that famous visit. It fell to the ground in a great storm some time in the late nineteen-forties; everyone was surprised with the ease at which it fell—and boy! Didn't it make a great crash as it came down.

When they went to examine it and cut it up for firewood, the local people found that it had been rotting from the top—just like the strange Dean who had come among them.

Eddie Landers sighed. He began to walk down the slope toward the castle entrance tower. Ronan followed him.

"See that big house down there? People called Fitzgeralds own it now. That used to be the dower house of the castle—the Mathew family owned it too, and every spring the daffodils still come up, tracing the initials of the family." He turned to Ronan. "I could stay here all day, but I have to go. What about you?"

"I don't know what to do."

Eddie Landers wrinkled his freckled face in thought.

"Well, you nearly had him here." Silence. "What would I do if I was you?" Silence. "I wouldn't know what to do. But this is a small country, everyone knows everyone else. So all I can do is hand you on to someone else who might help. If he's at their house, you're in luck—if not, ask them to send you to the next likely place."

Eddie Landers took Ronan from the deep countryside to a busier road.

"From here you'll get to the town of Callan in county Kilkenny. And you'll know the minute you cross the county border—I always do. Ask for a man called Mick Walsh; he's a builder, and they call him 'Mick the Brick,' but don't call him that to his face. He likes to be addressed as Michael. He may know where the man is. And when you find our old friend, tell him I said it's time for him to come in off the road. He's too old now for the traipsing and tramping. If he ever needs a place to live, I'm sure I could fix him up."

They shook hands. "Thank you," said Ronan.

"You know where I am," said the vet. "Any time. Have you enough money on you, do you need any?"

Ronan shook his head and thanked him again, and the car that had once been green and now sported widely the brown of rust, that had traveled two hundred thousand pell-mell miles, snorted away.

Mick the Brick had not seen the Storyteller, but he knew a woman in Kilkenny city who kept an eye on all of these things.

The woman in Kilkenny city did indeed "keep an eye" on many things, she said, but not on the current whereabouts of the Story- teller. A teacher of her acquaintance, she said, down in Mullinavat, was interested in such things, and he might know.

The man in Mullinavat told Ronan that the woman in Kilkenny city confused him with a man in Mooncoin, who lived by the river; and the man in Mullinavat said, "D'you know the song?" and he sang a few bars: "Where the thrush and the linnet their sweet notes entwine/With you, lovely Molly, the Rose of Mooncoin." Ronan thanked him, and the man said, "I think I got the words of that verse wrong, but 'tis the only verse I know."

In Mooncoin, he never met the man. Certainly such a figure existed; Ronan established that; but the man's wife said he had a headache and couldn't come to the door. She asked what Ronan wanted, and she said, "The old Storyteller? He was here, but not for a while. I know who'll know. There's a Mrs. Colfer in New Ross who always puts him up—she's easy to find, she has the bakery."

Mrs. Colfer's married daughter said her mother was gone to Lourdes on a pilgrimage and would not return for two days, but Ronan was welcome to stay, they did bed-and-breakfast. While he stayed there, they served bread mostly and some ham and many eggs. The stay restored him; by the time Mrs. Colfer returned from Lourdes, a full week had gone by since he met Eddie Landers and heard the tale of Jonathan Swift.

When Mrs. Colfer saw Ronan, she lit up.

"You met our Celia, she's the married one, but did you meet Catherine at all? She's about your age."

Mrs. Colfer evidently ate a lot of her own baking. Ronan made a polite noise, and Mrs. Colfer said, "I'll tell you what, Celia says you're a history student, there's a great piece of history on here tomorrow night."

Mrs. Colfer led Ronan to a poster in the hallway of the bakery: "The True Story of the 1798 Rebellion. In Song and Story."

The poster showed three happy men with dark hair and dark eyes, peas in a pod, and the words beneath them read, "Three Furlongs from Home."

"Who are they?"

Mrs. Colfer looked at Ronan as at an ignoramus. "Is it under a stone you live?"

"How do you mean?"

"How do I mean? They're famous the length and breadth of Wexford."

"But I've never been in Wexford before."

"Your loss."

"But—what are they?"

"They're triplets."

"No, I mean—are they historians?"

"What?! Why would they be that? They're country-and-western singers. Billy, Shane, and Ronnie Furlong."

"But—"

"You keep saying 'but.' D'you know what? You've more butts than a goat."

"What I'm asking is, how do country-and-western singers tell the story of the 1798 Rebellion?"

"Catherine'd love to go. She's a big fan. Catherine'll get the tickets, you can pay her. It starts at eight sharp."

At nine o'clock that night, Ronan sat squeezed tight on a backless bench beside Mrs. Colfer's daughter, in a "hall" with walls and roof of corrugated steel; bare earth was the floor. They had been there for more than an hour, but no performer had yet appeared. A "bar" (a series of naked trestle tables) ran the length of one wall and sold whiskey, gin without tonic, and bottles of lager beer. Ahead, on a "stage," men came and went, stopping to chat, laughing, fixing speakers and cables. Some blew into microphones—"One, two, three, four, testing, hallo-hallo"—and handled banter from the crowd.

"Are them suits coming back into fashion?"

"Make sure you finish every song together."

One or two men plunked a guitar and hustled short riffs; a bald man bruised the buttons of an accordion.

Finally, at ten minutes past ten o'clock, various characters slouched onto the podium and took up positions. Soon, one by one and each stopping to chat along the way, three men came to the fore. In their late forties at least, they wore check shirts with pearl buttons and dog-eared buckskin fringes, long blue dungarees, and cowboy hats. A smattering of applause broke out, pierced with two-finger whistles. For the life of him Ronan could not work out how he might come to hear from these men's lips the history of Ireland's most heartbreaking rebellion, the near-and-yet-so-far Insurrection of 1798.

The balding man with the accordion picked up a microphone and blew into it. "Testing, testing. Ladies and gentlemen. Hallo, hallo, hallo, and give a big hand to the singers you might think are racehorses, judging from their names. But they're thoroughbreds all right, here they are—the most famous triplets in all county Wexford, Ronnie, Shane and Billy—Three Furlongs from Home."

Under cover of the applause, Ronan said to Catherine Colfer, "Are there lots of triplets in all Wexford?"

"No—they're the only ones."

"So why did he call them 'the most famous triplets in all Wexford'?"

Catherine looked at him as at a wall and said, "Well, if they're the only triplets in county Wexford, they're the most famous triplets in county Wexford, aren't they?"

A Furlong stood forward.

"D'evening, ladies and gentlemen, or should I say boys 'n girls, we're all young inside. I'm Chet, this is my brother Brett, and over there on slide guitar is our brother Ever-*ett*—and we're the—Three Furlongs from Home!"

Loud applause and whistles.

Ronan said, "I thought their names were Shane and Billy and Ronnie."

"They are."

"But he just said they were called Chet, Brett, and Ever-ett."

"Ah, those're their stage names, no one takes any notice."

The three Furlongs, at a sign from Chet, whipped off their cowboy hats and shouted a wild. "Yeeeee-haaaaa!"

Ronan asked, "And where's 'Home'?"

"That's where they're from," said Catherine.

"You mean there's an actual place with the name 'Home'?"

"Yeah. We all have one."

"Have we?"

"Yeah. I'm from home. You're from home."

Ronan felt a rising irritation. "No. I mean—what is the name of their native place? Is their native place called Home?"

"You're very particular," said Catherine. "They're from Enniscorthy."

"So why don't they call themselves 'Three Furlongs from Enniscorthy'?"

She looked at him with matchless pity.

"Were you ever at the races? Because if you were, you'd know that when the horses are coming to the finish, they're four furlongs from home, and then they're three furlongs from home, and then they're two furlongs from home, and so on."

Onstage, the Furlongs began to pick at guitars and banjos.

Ronan thought aloud. "So—if there were only two of them, if they were twins rather than triplets would they be Two Furlongs from Home?" He broke off. "I don't think I understand this at all."

The Furlongs began to sing. Their renderings had a ruinous nostalgia; "Nobody's Child," followed by "Shall I Ne'er See You More, Gentle Mother?"

"Why are their songs so—mournful?" said Ronan beneath the everlouder applause. He felt too polite to say "terrible" or "maudlin."

"Shhhhhh-up, will you?"

Two more songs followed, about an emigrant girl with tuberculosis and the shooting of a beloved pet dog. A boy appeared with a tray and several full pint glasses.

Chet lifted his glass and looked at it.

"We must be careful not to get ineeberated."

Ronan said, "I think he means 'inebriated.' "

Catherine said, "If he meant it, he'd say it."

Chet, Brett, and Ever-ett swigged from their large drinks, put the glasses down, and walked together to the front of the stage. They assumed mournful expressions. Chet did the talking.

"Now, ladies 'n gentlemen or, should I say, boys 'n girls, we bring you the Wexford Trilogy, our famous rendition of the seventeen-ninety-eight rebellion in song and story. As some of you may know, this can be very heartrending, and we'd be grateful for no applause till we're finished. So" —he waved his hand expansively and rippled guitar strings—"Music, maystro, please."

The bald man on the accordion squeezed out eight bars of unmistakable lament. Each Furlong removed his cowboy hat and bowed his head; and each, Ronan saw, had identical bald circles. When the accordion ended its sobbing, Chet raised his head high, put on his hat, looked nobly into the distance, and began to intone.

I N THE YEAR OF OUR LORD SEVENTEEN HUNDRED
and ninety-eight, the people of Wexford rose up against the
oppressor, England, who had captured most of our land for
centuries. There are three Wexford songs that tell the story of the
Rising, "Boolavogue," "Kelly of Killanne," and "The Croppy Boy,"
and as I provide the verbal narration, my brothers and me will sing
these songs as musical illustrations of this gallant but tragic time.
Take it away, Brett.

At Boolavogue when the sun was setting
O'er the bright May meadows of Shelmalier
A rebel band set the heather blazing
And brought the neighbors from far and near.

Any of you here from the parish of Shelmalier tonight cannot but
feel a burst of pride oozing from your stout heart at the memory of
what your neighbors did when called to arms. But they weren't the
only ones. Take it away, Ever-ett.

It was early, early all in the spring
The small birds whistled and sweet did sing.
Changing their notes from tree to tree
And the song they sang was, Old Ireland Free.

Yes, that was surely the song they sang, because an Ireland not free
will always be a prisoner, because no prisoner is ever free. But the
Croppy Boy, who heard the birds changing their notes from tree to

tree, he knew those birds must have heard something—it was the call to arms they heard, and he answered that call.

A note of historical importance here, ladies 'n gentlemen, or should I say boys 'n girls, because we're all young inside; he went and got his hair cut—he got it cropped so that he would look like one of the French revolutionaries who, nine years earlier, had cast off the yoke of slavery and stormed the palace of oppression called the Back Steel in gay Paree. And that's why he and his comrades-in-arms were known as the Croppies, on account of the cropped hair. And he wasn't the only hero—here's the man we all adore, I'll sing this myself because the tempo is quicker.

What's the news, what's the news, O my bold Shelmaliers
With your long-barreled gun of the sea?
Say what wind from the south blows his messenger here
With a hymn of the dawn for the free?
Goodly news, goodly news, do I bring youth of Forth,
Goodly news shall you hear, Bargy man.
For the boys march at dawn from the south to the north
Led by Kelly the boy from Killanne.

Yes, all you boys 'n girls from Forth and from Bargy, you can all give yourselves a pat on the back and stand up there with the massed ranks of the people from Shelmalier and take your places among the nations of the earth.

Another historical note—the wind from the south was from France, who were sending an army to help us, but as we well know, not all wind is beneficial, and the French ships were blown off course. The gallant men of Wexford with their famous haircuts went ahead anyway and rose up guided by the hand of God him-self—or at least his representative here on earth. Take it away, Brett.

Then Father Murphy, from old Kilcormack,
Spurred up the rocks with a warning cry;

"Arm! Arm!" he cried, "for I've come to lead you,
For Ireland's freedom we live or die."

Thank you, Brett. The game was rightly on now. Father Murphy, a
horse of a man, was not alone in his valor. Sometimes I prefer to
speak the words because they're like poetry. So—

Tell me who is that giant with gold curly hair
He who rides at the head of your band.
Seven feet is his height with some inches to spare
And he looks like a king in command.

And everyone here from the slopes of Mount Leinster tonight
knows the answer to that question.

Ah, my lads, that's the pride of our bold Shelmaliers
'Mongst our bravest of heroes a man.
Fling your beavers aloft and give three ringing cheers
For John Kelly, the Boy from Killanne.

Shelmalier is getting a lot of mentions tonight—I hope the rest of
you aren't too jealous, that's history for you. And another historical
note, a beaver is a hat—here in Wexford, anyway. Wasn't John Kelly
some man? Seven feet was his height with some inches to spare—to
continue the poetry, he was as tall as a ladder and as golden as a
stack of corn. On with the story.

The rest of the country was supposed to break out in a rash that
same week—a rash of rebellion. But the rash wasn't widespread.
Isn't that funny? Normally you wouldn't want a rash not to
spread—and it would. And here was a rash people wanted to see
spreading—and it didn't. It spread in Wexford, though, and the red
color a rash usually has—it was blood this time, spilled by Father
Murphy and his men. Take it away, Brett.

He led us on 'gainst the coming soldiers,
And the cowardly Yeomen were put to flight;

'Twas up at Harrow the boys of Wexford
Showed England's regiments how men could fight.
Look out for hirelings, King George of England,
Search every kingdom where breathes a slave,
For Father Murphy from county Wexford
Sweeps o'er the land like a mighty wave.

A mighty wave is what he surely was. And he wasn't the only fish in the sea—here comes my boy with his gold, curly hair.

Enniscorthy's in flames and old Wexford is won
And the Barrow tomorrow we'll cross.
On a hill o'er the town we have planted a gun
That'll batter the gateway of Ross.
All the Forthmen and Bargymen march o'er the heath
With brave Harvey to lead in the van
But the bravest of all in that grim gap of death
Was young Kelly the boy from Killanne.

Another important historical note here—the brave Harvey was of course, Bagenal Harvey, a member of the United Irishmen, the revolutionary group led by Theobald Weolfe Tone who started this rebellion, and when I say "brave Harvey to lead in the van," I mean that he was up in front and not in a vehicle. And while my boy John Kelly was fighting, let us not forget Brett and his men. All yours, Brett.

We took Camolin and Enniscorthy,
And Wexford storming drove out our foes;
'Twas at Slieve Kilty our pikes were reeking
With the crimson stream of the beaten Yeos.
At Tubberneering and Ballyellis
Full many a Hessian lay in his gore;
Ah, Father Murphy, had aid come over
Our green flag floated from shore to shore!

Ronan looked at Catherine; she sat, hands folded, rapt and evidently in thrall; no support there. He glanced around the audience; all sat still and enraptured.

On the stage, a new development dragged his attention back to the Three Furlongs from Home. Brett and Ever-ett struck up a wild, throbbing strumming on their instruments, and Chet stepped forward a pace, freshly urgent.

ANOTHER HISTORICAL NOTE, LADIES 'N GENTLE-
men: a Hessian was an English soldier, German but English at the same time. But things are never what they
seem, and no man is safe till he's free; the tide turned against the
mighty wave, and the armies of Albion poured across our virgin
lands with the ruthless power of a helicopter and crushed us
once more beneath the heel of the mighty enemy. Take it away,
Brett.

At Vinegar Hill, o'er the pleasant Slaney,
Our heroes vainly stood back to back,
But the Yeos at Tullow took Father Murphy
And burned his body upon the rack.
God grant you glory, brave Father Murphy
And open heaven to all your men;
The cause that called you may call to-morrow
In another fight for the green again.

Yes, indeed, "God grant you glory, brave Father Murphy"—but
instead of that, you were hung, drawn, and quartered, and when
they were burning you on the rack, they stuck a pike through you
to make the point that this is what would happen to all rebels. And
I have a sad verse myself, for all good things were coming to an end
in the year of Our Lord seventeen-ninety eight.

But the gold sun of freedom grew dark over Ross
And it set by the Slaney's red wave

And old Wexford stripped naked hung high on a cross
Her heart pierced by traitors and slaves.

"Traitors and slaves"—never was a truer word spoke. Come in, Ever-ett.

As I was walking up Wexford Street
My own first cousin I did chance to meet
My own first cousin did me betray
And for one bare guinea sold my life away.

And he's not finished. More than the Croppy Boy's cousins betrayed him. Come on, Ever-ett.

As I was mounting the scaffold high,
My aged father was standing by.
My aged father did me deny
And the name he gave me was "The Croppy Boy."

And there you have it, boys 'n girls, that etipomizes the sadness of seventeen-ninety-eight—a man given a nickname by his own father. They say give a dog a bad name, and you can hang him—well, they hung the Croppy Boy, haircut an' all. Ever-ett, tell us the worst.

'Twas in Duncannon this young man died
At Passage East is his body laid.
All you good people, who may pass by
Breathe a prayer for the Croppy Boy.

The rising of seventeen-ninety-eight failed, and people died whole-sale. But it lives in our memories as another gallant episode in our history of breaking the English yoke. Join me and Brett and Ever-ett as we bring the house down in the last rousing four bars of our famous Wexford Trilogy.

Glory-oh, glory-oh to the brave men who died
In the cause of long downtrodden man.
Glory-oh to Mount Leinster's own darling and pride—
Dauntless Kelly, the boy from Killanne.

In the deafening applause, Ronan said, "They seem to be very popular."

"They deserve every bit of it," said Catherine. "All that history."

"Isn't the word *epitomize*—not *etipomize*?"

"Ah, things change," said Catherine. "This is Wexford."

Next day, Ronan left New Ross. Mrs. Colfer sent him to a priest in Enniscorthy who, she said, loved the Storyteller and liked to take care of him whenever he came through the town.

In the priest's house, he helped with the crossword and stayed for two days—"In case," said the priest, "our old friend turns up, like he did two months ago." It transpired that the priest's memory had certain failings—in fact, the Storyteller had not been there for two years; "But I know for certain he went to Arklow from here."

Ronan took this latest setback philosophically and headed up along the east coast. One burst of excitement eased the fruitlessness of his enquiries. Near Arklow he watched a stream flowing into the sea and suddenly recalled, with a shout, a detail from the Storyteller's account of Newgrange; the Architect had sailed into the hinterland of county Wicklow along such a river.

A quick inquiry took him inland along a riverbank, and he scrambled over rough country, through smooth fields, and then climbed a hill—there it was! He looked down at an old, overgrown quarry of small white stones; this was surely the place whence the Architect of Newgrange had ferried the stones "like the moon" for the facade of his tomb.

Ronan lingered, turning over in his hand one stone after another and finally slipping a beautiful specimen into his bag. He brimmed with excitement at this tangible proof from that glorious tale—yet in his elation, he felt a melancholy sense of having gone back to the beginning with nothing to show for his journey.

So it continued, day after day, week after week, into the tumbling blossoms of late May and June. This tall young man with spectacles and, now, a strengthening beard went from town to town, village to village. A large rucksack on his back, he walked or hitched rides in cars and trucks or sometimes took a bus. He met men and women who cooked him breakfast, some talking all the time, others remaining totally silent, yet others bending him with questions as to who he was and where he came from.

Of the beds he slept in, a few had concave mattresses, a few convex; some had nylon sheets out of which he gradually slid during the night; some had linen sheets of pure luxury. He stayed in houses that had fancy new bathrooms with elaborate tiles suggesting Egypt or the Incas, often in black and red, usually highly glazed. And he stayed in houses that had no bathrooms at all, where he washed his face in a basin on the landing and, when he asked for a bath, was told of the swimming pool in the next town.

The food remained more or less constant. Breakfast gave him wide strips of bacon with fried eggs, sausages like thick shiny glands, golden potato cakes, and doorsteps of toasted bread beside a pot of tea brewed so strong a mouse could stand on it. Lunch, when he took it, brought soup (very often unidentifiable), bacon, and cabbage followed by apple pie and cream. Dinner, called "supper" in some counties or "tea" in others, meant steak—succulent, thick steak, so large that the potatoes or cabbage or carrots had to be allotted a second, equally large plate. And, again, apple pie. Despite the fact that he walked many miles a day, he grew heavier, his beanpole frame gone forever.

Slowly he allowed the journey to gain an importance in itself, rather than continue to be dominated by the desperation of the quest. The weather brought him great fortune. That spring and summer of 1961 had a long-lasting sweetness, and the fields and the hedgerows grew many shades of green and white. He began to savor his surroundings; this seemed the only measure he could take to ease his disappointment. Sightings of the Storyteller grew fewer and farther apart, and he had almost exhausted all associations with the stories he had heard—though as yet he had not seen hares dance nor spent the night in the warm arms of a stone circle.

But by now, as part of the mental exercises he demanded of himself, he had created in his own mind a hierarchy of all the stories. The one that remained the most magical and the most important was the one told, he felt, especially for him—the roadside tale of Brendan the Navigator. "Look to the west," that story had said—the west was where Brendan, after many difficult journeys, had found his own destination. And so, with a fresh urgency, he let the journey lead him in that direction.

Ronan's map reckoned him a hundred miles from the Kerry coast. He walked for half a day, then increased his pace by catching a bus to Limerick. The bank there told him he still had "good money" left, so he bought a clean shirt and new underwear; too many days of being washed in streams and boardinghouse basins had reduced his existing possessions to lifeless gray.

He took another bus to Killarney. Sensing that his journey was coming to an end—and fearing too that he might not get what he wanted—he spent more than he had so far done on any one night's accommodation. It gave him a helpful result.

The hotel, though small, had high standards; excellent room, deep bath, and the best food since Dublin. He sat alone, as spruce as he could make himself. During dinner, as he jotted down his nightly record of the day, a man at the next table said, "Are you a writer?"

Ronan, though flattered, laughed. "No, I'm afraid I'm not."

"You look the part. The beard, the glasses, all that. And there's always writers coming to Killarney."

"I'm just passing through."

"But you're a writer at the moment; I saw you writing in your notebook. That makes you a writer, doesn't it?"

Ronan laughed again. "Just—notes."

"That's not a local accent?"

"No. I'm studying in Dublin."

"Not tonight you're not." He seemed about forty or more, suit, white shirt, tie, exceptionally large earlobes.

"Ray Cashman. Who're you?" He leaned over with a handshake.

"Ronan O'Mara."

"Will you have something, Ronan?"

"No, I don't actually drink."

"You're bad for my business, I'm a traveler in whiskey. Ah, well, I'll just have to support my own industry," and Ray Cashman ordered another drink.

They talked until one in the morning. Ronan found himself telling of his search for the Storyteller, and Ray Cashman proved an excellent audience. He asked for a story or two; Ronan told his best version yet of Newgrange and then of Strongbow's arrival in Ireland.

"Wish they taught us like that in school. Jesus, our history teacher was so bad, I can't remember the date I was born."

Three other people in the small bar (to which they had by then moved) listened keenly. One of them, with a white cyst on his forehead and an accent broad as a cliff, said, "There's a man with stories like that going to be in Derrynane tomorrow. He was invited there, and I know the man who invited him." The man nodded repeatedly to confirm his own story: "Derrynane House. I know the man who invited him. Derrynane, you know where I mean, O'Connell's old place."

Ray Cashman said to Ronan, "Right, we'll hit the hay, and tomorrow we'll hit Derrynane."

Over the mountains they went into deep Kerry, through towns with magical names—Killorglin, Glenbeigh, Caherciveen.

"Notice," said Ray Cashman, "we're taking the long way round because the scenery is nicer. And everyone knows the longest way round is the shortest way home."

Ronan said, "But this is taking you away from your work. What will your boss say?"

"I had cancer last year. They go very easy on me."

Nobody answered the doorbell at Derrynane House. They looked for a side door but at twelve noon, no life did they find.

"I need strength for this," said Ray Cashman, and they found a pub. After an hour in which he drank four whiskies and Ronan two lemonades, they went back. Now a car stood in the mossy forecourt, and the front door had opened.

Inside, a man sat polishing his shoes.

"Hallo," said Ray Cashman.

"Is it raining yet?" said the man.

"I don't know," said Ray Cashman. "We're not from around here."

"Then you won't get wet, I suppose."

"I'll tell you—we were hoping to meet a storyteller here. A tall man, isn't that right?" he confirmed to Ronan.

"So was I. But none of us'll be meeting him. Look."

The man reached to the floor and picked up an envelope.

"This was handed in. He was here, and I wasn't."

The envelope contained a note and some papers.

"Dear Mr. Kavanagh, I had hoped and intended to meet your audience in Derrynane. But my health is not good, and I am trying to find a place that will have me. I don't like the idea of going into the county home, for whatever name they use, it is still the poorhouse. But it grieves me to let people down, so I wrote out a little of something resembling what I was going to say. Maybe you could read it out to them. I'm sorry I'm not there to give a great deal more, and I hope you'll forgive me."

No signature; Ronan needed none when facing the broad, strong writing, with the tough, yet ornate downward strokes. Ronan began to read.

"Stop." Ray Cashman tapped his shoulder. "Shouldn't you do him the honor of reading it aloud? Who better than yourself?"

E VERYONE WHO HAS HEARD THE NAME DERRY-nane knows that it is associated indelibly with the name of a very great Irishman, Daniel O'Connell. He was a lawyer, a politician, an orator of remarkable might, a fighter against injustice, and a man who liked ladies very much indeed. Altogether a man to be treasured. He was born here in seventeen-seventy-five, and he died in eighteen-forty-seven, after a life of magnificent achievement.

It would take me ten nights to list out for you all the man did in his seventy-two years. For the first forty years of the last century, anything to do with Irish politics had to do with Daniel O'Connell. He broke down all sorts of barriers, he got the Penal Laws repealed, he held the biggest political meetings ever seen. Nobody else ever got half a million people in one place at one time; and he became not only Lord Mayor of Dublin but that rare species, a Catholic member of the English Parliament.

O'Connell stood well over six feet, a burly fellow with curly hair and a great wit about him. Bitterly opposed to the way England treated the Irish, he described the British prime minister, Robert Peel, as having a smile like moonlight glinting on the brass plate of a coffin. If ever a man could have made his way in the world by personality alone, that man was Daniel O'Connell.

He fathered a large known family, eleven children I believe, and since I am addressing an audience of adults, with no children present, I may tell a story of one of the many other children of Daniel O'Connell, who were born on what we call the wrong side of the blanket.

O'Connell was a famous courtroom defender; he understood all the niceties of law, the little twisty points on which a case may win or fail. Never blatantly obvious unless he had to be, always canny when he needed to be, he was reckoned to be a man who knew just when too much was too much, and maybe even more important, when to say very little.

One day he was coming back to Derrynane after winning a long court case; the prisoner had been in the dock for six weeks with the shadow of the noose hanging over him, and O'Connell got him off. Driving in his carriage over the mountains, he came to a house that he thought he had visited about eleven or twelve years before. The lady in question, if he remembered aright, was very good-looking, and her husband was an officer in the English army and away a great deal of the time.

O'Connell told his coachman to stop, and he walked into the house. It was dark enough inside, and the only person he saw was a boy of about ten or eleven tending a pot on the fire.

"Is the woman of the house here?"

The boy said, "She's out feeding the hens."

O'Connell said, "Is she your mother?"

"She is." The boy was very cool and composed.

"Will you please go out and tell her that Mr. Daniel O'Connell is here to see her?"

The boy replaced the lid on the pot and ran out. While he was gone, O'Connell darted over to the fire, lifted the lid, took out a potato—they hadn't boiled yet—and put it in his pocket. By the time the boy came back, our man Daniel was standing by the doorway again, looking as if butter wouldn't melt in his mouth.

"My mother said she'll be here in a minute"—and the boy went back to his potatoes. He lifted the lid off the pot, looked at the potatoes, looked at O'Connell, and looked at the potatoes again. He sat back on his haunches, leaned forward once more, and looked into the pot.

"Is there anything wrong?" said O'Connell, nice as pie.

The boy said, "When I left this kitchen a minute ago, there were twelve potatoes in this pot, and now I have only eleven left."

"What are you trying to say?" said O'Connell.

"I'm not trying to say anything, I'm saying it. When I left this kitchen a minute ago, there were twelve potatoes in this pot, and now I have only eleven left."

"I was the only one here."

"I know that," said the boy.

"So are you accusing me of stealing one of your potatoes?"

"I'm not accusing anyone of anything. All I'm saying is—when I left this kitchen a minute ago, there were twelve potatoes in this pot, and now I have only eleven left."

O'Connell went over to the boy, patted him on the head, handed him back his potato, and said to himself, "Yes, he's a son of mine all right."

Here's another story about Daniel O'Connell. One of his most controversial statements was that the freedom of Ireland wasn't worth the spilling of one drop of anyone's blood. He was very heavily criticized for saying that. But what people don't know is why he said it and how it is connected with the way he wore gloves.

His power as a lawyer and a parliamentarian put fear into the hearts of his enemies. They knew he could best them up and down—in talk, in any argument or debate. They tried every way to outsmart him, and they failed. Finally he was challenged to a duel.

The man who challenged him was called D'Esterre; he was a loyal and strong Orangeman, meaning a staunch Protestant supporter of the English king. D'Esterre and his sort feared and loathed the idea of giving any power to Catholics, and O'Connell stood for nothing else but getting Catholics back their rights. O'Connell had built a great political movement out of something called the Catholic Rent, which meant that every Catholic in Ireland gave a penny a month to O'Connell's political movement. O'Connell used that money to get Catholics standing for elections in Ireland, and so many of them won that the English had to change all the bad laws they had passed against Catholics.

One day, in addressing a political meeting, O'Connell said harsh things about Dublin Corporation, the body that governed the city. He said the corporation refused to debate the rights of Catholics, even though Dublin was a predominantly Catholic city. D'Esterre, who was a member of the corporation, said he took this as a personal insult and threatened to horsewhip O'Connell—that was one of the ways you challenged a man to a duel.

O'Connell ignored the threats and continued to ignore them— until D'Esterre, with a whip in his hand, turned up at the courts where O'Connell was practicing law. Then O'Connell had to fight the duel.

They met on a winter Thursday, the second of February, eighteen-fifteen. Someone had chosen a hill outside Dublin as the place they should fight with pistols, and you can still see the site—it's on the road to Naas on the right-hand side going south.

Duels were fought very differently from what people imagine. There wasn't much of this lining up back to back, walking ten paces away from each other, and turning and firing; the guns were too uncertain for that. Instead, they tossed a coin, and one got the privilege of first shot. In this case, it was D'Esterre.

He missed—but O'Connell didn't. His bullet hit D'Esterre just above the hipbone and went into the soft flesh. They shook hands, and O'Connell was deemed the winner, because D'Esterre didn't have the strength to continue. They all made their way back to Dublin, where D'Esterre's people took their man to the hospital.

The foolish and unfortunate fellow developed blood poisoning, and he died a few days later, leaving a widow and children. But he had enough decency on his deathbed to tell everyone it was all his fault and not to blame Dan O'Connell.

"The Liberator," as O'Connell is always called, felt mortified that he had been responsible for the death of a husband and father. For the rest of his life he supported members of D'Esterre's family financially. And for the rest of his life too, whenever he appeared in public, he wore a black glove on his hand, the hand that fired the gun in the fatal duel. And that's why Daniel O'Connell, the Liberator, said the freedom of Ireland wasn't worth one drop of blood.

Slowing down, Ronan read the last paragraph:

"Once more I ask your pardon for letting you down and for offering you only a missive of brief proportions and at such short notice. I was never a man to worry about myself until now, and that is why I must go and try to get myself looked after. I hope you'll forgive me."

Ronan handed back the sheaf of papers. Ray Cashman looked equally disappointed.

"I'm afraid your old friend mustn't be in great shape."

With expressions of regret, they left Derrynane, drove back to Killarney, and said good-bye. This time, Ronan found a bed-and-breakfast place where, to his delight, no one spoke to him all evening. In his room he opened out his rucksack and repacked all the contents. He had decided it was time to go home.

On the way, he could yet pay homage to Brendan the Navigator; next morning, he caught a bus to Tralee. He walked seven miles to the village of Ardfert and, on a long strand with some cattle cooling their legs in the sea, he looked out to the west.

No towers did he see, no golden fountains, no flocks of white seabirds who could speak like humans. No whales disguised as islands swam close; no icebergs shone their blue crystals across the surface of the waves. But he did see the green ocean, and he did watch its rolling waters, and he did envisage a boat round as a leather belly, full of men in dirty white robes, men with genial faces and brawny arms rowing into eternity. And he did make a decision to have one last search, one more try at finding his man.

He stayed the night in the coastal village of Ballyheigue, where they told him stories of a graveyard out beneath the waves. People still buried their dead in it; at sundown they took the coffin down to a ledge on the cliff, and at dawn next day, high tide or not, the coffin had been taken out and rested gently in the cemetery under the ocean. And they told him too that in a nearby family burial plot sat a stone amulet; every time a member of that family died anywhere in the world, a blue light shone over the plot, and the stone amulet grew mysteriously wet for seven days and seven nights.

In the morning, a truck full of bacon took him to Killimer, where the ferry crossed from north Kerry to Clare.

"You'll have an easy journey," said the driver. "Although the Shannon can be choppy enough."

Few cars drove onto the ferry; the crossing took twenty minutes. The ferryman, who had a face like an ancient angel, said, "I'm Matt Doyle." He took Ronan's fare, cranked out a ticket from a hand machine, and then leaned against the rail, talking.

"D'you see that man over there?" He pointed to a figure in a bright yellow waterproof. "He's on this ferry every day. They call him 'the Weather'—watch!"

Matt Doyle called, "How're you today, Maurice?"

The man turned. "Hallo, Matt."

"How're you keeping? I didn't see you yesterday."

"Did you see that rain yesterday?" said the man they call the Weather.

Matt nodded and turned back to Ronan. "He never lets me down. If I said to him, 'Listen, Maurice, I'm after strangling your father and mother,' he'd say to me, 'This fine spell will never last.' Where are you going to yourself?"

Ronan said, "Toward Ballyvaughan."

"Someone said they have new potatoes over there—very early altogether, new potatoes at this time of the year. But they're strange people in Clare—I'm allowed to say that, my mother was from Clare. D'you know anything about potatoes?"

"Not much."

"Oh, the potato is a very interesting animal. They say that the English adventurer Sir Walter Raleigh brought the potato to us. He had a house in county Cork."

"In Youghal?" said Ronan, recalling Mrs. Cantwell and "Yaww-ll" and Theresa who always interrupted.

"That's right, the very place, and maybe 'twas to that house he also brought back the tobacco. But you can't eat tobacco and you can eat potatoes; what would we do without them? D'you like them yourself?"

"Very much."

"So do I," said Matt Doyle. "I think if you don't like potatoes, you can't call yourself an Irishman. D'you know why the potato grows well here? Moist and moderate temperatures, they told us at school, moist and moderate, that's what we are. And of course, they're great for all kinds of things. Look."

From a coat pocket Matt Doyle took a potato. He held the lumpy, washed tuber up to Ronan and pointed to four or five of its nodes.

"These are the potato's 'eyes,' and if you cut the potato in a certain way, leaving a number of these eyes in each half, you'll have as many new potatoes as there are eyes. If I cut this diagonally, and in one half I have four eyes, and in the other half I have six eyes—where previously I had this one potato in my hand, now I'll have ten. Now—ask me why I have a potato in my pocket. Go on, ask me."

"Why have you a potato in your pocket?"

"I'll show you."

Matt took from his other pocket a yellow tobacco pouch and opened it. Nestling in the tobacco lay a wet slice of potato.

"Tobacco'll never go dry if you put a slice of potato in it. A great article altogether. A potato is like a chicken. You can boil it, you can roast it, you can fry it, you can bake it, you can mix it with cheese or onions or eggs, you can put it in stews with meat. Not only that, you can feed it to pigs. If the Chinese had potatoes, they wouldn't need rice. What's the odd one out between an egg, a drum, and a potato?"

Ronan shook his head, mystified.

"You can beat an egg. You can beat a drum. But you can't beat a potato. D'you get it, do you?"

Matt relaxed and looked out across the rail to the west.

"There was a woman here who gossiped a lot, and they used to say that she had a mouth as wide as the mouth of the Shannon. Well, that's the mouth of the Shannon. She must have been some woman. That's America out there, by the way, straight out from here."

He walked away and began to talk to some other passengers. Ronan watched him and saw that the other people paid Matt not nearly as much attention. Within minutes, Matt had come back. This time, he could not be stopped.

"God in his heaven only knows—how did any Irish people survive without potatoes? See that hill over there? Where we'll be landing? In eighteen-forty-five, that parish had a population of nearly six thousand people, a big parish. Between them they owned about twelve beds, and two hundred chairs. Half of the houses were one-roomed cabins that had no windows. Those people lived on potatoes.

"My grandfather was a man called Laurence, that was his first name. Laurence was born in eighteen-thirty, in a small village called Ballykill, a village that's not there anymore, everyone left it. D'you know what the name Ballykill means?"

Ronan said, "Doesn't 'Bally' mean a town? And 'Kill' means a church?"

"Yeah. Churchtown, it might be called now."

Matt took out a pipe and began to fiddle with it. He put it away again.

"Ah, Jesus, I'm always forgetting it's 'No Smoking' on the ferry. Anyway—Laurence—my grandfather."

ON THE MORNING OF THE SEVENTEENTH OF JUNE, eighteen-forty-five, the day of his fifteenth birthday—it was, I believe, a Wednesday, and four days before the longest day of the year—Laurence set out from his home to walk the three miles into the town of Ennis. It was a beautiful day. Some days down here in the west of Ireland the weather can come straight from Paradise.

Laurence had a sharp brain. They say that very intelligent people usually have one of the five senses more sharply defined than all the others, and that's the true source of their intelligence. Well, Laurence had a very keen sense of smell, and furthermore he had a scientific interest in the world—he liked to know what caused clouds and fog, why some flowers bloomed in spring and some in winter. A bit like myself—I have a keen interest in the potato, for example. And the way birds migrate.

Swinging his arms, full of the joys of life, Laurence walked along this ordinary road, a happy boy. And then, as he passed a field of potatoes, where the crop had well developed, he wrinkled his nose. A peculiar smell caught his attention, a sickly smell, not strong but a definite stink, and even maybe a little sweet. He stopped and looked over the hedge at the crop in the field. The smell seemed to come from within the potato rows, whose leaves stood well above the ground and whose farmer had already been gardening carefully.

Laurence climbed through a gap in the fence, walked into the middle of the field, and squatted down. He couldn't say for certain if the smell came from nearby or from the air above his head or from some distant quarter of the field. But he had been hearing disturbing tales among his father's friends, and so he reached down and gently pulled up a single potato stalk.

At its root, white as little babies, he saw what he should have found—a crop of tiny potatoes, perfect and ready to mature. Laurence left that field puzzled; everything seemed all right with the little potatoes, but yet the smell still hung in his nostrils. Then he realized that something else had bothered him about that first field—it was unnaturally silent; no birds, not even the crows who are usually everywhere, no insects buzzing.

Half a mile or so along the road, he came to another field of potatoes, and here he found no smell at all. The birds chattered and warbled in the trees, and the butterflies flitted along the hedges. He tried that field too, and the potatoes were as perfect as the first ones.

Laurence's journey that morning was to take him to the doctor in Ennis, an English gentleman called Crawford, who came from Yorkshire. Dr. Crawford, married to a local lady, had been looking for an intelligent boy to help him with such matters as delivery of medicines and the like and interpreting into English the Irish language of the local people. Laurence had taught himself English and could read and write it, very unusual in a country where education of the Catholics was forbidden by law.

Dr. Crawford liked Laurence the moment he saw him, and after a few questions and answers he hired the boy—who at that moment became the sole breadwinner for his family.

He says to him, "I like the name Laurence, and we won't have it shortened to Larry or anything like that. Do they call you Laurence at home?"

"They do, Doctor," and Laurence went about his work tidying Dr. Crawford's office.

After a morning of observing the doctor at work, Laurence approached him.

He says, speaking up and speaking brave, "Doctor, I saw something on the way here today that troubled me." The doctor looked at him; Laurence had a very arresting manner.

He says, "And what was it?"

Laurence says, "Doctor, I was passing one field of potatoes, and I got a bad smell—and then I was passing another field of potatoes not far from the first and got no smell. And the first field had no birds in it, and no bees buzzing, but the second field was business as usual."

Dr. Crawford stopped what he was doing and says, "Why are you telling me this?" and him looking straight at Laurence.

And Laurence says, "Sir, I heard some men talking to my father, men from Limerick, and they were talking about a potato failure. So I looked at the potatoes in the field with the bad smell, and there was nothing wrong with them. But these men, they were saying, the blight zigzags across the country, that it can hit one part of a field and ignore another."

Without a minute's hesitation, Dr. Crawford put on his hat and called his coachman. Five minutes later, he and Laurence were rattling along the road to Ballykill in the doctor's coach.

They stopped first at the "clean" field, and Doctor Crawford went in among the potato stalks with a notebook in his hand. He walked up and down the drills, pulling up a stalk here and a stalk there, examining the little baby potatoes and making notes. Laurence watched him.

After half an hour the doctor climbed back into the coach, and they went on to the field where Laurence had found the odor. If anything, it smelled stronger than before, and Laurence was relieved in case the doctor thought he was making it up.

In fact, the doctor says to him, "Very well observed, Laurence. We'll make a medical man out of you yet."

Into the field they went, and this time the doctor made many more notes, asking Laurence to pull up the stalks for him. As they progressed, and as they moved into parts of the field where the smell seemed sickliest and sweetest, Laurence observed that the doctor peered ever closer at the little white tubers. At last he held one up between thumb and forefinger.

And he says, "Laurence, I can scarcely praise you enough—even though for very sad reasons." He handed the little potato to the boy and said, "Examine this, Laurence, and tell me what you see."

A wee bit anxious, lest he not find what he was supposed to, Laurence turned the potato over and over in his fingers.

And he says, "Is it this, Doctor?" and he pointed to a number of small bumps, like tiny hard brown blisters on the skin of the little tuber.

And the doctor said, "Yes, Laurence, and now I'm afraid we must look at the leaves."

Even though he was wearing his good clothes, Dr. Crawford went down on his hands and knees and began to crawl along through the potato furrows. "Come on, Laurence! Join me!" says he.

Laurence dropped to his knees too in the next furrow, much more worried about his clothes—Laurence didn't own a second pair of pants, and he was sure the doctor did. In order to learn what he should do, he watched Doctor Crawford, who was peering up at the underside of the leaves on the stalks. Laurence did likewise, and for many yards of crawling he saw nothing but the nice blue-green leaves that he had known as potato stalks since he came out his cradle.

Then his nose began to sing again—and he saw that the leaves of one plant had begun to turn black. Laurence bent close and sniffed. That was the smell! Sickening, too sweet to be wholesome, a wrong smell!

He said, "Doctor!"

The good man looked up, a bit comical with his hat peeping over a row of potatoes that were no more than a couple of feet high. Laurence held up a blackened leaf between his thumb and forefinger.

Said he, "Is this what you're looking for, sir?"

Dr. Crawford thundered on his hands and knees through the stalks. He took the leaf from Laurence's hand and ripped it from the plant.

Well—did that man wail! "My God!" says he. "My God in heaven!" and he began to cry—real, deep sobs. He sank back on his haunches and covered his hands with his face, and he sobbed like a little baby. When he took his hands away, brown clay was stuck to his face.

In a minute he lifted his head and he said, "Laurence, would you go to the carriage, please, and bring me that wooden box I left on the seat. And my medical bag."

From the bag Dr. Crawford took some scissors, and with Laurence holding the box open, they went along the rows of potatoes, the doctor snipping black leaves from here, from there, from everywhere, and dropping them into the box. They did this until he had collected about thirty leaves, and all the time Dr. Crawford tried to restrain his sobbing and said out loud, over and over again, "These poor people! What's to become of them?" Eventually he calmed himself, and they left the field.

That was the first discovery of the potato blight in the west of Ireland. And we know what happened after that. Millions of people died. The road from here to Ennis was soon lined with people looking like skeletons, their big dying eyes full of hope that a food cart would go by. Eventually it got so bad the government dug long trenches on the roadside—so that when the people waiting for the food dropped dead of hunger, there was a grave already waiting for them; they just had to fall backward.

The ferry klaxon blared, calling Matt back to the present.

Ronan said, "What happened to your grandfather?"

"He stayed working for Dr. Crawford, and because they were Protestants, they got all kinds of food—flour to bake with, food from England, all of that. My grandfather kept every one of his family alive, out as far as second cousins."

Matt Doyle stopped talking, and Ronan stopped writing.

"And what'll you do with those notes?"

Ronan said, "I'll sit down tonight and fill out the story as I remember it."

"In that case," said Matt, "let me add something to your immortal record of me. Everybody talks about the Great Potato Famine. And everybody thinks they know how terrible it was—and it was terrible. Here's how I know it was terrible. There was an old lady up here in Killimer, just up the hill from where we're landing. Her father worked for the British government. When I was a small boy I heard that old lady telling my mother something her father told her. He went into a house near Kilrush, a small cottage, a kind of a mud cabin. There was a hen lying dead on the floor, dead of hunger, a scrawny hen, feathers all loose and raggedy. Hens don't die of hunger. That's how bad the famine was—even the food was dead."

The ferry nosed to the Killimer pier. Matt Doyle said, "Good luck now. Don't walk across the Burren at night, 'tis very easy to lose your way."

At Hanafin's, no light showed, no door opened. Ronan walked around the back; no one there. He felt he had come full circle. In boyhood, helped by his father, his first true search for the Story-teller had begun here, the pub where the Storyteller sometimes wintered. Now here he was again, still searching, still, as it were, knocking on a closed door. A woman in the next house watched his movements, and he walked over to her. He had no need to ask; she wanted to tell.

"Him and the wife had a row. She's gone off to her sister's in Galway."

"Is he gone away too?"

"They fall out every year."

"Where would I find him?"

"On the floor, I'd say."

Ronan went back and knocked again, louder.

An upstairs window opened.

"Hallo." The hairy face appeared; the wary eyes looked down; "What'd you want?"

"I was looking for—"

"Hold on, I can't hear you." The face disappeared, and moments later the poet opened the front door; he swayed a little, in a gray suit jacket with the remains of a flower in the buttonhole, a long shirt, a blue tie, and socks; no trousers. He looked like a fugitive from a riot.

"I was having a bit of a lie-down—come in, I'm a bit sleepy today."

"Ah'm—I was here once before."

The poet, his face red as a furnace, stared at Ronan.

"You were, you were—with that fella, what was his name, he tells everybody he's a great friend of mine, the teacher?"

Suddenly Hanafin held out his hand. "I'm sorry for your trouble."

"How did you know?"

"There was a man staying here who was at the funeral. Very sad he was, too, about it, very sad, decent man your father was, he said."

"Who was the man?"

"He's the man I told you about before. Him and his stories. He stays here, gives us great value."

"How long ago? Is he here now?"

"No, no, hold your horses." Hanafin saw the force of Ronan's interest. "He's gone outta here."

"Where?"

Hanafin paused. "He's not that well."

In the dim bar, he righted an overturned chair. Everything smelled musty; the poet poured himself a gigantic whiskey, cleaned a spoon on his shirttails, and began to stir the whiskey.

Ronan had to ask; "Why are you stirring it?"

"No apparent reason. D'you want the old guy for something?"

"I do."

"And it's nothing bad you want him for?"

"Oh, Lord, no!"

Hanafin drank deep. "I don't like saying it, but you might have to hurry. I got the doctor for him. He had this bad wheezing—I s'pose the years on the road, and the damp and that."

"When did he go?"

"What'll you have?"

"No, no drink, thanks." Ronan almost shuddered.

Hanafin eyed him. "You seem like you want him real bad?"

"How long is it since he was here?"

"Two months. More. Maybe three. Jan was here at the time, she's'n't here now."

Suddenly Hanafin began to sob. He put his head down on the bar and wept like a child.

"We were at a wedding—and she went. That's why she's'n't here now. I mean—she's'n't here at all. She's gone, and she'll maybe never come back, she might go off with some fella, it'd be like a death."

Ronan, untrained for such events, had no words. He wanted to say something, anything, but Hanafin prevented him with wilder crying.

"It might be a fella I know. Would that be worse than if it was someone I didn't know? Which is the worst, huh, what we know or what we don't know? Look at us, you and me, and the things we know that we don't want to know. There's you and the sadness of your life and your father cold in the ground and your mother your aunt and your aunt in actual fact your mother and there's me and I've no wife 'cause she's'n't here now. She's'n't here. Maybe she'll never be here again."

Ronan looked at Hanafin, wild-eyed, hairy, tearstained Hanafin. In his mind, the words clanged like bolts in a metal tunnel—"and your father cold in the ground and your mother your aunt and your aunt in actual fact your mother and your father cold in the ground and your mother your aunt and your aunt in actual fact your mother and your father cold in the ground and your mother your aunt and your aunt in actual fact your mother . . ."

He picked up his knapsack, felt the old bleak red colors descending, fought them off, and walked to the door.

"Here, listen, have a drink for Jeezus' sake, you're lookin' at a man whose own wife isn't here, the least you can do is drink with him, don't leave him on his own."

Outside, everything had turned to gray—gunmetal gray; father cold in the ground and your mother your aunt and your aunt in actual fact your mother; the clouds lowered but threatened no rain; father cold in the ground and your mother your aunt and your aunt in actual fact your mother; the house of the gossipy neighbor had no color of any kind except gray; your mother your aunt and your aunt in actual fact your mother; the universe had grown gray.

Ronan put one foot in front of the other—at least, that was what it felt like. In his brain, tumblers kept clicking into place like the locks of a massive safe vault being opened—clunk, clunk, CLUNK! And he was wrong too about the sky threatening no rain; it swept in, a sneering, dense rain, swiping his face.

He pushed up his parka hood up, and once more, as before in awful times, his mind raced with ridiculous, incongruous thoughts. I wish I had windshield wipers for my glasses. The hen must have died in the famine because nobody had enough strength to wring its neck. Barry Hanafin, under his long shirttails, has legs as young as a girl's.

Ronan headed east. The white stones at the edge of the Burren moonscape kept the light alive long enough to guide him to a village. No buses tonight, not coming through here, a woman said; wait until tomorrow. He nodded, numb as a stone. The lone pub also offered bed-and-breakfast—and an evening of music and song. He tried to eat the meal he had ordered, but the potatoes contained spring onions, the way his mother made them, and that shut off his escape. His mother? Alison? No, his aunt. No, that was Kate. Alison. Kate. Kate. Alison. Time after time he closed his eyes, desperation rising like a tide.

Around nine o'clock a very old concertina player struck up, and then two fiddlers joined in, one of them a seven-year-old girl. Ronan watched them, envying the child her talent, wondering if he could ever reach such a visible plateau in any skill. She had dark curly hair, intense concentration, and her fingers moved faster than he could see.

After the third tune, two couples, deep in middle age, swept to the floor and began to dance. They also concentrated hard, and he watched their feet—more delicate, he thought, than their faces. Nausea began to curdle in him, and he felt sweat trickle down under his arms.

At his shoulder, a girl in her late twenties said, "C'mon. C'm'out here," took his arm, and steered him onto the dance floor.

He did not resist, and he looked as ungainly as he felt; but nobody laughed or mocked as she began to teach the rudiments.

"You're in Clare, so this dance is a Clare Set, and you can follow me, I mean your feet can do what my feet are doing, look down until your feet can do it by themselves."

It took some moments; he could not seem to push the rhythms he felt in his body through his ankles into his feet.

"Give yourself time, don't rush at it." The music stopped. "We'll hold on here for the next one." She held his hand in her warm dry fingers. "I'm Lelia."

"You're doing grand," said one of the women dancers to Ronan. And, "God, Lelia, you always had an eye for the Yanks."

"He's not a Yank, are you?"

Ronan said, "No."

"You're too silent for a Yank, aren't you?"

The music started again, and this time Ronan moved easier. Other couples came onto the floor, but nobody bumped, such was their gracefulness. He had never been in a milieu like this; he had a vague knowledge that music got played in pubs, but the life at home and then in Dublin had been almost monastically enclosed. Now he thought he knew why he had been so protected; Alison, Kate, even his father—they were also protecting themselves.

"You enjoying yourself?" asked Lelia.

Ronan nodded, afraid to look in her eyes.

"You've'n't said a syllable. What you doing here, anyway?"

"I'm—sort of going on somewhere."

"Where?"

"Can we stop dancing and talk?"

"You're direct anyway," said Lelia, but not unkindly.

They went to a quiet end of the bar. Lelia looked at him, "No. Come on outside. That's not good sweat that you're sweating."

In the open air she made him lean against the wall and said, "Now—ease yourself."

"Ah'm—listen—"

"Stop for a while, will you? Cool yourself down."

"But I've just had very bad news."

"What's the good news inside it? There's always good news wrapped up in bad news."

"Jesus God, I don't know."

"But there is."

"That's ludicrously optimistic."

Lelia said, "You'll have to use smaller words, you're in Clare now."

Ronan wanted to laugh but could not.

"C'mere," she said. "You've a nice hand, give it to me."

She took his unproffered hand and warmed it with her own two hands.

"Are you dying of anything—anything urgent, I mean?"

Ronan shook his head.

"Is anybody who matters to you dying of anything urgent?"

"No."

"If you're not dying of anything urgent and if anybody who matters to you isn't dying of anything urgent—that's good news. Now—close your eyes and stand still and you'll be all right."

Two days later, in the early morning, he stood outside the apartment in Dublin. He had traveled rough, by bus, on foot, by night train, his heart in his hands, through swinging moods of calming and raging, easing and fretting, sinking and elation. No sign of life; the curtains had not been drawn closed in any of the rooms for the previous night, and Kate always closed all curtains; the air seemed cold.

A milkman came by—Ronan knew him, a bandy-legged, cold little man.

"Are youse signing on again? We've stopped doing eggs."

"I don't know, I mean about signing on."

The milkman looked at him oddly. "Weren't youse away in England or sump'n?"

"When did she cancel?"

"It'd be four or five months ago, last March, I'd say, from memory, I'd hafta look it up in the ledger, like. I hear there's new people coming in next week. Did youse not pay your rent or sump'n?"

On Earlsfort Terrace he hesitated; to focus his mind, he counted the steps up to the main door but stopped after ten. A secretary whom he recognized passed by, and he followed her.

"Professor Ryle—is he away?"

"How could he be, and he doing the summer school?"

"Ah."

Inside, he checked the summer school notices on "Victorian Ireland"; later that day the schedule would include "Charles Stewart Parnell. Lecturer, T. Bartlett Ryle."

Two hours later he slipped into the back of the packed, all-adult summer school in his old lecture theater.

L ET ME ASSUME THERE ARE MARTIANS AMONG you who have never heard of Parnell or the Land War in Ireland or Irish republicanism or Kitty O'Shea or any of the whole damn boiling.

And why should you have? Many of you have come here from overseas and the only thing you know about Ireland is that we have ugly little men here, tricky fellows in green hats, who'll look you in the eye and promise you a crock of gold. But then, when your glance is distracted even for a second, they vanish and take the gold with them.

Yes, we do have such figures here—I can show you several. We call them "elected politicians."

Or you might have heard that our horses are fast and our women are beautiful. Or have I got that the wrong way round?

And someone may have told you that this Irish Republic of nineteen-sixty-one is a land of tolerance and peace. It is indeed—we're tolerant people. Tolerant provided you're not a Jew—or "Jewboy," as we prefer to say—who wants to play golf, in which case you had better found your own golf club. And we're peaceful, unless you happen to be a harmless Protestant farming land along the Irish border, in which case you might just get yourself shot in the head on your way to the creamery for no better reason than the little church you worship in or the fact that your wife had a second cousin who joined the British army.

But we're here to discuss Victorian Ireland, and my role today is to tell you about a man called Charles Stewart Parnell, born eighteen-forty-six, died eighteen-ninety-one, and if you go to the top of O'Connell Street, Dublin's grandest thoroughfare, you will see his words stamped on the obelisk there: "No man shall have the right to fix the boundary to the march of a nation." We could debate that for a while, but we won't, not today anyway.

Let me start you with a thumbnail sketch of Parnell. He was a tall, bearded man with a passion to get justice for the ordinary people of Ireland—of whom he was not one, he was privileged, a wealthy landlord. He rose to power in the second half of the nineteenth century and damn near got Ireland the right to govern itself and then lost it all for fancying a married woman. Of all the characters across the landscape of Irish history, he is one of the most interesting—powerful enough to arrest the rolling machinery of a great empire, and weak enough to be brought down by wearing his heart too low down on his body.

No wonder he became a huge mythical figure, because in Ireland all politics is myth anyway. And so prevailing was the Parnell myth, which is the same as the Parnell reality, that there are people alive today who, if you pinched them hard, would weep salt tears for him.

But that's a feeling I loathe. Forget the popular Parnell you may have heard of—the man who let his heart rule his head; the man who chose the love of a woman over personal glory; "the Uncrowned King of Ireland." Forget that. Cast aside the sickly nineteenth-century sentimentality that mourns "the Lost Leader." Drop the pity for a man more sinned against than sinning, ruined by a sidelong glance from a beautiful siren.

God, can't you hear the heartstrings and the ballads! Bypass those who linger on the what-might-have-been. Instead shine a different light, and under it, what you see is different, and in fact, I believe a more admirable and significant Parnell emerges.

There are three essentials in politics: getting power, using it, and keeping it. Parnell cleared the first hurdle in style. In the wake of the Great Potato Famine, he had grasped that a people treated too badly is the beginnings of a power base. He understood the anger that the Irish people felt at not having enough resources to keep themselves alive, and at the pisspoor efforts of the rich Protestants and the English government to ease the worst of the famine.

Second, he used power well—his associations with the newly formed Land Leaguers gave him a base that also roped in the people who underpinned a newfound republican movement, the Irish Republican Brotherhood, and that would eventually lead to the armed Irish Republican Army. In fact, you can point to Parnell's moment as the time when it became likely that the desire to own their land again would put bullets in Irish guns—although he had nothing to do with that. But as to keeping power—that's where he goes Greek on us, by which reference I mean tragedy.

Parnell was born at the height of the famine, in eighteen-forty-six. His father owned land in county Wicklow, a house called Avondale, and the children of Ireland, God help them, have grown up listening to a mournful old song—"Oh have you been to Avondale and lingered in her lovely vale. Where tall trees whisper low the tale of Avondale's proud eagle. Where pride and ancient glory fade; such was the land where he was laid; like Christ was thirty pieces paid for Avondale's proud eagle."

Give me a head start myself and a strong following wind, and I'd sing it for you, but I'd have to have vessels of a certain liquor line up in front of me. And I'd drink them fast, because I'd regret singing it—that song contains exactly the kind of maudlin expressions that obscured Parnell's importance.

His motive forces are much more interesting than any public reaction to him. Parnell's mother was an American, and twenty years after the famine she had a good sense that if anything in Ireland was to change politically, the power for it would come from the States.

Why? Because half of Ireland was over there, escaping from the Famine or, earlier than that, because they had no place else to go once their lands—and their language and their religion and their dignity—were taken from them. If they survived the journeys in the coffin ships, they got their snouts in the great gold trough of America, and some would say their snouts are in there still.

Twenty years makes a generation, and by the time the children of those coffin-ship emigrants grew up, they had imbibed a hatred of England with their mother's milk. They were looking day and night for ways to pay back the English—who by then owned, it is said, in excess of eighty-five percent of the surface of Ireland, although I myself believe that figure somewhat unreliable; it might have been higher, it might have been lower—the measuring devices were unsophisticated and subject to the alterations of vested interests.

The timing of Parnell's arrival on the political scene is no accident and should be no surprise. No accident because conditions already existed for such a figure; even though England governed Ireland absolutely, Irish affairs were now represented by Irish-elected members to the English Parliament in London. It was our foot in the door since before Daniel O'Connell's time. And at the age of twenty-nine, Parnell got himself elected as a member of Parliament for Meath.

As to this being no surprise, the precedent also existed for a big, flamboyant man speaking Irish concerns to the heart of the British Empire and tweaking their noses. Daniel O'Connell rightly gets a lot of praise for having freed Ireland from the Penal Laws that hammered Catholics and for campaigning for Irish self-determination. He should be praised more, though, for paving the way. If there hadn't been an O'Connell, I wonder if there would have been a Parnell; O'Connell demonstrated that there was a place for a powerful, distinguished Irishman in the politics of England, and he had proven that such a figure could make a mark.

Incidentally, a note here about Parnell's name—Charles Stewart Parnell. Stewart was a family name and spelled differently from the "S-T-U-A-R-T" of Bonny Prince Charlie, that poxy old dipsomaniac who came across from France to Scotland, ignored the advice of the most hardheaded people on this earth, namely the Scottish clan leaders, and fought a futile war. And when his cause was lost in seventeen-forty-five—as it was always going to be—he had to be smuggled away out of Scotland disguised as a woman. Very appropriate.

Not like our fellow here at all. Our Charles Stewart had a sharp political eye, and he knew perfectly well that in Ireland the source of power always had been and always would be—land. Before he ran for election, he had been observing the ground-roots political movements, and among all the splinters and rebels and passionate groups, the feelings—and all politics come from feelings—the feelings were clearly definable in two ways; revolution and land reform.

Parnell had enough sense to know that armed revolution had little enough chance of success against so mighty a power—this was by now the huge British Empire. But the land factor embodied a great deal of useful thought and feeling, and that's the direction he took: political agitation with a weather eye on those who would use arms. In eighteen-seventy-nine, four years after his first election, he helped found something called the Land League. At more or less the same time he consorted with chosen agitators—the Fenians, who openly preached the violent removal of England from Ireland. Parnell knew the value of having a cake without yet eating it.

Not enough understanding exists regarding land and its place in the Irish soul. There's a primitive feeling for acreage on this island; there always was, there always will be. A man will still kill for a field more than he'll kill for money, revenge, or a woman.

Maybe it was the losing of the land that caused that passion in us—especially losing it to foreigners who just came in and took it. I think that connection was always there: I think our deepest ancestors who wrestled patches of soil from the Atlantic and then felled the forests and opened up the interior of the island—I think they built that gut passion into our spirit. After all, in some of our earliest and wildest mythologies, our gods mated with the earth, and our ancestors chose to lie in the earth after they died.

The losses, the evictions, the colonizations, simply intensified our land hunger. So the Land League knew what it was doing emotionally; it was politicizing this visceral issue. And it knew what it was doing intellectually; by then English landlordism—most of it absentee, by which I mean they ran their estates from tall houses in fashionable London—had become so corrupt that someone needed to speak of reforms. Here, a great advantage existed; almost any reforms would have seemed reasonable to any outside eyes, because the existing systems were so unfair.

The outside eyes that the Land Leaguers wanted to catch were, of course, American—that's where the money was likely to come from in the long term, because politics costs money, and revolution costs even more. Now, thanks to the new Irish-American generations, all they had to do was cry "unfair" loud enough in Ireland, and the cry would be heard across the Atlantic.

So—what was unfair? It was unfair that no Irishman knew what day or hour he might be thrown off the land that he farmed. Mark you, this was land he probably once owned, and for which he now paid a steep rent. A lot of the imported settlers—what we call planters—had left in fear, and the landlords had to have someone who worked the land, so they got the local Irish to tenant the estates.

It was unfair too that such a tenant farmer's rent could be jacked up sky-high at a moment's notice and bear no relationship whatever to the yield from the land. And—he was expected to pay his rent out of that yield. And it was unfair that a man could never expect to own the land he tilled year in, year out. In any reasonable eyes, as I say, these facts were unfair—especially if you were an embittered Irish emigrant looking back from the chunk of prairie you had just been given free by the American government. Who the Yanks took it from is not a subject I care to get into.

This is a good moment to build a bit of context. I love context—it's the spine of history. We're addressing in this summer school "Victorian Ireland," and we can assume that we mean the period the little old German lassie was on the throne, eighteen-thirty-seven to nineteen-hundred and one. An Irish landlord, Lord Castlebar, met Queen Victoria at a gathering in London one day, and he said to her, "Upon my soul Madam, your face is awful familiar but I can't put a name to you." Excuse the digression.

In every new development it attempts, Irish history has a strange way of summarizing all its previous existence. This is what I mean by context. Over the centuries, the following major phases shaped the country into which Parnell was born. The twelfth century brought the Normans under Strongbow and King Henry the Second. They weren't long here when they enacted laws to take over Irish land and keep their identities separate from the natives. That happened in the thirteenth and fourteenth centuries with such measures as the Statutes of Kilkenny and the taking of land to give to Norman barons so that they could settle here and have power.

And at the same time they tried by law to keep the sides apart, conqueror and conquered, so that the Irish would lose their identities as the new rulers became more and more widespread; domination by assimilation.

But that backfired; in fact, it went the other way. No matter what was tried, the Normans soon became indistinguishable from the Irish—especially the old Irish families. So, we had the next wave of English attempts to keep the island under control, again with land measures being the motive force. In the late fifteen hundreds and on into the sixteen and seventeen hundreds, the English monarch and the Parliament sent in ordinary English and Scottish families to take over the Irish lands. So numerous were they that London hoped they would outbreed and in time wipe out the native Irish. They underestimated our breeding powers. That's why the Irish are so loved by the Vatican—we can always be relied upon to turn out lots and lots of little Catholics.

At the same time the colonizers attacked the Irish identity once more—outlawing the religion and the language and the possibility of ownership or education.

To counter these recurring measures, recurring skirmishes of uprisings broke out—and don't let anyone tell you they were much more than that. In almost every generation since the Battle of the Boyne, some individual or some handful of men have had a go at being heroes. Seventeen-ninety-eight remains the most colorful example, when brave men with pikes and pitchforks took on soldiers with guns, mostly in county Wexford. Five years later, Robert Emmett, a handsome romantic lad, tried it here in Dublin and got hanged at the age of twenty-five. That stopped his gallop. Then, to show the Irish that there were other possibilities, along came Daniel O'Connell, with big shoulders, big brain, and big talk.

What O'Connell knew and what Parnell observed—and this was the cleverness of both men—was this pattern of failure on both sides. The English hadn't succeeded in their different eradication attempts, which ranged from assimilation to would-be genocide, because somehow the Irish clung on to who they were. And the Irish failed to throw them out because the country was simply too small to get anywhere by force of arms.

So: from the Irish point of view a political system had to be laid down—O'Connell had proved that we're among the world's most effective talkers. Given the volatile nature of the Irish, there would have to be guns somewhere too. But O'Connell and Parnell knew that someone else could—and surely would—look after that. O'Connell, therefore, sought to restore identity through the abolition of the Penal Laws and the restoration of ordinary decent rights to the Irish people. And Parnell sought to get them back some measure of control over their land.

That's what I mean by everything in Ireland always summarizing what went before.

All-right-very-well-so: those are the contexts and core values through which to view Charles Stewart Parnell. After all that, what is there to say about him? There's a lot to be said, even outside of the romantic fact that he was that most interesting of figures—a man who acquired great power and then allowed it to slip away.

We know he was a man who could get himself elected—that's a politician for you. And we know that once elected, he used his power to get a broader base—he commanded the Irish party of politicians at the English Parliament in the House of Commons in London. And that added unmistakable power to the way in which the Irish could have a say in governing themselves; Parnell was capable of disrupting the whole parliamentary debating system on which England so prided herself.

He also did something that makes me personally fond of him—he caused a word to be entered into the English language. Parnell and his Land League associates wanted to develop a system of civil disobedience, and they worked out that a policy of ostracization might prove very effective. But the word *ostracism* was always going to prove difficult for a people whose first language was not yet English. So they needed a different word, a headline term.

There was a property on the east side of Lough Mask in county Mayo owned by the absentee Lord Erne and managed out of Ballinrobe by an Englishman with a very bad name for cruelty—and this man's name was the word Parnell made into an everyday word.

In the summer of eighteen-eighty, the Land League asked several of its members to approach this agent and ask for a reduction in their rents. You can imagine the response—the agent gave them short shrift, angry contempt, and instead of a reduction, a crude and immediate increase. This was exactly what Parnell had foreseen—and actually wanted—from this rude, despotic steward.

So: the Land League instructed all the steward's neighbors to withdraw all services; they stopped working on his land, in his household, on all of the properties he managed; they refused to deliver his letters, sell him anything in the shops, saddle his horse, wash his crockery, or, most important of all, help with the harvest on which the estates depended for a slice of his income. The distracted agent brought in teams of Protestant laborers from northern counties, but that made the harvest impossibly expensive, and eventually the agent went back to England, his tail between his legs.

The man's name was—Charles Cunningham Boycott. And his name became a practice that is known to this day—to boycott someone means to cut them off from all essential services, to ostracize them within their own society. Some of you who live here may recall a recent murder investigation where no perpetrator was found. But the local people made up their own minds as to who had done it, and they boycotted a certain man and his family, and he had to leave the neighborhood.

The word *ostracism*, by the way, comes from an old Greek social rite. Its root word is *os*, "bone"; it has a cousin in the word *oyster*, and when the Greeks wanted to banish someone, they wrote his name on a shell or a bone or a shard, and that's where *ostracism* comes from.

In nineteenth-century Ireland, the ostracism known as the boycott went on to form the basis of an effective political campaign. For example, if a landlord evicted a tenant farmer for nonpayment of rent, no other farmer would work that land. I myself saw a case of the same thing ten years ago where a bank foreclosed on a farm and nobody turned up to the auction. And the auctioneers knew too that whoever bought that place might well be boycotted in the locality. In Ireland history never ends.

Captain Boycott left Ireland in the autumn of eighteen-eighty. Charles Stewart Parnell was riding high—intelligent, magnetic, astute, and increasingly powerful. He drove the Irish members of Parliament in London like a cattleman with a herd; he spoke brilliantly, and he was followed by admirers everywhere he went.

But he had a colleague whose wife was a beauty, the wondrous Kitty O'Shea, and she began to flutter her eyelashes at him. Handkerchief-pandkerchief followed. There was tumbling in the hay, bosoms heaved, palms grew sweaty—and bang! The word got out; they're tumbling in the hay! Parnell is introducing her to Fagan, a good old Dublin slang term for the compelling act of reproducing the species.

And we all know what happened next. Parnell's core followers were Irish Catholics, at their most devout since having permission restored to them to practice their religion. And they disliked adultery and divorce, two factors of life that now came into Parnell's life as friskily as a donkey will trot through an open gate into a fresh meadow.

The word got out. Mr. Kitty O'Shea was pushed out of the nest, and Charles Stewart Parnell, because he married a divorcée and lost the Catholic vote, went to his doom in a featherbed. Thus, between the sheets, ended the parliamentary career of the uncrowned king of Ireland.

In the laughter, a nun jumped up from her bench and began to leave the lecture theater; a second nun followed her, blushing and muttering. Ronan had hidden himself by sinking low in the hindmost of the packed benches and keeping his hands studiously tented to his face—but the nuns' departure exposed him to Ryle's attention.

The professor, long the star of every summer school and much loved for his salty views, looked at Ronan. Then he looked—then he looked again. To everybody's astonishment, he bounded crane-legged up the steps.

"The beard won't hide you. It is you, isn't it?"

Ronan nodded, suddenly in tears.

"Don't move out of this seat, O'Mara. Not a muscle. I want to talk to you."

Ryle returned to his podium. "I'll take some questions, and you can ask me anything you like. Even about hanky-panky."

He replied at some length to a statement about the Land War and the secret societies who slaughtered landlords' cattle in the fields and crippled their horses by cutting the tendons in the hocks.

"If you like, you can see it as symbolic. They were hobbling the conveyances and the power of the British Empire. You could also see it as cruelty to animals."

Another questioner asked how lurid had been the accounts of Parnell's dalliance.

"Well, I don't know what you'd think of as lurid, but there was no doubt that shanks were bared and people bounced around a bit, if that's what you mean."

This proved too salty for some more students, who weren't even nuns. The class, all mature, began to disperse, to the sadness of the many who relished the salty prof. When the last one had gone, Ryle raced long-legged again up to Ronan's seat and directed him along the bench to make room. "You heard it, so?"

"I did, sir."

"And is that why you're here?"

"Sir, I didn't know you were lecturing."

"No, you fool! I'm not talking about the bloody lecture!"

"Sir—I came—I came because I want to get things back in order."

"What about the bloody announcement?"

"Sir—what announcement?"

T. Bartlett Ryle took off his glasses and wiped his face like a monkey.

"God Almighty! Listen. D'you know when you're waiting for the wireless news to come on at half past six in the evening? Haven't you ever heard announced 'Will So-and-So, believed to be traveling in Cork and Kerry, please contact the nearest police station for an urgent message.' They put out one for you too—it said, 'Will Ronan O'Mara contact the nearest police station.' Or maybe lunatic asylum? Where were you, driving everybody mad with worry? Your mother's nearly demented."

"She's not my mother."

"Ah—is that what did it? You found out?"

"No. I only found out two days ago."

"Well, it took you long enough."

"Has everyone always known except me?!"

"Explode all you like—this is Ireland; no family worth the name is without a secret. And you should know that in this country a secret is something that everyone else knows."

"Why wasn't I told?"

"If this is how you handle things, I wouldn't blame them for not telling you."

"Sir, it isn't fair!"

"Stop shouting. And fair is a body pigment, that's all it is. Where were you? Why didn't you write to your mother?"

Ronan sank back. "I was—all over the country."

"Bloody thoughtless of you. What are you going to do now?"

"What should I do?"

T. Bartlett Ryle said, "Are you expecting me to tell you? If you are, you'll have a long wait."

"But—you're a teacher."

"A farmer can't sow potatoes on hard ground."

Ronan subsided. "What should I do?"

Ryle clapped his hands. "That's a dangerous thing—asking me for advice. I could keep you here all day, giving you advice. But I'd say, for a start, go home and apologize to your mother and your aunt. And"—he leaned forward for emphasis—"it doesn't matter which is which."

"I don't, I can't—understand any of this."

"Then I'll spell it out for you. You're eighteen, and I'm told you came into a lot of money when your father died, and then you behaved without an ounce of consideration for the two women who brought you up. You took off around the country like a tinker and never so much as sent a postcard or made a phone call. You walked out of what is thought one of the best history faculties in western Europe, even if I say so myself. And in this college we could fill your place fifteen times over with people who'd behave better."

The professor stood up; Ronan rose with him.

"O'Mara, if you waste the gifts you have, I'll personally scourge you. That's a warning."

Ronan hoisted his rucksack feebly. "And if I don't?"

"I'll say, 'Good man.' Now go and mend the holes in your life. And do it decently, for Christ's sake. Don't act like a boor. Piss out any vinegar in your bloodstream. No one meant you any harm."

At Kingsbridge the platforms echoed to the clank of shunting. Not more than ten people boarded the train. Ronan slumped in a deserted carriage, still wincing at Ryle's remarks. Bloody thoughtless. Don't act like a boor. Without an ounce of consideration. Thank God the train's empty. Rode this train with Kate. Kate!

What's she going to say? And Mother—or Not-Mother? Jesus God! What to do? Right! If they attack—attack them. But if they don't attack? They deserve some punishment. Perhaps a coolness. Or— wait and see? Will they tell the whole story? *Will they tell?* What will they say?

At six o'clock, Ronan walked through the little wooden gate. Tresses of sweet pea tumbled by the climbing roses. All the windows of the house had been opened; the heat of a warm afternoon lingered; he could hear bees—and a piano, meaning Kate must be home. His own calm surprised him. He knocked. No answer—he knocked again, and was rewarded with footsteps.

Josie appeared. "Yes?" and then, "Oh, Mother of Jesus!" and, louder, "MA'AM!"

"Yes?" Alison's cool voice echoed in the hall. She looked at Ronan, and he saw her guard go up in a way he knew well, the eyes slightly hooded, the head turned a little to one side. Then she smiled.

"Your father had a beard for a while." And now she did the call-ing: "Kate!"

Josie made way for him, and Ronan stepped into the hallway. The piano music stopped; he heard Kate's footsteps. His heart did not race, his vision did not blur.

"Oh! Oh my!"—that was Kate's most excited term. "But are you taller, and look how—how big you are."

She hung back; nobody touched him—no hugs, no kisses; he felt massive relief. At the foot of the stairs he took off the rucksack and said, "I need a bath."

Now the sisters let go a little of their control and put their hands to their mouths. For the first time he observed how alike they looked above the nose—twins almost. Each, at exactly the same moment, looked directly at the other, then at him, reached for-ward, and touched his arm.

Alison said, "Thank God you're all right."

Kate said, "When did you eat?"

Alison said, "We're glad you're here."

An hour later, sitting down at dinner, he looked at the two women facing him, and for one brief moment he was able to see them as a stranger might. He knew their ages—Alison was forty-seven, Kate thirty-nine; dark-haired, comfortably off, attractive women of some polish, who took care with their looks and their clothes. During that single objective flash he almost could not view them as his mother and his aunt, no matter which was which.

Then their old roles took over, and he saw that they both looked at least expectant and probably nervous—he found he could not judge how agitated, how apprehensive, they were. But if anything good were to come out of this, he had to lead it—and to do so, he had to say something. He looked from one to the other, he looked down at his plate, and he looked at them again—straight into the eyes of each, not flinching.

"I didn't find him," he said.

They nodded.

"But—I learned a lot. And"—he never knew how he cranked out the next words evenly—"and I learned nothing but good things. Interesting things. Things that harm no one."

Kate said, "Your father had a proverb; 'Time is a fair and just teacher.' D'you remember?" She looked at her sister; they both looked at Ronan, who frowned.

"If you say so."

Now the sisters looked down at their plates. But that was the only jab he ever allowed himself to deliver. Knowing they felt stung, he took a deep breath and looked to the future.

"The two of you—you look exactly the same as you were."

Fatigue, the high emotions of the last few days, and the return from a kind of wandering exile had, he suddenly realized, made him desperate for a "normal" life, and they heard the ice break.

"Well, I should hope so," said Alison. "It's only been six months."

Kate said, "And Toby—he was a help."

"Oh, yes, a big help," said Alison tartly, at which all three laughed.

Dinner filled up with conversation about events since his departure. They stinted nothing and raced each other to give him juicy details. In return, he gave them snatches of his experiences; the thaw had begun. By tomorrow, he felt, he might be able to regale them with the Wexford Trilogy.

At ten o'clock, with generosity once again a member of the household, everyone went to bed. Ronan slept for fifteen hours.

Ronan spent the rest of that summer of 1961 doing little. Sometimes he lay in the sun on the lawn, thinking, reflecting, his father's old panama hat tipped over his eyes. He had not lived in the house since the funeral, and he had dreaded the experience; but John's absence materialized as a vague and lonely ache, not the sharp pain he had dreaded.

Over the weeks he correctly guessed at essential connections. Alison and Kate must have known of his meeting with Professor Ryle; Kate had mentioned telephone calls from Father Mansfield, Ryle's good friend. Thus the women had evidently been primed that Ronan knew about his parentage and that he was on his way home. This had given them time to prepare their attitude, to ease him back into their lives. Somewhere along the line they had decided not to reproach him, not to reprove, merely to welcome and accept, to let him be, to give him time.

In general, too, they altered in their attitudes to him. Alison grew warmer, easier; she began to stir memories and tell anecdotes of John. Kate had not exactly grown cooler, but she did not patrol his life so intently; he saw that she watched over him, sometimes made suggestions, never issued directions. The house itself gave off an undeniable and completely new air of calm; Alison smiled more easily, and Kate's music and songs had lost their madcap quality.

Ronan now had to figure out his own position. What was he to do? Should he raise "it" with them? What exactly had happened around his conception and birth? Why were his origins portrayed falsely to the world? Professor Ryle had said it didn't matter which was which. Did it? It did. No, it didn't. As a boy he had read a thriller where, with a soft rumble of powerful machinery, the walls of a locked room began to press toward the trapped hero. The inside of his mind felt like that. Did it matter? Yes, it did; no, it didn't. Yes, it did matter; no, it didn't matter. And the ordinary, bloody practicalities: what to call them—"Mother"? "Aunt"?

The solution to that problem gave him another little breakthrough; he already addressed her as Kate; now he'd call them both by their names: Kate and Alison; Alison and Kate; and the very gesture would tell them that he knew. The rumble of machinery stopped; the walls stopped closing in.

His next practical step pushed the walls back a little; he invested a new energy in his own appearance. He shaved off his beard, a little at a time, and then he slowly built up a new, very different wardrobe, reminiscent of his father's style. He even wore some of the clothes; John's waistcoats, the pocket handkerchiefs, an old linen jacket. With Alison's permission he made John's desk and bookshelves his own and reorganized the thousand or so volumes. And eventually he forced himself to face his great search again—but only by bringing all his notebooks up to date.

From boyhood enquiries to the jottings made on the road, he fleshed them out and turned them into a comprehensive record of all he had done. Not for a second did he feel he should abandon his obsession; every day he checked the newspapers for any trace or mention of the Storyteller. A festival somewhere? A broadcast, radio or television?

But the anxiety of that inner register had dropped; its tone inside him had grown less shrill. A wistfulness had replaced the urgency, and he began to accept that he had long feared the worst, that the Storyteller had died. He surmounted this fear and its potential to cripple him by telling himself that at least he had made a good record of it all, and that now he had other things to do. But still he remained somewhat becalmed; still he seemed unable to command his moods and reorganize his life.

At last, at the end of the long and reflective summer, he resolved the most demanding of his problems—how to address the two women, the whole issue of "it." Other than changing the form of address from "Mother" to "Alison," he would never register with them the matter of his parentage. It would have to evolve into his own private history, dwell inside him as a kind of mythical beginning. He had no idea how it would play out—all he knew for certain was that it needed time. And time was something he had in plenty. Besides, by not raising it head-on, he sensed, he was doing them a kindness—and that would atone for his absence and silence.

As if this new resolve had somehow communicated itself to the entire household, the two women now found a way to tell him of his full inheritance—where it reposed (in banks and investments), how much it was worth (he need never work again), and when it came to fruition (three years on, when he reached twenty-one).

The decision and then the sense of security finally released him. In the first serious view of his future that he had managed to take since he came home, he wrote to Professor Ryle, who, in reply, introduced him to the sister faculty of history in the university at Cork, forty miles away. That October, Ronan enrolled in college all over again and embedded himself in his beloved subject more intensively than any tutor there had ever seen.

Three years later, three driven, intensive, committed, focused years later, in the summer of 1964, Ronan O'Mara graduated from University College, Cork, with the highest honors in history that the college had ever awarded in a bachelor degree. His examiners especially acclaimed his "capacity to convey the reality of history while losing nothing of the required formal interpretation." Learning had become his mature emotional outlet, as it had been his youthful one. And that October he came into his inheritance from his father.

His career, which had never perhaps been in doubt, merely in abeyance, now began to take shape, and he built his life toward it. Alison had taken over the management of John's practice, purely the business affairs; not herself a lawyer, she hired the best she could find, and matters throve. Kate had taken a teaching job two towns away and bought land there to build her own house. Father Mansfield had begun to appear in her life more and more; since nobody dared ask questions, no explanations were offered.

Ronan took his own cue from these developments. After his bachelor's graduation and before he commenced his master's degree studies, he bought a house near Fermoy on the river Blackwater, an equidistant hour away from Kate and Alison; he visited each on alternating Sundays. He learned to drive, owned a car, ran his life like a man. When he balked initially at doing all these things, Alison repeated what she had said at his father's wake; "At your age men have led regiments into battle, been crowned kings, written everlasting poetry."

The year of his master's studies brought Ronan new peace and confidence. A gentle fame arising from his degree results had given him greater personal comfort among people. Professors and lecturers included him in their social lives; eligible girls stepped forward like dancers; but none caught his sleeve. Those who watched over him—his academic supervisor; Kate and Alison; the housekeeper from the town—they all urged him to "live a little more."

By way of response Ronan threw himself into the establishing of a local historical society, canvassing a wide membership and finding contributors for the journal he intended to edit. He convened and chaired meetings, inviting distinguished colleagues as well as local people to give papers. This, with formal study, dominated his life, and he kept himself busier than anyone he knew. Shrewd observers might have wondered whether it was his means of filling some painful void.

On the day his professor called to tell him that he had handsomely won his master's degree—"the surest bet in history, Ronan"—he drove the hour-long journey into Cork. Having congratulated him, the professor showed Ronan a letter from the outside examiner: "If you don't want him, we'll give him the chair of history here now, tomorrow—I'll retire to make room for him, and the devil take the hindmost." It was signed "T. Bartlett Ryle."

Ronan's own professor laughed and said, "But I'm retiring in two years—by which time I expect you'll have completed your doctorate."

Ronan said, "Is that a job offer?"

"It's a promise."

In fact, the doctorate studies had already begun: he called it "Blood on the Page: The Value of Myth in History," and everything he had thus far accumulated proved of direct or tangential use. By now he truly knew how to study; by now he knew instinctively which paths of scholarship led to caves of treasure and which halted at walls of rock.

Nor did he abandon the old trails. Time and again in his four years of study, he had written to all the people he had met, asking for any trace of the Storyteller, any sightings, any information. All, without exception, replied—and all, equally without exception, had no new trace. Even Ray Cashman answered, letters (on distillery invoice forms) that always began, "I'm still alive," but had nothing to report on "the old man."

Slowly Ronan allowed himself to grasp that, one by one, they all seemed to be suggesting that the Storyteller had died. Mrs. Cantwell knew the old man's age (as she would have done), and she pointed out, "He was born in eighteen-eighty-eight, and he would now be in his late seventies if he lived. And that hard life he led won't have made him any younger."

Such letters Ronan filed away with a sigh, followed by a speedy return to work. As a graduate student, he had begun to teach in the university, and his reputation packed his lectures to the brim. His life's pattern was now fixed in its groove, and bit by bit, he became content, like a sea calming.

Then—it all changed again.

One day, one November day in 1965, Alison telephoned. Their conversations had grown far beyond cordial; he allowed her to express interest in his life; she had even come to a lecture or two. The old wariness between them had more or less dissolved; a true warmth had grown up, based on their common love of his father.

She said, "I hope you don't mind, but I've given your telephone number to a girl you were in school with."

"Are you matchmaking again?"

"No." Alison laughed.

"Who was it?"

"D'you remember Deirdre Mullen?"

Green ribbon, red hair, sent to fetch him back to school the last morning of the Storyteller—how could he ever forget?

"God, yes. What does she want?"

"She lives near you—she'll tell you herself."

That night, the phone rang, and a woman's voice said, "Could I speak to Professor O'Mara?"

Ronan laughed. "I'm not a professor yet."

"Well, when you are, I hope you'll remember your old friends. D'you know who this is?"

Ronan decided to play. "No-oo."

"I'll give you a clue. Brendan the Navigator."

"Deirdre Mullen."

"Aah, your mother probably told you. I thought you'd have forgotten me. I'm Deirdre Carroll now—I married Harry Carroll, d'you remember him, you mightn't have known him. I remember trying to put on your coat in the rain. You were a stubborn little divil."

"I probably still am."

"Listen, you're living near Fermoy, aren't you?"

"I am."

"I'm living very near you. Are you at home this coming Saturday?"

At half-past three she arrived—unchanged; the same frizzy hair, the same level calm.

"Imagine us living so close!"

"Is your husband working here?"

"He's a job in the cheese factory over in Mitchelstown."

They drank tea, and reminisced. Soon Deirdre said, "Now. Tell me. Have you ten minutes to spare?"

"Why?"

She put a finger to her lips. "You'll see."

In her car she told him, "I'm a nurse. I'm taking you to where I work."

Less than two miles from Ronan's house, on the outskirts of Fermoy, she drove into the car park of a large, gray Victorian house.

Inside, all was still and pleasant. Deirdre led the way along two quiet corridors and into the garden.

"We'll go in that way, through the French windows—it'll disturb fewer people." They walked a path to an annex, and she began to whisper. "Now," she said. "This'll be a surprise for the both of you. We have to be quiet—we're a little late, he starts every day at four. In here—go on tiptoe."

Deirdre opened a tall French door, and Ronan stepped into a large, airy room.

Ahead of him in a semicircle sat fifteen, perhaps twenty people, all considerably old. One or two had fallen asleep, mouths gaping. But most were bright-eyed and alert in institutional blue or pink cotton pajamas, nightdresses, and robes; they were in thrall to a seated man behind whose back Ronan now stood.

And yes, he was in full flow; no hat this time; no long black coat; institutional blue, too. But the stoop of the shoulder, the shape of the head—unmistakable again; and the voice—it seemed to have lost little, the same brown richness, the love of words. Ronan almost turned and ran, ripped open by delight and relief; he pressed himself against the wall to listen to the story.

HE WAS ABOUT TWENTY YEARS OLDER THAN ME, and believe it or not, he was a bigger man. I wasn't small; we were about the same height—but Yeats was bulkier, broader everywhere. War had just been declared, it was September nineteen-fourteen, and I think he was under the impression that I was walking into the town of Sligo in order to enlist.

"Don't do it!" he said to me.

Those were the first words I heard him speak, and whatever his reputation, I have never considered that he meant it as a poetic utterance.

"Don't do what?" said I.

You can well imagine how flummoxed you'd be if you were walking along a road overlooking the sea, the magic mountain of Ben Bulben in the distance, and a tall, floppy-haired man in a tweed suit and spectacles suddenly barks at you from where he's perched on a gate, "Don't do it."

"Come over here and sit by me," Mr. W. B. Yeats said—and I did.

It gave me an opportunity to look into his eyes, and I want to tell you, I saw the world in there. I want to say that in his eyes I saw Michael Robartes the dancer, and the boy who spread dreams at his true love's feet, and the bird's nest beneath the window, and the old men playing at cards with a twinkling of ancient hands, and the rough beast slouching through the desert to be born, and the falcon turning and turning in a widening gyre, and even his own newborn daughter—all the creatures of all the poems he had already written and was about to write.

Of course, I didn't see them that day, and I certainly didn't see them at that moment. All of that came to me later, when I contemplated him as his fame grew. That morning, there were three things that went on between us; first of all, he clarified what he meant when he addressed me; secondly, he gave me a short lecture; and finally, I'm afraid, I played a little trick on him. This is how our meeting went.

"When I said, 'Don't do it'—the 'it' I don't want you to do is go to war."

I said, "Sir, I'm not going to any war."

By the way, I knew who he was; and, if I hadn't, the ring he was wearing would have told me—a great, bright scarab on his finger. A woman in Portumna said to me that she had seen the same ring on Yeats, and that it was the only piece of jewelry she had ever coveted—you hear strange things when you travel the roads.

I also knew that his mother's family, the Pollexfens, came from Sligo, that he spent a lot of time over there, and that his family solicitors had their office in the town, with a most suitable name perhaps for a firm of lawyers, "Argue and Phibbs." They're still there, so far as I know.

"I'm glad to hear you're not going to war," he said. "Man shouldn't make war, it opposes the natural spirit, and don't let anyone tell you otherwise."

Now, I like it when people talk like that; I believe the world of the spirit is in general greatly neglected and not at all served by the practice of faith as we know it, because religion isn't individual enough. So I said to him, "I'd love to hear a little more of what you mean."

"War," he said, "goes in the direction opposite to that in which man naturally wants to aim. Man wants peace and ease, so that he can work out the mysteries of life, but war introduces such chaos and actual physical pain that man can't think. And that, of course, is what politicians want—they want us not to think."

"So—how would you counter it?" I said.

"If we can only look away from this world," said Mr. Yeats, "we'd find such wonders elsewhere that we'd never want to fight."

"What kind of wonders do you have in mind?"

He said to me, "Turn around, young man, and look at that mountain over there. D'you know what it's called?"

I said, "Ben Bulben," a fact that everyone knows because the mountain isn't shaped like any other mountain in Ireland—it's high and flat, a genuine plateau.

Mr. Yeats said to me, "Screw up your eyes hard and tell me—can you see up there, halfway up the side of Ben Bulben, any traces of a door?"

I narrowed my eyes and peered hard—it was a bright sunny day—and I said, "Yes, I believe I can."

"Now," said he, "look over there." We turned in the opposite direction. "What's that mountain called?"

"I believe it's Knocknarea."

"It is," he said. "And d'you see that pile of stones on top of it?"

"I do."

"That's the grave of Maeve, the Queen of the Fairies. Now, at midnight every midsummer, that door on Ben Bulben opens, and out across the sky, on little fairy horses, ride the hosts of the air. Out and out they ride, high across the sky in a great wide loop, until they land at that cairn of stones on Knocknarea. They pay homage at Queen Maeve's grave, they hold a full wake with music and dancing, and then, just before dawn breaks, they ride back and return to the world they were given long ago—all of Ireland beneath the earth."

Now: I had known this story for some years; the old storyteller from whom I learned my trade often told it when he was in Sligo or south Donegal, because it connected with the people who lived in sight of these two mountains. To my great sadness, though, I have never met anyone who actually saw the hosts of the air on their midnight ride. But now I had met a man who believed it happened every year.

I said to him, "Do you derive comfort from the fact that such a thing takes place?"

"Oh, I do," he said. "And more than comfort. I feel it places me squarely within the fellowship of the world."

That was a mysterious saying, and I asked him to explain it a little. Mr. Yeats said to me, "You know about leprechauns, I suppose."

"Oh-ho," I said. "I know a great deal about leprechauns."

"Well," said he, "if ever there was a definition of the fellowship of the world, then the leprechaun embodies it," and he launched himself into a little lecture on the subject.

"We may think the leprechaun exists solely for the entertainment of visitors to our shores—but not at all. He's not unique to Ireland. Every society in the world has a little green man somewhere in its soul, who usually appears under the influence of too much alcohol. It even happens in Mexico, I'm told. And in Africa and Hawaii and Lithuania. He first appeared in Irish lore around the year sixteen hundred, and there are two explanations I give for his name. This is the first explanation: to those who have seen him in Ireland, he has always appeared as a little shoemaker—maybe they were walking home from a good, lubricated evening, and the roads were wet, and they had leaky boots. Anyway, there he sat, and this is the point—he was always working on just one shoe at a time. Now—the Irish-language word for 'half' is *leas* or *leath,* pronounced 'la.' And another word for shoe is *brogue.* So, as he was working on half a pair of shoes at a time, he was a 'la-brog-awn.' That *awn* suffix means 'little,' but it also got tagged on for the sake of making a word sound musical.

"And here's the second explanation: the word *leprechaun* came from *lucorpawn*—*lu* meaning 'little' and *corp* being a body—and again you have the *awn* diminutive suffix. Time expanded the feelings and imagination of those who saw the leprechaun, and all factors conspired to resolve in the image of a little man with a green hat and a face like a potato, hammering on a pair of boots."

I said to Mr. Yeats, "That's most interesting."

He agreed with me. "What's more," he said, "I intend to give a paper on the subject to a gathering of important doctors in Switzerland early next year. I hope this war doesn't prevent me from traveling."

He was very serious about all this—and that was when I decided I'd play a little trick on him.

"Did you ever see a leprechaun?" I asked him—and this is where my little trick came into it.

"No," said he. "Did you?"

"Only last night," I said. "Only last night."

Well! He nearly fell off the gate.

"You did? Where?"

"Up the road a bit," said I. "Just inside the avenue at Lissadell."

His face lit up. "I know Lissadell; I have the honor to be called a friend of the Gore-Booth family. Tell me more."

"I was walking past the gate," I said. "It was just gathering dusk, and I heard this little voice singing. Very melodious, very true, every note like a small bell. It was a merry little song, without words, keeping time to something tapping. So I strolled over—in fact, I went on tippy-toes—"

"Very wise," said Mr. Yeats.

"—and I looked in through the gate. Now you know there are lovely shrubs lining the drive of Lissadell, and in there, under an arbutus tree, sitting cross-legged on a large stone, was the neatest little man you ever saw. He was about two feet high, and he was repairing a shoe. The shoe had a silver buckle on it, and I realized it must have been his own shoe—because he was only wearing one shoe, and that had a silver buckle. And there he sat, tapping and making lovely mouth music."

Mr. Yeats's eyes were now as round as twin moons in the sky. "You see! Half a pair of shoes! What did you do?"

"I had a good look at him, I took in everything—the ginger hair sprouting out from under the hat, the green jacket and darker green pants, the big nose and the dancing silver hammer, the hands twinkling at his work, the skin weathered by all those rainbows. I have to say he was no film star, no oil painting."

"Did he see you?"

"Oh, sure he did. He looked up at me and winked, a big broad wink—with his right eye. I raised my hat and said to him, 'Good evening, sir, God bless the work.' "

"Oh, no! You didn't!" said Mr. Yeats. "Oh, no!"

"Did I do wrong?"

"Ohhhh! You must never mention God to them, that's a rival power, a different system altogether."

I allowed myself to have light dawn on my face.

"Ach, that explains everything," I said.

"What happened? What happened?"

"Well," I said, "as I was replacing the hat on my head, I passed it briefly before my face, blocking my line of vision for an instant. In that second—he was gone. By the time I had the hat back on my head, he had disappeared."

Mr. Yeats sagged back, very disappointed.

"And left no trace?"

"No trace."

He sat back on the rail of the gate, and he looked into the distance and thought very deeply.

"Would you mind," said he at last, "if I went looking for the same leprechaun?"

"Of course I wouldn't," said I. "Leprechauns belong to us all. Why would I mind?"

"Ah," he said. "You must be a true gentleman—you understand that we must all share in each other's visions if the world is to become civilized."

He climbed down off the gate and shook my hand with both of his big hands. That was the way William Butler Yeats and I parted company, expressing all the good wishes gentlemen like to convey to each other.

I have it on good authority that the great poet, William Butler Yeats, was seen that same evening, and many evenings thereafter, hovering on tiptoe just inside the gates of Lissadell. Local people thought he was summoning up courage to ask either of the Gore-Booth girls to walk out with him because, as he wrote later, one of them was beautiful, and one moved like a gazelle. But I know different—I know what he was looking for.

Nurses and orderlies came flooding in, and the Storyteller drew his tale to a close.

"I hope you've been paying attention, because tomorrow I'll be asking questions."

The elderly audience laughed. As they dispersed, the Storyteller sat without moving, watching them until the last one had left the room.

Deirdre watched Ronan closely, then whispered, "He came in here three years ago; they sent him up from Cork. They have no records for him, and he wouldn't give them a name. Isn't he the same man? He asked me to try and find you."

"Does he have a name?"

"He never told us. We call him Pat, but we do that with all people who can't remember their names."

The Storyteller heard the whispering and half turned his head—but not so fully that he could see who stood behind him.

He said, "Is that who I think it is?"

Ronan stepped round, into the man's eye line.

"How are you, sir?"

Deirdre withdrew, leaving the old man and his young pursuer alone in the wide, bright room. Ronan sat and scrutinized the face. All those lines—and now so pale; the eyes seemed sunken in the head, the whole presence so lacking in vigor. Both hands lay resting on his knees—the long bony hands, surprisingly smooth, with trimmed and clean fingernails.

Ronan, with no cogent thought in his head, reached out, and gently took one hand in a handshake. The Storyteller blinked, blinked again, then shook his head; he looked around the empty room and back at Ronan; he looked at Ronan's hand holding his own hand.

"I told you I'd send for you," he said.

Within two weeks Ronan had finalized arrangements. He brought the Storyteller into his house and gave the Storyteller his own bed. But once he had moved in, the old man's health sagged alarmingly; he developed infection after infection—sinus, bronchial, ear. The doctor said it seemed as if, having fought off everything during his years on the road, and held himself together in front of others at the old people's home, he now felt it was safe to succumb. Day by day the Storyteller fell into deeper and longer sleeps.

He refused to go to hospital, and Ronan approved of the decision. Deirdre Mullen said she would be glad of the extra money to nurse him; she knew others who would join a roster of care. Until the Storyteller recovered fully, and began to sit up, then walk, then go outside, Ronan felt he could ask none of the questions he had planned.

But the old man's mood sank in parallel with his physical decline, and he spoke less and less. He shied away from contact; intimate conversation seemed to faze him. Many times Ronan asked him his name and received no answer; to any other queries he answered at best perfunctorily.

Kate came to see him, and the Storyteller, though he seemed to recall her easily, scarcely spoke to her. She visited again and again, and always reported that he seemed close to catatonic, or afraid of something. (Alison put in no appearance, and when Ronan told her of his new house guest, she merely said, not unkindly, "Well, that will please you.")

The doctor began to take a keener interest. More progressive than the typical medical man of 1966, he opined that the old man needed some psychological help or perhaps had something locked in him that was hindering his recovery. Ronan resolved to conquer the baffling melancholy, and he knew of only one thing that might do it—get the Storyteller back into his most familiar mode, get him to perform again.

In early February 1966, by the fire on yet another generally silent evening, Ronan said to the Storyteller, "Pat—how much do you know about the Easter Rising?"

The old man looked at him. "I was there."

"How do you mean?"

"I was in the General Post Office in Dublin on Easter Monday and Tuesday."

"Would you tell it to some people?"

A shake of the head. "I'm done with telling stories." And down once more came the silence.

"I think it would cheer you up."

The Storyteller shook his head.

"All right," said Ronan. "There's something I have to tell you. The year my father died, in nineteen-sixty, even though I was broken-hearted, I gave up my life, and for six months and more I followed you all over Ireland, trying to find you and, when I failed, trying to be like you. I don't quite know why I did it. The letters you wrote to me—and I know they came from you—I read them very closely, and I felt as I was being driven by you for, I don't know—some mysterious reason. In the end I gave up and went back to my studies. When I reached the age of twenty-one, my father's will gave me all this comfort that I hope I can now share with you."

For the remainder of the evening he told the Storyteller of his travels through the counties, of the people he had met and the stories he, Ronan, had heard and told. "Pat" listened, growing more and more moved. At the end he said, almost in a whisper, "And you say you came into your inheritance?"

"Every penny."

The Storyteller thought for a moment. "And you say you went on all that traveling to try and find me?"

"Every step."

"I don't think I can refuse you one last story."

Ronan said, "Suppose we call it—one more story?"

The old man smiled, thin and lost. "I remember—Saint Brendan, wasn't it?"

"Yes."

"Thank you."

"But I have two favors to ask. The first is—if I'm to speak like that, can it be somewhere bigger than a kitchen? I easily get feelings of being crowded these days, being unaccustomed to indoors, I suppose."

"Fine," said Ronan. "We'll do it in a hall or a theater, so that the people aren't sitting too close to you. And the second favor?"

"I'll tell you nearer the day."

In Ireland in 1966, the country celebrated the fiftieth anniversary of the Easter Rising, the final rebellion that led to the War of Independence, that led to the Anglo-Irish treaty, that led to the two states of Ireland—the twenty-six counties of the republican south, and the six counties of Northern Ireland, governed by Britain. Ronan wrote to everyone who had ever been part of his Storyteller search and invited them to a special evening in the main lecture theater of University College, Cork. He also wrote to another host of names that the Storyteller gave him; houses he had stayed in, people who had sustained him, old friends.

So many replied and with such enthusiasm that they had to move the event to a public theater in the city with a capacity of six hundred seats, each one of which they filled.

Ronan took all necessary measurements, and in the shops of Cork bought the Storyteller his old "wardrobe"—the long black overcoat, jacket, waistcoat and stovepipe trousers, excellent boots. And a new homburg hat.

The old man smiled. "I've only one criticism—they're not shabby enough." He seemed more animated, readier to recover; he began to sleep better, and the doctor reported improvements.

On the night before the event, the old man said to Ronan, "You and I have much to talk about."

"I have a hundred questions."

The Storyteller said, "And I have a thousand. And—" He hesitated. "D'you remember I said I have a second favor?"

"Yes?"

"You wouldn't be surprised to hear—from your knowledge of me—that I have a box buried in the ground. As you yourself had."

"That was one of my main questions: How did you know about mine? You left one of your chronicles in it for me."

"I used to see you as a small boy—I was often in those woods near your house."

Ronan felt surprised not to find the information sinister.

"My own box isn't too far from here, and tomorrow I want you to get it."

"But I have to take you to the theater in Cork."

"Let someone else do that. Inside the box, the only thing in it, you'll find the last piece of the document I wrote for you."

"The chronicle?"

"Read it. It's not very long."

Kate arrived early next morning and helped to prepare the old man for his public. He allowed himself to feel excited and had kept abreast of every invitation and every acceptance.

"This is like giving me back the best parts of my life," he said. "I don't deserve this—but it'll be lovely to see them all."

Ronan had previously explained his chore to Kate. He then left the two of them, having worked out detailed timetables of every-one's arrival at the theater. Following the Storyteller's directions, he drove to the riverbank; no swans appeared, but he found the essen-tial tree and shivered as he dug up the box wrapped in sacking—it felt to him like exhuming a body.

Prizing open the rusted lid required a screwdriver from the car and finally a stone to hammer in the sides. In an old oilcloth, like a tobacco pouch, he found the small stash of blue pages; the title page read, "A Storyteller's Chronicle—Final Installment."

Ronan sat in the car and read.

Of LOVE AND TRUTH

For many years I have had two powerful loves in my life; I have had them for as long as I have been able to think clearly about my feelings; I have carried them in my heart, and they have defined my existence. When they were joined by a third love, my life felt completed, a circle closed. My feelings for these three—I shall call them "entities"—have been my salvation, although it has taken me until now to understand that fact. This realization broke upon me gradually; I had no epiphany, no blinding light, no voice booming down from on high. Slowly I began to grasp what they have meant to me.

The first love is my country. I describe it to myself as like one of those wells I know, out in the land somewhere, miles from anywhere, on a mountainside, or beneath ferns in an old forest. There it will sit, alone and untroubled, secluded and quiet, yielding pure and cool water that has risen to the surface from deep in the earth.

I have a number of such wells in mind. In county Longford, not far from the town of Granard, a spring bubbles in some rough ground a few yards from the roadside. Climb the old wire fence where it ties into a tree, walk in a northwesterly direction, and look out for some unexpected ferns and water fronds; the big green blades will catch your eye. The water in that spring, which bubbles up by some stones, has as lovely a taste as water may ever have.

Just off the road between Cashel and Tipperary, beyond the hamlet of Thomastown, you will find, along a broad avenue going north, a deep well, lined with stone, a dark and excellent spring that once serviced the great local houses.

And, out in the plowed fields of Kildare, near the town of Newbridge, there is a well so hidden in an old grove that I may be the last person alive who knows of its existence.

My love of country feels like those wells; I go to it for refreshment. The springs may rest in brackish land, but their waters rise up from a source deep as the soul, and to drink it is private and renewing.

And love of country must remain a private matter. In Ireland, to love your country requires a political statement, which I refrain from uttering. Worse than that, it is a political statement measured only by the hostility expressed against England. As I believe that no love can have enmity as a component; therefore I say nothing, and I continue to love my country more than I have words to tell. Besides, to express such powerful emotion in public smacks of vulgarity.

That is partly the reason that, in my stories, I never directly mention my love of country. The other reason is—my eyes will fill with tears. But when I come out on the road of a morning, when I have had a night's sleep and perhaps a breakfast, and the sun lights a hill in the distance, a hill I know I shall walk across an hour or two thence, and it is green and silken to my eye, and the clouds have begun their slow, fat rolling journey across the sky, no land in the world can inspire such love in a common man.

Or when I sit by the weir on a river and watch small birds fly, busy, busy, in and out of the hawthorn bushes, or a peaceful man in the distance flicking a line onto the water, or touch a horse's velvet muzzle over a fence in county Limerick—then I know that I love this land down to its limestone bones.

My second love had flesh and blood. Her name was Sylvia; I miss her still, as I have missed her every day of my life, and I vowed when I began to keep this ramshackle record of my existence that I would conclude by honoring her and her memory and her descendants. Sylvia was my only true love. I met her in a house in county Monaghan that first year I took to the road. Other than a wild woman in Rome one night, she was the only girl with whom I lay. It happened like this. We stayed, my old storytelling mentor and I, in Sylvia's family home, telling stories for four days. She sat facing me each night in the kitchen, and I began to dream of her. When the time came for us to leave and take to the roads again, I found I could not go. Back I went and found her, and we sat on the hillside. She enchanted me, and she said I enthralled her. We wrapped our arms around each other, and no other world existed. I lingered in the neighborhood for weeks, seeing her every day.

Inevitably it transpired that Sylvia had conceived a child. When her body could not be masked anymore, our world caved in. Priests were called; I was whipped and kicked by her family and told what shame I had brought to a lovely girl—and banished from her sight forever.

It is probably impossible to imagine today how much shame a pregnancy outside wedlock could bring down on a girl and her family. Sylvia's distress, and the fact that I had caused it, broke off a part of my heart; that she and I had to part, and would never live our lives with and for each other, destroyed part of my soul.

The church, the priests, forced the pace. They made her marry the well-to-do local man whom her parents had always wanted to bring into the family. And the world was told to assume that he was the father of her child. He was a man called O'Mara, and the boy Sylvia bore under his name was my son—my son, John; I believe she named him after me, even though John was also her own father's name. Later, she had a son by this Mr. O'Mara, whom she named Tobias.

I managed through the years to keep track of my son. Sylvia's closest friends helped secretly; they told me where John went to school, what happened to him next, and so on. Year by year I kept in touch with his life—and one day, not long after he married, I visited him and his new wife, down in the south.

My son John knew about me and received me with a kindness that made me proud of him. His wife, however, feared the disreputableness of her husband's bastardy, and I was never truly welcome in that house. Were we ever to meet in public, she told me, I would not be acknowledged.

My life changed again when my third love came to earth—when my grandson was born. I learned that a child of my son had come into the world, healthy and strong. He was an infant when I first saw him—a snatched glimpse in his father's arms on the streets of the nearby town.

Thereafter, I found ways of learning his progress, largely through Sylvia's other son, Toby, who was always kind to me. As the boy grew, I was able to keep a kind of watchful eye over him, and from time to time I was even able to observe him at play in the woods among the badgers and the deer. But I knew that were I to try and make him truly part of my life, he might suffer from my past, and so I have had to be content with a few days spent in his company as a little boy and a few hours after the funeral of his father, my dear son.

And through Toby too I was able to return Sylvia's ring to our son's finger; Toby gave it to me when his mother died, and in his kindness he never felt overlooked when, years later, I asked him to put it on his half-brother's hand.

This, then, has been my life's secret—a hidden and surely unpopular love of country; an unrequited passion for the only woman I ever loved; and a son and grandson observed from a distance. And to think that my loss of family came from love.

It probably could not happen now; Ireland is more elastic, and these matters do not weigh so gravely. Back then, in 1912, it amounted to a black disgrace; there was no shame like shame, especially if it involved a former aspirant priest such as I was.

If I have a dream left, it is that my "family" (I feel only a hesitant right to call them so) will one day understand that for this love and this disgrace I committed myself to a life on the road and to teaching the history of my country by means largely of my imagination—facts alone have always been too painful for me. There were times when I knew this was an extreme decision—but all in all I have gained inner riches beyond measure. I hope I have brought light into people's lives; to love of woman I have added love of country and, now, love of a generation that will carry my blood— and my name, which is the same as my grandson's.

I, the writer of this entire account, am the young Ronan O'Mara; I am the one who has been telling you this story, which began in 1951 when my grandfather came across the fields to our house.

Now I know why my father had always told me about the old story-tellers and that I should look out for one; what was it he said? "I wouldn't be surprised if one of them came here one day." The picture he painted was, of course, that of his own father; I remember the words so well; "He'll probably be tall and old, with boots and a hat, and he'll enchant us all." And again, on the night we first saw television, he pressed me further; "This is my advice. Go look for him."

For the rest of my life I shall remember that time, that April day when I learned the Storyteller's identity; the texture of the weather, sunshine trying to break through; how the windscreen of the car misted up as I sat inside reading; the kind air when I got out again to lean on the car and weep; the farmyard geese tugging at the grasses of the field where I dug up the box.

And I remember every moment of the drive to Cork—how every-thing fell into place, above all my "mother's" rejection of the Story-teller. Alison, to whom appearances and moral respectability had such critical importance, evidently feared that her husband's illegitimacy might become public. Then, had I found the old man in my travels and brought him back into the family, as I would surely have done, she might have threatened my inheritance; was that why he had so clearly wished to evade my company—to keep me safe? He certainly altered when I told him my father's will had been discharged.

But—did Alison not know that in all secretive communities, such as the Irish countryside, there is no such thing as a secret, except to the people who live it? Suddenly I recalled how the people after the funeral looked at me when the Storyteller told of Hugh O'Neill in that cottage; did they all know he was my grandfather, did everyone always know? I have no doubt that they did, as they most certainly knew of my parentage.

As for Sylvia: now I understood too why the details of my father's mother had been so vague. Toby was the only member of his family that I knew—Toby was all I would ever have been allowed to know. Now his role was clarified too; that's how I was able to receive a letter from my grandfather at the bank; he had obviously kept in touch with my grandfather, fed him news of Dad—and of me. By the time I drove by the ribbon of the river Lee into Cork city, my questions had begun to evaporate like mist in sudden sunlight.

Fifteen minutes before curtain time I slipped in at the stage door. In the wings Kate stood beside my grandfather, who sat on a stool and looked away when I approached; Kate stepped aside from us.

"Did you find it?" he said.

"I did."

He lifted a cautioning finger. "Say nothing to me now, not now." His eyes looked desperate, and I felt indescribable, almost panic-stricken sorrow for him—all those years; all that displacement; his and my father's loss of each other; the loneliness implicit at the thought that I would have dearly loved to have lived my life never more than five feet away from him.

I said, "Please. I'm trying to cope with shock."

With worry his ears seemed to draw back like a frightened dog.

"One question," I said.

He nodded.

"If you already knew that Alison was so hostile—why did you come to our house that evening in nineteen-fifty-one?"

He had a habit of gnawing his lower teeth on his upper lip. Now he did it—but he had such bravery; he never took his eyes off mine.

"Because," he said, "I couldn't bear it any longer. I contacted your father, and I told him I'd die if I didn't meet you."

A stagehand strolled forward, in shirtsleeves; "Any time you like, sir, we're all ready for you."

I was by now thoroughly flummoxed. For something to say, I asked Kate, "Should someone introduce him?"

She calmed my fretting; "It's an invited audience—they all know him or know of him. And they're not expecting to see anyone else."

And now I certainly would not have been capable of any coherent few words.

My grandfather rose to his feet, took off his hat, and put it on again. Kate fixed his lapels, brushed him down a little, tweaked his waistcoat, and, not a little quavery, he strolled onstage and in the center sat on the simple kitchen chair he had requested.

The curtains rolled back, and the applause built up and up, almost into a roar. As Kate and I watched, the quavers in his hands vanished; like an old stage trouper, he sat there calmly and went through all the familiar motions.

"I'll be with you in a minute," he said to the audience, fixing the hat, the pipe, the opening out of the coat, the settling back in the chair, the surveying. Finally he cleared his throat.

I'M TO TALK TO YOU, THIS ANNIVERSARY YEAR, ABOUT the insurrection of nineteen-sixteen. The Irish Rebellion, the Easter Rising, the Poets' Rebellion—people have given it many names. Let me be clear immediately as to how I think of it: it was the final movement that gained the Irish people back most of their country from the English. On a personal level, it made me look at people and their capacity for bravery in a way I have never since forgotten to do.

Often I make up the stories I tell, especially if they refer to times before history was written down. If I'm within the bounds of history, I invent little, only what I need for color and atmosphere—but otherwise I follow the historical facts largely as I was taught them. Which doesn't mean they're always right, and which doesn't mean I always tell them as they were meant to be told.

Tonight, I'm certainly going to tell you a story, but 'tis a story with a difference because, unlike virtually every other tale I tell—in this case, I was there. And yet I know that although I was there, and I saw people who were real, they have since become somewhat imagined—because I now view them through my memory. That's something every human being does—but storytellers live by it.

The building that housed the Easter Rising was the General Post Office in Dublin, and it must be the largest building ever constructed in the world, to judge from the number of people who claim to have been in it on that famous Easter Monday, the twenty-fourth of April, nineteen-sixteen; I was twenty-seven and a half years old when I entered its carved portals.

Let me begin by describing the morning, the way the world felt.

It was mild; the weather was what we'd call "soft"; people were still in an airy mood after Easter Sunday.

I had been in a good billet outside Dublin in the village of Chapelizod on the river Liffey. After five hospitable nights, I found myself on the Monday morning walking in the tranquillity of Phoenix Park. More than a few carriages clopped by on their way through the park, heading off to be in plenty of time for the first race at Fairyhouse, which as you know is about twenty miles outside Dublin. Some of the carriages were lovely, elegant broughams and painted sidecars, and I stood to watch them drive by, with the spokes of their wheels flashing. The ladies in them wore bonnets and looked grand.

For myself, I resisted anything that looked like an omnibus or a tram, and soon I reached Kingsbridge. I kept on walking east toward the sun, following the river along the quays toward the center of the city. Tongues of bright water gurgled from pipes pouring into the river Liffey; now and then someone went past me on a bicycle, whistling; a man on a horse and cart delivered milk to a high doorway behind which everybody was asleep; you could tell from the blindness of the windows.

The odd thing was—and I can capture this feeling now—something in my heart had begun to stir. I didn't know what it was; I could call it excitement, but it was more than that. Was it elation, a sense of triumph, or something dark? Yes and no to all of those things; it was a strange feeling; it hurt me, worried me, and made me happy at the same time. I might have been as near to tears as to laughing.

At the next bridge I stopped to admire the view; the sky was clear, except for a lovely wisp of cloud like the tail of a white mare. In my reverie, I thought I heard something very definite approaching, something considerable, but I could see nothing. Remember, banks, shops, and offices were to stay closed that day, a public holiday. A woman walked by; she looked thoughtful; she was wearing black, and she was probably going to half-past-eleven mass somewhere in a church along the quays.

The kind morning air seemed to grow clearer. Then I heard it again—from behind me, steady and in a rhythm. I still couldn't see anything, and the noise puzzled me. I walked to the far side of the bridge, and round a corner they came; I shall never forget it.

A troop of armed men marched along that quayside toward me, about eighty of them, a people's army, you'd call them, mostly in civilian clothes. "Country boys," I thought immediately; they had complexions ruddy from fields, not pale from offices; they lacked the general smoothness to which a city rubs its dwellers. A few, not more than nine or ten of them, wore a green uniform with a slouch hat—that is to say, a hat with one side of the brim standing up at right angles.

Who were these men, these boys? I think of them now as Irish tribesmen, with names such as Dolan, MacEnroe, Cusack, Egan, O'Donnell, Keogh, Brady, Daly, Lahiffe, Curran, MacMahon, O'Loughlin—any and all of the names in Ireland's long genealogy, names from before the time of Saint Patrick, names you have all known and heard, the music of our daily lives.

They had faces like priests, and they had faces like pikers—by which I mean they looked like everybody else and nobody else; simple faces, anxious or excited or resigned faces, some with little experience of life evident, some with eager attitudes, some afraid, some apprehensive, some grim.

Almost all carried guns, mostly bolt-action rifles; I saw one submachine gun and a number of double-barreled shotguns, more suited to shooting wildfowl. Most had Sam Brown belts or some other harness for carrying ammunition. But no matter how briskly they marched, how hard they tried, they looked anything but military; two lads in the middle of the ranks had no weapons, but oh, how they swung their marching arms.

They, like all the troop, had something about them. Was it determination? Or had they embraced the idea of blood sacrifice? I doubt it—these were lads who, in part, were caught up in the romance of a patriotic idea; it has happened across the world over and over again. I will say that what I think I saw in their faces was a genuine and modest nobility. Maybe they truly so loved their country they would have done anything for it, and that patriotic light was a fire inside them. Or is that memory again? Memory is the best tailor in the world.

I was immediately engaged with what I saw, with no idea of whether this was some isolated, crackpot, stupidly brave troop of rebels, or whether an insurrection was taking place. There had been talk of it for months—that one day men from each of the thirty-two counties of Ireland would march on Dublin and throw out the British. Somehow it didn't matter to me if these men were the only ones rebelling—their bearing, the expressions on their faces, a mixture of strength and tranquillity, that all captured my spirit.

They marched right in front of my face; I stood two feet or so above them, owing to the height of the bridge. A number of them glanced up at me—nothing in their look other than serene friendliness. They were dressed mostly in workingmen's clothes—rough jackets, many in dungarees, corduroy pants, mostly boots, those big strong working boots with broad thick soles that I myself like.

The officer who led them—I saw him many more times that day and the next, and you will hear more of him—was a tall young man with a powerful presence; he had a rangy build, no flesh on him, and a head of tawny hair and a moody face. His sandy coloring suited the green uniform, and he had polished his brown shoes and gaiters to a bright shine. Somehow I expected him to have an officer's sword, but he didn't; he had a revolver at his waist, in a holster whose flap had lost its button; it's strange the details you remember from such a moment.

I watched them out of sight—they disappeared into a side street, and I wondered where they were going. Then I decided to follow them and began to run. A man standing in a doorway grabbed my arm to halt me, so hard that I almost fell.

"What'n the hell are youse thinking of?" he said.

He had a cigarette and wore blue suspenders over a working shirt.

"What are they? Where are they going?"

"Leave 'em alone," he said. "Buncha clowns. Uniforms! Guns!

Jesus!" He hadn't let go of my arm. "Leave 'em go, they're going to jeopardize the whole bloody day."

"Are they rebels?"

"They're jackasses. Have youse a light on you?"

"No."

"What kind of a man goes out without a box of matches?"

He let go of my arm, and off I went after the troop. After a few minutes of quick walking, I saw them again in the distance, on the wide boulevard then called Sackville Street. As I hurried to catch up, some members of the Dublin Metropolitan Police, who had evidently not been alarmed by the marchers, watched me too but did nothing and said nothing. At the next bridge I stopped and asked a lady what was happening; she and the people near her said gruff, unpleasant things.

"Oh, a bunch of loonatics has gone into the General Post Office with guns, and they've locked the doors. And that crowd"—indicating my marchers—"they're going in there too."

A man near her pointed vaguely. "And there's more down at Liberty Hall. But the military'll rout them out soon enough."

"Disturbing us all," said someone else. "D'ja ever hear anything like it?"

Then a peculiar thing happened; such few police as stood about went away. A man called after them, "Where are youse going?" and a policeman shouted back, "We're leaving it to the soldiers."

I hurried on and caught up with my band of marching men, who by now were hearing shouts of abuse from the passersby; "Ah, would youse go home outta tha'!" and, "Leave us alone, would'ja?"

In short, Dublin had little encouragement for these rebels. A woman in a shawl threw a cabbage at the back of one of the armed men, but it didn't hit him; it fell in the street, and she retrieved it.

"I'm not one to waste my dinner on the likes of them," she said. Those around her laughed and approved.

By now I was abreast of the troop, and we had reached the post office; it was past noon. The marchers halted, performed what seemed like a fairly correct military maneuver, and turned left into the building.

As I made to follow them, a man stopped me and said, "If I was youse I wouldn't go into the GPO."

"Why?" I said.

"There's a bad crowd gone in there, guns 'n all. They went in about twenty minutes ago. And you know who they went in with— that fella, that bloody rabble-rouser, Connolly."

"But—" I began to say, and he cut me off, very angry.

"Ah, that's it, that's it! That's what the fault of the country is today, we don't know when we're well off—most of us are happy to be subjects of the king, but there's always some smart few donkeys who think they're better than that."

I tried to speak again, but he went on berating me.

"Go ahead! Go on! On your own head be it!"

Bear in mind that I had never seen this man in my life, and I never expected to see him again.

"Well?" said he. "Are youse going in there? You're not to, d'you hear? You're just not to."

He made my mind up for me. A life on the road, however lonely it may be at times, gives you certain gifts of independence, and I couldn't see that it was any of his business what I did. But that's Dublin for you, someone always on hand to tell you what they think you should be doing. I walked away from him and straight at the GPO.

The first door was locked tight, and I went along under that fine portico to the second door—but it was also locked. I could hear much commotion inside, but nobody would answer my knocking, so I decided to wait for a while and see if a door would open. Quite a few people were now gathering under the grand columns, wondering what was going on.

Well, I had to wait for about half an hour. In those days, I carried no watch; I took my time from the sun in the morning and the moon at night. But there was a clock across the street on a jeweler's shop, and when it said a quarter to one, a door opened and a group of men came out of the post office. Some wore the uniforms I had already seen, and some wore their own clothes. A slightly built, pale man led them; he had a crossed eye and a gentle face.

"Who's that?" I asked a man near me, and he said, "He's a fellow called Patrick Pearse, he's a bit of a poet, like."

All of you here tonight know who I mean; no doubt you learned his poems in school. "The beauty of the world hath made me sad, This beauty that will pass; Sometimes my heart hath shaken with great joy To see a leaping squirrel in a tree Or a red lady-bird upon a stalk." That was his last poem, and you'll understand why it always mattered a lot to me; its name is "The Wayfarer."

I edged closer to see and hear what was happening. This man Pearse stood there until his small group had assembled around him. Mr. Pearse had a piece of paper in his hand, and after looking around to see that his comrades were listening, he began to read out loud. The ordinary people around and about, who had been inclined to jeer, fell silent.

"Irishmen and Irishwomen, in the name of God and of the dead generations from which she receives her old tradition of nationhood, Ireland, through us, summons her children to her flag and strikes for her freedom."

Every schoolchild in this country has long since heard those words. Without any fear that I'm exaggerating, I can tell you now that when I heard them, I knew I'd never forget it. This was momentous, and I, whose lot had been dusty roads and rainy fields—I knew I was privileged to be there. It was the Proclamation of the Irish Republic, and Mr. Pearse was the first president. He was an idealist, an educated man. In his writings and speeches, he had tried to fight England intellectually as the founding fathers of America had done, but he too was forced to take up arms. Now he had written this proclamation, which was signed by him and six others.

Someone gave a kind of cheer when he had finished, and the men with Mr. Pearse reached across and shook his hand—very solemnly and respectfully, I thought. One man, with a mustache, wearing a green uniform, said to him, "Pearse, thanks be to God that we lived to see this day."

In the crowd someone said, "Look—up on the roof!" I still regret that I didn't step out onto the street and look. They had taken down the Union Jack and raised the Irish flag. Incidentally, I suppose you all know the symbolism of the green, white, and gold tricolor? The way I've heard it, the white is the peace between the green factions of the Irish Catholics and the orange factions of the Ulster Protestants, who were followers of William of Orange, the victor at the Battle of the Boyne.

The little party with Mr. Pearse slipped back into the post office, and in I went too—I squeezed inside just as the man with the mustache was telling a soldier to close the door. He had a very direct way of dealing with people.

"What do you want?"

I said, "I don't know, sir. To be here, I suppose."

He looked at me very straight and said, "Are you a working man?"

And I said, "I tell stories, that's my trade."

"As long as you've a trade," he said. "And there'll be a story to be told here today. And tomorrow and the day after that, and forevermore if I get my way."

A man in civilian clothes came up and addressed him with great deference as "Mr. Connolly." And that's how I found out that I had been talking to the great champion of the working man, James Connolly, one of the firebrands of the Easter Rising. He had been a union organizer in Dublin and had trained a little militia all of his own, the Irish Citizens' Army, which, under Mr. Connolly's command, had just taken over the post office that morning.

So in the space of a few minutes I had met two of the people who would become cornerstones of our country's history.

I mentioned earlier a tall young man with tawny hair, leading the men of the morning along the quays. Within the first hour of my arriving in the post office, I saw him again—he had become a force all unto himself. I watched him for several minutes; he had pushed the slouch hat back off his head so that it hung down his back by its lanyard. Everything about him mesmerized me—he had a natural power and superiority.

I said to someone near me, "You see the lanky man with the big head of tawny hair—where's he from?"

"He's from county Meath."

In the past, in the ages after the ice pulverized us, had his ancestor been a great figure in the Boyne Valley, I wondered, where even now, as I speak, they're opening up day by day the marvels in the great passage tomb of Newgrange?

Remember that I arrived in the post office shortly after the first soldiers who occupied it. They had scarcely had time to see what the building was like. None of these men had ever been to war, and none of them had ever taken over a building from which to launch a revolution.

To look at this young man, you'd never think that. He was striding the inside length of the building, inspecting every possible point of access—doors, windows, even skylights. So, by the way, was Mr. Connolly, on the other side of the building. Each of these two men pointed with his hands and spoke to himself, as though fixing each position in mind. When he had assessed the entire wall space, my tawny-haired young man walked over to Mr. Connolly, and he obviously asked permission to undertake some measure or other. James Connolly granted it; the young man saluted and immediately ordered two, four, six, eight—fifteen—young men to jump to it.

He directed them to shutter most of each window, but to poke holes in the glass for the riflemen's muzzles. Then he told them to push furniture here, there, and everywhere. First of all they dragged a huge table over to the very door through which I had come. Then they tipped the table on its side, so that anyone who came through that door was faced with a large surface of wood. He and Mr. Connolly then got men to pile tall cabinets above and behind that table, and when the structure was finished, it looked like as good a high rampart as a man could fashion.

By the way, I should remember to tell you that many women formed part of the occupying force; bright, busy women they were, who even in the heat and nervousness of all that was going on— and what they knew was likely to come—still bantered with the boys and shirked no hard physical work.

FRANK DELANEY

The ramparting measure was repeated on all of the post office doors. Every major point of access from the street outside was so fortified that it would have been very difficult for anyone to force a way through.

After that, again in consultation with James Connolly, the young tawny-headed fellow got his men to drag other furniture into place—desks, more chests and cabinets, tables—and he placed these about fifteen feet back from the front wall of the building. He then directed three soldiers to the top of each of these furniture piles, and they had been constructed so that men could lie or crouch on them and have full cover.

By now I could see his plan; if a door was breached, the attackers would walk into a hail of fire from the soldiers on top of these vantage points. He had also arranged things so that a long passageway led from the darker front of the building through this furniture to the very rear, where the lights shone brighter than anywhere else.

When he had all of these settled, he inspected each one, both the barricades and the vantage points, reordering something here, giving a direction there until he was completely satisfied. He walked along the tight passageway to the lighted sector, approving what he saw—and then he looked around for something else to do.

What struck me was this; he was no more a trained soldier than myself, and about the same age. Watching that young man gave me a belief that some people are born with a destiny inside them, waiting to make itself manifest. All we have to do is quarry down into our souls until we find it. Such people are the stuff of my tales.

My grandfather paused, rose for a moment from his chair, straightened his back, sat again, and spread his coats around him like a skirt. Not a sound came from the audience—not a cough, a sigh, a rustle. Though he had made himself more theatrical than he ever did in a country kitchen, the performance was better than ever, and the old spell had fallen across his listeners like a magic blanket.

Kate whispered, "Should I get him some water?"

As the words left her lips, the stagehand in shirtsleeves emerged from the far wings, sauntered across the stage, and put a glass of water on the small table. My grandfather picked up the glass, held it to the light, and said thoughtfully, "It seems—regrettably—clear."

Such a performer—he knew exactly when to release the high emotion, and the audience, as one voice, laughed.

With perfect timing, he worked the gag twice more. First, he sniffed the glass.

"No aroma either," he said.

Loud laughter.

Then he sipped. "And now—no taste."

The audience roared with delight and applauded. They applauded even louder when the man in the shirtsleeves reappeared, and this time placed a full glass of whiskey on the small table. With no trace of shame, my grandfather milked it again; he sat and looked at the glass for a long moment. As he picked it up he said, "They say the theater is where inspiration dwells. Perhaps . . ." and let it die.

The audience stamped its feet in delight.

"Was that rehearsed?" said Kate.

INSIDE THE GENERAL POST OFFICE THAT EASTER Monday morning, everybody meant business—the business of insurrection. I stood looking around me. The men I had first seen marching along the quays had stayed together. Some toiled to order, some helped with barricades, others had spread their ammunition on the ground beside them and held their rifles at the ready as sweetly as dancing partners.

In the middle of the floor, Mr. Pearse stood in deep conversation with two of the men who had been with him at the Proclamation. I wandered across toward him, making myself as unnoticeable as I could, expecting to hear some considerable discussion about war and strategy and patriotism. Instead, they were discussing the races at Fairyhouse.

It seemed a letdown, but then I listened closer; they were debating the fact that all the leading British officers were known to have gone to the races, and therefore very few remained by way of commanders to pitch forces against the rebels. Mr. Pearse was agreeing with a man who said this gave them time to have a real chance of taking over all Dublin; this man, who had recently come back in off the street, said there was fighting in many parts of the city.

"Thanks be to God," said Mr. Pearse.

The man who gave him the news seemed very intense, very urgent, insistent on what he was saying; he spoke quickly, and I looked at him closely.

Not tall, about five feet nine or ten, he had a sharp face, a Cork accent, and a pugnacious expression, though he seemed very deferential to Mr. Pearse. The man was unknown to me—as were all these people. When he became famous later, I recognized him from the photographs as Michael Collins, perhaps the most potent revolutionary we ever bred. I watched him as he walked around the place, giving orders, mock-wrestling with a comrade, checking a rebel's gun; it was clear that the men who knew him loved him; all responded to his gift of leadership.

The post office began to look very disheveled inside. Rows of men stood near windows, guns lying in their arms. Others bedded down, and I remember the scene as that of an august building being occupied and barricaded from within against its wishes. Not much light shone anywhere except in that one pool at the rear, and people teemed all over the place, rationing out the food that had been brought in.

And then, all of a sudden, everything went quiet. Still. Silent. I heard a seagull somewhere—and then some gunfire somewhere else—it was like a dream. But I know now that it merely amounted to a moment in which nothing took place; it was as though all the work had been done and nothing else needed to happen—the night before the battle, so to speak.

In the silence I saw two monks in their robes. One man was long and thin, one was short, fat as butter, and from the ease they showed to each other, even in that grim circumstance, it was clear that they were great friends. A man and a woman, comrades-in-arms, it seemed, stood side by side—quite military in appearance, except for the fact that every now and then she looked up at him with a tender gaze. Most remarkable of all, a boy of about eighteen had a drum, and he began a soft hypnotic beat; I would guess it kept time with the human pulse.

When all is said and done, the business of telling stories—call it an art, call it a trade, as I do, or a profession—depends principally upon one matter. It depends on making your listener ask all the time, "What's going to happen next?" As I wandered through the GPO that day, I couldn't answer that question for myself. As far as I could see, the answer, for some hours, was, "Nothing." No gun was fired, no glass was broken, no band struck up, nobody died.

Then, in the middle of the afternoon, I was talking to two brothers from the Naul, that easy place north of Dublin—they were twins with curly hair the color of brick—when the boy with the drum shouted.

"Shut up, everyone! Listen!" and then he got embarrassed at what he had said. It seems that like many musicians he had a keen ear. Through the thick walls and in all the noise and hum of chatter and the lugging of things around those hard floors, he had heard something.

Men rushed to the windows, I ran with them, and, peering through the rifle holes, we saw a thrilling, frightening sight. Down the wide and now almost empty street rode a big party of Lancers, troops of British cavalry. Who in God's name sent them in? It's not a difficult question to answer. The cavalry had won many a battle for king and country, and the British commanders tended to come from the cavalry, especially here in Ireland—they came over for the good hunting and the great horses. But they had never faced a circumstance like this—a huge building, locked against them, fortified from the inside by men with guns that were as up-to-date as Germany could supply.

Some of the Lancers, poor fellows, waved their swords in the air and shouted. At a given moment, all the rebel commanders gave the same order. The young Irish boys poked their rifles out through the holes in the panes of glass and opened fire.

In front of my eyes I saw a horse go down. One bullet had hit him, and another had hit his rider. Both of them died. All across the range of these riders the bullets hit again and again. Men flung their hands to their faces and then fell off their horses, and the lucky ones were those who didn't get shot. They were also the reckless ones, because you have to say it—those Lancers were brave men. The rebels inside the post office kept firing, but the Lancers came back at them again and again.

Of course they got nowhere—they never could have done—and eventually some officer found a little bit of sense somewhere in his addled brain and called them off. They retreated, and we saw them galloping away along Sackville Street. Outside the windows, people picked themselves up off the paving stones, surprised that they were still alive.

Inside the post office you never saw such jubilation. Men cheered and clapped, and heroes were born instantly. The more thoughtful ones went back to the windows and wondered which of the bodies they had been responsible for. When they saw that so many horses were there as well, they grew morose. At least four of the horses had been killed outright. Three more had been wounded, although only one of them had to be put down. Four or five more reared and bucked about the place because their riders were dead.

Then a man appeared whom I'd like to have met—he was the fellow who came in and collared some of those horses. He had black, black hair and a tweed waistcoat. I watched him; he came out of Henry Street at the side of the post office, and he ran over to where two horses had begun to ease down a bit. Brazen as you like, he grabbed one bridle and then the other one, soothed the two agitated beasts, and led them away. I bet he sold them back to the British Army as good Irish three-quarter-breds.

It was plain to see that the leaders in the post office, while pleased at the repulsion of the Lancers, remained puzzled that no greater attack came. And none did that day. Outside the windows, the people who had hid when the Lancers came in now dispersed, and we could see them across the street, looking for doorways to hide in, watching to see what would happen next.

There had been such talk for months of a new rebellion. But nobody believed it, and even though rebel volunteers from the IRA and Mr. Connolly's Citizens' Army had been patrolling openly, the police didn't bother with them anymore. That was why they were able to march so freely that morning. Now they had put their rebellion into operation, and I think everyone was shocked—including themselves.

The post office now felt as still as a church. I took advantage of the lull to get into conversation with Mr. Pearse. From time to time he would walk around by himself as if in contemplation, and when

he was coming out of one of these reveries, I made sure I was standing by.

He looked at me with a question on his face.

"You're not a soldier?"

"No, sir, I'm not, and I'd make a poor soldier."

"And even though you're somewhat dressed as a cleric, I judge
that you're not a priest either."

"Oh, sir, as a priest I'd be even poorer than a soldier."

He laughed; he had an accent that was unusual—soft it was, certainly, but it had a slight twang in it—and later in the day somebody told me his father was an Englishman, which would account
for the twang.

"So what are you?"

"I'm a man passing by, sir. That's what my life is. I spend my time
traveling the roads as a storyteller, but somehow my heart was
caught on this bush here this morning."

He shook my hand, and I shook his.

"Well," he said. "I'm not sure I have the makings of a soldier
either. Those young men who died out there were true soldiers—
riding into the jaws of death. But I suppose you could argue that
they are also contributing to the freedom of a nation, even though
they certainly didn't mean to."

"All wars kill the young, sir," I said to him.

"Where were you educated?"

"I went to Rome."

He looked at me again. "They—my friends here and my brother,
he's over there somewhere—they tell me I'm too soft to be a soldier
and too innocent to be a politician."

Here I must tell you what one of the men told me later. A few
nights before the Rising, a group of the lads took Mr. Pearse to the
Gaiety Theatre, where they saw dancing girls in a chorus line. They
watched him to see whether he'd feel any excitement at these high-
kicking fillies, and all he said was, "How good of God to give them
such lovely legs." Not what you'd call a raucous man.

As night began to fall, I made my way through the narrow passageway to where the lights shone at the rear. There I found something that greatly surprised me; leaning back against a pillar was a man in a British army uniform. I looked at him, and he looked at me, and I said to him, "In the name of God what are you doing in here?"

He laughed a little, and then I realized that he was tied to the pillar.

"What's your name?" I said to him.

"Chalmers, sir."

"Mr. Chalmers, this is no place for you to be."

"It's better than where I was, sir."

"And where were you?"

"They had me tied up in the telephone booth. Very painful, sir, that was."

Apparently Mr. Chalmers was a Royal Fusilier, and he had been captured when Mr. Connolly's men stormed the post office.

"Are you all right?" I said to him.

"Oh, yes, sir, I've been treated very well, thank you."

I liked him; he was a sprightly fellow, good sense of humor.

That night I slept on the floor—it was no hardship to me, floors were nothing new in my sleeping experience, and I was accustomed to wrapping myself in my coat. During the night I woke more than once and realized that the guard watch was being changed, and I began to get the feeling that here, in front of my eyes, this was a real war. In the morning, big slices of bread and jam were handed around and mugs of tea, and nobody tried to exclude me on the grounds that I wasn't a soldier. Nurses had arrived, which surprised me; they must have slipped in on their way home from night duty.

On Tuesday morning, we knew that the English had begun to address the situation afresh. Through the windows, we could see barricades going up, and all the buildings across Sackville Street being emptied of people. Some of the folk over there were as touchy as hornets, and they called the soldiers and police every name they could think of for disturbing them.

Some time later, I was standing about five feet away from Mr.

Connolly; his uniform was a darker green than the others, and he had feathers in his hat. I heard him say, "I think, boys, we can expect a bit of a tantery-ra"—meaning commotion. A minute later, a shell landed on the roof above, and big guns began to pound us. I was never so frightened in my life—I didn't want to die. And I don't want you to think that I was ashamed of that feeling; I wasn't; in fact I began to chide myself for not having had the sense to keep out of this danger. But a few minutes after that, I stopped worrying about myself and began to worry about someone else.

During a lull in the shelling—and I must tell you, there was furniture cracking and glass breaking and sounds on the roof like the end of the world—someone opened a side door. To the alarm of everyone who saw them, a woman and a young child slipped in; I was near that door and I too was consternated. The young rebel who let them in was too concerned with the door to pay them any attention, so I went over to them.

The woman was about thirty, I'd say, brown-haired, pretty as a garland, and the child, a small girl, wasn't any more than six or seven, a little blond girl, with her thumb never far from her mouth.

The child looked up at me with big eyes. And so did the mother. I think she guessed that I was about to say to her, "This is no place for women and children," and she forestalled me.

She said, "Sir, I'm looking for Jerry Quinlan, do you know him? I'm fairly certain he's here."

I said to her, "If he's here, he's all right, because so far everybody's all right. What does he look like?"

"He's easy to find—he's tall, with a head of straight black hair."

"Does he wear very big boots?"

"Big as boats," she said.

"Then he's over here," I told her, and I led her across the floor to a group of men who were cleaning guns and laying out belts of ammunition.

"Jerry Quinlan," I said, and when he turned around, I knew that I had already marked him out; he was the one man in whom I had seen real fear. When the gunfire started with the Lancers, he hadn't known what to do with himself, and there was a moment in which I felt he was about to burst out into tears. And that was the last thing he should have done, because he'd have been mocked to high heaven by the others—who were probably just as afraid themselves, but had managed the knack of not showing it. As I was watching him the previous day, he grabbed his gun and held it crosswise across his chest, as if putting a bar across his heart to protect it.

Now, when he looked at me and then saw the woman and the girl behind me, I understood why he was afraid. This was his wife and their little daughter, and he'd feared he'd never see them again, and that if he died, they'd starve without him to support them.

The wife didn't run to her husband's arms, like they do in books; instead she said to him, "Jerry, in the name of God come home out of this."

The little girl, however—she ran over to her father, and he bent down and picked her up. She planked her face right against his cheek and kept it there as though it were glued. He kept patting the child on the back, saying, "Well, well, what's this, what's this"—because of course the child had started to weep.

"Jerry," said the wife, "can you come away home with us?"

"I can't, Noreen, I told Mr. Connolly I wouldn't let him down."

Their accents told me they came from Dublin city, which is where James Connolly had recruited his Citizens' Army.

"But what about letting us down?" she said.

I stepped back a little, not wanting to intrude on their privacy, but, God forgive me, I stayed within earshot—I'm a storyteller, and a story's a story.

"Noreen, if there's one thing you know, it's that I'd never let you and Ivy down."

Up to that moment I had never heard the name of Ivy—who grabbed her father even tighter around the neck and tried to wrap her little legs around his chest.

"Well, what're we going to do, Jerry? The people down the street, they're saying youse're all goin' to get killed."

"Noreen, sure there's too many of us here to kill us all. They'd need an army."

"Isn't that what they have, an army?"

"No, I mean a big army."

"Jerry, the king has the biggest army in the world, everyone knows that."

"But Mr. Connolly told us, he told us, Noreen, most of that army's over in Germany."

At that moment, an almighty shell hit the building, and everybody ran to some kind of shelter. Little Ivy started screaming, and not even her father could calm her down as the bits of the ceiling fell down all around us and terrible gray dust billowed everywhere.

Noreen Quinlan was a steady woman, so steady not even the cannon of the king of England could knock her off her stride. She confronted her husband again.

"And who d'you think is doing that, Jerry, only an army?"

I intervened and said, "You should be looking to stand somewhere safer."

Noreen Quinlan looked at me and said, "Where's safer? If we go under a table, it could fall on us and crush the life out of us. If we stand by a wall, the wall could come down on us. We'd be safer outside."

"There's nowhere safe this minute," I said. "But I'm going to move over to one of these pillars, they seem to me strong enough."

She followed me, and so did her husband, still carrying little Ivy. The group of us stood there; I'd say we looked like something in a painting. Three more shells landed on or near the building; one wall shook very badly; a main window crashed in—the glass came in like a wave breaking over a rock, all green and glinting. Nobody, anywhere, moved; everybody was hunched down, crouching, huddled. At least as far as I could see that's what they were doing—the dust was like a fog that had gathered grit.

When I look back on that moment—and there were other moments I'll come to presently—I remember it for two things. It brought home to me the experience of fear, not so much for myself, though I was very frightened indeed, but as seen through the eyes of others. And it told me a principal fact about revolutions—they truly do come up from the people. I'll talk about the fear first, and then I'll come back to the revolution point.

Many times in my life, I have been afraid. Before the nineteen-sixteen rising and the GPO, I had been afraid for moral reasons, when I wanted to do something others didn't want me to do. I had also experienced physical fear. In my home village of Ballinamore, when I was twelve years old, a horse bolted one day, pulling its cart, which had high sides on it, for ferrying calves. Like a mad chariot it went tearing down the main street, the cart swinging from side to side. Someone later said it was a goose that had flapped across the horse's eyes and scared it.

I was crossing the street and got nearly paralyzed with fright, but I managed to find my legs, and I ran into a doorway. The poor creature—its head was rolling and its mouth was foaming and it was altogether going crazy.

The next thing I saw was a man at the side of this horse, running along with it. He had to run fast, I can tell you, because this horse was fairly galloping, but he got hold of the trailing reins and, clever fellow that he was, he dragged it down until eventually his weight slowed the horse.

It came to a full stop, and the man walked up to its nose. The creature reared its head, and the man did a very clever thing—he untackled the horse's blinkers. That caused a lot of debate later; many people said it was the wrong thing to do to quieten a horse—but the horse calmed down, and then the man rubbed its nose and led it back to its owner.

I've two surprises for you in that story. When they found the owner, a farmer from Drumsna, he went pale in the face and ran to the cart, brushing everyone aside. And when he opened the back, we saw his little child in there, lying curled up in a ball. We thought the child had been knocked unconscious by bouncing off the sides or something. Not at all; the child had slept through the whole ordeal.

Here's the second surprise, which nobody found out for some time—and it's my main point; the man who caught the reins and brought the runaway horse under control had been dismissed from the British Army on suspicion—never proven—of cowardice.

Now, was he a coward? Or was he someone who overcame his fear that day? Because, perhaps, he could no longer live with the accusations of being a coward? I'm told he used to see people looking at him in an odd way, because however much people disliked the king's soldiers, to be a coward was worse than anything. Nobody ever thought that man a coward again.

So that was one of my earliest encounters with fear—both feeling it myself and observing someone else overcoming it. It has given me the greatest respect for people who find themselves in dangerous situations, even if they find themselves frightened. The people in the post office that Easter must have felt terrible fear. And they must have overcome it, and it is not possible to admire that achievement more than I do.

Because they were ordinary people! Among my friends up and down the country have been many librarians. Being of no fixed abode, I have never been able to possess a library ticket. But I have been lent books by librarians who have broken the rules. In most towns I used to make a beeline for the local library, and I'd get into conversation with the librarian.

I never met a librarian worth his or her salt who didn't perceive my passion for books. And without exception, each one would lend me a book on a subject we had been discussing. No paperwork, no formalities of any kind, no rules or regulations.

My unspoken side of the bargain was to protect them, in two ways; first, by keeping the book unharmed—not that easy, especially in bad weather, but when it rained, I carried the book next to my skin. I can tell you now that carrying *Gulliver's Travels* or *Lays of Ancient Rome* or Mr. Oscar Wilde's stories or Mr. William Yeats's poems next to my heart gave me a kind of sweet pleasure.

The second half of the bargain often nearly broke my heart, but I always kept it—and that was to return the book safe and sound to the library that had lent it. To part company with Mr. Charles Dickens or Mr. William Makepeace Thackeray and his lovely name!—that was harder than saying good-bye to a dear flesh-and-blood companion. But I always did it—and I sent the book by registered post, no small consideration of cost given the peculiar economics of an itinerant storyteller.

I'm straying too far—here's my point concluded. Often I asked for books about revolutions and the men who led them, because I'd seen our country come of age, and the rebel process interested me mightily. After many years of reading about it, I was able to look back on what I saw in the Easter Rising and come to an important conclusion.

When historians write that revolutions are made by the people—that is completely accurate. Something happens in people's hearts and then in their stomachs, down there where they have had too much or have heard of their ancestors having had too much. Then, up they rise. It seems to me that it's unstoppable, because people don't give up—and that's what happened in nineteen-sixteen.

It wasn't the first rebellion in Ireland, as we all know—there had been everything from skirmishes to out and out insurrections. From what I saw of the men fighting in the GPO, they knew they were in that tradition. But they also knew that they were ordinary men and women who wanted the right to own and run their own country. It was as simple as that, and of course it was as complicated as that. And to do so they had to overcome their fear. As I say, no small matter.

The second bout of shelling stopped. Jerry Quinlan and little Ivy and Noreen stretched a little, and she said to him, "Now what're we going to do, Jerry?"

He said, "I doubt Mr. Connolly is going to let anyone out of here."

"I'll ask him," she said, and over she goes, Jerry following after, with little Ivy still in his arms. Naturally enough, I wasn't far behind myself.

James Connolly was standing by a high desk, reading what I discovered was an inventory list of supplies, weaponry, and ammunition. He was arguing with someone about what should be in their
possession but which someone seemed to have mislaid; my goodness, he had a blunt manner.

"Mr. Connolly," said Noreen Quinlan. "Can I ask youse a question?"

James Connolly looked at her, he the hardheaded working man's
hero, she the working man's striving wife.

"And I'll ask you one—how did a woman and child get in here?"

"Never mind that. Here's my question. Which do youse think is
the most important—a man's country or his family?"

"I can't separate them," said James Connolly.

"I want my husband out of here," said Noreen Quinlan.

"Your husband is a soldier."

"He's not. He's a printer's apprentice."

Jerry, meanwhile, looked like a man caught between the devil
and the deep blue sea.

"In the next lull of bombardment, ma'am, I'll have you and your
child escorted to safety."

Noreen Quinlan said, "I'm not leaving without my husband."

"You'll have no choice, ma'am. I'm very sympathetic, but we're
fighting a war."

James Connolly called over two soldiers; they detached little Ivy
from her father's arms and hustled Noreen and the child to wait at
a door. Jerry was dispatched to another part of the scene, and when
next I looked, the woman and the child were gone.

For an hour, things quietened down a fraction—maybe the British
Army was at lunch. I roamed around a bit. The stronger men, by
which I mean the leaders, like Mr. Connolly and Mr. Pearse and his
brother—they talked to everyone. They checked for injuries, they
looked at supplies, and they gave permission for some timbers to be
loosened from walls for the windows to be boarded over again
where shells had come through.

My eye fell on a man sitting by himself, in at the back where the clerks' desks were, hunched against the wall, all on his own. Something about him caught my attention, and I strolled over to him.

His face was as gray as a grave. He was half sitting, half lying, as if he had been thrown there by a blast as strong as the one that blew in the windows.

I said to him, "Are you all right?"

He made no answer, just looked up at me, eyes as wide as an animal's.

"What's your name?"

He answered so quietly I couldn't hear him, so I had to ask him again.

"Tony Fallon," he said

"How old are you, Tony?"

"I'm twenty." His breathing seemed hard and slow; he was wearing a suit with a shirt and a tie, and they were obviously his Sunday best clothes.

"Are you all right, Tony?" I said to him.

"I don't know, sir."

"Did you get hit—or shot or something?"

And he said, "No, I don't think so. Mr. Pearse asked me the same question."

"Have you a pain anywhere?" I said to him, and with his right hand he drew a line across his chest and down his left arm and up into his jaw.

"Where are you from, Tony?"

"Ringsend. I'm with Mr. Connolly." He kind of propped himself up a little, got into a better sitting position, and I helped him. The rifle he'd been carrying lay over to one side, the muzzle pointing at us, so I turned it away a little in case of accidents—you never know with guns. He had those dark eyes that you never forget, like pools.

I said to him, "How're you feeling now?"

"Sir," said he, "I'm feeling a bit afraid."

"We're all feeling that, Tony. How're you feeling physically?"

"In my body, like?"

"Yes."

"This pain, it's starting to hurt again."

"Can I get you a drink of water? Or a drink of milk?"

"Sir, no, if you do that you'll have to go away from me, and I don't want that."

I said to him, "All right, I'll stay here and I'll wave to someone, and when they come over I'll ask them to get you a drink of milk."

He leaned back against the wall.

I said to him again, "Are you sure you weren't hit by something? Glass or something like that?"

"No, sir. I was hit by fright. That's what hit me."

I sat down beside him, and he dozed off; he seemed restful enough.

Somewhere, through a high window, the sun streamed in, and I stood and had a good look at Tony Fallon and didn't like what I saw. A nurse walking nearby came over and looked at him too, and she went off to get a drink of milk. Tony Fallon woke up, but he was worse than before. He couldn't talk much by now, and when the nurse arrived with the milk I held the tin mug to his blue lips and helped him to drink it. I whispered to her, "Have we a doctor in the building at all?"

"We've no doctor yet."

She went away, and I helped Tony Fallon to drink a little more. He had little control, and the milk was slobbering down his lips. I put the mug down, and he caught my hand.

"Don't go anywhere, sir," he said to me, "stay here."

"I will," I said, and I sat down beside him; up to then I had been crouching.

His eyes were falling closed, and I kept talking to him—I don't know why, I think I must have heard somewhere that when people's lives are in danger from natural causes, you must never let them fall asleep. When they're awake, they can fight for life; when they sleep, they can't. I said to him, "I'll tell you a story about a man I knew up the country who was afraid the way you're afraid now. A man with a runaway horse. And I'll tell it to you just to prove there's no shame in being afraid."

His grip tightened on my hand. "You won't tell Mr. Connolly that I'm not able to fight, will you?"

"Of course I won't, Tony."

"Tell him I was wounded; he won't find out because I'd say there'll be many wounded."

I said, "Well, you are wounded—I mean, this wouldn't have happened to you if you weren't caught up in all that's going on here."

He said, "But if I'm to be a soldier, don't I have to have wounds with blood and everything?"

"There's all kinds of wounds," I said. "The thing about wounds is that they can be healed."

He sat up a bit more, and his eyes brightened.

"They can," he said. "Wounds can be healed." Then he paused and said, "But my uncle died last year fighting in France, and they told us there wasn't a mark on his body."

By now I knew—as do you—the source of Tony's wounds; he'd had a heart attack. His family had a history of weak hearts, just like my family has a history of weak chests. But his eyes continued to brighten, and he went on straightening himself up.

He said to me, "D'you think you could help me to stand up?"

"Tony, I'd say you should take a little rest, just for a minute or two, get your strength back."

"No, I want Mr. Connolly to see that I'm all right."

I rose to my feet and bent down to help him.

"Wait a minute," he said. "My legs need a bit of a warning that they've to start working again."

From the street outside, a new fusillade hit the walls of the post office.

"Where's my gun?" said Tony Fallon. "Could you hand it to me, sir?"

He leaned back against the wall, he rested his head against the wood paneling, and he died.

For practical reasons, owing to time, I can't describe every shell that hit us, every shot we fired back, every shot they fired at us in those two days. In any case, I wouldn't be able to get through it without weeping. But that Easter, I became a man opposed to violence in any form—and committed to speech and its powers, in every form.

I saw boys with their heads split open, I saw a man's stomach open out like a red flower from shrapnel. One soldier I knelt beside asked me to tell his mother he believed in what he was doing, and then he died. Another said to me, "I'm supposed to be playing football next Sunday," and he had lost a leg; he died of gangrene.

The damage to the building was bad. By five o'clock we had many people suffering. I made myself useful in an odd way—I held the hands of men who feared they were going to die or who were badly wounded. Some of them wanted to pray, and God knows, I had enough prayers in my head after six years at the Irish College in Rome. And if I didn't believe in those prayers anymore, I wasn't going to let those people see that—especially if what I recited with them brought them any comfort.

Then the thing happened that I feared most. English soldiers—the Sherwood Foresters, I think, or were they on Mount Street Bridge? I can't remember—anyway, they were so close we could hear the officers' commands; in fact we were able to duck when we heard them shout "Fire!"

But poor Jerry Quinlan didn't duck quickly enough. Out in the middle of the floor, the emptiest part of that hell's half-acre, I saw him spin around as a bullet or a splinter of glass or shrapnel or something hit him on top of the head. Some flesh blew away from his cranium, and he was dead before his lanky body hit the floor.

My stories often dwell on heroism. Heroes make powerful decisions, accomplish difficult tasks, explore new lands, defy kings, lead their people. What makes a hero? Oh, how often I have asked myself that question. Was Jerry Quinlan a hero? Perhaps—merely for being there. Likewise poor Tony Fallon. And the nineteen-sixteen leaders? Were they heroes? They were—but not for the reasons you think, and I'll come to that in a moment.

The tall young man with the shock of tawny hair—he was a hero;

in fact he's the one I think of as the bravest man in Easter week. I watched him a lot those two days, and he was everywhere at once. First he'd fire out one window, then he'd fire out through another. He seemed to answer to no particular commander. Some of the time he'd ask Mr. Pearse or James Connolly or Michael Collins regarding some exploit or other, but most of the time he acted on his own initiative. He propped up injured men, he distributed food, he cleared away debris from shell damage—he was a one-man natural force.

The odd thing was—nobody except myself seemed to take any notice of him. He surged here, he surged there, he never seemed to stop for food; there was a kind of mysterious air about him, and he had a power I had ever only imagined. Now comes the moment at which he intervened directly in my life.

On Tuesday evening, before the light faded, with Jerry Quinlan and Tony Fallon dead, the young man came striding over to me. I was looking into empty air, trying to steady myself after the deaths I had just seen, after meeting the men I had tried to console. The tawny young man grabbed my arm and said, "What are you?"

I said "I'm a storyteller. That's all I am."

"That's all?" He mimicked my words and the way I said them. "How can you say, 'That's all'?"

"What do you mean?"

"You may be the most important man here," he said.

"No, I don't think that's the case." I nearly laughed at the ridiculousness of this suggestion.

"Who else is going to create our memory?" he said. He waved his hand to indicate all around us. "What would be the point of all this if nobody told our generations to come what we meant?"

This was a man who would have no argument. Before I knew what he was doing, he steered me toward a side door and nodded to a young rebel to open it.

"We need you to live. You know what to do," he said to me. And I did.

Outside, guns looked at us everywhere. The tawny young man burst out of the door and ran at the barricades, firing his rifle. When the gun jammed, he swung it like a club, jumping up on the sand-bags, hammering the gun left and right at everyone he saw. Then he threw it away, drew the gun from the holster with the missing button, and fired it left, right, and center. That was the last I saw of him as he disappeared in all the smoke and dust.

He attracted such attention that nobody looked at me, and I went in the opposite direction; through some miraculous circumstance I merged into the situation as a passing civilian—and left the city that night.

We all know what happened next: the true heroism emerged. The center of Dublin was all but destroyed by British guns. Buildings all up and down Sackville Street burst into flames, and at last the post office had to be evacuated. James Connolly was badly wounded, and on Saturday morning he and Mr. Pearse and the other leaders decided to surrender; the terms they argued for—and won—meant they, the rebel leaders, would be shot, but their rank and file would be spared. That was the heroism of which I spoke.

On Saturday afternoon Mr. Pearse handed over his sword to General Lowe, and the two men walked away together. Four young rebels carried James Connolly on a stretcher to the British lines, where he too surrendered. Some weeks later, he and the others were tried, and he was the last to be executed—by a firing squad who had to prop him up in a chair, so bad were his wounds.

Around the country and around the world the sympathies went at last to the rebels. If the English commanders hadn't been so foolish as to carry out those executions, who knows what would have happened to Ireland? But that's an argument we've all heard often.

I've never told my story of Easter nineteen-sixteen until tonight, because I felt it had too many real, true facts in it to let me reach the truth of it. But now memory has invested it a little, and I always feel safer when that happens—it brings me closer to the core. I went back to the roads of Ireland, telling stories, remembering the young man with the wild head of tawny hair that looked like a tree on fire. Over and over I pondered what he stood for, and from that I began to ask myself what he meant to me, what we mean to each other in this country, where we have such wonderful natural assets, and yet we have so often failed to feed our children. I have no solutions; my task, I think, is to go on discovering these people inside me and let them tell me—and you—what they mean. But these are thoughts I will go on thinking—and rightly so—until I die.

In all those years since nineteen-sixteen, I have had many tribulations, but we'll pass quickly over them. However, I have had one constant joy, and to tell you what it is, I need to see your faces.

My grandfather was wonderful that night in Cork—
wonderful. I had been worried at his facing an audience much
larger than he was used to, and the fact that he couldn't see his listeners—I had feared he might find it all too much.

I had no need to worry; in fact I had private cause to rejoice,
because his performance once again—as in my childhood—seemed
also to have been directed specifically at me. How could I not recognize the figure of the Architect from Newgrange—to my grandfather he seemed to represent Life itself, a force of nature, as he said.
And the two monks—one tall and thin, one short and buttery?
Annan and Senan, of course! And, like the couple he mentioned so
casually in the post office, did Aoife not gaze adoringly up at
Strongbow as all the city around them fell into carnage?

At last I began to understand that beyond the blood ties, of
which I had known nothing, there had always been another, far
deeper reason why I had gone searching for him. From that very
first story of Newgrange he had, I now realized, given me one of the
greatest gifts available in humanity. Like a plowman opening a
field, he had carved out the beginnings of my imagination; he had
helped me to recognize instinctively the country and the people to
whom I belonged.

Remember his list of blessings and curses at Newgrange? They
had all appeared in some fashion or form in everything I had since
heard, read, or encountered. True to his words, I had been raised,
wandered through, and long lived in "a land full of milk and
honey." I had seen in my own studies that the country had produced "men of strength and wisdom, women of beauty and love."
And yes, we had been "conquered again and again," and our "seed,

breed, and generations" were "made subject to others." Also, our fighting men, from Brian Boru to Hugh O'Neill, had become feared "wherever water flows or birds fly."

That story had a violently relevant point too—which came back to nag me. Though I had had plenty of opportunity, I had not had the courage to uncover more about the IRA campaign that began in 1956 and ended in 1962; in fact I had fled the area of the Irish border and, like all my family and everyone I knew in the south, had not had the courage to explore the Six Counties of Northern Ireland. And I had been queasy and squeamish when faced with the couple near Banagher whose son was on the run.

No doubt I would have defended myself by arguing that any Irish "Troubles" would very likely "destroy the root of thought, the soul of reason," as the Silken Elder had warned, and I would have added, as he had, that "men will use the power of the past to give themselves the power of the future." But the Storyteller had at least given me benchmarks by which I could judge myself—delivered, it has to be said, in a most unusual way.

Most vividly of all came a fusion in my mind of the two strongest exhortations from the Newgrange hillside; since I became a teacher of history, both had echoed through me again and again.

The Chief Elder had said, in his "last and most wonderful blessing," that we would "spread our breed and our blood" across the world and that everywhere we went, we would be "known to come of this land." But his enemy had countered with an equal truth; "It shall indeed be the case that your children and their children and their children's children forever will go to other lands and be among other people. But your descendants will leave because this land will drive them out, drive them away. Will not be able to sustain them. Will not be able to give them enough food and drink." I mourned again a crucial statistic of my own life; of the fifteen children in my final class of primary school, 1954, I was the only one who had been privileged enough to avoid emigration.

All these reflections had been stimulated, all these seeds of thought had been planted in me, by the man out there on the stage.

He might have thought himself absent from my life—but he had grown me up.

When he rose and asked to see their faces, the house lights came up slowly. Now I also could see the audience, row after row, applauding delightedly; I began to recognize them, and my skin felt that shivering excitement. Here were the people I had met as a boy when I visited their houses, inquiring tactfully whether they had ever again heard of the Storyteller; and here too were the people I had called on during my long search up and down the country.

The poet Hanafin looked merry, some lively girl by his side, long hair and very red lipstick. Madge O'Callaghan (Mrs.) sat in the front row, with her excellent typist daughter; next to them sat the Three Furlongs from Home, all in suits and wide smiles, but wearing white kid shoes, and beside them Uncle Toby—he had flown in from Oxford.

And there was Ray Cashman in his suit and red tie, with Mr. Kavanagh, the man we found polishing his shoes at Derrynane. There too sat the tall Dutch family from Two Horse House by the lake, and Eddie Landers, the vet, and Daniel P. Kerry from Cootehill, and Mrs. and Mrs. McKenna, and Sean O'Sullivan from the Folklore Commission, and Matt Doyle the ferryman, and the man from Mullinavat, and Mrs. Colfer the baker, and Archie Halpin, though mercifully no trace of Morning Star of Slane. There was Mrs. Cantwell from Clonmel, whose great-great-great-great-great-grandmother had helped make an idiot of Oliver Cromwell.

Marian Geraghty and her husband Tom had come from the house called Boyne Water, and Dickie the barman was there, wanting, I expected, to be reimbursed for his coat. And, believe it or not, there also sat Myrtle O'Farrell and Uncle Bob, who seemed stooped and perky as ever; they and many more must have driven over a hundred miles to be in Cork that evening. And behind them—my heart rose a little further, because I had often thought of her—sat Lelia, who had tried to teach me to dance Clare Sets and failed.

Who were these people? Angels? Ghosts? No; they were listeners whose imagination had been fired by my grandfather's stories of

Ireland or my stories from and about him, and I felt my heart turn over when I looked at them.

The applause died slowly, and they settled back in their seats. My grandfather the Storyteller raised his whiskey glass in the manner of a toast to his audience and spoke, it seemed, to each face. I grinned, because I knew one dimension of what was about to happen—he was in a theater; so, like a good old trouper, he would make a dramatic speech.

WHAT I TOLD YOU TONIGHT—IT ISN'T MY story alone. It belongs to every Irish person living and dead. And every Irish person living and dead belongs to it. And to all the story of Ireland; blood and bones, legends, guns, and dreams, Catholics, Protestants, England, horses and poets and lovers.

Conveniently for me, I liken Ireland to whiskey in a glass—a cone of amber, a self-contained passage of time, a place apart, reaching out to the world with sometimes an acrid taste, a definite excess of personality, telling her story to all who will listen, hauling them forward by the lapels of their coats until they hear, whether they want to or not. But always, always—the story is the teller, and the teller is the story.

The one joy that has kept me going through life has been the fact that stories unite us. To see you as you listen to me now, as you have always listened to me, is to know this: what I can believe, you can believe. And the way we all see our story—not just as Irish people but as flesh-and-blood individuals and not the way people tell us to see it—that's what we own, no matter who we are and where we come from.

That's why I spent my life as I did—because that was all I have ever owned, stories. Indeed, our story is finally all any of us owns, because, as I once told my grandson, a story has only one master.

IRELAND

Statute miles

0   10   20   30   40

N
W   E
S

ATLANTIC
OCEAN

DONEGAL

Liff

FERMAN

Ennisk

LEITRIM

• Sligo

SLIGO

Carrick on
Shannon

• Castlebar

MAYO

ROSCOMMON

LONG

Longfore

Roscommon •

WE

GALWAY

Galway •

OFFA

Tullam

CLARE

• Ennis

• Limerick

TIPPERAR

LIMERICK

• Tipperary

• Tralee

WATERF

CORK

KERRY

Cork •